A Moment of Desire

As his eyes met Erin's in the moonlight, Kellen found himself suddenly flooded with desire for the beguiling creature who stood before him.

Very carefully, he lifted one hand to stroke her exquisitely structured cheek. Then, without truly considering his actions, he lowered his head to Erin's and covered her mouth with his own. Erin did not resist him, allowing him to revel in the sensation of her honeyed lips as they trembled slightly beneath his.

Kellen was soon lost in a passionate exploration of Erin's body—her neck, her shoulders, the swell of her breasts, and all that she had to offer . . . .

MORE TEMPESTUOUS ROMANCES!

GOLDEN TORMENT   (1323, $3.75)
by Janelle Taylor

Kathryn had travelled the Alaskan wilderness in search of her father. But after one night of sensual pleasure with the fierce, aggressive lumberjack, Landis Jurrell—she knew she'd never again travel alone!

LOVE ME WITH FURY   (1248, $3.75)
by Janelle Taylor

When Alexandria discovered the dark-haired stranger who watched her swim, she was outraged by his intrusion. But when she felt his tingling caresses and tasted his intoxicating kisses, she could no longer resist drowning in the waves of sweet sensuality.

BELOVED SCOUNDREL   (1259, $3.75)
by Penelope Neri

Denying what her body admitted, Christianne vowed to take revenge against the arrogant seaman who'd tormented her with his passionate caresses. Even if it meant never again savoring his exquisite kisses, she vowed to get even with her one and only BELOVED SCOUNDREL!

PASSION'S GLORY   (1227, $3.50)
by Anne Moore

Each time Nicole looked into Kane's piercing dark eyes, she remembered his cold-hearted reputation and prayed that he wouldn't betray her love. She wanted faithfulness, love and forever—but all he could give her was a moment of PASSION'S GLORY.

Available wherever paperbacks are sold, or order direct from the Publisher. Send cover price plus 50¢ per copy for mailing and handling to Zebra Books, 475 Park Avenue South, New York, N.Y. 10016. DO NOT SEND CASH.

Forbidden Flame
Luanne Walden

ZEBRA BOOKS
KENSINGTON PUBLISHING CORP.

ZEBRA BOOKS

are published by

KENSINGTON PUBLISHING CORP.
475 Park Avenue South
New York, N.Y. 10016

First printing: May, 1984

Printed in the United States of America

To Mother and Dad

I

The Intruder

Chapter One

March 22, 1865

The moon hung like a beacon in the heavens, its rays casting a brilliant sheen on the elegant mansion nestled midst the shadows of a dozen towering oak trees. How serene and stately the estate house appeared by the shimmering moonlight. At first glance, one would not suspect that its majestic splendor had been marred by the ravages of war, for the sturdy white pillars still stood proud and straight, as if to defy those who would do it harm. But upon closer inspection, one could detect the cracked, peeling paint, the loosened shutters and creaky hinges that were the result of years of neglect.

But these were merely surface scars, defects that could be corrected with proper maintenance. However, the scars that haunted the mistress of the impressive hall could not be so easily mended.

Erin Louise Richards slept fitfully; the frightening nightmare that had plagued her in recent months had returned to torment her. There were three of them, their eager faces hidden by the brightly colored bandannas. They had chased her to the barn, far away from the house and fields, where her screams would go unheeded.

She opened her mouth to scream, but no sound was expelled. Horrified, she watched as they approached her, stalking her as though she were a wild animal which might bolt at any moment.

Thinking to catch them off guard, she sprinted sideways in one frantic attempt to escape what she realized was about to happen. But it was for naught, for they surrounded her; three pairs of strong arms wrestling her to the hard, earthen floor.

One of them held her arms above her head and another pinned her legs to the floor to quell her struggles. The third one was on his knees straddling her, his hideous laughter echoing in her head as he ripped open the front of her dress to expose her youthful breasts to his callous manipulation. But the worst was yet to be, for her assailant then opened the front of his trousers to release the throbbing weapon he would use to violate her.

Tears ran uncontrollably down Erin's distressed cheeks as her fingers dug fiercely into the mattress beneath her. How utterly helpless she felt. To be a witness to such a depravity and yet to be a slave to one's dreams, unable to prevent the inevitable. It was as if she stood aside, a spectator at some cruel sporting event, helpless to prevent the occurrence, yet destined to observe it.

She watched in agony as the one astride her anxiously pushed her skirt and petticoats aside, and she heard the tearing of material as her delicate undergarments were ripped away. Then her assailant lowered himself deliberately over her trembling body and, with an evil chuckle, he lunged forward to plunge into the velvety passageway that had never before been explored.

Erin lurched upward in her bed, the scream that had been suppressed had finally broken free and now echoed hauntingly throughout the empty rooms of the mansion. She gazed down at her quivering hands which clutched the coverlets to her bosom and, as the tears fell freely onto the coarse woolen material, she tried to block the events from her memory of that fateful day, nearly four years past, that had changed her

10

life forever. God, but she hated the Yankees, all of them!

Erin slowly pushed the covers aside and laboriously climbed from her bed and made her way to the washstand. In a single motion, she shed the worn nightdress and, gripping the bar of harsh lye soap, she dipped her hands into the icy water and rubbed viciously, creating a generous lather. Then she cleansed every inch of her flesh that their loathsome hands had soiled. She rubbed with a vengeance that left her skin red and tender, scrubbing frenziedly until she was drained of strength to continue. Weakly, she pulled the linen gown over her head and, wrapping a robe tightly about her, she pushed open the French doors that led to the terrace. Walking numbly to the parapet, Erin gazed down at the moon-drenched lawn that stretched out below her and reconciled herself to await the dawn, for she knew that sleep would not come again this night.

Maisie, one of the few remaining members of the Richards' serving staff, was in the kitchen preparing a meager breakfast for her mistress when Erin slowly walked into the spacious room and sat down at the table.

"Yore breakfas' iz ready, Miz Erin. If'n you laks, ah'll serves you in de dinin' room." The servant lifted the heavy coffeepot from the stove and filled a cup for her mistress.

"I'm not very hungry this morning, Maisie," Erin mumbled softly.

"Jes' as well, Miz Erin, coz dere ain' much left in dis hyah house ter eat nohow." The housekeeper placed the cup of steaming hot coffee on the table before Erin and, noticing her mistress' beleaguered expression, she inquired, "Had dat bad dream agin last night, din' you? Ah can tell coz you always looks lák a whipped pup de mornin' aftah. Wuz it worse'n usual?"

"What?" Erin's thoughts had wandered during much of Maisie's talk. "Oh, *that*. It was the same, Maisie. It's always

11

bad." She absently sipped at the strong coffee. "Oh, Maisie," she cringed at the bitter taste, "is there no sugar?"

"No, chile." Maisie placed a saucer of biscuits on the kitchen table. "Ran out yest'dee an' dat's de last of de coffee. Dey's enuff flour ter make a couple moe batches of biscuits." She observed as Erin dunked the hard biscuit in her coffee, and continued to elaborate on their bleak circumstances, "We ain' had no decent food in dis hyah house in weeks, Miz Erin. An' de smokehouse wuz cleaned out months ago. What iz we gonna do?" The servant sat down opposite her mistress, hanging her head sorrowfully, for she was well aware of their dismal financial situation.

Erin regarded the faithful servant sympathetically, and the memories of the previous evening's nightmare temporarily vanished to be supplanted with the even more disturbing reality of their current situation. What *were* they going to do?

All of the household furnishings that Erin had been willing to part with had either been sold or bartered for food. Many of Erin's neighbors shared the same plight, having been forced to do the same and, consequently, the local shop-keepers had been obliged to adopt a *cash only* policy when dealing with prospective customers, due to the exorbitant number of once-cherished, personal belongings that were accumulating dust in their storerooms.

Cash, Erin mused and laughed cynically to herself. Where was she going to find cash to purchase the goods they needed, especially at the prices she would be expected to pay. And now that merchants were demanding gold coins rather than Confederate currency for payment, it was a near impossibility. Erin shook her head wearily and stood up, wrapping her arms tightly about her to ward off the early morning chill.

"Did you hear me, chile? What iz we gonna do?" Maisie repeated worriedly.

Erin gazed down fondly at the old, loyal servant and patted her shoulders reassuringly. "To be honest, I haven't a notion. But as soon as I get dressed, I'll ride over to Briar Cliff. Perhaps Aunt Lydia will be able to help us."

Erin turned to walk from the cozy kitchen, but Maisie's next question made her pause at the door. "Iz you gonna look in on Miz Debrah afore you leaves? You know how much she laks to visit wid you in de mornin'."

"Have you seen to her this morning?"

"Yas'm. She wuz in good spirits, but she kept askin' fer you. You know how she loves you." Maisie had busied herself with her daily kitchen chores and, in her preoccupation, she barely heard Erin's response.

"I'll check on her before I leave, Maisie." And the door was closed on the servant as she began to whistle an airy tune while she bustled about the kitchen.

Lydia Richards greeted her niece warmly and escorted her to the verandah, so they could chat comfortably and enjoy the early spring morning. Erin observed as Lydia poured each of them a cup of tea, and she could not help but notice how her aunt had aged since the outbreak of the war.

Lydia Richards was a proud woman who carried her tall and slender, aristocratic frame with a reassuring grace that immediately put her guests at ease. But the once regal brow now bore several wrinkles; the result of months of constant worry, and her thick, black hair had grown noticeably streaked with gray. But even though the stately shoulders had begun to slump and the brilliant blue eyes had lost much of their luster, Erin knew that her aunt still possessed the courage and inner strength to hold the Richards family together until the war reached its conclusion.

Erin gratefully accepted the hot tea and warmed her hands with the cup, for although the sun shone down upon them, the morning air was quite brisk. Erin sipped at the sweet-tasting, aromatic tea and, offering her aunt a sunny smile, she said, "I don't know how you manage to ration your supplies so carefully, Aunt Lydia. We ran out of sugar at Kilkieran this morning, and I haven't an idea as to how I'm going to gather the money to purchase more; not to mention the other staples we desperately need."

"There is no great secret to my management," Lydia confided in her niece. "Your uncle made arrangements with Mr. MacPhearson to supply us with whatever we needed before he left to fight with General Lee." She frowned a little as she drank from her cup and immediately reached for another spoonful of sugar to neutralize the strong taste. "I'll swan, but even extra sugar doesn't help make spicebush taste like *real* tea. You know that's what I long for most, Erin; a simple cup of tea. But that is one luxury I cannot afford these days, even if that stuffy old MacPhearson had any in stock," Lydia grunted sourly, then fell suddenly silent.

But Erin had read her aunt's thoughts as easily as if she had spoken them aloud. How ironic it was for one to consider a formerly insignificant item such as tea to be a *luxury*, especially when one was accustomed to attending lavish balls, wearing elegant gowns and dining on the finest food the land could provide. But the days of debutant balls, cotillions, and Sunday socials were gone forever. The Yankees had seen to that.

Erin placed her cup on the table before her and reached over to gently take her aunt's hand in hers. "It will get better," she assured the older woman.

"It will never be the same."

"No," Erin agreed. "But you must believe that this awful situation will improve. The war will end soon; *it has to,* for we cannot endure much more. Then our menfolk will come home to us and we can see about restoring order to our lives." She patted her aunt's hand comfortingly, trying to sound more optimistic than she truly was.

"But what of those who won't be returning?" Lydia reminded her niece. "Two of your brothers and my own precious Jeremy gave their lives for *the cause.* And the Lord only knows how many others this senseless war has claimed. Perhaps Kevin, or even my Philip." Her voice began to shake a little as she voiced her worst fears, that of losing her only surviving son and her husband, and Erin tried to ease her aunt's anxiety.

"You musn't think such thoughts, Aunt Lydia. Uncle Philip and Kevin are safe, you must believe that. Have you had word from them lately?"

"No, nothing. Christina went into town to see if anything came in the mail, but I'm not hopeful," she added sorrowfully. "And you, have you heard from your brothers, or Michael?"

"No, not in a very long time." Erin released her aunt's hand and retrieved her teacup. "This waiting . . . not knowing . . . is perhaps the most dreadful part. Sometimes I think I'll go crazy rambling around that big house by myself. Maisie and the others are a great comfort, of course, but it's not the same. Not like when Mamma was alive and she'd invite the entire county over for barbecue, and everyone would dance and laugh at Papa's funny stories. Our lives were carefree and uncomplicated then. And now . . . now everything and everyone that I have ever known, ever loved, is dying. I'm not certain that I'm strong enough to endure all of this." She paused suddenly, shocked by her own admission.

"Yes, you are," Lydia murmured softly. "You are perhaps stronger than the rest of us combined. You have to be, for you are all that is left at Kilkieran. And just as I must remain hopeful that Philip and Kevin are safe, you must remain strong for your brothers and Michael. For just as you say, our menfolk will be returning, God willing, and we must be prepared to help them readjust. The war has been unkind to us, to be sure, but we will never know the burdens they have had to bear." She paused to brush a tear from the corner of her eye and, once she regained control, she turned to Erin with renewed determination and said, "You will survive, Erin. You have already endured a great many sorrows. This war has claimed your parents and two of your brothers, then there was that horrible episode with the Yankees. And each incident has served to make you more resolved to show the Yankees that they cannot lick you."

Lydia paused to freshen her tea and, noticing the painfilled expression on Erin's face, she hastened to change the subject. "Well, I believe that we are in agreement that it will be a blessing when this awful conflict ends, but for now, let's try to concentrate on more pleasant things. For instance, you must get terribly lonely at Kilkieran. You have said as much," she reminded her. "Why don't you move in with Christina and me until Graham and Evan return? We have plenty of space, and I know that Christina would love having someone nearer her own age to chat with."

Erin was genuinely appreciative of her aunt's invitation, but deep within her heart she knew where she belonged and, turning to her aunt, she said, "Thank you, Aunt Lydia. It is really sweet of you to make such an offer, but I simply cannot leave Kilkieran, not my home. Why, there's no telling what kind of riffraff might try to scavenge the place without me there to look after things. Besides, I have to care for Deborah. She's so frail and vulnerable these days."

"I thought as much." Lydia nodded knowingly. "But if you can't agree to moving in with us, you must at least try to visit more often. I see you so seldom these days," she spoke with a soft, Virginia drawl. "Tell me, Erin, what brings you to Briar Cliff this morning?"

"I know that my visits have been infrequent, Aunt Lydia, and I'm ashamed to admit the reason that has prompted today's social call, but we're getting dreadfully low on food supplies at Kilkieran. I was wondering . . . that is . . ." Erin found the request she was about to make more than a little awkward. "Could you spare a few things?"

"I'll not listen to another word, Erin Louise. Of course, we can spare some things. Not that we have a bountiful supply, you realize, but I could never refuse food to family." Lydia stood and motioned for Erin to follow her.

"Just a few things until I can persuade Mr. MacPhearson to extend my credit," she insisted.

"That moneymonger," Lydia chatted lightly as she led Erin to the pantry, the seriousness of their earlier conversation apparently forgotten. "He's worse than any Yankee. I'll have a word with him tomorrow about your credit, and my Philip will deal with him when he gets home. Why, it's a crying shame for him to treat his own kind with such indiscretion. Imagine that, when he and your papa were such good friends, too."

Erin followed her aunt silently, grateful for Lydia's stream of chatter which required no response from her other than an occasional nod. Erin marveled at how rapidly her aunt had reassumed the cheerful mannerisms that were so characteristically Lydia; the brilliant smile, the lightness in her step, and the soft inflection of her voice that immediately charmed even the dourest of dinner guests.

Yes, Lydia had managed to come through the war virtually unscathed. Perhaps that would be a blessing for her Uncle Philip, but as for Erin, she knew that it would be a very long time before she would be able to laugh with abandon, or carry a joyful feeling in her heart . . . a very long time indeed.

Erin did not return home immediately. Instead, she guided her mount onto a lesser traveled trail that led away from the main road and deeper into the woods behind the Kilkieran plantation. Once on the new trail, the old mare adopted a livelier gait as if sensing Erin's destination.

Erin gave the horse an affectionate pat and leaned forward to say, "That's right, Lady, we're going to the waterfall. Can't fool you, can I?"

She settled herself on Lady's back and was content to view the passing landscape as they continued their journey. The forest foliage that had lain dormant over the recent winter months showed signs that it was preparing to spring back to life. The occasional warble of a bird intermingled with the other forest sounds to remind her that, thankfully, the complete ravages of war had not extended to this part of Virginia.

Spring was Erin's favorite time of year, when the dogwood and wild flowers bloomed and the air was filled with the clean, fresh scents of the season that had a way of cleansing her soul and making her feel like a young child again.

But a distressing frown suddenly flashed across her pretty face, bringing her back to realilty. The fact was, she no longer was a young child, indeed, she was very nearly twenty-two years old. By rights, she and Michael should have been man and wife by now with a family to care for. But the war had obliterated her dreams, as well as the dreams of countless others like herself.

"The war!" she exclaimed bitterly. "Why can I not have a single thought that isn't overshadowed by this accursed war?"

Her sudden outburst broke the spell of the daydream into which she had lapsed, and she realized that they had arrived at the waterfall. Lady stood at the edge of the pool into which the wall of water cascaded, as it fell over the cliff above them, before emptying into the stream that flowed past Kilkieran. Lady's head was poised contentedly over the water as she drank from the shimmering pool.

Erin dismounted and strolled about the clearing as if lost in a daze, her thoughts totally submerged in memories of happier, more carefree times. She and her brothers had spent a good portion of their youth swimming in the glistening pool and, in later years, she and Michael had used the secluded clearing as a private hideaway in which to picnic and plan their future together.

But of all the fond memories that came to mind, none provided her with more pleasure than her secret that had remained undiscovered all these years. As she reminisced, Erin's eyes came to rest upon the waterfall. Even now the cave remained hidden from view; the cave that had served as her secret hideaway whenever she sought respite from her brothers when they would tease her unmercifully. The cave had been her sanctuary for years whenever she needed to be alone to think, and it had remained her private haven. Even her brother James, who had been prideful of his ability to track down any quarry, had been unable to locate her when she went into seclusion.

"I wonder," she murmured aloud and instinctively walked toward the embankment. Yes, the path that led along the edge of the base of the cliff was still there. It was narrow and could prove perilous to one who was unfamiliar with it, but it had never been an obstacle to Erin.

On impulse, she walked along the bank to the opposite side of the pool and started to inch her way along the narrow path. But she had managed to go only a few steps when she became aware of the sound of traffic on the roadway. There were several horses and a wagon on the road that led to Kilkieran; the road which passed only a hundred yards or so from where she presently stood.

Erin was thankful for the heavy growth of trees that shielded the clearing from the view of the road. She could only wish that it was summer, for when the thick undergrowth was in full bloom, the clearing was virtually inaccessible. In fact, nature had managed to camouflage the clearing so successfully that only a handful of local residents knew of its existence.

She started to retrace the few steps she had taken along the path, but she stopped short and her heart pounded fiercely in her chest when she heard the shout that went up from one of the men on horseback.

"Yankees!" she whispered hoarsely. What were Yankees doing on the road to Kilkieran? What were they up to? "Surely, I must have imagined the voices."

But as quickly as the notion came to her, it vanished, for the continued sound of muffled voices made her realize that someone was definitely on the road and they were headed straight for her beloved Kilkieran.

Erin quickly retraced her steps and tethered Lady to a tree to prohibit her from wandering astray. Then she stealthily crept through the trees and the spring grass to secure a vantage point that allowed her to view the intruders without being detected. There were at least a dozen of them, all clad in the Union blue that had terrorized her dreams for these many months. Undaunted by the chance of discovery, Erin was resolved to hold her ground until she could determine what the Yankees were up to.

"Major," one of the men summoned the officer in command. "She's busted right enough. Now what are we gonna do?"

Erin could see that the men had gathered around a covered wagon. She correctly surmised that the wagon was the source of their concern, and she strained to hear the conversation.

"Well, private, logic dictates that we make every effort to repair the wheel and, if that fails, we shall enlist you to carry the freight on your back to our destination," the officer replied tersely. "That was a careless action on your part, and we're damned lucky the cargo wasn't destroyed and all of us killed. Where were your thoughts, man, that you could not see a chuckhole the size of that one? Now, due to your recklessness, this delay will cost us valuable time." The major concluded the stern reprimand, then knelt to examine the damaged wheel that lay on the roadside.

"I can tell you where his head was, Major," one of the other soldiers volunteered. "They was on that pretty little miss he seen on the road yesterday," he goaded the young private.

"Was not!" the private shouted a denial, infuriated by the uproarious laughter the jibe had created among the other men.

"Enough!" the major said firmly. "Unload the cargo, so that we can repair the wheel at least temporarily, and mind what you're doing lest you send the lot of us prematurely to our eternal resting place." He stood and walked with one of the other men away from the wagon toward the edge of the road, precariously close to Erin's hiding place.

From her vantage point, Erin was allowed the opportunity to better scrutinize the major who had led his band of Yankee intruders onto her homeland. He was tall, so tall that she knew she would barely reach his broad shoulders were they standing toe-to-toe. His hair was dark and unruly, and his eyes were blue; not an ordinary blue, but the shade of blue that colors the heavens after a hard rain washes the sky of impurities.

Erin's breath caught in her throat as she realized that the reason she could so clearly define the color of the Yankee's eyes was due to the fact that they were staring intently at the bush behind which she was hidden. She tensed, ready to dart into the woods should the major try to apprehend her, when she noticed that, even though the clear-blue eyes were fixed in her direction, they were quite obviously clouded with thought. Yet she gave a little jump when the major turned abruptly to the lieutenant at his side and began to speak.

"Tell me, Brad, can you fix it?"

"Kellen, you know I can fix anything given the proper tools. But out here, in the middle of nowhere—" He didn't bother to complete his statement.

But just then another soldier came toward the group, riding from the direction of Kilkieran. The soldier was obviously excited because he leaped from his mount before it had come to a complete stop. He rushed toward the major and the two exchanged salutes before the soldier addressed the officer.

"Major Sinclair?"

"Yes, Gates. What did you find?"

"There's a plantation house about a mile up the road, sir. I took the liberty of checking out the barn. There was a metal-works area, though from the looks of things, it hasn't been used in some time. But we should be able to mend the wheel there, sir." The private seemed pleased that he was able to report such agreeable news to his major.

"I've been through this area on assignment before, and I'm

21

somewhat familiar with the place. It should do nicely," the lieutenant advised the major.

"Good work, Gates." The major dismissed the soldier and turned to the man at his side. "Well, Brad, let's see if we can get the wheel back in place. Perhaps it will last until we reach the plantation. I'll take a detachment and ride ahead to see what sort of arrangements can be made with the owners."

The two men turned toward the wagon, and the remainder of their conversation fell unheeded on Erin's terror-stunned ears. Yankees invading Kilkieran again! No, she simply would not allow it to happen . . . not again . . . not like the last time.

Erin flew like the wind back to the clearing where she had left Lady and hurriedly mounted the animal. She could not remember a time when the old mare had responded so swiftly to the heel of her shoe. It was as if the horse sensed her mistress' anxiety as she sped along the narrow backwoods path to deliver her mistress to safety. Erin deposited Lady in the barn, then ran as fast as she could to the house to warn Maisie and the others of the impending danger.

"Lawdy, Miz Erin." Maisie turned abruptly from the mantel she was busily polishing when Erin bolted into the front parlor. "You knows better'n ter gallop into a room lak some wild thing what doan know no bettah. What'd yore poor mamma say if'n—"

"I'm sorry, Maisie, but you'll have to wait and scold me another time. Right now, you need to warn the others." Even as she spoke, Erin hastened to the window to see if the soldiers were in sight.

"Warn do othahs?" Maisie repeated confusedly. "What *iz* you talkin' 'bout, chile? You ain' makin' much sense."

"Listen to me, Maisie." Erin turned from the window and took the servant anxiously by the arm. "Yankee soldiers are on their way here. I overheard them in the woods, and they'll be here any moment, so we haven't time to spare. Tell Ruth and Lily to take the children into the woods and hide. Take Deborah with you and don't let her get away. Tell her it's a game and she has to be very quiet." Erin released the old woman and again turned to the window. The cloud of dust in the distance warned her that the enemy was rapidly approaching.

"They're coming!" she exclaimed. "Now, do as I say, Maisie. Hurry and warn the others. I'll sound the signal when it's safe for you to return to the house."

"But what 'bout you, chile? What iz *you* gonna do?"

"What should have been done the first time those dirty blue-bellies dared to invade Kilkieran." She walked determinedly to the fireplace and removed the rifle that hung above the mantel and, gathering the powder and bullets from a desk drawer, she issued one final order to the faithful servant, "Go now, and don't come back till I summon you. You hear?"

"Yas'm, but—"

"Go, Maisie, *now!*"

The servant scurried from the room and Erin could hear the soldiers riding up the graveled driveway as she meticulously loaded her father's rifle. The fear that had gripped her stomach earlier had been replaced by a grim determination, and it was this resolve that led her onto the porch to *welcome* the Yankee intruders to Kilkieran.

Chapter Two

Major Kellen Sinclair regarded the young woman who stood defiantly before him with a somewhat perplexing frown. Indeed, were it not for the rifle that was confidently leveled at his chest, he might have found the scene to be quite amusing. Imagine, a young miss thinking she could intimidate a detachment of the Union Army with an antiquated, single-shot rifle. Yes, given different circumstances, the major might have found the situation engaging. But the weapon pointed at him, coupled with the lethal glare with which the young lady favored him, made Major Sinclair realize that this was no laughing matter.

"Good day, miss," he began cordially, tipping the brim of his hat in a gentlemanly gesture. "I'm —"

"I'm not interested in your name, Yankee," Erin informed him bluntly.

"Yes, I can see that." He looked pointedly at the rifle and, clearing his throat, he began again, "Perhaps you will allow me to explain the reason —"

But his entreaty went unheeded, for Erin again interrupted. "Nor am I interested in your explanation."

A whoop went up from the soldiers in response to this caustic reply, but Erin ignored the outburst, for her resolute gaze was doggedly fastened upon the young major. It was only when one of the soldiers offered to "teach the sassy little rebel a lesson in manners" that her resolve wavered for an instant.

The major noticed the frightened expression that briefly crossed her anxious face, and he hastened to caution the soldier, "As you were, sergeant."

Major Sinclair did not know if the girl was capable of firing the weapon voluntarily, but he certainly did not want his men to provoke her into discharging the gun out of fear. With his thumb, he positioned his hat a little further back on his head and, leaning forward in his saddle, he calmly matched her determined glare.

"You've made it abundantly clear that you are not pleased with the notion of receiving this assemblage." He nodded purposely at the weapon still aimed at his chest. "And were it not for extenuating circumstances, I can assure you that we would not have darkened your door. However, the fact is, we have a disabled wagon and will require the use of your forge to make the necessary repairs. Now, I'm more than willing to strike some sort of bargain with you, miss, but first, do you think you could lower that weapon? It just might go off . . . *accidentally*." He offered her a wan smile, but Erin was not to be cajoled.

"I'm not likely to strike a bargain with any no-account *Yankee*," she snapped at him coldly.

"Now, see here, there's no need to be unreasonable." The major's amiable disposition was beginning to wane considerably and, filled with a sudden distaste for the course the conversation had taken, he started to dismount, heedless of the rifle in Erin's hands.

Taken aback by the major's overt action, Erin took an abrupt step backward. But in her haste to avoid the soldier's advance, her foot caught on a loose floorboard, causing her to stumble clumsily. In the ensuing confused instant, during which she tried to regain her footing, the weapon discharged sending the major's hat swooping from his head.

Major Sinclair ducked instinctively at the sound of the explosion, but he jerked his head around in time to see his hat swirl to the ground several yards behind him. The major turned on Erin furiously, but his anger quickly abated when he discovered her present state of mayhem.

She was on her backside, evidently due to the recoil action of the rifle. Her skirt and petticoats were flung about wildly as she kicked at the soldiers who had surrounded her in an attempt to relieve her of the weapon.

The major started to rush forward to ensure that his men did not harm the girl, but the painful howl that went up from one of his soldiers made him realize that he had been premature in his concern. One of his men was bent over, clutching his midsection, for Erin had shoved the butt of the rifle into the private's stomach, leaving him momentarily breathless. Another was examining his wounded hand after he had carelessly positioned it too close to Erin's mouth, thereby letting her sink her sharp teeth into the hand.

A slight grin twisted the major's mouth as he surveyed the ramshackle condition of his men and, shaking his head unbelievably, he sauntered toward the porch. "All right, men. Leave the miss alone and go help the others with the wagon. I'll handle this," he said firmly.

Upon receiving this command, the soldiers scattered to their respective mounts, with the exception of one. The sergeant who had offered to teach Erin a lesson in manners had managed to wrestle the gun from her, and now he was on his knees straddling her stomach. He had pinned her arms to the ground above her head and his sneering mouth was poised just inches from her lips. The sergeant was preparing to claim the frightened lips that strained to avoid his caress when he received a sharp tap on his shoulder.

"Keep yer shirt on, fella. You'll get a go at her," the sergeant snorted gruffly.

"Will I?" Major Sinclair could barely restrain the rage that swiftly rose in his throat. "Get to your feet, soldier, and do as you were told. We're here to ask a favor of this young woman, not terrorize her."

The sergeant stood up begrudgingly and turned to face his major. "I meant no harm, sir." He offered the major a wily grin. "The little lady didn't have a hankerin' to converse with us, so I just reckoned she might be lookin' fer a little funnin' instead. That's all."

"You were obviously mistaken, Sergeant Taggart," Major Sinclair replied tersely. "Now, I believe I issued an order."

"Yes, sir." The sergeant bent to retrieve his hat. "I'll see that the wagon is delivered safely. You can count on me, sir."

Major Sinclair watched the man mount his horse before turning his immediate attention to Erin, and he was quite taken with the disheveled scene he discovered. She certainly was a comely young woman. He studied her thoughtfully as though truly seeing her for the first time. His appraising gaze swept over her, taking in everything from the thick strands of chestnut-brown hair that hung about her shoulders in wild disarray, to the brilliant green eyes that were wide with anticipation, to the slim ankles that still remained exposed to his wandering and appreciative gaze.

Erin noticed the direction of his pensive gaze and, feeling suddenly self-conscious before the irksome Yankee, she hastily rearranged her appearance.

"Yes, lovely indeed," the major murmured to himself, his eyes still fixed on Erin. He could easily understand how a man could be driven by desire to hold this enchantress in his arms and kiss the defiant glower from her lips. For one impetuous moment the officer contemplated doing just that, but an impatient whicker from the man's horse reminded the major of his immediate purpose, and he reluctantly pushed the tempting image from his mind.

Instead, he stepped forward and gallantly proffered his hand to assist her from her rather humbling position. "If you will permit me," he said formally, struggling all the while to restrain the amused grin that tugged at the corner of his mouth.

"I don't need your help, Yankee." Erin angrily slapped his hand aside and, as gracefully as she could, she climbed to her feet and assumed an unyielding stance before him.

"Yes, you have adequately demonstrated your resourcefulness, Miss . . . uh . . . you have a name, I presume."

"Yes, but I don't anticipate your staying long enough to have the occasion to address me by it. *Good day,* Yankee." She presented her back to him and started to enter the house, but the hand that reached out to capture her wrist prevented her from executing a clean escape.

"Sergeant Taggart usually displays an uncanny knack for inaccuracy, but in this instance, he has exhibited exceptional insight; you *are* sorely lacking in manners." He turned her so they were facing again. "My name is Major Kellen Sinclair. Now, I fully understand your reluctance to have the *enemy* set up camp on your property, but I assure you that we are not here to pillage and plunder. I have an assignment, and I cannot conduct it properly with a disabled wagon; therefore, I shall require the use of your barn in which to repair it. I am, of course, willing to compensate you for your inconvenience. We have our own provisions, so there will be no need for my men to disturb your home while we are here. We shall make camp in the barnyard and, if all goes as planned, we'll be gone before you rise in the morning." He released her arm and looked down into the skeptical face he knew to be summing him up.

"How much?" she inquired matter-of-factly.

"What?"

"You said you were willing to pay. How much?"

"Ten dollars sounds like a fair price, don't you think?" he replied.

"Twenty," Erin informed him staunchly, and from the determined set of her jaw, he knew that further haggling was useless. "In gold *and* in advance," she continued, stretching out her hand beneath his nose and impatiently tapping her foot while she waited for the Yankee to locate the money.

"Twenty, huh? That seems like a rather steep price for one to pay to bunk with the stable creatures," he grunted sourly.

"You flatter yourself, sir. I shall see that the animals are moved from the barn before your men inhabit it." She turned up her nose at him in obvious distaste. "Besides, I'm not certain it's healthy for them to breathe the same air as *Yankees.*"

"Yes, well, I have similar reservations about the welfare of my men." He reached into his pocket and pulled out a twenty-dollar gold piece. The major started to drop the coin into her outstretched hand, but he paused and regarded her speculatively. "Tell me, this sudden change of heart . . . you wouldn't be contemplating some crazed attempt to murder us dirty old Yankees in our sleep, would you?" He had aired the notion facetiously, but Erin's reply left him completely stunned.

"That's a chance you will have to take, isn't it, Yankee?" She snatched the gold piece from his hand and, recalling how her father would check the authenticity of a gold coin, she placed it between her teeth and bit down. If the truth were told, Erin had no idea how one determined a real coin from a phony, but the Yankee was unaware of that.

She deposited the precious coin in the pocket of her dress and with a saucy shake of her head, she started to enter the house. But just before she closed the door, she turned to focus a cold glare on the major and issued one final declaration, "See that your mangy crew is gone at sunrise, or you'll owe me another twenty dollars, Yankee." And before the major could find his tongue, the door was slammed in his face.

Major Sinclair stood staring at the house for a full minute before he whirled and stalked to retrieve his fallen hat. He solemnly examined the damage that had been inflicted upon the headgear, then muttering something about irresponsible, trigger-happy, young women, he jammed the hat upon his head. Whistling for his horse to follow, he marched toward the barn to await the arrival of his men.

Erin surveyed the major from the parlor window. How could she have allowed Yankees to spend even one minute on Richards property? Her poor father had probably turned over in his grave when she had relented to the major's demands. Oh, well, there was little she could do about it now. The major had seemed determined to stay at Kilkieran and her protestations had only served to make him more relentless. At least he had been willing to pay, she sighed thankfully as her fingers absently fondled the precious gold piece. Now she could buy a few desperately needed supplies, and they could prolong starvation a little longer.

She glanced up from her hands to again focus on the major. He was leaning against the barn, one foot propped up behind him, his arms crossed as he thoughtfully scanned the heavens. Erin surmised that he was waiting for his men, and she remembered her threat to remove the animals from the barn. Not only that, but the provisions she had brought from Briar Cliff were still in the saddlebags on Lady's back. In her haste to warn Maisie and the others about the Yankees, Erin had forgotten them.

Well, if they were to have dinner that night, she would have to get them before the other Yankees arrived. Besides, the major was positioned at the front of the barn. She could easily slip in the back way and he would be none the wiser. Without a moment's hesitation, Erin hurried to the back door and scurried across the lawn without attracting the officer's attention, or so she thought.

First, Erin removed the Richards' milk cow, then she returned to collect Lady. "Hello, girl," she cooed lovingly to the old mare. "I didn't mean to leave you in such a snit, but I had to warn Maisie about those nasty Yankees. Come on." She took the reins and started to lead the horse out the back way. "I'll put you in the lean-to behind the smokehouse and give you a proper brushing."

"You know, this really isn't necessary."

Erin spun around at the sound of the Yankee's voice. He

had evidently slipped into the barn unbeknownst to her while she was preoccupied with Lady.

"My men won't harm your animals," he continued. "Nor will they steal them when we leave in the morning."

"Really? And what guarantee do I have of that?" she demanded.

"Why, my word, of course," he replied smugly as he sauntered over to Lady and scratched her affectionately behind the ear. Then, reaching into his pocket, he slipped the old mare a sugar cube. Lady eagerly ate the confection and sniffed at his pocket for more. "Ha, liked that, did you?" The major laughed good-naturedly and started to repeat the gesture when Erin angrily jerked Lady's reins and tugged the reluctant animal toward the door.

"No need to spoil her, Yankee. There will be no special treats after you're gone," she snapped.

"Perhaps her mistress would care for a confection then." The major deliberately extended his hand toward Erin. "For it is apparent to me that your disposition could certainly do with a little *sweetening*."

"Humph!" Erin grunted and turned on the major bitterly. "Look, Yankee," she began hotly, hands on hips, "you weren't invited here, so don't expect any hospitality from me. Just mend your accursed wagon as quickly as possible and get your men off my property."

"Okay, okay!" Major Sinclair threw up his hands in mock surrender. "I didn't expect a royal welcome, you understand." He came to stand directly in front of Erin and, impulsively, he tipped her chin back until their eyes met. "Nor did I expect to encounter such a high-spirited little rebel." He offered her a genuine smile, but Erin would not yield in her resolve to disregard the Yankee. "You know," the major sighed impatiently, "a simple smile would not be an admission of defeat, nor would it mean you were traitorous to your cause."

"I've not had much reason to smile as of late, Yankee," Erin mumbled sourly.

Discerning that the girl was determined to maintain this stand-offish attitude, Kellen Sinclair released her from his gentle caress and walked away from her. "I'll not detain you any longer. My men will arrive soon, and I'm certain you would rather avoid them if possible."

"You are quite right." Erin again started to lead Lady from the barn, but the major's next words stayed her movement.

"There is no need for your people to spend the night in the woods."

Erin gazed at him in total bewilderment, silently wondering how he had known about Maisie and the others.

"I hold myself personally responsible for the actions of my men, and I promise that you and your people will not be molested," he assured her.

Erin regarded the major with a skeptical frown. She was reluctant to believe the Yankee's words, but realized that there was literally nothing else she could do. Besides, he had really done nothing to intimidate her except, of course, commandeer the use of her barn. Perhaps this particular Yankee was not like the others who had terrorized Kilkieran. Perhaps this Yankee could be trusted.

A cold shiver ran down Erin's spine as she pondered this remote possibility, and she silently reprimanded herself for having considered such a ridiculous notion. A Yankee could *never* be trusted.

Turning from the major, she muttered awkwardly, "Well, I suppose I should thank you for that small blessing." And without a backward glance, she led Lady from the barn.

Erin sat on the back stoop of the mansion for a long time after her encounter with the Yankee. The other soldiers had arrived with the disabled wagon and, from the sound of things, had begun to make the repairs.

Good, she sighed inwardly. If all went well, and the major kept his word, the soldiers would be gone by sunrise. "Sunrise," she mumbled forlornly, silently dreading the long, lonely night that lay before her.

But there was no need for her to be alone. Had the Yankee . . . what was his name . . . she struggled to remember. Oh, yes; Sinclair. Had Major Sinclair not guaranteed their safety? Well, she had never met a Yankee who could be trusted, but there was something different about this one. She had nothing upon which to base her rationale; it was just a feeling she had and, of course, his eyes. Those eyes had already laughed at her anger and mocked her courage, but not once had the crystal-blue orbs made her feel that she should be apprehensive of the major's intention.

It was in that instant that Erin jumped to her feet and ran to the bell that hung on a pole just off the porch. She tugged on the rope, sounding the prearranged signal that she and Maisie had devised for such an occasion. The bell had barely stopped echoing in her ears before the first of the slaves started to wander back from the woods.

Maisie was the last to appear. She was leading, what appeared to be a young girl; no more than a child. But a closer examination revealed the eyes and features of a much older girl, probably in her mid-twenties. Her black hair was cropped short and, from its appearance, had not been combed in days. The girl was clad only in a white linen nightdress and seemed to be in a trance as Maisie led her along by the hand.

"Maisie, take Deborah upstairs," Erin whispered anxiously when she saw the girl. "Wrap her in a warm blanket and see that she is comfortable."

"But, Miz Erin," Maisie protested mildly.

"I'll explain everything, but first, see to Deborah." She shooed the housekeeper toward the house.

Erin then quickly explained what had transpired to the other slaves and instructed them to stay close together and to summon her if any of the Yankees got out of hand. As the slaves started to wander to their respective lodgings, Erin motioned one of them to her side.

"Ruth, I brought provisions from Briar Cliff. Maisie will probably be busy with Deborah for some time, so would it be a bother to ask you —"

"Not 'nothah word, Miz Erin, ain' no bothah ter help out," the servant said kindly.

Erin favored the servant with an appreciative smile and hurriedly made her way to the front parlor where she again took up vigil at the window, so she could monitor every move the Yankees made. Everyone appeared clustered around the wagon and much of the activity centered around the disabled vehicle.

Erin watched curiously as the soldiers carefully, almost lovingly, lifted the crates and boxes from the wagon. Her curiosity was further piqued when she observed the slow, measured strides the men used when walking away from the wagon with their burdens, almost as if they were trying to sneak unnoticed past enemy lines. For the first time since viewing the vehicle on the road, Erin's inquisitive nature was aroused, and she wondered at the contents of the Yankees' wagon.

But by early evening, Erin had grown weary of her surveillance from the parlor, so she bravely positioned herself on the front porch in full view of the pesky Yankees. But if the soldiers were aware of her presence, they gave no indication. Apparently, the major was a man of his word.

Erin's silent deliberation of the situation was suddenly interrupted as she became acutely aware of the delicious aromas of frying bacon and strong, black coffee as they drifted from the Yankee camp to envelop her nostrils, making her empty stomach rumble hungrily. She could not recall the last time she had eaten a piece of crisply fried bacon, but Erin could well remember the taste of the hickory-flavored meat upon her tongue. That memory, coupled with the dull ache in her stomach, reminded her that she had not eaten since breakfast.

"Oh, well," she moaned softly. "Perhaps I should see what

Maisie and Ruth managed to scrape up from the supplies I brought from Briar Cliff." She rose from her chair and slowly walked to the door, but as she turned to enter the house, she caught a glimpse of a figure approaching her in the dim twilight, and Erin braced herself as she turned to confront Major Sinclair.

"Evening, ma'am." He tipped his hat and offered her a friendly grin. "I thought you would be relieved to know that the wagon has been repaired, and we will be leaving bright and early in the morning."

"Good," she replied brusquely. "Tomorrow isn't soon enough."

"Yes, well, I'm afraid tomorrow is the best I can do," he responded testily, perturbed by her steadfast hostility. But his manner softened a little when he detected the exhausted expression that darkened her pretty face, and he continued more calmly, "I just thought you might rest easier tonight if you were reassured that we will be gone when you awaken in the morning."

Erin heaved an impatient sigh at the persistent Yankee and was about to unleash a flurry of angry oaths on the major when Maisie appeared at the door to summon her to supper.

"Tain't much, chile," she sadly informed her mistress. "But ah sposes dey's bettah'n no vittles at all."

"Yes, Maisie. I'll be along directly." Erin waited until the servant had departed before she returned her attention to the Yankee, and her fiery temper had cooled considerably when she said, "Thank you for that bit of good news, Major, but I fear that I shan't *rest easy* until this horrible war has ended and some semblance of order has been restored to my life."

The major accepted her reply, nodding his head in silent agreement, realizing that there was no adequate response he could offer which would ease her mind. Lord knows, we shall all rest easier when the conflict ends, he mused silently. But something the housekeeper had said troubled him greatly yet, when he would have questioned the girl about the matter, he found that she had entered the house. Unthinkingly, he stepped across the porch and opened the door to let himself into the expansive mansion.

"Miss," he began, but Erin spun on him viciously and swiftly retraced the few steps she had taken down the long corridor.

"Sir! You forget yourself." She lashed out at him bitterly. "But then what is one to expect from a mangy, low-life Yankee?"

"Now, hold on!" Kellen had endured quite enough of her spiteful tongue, and he planted his feet firmly and returned her harsh glare in full. "I've suffered just about enough of your foul disposition for one day. My entrance into your home is not an attempt to loot the place. On the contrary, not all of us good-for-nothing Yankees are hell-bent on returning home brandishing the spoils of our victories."

"Victory . . . humph!" Erin spat severely. "It's no great accomplishment to run roughshod over helpless women and children," she scoffed.

"*Helpless!*" the major bellowed, genuinely amused by her statement. "I'd wager that if half the Confederate Army wielded a rifle as courageously as you did today, this skirmish would have ended months ago, and most likely in your favor." Impulsively, he cupped her chin in his hand and tilted her head back, so he could better analyze her face, but her mouth was forever shadowed by an unbecoming frown.

"Will *nothing* serve to lighten your heart and coax a smile upon your lips?" he asked softly.

Erin quickly averted her gaze from the piercing blue eyes that regarded her closely, and she pulled away from the hand that lingered along her cheek. "I have little reason to be joyful, Major, I assure you," came her mumbled response.

"Yes, I can imagine, miss. Uh . . . you know, it's damned awkward trying to carry on a conversation with you when I don't know your name." He paused purposefully, but when it became apparent that she was not going to acknowledge his request, he continued, "Very well, have it your way. Perhaps I should reaffirm my position. As I told you, I am responsible for my men. I'm not like some Union officers who encourage the looting and destruction of private property, nor do I allow them to molest innocent civilians. *I* do not tolerate such behavior from my men, and they well know it.

"I am not a pauper; therefore, I don't find myself in need of appropriating your family treasures. And I seldom find myself wanting for female companionship," he added a little arrogantly, "so *you* are quite safe, I assure you." He ignored the lethal glare she leveled at him and, suddenly recalling the concern that had brought him inside the house, he said, "Now that I've guaranteed your safety for the hundredth time, may I finally suggest the proposal that prompted me to follow you into your home?"

"What?" Erin inquired petulantly, genuinely irritated that she be subjected to such a scolding from a stranger, and a *Yankee* at that.

"Food supplies," he stated simply. "It's apparent that yours are sadly inadequate; just look at how thin you are. You see, I took the liberty of rummaging through your smokehouse. It's obviously been empty for some time, and I'd wager the kitchen pantry is no better. Your housekeeper said as much when she summoned you to supper," he reminded her.

"We get by, Major," she informed him tartly, self-consciously hugging her arms to her slender waist in defense of his comment about her scrawny appearance. "Besides, our situation is really none of your concern. Now, if you will excuse me, my paltry supper *is* waiting."

"Precisely, and if you'd but permit me to finish, I would gladly leave you to it," he informed her shortly. "I was about to offer you some provisions from our supply wagon to augment your pantry."

He noticed the suspicious slant of her eyebrows and hastened to explain, "I've no ulterior motive about me, I swear. It's just my attempt to alleviate your circumstances somewhat. I know that the war has caused you great anguish—"

"Forgive me, Major," Erin interrupted impatiently, "but you cannot sufficiently imagine the hardships we have endured at the hands of you Yankees. Had you known, perhaps you would have left us in peace."

Kellen was growing accustomed to the girl's embittered attitude and, shrugging aside her unwavering coldness, he inquired, "Will you accept my offer?"

Erin stared at the major a full thirty seconds before she formulated her reply, and when she spoke, it was in a direct, straightforward manner; not once did her voice reflect that she was appreciative of the major's generous gesture.

"I may be stubborn, Yankee, but I'm no fool. There are others for whom I am responsible, and I must see to their welfare; therefore, I am forced to accept. But you may well believe that were I the only one involved, I would *starve* before I accepted a Yankee handout," she hissed at him scornfully.

Kellen bristled at her terse words and it took a great deal of self-control to keep his rising temper in check. Indeed, had he known the girl better, he might have been inclined to turn the impudent creature over his knee in an attempt to mellow her offensive disposition. But one could hardly handle a perfect stranger in such a familiar manner, even though the girl's churlish attitude vexed him sorely.

Erin studied the play of emotions that danced across the major's ruggedly handsome face, and a wry, self-satisfied grin quickly spread her lips as she realized that she was getting the better of him.

"You may deliver the goods to the kitchen at your leisure," she instructed him haughtily. "Oh, and be sure to use the *rear* entrance. I fear that the foyer shall have to be thoroughly cleansed if I ever hope to eliminate your foul Yankee stench." She wrinkled her nose distastefully and, turning her back on him, she started to move down the corridor.

Erin had taken no more than two steps, however, when she found her arm clutched angrily in a relentless grip, and she was whirled around to face a red-faced Kellen. She could not restrain the frightened squeak that rose in her throat, and her pounding heart seemed to cease beating altogether when she saw the primitive fury that flashed behind the brilliant blue eyes. In the next instant, Erin was dragged into a bone-crushing embrace and her chin was tilted back, so she could observe those brooding orbs at a more intimate angle.

"You shall pay for that insult, my fiery-tongued vixen," Kellen breathed hoarsely.

"No, Yankee! *Don't!*" Erin gasped brokenly, as she frantically grappled for her freedom.

But her struggles proved to be futile, for Kellen aptly rendered her defenseless by lowering his head and covering her protesting lips with his mouth. His kiss began as a harsh and demanding caress, as though he meant to break her spirit through this exhibition of his superior strength. Yet, as Kellen's mouth lingered against the sweet tasting flesh, the need to punish this ravishing vision was swiftly supplanted by a burning desire to possess her. Accordingly, his kiss grew more persistent, and he pulled her so tightly against him that her breasts were crushed against his chest, and Kellen swore that he could feel her taut nipples through his jacket.

This last thought prompted a tortured groan from Kellen which, in turn, caused Erin to flinch. Consumed with a nagging fear that the Yankee was about to lose himself to his passion, Erin maintained the presence of mind to take advantage of the major's somewhat flustered condition. Bracing her hands against his shoulders, she summoned all her strength and managed to push herself free from the menacing Yankee.

She quickly retreated several steps backward and, with a childish gesture, she wiped the back of her hand across her mouth as if to obliterate any memory of the hated man's caress. While this action provided Erin with immense satisfaction, it merely served to amuse Kellen, and he gave a hearty laugh.

Infuriated by the scoundrel's effrontery, Erin plucked a ceramic figurine from the whatnot table beside her and heaved it at Kellen's insolent head. To her dismay, he effortlessly side-stepped the airborne projectile, and took an ominous step toward her.

"*No!*" Erin screeched at him, her breasts heaving violently. "*Get out!*" she screamed hysterically, clutching at the table for support.

"With pleasure," Kellen replied tersely, doffing his hat to her in a mocking gesture. He turned and strode determinedly toward the door, but he paused on the threshold to deliver a staggering setdown. "By the way, you may well believe that were you indeed the only one residing here, I would happily leave you to starve." Then returning his hat to his head, the major presented his back to her and marched angrily from the house.

Erin slept peacefully for a change. The horrifying nightmare that frequently tormented her showed no signs of disturbing her slumber this night. Instead, the face that haunted her dreams belonged to the Yankee major who had proven to be little more than a thorn in her side the livelong day.

She shifted in her sleep and a disturbing frown suddenly wrinkled her brow. Why must her dreams forever be of Yankees? Her unconsciousness again focused on the figure of Kellen Sinclair. He was standing before her, resplendent in his uniform and, as usual, they were arguing bitterly. But just as Erin was about to attack him with a scathing retort, Kellen clamped a hand over her mouth to forestall her verbal attack. Not to be outdone by the annoying major, Erin struggled to remove the restrictive hand, but somewhere in the drowsy recesses of her mind an intense fear was born as she became suddenly aware that this was no dream.

Her eyes snapped open to reveal Sergeant Taggart leaning over her, his leering face illuminated by the bright moonlight. Instinctively, Erin tried to scream, but it was then she discovered the sergeant's hand securely placed over her mouth to prevent her from summoning assistance.

"Well, hello there, Missy," the man snickered hoarsely. "Bet ya didn't reckon on meetin' up with me agin so soon, now, did ya?"

Erin tried desperately not to let the soldier know how truly frightened she was, but she had been brutalized by Yankees before and that memory tormented her constantly. Dear God, she prayed silently. You cannot mean to let it happen again!

But the lustful expression on the Yankee's face warned Erin that her worst fears were about to be realized.

The sergeant recognized the panic in her eyes and he grunted smugly, "Scared, ain't ya, Missy? I see it in yer eyes. But I seen how ya handled the major today, so's I reckon you'll put up a ruckus once we get on with the sportin'. And that's just fine with me cause I like a spirited lass." His free hand deftly crept along her slender waist, slowly inching along till it captured one firm, quivering breast.

Erin recoiled from the sergeant's intimate caresses that did little more than disgust her, threatening to cause her to become physically ill. But she fervently struggled to remain level-headed and, when the soldier became overcome by his consuming passions, Erin instinctively bit into the hand that had carelessly slipped from her mouth. This brought about immediate results, as the sergeant yelped and jerked away from her to see to the injured appendage.

Erin immediately climbed to her knees in the middle of the bed, and when the sergeant turned on her furiously, she was ready for him. Locking her hands together to form a tight fist, she swung with all her might, catching him squarely in the jaw. The sergeant staggered backwards, visibly shaken by the unexpected blow. It was then that Erin saw her chance to escape, and she scrambled from the bed and darted past the dazed man.

But her actions were not quick enough, for Sergeant Taggart swiftly recovered. With lightning speed, his hand shot

41

out to capture a fistful of Erin's chestnut-brown curls, thereby thwarting her escape. Cruelly, he dragged her back to stand before him, and he mercilessly leveled a blow across her cheek that sent her sprawling to the floor.

"Bitch!" he spat. "I'll teach ya to raise a hand to me." He straddled her, and the cast of the moon caught the foreboding glint of a knife that had somehow appeared in the sergeant's hand.

Erin could not restrain the terrified gasp that escaped her mouth when her eyes beheld the sinister-looking weapon, and it took all the courage she could muster to say firmly, "Get out of here, or I'll scream for the major."

"Go ahead, Missy." The sergeant methodically unclasped the belt buckle at his waist, as he started to remove his restrictive garments. "The major ain't likely to hear ya from here nohow, and yer coloreds done gone to their quarters fer the night."

He had successfully removed his coat and shirt and was now on his knees astride her stomach. "So, go on and holler yer pretty little head off, but I figure you'll be beggin' fer more before it's over."

Erin watched in horror as he brought the point of the wicked knife dangerously close to her cheek, and she strained to move her face away from the blade. She heard his evil chuckle as he ran the dull edge of the weapon along her cheek to her throat till it finally came to rest near the delicate ribbons that tightly secured the opening of her nightdress. In less than an instant, he severed the ribbons with the knife, then hastily gathered the garment in his rough hands and ripped the flimsy material apart to reveal her youthful, naked splendor to his greedy eyes.

Erin began to weep, and as the huge tears of anger and humiliation rolled down her cheeks, she moved her head aside to avoid the sergeant's revolting kisses. But the soldier was not to be denied, and he forced her to submit to his demands.

"So, ya don't care none fer my kisses, Missy." He carelessly allowed the knife to slip from his fingers onto the floor, and he gathered her face between his cruel hands and covered her lips with his.

His kiss was harsh and brutal. It was not meant to convey pleasure, only to seize that which was not freely given.

"The kissin's the best part. Well, next to this." He stood up then, and his hands went to his trousers to release his already stiffened manhood, but his eyes never wavered from Erin's panic-stricken face.

The triumphant leer abruptly vanished from the sergeant's face, however, when he heard the familiar sound of a gun being cocked dangerously close to his left ear. The sergeant did not dare move, not knowing the identity of his would-be assailant, and the blade of his discarded knife caught his eye in the moonlight, taunting him invitingly.

"Go ahead, Taggart." Major Sinclair saw the direction of the soldier's nervous gaze. "I'd welcome a valid excuse to send you to the fiery depths of hell," he whispered hoarsely, his face white with fury.

The sergeant quickly refastened his trousers and cautiously turned to face his commander. "I . . . I'm sorry, Major." He fumbled awkwardly for the words to say. "I didn't realize you'd set yer eyes on the filly. Go ahead, sir, you take her. She's a right feisty gal, I'll give her that." He gingerly fingered his throbbing jaw. He then started to retrieve the clothing that he had hastily discarded, but Kellen suddenly thrust him against the wall and pinned him there.

"It's lucky for you, Taggart, that I happen to need your services until we make the rendezvous and deliver our cargo. I'm uncertain of the opposition we might encounter the next few days, and I need every available man." The major collected the sergeant's shirt and coat and shoved them into Taggart's hands. "Because, were I not in need of your cooperation, I would have put a bullet through your disgusting head the moment I saw you forcing yourself on the young lady."

"She's the *enemy*, Major Sinclair," Taggart offered lamely, struggling back into his shirt. "I had a right —"

Kellen favored the sergeant with a severe look that was meant to silence him. It did.

"No one has a *right* to treat another human being in such a demeaning manner. Besides, I was not commissioned to make war on women," he fairly shouted at the sergeant. "I do not tolerate such behavior from the men in my command, Taggart, and you would do well to commit that to memory. For if you ever dare to defy my orders again," his blue eyes narrowed angrily, and his voice was barely an audible whisper when he delivered the remainder of his stern warning, "I shall horsewhip you to within an inch of your life and cast your worthless hide to the buzzards.

"Lieutenant Petersen!" Kellen abruptly summoned another officer to the room. "Escort Sergeant Taggart back to the campsite. And, Brad, secure him to the wagon to ensure that he doesn't attempt to molest our hostess again."

He waited until the men had vacated the room before turning his attention to Erin. He half-expected to be greeted by a flurry of bitter oaths from her spicy tongue, therefore, he was more than a little surprised by the pitiful picture that greeted his eyes.

She had gathered the shreds of her tattered nightgown about her and crawled to a far corner of the room. There she sat, knees drawn up to her chest, head resting tiredly on her crossed arms, shoulders slumped forward in total defeat. His heart melted a little as he realized how frightening an experience the sergeant's assault must have been for her, and he sought to comfort her.

"Miss," he murmured softly and stepped forward, his hand outstretched to console her.

Erin's head snapped back at the sound of his voice and the major could detect the desperate tears that shone brightly in her wide, green eyes, as well as those that moistened her cheeks. "Don't, Yankee!" she hissed hatefully. "*Don't touch me!* I

44

cannot stand to have Yankee hands paw me." The tears began to slide freely down her distressed cheeks.

For the first time, Kellen noticed that she clutched Sergeant Taggart's knife to her bosom and, fearful that she might harm herself, he attempted to relieve her of the weapon. He inched forward carefully, talking to her in a low, soothing voice, his eyes never wavering from the knife. "Give me the knife, ma'am," he urged gently. "I sent the sergeant away. He won't harm you again."

"The others," Erin mumbled faintly, reaffirming her hold on the weapon.

"No," he quietly reassured her. "I won't let them. I was careless with Taggart, and I'm truly sorry that you suffered by his hand. But I will personally guard your door for the remainder of the night to ensure that you are not further molested. Now, please give me the knife."

Erin stared at the major, her mind a whirligig of confusion. One Yankee had just tried to rape her, to violate her body and strip her of all dignity. Now this one stood before her, offering her his help. What was she to believe? Why should *he* want to offer her kindness; especially considering his own despicable behavior toward her. *Could* this Yankee be trusted? But before Erin could reach a conclusion of her own, Kellen took advantage of her indecision and leaned forward to gently pluck the knife from her hands.

As if totally undone, Erin fell victim to a wave of spasmatic sobs that shook her entire being. She felt so alone. There were no familiar allies to hold and comfort her and ease her troubled mind, and she suddenly yearned for her mother's reassuring embrace; the loving arms that had often enfolded her and kept her safe from harm. She had always felt secure when held in her mother's protective, soothing embrace and, quite involuntarily, she sobbed, "Mother . . . I want my mother."

Kellen removed his coat and considerately wrapped it tightly about Erin's shoulders. He then resisted her meek struggles and lifted her effortlessly in his strong arms and carried her back to the security of her own bed. It was then that he saw the ugly bruise that blemished her otherwise flawless cheek and the dribble of blood that oozed at the corner of her mouth.

"Swine!" he spat thickly, placing her gently upon the crumpled sheets. "I should have the bastard drawn and quartered."

He crossed to the basin and dipped his handkerchief into the cool water and returned to blot the blood from her injured lip. Then he tenderly pressed the compress against Erin's swollen cheek. Kellen sat down on the bed and carefully pulled the coverlets over Erin and, unthinkingly, he brushed the errant strands of hair away from her tear-streaked face. The eyes that regarded him were wide with uncertainty and apprehension, but their anxious cast seemed to dim somewhat when he stood up.

"Hush, little reb," he spoke softly. "Go to sleep now." He clasped her hand for a brief instant. "Don't fret." He correctly interpreted the basis for her worried expression. "I shall not force you to suffer my advances again . . . I promise." He gave her hand a reassuring squeeze, then turned and sauntered from the room.

Chapter Three

Erin awakened early the following morning to the sound of birds chirping outside her window, and brilliant rays of sunshine cascading across her pillow. And, if she was unnerved at finding Major Sinclair standing at the foot of her bed, the most intriguing expression fashioned upon his roguish face, she gave no immediate indication.

"Good morning, little reb," he called her by the pet name he had obviously selected for her.

His attitude was casual, as if he were quite accustomed to addressing young ladies in their bedchambers. The major recognized the dark scowl that instantly shrouded Erin's lovely face, and he quickly stepped forward.

"Please," he threw up his hands to forestall the assault he thought to be imminent, "let me explain my presence in your chamber. Perhaps I can prevent you from assuming such a gloomy disposition, for certainly a comely vision like yourself does not easily succumb to a devilish mood. Unless, of course, she has been provoked by a group of pesky Yankees."

He offered her a genuine smile, and Erin felt her skin raise with prickly gooseflesh as she became acutely aware of his appraising gaze, and she self-consciously pulled the sheet tighter about her chin as he continued, "For you appeared quite angelic just now as you lay sleeping, and I cannot believe that you would condemn me when I have but returned to collect my property."

"What?" she inquired hesitantly, her voice raspy in the cool, morning air.

"My coat," he replied softly, gesturing toward the garment that was nestled comfortably about her shoulders. "I fear you were more in need of its protection last night than was I."

Erin quickly removed the coat and held it out to the major. "Here. Take it," she said shortly, wishing very much that he would take the accursed rag and leave her in peace.

"Forever the stalwart rebel, I see," he chuckled amusedly and slipped into the garment. "Actually, the coat was of minor importance, for my true interest lies in your welfare. How do you feel this morning?"

"How do you *expect* me to feel, Yankee, after being mauled by your man?" she asked coldly.

"Tch, tch," he patiently scolded her. "An *angel* is not apt to be so surly upon first awakening."

"An *angel* most likely would not awaken to find the *devil* loitering about her chamber," she countered.

"Touché," Kellen conceded.

Just when Erin thought he was about to take his leave of her, he boldly stepped forward and sat down on the edge of the bed. His actions were innocent enough, but she was on her guard at any rate. Yet she jumped instinctively when he reached out to finger her injured cheek.

"Looks as if you'll have a little remembrance for a few days." He examined her carefully, then his eyes settled on hers and his next statement was issued in such a solemn manner that Erin knew he sincerely meant every word. "I am truly sorry for what happened last night. I know that an apology cannot erase the memory of those frantic moments, but unfortunately that is all I have to offer. However, I can promise you that Sergeant Taggart will be severely reprimanded once our mission has been completed."

Erin's resolve seemed to dissolve a little, and she sighed,

"It was not your fault, I suppose. Indeed, I should like to thank—" Her voice suddenly trailed off as she caught a movement near the door out of the corner of her eye.

Kellen was understandably puzzled by the startled expression that suddenly adorned Erin's face, especially since he had done nothing to warrant her abrupt behavior. But the unmistakable clicking sound of a hammer being pulled back, rotating a revolver's cartridge into firing position alerted him to the impending danger. Instinctively, his hand flew to his side to retrieve his gun. Only then did he realize that he had left his holster and revolver on the chair outside the door when he entered the chamber.

Kellen half expected that the intruder was a Confederate soldier; perhaps an outrider from a detachment that was canvassing the area. Also, the remote chance that Taggart had broken free of his bonds and had come looking for him fleetingly crossed Kellen's mind. But he was in no way prepared for the image with which he was confronted when he stood and slowly turned to come face-to-face with his would-be assailant.

There before him stood a young woman, perhaps twenty-three or four, clad only in a nightdress, her bare feet planted squarely on the floor. Her black hair was cut in short, uneven layers and lay in wild disarray about her head. She was tiny, just a mite of a thing, but the lethal glare she leveled at him through dark brown eyes unnerved the usually unflappable major.

Upon closer examination of those intense eyes, Kellen thought he detected a glassy, faraway cast that led him to believe the girl to be mentally unbalanced. The seriousness of the situation in which he found himself seemed to be growing bleaker with each passing moment. Kellen's eyes then fell to the barrel of the weapon she purposefully aimed at him, and he was none too surprised to find that the gun was his own.

"Damn fool," he berated himself under his breath.

"Deborah." Kellen heard Erin's voice gently call out to the

49

pathetic-looking girl. "Put the gun down, honey."

But the girl did not respond to Erin's softly spoken command.

"Damned blue-belly!" she cursed loathsomely at Kellen and stretched the gun out in front of her, taking careful aim.

"No!" Erin shrieked. "It's not what you think, Debby. He didn't hurt me."

Deborah seemed reluctant to accept Erin's declaration, and she glanced away from Kellen to focus on Erin uncertainly, as if to say; if the Yankee had not hurt her, then why was he in her room?

Kellen took advantage of the girl's obvious indecision, and he lurched forward in an attempt to extract the weapon from her hands. But Deborah responded quickly to his assault, and the room suddenly reverberated with the thunderous sound of the gun's blast as it discharged, sending Kellen staggering sideways into the chiffonier.

Erin stared at the scene before her in confused disbelief, her mind not willing to accept the amazing turn of events. Then she became like a whirlwind, engaged in a flurry of activities. She darted from the bed and hastily struggled into a dressing gown to cover the shreds of her ruined nightdress. Then she flew to the landing and summoned Maisie and Ruth. Finally, she returned to the room and gently removed the gun from Deborah's trembling hands and seated her on the edge of the bed. At last, she turned to the injured major.

He stood clutching at the chiffonier for support with one hand while the other tested the damage inflicted upon his right thigh. The bullet had exploded like fire upon impact, and he was losing a good deal of blood. Kellen was unsure how much longer he could maintain consciousness, and he bit into his lower lip to keep from screaming at the agonizing pain.

Erin jerked the sheet from the bed and hurried to his side. Gently, she helped him to a sitting position on the floor, resting his head against the chiffonier for support. One glance at the leg was enough to warn her that the wound was serious, and she realized that the bleeding would have to be stopped quickly, or he could die.

By this time, Maisie and Ruth had arrived in the room, and dogging their tracks were two of the major's men who had been alerted by the gunblast. Erin did not once look up from her task as she ripped the sheet into bandage strips and began winding one around the major's wounded leg. Instead, she shouted out orders as she worked.

"Ruth, send Paulie for Doc Wilson. Tell him to fly like the wind and not to dally, or I'll tan the backside of his britches so he won't be able to sit for a week.

"Maisie, return Debby to her room and stay with her until I can come to her. Don't leave her alone for any reason," she added firmly.

"Yas'm." The servant obediently took Deborah by the arm and guided her toward the door.

"And you two," Erin stood up suddenly and, placing her hands on her slender waist, she turned to the soldiers, "pick up the major and follow me."

"Carefully," she cautioned when she witnessed the pain-filled grimace that appeared on Kellen's distressed face when the soldiers hoisted him into their arms. "This way." She stepped through a side door to the connecting chamber and, whisking the coverlets aside in a single motion, she instructed the men to lay the major on the chamber's massive fourposter.

But when she started forward to check on Kellen's condition, one of the soldiers seized her roughly by the arm and spun her away from the bed.

"Looks as if you've done enough already, little lady. We'll see to the major until the doctor arrives," the one wearing lieutenant's stripes addressed her coarsely. "And you better pray that he gets here quickly because, if Major Sinclair dies, we'll bring this fancy palace down around your head so fast it will spin," he delivered his threat exactly, then released her and stepped to the bed.

51

"Don't, Brad," Kellen managed painfully. "Don't blame her. It was the other one."

"Other one?" Lieutenant Bradley Petersen repeated vaguely.

"Deborah," Erin offered faintly.

Completely disregarding the lieutenant's stern glance, she pushed him aside and sat down on the bed to get a better look at Kellen's injury. The bleeding had subsided for the most part; only a little trickled near the opening where the bullet had penetrated the leg. She emitted a low sigh of relief, for at least the major was out of immediate danger. She removed the blood-soaked bandage that she had placed about the leg only moments before and replaced it with a fresh dressing.

Kellen was genuinely surprised at her attentiveness and, when Erin noticed his curious perusal, she hastened to account for her actions. "Don't misinterpret my conduct as concern for your worthless hide, Yankee. I owe you a favor from last night is all, and I'll not have you die here at Kilkieran and give your friends an excuse to wreck the place and . . . and, well, Lord only knows what else." Her voice trembled a little as she realized for the first time the full implication of the delicate situation.

Major Sinclair had been the one controlling factor during the Yankees' brief occupation of Kilkieran. Only the sergeant had dared to oppose the major, and he had suffered his commander's wrath. The Yankee evidently maintained strict discipline over his men and had justly earned their respect and loyalty. What would their reaction be if Major Sinclair died? What sort of revenge might they perpetrate against Kilkieran and its inhabitants?

Kellen's perceptive eyes recognized the distressed slant of her brow, and he took her hand in his to reassure her. "Don't worry, little reb, I'm too stubborn to let a Rebel bullet keep me idle for long."

"It was a *Yankee* bullet that did this." She snatched her hand away. "And from your own gun no less. Oh, how could you have been so careless? Now look what you've caused." She stood up and shook a stern finger at him as she delivered her next statement, making it sound very much like a command. "Don't you dare die here, Yankee! I could care less what happens to your mangy hide once you have left Kilkieran, but don't you go dying here and make trouble for me and mine." She stamped her foot angrily and scurried to the window to watch for the doctor.

"Kellen, what the devil happened anyway?" The lieutenant had overheard their conversation and his curiosity grew more intense with each word that passed between them. "Who is this Deborah, and why would she assault you? And what's this about being shot with your own weapon? How can that be?" He looked to the major for an answer, but it was not Kellen who responded.

"Because he is a simple-minded blue-belly, and he thoughtlessly left his weapon unattended," Erin snapped at them tersely.

"Believe me, miss, had I known there was another female about who entertained your particular penchant for firearms, I would have joyfully left the pistol strapped to my leg when I came to inquire about your welfare," Kellen addressed her curtly, quite obviously put out with her continued ill-humor.

After all, *he* had been the recipient of the attack and now lay bleeding, possibly dying, in a stranger's bed. He had been a fool to try to set things right this morning; there was just no reasoning with the girl. And for the little imp to behave as if he had arranged to be shot just to inconvenience her, well, the whole situation was utterly ludicrous. He shifted a little, forgetting about his leg, but the sudden movement brought an agonizing moan from his lips. The pain in his thigh throbbed unmercifully, making it exceedingly difficult to concentrate on anything else. But he feared that if he gave in to the relentless ache, he might lose consciousness, and he wanted to remain alert until the doctor arrived.

"It was all an unfortunate misunderstanding, Brad," Kellen

went on to explain. "The one called Deborah happened upon us and, thinking I had *compromised* little reb here, she opened fire."

"I see, Kellen. And does the major wish to prescribe some form of suitable punishment?" With his back to Erin, she did not see the playful wink the lieutenant offered Kellen.

"*No!*" Erin shrieked.

Kellen directed a severe look at Erin which plainly said he would not tolerate her interference. Then he spoke to the lieutenant, "No, Brad. It *was* my fault. I should never have left the gun unattended.

"But if that one," he leveled a foreboding finger at Erin, "calls me a blue-belly one more time, you have my permission to soundly wallop her cantankerous backside." And any reply that Erin might have made to this blatant threat was preempted by the arrival of Doctor Wilson.

Erin and the two soldiers stood aside while the doctor examined Kellen. Doctor Allan Wilson had been very surprised to learn that his patient was an officer of the Union Army, and more so, that Deborah had been his assailant. But there would be time enough for explanations, he reasoned, turning his immediate attention to the wounded leg.

"Ah, just as I thought," the crusty, old doctor grunted and, returning his medical instruments to his leather bag, he stood up. "The bullet penetrated the bone. It appears to have shattered upon impact, for there are a number of bone fragments imbedded in the neighboring tissues." He removed his spectacles and began to polish the smudged lenses with the edge of his coattail. "I won't sugarcoat it for you, Major, you've got yourself a very nasty injury."

"I suspected as much," Kellen informed him calmly. "Where do we go from here?"

"Well, there are three options, really. I can remove the larger pieces without administering an anesthetic, then sew up the wound and allow it to mend by itself. However, the leg will likely be a menace to you for the rest of your life; it will severely hamper your mobility and cause you a great deal of discomfort. You'll most likely develop a visible limp and probably require the use of a cane." The doctor safely anchored his spectacles over each ear before continuing with his explanation. "Or, it's my considered medical opinion that we proceed with the one option that will be the safest and ultimately cause you the least discomfort."

"And that is?"

"Amputate," the doctor said simply, watching the major closely for his reaction.

"*Amputate?!* Bah!" came Kellen's thunderous reply. "Leave it to this imp to summon a butcher to care for my wound," he fairly shouted, pointing an accusing finger at Erin. "Let's strike a bargain, shall we, Doctor? You keep your *considered* medical opinions to yourself, and I'll keep my leg, thank you. Besides, you'll quickly discover that it will take a good deal more than a Rebel bullet to do *me* in." He puffed up indignantly, folding his arms across his chest; unsuccessfully masking the sharp pain his outburst had ignited.

"*Yankee* bullet," Erin patiently reminded him again as she moved from the window and took a seat on the edge of the bed. "Calm down, Yankee," she cautioned reproachfully as she casually examined his leg to see if the abrupt movement had caused the wound to seep again. Satisfied that everything was all right, she said encouragingly, "After all, Doc Wilson did say there were three options to be considered, and we've heard but two."

"Yes," Kellen readily agreed. "Tell me, Doctor, what other charlatan notions have you tucked away in your little black bag?"

The expression that Kellen offered the doctor was venomous, but Doc Wilson ignored the snidely phrased question as he continued, "Naturally, the most logical recourse is to operate to remove the bullet and bone fragments, but . . ."

"Capital notion!" Kellen interrupted, his voice richly laced with sarcasm. "At last we concur."

"*But*," Doc Wilson repeated purposefully, giving his patient a silencing look, "that would require an anesthetic; ether or chloroform, and those precious items are hard to come by these days."

"But can't we give him liquor, or . . . or *something* to deaden the pain long enough to remove the bullet?" The question was aired by Erin who was growing increasingly uneasy at the prospect of having the Yankee remain a house guest any longer than was absolutely necessary. For certainly the major would be bedridden for some time to come if the leg had to be removed.

"No, Erin," the doctor answered her kindly. "It's a very serious injury. And though the major looks to be a strong healthy, young fella, I seriously doubt that even he could withstand the tremendous pain such a procedure would create.

"That's why I suggested amputation, lad." The doctor turned to address Kellen. "I'm not a butcher. I was only trying to spare you some agony. Can't say as I blame you though. I'd fight tooth and nail if a stranger told me he wanted to cut off my leg, especially if that man was considered to be the *enemy*. But the devil of it is, son, if I attempt the surgery and, for some reason, begin to lose you, I'll sacrifice the leg to save your life."

"That won't be necessary." Lieutenant Petersen, who had remained silent throughout the exchange, joined the conversation. "We have a wagon load of medical supplies at your disposal, Doctor."

"No, Brad," Kellen said sternly. "Those are meant for others more unfortunate than I."

"Forgive my bluntness, my good friend, but you look pretty unfortunate at the present. Besides, you're a Union soldier, and that entitles you to make use of the supplies as well," the lieutenant said grimly.

"Come with me, Doctor, and select the things you'll be needing." He and the private escorted the doctor from the room, closing the door on Kellen's protests to the contrary.

"So, it's Erin, is it?" Kellen said softly when they were alone.

"What?" she murmured low, still dazed by the morning's disastrous occurrence.

"Your name. Faith, I was beginning to doubt that you had one, and was prepared to give you one of my own choosing. But Erin suits you; what with your flaming green eyes and the reddish cast of your hair." He considered her thoughtfully. "You're of Irish descent, are you not?"

Erin nodded.

"I guessed as much. Now I can better understand your stubborn, argumentative, and all-round unsociable disposition." He could not restrain the chortle that escaped him as he observed her face grow scarlet with fury.

But Erin let the jibe pass, for she was more intrigued by the lieutenant's announcement concerning the mysterious wagon's cargo, and her natural curiosity compelled her to go to the window. With her back to the major, he did not observe the confused pout that crinkled her face as she watched the soldiers who stood guard over the wagon.

"Humph!" she finally grunted. "Your men seem mighty protective of a bunch of silly, old medicines," she muttered indifferently, turning slowly from the window.

"What?" Kellen tried to camouflage his surprise, but her statement had caused him some concern.

Was it possible that the girl had discovered the true reason for their mission? Not that she would be any the wiser at the implication of such a discovery, but even a causal slip of the tongue to the wrong people could prove to be disastrous at this crucial point. He had to know how much she knew.

"What did you mean by that?" he persisted.

"I simply meant that you Yankees are a peculiar lot. What with the careful way in which your men treated the crates when they unloaded the wagon yesterday, I just expected it to contain something more precious that *medical* supplies is all." She shrugged her shoulders carelessly.

"But these *are* precious, my dear." Doc Wilson had reentered the room in time to overhear her last declaration. "And I'd wager that many of my colleagues who are situated closer to the actual fighting would sell their souls to have access to the wealth of medicines parked outside."

Kellen breathed an intense sigh of relief as the doctor's explanation apparently satisfied the inquisitive girl, and he folded his arms behind his head and relaxed against the pillow while he awaited the doctor's next statement.

"Change quickly, Erin. I'm going to need you," he instructed the bewildered girl.

"But . . ." she started to protest, but the doctor waved aside her objections.

"I've instructed the major's men to set up a table in this chamber. It will be better if I operate here, so we don't have to move him far afterwards," he explained as he went about preparing his instruments. "Have Maisie bring fresh water, so I can wash up. Oh, and we'll be needing plenty of bandages."

"I can do that," Erin offered eagerly, not sure that she was strong enough to witness the actual surgery. "Maisie is with Deborah and—"

"I'll give Deborah a mild sedative." He took her by the hand and led her to the door. "Now hurry; the surgery will likely take a while, and I want to get started while the sun is with us."

Erin ran from the room and hastily donned a modest gown, then went to instruct Maisie to carry out the doctor's request for fresh water and bandages. She likewise made certain that Deborah was comfortable before returning to assist the doctor.

When she entered the room, she discovered that the major's men had set up the make-shift operating table and Doc Wilson was preparing to begin the surgery. Kellen's clothing had been removed, and he lay in peaceful repose on the hard table, a clean sheet draped over him, and an apprehensive look adorned his face as he carefully studied the doctor who was preparing to cut into his leg.

"Nervous, aren't you, Yankee?" Erin could not resist the temptation to harass the major.

"No more than you would be were our positions reversed," he countered.

"Don't worry, Yankee, Doc Wilson is the best," she assured him a little more kindly.

"She's a mite prejudiced, Major, seeing as how I saw that Erin and her four brothers were safely brought into this world," the doctor joined them, "but I promise you that I'll do my level best to save your leg.

"Now, Erin," he directed his remaining comments to her. "Take this cloth and place it just so." He held the folded cloth over Kellen's nose to demonstrate how the procedure should be carried out. "Then shake a few drops of the ether onto the cloth until he becomes more relaxed and his breathing is regular." Doc Wilson moved to the side of the table and lifted the sheet to reveal the ghastly looking wound. "Go ahead." He nodded toward Erin.

Erin started to follow the doctor's instructions, but Kellen's hand on her arm stayed her movement. "I suppose this means I owe you another twenty-dollar gold piece." He offered her a wan smile, but Erin quickly administered the anesthetic, prohibiting any further comment from the Yankee.

From the looks of things, she sighed to herself dismally, his stay was going to be quite an extended one. And Erin seriously doubted that any monetary reimbursement the major might be willing to pay would be worth the aggravation his presence at Kilkieran would create.

"Twenty dollars, indeed," she muttered forlornly, then devoted her attention to the doctor and the surgery that was taking place.

Chapter Four

Erin sat in a chair beside the window in Kellen's room, numbly staring out into the abysmal darkness. The operation had been successfully completed several hours earlier, but still the patient slept. She shook her head a little to clear it of her jumbled ruminations, then her gaze fell on the major who lay unconscious upon her parents' bed.

"What you must be thinking of me now, Papa," she mumbled morosely, and her eyes glanced fleetingly toward the star-speckled heavens before returning to their original target.

"Is . . . is that you, little reb?" Kellen's voice called to her weakly in the darkness.

The sudden utterance startled Erin for an instant, but she quickly recovered her equanimity and stepped from the shadows to be illuminated by the soft glow of the bedside lamp. "Yes, Yankee. I'm here," she whispered faintly.

"Well, I never thought to see . . ." Kellen began lightly, but he suddenly became overwhelmed by a violent wave of nausea, and he lurched upward in the bed coughing uncontrollably.

"Here." Erin hurried forward and extended a small basin to Kellen and helped support him until the retching subsided. Then she eased him back against the pillows and set the basin aside before turning to witness the expression of acute embarrassment that crossed Kellen's handsome face.

"Forgive me—"

"There is really no need to apologize, Yan . . . uh . . . Major," she corrected herself, deciding there was no need to intimidate him in his weakened condition. Besides, she no longer derived pleasure from their bantering; she only longed for his rapid recovery, so that he could rejoin his comrades. "Doc Wilson warned that this might happen. It's a side effect from the ether," she explained, bending down to rearrange his pillows in a more comfortable position. "How do you feel?" she inquired considerately.

Kellen's face came alive with expression as if at that very instant he fully remembered the incident that had rendered him into his present condition, and his hand flew to his leg. Satisfied that everything was as it should be, he breathed a sigh of relief and relaxed once more against the pillows.

"I'm feeling much better *now*," he freely admitted.

"Doc Wilson is a competent surgeon, Major Sinclair. He worked diligently to save both your leg and your life."

"I find myself indebted to the good doctor."

"As well you should," Erin informed him tartly. "And you owe him an apology as well for all the abusive things you said prior to the surgery."

"Yes," Kellen agreed. "I *was* hasty in my judgment. Perhaps I can persuade you to extend my sincerest apologies to the doctor, for I'll no doubt be leaving with my men when the sun rises."

Erin grew suddenly somber and, taking care to avoid disturbing the injured leg, she sat down upon the edge of the bed. "No, you won't," she murmured softly.

"*What?* Of course, I will. My mèn can make a space for me in the wagon—" He looked up to observe the negative shake of Erin's head and demanded roughly, "Damn it, girl, who are you to say what I may or may not do?"

"At the present, I am your nurse and hostess, albeit I am reluctant to assume either responsibility," she assured him.

"You cannot be moved right now, especially in a rickety old wagon. It would only serve to undo all of Doc Wilson's fine work, and you would most likely bleed to death," she explained patiently.

"But, when?"

Erin shrugged her shoulders uncertainly. "Doc Wilson said your recuperation could take several days, perhaps weeks."

"Impossible!" he thundered. "I have a mission to complete. My men cannot lounge about while I pamper this scratch." He impatiently indicated his bandaged leg.

"Your injury is a serious one," she reminded him. "Further argument is for naught, for your men have already departed. After your lieutenant determined that you were going to recover, yet be incapacitated for some time, he decided to carry out your assignment."

"*What?!*"

"Settle down," she cautioned him. "It's no surprise, really. You would have been more of a hindrance than an asset in your present condition. The lieutenant left you a rather lengthy message." She stretched tiredly, unsuccessfully trying to smother a sleepy yawn. "I'll bring it to you in the morning. Right now, you need to get some rest."

"So do you," he said softly. "What time is it?"

"One o'clock, or two. I'm not certain." She stood up and started to move toward the connecting chamber. "I'll explain everything tomorrow, and Doc Wilson said he would drop by to check on your progress. I'm just in the adjoining chamber should you require anything."

"But . . ." he began.

"No. Whatever it is can keep till morning." Erin gently chastised him, then she stepped through the doorway, leaving Kellen to ponder the circumstances in which he currently found himself.

Erin sighed languidly from her sanctuary, nestled beneath

the clean smelling sheets, and she stirred a little, her eyes flickering open to greet the bright sunshine that illuminated the spacious room. She yawned and stretched sleepily, then rolled over to snuggle her pillow against her, and it was then that she discovered she was not alone.

"'Bout time you wuz wakin' up, chile." The warm smile that Maisie bestowed upon Erin belied the sternness of the accusation.

"Please, don't scold me, Maisie. I had such a dreadful day yesterday, and I'm so very, very tired." She burrowed further down under the coverlets and cradled the pillow to her bosom.

"Ah knows dat, honey-chile," Maisie replied considerately. "Dat's why ah brung yore breakfas' ter you hyah, sose you can rest a spell longah."

She waited while Erin assumed a more comfortable position. Then Maisie plumped up the pillows behind Erin's back and placed the breakfast tray across her lap.

"Oohh, Maisie, this smells scrumptious." Erin lifted the cover and savored the delicious, hickory-smoked aroma of the thick slice of ham that tantalized her from the plate.

"Since we ain' got no buttah, ah fixed some gravy from de drippins' sose you could sop yore biscuits in it. An' dat dere's *real* coffee, not de chick'ry you iz used ter lately. Yep, dem Yankees done cauzed a pack o' trouble, Miz Erin, but it done turned out ter be a blessin' in disguise, coz dey done left plenny o' vittles ter makes sho dat de maj'r gets fed propah." As she spoke, Maisie fiddled about the room, straightening bottles on the dressing table, and dusting an already spotless table top.

Erin had just taken a bite of the succulent ham, and she chewed the morsel slowly, thoughtfully contemplating Maisie's statement. "Just how is our Yankee houseguest this morning?" she finally queried. "I didn't hear a sound from him the entire night."

"Well as can be 'spected, ah spose. De doctah iz wid him now. But doan worry none 'bout dat, honey-chile. You jus' eats yore breakfas'; dey'll be plenny of time ter check in on de maj'r. He ain' gwine nowheres."

"That's for sure," Erin muttered dismally, then shrugged her weary shoulders and continued with her meal.

The dirty dishes had been cleared from the room, and Erin had washed and donned a fresh gown before she made her way to Kellen's chamber. She half-expected to be chastised by Doc Wilson for having left his patient unattended for so long, but she was genuinely surprised to discover that Kellen was alone in the room.

"Good morning." She forced an airy lilt into her voice once she ascertained that Kellen was awake.

"Good morning," he returned the greeting.

"Maisie said that Doc Wilson was here. I am sorry that I missed him." She stepped to the window and pulled the draperies apart to allow the bright sunshine to fill the dreary sickroom. "Is he satisfied with your progress?"

"I suppose, but he seemed to be concerned about the possibility of infection," he explained casually. "I guess it is too soon to tell."

Erin crossed to the bed and pulled the sheet aside to get a better look at the bandaged wound. "Did he leave any instructions for me?" She grimaced a little as she observed the red, swollen area around the dressing.

"Just to keep fresh bandages on the wound," Kellen offered. "He'll be dropping by from time to time to check on things, but he did not wish to disturb you this morning, considering the *eventful* day you suffered yesterday."

Kellen pensively studied the ragged expression that adorned her pretty face, and he found himself suddenly consumed with a longing to enfold this fragile creature in his arms and kiss away the lines of fatigue that haunted her beautiful eyes. The enticing notion vanished upon its conception; however, for Kellen knew that the proud girl would not welcome his solace. Yet he realized that his presence in her home must be placing a tremendous strain on her nerves.

Therefore, it was genuine concern for her welfare that prompted him to inquire, "How are *you* feeling this morning?"

"Rested," she stated simply and set about rearranging the bedclothes into a more comfortable position for him. "Have you an appetite this morning?"

"No, not really."

Erin stood up from her task and glanced about the room, looking for something with which she could occupy her hands. She had been very much aware of Kellen's lengthy perusal; had felt herself grow inexplicably breathless as the intense blue eyes had caressed her. Consequently, she now felt ill-at-ease with the major, and she believed that an activity would help alleviate the tension. But the room was spotless and, finding nothing that required her immediate attention, she again turned to Kellen.

"Are you certain that there is nothing I can get you? Coffee, perhaps?" she suggested.

"No, nothing," he assured her.

"Then I suppose I should see about changing this soiled bandage." She started to move away from the bed, but Kellen reached out to take her hand, and he gently pulled her down on the bed beside him.

"Erin," he began softly. "I realize how awkward this must be for you. I'm certain it must be tedious to care for any bedridden patient, but an officer of the Union Army is sure to be an intolerable ordeal for you. And," he sighed deeply, "I know the risk that you're taking must prey on your mind constantly, but—"

"Risk?" Erin interrupted. "What risk?" The puzzled look she offered Kellen truly surprised him.

"Surely, you must realize that this," with a sweeping gesture he indicated himself and the bed in which he lay, "constitutes aiding and abetting the enemy. If a patrol of Confederate troops should happen upon me, or one of your neighbors learns that I am here and notifies the proper authorities, you could be accused of treason," he patiently explained the graveness of the situation.

"*No!*" she cried. "I'm not a traitor!"

"Not in your heart, little reb, but you would be hard pressed to explain my presence were I to be discovered by someone who did not fully understand the circumstances," he pointed out. "Therefore, it's imperative that as few people as possible know about me."

"Yes, I see." Erin thoughtfully considered all that Kellen had said. "Doc Wilson is the only one away from Kilkieran who knows about you."

"And it's unlikely that he would say anything since he was charitable enough to save my life," Kellen murmured speculatively.

"No," Erin agreed, biting her lower lip pensively. "And he would not wish to do me harm. But I need to caution Maisie and the others."

The sound of thudding hooves along the front drive alerted her to the arrival of visitors, and she scurried to the window to determine the identity of the callers.

"Oh, bother!" she sighed in complete exasperation.

"What is it?" Kellen raised himself on one elbow to enable him a clearer view of her beleaguered face. "My gun. Where is it?" he asked anxiously.

"There's no need for that," Erin assured him as she turned from the window. "It's only my cousin, Christina, and her friend, Jennifer. And, while both of them can ofttimes prove to be enormous trials, I hardly think that warrants violence." She offered him a slight smile.

Kellen relaxed again, relieved to know that there was no immediate danger.

"I'd better see what they want." She crossed to the door. "Get some rest, Yankee. I'll come back after they leave and see to your wound," she promised, then exited the room before Kellen could make a reply.

Erin scampered down the wide, hand-carved mahogany

staircase and intercepted Maisie in the main hallway as she was about to admit the visitors to the mansion. Motioning the servant away from the door, she cautioned, "Not a peep about our houseguest, you hear?" She then paused to smooth the folds of her gown and, after checking her coiffure in the hall mirror, she opened the door and greeted the arrivals with a dazzling smile.

"My, what a pleasant surprise," she announced in her cheeriest voice. "Good morning, Christina, Jennifer." She welcomed each girl cordially and escorted them to the sitting room and saw that they were comfortably seated on the sofa. "May I offer you some refreshment?" she inquired graciously. "I fear that our pantry is dreadfully inadequate these days, but I'm certain that Maisie could prepare some sort of treat."

"Thank you, Erin, but gracious, no. I simply couldn't eat a single bite." The words came tumbling from Christina's lips in such rapid-fire succession that the unfamiliar listener would have been quite bewildered by the young girl's manner, but Erin was accustomed to her cousin's ways and accepted her accordingly.

Erin dismissed Maisie and positioned herself in an upholstered armchair opposite the duo. "Well, what brings the two of you to Kilkieran this morning? Is this not the day you usually assist the Widow Breckinridge with the orphans?"

"Oh, yes, yes," Christina replied hurriedly. "We're on our way there now, in fact." She leaned forward in her chair and glanced about the room as if she feared her next statement might be overheard and, in a hushed voice, she said, "But we just *had* to know if it was true."

"You had to know if *what* was true, Christina?" Erin asked slowly, regarding her cousin with a cautious frown.

But it was Jennifer who impatiently blurted out, "About the Yankees, Erin. Is it true that Yankees ransacked Kilkieran again?"

Erin tensed a little, but as she relaxed her rigid spine against the back of her chair, she carefully scrutinized the two faces that eagerly awaited her response. The two girls were as different as night and day in appearance.

Christina was tall and slender; a strawberry blonde with bright blue eyes that had captivated many a beau. She had a winning personality, and it had been said that she could charm the honey from the bee. Consequently, few people were strangers to Christina.

Jennifer, on the other hand, was short and plump; not fat, but her weight was a constant dilemma for her. Her eyes and hair were a deep brown and, unlike Christina, she was almost painfully shy. Therefore, it was often awkward for her to make new acquaintances.

Actually, the two complemented each other quite nicely. Christina would guide Jennifer through nervous introductions and, likewise, Jennifer would rush to her friend's rescue when Christina's harmless flirtations would draw undue advances from one of her many beaux.

The two girls had been fast friends for as long as Erin could recall. In fact, all three of the girls had been constant companions for years, but since the outbreak of the war, Erin had felt herself drifting further and further away, and the bonds of friendship had weakened considerably. Consequently, Erin was undecided as to how many of the events of the preceding two days she should recount to her curious friends.

She studied the girls for several seconds, and it was obvious that she had weighed her response carefully before saying, "No, Yankees did not *ransack* Kilkieran."

"But Amanda Hilliard said—" Christina began.

"Amanda Hilliard is a foolish old toad," Erin snapped impatiently.

"But she *saw* them on the road to Kilkieran," Jennifer insisted.

"I don't doubt that." Erin's tone was rich with sarcasm. "Amanda has the uncanny ability of minding everyone's business except her own." Her disapproval of the local busybody was apparent in the agitated tone of her voice.

"If you *must* know, girls, a detachment of Yankees did pass by here two days ago. They had some sort of trouble with their wagon and, unfortunately, Kilkieran was convenient for them to make repairs. They departed yesterday morning," she said simply and gestured as if to say the experience had been quite mundane; nothing out of the ordinary.

"But Amanda was at Doc Wilson's yesterday morning—another one of her flare-ups, don't you see—when your boy, Paulie, dragged him over here for some sort of emergency," Christina persisted. "I'll swan, Erin, *something* happened here, and it's positively mean of you to behave like such a goose. After all, I *am* family; there's no need to be so closemouthed." Christina's mouth dropped into a petulant frown, and her dissatisfaction at not being included in the secret was apparent on her face.

Erin again scanned the faces of the two girls and, with a sinking heart, she realized that she would have to offer them some plausible explanation if she were to rid herself of the inquisitive pair. Then, without giving the matter excessive consideration, the ideal solution sprang to mind.

"Oh, *that*," she droned indifferently. "It's nothing noteworthy, I assure you. One of the soldiers suffered a minor injury when his gun discharged while he was cleaning it." Erin absently toyed with a lace doily that decorated the triangular-shaped table at her side.

With a casual glance, she looked toward her visitors to see if they had accepted her account of the incident, and, from the disillusioned expressions that shrouded the faces that returned her stare, she surmised that they had.

Erin swallowed the titter that threatened to escape her lips and, with a forced air of nonchalance, she continued, "I had quite forgotten the entire episode."

"That's *all!*" Jennifer huffed sourly. "You mean to tell us that you summoned Doc Wilson over here to mollycoddle some dirty ol' Yankee!" She turned up her pug nose in obvious distaste. "What a waste of time," she sighed disconsolately.

"Precisely," Christina concurred with her friend's apt appraisal of the situation as she stood to leave. "Thank you for your hospitality, Erin, but we really should be going."

"We mustn't keep Mrs. Breckinridge's darlings waiting any longer," Jennifer explained politely, standing beside Christina, and the two girls started to move toward the sitting room door.

"We've dallied long enough as it is," Christina added and turned to offer her cousin a parting smile, but the expression she discovered on Erin's attractive face was far from amicable.

Erin had stood up with the girls to escort them from the house, and she had endeavored to dismiss their insensitive chatter for the most part. But this blasé, almost *disappointed* attitude at not having discovered Kilkieran in ruins infuriated Erin, and she found that she could not hold her tongue.

"I'm truly sorry to disappoint you, Christina. It would seem that you had hoped to find Kilkieran pillaged and burned, and its residents raped and slaughtered." They had arrived at the main entrance, and Erin pulled the barrier open in one, swift motion.

"Don't be such a goose, Erin," Christina chastised her cousin, and she appeared genuinely affronted that Erin would misconstrue the meaning for their visit. "It's just that it's so frightfully dull with the menfolk away. And the chance that *something* exciting might be happening in this dreary place," she stepped across the threshold, "well, I just *had* to be a part of it."

"I'm sorry if I offended you, either of you," Erin quickly apologized for her terse behavior. "But even though the Yankees did not cause trouble this time, their brief occupation of Kilkieran did prove to be an unsettling experience for me."

"I'm sure," Christina barely acknowledged Erin's apology, for her feelings had been bruised, and she would not likely let Erin forget her rude conduct for some time to come. "But you

70

needn't unleash your hostilities on us. Good day, cousin." She turned her back on Erin and stiffly made her way to the post where she had tethered her mount.

Erin emitted a long, dismal sigh as she watched her cousin's hasty retreat. She had not meant to behave badly, but Christina and Jennifer had provoked the chilling reception with their incessant questions.

Oh, well, she thought to herself wearily, I'll ride over to Briar Cliff in a day or two and try to make amends.

"Don't fret over Christina." Jennifer's soft voice penetrated Erin's troubled musings. "You know how fickle she is. She'll have forgotten the entire episode by tomorrow and come running over to fill you in on the latest gossip." She gave Erin's arm an affectionate pat and stepped from the porch.

"I *am* sorry that I snapped at you," Erin again apologized.

"Don't give it a second thought." Jennifer offered her a sincere smile. "It was beastly of us to have forgotten what a terrifying ordeal it must have been for you to have Yankees invade Kilkieran again. Take care, dear, and do come for a visit when you get a chance," Jennifer encouraged before she went to join Christina by the horses.

Erin slowly closed the door and, with a downhearted sigh, she turned to rest her shoulders against the sturdy barrier. Her eyes instinctively fell upon the staircase that led to the upper regions of the stately mansion, and her thoughts irrevocably returned to the Yankee who lay helpless in her parents' bed. As if drawn by some sense of duty, she mechanically made her way to the stairs, but as she started her ascent, Erin suddenly realized that she was not ready to face the major so soon after her confrontation with Christina. Instead, she turned and made her way to the kitchen for a cold glass of milk, and some cheerful conversation with Maisie.

Outside the expansive mansion, Christina angrily jerked the reins of her mount from the tethering post and led the animal toward a tree stump beside the house where she prepared to mount the mare. "I do declare, Jennifer, but that cousin of mine can be such a ninnyhammer."

"You don't mean that, Christina Richards, and you know it," Jennifer softly scolded her friend. "Come along. Mrs. Breckinridge is sure to be wondering where we've gotten to."

Christina started to climb upon her horse, but a sudden movement among the shadows of the oak trees caught her eye, causing her to pause. Upon closer investigation, she discovered that Deborah was running in and out of the shade of the gigantic trees, almost as if she were a child playing some sort of game.

"Of course," she murmured beneath her breath; Deborah would know what had occurred with the Yankees. And Christina was thoroughly convinced that she could extract the details from the girl with minimal effort.

"Christina," Jennifer firmly prodded. "We've got to be going."

"Then go on without me," she replied testily. "I haven't chatted with Deborah in ages."

"*Christina*," Jennifer said disapprovingly. "You're up to no good, aren't you?"

"Don't be such a ninny. You're beginning to sound very much like my dowdy cousin, Jennifer, and I don't like that one bit," she severely censured the girl. "Poor Deborah hasn't been right—you know; in the head—ever since the Yankees pillaged Kilkieran, and Graham went off to war. Why, it would be downright unneighborly of me if I didn't at least inquire about her welfare. You run along, Jennifer." She shooed her friend away with a pointed gesture. "I'll only be a few moments." She observed as Jennifer spurred her mount away from the house and across the rolling lawn, then she approached Deborah.

"Deborah," she called sweetly to the girl who still played among the shadows, and she was somewhat taken aback by the frightened face that whirled to greet her.

"Don't be afraid, honey," Christina cooed in her most appealing voice. "You remember me, don't you, Deborah?" But Christina could tell by the blank expression in Deborah's eyes that her face did not register in the girl's memory. "I'm Christina; Graham's cousin," Christina explained patiently as though she were talking to a small child.

"Graham?" Deborah repeated vaguely.

"Yes, your *husband*," Christina said the word distinctively, trying to spark some recognition in the girl's feeble mind.

"Hus . . . band?" The thumb of one hand instinctively found its way to her mouth, and she chewed thoughtfully on the nail as she mentally struggled to recall a husband, whatever that was, named Graham. Then as suddenly as the contemplative mood swept over her, it vanished, and she again submerged into a childlike behavior.

"Would you like to play with me?" she asked shyly.

"Perhaps." Christina humored her. "What game are you playing?"

"I'm killing Yankees," Deborah replied excitedly.

"You are! What on earth for?"

"'Cause they're no good critters, and I hate them!" She favored Christina with a reproachful stare; didn't *everyone* hate Yankees? "I almost killed one yesterday, too, but Erin stopped me."

"*She did?*" Christina leaned forward, her interest obviously piqued with this piece of information, but she could not yet determine how much of the tale was factual and how much was make-believe. But she resolved to play along with the girl until she could make a rational judgment.

"Uh huh. Don't ask me why, but she did. Even had Doc Wilson come and fix up his busted leg. She's probably up there with him now, pampering him, and him a no-account *blue-belly*," she spat the word bitterly as though it left a sour taste in her mouth.

Then suddenly, as would a small child, she became bored

73

with the whole thing and, placing her hands on her slender hips, she demanded, "Well, Christina, are you going to play with me, or not?"

Christina had focused a concentrated gaze on an upstairs window, but Deborah's childish question roused her from her reflections. "What?" she inquired distantly, her thoughts still plainly centered on the Yankee she now knew to be cloistered within the huge hall. "Oh, goodness, no. I haven't time to play today, Deborah. Perhaps another day. You run along now." She dismissed the girl with an impatient gesture.

"It's just as well," Deborah mumbled glumly. "You probably wouldn't be any good anyway. You don't look like the type that could kill Yankees." And with that, she scampered away to continue her childlike gamboling.

But Deborah's final words had fallen upon deafened ears, for Christina's concentration was focused solely on that which she had just learned. Erin was concealing a soldier of the Union Army in her home; a *Yankee!* But, why?

Christina slowly moved toward her horse as she silently deliberated every conceivable notion that would compel Erin to do such a thing. But try as she might, she could conjure no plausible explanation. Consumed with curiosity, Christina had to forcibly restrain the impulse to march straightway to the house and confront Erin with the information that had just been made known to her.

But, no. *Now is not the time,* she reasoned shrewdly, calmly pondering the situation as she strolled along the lawn. She had arrived at her horse, and she quickly mounted the mare and directed it down the long driveway. *Besides,* she continued her silent musings, *she would like as not try to appease me with another one of her lies. I'll have to think of something else.* Her eyes narrowed cunningly as she considered the options available to her.

"You haven't seen the last of me, Erin Richards," she vowed aloud. "Something's going on that you obviously are

74

determined to hide, but I'm as equally determined to find you out, little cousin." She turned to cast a resolute frown at the mansion before kicking the mare into a lively gait, leaving Kilkieran, and its secret, behind her . . . for the time being.

Chapter Five

It was late afternoon before Erin again climbed the stairs to monitor Kellen's condition. Maisie had checked in on the major from time to time throughout the day, and she had carried him cold beverages and seen that he was comfortable. But Erin had been unable to force herself to confront the stricken soldier until now. To be sure, were it not for the fact that Maisie had reminded her that Kellen's bandages needed to be replaced, Erin would have been in no great rush to face the Yankee again.

After all, *he* was the uninvited guest; the intruder in her home. She had played no part in the events that had brought about his dilemma, yet she was saddled with all the responsibility. It simply was not fair, she paused on the stairway and stamped her foot in total frustration. Erin could but pray that the good major enjoyed a speedy recovery, so that he could rejoin his men and leave her in peace.

Erin had arrived at the chamber door and, taking a deep breath, she solemnly swung the barrier open and stepped inside the room. At first, she thought the major was dozing, for his eyes were closed in quiet repose. But the click of the door being shut brought the crystal-blue orbs to immediate attention and, when Erin again looked at him, she discovered them curiously trained upon her.

"I was beginning to think that you had forsaken me," he said readily, forcing a smile on his lips as he tried to ignore the sharp pain that throbbed relentlessly in his leg.

But Erin was not to be duped by the major's noble effort to conceal the discomfort he was experiencing, and she immediately crossed to the bed to get a better look at him. From the restrained cast to his face, Erin determined that she had correctly assessed the situation. The man was suffering with excruciating pain yet, for some insane reason, he seemed resolved to bear his misery in agonizing silence.

"Don't be a fool, Yankee," Erin said bluntly. "You're quite obviously in pain; go ahead and give in to it. I promise that I shall derive no pleasure from your discomfort," she assured him. "Besides, it will make you feel better."

"Oh, and can you explain how screaming my head off like some lunatic will help ease my agony? Tell me, ma'am, what makes you such a bloody expert on the subject?" he grunted sourly, not the least bit charmed with their conversation.

"I'm not an expert," she admitted, sitting down on the bed beside him; quite amused with his banter and continued stubbornness. "Thankfully, I have seldom had the occasion to experience severe, physical pain. But I am told by those who have that it is best to get it out of one's system," she imparted this bit of wisdom to him. "But then, please feel free to deal with your problem as you see fit, for I assure you that it matters precious little to me, Yankee."

"Thank you, I shall," he informed her curtly.

"My only pressing concern is to see that you recover, so that you may be on your way." She stood up suddenly and stepped through the adjoining door to collect the bandages that Maisie had placed in her room. But the abruptness of her movement so jolted the bed that Kellen could not contain the anguished yelp that rose in his throat.

"There now, don't you feel better?" Erin giggled jubilantly as she poked her head back through the doorway, unable to resist the opportunity to badger the menacing Yankee.

"Come here, you little imp," Kellen bellowed in a stern voice, though in actuality, he was quite taken with her gay antics, "so I may reward you with the proper thrashing you have justly earned."

Erin reluctantly reentered the room and tentatively examined the major. She did not truthfully believe that the Yankee would attempt any such stunt in his weakened condition, but she was wary of this outspoken intruder just the same. Placing the bandages on the bed, she quickly crossed to the washstand and gathered the materials she needed to care for the wound. When she returned to him, she had forgotten his threat of moments before.

Erin placed the basin of fresh water and other items on the bedside table, then she dragged a straight-backed chair from a corner of the room and sat down, prepared to play nursemaid to the injured major. She carefully pulled the sheet aside and seriously examined the wound. The swelling and inflammation had grown noticeably worse since she had last inspected the area, and her brow instantly assumed a worried frown.

"Something troubles you?" Kellen ventured.

He had been watching her intently, and the sudden forbidding scowl that marred her otherwise flawless face gave him reason to feel concerned.

"What?" She glanced at his watchful face for an instant, then shrugged her shoulders indifferently. "I'm certain that it's nothing to become anxious over. I'll summon Doc Wilson in the morning should there be no marked improvement."

She started to unwind the soiled bandage, but Kellen's sharp intake of breath caused her to pause and look at him. The sympathetic gaze she turned on him was sincere, and her surly disposition softened considerably when she beheld the tortured grimace that twisted his rugged face.

"I'm sorry," she whispered faintly. "I know it must be quite painful, but I fear there is no way to avoid it." She suddenly thrust her hand into her pocket, recalling the message that Lieutenant Petersen had left for Kellen, and she extended the sealed envelope to him. "Read this," she suggested. "Perhaps if you concentrate on its contents, the pain won't be so severe."

Kellen accepted the missive, and Erin returned her attention to his injured leg, cutting away the stained bandage to reveal the repulsive looking wound. Erin thoroughly scrutinized the wound for signs of infection and, though the area around the incision was red and tender, she did not yet detect any discharge that would be a sure indication of infection. She then lathered a washcloth with soap and meticulously, but gently, cleansed the area surrounding the incision.

Erin had just concluded applying a clean bandage when she looked up to find Kellen's warm, appreciative gaze fixed intently upon her. Becoming suddenly self-conscious about being alone with him, her nervous fingers began to clear away the articles she had just utilized to complete her task.

But Kellen reached out to capture her hands, and his voice was soft when he said, "You have gentle, soothing hands. I felt nary a twinge." He squeezed her hands affectionately before releasing them.

Erin was speechless. Frankly, she did not know how to react to this accursed Yankee when he adopted such a congenial manner. She much preferred him when he behaved like the loathsome blue-belly that she knew him to be; she could deal with him much more capably then.

Erin tore her eyes from his and quickly finished clearing away the mess. She then returned the chair to its corner and, when she turned, she discovered that Kellen's appraising gaze still observed her every move. Erin paused uncertainly, quite put out with herself that she would allow the major's somewhat sensual perusal to unnerve her. After all, the man *was* bedridden; he was not a threat to her.

She unconsciously hugged her arms to herself as she retraced her steps to the bed. "Well, that's out of the way for now, and there are other matters that require my attention. Maisie will bring your dinner—"

"Must you go? I was hoping that we could chat for a while

and get to know one another better." He aired the suggestion expectantly.

"You're a Yankee," Erin reminded him simply. "That's all I need or care to know about you, Major. I'm quite sure there is nothing about your Yankee way of life that would interest me in the slightest," she informed him haughtily and started to withdraw from the room.

But Kellen's hand flew upward to grasp her arm, and although he was severely weakened from the surgery, his hand clutched her arm with a firm but gentle pressure. The expression that settled on his handsome face reminded Erin of her twin brother, Evan, when he would plead with her for some trifle. Suddenly, Erin felt very lonely, and the notion of sharing a few moments with the Yankee was not as displeasing as it had been only seconds earlier.

But she would never allow the major to know that she actually welcomed the opportunity to chat with him. "What now, Yankee? Can't you take *no* for an answer?" Erin sighed heavily, but she nevertheless allowed him to pull her down onto the bed beside him.

"No," he replied honestly. "That's one response I've never been able to accept graciously, especially from a beautiful woman." He admired her fondly.

Kellen's hand still rested on her arm, making Erin extremely uncomfortable, and she shifted restlessly on her perch on the edge of the bed. "What do you want to talk about?" she asked vaguely, her eyes glued to the hand that softly stroked the flesh along her arm, and she fervently wished he would remove the disturbing hand.

As if reading her thoughts, Kellen carefully pulled himself to a more comfortable position and, crossing his arms behind his head, he began to speak, "Since you find me to be such a bothersome topic, perhaps we should focus our conversation on you. For I assure you, I find myself becoming more intrigued with each moment we share together."

"Intrigued?" she questioned.

"Yes, and curious," he admitted. "For instance, I couldn't help but notice the pictures on the mantel." He nodded toward the fireplace. "You seem to come from a rather large family yet, here you are, completely alone. Surely, not all of your menfolk abandoned you, leaving you to fend for yourself."

"I was not *abandoned*, Major. The South was in need of every able-bodied man, and my brothers are not the type to shirk their responsibility," she informed him gruffly.

"It was not my intent to imply otherwise." Kellen observed her petulant face with mild disdain.

The conversation was not progressing as he had hoped. He had not meant to ignite her ready temper, only draw her into a leisurely dialogue in an attempt to lessen the tension that existed between them. After all, if the doctor's prognosis was correct, he would be a house guest for some time to come, and they might as well try to make the best of an awkward situation.

He swallowed slowly, deciding upon another approach, but before he could voice his next question, Erin stood up abruptly, evidently concluding that her decision to humor the major had been a poor one. The suddenness of the movement, coupled with the severe look she cast in his direction, made Kellen realize that she had lost all interest in their discourse. Her next statement merely served to reaffirm his supposition.

"Look, Yankee," she had positioned herself at the foot of the bed, "I knew nothing would be gained from this. I cannot think of a single thing we could have in common, therefore, this entire conversation was senseless."

The door to the chamber had opened, but Erin continued her tirade, oblivious to the onlooker who now stood witness to her fiery attack on the major.

"You're an enormous burden, Major," she confessed bitterly, "and I'll not pretend that you're anything less. So I'll continue to tend your wound and bring your meals, but my affability ends there. You, in turn, would do me a great service if you concentrated on your recovery, for the sooner you are able to leave Kilkieran, the better it will be for all concerned."

"Erin Louise Richards!" Doctor Wilson's stern voice drew her attention away from the major. "Step out here in the hallway, girl. I'd like a word with you."

Erin was indeed startled by the doctor's sudden appearance, but the harsh look and the stiff command he directed at her gave Erin reason to wonder at his purpose. Without a word, she hurriedly made her way to the hallway and the door had barely closed behind her before the doctor turned on her heatedly.

"Have you taken leave of your senses, girl?" he began hotly. "That man has just suffered through a serious operation, and he isn't out of the woods yet. Are you trying to undo everything I've accomplished thus far?" he demanded roughly.

The doctor, considering his slight stature, had assumed a dogmatic stance before her, and Erin could surmise by the dark cast of his eyes that he was genuinely perturbed with her. Erin was crushed. Doc Wilson had been a lifelong family friend, and she could not recall the man ever raising his voice to her.

"How can you defend a . . . *Yankee* after all that they've done to the South?" Bitter tears of confusion and anguish burned at the corners of her eyes, but she brushed them aside impatiently, determined not to yield to the emotion.

"I'm a doctor, Erin. That man is a human being to me, and a mighty sick one at the present." His mood had softened in view of Erin's distraught reaction to his scolding. "The last thing he needs is to have you raving at him like a madwoman. You want him to get well, don't you?"

Erin nodded numbly.

"Then why not try to exhibit a little friendly compassion when dealing with the man?" he suggested. "Erin, do you remember the time you came to me with an injured baby raccoon that you had found while playing in the woods? You

82

were no more than a tyke at the time," he reminded her. "The animal could have scratched or bitten you, yet you weren't afraid. I patched up its busted leg and you cared for it until it was well enough to return to the forest."

Erin shook her head uncertainly. "I don't understand."

"Just think of the major as that tiny raccoon you brought to me all those years ago," he explained. "You don't have to *like* him, but at least try to exercise a modicum of human kindness when you're forced to be with him." Doc Wilson reopened the chamber door, and he gave her shoulder an affectionate pat before entering the room. "Heed my advice, and I think you'll find that the major's recuperation will pass by much more to your liking," he whispered kindly then disappeared within the sickroom.

Erin stared at the closed door for a full three minutes as she considered the words that Doctor Wilson had spoken, and her shoulders dropped dismally as she realized that his advice had been wise; though Erin seriously doubted her own ability to carry it out. Major Sinclair was not like the baby animal she had found in the wilds and nursed back to health; he was more like the plague.

The Yankees had been a plague that swept the South with a deadly force that vanquished and destroyed everything in its path. And now that this pestilence had settled in her own home, was she expected to welcome it to her bosom with open arms?

Erin turned away from the door and started to ramble down the hallway, but she paused at the top of the staircase and threw a resolute look at the major's door. After all, she had already survived a great many adversities that had been a direct result of Yankee involvement in the South, and she could certainly withstand this *minor* inconvenience.

With renewed determination, Erin descended the majestic staircase. As she was filled with a new sense of confidence, she murmured, "If a little, old-fashioned pampering will serve to improve the scoundrel's condition and quickly send him on his way, then he'll soon find that the South does not possess a more affable belle."

Meanwhile, Doc Wilson had begun his routine examination of his patient, and he was not entirely pleased with his findings. He was immensely relieved to see Kellen looking so alert and sitting up in bed, but the inflamed skin around the wound gave him reason to be concerned, and he again cautioned Kellen about the possibility of infection.

"When do you think I'll be able to travel?" Kellen inquired when Doc Wilson had completed the examination.

"I can't say just yet. I should be able to tell you more in a day or two." He returned his medical instruments to his bag and offered Kellen an encouraging smile. "If all goes well, we'll get you up on that leg the first of the week to see how it's progressing."

"That should please the mistress of the manor," Kellen droned icily.

"Don't be too harsh with her, Major," the older man reproved him kindly. "I overheard most of Erin's remarks, and I'll admit they were uncalled for, but she has a reason for her bitterness."

"She has implied as much." Kellen nodded knowingly. "I take it that she has encountered Union soldiers before."

The doctor studied Kellen thoughtfully before he replied. Perhaps if the major was made aware of the circumstances that had sharpened Erin's antagonism, he might be better equipped to deal with her erratic moods. The doctor leaned back in his chair, suddenly weary, and ran his fingers through his graying hair. He had not thought about the incident for a long while, and he was uncertain as to how much of what was known about the tragic affair he should recount to the stranger.

"Yes," he finally sighed. "There was an incident."

"What happened?"

"To be truthful, we may never know the entire story, for the only two surviving witnesses have been unable to recall much of what transpired that day," the doctor began. Then, noticing the question that had formed on Kellen's lips, he held up his hand to forestall the interruption. "I'll explain everything in due course, son.

"Erin and Deborah are the witnesses I referred to," he continued. "You've met Deborah," he looked pointedly at Kellen's leg, "so you see how she has dealt with her memories. As for Erin, well, it seems that she has wiped the entire episode from her mind. Oh, she remembers the Yankees and her mother's death, but she has refused to talk about it for so long that all that remains in her subconscious is an intense hatred of all Yankees."

"Her mother was killed?" Kellen prompted.

Doc Wilson nodded sadly, for he had been friends of Maura and Joseph Richards since he had arrived in the area to establish his medical practice. He had presided over the delivery of each of the Richards children and, unhappily, had lived to see his dear friends laid to rest in the family cemetery. The memory of these disturbing events filled the doctor with deep sorrow, and it was with some difficulty that he managed to resume his narrative.

"Yes, Maura was killed and Deborah was viciously assaulted. That's why she's the way she is."

"And Erin? Was she assaulted?" Kellen asked gravely.

"I've always suspected it," he admitted, "but Erin has never confirmed my suspicions. I questioned her after the occurrence, but she refused to discuss the matter, or let me examine her." The doctor stood up slowly and, retrieving his medical bag, he prepared to leave. "Perhaps, one day, something will happen to jolt her so badly that she will unburden herself of those pent-up memories. Until then, she'll most likely continue to be tortured by that recurring nightmare."

"Nightmare?"

"Yes, and from what Maisie tells me, it's pretty intense.

She's never confided its contents to anyone either."

"Likes to handle things her own way, does she?" Kellen noted admirably.

Doc Wilson nodded. "Erin was raised with four brothers, and she always took pride in her ability to hold her own with them. But this is a grave matter, and I'm not certain she'll be able to deal with it much longer before her resilience is shattered." He paused and glanced at the major apologetically. "I've rambled on, haven't I?"

"Not at all," Kellen replied. "Indeed, you've helped me understand the reason for that intense bitterness that burns behind those provocative green eyes. At least now the keen desire to strangle her every time she calls me *Yankee* won't arise in me so readily," he chuckled softly.

"I've other patients to see." Doc Wilson crossed to the door. "It might be a day or two before I can make it back here so, until then, try to maintain a harmonious rapport with my reluctant nurse." He offered Kellen a wan smile before departing.

Kellen stared at the door as he contemplated the final words the good doctor had spoken. "Humph!" he snorted. "How can I be expected to be cordial with an impossible minx who scorns my very existence?" He folded his arms across his wide chest and a sour expression settled upon his rugged face.

But his mood sobered considerably when he recalled the doctor's account of the events that had served to instill such rancor in his hostess, and his thoughts were predominantly cluttered with this subject when he finally succumbed to a tranquil sleep.

Following her evening repast, Erin made her way to the barn to tend to the animals, for with the presence of the Yankee, she had the added responsibility of caring for his horse, too. Erin did not truly dislike this particular task, for she had often assisted the stable hands over the years. But since the

Confederate Army had seen fit to enlist the assistance of Kilkieran's able-bodied slaves, Erin had been forced to assume the burden of performing many menial chores that had heretofore been alien to her.

Erin emerged from the barn and, on impulse, she decided to walk down to the slave quarters to visit with Ruth before retiring for the evening. She had turned toward the cabin when she noticed that Maisie was hurrying toward her. Even in the dim shadows of twilight, she could detect that something was amiss, for the elderly servant seldom maneuvered her bulky frame at such a quickened pace unless spurred on by some emergency.

Erin stopped short to wait for Maisie to join her and emitted a long, forlorn sigh. What was wrong now?

Erin's mouth immediately fashioned into a cynical frown as she patiently waited for the servant to catch her breath before imparting the nature of the distressing news. But her endurance proved to be transitory and, folding her arms tightly across her bosom, she turned a stern look on the old woman.

"Yes, Maisie," she began shortly, unaware of the severe inflection of her voice. "What's happened now? And, whatever it is, couldn't you have handled it?" she added tiredly, growing increasingly disenchanted with the responsibility of managing the affairs of the plantation.

Maisie was aware of the pressure her mistress had been under since the arrival of the major; therefore, she attributed the surly welcome to this and hastened on with the somber tidings that had led her to seek Erin's counsel. "You bettah come quick, Miz Erin. It's de maj'r. He done come down wid a real bad fevah an'—"

"*What!*" Erin's hand shot out to grip the servant's arm. "Are you certain?"

"Ah jest went up ter take him his suppah. He wuz sleepin' lak a baby sose ah went ter shake him awake an' he lak ter burnt mah hand, he's dat hot," Maisie confirmed Erin's worst fears.

Without a backwards glance, Erin released Maisie's arm and sprinted toward the house, shouting a list of instructions to the servant as she ran. The fact that the majority of her words were lost on the wind was oblivious to Erin, for her immediate concern lay with the Yankee. But Maisie had dealt with this type of ailment on numerous occasions and knowingly scurried off toward the kitchen to gather the necessary items for her mistress.

Erin's heart was thumping wildly by the time she reached the major's side, and her hand was trembling as she gently placed it against his forehead to test its warmth. The dismal scowl that appeared on her face was an instant indication that she was not at all pleased with her findings. Intuitively, she ran her hand along the muscular contour of his arms and chest to determine if these areas' heat intensity matched that of his forehead.

Much to her chagrin, she found that his arms and chest were alive with fire as well. But her dismay turned to genuine consternation when she heard the contented sigh that came from Kellen's lips, indicating that he had awakened. Erin did not have to look at him to know that those menacing blue eyes, though they might be clouded with fever, would be focused directly on her.

She looked at him anyway and was none too jubilant to discover that she had been correct in her assumption. The crystal-blue orbs danced in gay anticipation at awakening to such an interesting distraction and, though their brilliance was overshadowed considerably by the fever, they still sparkled with mischief.

"You . . . you have a fever," Erin stuttered a little as she began to explain the rather awkward situation in which she found herself.

"Indeed," he murmured thickly. "What man would not burn upon receiving such a gratifying *arousal*?"

Erin's mouth dropped open in unquestionable mortification at his scandalous insinuation, but it was not until she felt the rumble in his chest, as he chortled heartily at her reaction, that she realized her hand still rested amidst the plentiful, curly hairs of his broad chest. She instantly snatched her hand away and covered him with the sheet.

Swallowing the bitter words that sprang to her tongue, she recalled her decision to pamper the major and resolved that she would endeavor to enforce her plan. Besides, if the Yankee insisted on playing the role of the unceasing prankster, what difference should it make to her? She shrugged off the urge to scratch from his lips the infuriating grin that mocked her embarrassment and, pulling herself up to her full height of five feet, three inches, she looked the major squarely in the eye, showing him that she would not be intimidated by his shenanigans.

"If you'll permit me to continue." She cleared her throat for effect. "You truly have developed an infection which causes me some concern. And, if you had a lick of sense, you'd be worried, too," she chastised him, though not unkindly.

Kellen surveyed her thoughtfully as he mentally considered this decided change in the girl's attitude. He had witnessed the myriad of emotions that had danced across her face, and had accordingly wondered at the control she had subsequently exhibited. Perhaps the good doctor's words had been absorbed by that stubborn, rebel heart, and this was her dauntless attempt at cordiality. Well, he would not allow her valiant endeavor to be for naught. Besides, it would please him beyond belief to be able to engage in spirited discourse with the girl, especially if he could do so without having his head snapped off by the impetuous imp at every turn.

"I assure you, Erin," he began softly, "the status of my health is a constant concern, particularly now that I am reduced to such an enfeebled position."

For the first time since setting eyes on the major, Erin regarded him with a truly considerate gaze. Until this very moment, she had thought of him as nothing more than a fragment of a disgusting breed that should be wiped from the face of the earth; a Yankee. But at some point during the course of her rather lengthy perusal, the demonic aura that had heretofore hovered about the major seemed to dwindle substantially, and Erin viewed Kellen for what he was; a man. A man who, through no real fault of his own, had found himself at the mercy of a stranger who had done little more than condemn him since his appearance at her door.

Erin's eyes conducted a careful examination of the powerful physique that lay shielded beneath the bedclothes. From the wide shoulders to the muscular arms and broad chest to the long legs that nearly stretched the full-length of the bed, she could determine that he was accustomed to a rigorous, physical routine, and that being confined to a sickbed must be a tremendous ordeal for him.

Her eyes instinctively climbed to scrutinize the rough lines of his ruggedly handsome face, totally oblivious to the amused grin that shaped his mouth as he secretly pondered her curious behavior. But, to Erin, the figure on the bed had acquired a very different perspective and, in her mind, the image of another appeared; Michael, her childhood sweetheart.

Erin's eyes misted over with tears as she recalled the lightness of his laughter and the comfort of his reassuring embrace, making her long for him. Suddenly realizing that if Michael had fallen victim of a Yankee bullet behind enemy lines, she would pray that some Northern girl would demonstrate a more benevolent disposition while caring for her beloved.

It was this notion that caused her to reevaluate her halfhearted musings of the afternoon and, deciding that the major would like as not see through any lame attempt to appease him, Erin resolved that any action on her part would have to come genuinely from the heart. Shaking her head clear of her silent ruminations, she again focused on Kellen.

Without a trace of bitterness lacing her voice, she said, "Maisie said that she brought your dinner, but it's certain to have grown cold by now. Would you like me to warm it for you?"

"Thank you, but no. I haven't much of an appetite this evening," he replied slowly, his watchful eyes never wavering from her face.

"I feared as much," she stated frankly. "Actually, it's quite common for one's appetite to wane when succumbed with fever." She endeavored to ease his mind. "But we need to do what we can to combat the infection and keep it from getting worse." As she spoke, Erin moved to the washstand and, retrieving the pitcher, she walked to the door. "I won't be but a moment," she promised him.

True to her word, Erin returned shortly lugging the pitcher that had been made considerably heavier by the addition of a huge chunk of ice from the icehouse. Kellen observed in contemplative silence as Erin collected the basin and washcloth and placed them on the bedside commode. Next, she filled the basin with the cold liquid and took a seat on the edge of the bed, quite obviously preparing to administer a bath.

Erin caught the playful twinkle in the eyes that monitored her every move, and quickly decided that she should explain her intentions lest the major interpret her actions to be of a more personal nature than she actually meant.

"The cool water will help diminish the fever's severity," she said simply.

"I would not count on that, were I you," came his shameless taunt, as his ever admiring gaze mapped a sensuous trail from her face to her amply proportioned breasts.

It was almost as if Erin could feel the fire from those intense blue spheres penetrating the thin material of her gown to caress her silken flesh. But she was completely shaken when she realized that the warmth she experienced was her own awakening desire. For despite her efforts to disregard the perturbing Yankee's dauntless scrutiny, Erin could not control the brilliant flush that instantly overwhelmed her.

What was even more remarkable was the fact that Erin suddenly found herself wondering what it would be like to be embraced by Kellen's powerful arms, to feel the pressure of those wondrously full lips against hers. Oh, not the way he had kissed her in the foyer that fateful day he had arrived at Kilkieran, but a genuinely affectionate— Her reverie broke off abruptly as Erin became acutely aware of Kellen's knowing chuckle, and she hastily put her romantic musings from her mind.

Fearing that Kellen had guessed the essence of her thoughts, Erin wisely avoided his curious expression. She gave a nervous cough and hurriedly plunged the cloth into the icy water, thankful for the excuse to avert her eyes from his maddening gaze.

She then squeezed the excess moisture from the washcloth and, turning back to Kellen, she began to gently rub the cloth along his arm. Erin felt the tenseness in his muscles as her fingers ran along his shoulder and, beginning to grow self-conscious at the rather intimate aspect of her task, she decided to draw him into conversation; thinking that if they devoted their attention elsewhere, neither would be embarrassed by her undertaking.

"Major," she began.

"*Kellen*," he whispered hopefully.

Erin paused as she again dipped the washcloth into the icy water and, when she resumed the application of the cool towel, she reformulated her comments. "Kellen," she murmured softly, surprised at how easily the name rolled from her tongue. "I behaved badly this afternoon. I . . . I realize that I haven't been a very gracious hostess, but I shall endeavor to remedy that oversight for the duration of your stay." She halted the movement of the cloth along his chest and glanced up into his doubtful face. "Would you still like to have the chat you suggested earlier?"

"That would be nice," he admitted honestly.

And the familiarity of the task she was performing became suddenly less awkward as they began to engage in a lighthearted conversation. A conversation that came surprisingly easier than Erin had anticipated. Erin was to repeat the procedure of the cool, refreshing sponge bath several times throughout the night, and it was not until the predawn hours that the tension along her neck and spine dwindled, allowing her to relax and succumb to a richly deserved, unencumbered slumber.

Kellen awakened early the following morning and shifted uncomfortably against the pillows of his unwished for prison. The pain in his tortured thigh had subsided a little, but the dull ache that remained was an incessant reminder of his present fate. All this, coupled with the fact that his flesh still burned with a raging fever, would have been sufficient cause to drive a normally idle man to despair. But for Kellen, who was accustomed to a highly rigorous schedule, this imposed inactivity was unbearable.

Thus far, the sole modicum of respite he had experienced from this intolerable boredom had been the moments he had spent with the mistress of the manor. And, for the most part, those encounters had proven to be far from enjoyable distractions . . . until last night, that is.

A thoughtful frown crinkled his brow as his eyes fastened on Erin where she slept contentedly in a leather wing chair just a few feet removed from the bed. Vaguely, he recalled her gentle ministrations throughout the night, and a somber expression settled on his face as he recounted the revelations of the past evening's conversation. He had again questioned her about her family, but this time she had offered willing responses to his queries.

"I had four brothers," she had begun quite naturally, as if talking with an old family friend. "James was the eldest; he was killed at Sharpsburg," she had added a little sorrowfully. "Then there's Graham, Matthew, and Evan. Matthew was killed at Gettysburg. Poor Matthew," she had lamented. "Of all my brothers, he was the least suited to go to war. He was the gentle one; not much of a fighter, I fear."

"Unfortunately, war is often imprudent in the victims it claims," Kellen had offered consolingly.

"I know. It's just that this whole war seems so senseless at times." She had concluded the sponge bath, yet continued to sit on the edge of the bed, genuinely involved in their discourse.

"And what has become of your other brothers?"

"They're safe. At least, I've had no word to the contrary. The last time I heard from them, they were with General Lee, trying to keep your General Grant and the other Yankees out of Richmond."

Erin had preoccupied her hands by straightening the wrinkled sheets of his bed; therefore, she did not observe the sudden intense expression that shadowed his brow with the mention of this particular theater of action. But he quickly masked his surprise when Erin again turned to him.

"Graham is simply too stubborn for anything to happen to him," she had continued, unaware of Kellen's apprehensive reaction to her declaration. "And Evan, well, Evan is safe. I'd know if anything had happened to him," she had stated confidently.

Kellen had been understandably intrigued by this statement, and he promptly questioned her.

"Oh," she had bestowed upon him a winsome smile, "Evan and I are twins. We've always been close, perhaps more so than the others. I mean, I loved all my brothers, but there's a special bond that is shared between twins."

Kellen shook his head to clear it of these reflections and he became preoccupied with thoughts of his men, the mission they were in the midst of completing, and the precarious cargo they carried. Again, Kellen's pensive eyes settled on Erin, and he regarded her sympathetically, for if plans proceeded accordingly and his men performed their mission successfully, there was an excellent chance that her brothers might not be as secure as she suspected.

Erin came fully awake as the abrupt sound of porcelain shattering against the fireplace summoned all her faculties to consciousness. Hastily brushing the sleep from her eyes, she quickly scanned the room for the source of the commotion and was quite puzzled by the scene which welcomed her drowsy eyes.

The pieces of one of her mother's everyday china cups lay strewn across the hearth, and a strong, distinctive odor of herbs and spices pervaded the chamber. Her gaze somberly moved from the fireplace to the major who openly struggled with Maisie as the servant valiantly tried to force a spoonful of some concoction into the Yankee's mouth. Erin had to forcibly restrain the giggle that arose in her throat at the comical spectacle and, stepping forward, she cleared her throat sternly.

"All right, Maisie. What is this about?" she demanded, fighting to control the grin that twitched at the corner of her mouth.

But Kellen was the first to respond. "I'll tell you what it's about," he volunteered and, wrenching the spoon from the old woman's hand, he flung it against the opposite wall. "Your . . . your *servant* is trying to poison me!" he fairly shouted.

"Tain't so, Miz Erin," Maisie hastened to deny the accusation. "When ah found out de maj'r had a bad fevah, ah done went in de woods to gathah de special fixin's fer mah bittahs. Ah wuz up all night brewin' 'em, too."

"Tain't no poison, Mistuh Yankee, suh, it's jest mah bittahs to hep you git well agin," the woman explained kindly, then started to clean up the mess that Kellen had made.

But Erin walked over to the old servant and patted her shoulder sympathetically and, assuring Maisie that she would see to straightening the room, Erin dismissed the domestic. She had knelt by the fireplace to gather the pieces of broken china when Kellen's rather humbling voice interrupted her task.

"I'm . . . I'm sorry. I truly don't know what came over me," he apologized.

"It's the fever, Yankee," she stated simply. "No need to apologize."

Erin had collected all the remnants of broken china and retrieved the discarded spoon before she turned toward the major, a full grin blossoming on her pretty face. Stepping to the tray that held another cup of Maisie's infamous bitters, Erin deposited the debris thereon and sat down on the edge of the bed.

"You should have seen yourself," she laughed openly. "You projected quite an image, I assure you. Struggling with Maisie, as though she was trying to take your very life," she continued to giggle airily.

"Have you ever tasted that wretched stuff?" Kellen cast a rueful glance toward the tray. "I thought that was precisely what she was attempting to do! But it's of little consequence." He waved the incident aside casually.

For when his eyes fastened on the lovely face that smiled down at him, his irascible disposition mellowed instantly. And when Erin gently reached forward to place her hand against his forehead to test his fever, Kellen captured the graceful appendage in his hand when she would have pulled it away.

"Your fever has . . . has worsened," she stammered clumsily, uncertain of the major's purpose.

"I know, but at least you're laughing, and it's quite a delightful sound." He ran his fingers gently along her arm, giving rise to a multitude of tingly gooseflesh along her erect spine. "Much more appealing to the ear than when you call me *Yankee* or *blue-belly*." He softly brushed his lips against her hand in an appreciative gesture.

Erin could not control the blush that immediately colored her cheeks, and the alluring eyelashes dropped automatically to shield her eyes from his ever-penetrating gaze. She withdrew her hand from his demurely, and she struggled to suppress the tremulous stirrings that his tender caress had mysteriously aroused.

"Well," she shrugged her shoulders indifferently, giving her chestnut-brown tresses a careless toss, "have you not constantly rebuked me for my lackluster attitude? I am but merely demonstrating my aptness at portraying the charming and efficient hostess."

"By mocking an invalid's misfortune?" He pretended to sound affronted by her antics, but Erin caught the glint in his eye that refuted his anger.

"Oh, fiddlesticks!" she sighed impatiently. "*You* would have *howled* had our positions been reversed." Thinking to draw the conversation back to her more pressing concern, that of his health, she said, "And to answer your earlier question; yes, I have tasted Maisie's bitters.

"There is no avoiding it, actually. Every spring, just as sure as the dogwood is going to bloom, one can count on Maisie brewing a batch of her bitters." She dunked her finger in the cup that sat on the tray beside his bed, then placed it to her lips and tasted the odorous brew. Instantly, her mouth puckered and her brow crinkled into an unpleasant grimace. "Hmmm," she thoughtfully considered the potent flavor, "milder than usual. It probably needs to ferment a day or two."

"You're joking!" he bellowed incredulously.

"No, it *ripens* with age," she spoke knowledgeably. "And it would do you more good than harm if you would stop being so stubborn and drink a little of it. After all, I've had an annual spring dose ever since I was old enough to walk, and I have never suffered from as much as a sniffle," she told him matter-of-factly, then winked at him and playfully admitted, "Of course, *had* I become ill, I realized I would have been forced to consume a whole cup of the awful stuff instead of an occasional spoonful."

The two of them laughed gaily at her amusing anecdote before Kellen inquired, "What's in it, anyway? I must admit that it possesses a rather *interesting* bouquet."

"Oh, ginseng, sassafras and some of Papa's homemade spirits. Then Maisie adds some of her secret roots and herbs and, by the time she's finished, this is what you have." She extended the cup toward him, but he quickly threw up his hand in protest.

"No, thanks."

"You know, it isn't so terrible once you grow accustomed to the somewhat peculiar flavor. And, honestly, it could do wonders in helping to diminish your fever." She steadfastly encouraged him as one would coddle a reluctant child. "Although it's medicinal potency is reputed to be far more effective when it is hot *and* when it is consumed internally." She purposely indicated the dark stains that had splattered on the sheets during the earlier struggle with Maisie.

"I'll just run down to the kitchen and get you a hot cup of Maisie's *tea*." She gathered the tray in her hands. "Then, if you're feeling up to it, I'll get one of the servants to help me assist you to a chair and I'll put fresh linens on your bed." She stood up, prepared to carry out the self-imposed errand, but she was ill-prepared for the voice that shattered the air behind her, startling her so that the tray slipped from her fingers.

"There's no need to trouble anyone, Erin, dear. Why, I'd be more than happy to help out," the voice informed her with a soft, self-assured hauteur.

Chapter Six

Erin wandered aimlessly along the bank of the James River; her thoughts thoroughly jumbled and askew. Consequently, she barely noticed the panoramic view of the Piedmont region of the Blue Ridge Mountains that lay in breathtaking, blossoming splendor before her. Instead, she paced purposelessly back and forth, staring emotionlessly at the swift current of the blue water, or a brightly colored wild flower; visualizing all, but truly concentrating on nothing. For Erin's thoughts were focused inwardly these days, and the purpose of this excursion had been to leave the tension and strain of Kilkieran behind her for one afternoon while seeking temporary respite from her responsibilities at home.

Ten days had passed since the fateful morning that Christina had discovered Erin's guarded secret. Though she usually detested her cousin's often demanding and overbearing demeanor, Erin had to admit that Christina had proven to be a godsend in this particular instance. For Christina considered the Yankee's presence at Kilkieran to be quite an adventure and, after severely chastising Erin for neglecting to include her in the daring escapade, she had eagerly appeared at Kilkieran every day to help care for Kellen.

Erin smiled wanly as she mentally recounted the picture of Christina energetically bustling about the major's chamber, performing a multitude of trivial tasks that she usually considered to be quite beneath her. All the while, regaling Kellen with a barrage of girlish chatter involving beaux that the invalid could not have possibly found entertaining.

A genuine smile parted Erin's lips as she remembered the day she had entered the room to relieve her cousin to find the beleaguered major unsuccessfully feigning interest in one of Christina's ridiculous tales. After the girl had departed, Erin had been mildly surprised when Kellen calmly requested that his revolver be brought to him.

"I realize that Christina can be a great trial, but you cannot mean to *shoot* her!" Erin had exclaimed.

"The gun isn't meant for Christina!" he had bellowed. "I'm merely going to finish the job your friend Deborah began, and release myself from this insufferable misery," he had cried in utter desperation.

But the smile abruptly faded from Erin's pretty lips as she recalled the current grave status of Kellen's condition. He had suffered with a fever for several days; the severity of which had fluctuated almost daily. But shortly following this rather amusing encounter, he had succumbed to the raging fever and slipped into unconsciousness; a deep sleep that had imprisoned him ever since.

Erin paused and stretched, placing a soothing hand to the small of her aching back. Lifting her eyes heavenward, the position of the afternoon sun cautioned her that it was time to return to Kilkieran and relieve Christina of her vigil. She walked slowly to where Lady stood contentedly grazing on the spring grass and, mounting the animal, she directed her across the rolling meadow to the road that would take them home.

The old mare moved leisurely along the familiar path and Erin appeared content with the sluggish pace, obviously uneager for the tranquil afternoon to come to an end. In fact, by the time Erin had arrived home and brushed and settled Lady in her stall, she estimated that it was well past five o'clock. Not wishing Christina's late departure to arouse unwarranted suspicion from her Aunt Lydia, Erin quickly made her way to the sickroom.

"I'm sorry that I'm late, Christina," she apologized, removing her bonnet and tossing it on a chair. "It's just that the sky was so blue and the sun was so warm that I simply couldn't tear myself away any sooner.

"Has there been any change in the major's condition?" she inquired hastily.

"No, he's still the same." Christina stood up and crossed to the mirror to check her appearance, preparing to leave. "But you're the one that concerns me, cousin. Why, you're beginning to look quite peaked after staying up till all hours while looking after our Kellen. I do wish that you'd consider letting me stay through the night."

"You're a dear to make such an unselfish offer, but I'm certain that Aunt Lydia would miss you awfully." Erin quickly tried to discourage her cousin from pursuing the notion. "Besides, Aunt Lydia must be agog with curiosity as it is, what with you traipsing over here every day. Tell me, what does she think of our newfound friendship?" Erin attempted to steer the conversation to a more favorable subject. But as she awaited her cousin's reply, a commotion along the driveway caught her attention, and she casually sauntered toward the window to determine the source of the ruckus.

"Oh, Mamma's just as please as punch, so I just know she'd understand if I said I wanted to spend the night," Christina chatted on, but when her eyes settled on her cousin, she was more than a little confused by the anxious look that suddenly crossed Erin's face.

"Good heavens!" she exclaimed. "What's happened, Erin Louise? You look as if you've seen a ghost."

"Worse," she whispered hoarsely, her delicate hands gripping the back of the rocking chair so fiercely that the knuckles were stretched white. "*Soldiers*."

"What? More Yankees!"

"No, they're ours, but with him here," she jerked her head toward Kellen, "what might normally be considered a blessing is more like having the devil himself come to call."

Erin turned abruptly from the window and started to run to the chamber door. But before she reached the barrier, it was flung open from without, and Maisie and a number of the other servants bolted into the room.

"Miz Erin!" Maisie began excitedly.

"I know, I know! I saw them from the window. I was just about to ring for you, for I'm going to need everyone's cooperation, and we haven't much time to formulate a foolproof plan. But one thing is for certain, our soldiers simply cannot learn of the Yankee. There's no telling what they will do if they find him here, even if they are Southerners like us," she said worriedly.

"Paulie," Erin summoned the young lad, and he stepped forward, eager to serve his mistress.

"Yes, ma'am."

"Run down to the barn and get the major's horse. Take him upstream to the old sawmill and hide him. Be sure to gather all his gear, too. If the soldiers go into the barn, they shouldn't be too suspicious to find Lady, but the major's mount is another story. Be very careful, and be sure to go the back way," she cautioned.

"I won't let you down, Miz Erin," the boy promised and scurried off to carry out the instructions.

"Whut can we-uns do ter hep out, Miz Erin?" Ruth asked anxiously.

Erin's calculating eyes surveyed the room in one sweeping glance and, with a fluttering heart, she suddenly realized that they would have to work rapidly if they were going to transform the sickroom back into an elegant bed chamber. Then her eyes fastened on Kellen, and her heart sank deeper when presented with the further dilemma of effectively hiding him. But as had been the norm of late when faced with adversity, an idea suddenly sprang to mind. Even though she was uncertain

102

as to its plausibility, Erin knew that they had to chance it, for they were quickly running out of time. Glancing toward the window to check on the advance of the soldiers, she hurriedly explained the plan to Ruth and Maisie.

"Perhaps they won't be interested in searching the house, but we need to be ready just in case," she warned the servants. "We'll try to stall them downstairs long enough to give you time to get things ready up here."

Then grabbing Christina by the arm, she ushered her cousin toward the door. "Quickly, Christina. Come with me. I'm going to need your assistance."

And amidst a flurry of swaying skirts, the two girls disappeared down the corridor.

"I'll swan," Christina declared as they hastened down the long staircase, "but this is turning into the most divine adventure. And *you*. Why, you're just the cleverest thing, cousin. I never should have thought of such a brilliant scheme. Do you think it will work?" she chatted on breathlessly.

Erin paused at the foot of the stairway to catch her breath and poise herself. "It's up to us to *make* it work," she informed her cousin. "You know what to do?"

Christina nodded enthusiastically.

"Good." Erin smoothed the skirt of her gown with trembling fingers and, willing her thundering heart to become calm, she crossed to the door. "Act naturally, Christina. We don't want to arouse undue suspicion," she cautioned, then swung the door wide and stepped onto the porch to welcome the Confederate soldiers.

The small patrol of soldiers had already arrived in front of the spacious plantation house, and their commander had dismounted and was approaching the porch when Erin and Christina emerged from the mansion.

"Good afternoon, ladies," the soldier doffed his hat and offered them a friendly but haggard smile. "I'm Captain Winston Beddows. There have been reported sightings of enemy soldiers in the vicinity, and my men and I are conducting a routine search of the area. I trust that you lovely ladies have not been victimized by the treacherous marauders."

"*Yankees!*" Christina emitted a horrified gasp and clutched a hand to her bosom in a dramatic gesture. "Thank heavens you men have arrived to keep us safe from those nasty varmints."

"Well, ma'am," the captain's chest swelled visibly at Christina's lavish display of helplessness, and Erin had to squelch the triumphant smile that threatened to spread her lips as the soldier fell for Christina's innocent charade, "the truth of the matter is, we're just scouting for Yankees; we won't be staying long. Have either of you ladies encountered any enemy soldiers?"

"Do you honestly think that I'd be standing here before you if I had?" Christina exclaimed. "Surely to goodness, I'd have been forced to take to my sickbed if subjected to such a ghastly experience. Why, just talking about the foul blackguards makes me positively giddy. In fact, I'm feeling quite faint at the moment." She placed the back of her hand to her forehead and allowed her eyes to roll up in her head for effect.

The response was immediate as the captain rushed forward to seize her arm and offer his support. Then he led her to the porch swing, so she might sit down and recoup her faculties. After seeing that Christina was comfortably seated, the captain turned to Erin.

"I must apologize for my cousin, Captain Beddows, but she is quite frail," Erin explained.

"I understand, miss, what with the menfolk at war, the South's ladies have had to weather many a hardship alone. Hopefully, that won't remain the circumstance much longer," he sighed heavily, and Erin noted that beneath the lines of intense worry and fatigue that creased his face lay the features of a younger man than she had originally suspected. "Do both you and your cousin reside here, miss?"

"No, my cousin is from the Briar Cliff plantation; about eight miles due east. Would it be an imposition to ask that some of your men escort my cousin safely home?" Erin posed demurely, summoning the coquettish charm that she had, at one time, used so effectively with Michael.

"It's not an imposition, miss. In fact, my men are sure to find the assignment a most pleasurable distraction." He summoned four of his men from the group that loitered nearby and curtly issued a command. "And be certain to conduct a thorough search of the area for signs of enemy troops. Then return here, and we shall find a suitable place to make camp for the night. That's all," he dismissed the men.

Erin watched in silence as the men carefully assisted Christina to her mount. Though her attention seemed intently fixed upon the scene before her, the look of apprehension that wrinkled her fair complexion was not out of concern for her cousin's welfare. Instead, her thoughts were implanted in the upstairs chamber that sequestered her injured house guest. She knew that the room had to be a jumbled flurry of activity, what with the servants furtively trying to restore it to order. And Erin could only pray that Christina's little escapade had allotted them the necessary time to successfully execute her hastily devised scheme.

"Excuse me, ma'am," the captain said, tapping her lightly on the shoulder to interrupt her suppressed musings, "but there's no need to worry about your cousin. My men will see her safely home." He falsely interpreted her anxiety as solicitude for the departing girl's well-being.

"Thank you, Captain. I know they shall." Erin forced a warm smile to her lips and turned to reenter the house. "I suppose your men will wish to conduct a search of the premises," she suggested nonaccusingly.

"Yes, miss." The soldier followed her into the house at her indication. "I'm sorry to inconvenience you like this, but it's for your own protection. For all we know, some of them no-account Yankees might be holding members of your family prisoner, threatening to do them harm if you turn them over to us."

"I understand," Erin replied quietly, leading the officer to the parlor. "But I assure you, if there were Yankees about, I would not hesitate to inform you. In fact, I had truly hoped not to be bothered about Yankees ever again after the last time."

Erin had silently pondered whether she should mention the incident that had ultimately left her with a bedridden patient. Then, deciding that it might create less suspicion to apprise the captain of the encounter with the Yankees, she carefully broached the subject.

"Last time?"

"Yes." She took a seat near the window and motioned the captain into a chair opposite hers. "About two weeks ago a patrol of Union soldiers stopped here to repair a disabled wagon. I was not keen with the idea of having the scoundrels on my property, but what was I to do?" she sighed tiredly.

"Did they cause you any trouble, or harm you in any way?" the officer demanded.

"What? Oh, no," Erin quickly explained. "They stayed only long enough to mend the damaged vehicle, then departed the following morning. The entire episode was quite . . . uh . . . uneventful," she lied convincingly, at least she prayed the captain had not detected the shaky inflection of her voice. "Although it was a thoroughly despicable ordeal, the Yankees caused us no misfortune."

"That's good to know, miss . . ."

"Richards," Erin offered. "Erin Richards."

"Well, Miss Richards. If you'll excuse me, I'll dispatch my men to search the barn and outbuildings, then perhaps you could show me through the house." He stood and exited the room without waiting for a formal response to his suggestion.

Erin sat stiffly in her chair as she awaited the captain's return. The only outside sound that penetrated her thoughts was that of the imported clock that sat upon the mantel. The minutes ticked away at an excruciatingly slow pace, and the noise drummed in her ears so persistently that Erin was certain hours had slipped away when, in actuality, the captain had been gone but a few moments. But when he again entered the parlor, she stood on remarkably sturdy legs to escort the captain through the august mansion.

The officer diligently followed Erin as she led him through the main floor rooms. He painstakingly reviewed both parlors, the dining room, library, and ballroom before they moved along the spacious corridor that led to the grand staircase that would carry them above stairs.

Erin chatted amicably with Captain Beddows during the inspection, speaking mainly about the weather and the war; making general small talk. But if the truth be known, she was scarcely aware of the context of the words that flowed so freely from her lips. By the time they reached the top of the staircase, her heart was pounding so fiercely that she had to mentally restrain from clutching her hands to her bosom to calm its turbulent beating.

Erin avoided the master chamber at first, choosing instead to show the captain the guestrooms, upstairs sitting room, and the family chambers. But at last, she found herself left with no alternative and, as she stood poised before the sickroom door, her fingers hesitating slightly over the knob, the door was swung wide from within and Maisie emerged to greet her with a confident smile.

"Ah wuz jest comin' ter git you, Miz Erin. Yore gran'ma wants to have a word wid you befoe ah brings her dinnuh and gits her ready fer bed." The servant lowered her head, so as not to be observed by the soldier, and gave her mistress a sly wink.

Erin's eyes were drawn immediately to the rocking chair that had been placed on the gallery; the back of the chair facing them. She was thoroughly pleased with the transformation of the room, to be sure, but Kellen's hastily contrived disguise had proven to be sheer genius.

Ruth and Maisie had dressed him in one of her mother's old dressing gowns and placed him in the chair. A shawl had been draped around his shoulders to camouflage their width and a thin blanket lay across his lap, and had been tucked in around his ankles to hide his less than effeminate feet. His large hands were positioned beneath the blanket as well and, of course, his unruly black hair had been hidden from view by one of Erin's summer sun bonnets.

The major was slumped forward in the chair, creating the aged, enfeebled picture that Erin had hoped he would emulate. The captain observed the scene with a casual demeanor, and stood patiently aside while Erin excused herself to have a word with her *grandmother*. The captain watched as the girl stepped through the French doors and knelt before the grandparent and, since it was unlike the captain to eavesdrop on private conversations, he occupied his time by conducting a cursory inspection of the room and the adjoining chamber.

Erin pretended to talk with the occupant of the chair while, indeed, her attention was focused on every movement the captain made. But when the officer completed his search of the connecting room and reentered the master chamber, Erin scrambled to her feet, placed a perfunctory kiss to her *grand-mother's* brow and rejoined the captain, lest he decide to amble out onto the gallery.

"Well, are you satisfied that none of those Yankees have sought sanctuary here at Kilkieran?" she asked as she closed the door of the chamber and walked along the corridor toward the staircase.

"Yes, Miss Richards," the officer replied. "I suppose the reported sightings must have been the patrol that you saw a couple of weeks back. I sure wish we had happened along then. Perhaps we could have spared you some grief."

"Thank you, Captain. Your concern is most gratifying, but as I explained, while the Yankee occupation was an unsettling experience, they did us no actual harm." They had started to descend the staircase and, as Erin silently applauded their successful deception, a small smile appeared on her face.

But the smile vanished instantly when she glanced toward

the foot of the stairs and recognized the slight figure that shyly approached them.

Deborah! Good Lord, how could she have forgotten about Deborah!

Erin's heart jumped and seemed to form a constrictive vise about her throat, and it was several seconds before she could find her voice. But before she could speak, Deborah had reached them, and Erin tried to dismiss the girl as quickly as possible without giving rise to the captain's suspicions.

"Hello, Deborah," she greeted her cheerfully. "This is Captain Beddows. I've just been showing him the house. Say hello, then run along and wash up for supper. I'm certain that Maisie will be wondering about you."

But Deborah was not to be so easily disposed of and, looking the soldier up and down, she settled her disturbing brown eyes squarely on the captain. "I suppose you came for the Yankee," she stated candidly.

"*What!*" the captain blurted unbelievably.

"Deborah," Erin said severely, praying that her voice did not tremble. "What have I told you about badgering others with your little games? Now run along like I told you." She continued a step or two downward, hoping that the girl would yield to her behest. But much to Erin's chagrin, Deborah remained staunchly fixed before the captain.

Erin was driven to the point of tears. Though outwardly, she successfully managed to camouflage her apprehensive misgivings, inwardly, a multitude of jumbled nerves formed a taut knot in the pit of her stomach, threatening to cause her to become physically ill. What was she going to do if Deborah convinced the captain that a Yankee was indeed safely ensconced in an upstairs chamber, and he decided to conduct a second, more thorough, examination of the house? That must not happen!

"Deborah," she repeated firmly.

"Oh, don't listen to her," the girl snapped impatiently. "I think she actually *likes* the varmint, what with the way she

109

dotes on him night and day," she added disgustedly.

Erin frantically tried to give the captain some sort of signal which would indicate that the girl was not entirely in control of her mental faculties, but she need not have bothered. For the captain had detected the faraway cast of her troubled eyes, and the general disheveled, unkempt condition of the girl made him realize that all was not right with her.

Here was most certainly another tragic example of the way the war had inflicted suffering on the South; the heartless devastation of its gentle women.

"Oh, and just how did this awful Yankee happen to end up here?" He decided to humor the girl.

"I shot him!" she boasted proudly.

"You did? And did you kill the scoundrel?"

"No," she said slowly, her face turning into a confused pout. "Didn't you see him? He's right up there." Her finger shot upward toward the door behind which Kellen was hidden.

The next moment seemed more like an eternity to Erin as she held her breath and waited for the captain's reaction to Deborah's declaration.

At last, Captain Beddows said, "Oh, *him!* I shouldn't worry, if I were you. It's doubtful that the cur will last through the night." He gave her an official looking salute and continued to gently mollify her. "Now you be a good, little soldier and march on up these stairs and do as Miss Richards said."

Erin slowly exhaled, but she watched sadly as Deborah's shoulders slumped in disappointment at not being believed by the captain. As Deborah dejectedly climbed the steps, Erin suddenly realized that she had spent very little time with her sister-in-law since the major had invaded their lives. Reproving herself for having neglected the girl, she silently vowed she would somehow try to make her understand their precarious situation.

"How long has she been like that?" the captain's question interrupted her private thoughts.

"Since my brother . . . her husband . . . left for the war," she replied in a low voice.

The captain said nothing, but shook his head glumly as he continued down the staircase. When he reached the front door, he turned to Erin. "Thank you kindly for cooperating with us, ma'am. And now, if I may be so bold, I have a favor to ask of you."

"Yes?"

"My men have ridden hard all day, and I don't want to push them unduly. Would it be an imposition if we made camp among the trees that line the driveway?" he asked politely. "The landscape puts me in mind a little of my own home," he added wistfully. "I'm sure the others feel the same."

"Of course, it's no imposition, Captain Beddows," she murmured softly. "Tell your men to set up camp, and they're free to roam as they wish."

"Thanks, ma'am, but I'll keep them close to camp. We'll be leaving at sunup, and there's no need for them to be pestering you. Good day." He tipped his hat, then exited the house.

Despite the captain's orders to the contrary, Erin instructed Maisie and Ruth to utilize some of the provisions that the Yankees had given them in order to prepare a dinner that was shared among the appreciative soldiers. A table, laden with food, was erected on the bluff overlooking the stream that flowed past the mansion, and Erin strolled among the soldiers, performing the social amenities that would normally be expected of a hostess.

She realized, of course, the risk she was taking by allowing the Confederates to spend the night at Kilkieran. But she could not, in good conscience, grant refuge to an enemy soldier, then turn her fellow compatriots aside. Besides, she reasoned, the major had been literally unconscious for several days, and the likelihood of him creating a distraction that might invite discovery was practically nonexistent.

Even if danger was imminent, the fact that one of the soldiers had served for a brief time with Michael, and was able to tell her a little about him, made flirting with the chance of discovery worthwhile. But later, after the festivities had ended and Erin retired to her room, she was given just cause to regret her decision.

She had just concluded her evening ablution and had sat down before the mirror to brush the tangles from her long, satiny tresses when she became aware of a commotion in the abutting chamber. The brush halted in midstroke as she jumped to her feet, hastily wrapping her robe about her to cloak her nakedness, and she veritably flew into the major's room to determine the source of the disturbance.

Erin was quite surprised by the scene that she discovered when she entered the chamber. For the most part, Kellen's reaction to the fever had been mild. He had suffered with intermittent bouts of chills and perspiration, and the intensity of the fever had fluctuated from abnormally high to moderate. But ever since he had fallen victim of this deep, almost impenetrable sleep, it had appeared as if he rested comfortably. Therefore Erin could not fathom the reason for his current behavior.

In reality, the explanation was a simple one. Kellen was in the midst of a delirium which had been ignited by the nagging fever that had tormented him for days. He thrashed about uncontrollably on the bed as if it were a berth of fiery embers rather than the downy soft mattress. He was totally oblivious to what was taking place around him, and he groaned incoherent mumblings, at last emitting an anguished cry that brought Erin across the room in an instant to soothe him, and quell his unrestrained ravings.

"Oh, do be quiet, Yankee!" she whispered hysterically.

The windows were open part way, and Erin could hear the rhythmic creak of the porch swing directly beneath the front gallery, and she realized that if Kellen's cries grew much louder, they would be easily heard by the soldiers who still

112

lounged near the front of the mansion. Realizing that detection must be avoided at all costs, she climbed upon the roomy bed beside the major and grasped his large hand in hers.

She brushed her other hand along his chest, and was alarmed by the severity of the heat that burned her delicate fingertips. Thinking that a cool sponge bath, and another dose of Maisie's bitters might serve to alleviate the sudden crisis, Erin started to leave to collect the necessary materials. But the hand that surrounded hers tightened instinctively, and Erin could not free herself from its persistent grip.

"Major," she hissed desperately, hoping that somehow she might break through his cloudy memory and make him understand her, "there are Confederate soldiers on the lawn. You *must* be quiet!"

"Vanessa?" he mumbled vaguely.

"What? Who?" Erin murmured in a hushed tone, completely mystified by his utterance.

The sudden increased activity of the soldiers outside the house caused Erin to move abruptly, and she cocked her ear toward the window to hear the faintest sound. Again, the major would not relinquish her hand and, to Erin's profound horror, she found herself being pulled to a reclining position beside the Yankee. Impulsively, she tried to jerk away from him.

"Vanessa!" he sternly reprimanded her.

"*Shhh!* They'll hear you!" Erin pleaded with the delirious major.

She was nearly in tears; afraid that they might be discovered, yet terrified at what the major might be contemplating in his irrational state of mind, especially now that he thought her to be someone named Vanessa. Lord only knew what he expected of her, and only her passionate desire to keep Kilkieran and its people safe from harm forced her to lie sanguinely in the major's arms.

"Don't leave me, Vanessa," he urged, softly nuzzling his face

113

in the silky strands of hair that flowed across the pillow. "Not yet."

"I . . . I won't. I . . . I'm here," she stammered. "Rest now, and try to get some sleep," she whispered softly, not knowing exactly what she should say to ease the major's troubled thoughts.

Even in his present state of delirium, Kellen seemed to find her statement amusing, and a soft chuckle resounded in his chest. For Erin was to quickly learn that *sleep* was not the predominant concern of the feverish major.

Very carefully, he turned her face toward him and, while his lips claimed hers in a tender caress, his hand crept down across her bosom till it found the sash that bound the restrictive garment to her. Before Erin could offer a protest, he untied the belt and spread the robe apart, so that she lay naked beside him. Then one hard, yet surprisingly gentle hand began to roam over her flesh, causing her to gasp at his familiar and intimate exploration of her body.

Erin somehow managed to pull away from his kiss, and she placed her hand over his to halt its inquisitive plunderings. But the Yankee was persistent and, gently the knuckles of his workworn hand caressed the fineness of her cheek, and his feverish lips again claimed hers in a tender embrace that left Erin quite bemused. Once again, his hands resumed their curious probing of the enticing flesh beneath them.

They roved expertly along the gentle, tantalizing curves; pressing here, touching there, leisurely mapping out a course that left not an inch of the stimulating flesh unexamined. Finally, the wandering hands found her youthful breasts and, as they began their skillful, unhurried fondling of the voluptuous mounds, Erin stiffened in his embrace.

As she lay there, her body rigid and tense, Erin became suddenly aware of the hard, masculine body that held her in such an intimate embrace. She was pressed so close to him that she actually burned from the personal contact of her naked flesh against his feverish skin and, unthinkingly, she frantically tried to push him away from her.

Sensing his companion's reluctance to his lovemaking, Kellen pulled her even tighter in his powerful arms, and snuggled his lips to her ear and muttered some unintelligible endearment, as if to help alleviate her tension. But his next maneuver was to completely unnerve Erin. For Kellen lightly placed a kiss against her petulant mouth then, ever so gently, he began to trace a pattern of feathery soft kisses along her neck and shoulder, zigzagging until he at last captured the treasure his fiery lips sought. But when the resolute lips finally encircled the taut peak of her breast, Erin began to weep.

She wept out of fear and shame and confusion. She feared what the major might ultimately attempt, for regardless of his weakened state, she had felt the urgent prodding of his aroused manhood along her thigh. She was ashamed that her body was being the subject of such ill-use by a veritable stranger who, in his delirium, did not even realize who she was. And she was confused. For although she despised the Yankee and thought his actions to be thoroughly despicable, she could not clearly understand why she was not completely disgusted by his sensual overtures.

Indeed, she had become rather accustomed to being manhandled and brutalized by Yankees; therefore the major's conscientious and affectionate behavior was a most perturbing surprise. As she lay quietly in his arms, Erin became acutely aware of the lips that still fondled her quivering breasts and, uncertainly, she placed her shaking fingers in the thick strands of his hair and diligently nudged his head away from the distracting spheres.

She could see his eyes by the moonlight that flooded the chamber and though they were open and scrutinizing the face that observed him with genuine apprehension, Erin could ascertain by the glassy cast that they held no comprehension of what was taking place.

He was above her in the darkness, the crystal-blue eyes now enflamed with fever and passion, and he poised, ready to claim the ultimate prize. His breathing had become heavy and labored as he positioned himself above her, his throbbing manhood anxious to proceed with the pleasurable encounter.

But when Erin felt the pulsating organ gently prodding against the most intimate and secret regions of her femininity, she could no longer endure the torment and, with a resurgence of strength, she again tried to push the major away from her. When this failed, she pounded furiously against his muscular chest with her determined fists.

"No, Yankee!" she whimpered desperately. "Please, remember who I am, and let me go. I'm not your Vanessa."

Kellen, of course, could not interpret her hysterical ravings, but something clicked in his unconsciousness, making him abandon his amorous advances. And though he did not release her entirely, he did ease himself down beside her on the wide berth and, placing a fleeting kiss upon her lips, he pulled her into his protective embrace and settled into a restful slumber.

But sleep was the furthest notion from Erin's distressed thoughts. Time and again she attempted to extricate herself from Kellen's stalwart grip, but whenever she moved, his hold tightened instinctively, thwarting her futile attempts at escape. Finally, with her ear resting against his chest, she became more relaxed by the rhythmic cadence of the even beating of his heart. Her primary objective of escape was quickly forgotten as Erin, too, fell victim of a deep, comforting sleep.

Erin stretched and yawned as she stirred in the early morning hours following her peaceful slumber. Eyes still closed, and not yet fully aware of her surroundings, she rolled to one side, arms reaching out to enfold her pillow. But when she burrowed her face into the fluffy bolster, her delicate cheekbone came into contact with a multitude of prickly chest hairs rather than the smooth fabric of a pillow slip, and her eyes snapped open as her semiconsciousness abruptly remembered her whereabouts.

Thinking to remove herself to her own bedchamber before being discovered by Maisie or another servant, Erin stealthily unwrapped her arms from Kellen's broad chest and, without glancing in his direction, she started to roll away from him. But she halted suddenly when, as she rolled, she bumped into the arm that had hastily braced itself beside her shoulder. She turned hesitantly, distressed to find Kellen's curious eyes, completely devoid of fever and sleep, fixed squarely upon her.

Momentarily forgetting the awkwardness of her circumstance, Erin quickly pressed her hand along his forehead. And a look of genuine relief spread across her circumspect face when her fingers came into contact with the coolness of his flesh. Her eyes intuitively darted toward his face for a fleeting instant, too ashamed to maintain eye contact with his inquisitive eyes for any length of time.

"Your . . . your fever has apparently broken," she murmured softly.

"Apparently," he replied huskily, his throat hoarse and dry from days of his bout with the raging fever.

The room grew unbearably quiet; Erin obviously too embarrassed to conduct a verbal exchange under such inappropriate circumstances. Yet Kellen apparently was waiting for some explanation as to the reason for her most perplexing, albeit, pleasurable presence in his bed.

Erin, her eyes still lowered, refusing to look at him, started to gather her robe about her, and moved as if she intended to vacate the berth. But Kellen's firm hand on her shoulder, pressing her against the pillows, warned her that she would not be permitted to so nonchalantly cast the situation aside. Swallowing hard, she finally forced her eyes upward to meet the pensive, blue orbs that stared at her in absolute confusion, and Erin knew that she would be expected to account for her actions if she were to satisfactorily appease the befuddled major.

Erin had correctly assessed Kellen's mood. To say that he was surprised to discover his provocative bedmate was a gross underexaggeration. Therefore, his astonishment would account for the gruff inflection of his voice when he addressed her.

"Pardon me, but you will, I think, understand the basis for my bluntness. But what in blue blazes are you doing here?" he demanded, oblivious to the rising crescendo of his agitated voice.

"*Shhh!*" she hissed desperately, and bolted forward to a ramrod straight position on the bed, clutching the sheet to her bosom. "They might hear you."

She craned her neck toward the window, but from her vantage point she could see only the tops of the trees and the distant horizon. She had no way of knowing if the soldiers had departed.

"*Who* might hear?" he asked softly, his eyes following a trail from her naked back and shoulders to the slender hand that gripped his arm with surprising ferocity.

"The soldiers," she whispered hurriedly.

"Rebels?"

"*Confederates*," she prompted impatiently, favoring him with a critical scowl.

Kellen threw a cautious look toward the door, half expecting to be set upon at any moment. But when it appeared that no disturbance was forthcoming, he gently persuaded her back against the pillow and raised himself on one elbow above her as his piercing eyes searched her anxious face.

"Tell me what happened," he urged.

Erin briefly explained the appearance of the Confederate soldiers, and their purpose. She went on to recount how she and Christina had stalled the soldiers while the chamber had been straightened, and he had been successfully disguised as her grandmother. Only then did the serious tint of his face mellow into an amusing grin, and he congratulated her on her quick thinking and cunning imagination.

118

"You mean you are not angry with me for dressing you up in women's garb and passing you off as my grandmother?"

"Not in the least," he replied candidly, then as an afterthought, he inquired, "Should I be?"

"No. It's just that some men might have felt, well, that their masculinity had been threatened by such a charade," she offered frankly.

"Nonsense. It was your alert thinking that prevented my being captured." His voice trailed off and, uneasy by the subdued silence, Erin glanced up into his attractive face to better scrutinize the major's ponderings. "And, I assure you, " he continued after a lengthy, contemplative pause, "my . . . uh . . . *masculinity* was not endangered by the masquerade. Indeed, your nearness is a very pleasant reminder that my virility remains, shall we say, *intact*," he murmured wickedly, chuckling heartily at Erin's startled gasp.

Even though he had dared to verbalize such a bold insinuation, Kellen made no improper advances toward Erin. Instead, he continued to question her.

"Far be it from me to appear prudish, Erin, but you must understand that it isn't often these days that I awaken to discover my bed festooned with such a captivating wench." He absently stroked a strand of hair as it fell across her naked shoulder, making her flesh tingle, and setting her stomach to churning nervously. "And knowing as I do your rather passionate dislike for us good-for-nothing Yankees, I'm certain that *you* can appreciate my curiosity. I'll admit that the tale about the Confederate soldiers makes for an adventuresome story, but that hardly explains this." He spread his arm in one sweeping, elaborate gesture to indicate the bed in which they lay.

Erin looked up at him in bitter disbelief, and had to bite back the spiteful retorts that burned at the corners of her mouth.

Damn his insufferable hide anyway, she thought angrily. It would be just like the Yankee to taunt her unmercifully when

119

he had her at such a humiliating disadvantage.

But, determined not to let Kellen know that he could annoy her, Erin met his smugly amused gaze and held it throughout the ensuing narrative.

"You've been unconscious for days; quite docile actually. But last night you became delirious with the fever and, when I tried to . . . to," she faltered uncertainly, "*comfort* you in an attempt to keep you quiet, you mistook me for someone named Vanessa."

"*Vanessa!*" he fairly exclaimed.

"Shhh!" she pleaded. "Yes, Vanessa."

Kellen pulled away from her then to study her face more seriously, and he was none too pleased with the findings of his lengthy perusal. Surely to goodness, he could not have been so wretched as to have forced himself upon this innocent creature; not after all she had already suffered. What with his fever and all, certainly he would not have been capable . . .

His eyes again strayed to the face that considered him with wide, cognizant eyes.

Damn it! he swore silently. If I thought her to be Vanessa, *anything* was possible.

Kellen again drew close to Erin and, placing a questioning hand with surprising tenderness against her cheek, he asked, "Did I hurt you, little reb?"

Erin understood the hidden implication behind his question, and she swiftly put his mind to rest. "No," she hastened to explain. "You . . . you kissed me and . . . and touched me a little, but that was all." She quickly averted her eyes, lest he ascertain more from her distraught expression than she wished. "It was all quite unpleasant, to be sure, but you did not *hurt* me," she assured him.

"Unpleasant, was it?" Kellen feigned indignation at the insult. "You must certainly realize, Erin, that I was at the disadvantage last evening."

He pulled her into his rugged embrace to purposely intimi-

120

date her, and, nuzzling his nose in the chestnut-brown tresses, he breathed in the fresh scent.

"Ah," he sighed luxuriously. "Perhaps now that I am, shall we say, more capable of conducting a proper interlude, you would permit me a second chance." His lips nibbled a sensuous path along her neck, creating nervous chills that caused her to shiver uncontrollably. "I'm quite confident that I can promise you a more gratifying encounter," he murmured dauntlessly, his mouth hovering ever so near her anxious lips.

But, before she could muster the words to offer the major the scathing response that he had justly earned, a third voice joined the exchange, making Erin fairly swoon at the untimely discovery.

Chapter Seven

"Well, well, but this certainly is an enchanting little scene," Christina sneered as she strode purposely from the doorway and positioned herself at the foot of the magnificent fourposter. "No wonder you were so determined to save your precious Yankee from our soldiers, cousin. You've quite obviously grown partial to having the blue-belly about. Perhaps you've taken a fancy to his more *manly* qualities," she suggested boldly, as her eyes raked Erin up and down in bitter disgust.

"*No!* It's . . . it's not what you think, Christina," Erin began helplessly.

"*Oh?* Christina grunted snidely, her eyes burning into Erin's vulnerable flesh like hot coals. "Just what would you have me think? After all, here you are spread across his bed like some . . . some *hussy.* Why, your poor mother would positively—"

"That's quite enough, Christina," Kellen shouted roughly, throwing a chilling look in her direction. "There *is* a very simple explanation for this, and we'll gladly accommodate you . . . *later.* As for now, I think you should leave."

"I'll leave when it suits me," she snapped haughtily.

Erin felt the muscles of the arm that still encircled her tense menacingly, and she turned her guarded gaze toward the Yankee, not knowing exactly what to expect.

"I did not mean to imply that you have a choice in the matter," he told her bluntly. "Now, I should leave of my own accord if I were you, else I'll be obliged to escort you from the room."

"You wouldn't dare!" Christina challenged, knowing full well that he lay unclothed beneath the sheets. Certainly, no *gentleman* would parade himself in such a vulgar fashion before a lady.

But to her profound consternation, Kellen carefully pulled himself to a sitting position, indicating that he was fully prepared to carry out his threat. The pain in his thigh was intense, but, even so, he achieved his purpose much easier than he expected.

"You will very soon discover, madam, that I am likely to do pretty much as I damn well please," he informed her curtly. "Now, what shall it be?"

Realizing that the Yankee was just stubborn enough to carry out his outrageous threat, Christina quickly backed away from the bed and stalked to the door. "I'm leaving, Yankee," she replied bitterly, "but I'll be back. And don't think for a moment that you've heard the last of this, Erin Louise." She shook a foreboding finger at her cousin before storming from the chamber.

Kellen emitted a long, slow sigh of relief when the chamber door had closed, and he immediately turned his attention to Erin. He approached her cautiously, fully expecting her to attack him with her vicious tongue; therefore he was totally surprised when she offered no reprisal whatsoever. Indeed, she had withdrawn completely, her preoccupation devoted entirely to the task at hand as she fumbled awkwardly with the sash of her robe, apparently anxious to remove herself from the embarrassing situation.

"Here," he spoke softly, "let me."

Kellen easily pushed her hands aside and promptly secured the sash. But when he observed the huge, green eyes that were bright with unshed tears of pain and humiliation, he was moved to sincere consideration of her feelings.

"Erin," he began uncertainly. "I'm truly sorry this unfortunate incident occurred."

"Don't . . . don't patronize me, Yankee," Erin mumbled wearily, pulling herself to a sitting position on the edge of the bed, "Don't." She shrugged off the thoughtful hand that gave her shoulder an encouraging squeeze. "I don't blame you. It was foolish of me to allow the soldiers to camp here." She rubbed tiredly at the tight knot that had formed at the nape of her neck.

"No, you did the right thing. It was just unlucky that your meddlesome cousin happened along when she did. Although I cannot fathom the basis for her rather begrudging attitude," he openly aired the perplexing thought.

Erin had risen from the bed and, feeling much safer now that she had successfully removed herself from the major's grasp, she endeavored to explain. "You have to understand my cousin, Major. Before the war began, Christina was accustomed to having the majority of the county's eligible young men cluster about her skirts like lovesick puppies.

"The war has taken away all the attention and romanticism. Then you came along and, what with her playing nursemaid to you, well, I suppose she became enamored of you," she informed him candidly.

"*Me?*" Kellen was genuinely surprised by this revelation, for although Christina had tried to make herself useful during the initial stages of his fever, he had considered the girl to be little more than a nuisance. "But I'm the enemy."

"Yes," she agreed. "But you *are* a man, and you're not too awfully unattractive . . . for a Yankee."

"Thank you," he mumbled dryly.

"Oh, you know what I mean," she sighed, shamefaced by her bluntness. "To have discovered us together under such incriminating circumstances must have been a shattering blow to her pride."

"I see," Kellen murmured understandingly. "But what of you, Erin? Surely, you had your share of beaux."

"No," she replied simply. "There was and *is* only Michael."

"Are you to be married?"

"Yes, when he returns," she said confidently.

"Well." Kellen folded his arms across his broad chest and favored her with a thoughtful gaze. "My stay has caused you enough hardship. Perhaps it's time this *Yankee* gathered up his belongings and rejoined his troops." He offered her a warm smile. "Would that not please you?"

"Immensely," she confessed. "However, I fear that you might be pushing yourself unduly. After all, you've not used the leg in several days. You might discover that you're not as ready to travel as you imagine," she warned.

"Suppose we find out," he suggested.

"Shall we have breakfast first?"

"Capital idea. I do possess a fierce appetite this morning," he admitted.

"That's a good sign." She paused at the adjoining door and turned to him. "I'm afraid we had to cut away your trousers in order to perform the operation, but you look to be about the same size as was my brother, James. I'll have Maisie bring you something to eat, and I'll air out some of his things. Then if you're feeling fit this afternoon, we'll get you up on that leg."

And with that, she hurriedly left the chamber, silently thankful that her days with the annoying Yankee were apparently near an end.

Erin's prediction had proven to be correct and, though Kellen found that his maneuverability on the injured leg was substantially better than he had anticipated, he still was not ready to rejoin his men. But in the days that followed, Kellen inaugurated a rigid exercise schedule that was designed to quickly get him back in shape.

He began his routine slowly and carefully, for he did not wish to suffer a setback by reinjuring the ailing leg. With Erin's assistance, his first attempts involved little more than

125

hobbling about the chamber. But the stiffness rapidly disappeared and, within a few days, Kellen was able to maneuver without Erin's support.

The limp that had been obvious at first improved daily, giving Kellen easy access to the entire house. He was no longer confined to receiving his meals in his room, but had grown accustomed to sharing his repasts with Erin in the family dining room. Her coolness had waned a little as she watched his progress, for she realized that it would not be long before the major announced that he was well enough to leave.

Accordingly, Erin's irascible disposition mellowed toward Kellen and, admittedly, she found his companionship to be quite tolerable during the days of his recuperation. Even though she still detested the Yankee quite thoroughly, she did allow him to persuade her to accompany him on his morning walks along the James River, and rode with him through the meadows and pasturelands of Kilkieran.

It was during these outings that they began to talk more freely with one another, and they talked of what their future would be like after the war. Erin of course, would marry Michael and settle down to raise a family, and Kellen would return to Washington City to resume control of his various business enterprises. Aside from this revelation, Erin was unable to obtain much additional information about Kellen.

Despite her usual indifference toward the Yankee, she quickly discovered herself becoming more and more intrigued by the enigmatic man who had so suddenly entered her life. But Kellen had offered little insight into his personal life and, Erin, being well bred in matters of this sort, had not considered it appropriate to pry into his private affairs.

"In all likelihood, he has some dowdy old sourpuss, Yankee-girl simply pining for him up North," she mumbled half-aloud as she browsed through the merchandise along the shelf-lined walls of the local mercantile.

Not only had the major's leg shown marked improvement, but his appetite had returned as well. Heretofore, Erin had been accustomed to providing a somewhat meager fare for Kilkieran's inhabitants, but the major's ravenous cravings had prompted this excursion into town to replenish the plantation's dwindling pantry.

Erin had, at first, considered visiting Briar Cliff to see if her Aunt Lydia might be able to spare a few things, but she did not want to take the chance of running into Christina. Besides, Kellen had surreptitiously slipped some gold coins into the palm of her hand when he had learned that MacPhearson's store was her destination.

Erin had selected the most desperately needed items, and was making her way toward the counter when a display of cigars caught her eye. As she placed the merchandise on the counter, she recalled how Kellen had commented, following the previous evening's repast, that he longed for a cigar to accompany his after dinner brandy.

"I guess you'll be wantin' to stock up on those now that Graham'll be comin' home."

Erin had paused in front of the cigar display, her thoughts miles away. Therefore the shopkeeper's statement had startled her, drawing her attention away from the rolled tobacco leaves.

"I beg your pardon," she cleared her throat and stepped to the counter, hoping that her undue interest in the cigars had not aroused the merchant's curiosity.

On the contrary, the crusty old man was pleased to have someone to talk with, especially now that he had such agreeable news to impart. "The cigars," he continued amiably. "I seen you eyein' them. As I recollect, that's the brand your brother was partial to, and now that the war is over, and he'll likely be comin' home soon, I just thought—"

But Erin's hand shot out and clutched the sleeve of his shirt with such intensity that the man paused in mid-sentence to gape at her.

"What did you say?" she asked hoarsely. "The war is . . . is *over?*" The last word was barely audible from her astonished lips. "But when . . . how?"

"The first parolé from General Lee's Army came through here this mornin'. He exchanged the news I just told you for a plateful of my missus' flapjacks." As Mr. MacPhearson related the story, he began wrapping Erin's purchases in a heavy, brown paper. "Reckon he was tellin' the truth right enough, cause another young fella dropped in 'bout an hour or so after he'd gone. Surprised you didn't meet him on the road."

"No, no. I saw no one," she muttered numbly, hardly believing the words she had waited so long to hear. This awful conflict had finally ended.

"Yep, guess old General Lee decided that there'd been enough bloodshed, and he surrendered to Grant at Appomattox a few days ago. Of course, some of our boys to the South are still holdin' on, but it'll only be a matter of time before Johnston gives it up as well, I reckon," he speculated.

MacPhearson had completed his task and looked up at Erin, a friendly grin spreading his lips. "What about the cigars, Miss Richards?"

"What? Oh, yes. I'll take some." She grabbed a fistful from the tin box and tossed them onto the counter.

"I suppose you'll be wantin' to add this to your account till your brothers git home to settle up," the shopkeeper suggested slowly, obviously disenchanted with the notion of another credit purchase.

"No, I'll be paying now." Erin surprised the man by dropping the gold pieces into his outstretched palm. "That should more than cover these purchases, Mr. MacPhearson." Erin hastily gathered up her parcels and made straightway for the door. "You can deduct the remainder from my account.

"Good-day," she said shortly and, with that, she verily flew down the steps to Lady.

If she had noted the puzzled expression on the merchant's face in regard to receiving cold, hard cash from her, she gave no indication. For Erin was pressed to get home and tell the

Yankee the good news. She had no time to worry about the old shopkeeper's curiosity.

Kellen was in the barn when Erin rode up the long, winding driveway an hour or so later. He had ridden with her as far as the main road when she left to conduct her errand then, not wishing to be discovered by some passing neighbor, he returned to the barn to administer a firm brushing to his horse. He had just completed that task and fed and watered the animal when Erin flung the barn door open, causing it to crash against the side wall, startling Kellen's horse so that it reared.

"Whoa, Achilles!" Kellen commanded as he deftly sidestepped the huge hoof that came precariously close to his head. He reached out, and grabbed a handful of the rich, red mane and brought the animal under control. "There boy. It's all right," he gently soothed the beast and, settling the horse in his stall, he turned on Erin furiously.

"Just what in the name of all that's holy did you think you—" He stopped ranting when he observed the whitish pallor of her face, and he rushed forward to take her hand and offer his support. For one anxious moment, he actually feared that she might be about to faint.

"What is it?" he whispered hurriedly, peering over her shoulder into the barnyard to see if the reason for her anxiety was there. But discovering nothing out of the ordinary, he turned to her. "Did you see more soldiers?"

"No," she mumbled vaguely.

Kellen led her outside and seated her on a wooden bench beside the barn. He sat down beside Erin and, still holding her hand for reassurance, he questioned her softly, "What's wrong, little reb? Did someone hurt you? Has Christina been badgering you again?"

"No." She shook her head slowly. "I'm sorry, Major. I must apologize for my peculiar behavior. It's just that I'm somewhat numbed from what I've just learned."

"What?"

Erin gazed up at the major, her brilliant green eyes wide with a myriad of emotions, and she grasped him by both arms as she searched his puzzled face.

At last, she breathed, "It's over. I cannot truly believe it, but it's finally over."

Kellen did not at first fully understand the implication of her statement, but as the pent up tears of emotional relief, joy, and frustration began to trickle down the cheeks of the stunned face that was still turned on him, comprehension suddenly dawned on Kellen.

"Good Lord, you mean the war, don't you?" he murmured incredulously, and leaned back against the barn wall, shocked as thoroughly by the news as Erin had been.

Erin could but offer him a dazed nod in response to his question.

"Who told you this?"

"Mr. MacPhearson," she explained. "He said that some paroles from Lee's Army of Northern Virginia stopped in his store this morning. General Lee has apparently surrendered to your General Grant." She paused, as though suddenly cognitive of the significance of her words.

The war was over at long last, and the South had been defeated. Her brothers, James and Matthew, had given their lives in vain for a *cause* that was never meant to be.

Erin slowly pulled herself to her feet and smoothed at the wrinkled folds of her skirt. "I should tell the others." She started to walk toward the worn path that led to the main house.

"Are you all right?" Kellen questioned, a little concerned by her shaky appearance.

"Of course, I'm all right," she replied stiffly, pulling herself erect before the major. "The war is over, and my brothers will return soon, so we can start living like decent, Southern folk again. But best of all, Yankee, I'll soon be rid of *you*," she informed him tartly, then turned and ran the entire distance to the house.

Even in her hasty departure, Erin could hear the loud guffaw as he responded to her insolent remark, and she could feel the piercing blue eyes burn into her back as she scurried away from him.

However, the remainder of his reaction went unnoticed by Erin, for Kellen slapped his knee, folded his arms behind his head and, as his laughter subsided, he was heard to mumble fondly, "Yes, by God, that little spitfire is more than all right."

Kellen strode back and forth along the gallery outside his room and, as he paced, he puffed thoughtfully on one of the cigars that Erin had magnanimously brought to him from her afternoon excursion into town.

"Humph!" he snorted. "The little firebrand berates and condemns me at every turn, then she brings me gifts." He removed the cigar from his mouth and carefully examined the slender rod as though pondering some serious dilemma. "Bah! Women!" he snarled under his breath. "Just when I thought I was beginning to understand the little minx, she displays a whole new dimension to her character that I didn't realize existed."

His disposition suddenly sombered as he recalled the velvety softness of her skin against his on the morning he had awakened to discover her in his arms. Then he shook his head firmly to make the disturbing apparition vanish, and he deposited the cigar ashes over the parapet and jammed the rod into his mouth as he resumed his walk along the gallery. "Bah! Women!" he repeated. "Who needs them?"

Kellen continued his journey a little further along the terrace, then paused to lean against the railing as he mentally considered the decision he had made earlier in the day. That decision being to leave Kilkieran and rejoin his men, wherever they might be at this juncture. He was aware, of course, of their ultimate destination, but if a rendezvous was not meant to be, he would return to Washington headquarters and await further orders.

Kellen's thoughts were focused on some distant star, but as he stood there, his penetrating gaze fastened on the moonlit horizon, he became aware of voices behind him. His curiosity drew him near the open window, and he discovered that Erin had joined her sister-in-law for, what appeared to be, a friendly tête-à-tête before retiring for the night. Not wishing to eavesdrop on the girls' private conversation, he started to retreat, but Deborah's harsh statement made him linger near the window to hear Erin's response.

"I'll bet you're sorry that the nasty blue-belly is finally leaving." Deborah plopped down on the stool facing the dressing table mirror.

"No, Debby. It will be a vast relief to have him gone, so we don't have to worry about hiding him." But to herself she admitted that he had not been such a bad Yankee, considering the sort who had ransacked Kilkieran the first time. "We're very lucky that he didn't hold a grudge for what you . . . *we* . . . did to him," she said softly.

But she instantly regretted her words when she noticed the huge tears that welled up in the girl's eyes. "There, there, Debby," Erin soothed her. "I didn't mean to scold you, nor did I come here to talk about the Yankee."

"Then why?"

Erin picked up the gold handled hairbrush that lay on the table, and she began to gently pull it through Deborah's unevenly cropped tresses. "Well," she deliberately considered her words, "do you remember how it was before?"

"Before?" Deborah questioned vaguely.

"Yes, before the Yankees came the first time."

"I don't like to think about *that*." Deborah shook her head severely.

"No, nor do I," Erin murmured softly, and she halted the movement of the brush. "I don't expect you to remember that

132

dreadful experience, honey, but I do want you to try to recall some things . . . happy things," she said encouragingly.

"Like what?"

Erin returned the brush to the table and dropped to her knees beside her sister-in-law. "Look at yourself," she instructed, and Deborah raised reluctant eyes to the mirror. "You are very pretty, Debby, and you have a husband who is going to be coming home to you soon."

"You mean Graham, don't you?" A flicker of recognition brightened her eyes momentarily.

"Yes, do you remember him?" Erin asked hopefully. But her spirits dwindled when Deborah shrugged her shoulders indifferently.

"I suppose," Deborah muttered, then stretched her arms out in front of her and yawned tiredly. "I'm sleepy, Erin. Can I go to bed now?"

"Of course, honey," Erin sighed dismally at having her first attempt at reaching the girl and helping her face reality fail so miserably.

Erin stood up and moved to the bed to turn down the freshly laundered sheets. After Deborah had climbed into the comfortable berth, Erin sat down on the bed and reached out to smooth the hair that curled along the girl's cheek.

"Go to sleep, Debby, and we'll talk again tomorrow." She stood up and started to extinguish the lamp, but Deborah's softly spoken question made her pause.

"Erin, he won't like me very much now that I'm, you know, *different*, will he?"

"Of course, Graham will like you. It's going to be awkward at first, for you must remember that he has been away for a very long time," Erin patiently reminded her, though she did not know how much of what she was saying was truly understood by Deborah's disoriented mind. "And you're not *different*," she insisted. "You just have difficulty remembering certain things is all, and I'm going to help you remember.

"First thing tomorrow morning, I'll trim your hair and we'll

133

find some pretty ribbons for it. Then we'll search through your wardrobe and find you a more becoming frock. Why, you'll be your old self in no time at all," she said with a forced confidence.

Erin stepped to the lamp and blew out the flame, then exited the room through the French doors and emerged onto the terrace. She was feeling quite low after the disheartening encounter with Deborah, and decided that a breath of fresh air might cleanse her thoughts and help her relax.

She stepped to the railing and gazed down at the moon drenched lawn below her, and breathed deeply of the cool, April air. It was then that her nose caught the telltale hint of the aromatic tobacco, and she whirled to find Kellen observing her curiously from the shadows.

"I did not mean to startle you." He stepped forward, not the least bit concerned at being discovered.

"You didn't," she stated crisply, turning her back to him in contempt. "Although I know you to be a good number of things, I had not thought you to be a meddler. Or do Yankees routinely eavesdrop on private conversations?" she aired the question derisively, and set her fingertips to drumming impatiently against the railing.

Her shoulders drooped severely, and she heaved a weary sigh, wishing very much that the bothersome major would return to his room and allow her a few moments of peace. "Go away, please," she dismissed him curtly.

"Don't, little reb," he murmured softly.

"What?"

"Don't shove me aside. For after what I've just witnessed, it's obvious that you need to talk with someone and, like it or not, I'm the only convenient listener."

"I don't *need* —"

"Hush! It's been no easy task to hold this plantation together the past four years. Faith, a man would have been hard pressed to accomplish this much," he applauded her efforts. "So don't you think the time has come to lower that nettlesome barrier you have erected around yourself, and let someone share your burden? After all, the war *is* over; I'm no longer the enemy," he reminded her kindly.

Erin cocked her head so that she could gaze into the blue eyes that patiently awaited her reply, and she was surprised at the genuine compassion she detected in the brooding orbs. It would be a vast relief to be able to confide in someone, she admitted to herself. If only he wasn't a Yankee and, more so, a man.

For even though she and Michael had been terribly close, she had never confided in him the things she was about to disclose to this Yankee, a veritable stranger. But Erin somehow found the courage, and she turned to Kellen.

"You heard and saw her. What is my brother going to think of me for allowing his wife to deteriorate into such a childlike state?" she finally admitted her nagging fear.

"I sincerely doubt he will blame you for her condition." Kellen gently eased her away from the railing, and they walked to the stairway that led to the verandah below them, and they sat down upon the top step. "She was evidently *normal* when she married your brother," he reasoned. "What happened?"

Kellen, of course, remembered the doctor's version of the incident, but he speculated that it might be an emotional relief for the girl if she were to cleanse her conscience of the horrible episode.

Erin was reluctant at first, but at last, she breathed, "Yankees."

"Go on."

"It was the September after the war began," she explained. "My father and brothers had gone down to the sawmill. You know the one; we walked there one day," she paused uncertainly.

"I know the place," he nodded, "but if the war had begun, why were your brothers still here? Had they not yet enlisted?" he inquired curiously.

"No," she said slowly. "You see, Father had wished to remain neutral. James wanted to join up right away, but Papa had forbidden it. He blamed the war on the politicians, and he refused to send his sons to die for a *cause* he did not fully support."

"I see."

"Anyway, there was a problem at the mill, and my brothers went with Papa to check on the matter. Our workers were in the fields to the east, so the house was virtually empty except for Mamma, Deborah, a few house servants and myself." Erin paused for a moment and swallowed deeply.

She had relived the horrible nightmare in her dreams for many, many months, but she had *never* told anyone the frightening details. Erin glanced sideways at Kellen's somber face, and she faltered, uncertain if she could continue.

But Kellen's calm voice prompted her in the darkness, "Is that when the soldiers arrived?"

"Yes," she whispered hoarsely. "Deborah and I were in the nursery. There were only a dozen or so of them, but they rode up the driveway at such a furious pace that the horses' hooves pounding against the ground sounded like thunder. Indeed, that is what I thought it to be, until I ran to the window to scan the horizon and saw *them*."

"Nursery?" Kellen had been understandably intrigued by this revelation, for he had not encountered any children during his sojourn at Kilkieran.

Erin nodded. "Deborah was with child. She wasn't very far along, but she was so excited about the event that we had already begun redecorating the nursery."

"What happened next?" Kellen leaned forward to extinguish the cigar, yet he listened intently to her tale.

"I ran downstairs to warn Mother, but I was too late. They had already locked the servants in the laundry house, and Mother had confronted their captain on the front porch."

In the darkness, Erin did not notice the reflective smile that flickered across Kellen's handsome face as he mentally recalled a similar confrontation with genuine fondness; the day

136

when Erin had welcomed him to Kilkieran.

"At first, the soldiers did not act as if they intended to harm us. They raided the smokehouse and pulled up Mamma's shrubs and flowers . . . senseless destruction of things that were of sentimental value to us. But then something happened and everything got out of hand — "

"What was it, Erin?" Kellen interrupted. "What happened that caused the soldiers to react with violence?"

"I . . . I cannot remember," she choked back the sobs that had risen in her throat. "I used to try to remember, but it's no use." She shook her head helplessly. "All I see, when I close my eyes and think of it, is my mother snatching the bandanna from the captain's face and then . . . total mayhem."

"Bandanna?" Kellen again intervened, thinking that disclosure to be peculiar for some reason.

"Yes, all the Yankees had shielded their faces," Erin explained simply. "Then everything seemed to happen at once," she continued. "Mamma began struggling with the captain, and some of the other men grabbed Deborah, and . . ." her voice trailed off doubtfully.

Kellen had realized that her vivid description of the haunting ordeal would probably rekindle a multitude of terrifying memories for Erin. But his purpose in persuading her to recount the incident had been to help her unlock the door to that part of her consciousness behind which she had secured away the answer that could absolve her of the tormenting nightmare that haunted her; a constant reminder of the vicious assault.

"And?" he persisted.

"I escaped through the back door," she emitted a nervous sigh. "I had intended to run to the mill to summon help, but . . . but there was a soldier blocking the path, so I turned toward the barn instead." She paused again, unconscious of the solicitous arm that had encircled her shoulder.

Kellen's hand reached out to stay the frantic wringing of her hands as she revealed, what had been for Erin, the most terrifying part of the attack. "He chased you into the barn?" he offered.

Erin nodded stiffly. "He and two others."

"*Three!*" he cried in bitter anger, outraged that soldiers of a common cause had demonstrated such despicable behavior toward innocent civilians.

"Yes, they trapped me inside the barn." Her eyes were alive with terror. Though she desperately wanted to dispense with the narrative, something willed her to continue, and the remainder of her story tumbled uncontrollably from her trembling lips.

"They kept grabbing and pawing at me, and they spun me around from one to the other until I thought I might faint from dizziness. Then . . . then they pushed me down, and . . . and—" Her voice finally broke off, and she at last succumbed to the sobs that she had courageously held back.

"It's okay, little one," Kellen whispered tenderly, as he pulled her onto his lap, and securely wrapped her in his protective embrace. "Go ahead and cry." He smoothed the hair that hung loosely about her shoulders and pressed a comforting kiss to her brow. "Lord knows it's time you purged yourself of these dreadful memories and allowed someone to console you." He gently tilted her head back and pulled a handkerchief from his pocket to dab at her tear streaked face. "Better?" he murmured.

"Yes," she sniffled, genuinely surprised by his compassionate attitude.

"Did Deborah lose the child?" he inquired and, although her tears had subsided, he still held her close.

Erin nodded. "It was after that when she began to change; *everything* changed. My brothers were enraged by what the Yankees had done. You see, Mother also died during the attack."

"They murdered your mother?"

"No, not like you think, though they were certainly responsible. Mamma had a weak heart, and Doc Wilson said that the raid was just too much for her to endure," she explained. "Within a matter of days, my brothers enlisted in the army, leaving Papa and me to manage things."

"What happened to him?"

"He died," Erin replied simply. "He loved my mother very deeply, Major. Then when the news came about Matthew and James, well, he seemingly lost the will to live."

"Well, at least now I can better understand the basis for your hostility," Kellen said somberly. "I realize that it's of little consolation, but I am truly sorry that your family was victimized by *so-called* soldiers of the Union Army. But perhaps now that you and I have had this talk the nightmares won't torment you as frequently."

Erin pushed away from the major and scrutinized his face carefully. "How did you know?"

"My chamber adjoins yours," he reminded her. "More than once I have been awakened by your anguished screams. I wanted to approach you before, but was uncertain of the reception I might receive." His voice trailed off pensively and, as his eyes met hers in the moonlight, Kellen found himself suddenly flooded with desire for the beguiling creature that was nestled trustingly in his embrace.

Very carefully, he lifted one hand to stroke the exquisitely structured cheek, and he forcibly swallowed the tortured groan that obstructed his throat when he heard her gentle sigh. Without truly considering his actions, Kellen purposefully lowered his head and covered Erin's mouth with his own. To his pleasant surprise, Kellen encountered no resistance from Erin and, thus encouraged, he pulled her more tightly against him to revel in the delightful sensation of her honeyed-lips as they trembled slightly beneath his.

Losing himself to his passion, Kellen conducted a thorough exploration of those lips that melded so compatibly against his own. With a little moan, he pulled away to place a fleeting kiss against her closed eyelids. He kissed the tip of her nose, her brow, nibbled on her earlobe, and finally pressed his lips

139

against the little pulse that thundered in the hollow of her throat before returning to recapture their original prize.

Erin shifted on his lap and struggled to maintain her composure. At first, it had seemed quite natural for Kellen to kiss her. After all, she had just shared her most intimate secrets with him. It was inevitable that he would want to comfort her.

What Erin had not anticipated; what she found so disturbing was her own growing response to Kellen's touch. She had vague recollections of Michael's embraces, but she could not recall ever feeling so completely overwhelmed by a man's caress. Her skin positively tingled with sensitive gooseflesh, and a warm, exciting glow had begun to spread upward from the pit of her stomach.

She was about to lose all reason when she felt Kellen's strong hand separate the folds of her dressing robe and slide beneath her gown to skillfully fondle her breasts. Erin stiffened instinctively as she felt her nipples harden under his precise manipulation and, to her horror, she heard the soft whimper from the back of her throat that she could not withhold.

As Erin fought to curb her wildly escalating passions, she became aware of Kellen's abrupt movement, and she felt herself being lifted in his arms. Realizing that he was carrying her toward her room, she suddenly panicked, tearing her mouth from his.

"N-n-no!" she cried. "Please, Yankee, don't," Erin pleaded, desperately pushing against his chest for her release.

"Shhh," Kellen cooed soothingly. "Don't worry, little reb. Not that I don't consider you to be a captivating temptation, mind you," he admitted candidly as he stepped across the threshold and laid her gently upon the bed. "But I have never been inclined to take from a lady that which was not freely given."

He leaned down then and pressed a brief, affectionate kiss to her confused lips and, when he pulled away, his eyes met and held hers in the semi-darkness. "Another time, different circumstances perhaps, and who is to say what fate could have determined for us?" he whispered speculatively, almost forlornly. "Pleasant dreams, little one."

He left her then, leaving a very befuddled Erin to stare at the dark void his departure had created. In an emotional daze, Erin lifted her fingers to the lips that his had only moments before caressed. And his disturbing conjecture was still plaguing Erin's thoughts when she finally drifted off to sleep.

Chapter Eight

Erin stood before the full-length cheval mirror, clad only in a threadbare chemise, considering her reflection with a critical eye. She was notably distraught by the ragged image that returned her gloomy stare. Her gaze deliberately wandered over the figure that had grown thin and gaunt over the past four years and finally came to rest on the face that bore a distinctly troubled frown.

It was as though the likeness reflected in the mirror belonged to a stranger, such was the impact of her wan appearance. Erin emitted a long, desolate sigh as she stepped to the dressing table and sat down dejectedly on the padded stool.

"What have you done to yourself, Erin Louise Richards?" she muttered glumly. "Why, you used to be the belle of the county and now look at you."

She leaned closer to the mirror to scrutinize her colorless cheeks, which only caused her to lament forlornly, "You look more like an old dowager rather than the youthful sweetheart that Michael must certainly be expecting to find when he returns."

But the disturbing image of another unobtrusively inched its way into Erin's consciousness, driving away all thoughts of her intended and causing a disconcerting frown to tug at the corners of her petulant mouth. "I'm certain that *he* considers me to be quite plain. Not that I'm concerned with what that irritating Yankee thinks." She shrugged her shoulders indifferently and gave her head a careless toss. "It's just—"

But the dubious cast of Erin's eyes belied her nonchalant musings as her fingers mechanically climbed to her lips, and she wistfully recalled the gentle pressure of Kellen's mouth against her own and his softly spoken murmurings of the past evening. Quite involuntarily, her skin came alive with tingly gooseflesh, and she shook her head vigorously to rid her mind of the disquieting ruminations.

"Stop being such a ninny," she admonished herself, shaking a severe finger at her likeness in the mirror. "He's a *Yankee*; something to be loathed, not regarded with fondness.

"Still," she murmured thoughtfully, her eyes never wavering from her reflection, "that does not mean I must parade before the scoundrel looking like a homely spinster," she reasoned.

Reaching for the hairbrush, she pulled it through her hair until it fairly glistened, then she arranged the heavy tendrils in a charming style. Next she turned her attention to choosing a suitable gown, and she crossed the room and began rummaging through the clothespress that at one time had held such a vast assortment of dresses that even the most fashionable lady would have been envious. Presently, however, Erin had a somewhat more modest array from which to make her selection.

It was not until Erin had begun searching through the armoire that she realized how truly weary she had grown of wearing the modest, everyday gowns that Maisie usually laid out for her. With determination, she reached deeper into the clothespress and withdrew a dress that met her approval. She quickly donned the frock and stepped to the mirror to inspect her appearance.

The gown she had chosen was of a soft chintz material; the calico print consisted of tiny blue and rose colored flowers against a white background. The tight fitting bodice was modestly cut and trimmed with a blue lace that matched the blue of her gown, and the sleeves were short, coming just above her elbows where they fit snugly about her shapely arms. The skirt was full and billowed out over the crinoline underskirt to gently swirl about her tiny feet.

Almost satisfied with the results of her labor, Erin grasped her cheeks between slender fingers and pinched at the delicate flesh until it was a bright crimson. Then she turned and, feeling more lighthearted than she had in months, she bounded from the chamber to find the major and bid him a cordial farewell.

Erin learned from Maisie that the major had risen early, partaken of a hearty breakfast and withdrawn to the barn. Her immediate impulse was to join him, but the housekeeper was determined that her mistress should enjoy a nourishing repast before proceeding with her daily routine.

Maisie was surprised at Erin's voracious appetite as she observed her mistress devour a huge stack of her special flapjacks and wash them down with a tall glass of cold milk. She had been understandably concerned with the piddling meals that the girl had subsisted on as of late, so to see her mistress attack her meal with such vigor was a pure delight for the servant. She attributed Erin's improved appetite to the fact that the war had ended which meant that the young masters would be coming home soon to resume management of the plantation. But more predominantly, Maisie imagined that Erin was relieved because the annoying Yankee would finally make his departure today.

Erin hurriedly gobbled down her food, oblivious to Maisie's close scrutiny, then she scurried to the barn to see Kellen off on his journey. She pulled the huge barn door open and stepped inside, pausing for a moment to allow her eyes to adjust to the dark interior. Upon first inspection, the barn appeared to be empty and, for some unfathomable reason, Erin felt deeply saddened that Kellen might have departed without saying good-bye. But the sudden whicker from the stall where the major stabled his mount quickly dispelled her fears, and Erin stepped to the animal and lifted her hand to scratch him behind the ear.

"Good morning, fella," she cooed affectionately. "Haven't seen that ornery master of yours, have you?"

"He's right behind you," Kellen's deep voice interrupted her play with the animal, and she turned to offer him her most becoming smile. "And he's a trifle chagrined that his hostess continues to call him names on the day of his departure." Kellen feigned indignation at her remark, but Erin recognized the sparkle in his eye that belied his anger, and she continued to smile at him.

"Oh, you know what I meant," she began, but a sudden mishap left her completely bereft of speech.

She had turned her back on Achilles to converse with Kellen, yet she remained standing directly in front of the animal's stall. In a playful mood, Achilles extended his nose to nuzzle Erin's shoulder with such force that it upset her balance, sending her stumbling forward into Kellen's arms.

Erin's immediate reaction was to push herself free from his embrace, but when she gazed up into the contemplative blue eyes that studied her, the will to struggle abruptly vanished, such was the impact of his brooding expression.

"Yes, I know what you meant." He at last broke the awkward silence. "You know, little reb," his voice grew suddenly serious, and his lips were poised just inches from her own, "I think that I shall miss you a great deal," he crooned softly, and Erin tensed in his arms and, for one breathless moment, she feared that he might be about to kiss her.

That is precisely what Kellen wanted to do, but common sense prevailed, and he gently set her from him as he stepped around her to offer his horse a severe reprimand. "As for you, my friend," he shook a stern finger at the animal, "what nonsense is this; shoving our lovely hostess about?"

Erin righted herself and pressed a hand to her breast to steady the rapid thumping of her heart. She watched silently

145

while Kellen tended the animal and her nerves had calmed considerably when he again turned to her.

As if truly seeing Erin for the first time, his discerning gaze swept over her from head to toe. "My, but you are looking quite lovely today," he said admiringly. He stepped back a little and placed his hands on his hips. "Turn around and let me look at you," he encouraged.

Erin felt herself flush at his leisurely inspection, but it had been so long since she had been the subject of such an admiring perusal that she modestly obliged his request.

"Yes, lovely indeed," he continued when Erin once again faced him. "Tell me, is this the prevailing fashion for bidding *adieu* to pesky house guests?" he voiced the jibe lightly, not accusingly.

"N-n-no," she stuttered doubtfully, uncertain as to how she should respond to his banter. "Truthfully, I haven't a notion as to the latest styles. Faith, I haven't seen a fashion plate since the war began, but I'm certain the modes have changed drastically," she chatted on while he watched her fondly. "I'm so tired of the same drabby clothes; I just wanted to wear something that made me appear a little more feminine."

"Well, you certainly succeeded," Kellen conceded, and he stepped past her and sauntered toward one of the anterooms. "Although I've personally never experienced much difficulty in distinguishing you from the others. You do leave a rather lasting impression on one," he added thoughtfully before disappearing into the workshop.

Her curiosity aroused, Erin followed him. "What are you doing?" she asked when she saw the block of wood on the table before him and the wood shavings that were scattered about his boots.

Kellen sat down at the workbench and motioned her to his side. "Come closer and I'll show you. To be honest, I'd welcome some objective criticism."

Erin hugged her arms to her waist as she stepped to the worktable and took up a stance behind him. Leaning closer to

146

peer over his shoulder, she discovered an ornately carved sign emblazoned with the name of her beloved plantation.

"That's quite beautiful," she whispered lowly. "But . . . why?"

"Oh, I've needed something to help me pass the time these past few days," he stated simply. "When we were riding one day, I noticed that the signpost at the entrance had rotted. So when I found the necessary materials and tools here in the workshop, I decided to put my talents to good measure.

"I came out early today to brush on the final coat of varnish. It's almost dry," he noted. "Would you care to ride out with me while I post it in its proper place?"

"Oh, yes. I'd enjoy that very much," she responded happily. "I'll go saddle Lady."

"Whoa, little lady. *I'll* ready the horses. You take this." He handed her the sign. "Too heavy?"

"No," she assured him.

"Good. I'll meet you outside in a few minutes." He ushered her to the door, then went to prepare their mounts.

The ride along the winding driveway in the warm, April sunshine proved to be a refreshing and exhilarating excursion, and much of the color had been restored to Erin's cheeks by the time they arrived at the entrance to Kilkieran. They had chatted easily on the trail and, as Kellen reached up to help her from Lady's back, the words he had spoken in the barn kept floating through her head; "I shall miss you a great deal . . ."

Reluctantly, Erin admitted to herself that she would miss the Yankee as well. But only a little, she quickly justified her moderate interest in the major.

"It won't be much longer," Kellen said, misinterpreting the basis for her sudden pensive mood.

Erin's reflective musings vanished instantly, and she turned an inquisitive gaze to the major as she braced her hands on his sturdy shoulders while he lifted her effortlessly from Lady's back and placed her on the ground in front of him. "What?"

147

"This contemplative frown." He gently ran a finger along the contour of her face. "As soon as I hang this sign, I'll be on my way, and there will no longer be a reason for such an unbecoming expression to mar your pretty face."

"Oh," she muttered in reply.

Erin watched as Kellen collected the sign, hammer and pegs and moved to the fencepost and began removing the old marker that had deteriorated over the years. She clasped her hands loosely behind her back and paced back and forth in the shade.

"I suppose you *are* growing anxious to return home," she offered.

"Uh huh," he mumbled, never losing his preoccupation with his task.

"Your wife should be especially happy to see you again," she ventured shyly.

Kellen had positioned the sign to his satisfaction, and was preparing to anchor the final peg, but Erin's offhand conjecture caused his aim to be faulty, and he caught the side of his thumb with the head of the hammer.

"Damn it!" he swore, rounding on her, a look of total bewilderment crossing his handsome countenance. *"Wife!"* he exclaimed. "What wife? I've never mentioned a wife."

"No," she agreed. "But . . . Vanessa?"

"Oh, *her.*" Kellen abruptly dismissed the subject and, returning his attention to the signpost, he promptly completed the undertaking. "Vanessa is many things, little reb, but fortunately my wife is not included amongst them."

"I see," she muttered confusedly, mentally recalling how he had cried out the woman's name in his delirium, as well as his subsequent plunderings. Erin had naturally assumed that he and the woman were romantically involved.

"Vanessa is married to my cousin, Geoffrey," he went on to explain, and Erin could not help but notice how a distinct air of contempt had mysteriously crept into his voice.

"But?"

"Erin," Kellen sighed indulgently and, replacing the hammer in the saddlebag on Lady's back, he strolled over to her. "I'm flattered with your sudden interest in my personal life, but this particular part of my past is rather complicated and, quite frankly, not worthy of discussion.

"Do you think we might devote our last minutes together to a more pleasant topic?" he tactfully changed the subject. "Does the sign suit you?"

Erin nodded and, though her curiosity about his association with Vanessa had been duly piqued, she relented to his request to maneuver the discussion away from his private affairs. "It does make for an impressive enhancement to the entranceway to Kilkieran," she agreed.

"Kilkieran," he repeated the name thoughtfully. "That is a bit unusual. Would I be prying if I inquired as to its origin?"

"Not at all," Erin responded readily, favoring him with a dazzling smile. "Indeed, it is quite an enchanting tale, and I love recounting it, but I know that you are anxious to be on your way—"

"Correction. *You're* the one who is anxious to be rid of me," he accused and, taking her hand, he guided her toward the horses. "I'm in no great rush. Might I suggest that you regale me with the story while we stroll toward the house?" He gathered the reins in his hands and tugged the horses into motion, leaving Erin little recourse save to follow him.

"The name Kilkieran comes from a small bay near my mother's childhood home in Ireland," she explained. "Her name was Maura Shaughnessy, and she was quite beautiful; with hair as red as a blazing sunset and an alluring charm that bewitched many a young Irish lad," she informed him proudly.

"It sounds as though she was quite an enchantress," he commented admiringly.

"Yes, but don't be duped by my modest description, for Mother possessed a fiery temper that could intimidate even the sturdiest of constitutions."

149

"At least you come by it honestly," Kellen chuckled beneath his breath, ignoring the indignant scowl she cast in his direction.

"Anyway," she continued, "as fate would dictate, it was Mother's exceptional beauty that set into motion the chain of events that would ultimately lead her to America.

"You see, an aristocratic gentleman became enamored of her. He was an English lord; a powerful man who was accustomed to getting that which he desired, and he desired my mother. Well, you can sufficiently imagine his outrage when he was rejected by, what he considered to be, a mere Irish peasant."

"Indeed, a beautiful woman's rejection is something that a man finds most difficult to endure," Kellen mumbled, a rueful expression suddenly appearing on his face.

Kellen led the horses from the road and released them to graze on the fresh, spring grass. Then, taking Erin's arm, he coaxed her out of the sun to share the shade of a budding elm tree. Once they were comfortably seated beneath its sheltering limbs, he urged, "Please continue, I assure you that I am thoroughly intrigued."

"You're mocking me," Erin bristled defensively.

"Not at all," he countered. "How did the English nobleman come to terms wih his anger?"

"He kidnapped Mother," Erin resumed the story, "and took her to his residence in London. He tried everything in his power to make her submit to his demands of matrimony, yet she remained unswayed. Then one night in a drunken stupor, he confronted Mother and told her that he was determined to possess her and, if she refused to be his wife, he would have her for his mistress."

"A formidable sounding rogue," Kellen interjected his musings. "Tell me, was the scoundrel successful in his lecherous plunderings?"

Erin shook her head firmly.

"Somehow, I'm not surprised," he laughed. "Allow me to

speculate; they became embroiled in a struggle, and your mother was able to render her assailant senseless, thereby, allowing her to escape with her virture unscathed."

"That's correct." Erin nodded. "Mother feared retribution from her captor, so she fled before he regained consciousness. She made her way to the waterfront where she hoped to obtain passage on a ship back to Ireland, but she had no money. Through a series of misunderstandings, she ended up as a stowaway on a ship that was destined for America."

"The luck of the Irish had obviously forsaken your mother," he interpolated. "I trust it improved."

"Yes. The captain of the vessel discovered her and, since they were already several days into their voyage, he relinquished his cabin to her rather than return her to London." Erin paused in her tale, and stood up to brush the grass from her skirt.

She had noticed two figures turn up the driveway and, while it was not uncommon for soldiers who were returning home to stop for a drink, or a bite of food, Erin thought she detected something oddly familiar about the men who slowly approached on foot. But they were too far away to distinguish, what with the noon sun creating a blinding glare, and Kellen's next question drew her immediate attention away from the strangers.

"Am I to assume that your mother married her dashing captain?"

"What?" she asked distantly. "Oh, no; though he was smitten, to be sure. But I fear that the story of how Mother and Father met is a lengthy one. Suffice to say that after they wed they settled here. Mother was never to see her homeland again, but she kept a piece of it alive in her memory forever by naming her new home for the one she had left behind in Ireland; Kilkieran."

"That's a lovely story, Erin." Kellen stood beside her. "I gather that you still have relatives there."

"Yes; a grandmother, aunts and uncles, and literally scads

of cousins that I've never seen, nor am I likely to," she added a little sadly. "We used to correspond regularly, but since the war the letters come more infrequently." Her voice trailed off as she again turned her concentration to the two men that doggedly made their way along the path.

Lifting her hand to shield her eyes from the blazing sun, Erin was able to discern that one of the men struggled along with the aid of a crudely shaped crutch; the need for which was made painfully evident by the right pants leg that hung ominously limp from below the knee. It was then that her pulse began to race wildly, and the blood drained from her face and, quite involuntarily, her hand flew out to grasp Kellen's arm for support.

"What is it, little reb?" he inquired anxiously.

But Erin could not muster a response. Instead, her trembling legs started forward and, by the time she reached the roadway, she had lifted her skirts and was running as hard as she could toward the two men. Tears of elation were flowing uncontrollably down her cheeks when she at last flung herself into her brother Graham's waiting arms.

Kellen somberly observed the happy reunion between brothers and sister from his position in the shadows. Then, hesitantly, for he was doubtful as to the sort of reception he would encounter, he retrieved the horses and started toward the group. When he reached the trio, Erin had pulled away from Graham's embrace, but she still clung to his arm.

"Oh, Evan," she cried compassionately, turning to her twin brother. "Your leg. When did it happen? Why didn't you notify me that you had been injured?" She started to embrace him, and was infinitely puzzled when he avoided her outstretched arm.

"It's nothing. There's no need to fuss," he said curtly, leveling a foreboding eye at Kellen. "Where are your manners, Erin? Aren't you going to introduce us to your *friend?*"

"It sounds as though you already suspect who I might be," Kellen offered slowly.

"I can spot a Yankee easy enough. The stench permeates the air for miles," he spat disgustedly and, jerking away from Erin, he hobbled down the driveway toward the house.

Erin's immediate impulse was to run after him, but Graham's hand on her arm stayed her movement. "No, let him go."

"But, how did you know about—" she began faintly.

"We stopped by Briar Cliff," Graham explained.

"Well, you needn't say anymore," Erin snapped bitterly. "It's obvious that Christina has regaled you with her distorted version of what has occurred here, and you've condemned me unjustly."

"Calm down, Irish," Graham gently soothed his sister. "I haven't forgotten Christina's ways, nor yours for that matter." He stroked her cheek affectionately then turned to face Kellen.

"I apologize for my brother's abruptness . . . er," he paused and, noticing the distinguishing markings on the man's military jacket, he continued, "Major. . ."

But Kellen would have none of it. "It's *mister*. Sinclair. Kellen Sinclair. The war is over, Mr. Richards, and I consider myself as much a civilian as are you," he said curtly.

"Very well, Mr. Sinclair," Graham allowed. "I'm certain that my sister has what she feels are justified reasons for offering you sanctuary in our home, however, I think you can appreciate my brother's bitterness. After all, it was a Yankee bullet that cost him his leg," Graham informed him shortly, though there was no hint of malice in his voice.

"Graham, I *can* explain," Erin began urgently.

"And so you shall." He smiled down at the tense little face that regarded him carefully. "But first, I'd like to hold my wife in my arms and get settled in the parlor with a glass of Father's best whiskey," he confessed tiredly. "Let me talk to Evan. He'll be more reasonable once he's had a chance to cool down."

Erin felt a cold chill envelop her slender frame as she watched her brother hasten down the driveway toward Evan, and she was possessed with a sense of foreboding which warned her that the already foul situation was about to worsen. It was not until she felt the solicitous hand on her shoulder that she remembered Kellen still remained close at hand, and was watching her every move.

"They'll come around," he said softly. "What man could remain angry with such a lovely creature for any length of time?"

"No." Erin shook her head numbly. "Graham pretends that it doesn't matter, at least Evan is honest with his resentment."

"I think that perhaps you've misjudged Graham," Kellen disagreed. "Once we have fully explained the circum stances . . ."

"We?" she interrupted.

"Like it or not, I feel responsible for this mess, and I'll not leave you alone to fend for yourself." He picked her up and settled her upon Lady's back and, noticing the objectionable slant of her eyebrow, he threw up his hand to forestall her protestations. "I'm staying until this matter is resolved and that, my lady, is that."

Erin paced back and forth in the front parlor, nervously awaiting her brothers' arrival. She had been apprehensive about allowing Kellen to accompany her, but he had been stalwart in his decision. But when he considerately placed a glass of claret into her hands to help steady her nerves, she was silently thankful that he had remained to help her through this difficult ordeal.

"Relax," he murmured consolingly, coaxing the glass toward her lips, "and drink this." He automatically reached out to steady her hand.

"Oh, you don't understand," she sighed desperately. "I have explained what happened the first time Yankees came to Kilkieran. The only reason my family became involved in the war was because they loathed the Yankees for what they did to us. And for me to have offered you refuge, well that's —"

"*Unforgivable!*" came the harsh completion of her statement from a voice in the doorway.

Stunned, Erin whirled to find Graham's enflamed eyes fastened squarely upon the two of them, and she quickly disengaged her hand from Kellen's. She was familiar with her brother's explodable temper and, though he appeared calm enough, she started forward, her hands outstretched beseechingly.

"Graham," she began.

"Spare me your entreaties," he said stiffly, coming full into the room, swinging the door closed behind him. "I've just come from my *wife*. It's interesting to see how you've cared for her since I've been away."

"You cannot mean to blame me," Erin objected. "After all, it was you who became so possessed with killing Yankees that you refused any opportunity to return home on furlough."

"Oh, but I do blame you, little sister, but not nearly half as much as I blame your Yankee friend, and others like him," he informed her bluntly. "But I'll discuss Deborah's condition in greater detail *after* Mr. Sinclair has displayed the good sense to leave our home once and for all."

"Now see here," Kellen interrupted angrily. "I've had it up to here with this *holier-than-thou* attitude that every man who wore the colors of the Union was a no-account, ruthless bastard. I was a *soldier,* as were you, and I performed my job to the best of my ability."

"By raping and murdering innocent women!" Graham shouted incredulously.

"There's no reasoning with you people," Kellen spat bitterly. "Fate certainly played me a cruel trick by leading me to this accursed house." He jammed his hat on his head and stalked to the door, muttering all the while. "I would have likely encountered less trouble had I abandoned that rickety wagon and carried the cargo to Richmond on my back."

Erin watched helplessly as the man who had so abruptly

entered her life prepared to execute a similar departure. Without considering the repercussions of her actions, she rushed forward to stop him, for she could not allow him to leave harboring such bitter thoughts of her.

"Kellen," she blurted his name. "Please, wait!"

Kellen had already stepped through the doorway by the time she reached him and, when he felt her slender hand on his sleeve, he paused and turned a grave frown on her.

"Don't go away like this; not hating me," she whispered hoarsely.

"I don't hate you, little reb." He instinctively brushed her cheek with his hand. "I should have left days ago, then all of this could have been avoided."

"But your leg," she insisted. "You weren't ready."

"Excuses," he berated himself, but his voice was soft and the blue eyes grew somber when he continued, "I truly regret that you have to remain behind to suffer the consequences that my presence here has caused."

"She won't be staying long, Yankee," Evan's voice called to them sharply.

Kellen and Erin whirled simultaneously to stare in confusion at Evan who stood clutching the rail at the top of the long staircase.

"Would you care to explain that remark?" Kellen asked dryly.

"Not to you," Evan replied snidely.

Graham had joined them in the wide corridor, and Erin glanced helplessly back and forth between brothers, breathlessly awaiting an explanation of Evan's perplexing declaration.

"Go on, Graham," Evan encouraged, his handsome face twisted with rage. "Tell our little sister what we've decided."

"Graham?" Erin turned to her older brother tentatively.

"I *had* hoped to discuss this sensibly; just the three of us," Graham began purposefully. "But, if you insist . . ."

"I do," Erin said staunchly.

"Very well," Graham sighed wearily. "Evan and I have discussed the situation and, considering the circumstances, we think it would be wise if you left for a while; just until the scandal dies down."

"Scandal!" she cried.

"Christina told us some pretty shocking things—"

"Christina again!" Erin set her hands on her hips and stamped her foot furiously. "That snippy cousin of ours wags her tongue recklessly. You know how she misconstrues things."

"Oh, and did she misconstrue the facts on the morning she found you abed with this blue-belly?" Evan asked haughtily.

"As a matter-of-fact, she did," Erin returned pointedly.

"Then you don't deny it?!" Graham demanded fiercely, favoring Kellen with a fulminating glare.

Erin went rigid. She had not realized that even Christina would stoop so low as to intentionally shame her before her own family. But for her brothers to condemn her on the circumstantial platitudes of their innocuous cousin, well it was more than she could bear.

Her countenance grim, Erin said icily, "No, I don't deny it, but I *can* explain."

"That won't be necessary, thank you," Evan replied. "I fear we've quite decided the matter."

"You see, Erin," Graham took up the exchange, "Christina is sure to make the whole countryside aware of your . . . uh . . . indiscretion. We're thinking only of your welfare, Irish," he tried to sound encouraging. "You know how spiteful some of the local biddies can be."

"To be sure," Kellen's sardonic voice muttered wryly. "If this is a sample of the charity she'll receive from her own family, I can just envision the reception that her condescending neighbors will arrange."

But Erin did not hear his caustic rejoinder. She was livid that her brothers, flesh and blood, would dismiss her in such a thoughtless fashion. "Where shall I go?" she demanded.

"We had considered Aunt Julia's," Graham offered.

"Is that far enough?" Erin scoffed. "Won't my sullied reputation follow me to Savannah?"

"Erin," Graham scolded. "Try to understand—"

"No, *you* understand," Erin shouted vehemently. "The single thing that has sustained me these past months has been the fact that you and Evan would be coming home, and we could become a family again." Tears welled up in her beautiful green eyes, and her voice crackled as she continued, "I'm going to try very hard to forgive both of you for spoiling this homecoming, but believe this; I'll not be leaving Kilkieran because of the unfounded gossip that Christina will spread.

"Michael will be returning soon, and I intend to be here to welcome him home." She gathered her skirts in her hands and swept past Graham, but as she reached the foot of the majestic staircase, Evan delivered a crushing blow.

"No, he won't. *He's dead!*" he said ruthlessly.

"*Evan!*" Graham stepped forward to admonish his brother's thoughtless words, but Evan stayed him with a sinister leer.

"*No!*" Erin's anguished cry echoed pitifully down the long corridor, and she sank to her knees clutching the staircase railing with taut fingers.

Erin was obviously distraught yet, surprisingly, the tears that glistened in her eyes did not immediately flood her cheeks. Instead, she began to laugh; hysterical laughter that momentarily stunned the three men that watched her carefully.

But Erin was hardly aware of the fact that she was the object of their close scrutiny. She only knew that with the utterance of a single sentence all her carefully planned dreams had been completely shattered. Michael, her one true love, was dead.

Erin felt the compassionate hands on her shoulder, and she knew without hesitation that Kellen, a virtual stranger, and not her brothers had come to offer her comfort. She gratefully accepted that hand he extended and slowly climbed to her feet.

"They're lying," she rasped. "They *must* be lying about my Michael." She lifted sorrowful eyes to Kellen and gripped both of his arms with surprisingly strong fingers.

"I'm not lying, sister," Evan continued heartlessly. "I *saw* him shot down by one of your Yankee lover's comrades. Would you care for me to describe how he looked when they carried him from the battlefield?"

"*No!*" The tears fell freely then, and she placed her hands over her ears to block out Evan's bitter words.

"By God, that's enough!" Kellen bellowed angrily, taking a step toward the stairs, but Graham sprinted past him to firmly usher his brother to his bedchamber.

Kellen gently pulled Erin into his arms and held her until her anguished sobs abated. "Here." He tenderly set her from him and considerately offered her the use of his handkerchief. "Fix your face, then walk with me outside, so we can say good-bye privately."

Erin did as he instructed, and she offered him no resistance when he escorted her from the house. Once they were on the verandah, Kellen turned to her. "What will you do, little reb?"

"I-I d-don't know." She shrugged her shoulders in dismal defeat.

"Will you go to Savannah?"

"No," she admitted. "Father's sister was never overly fond of me. If I must leave, then I will go far enough away so I won't be tempted to return."

"Where?" Kellen had strolled over to his mount, and he thoughtfully stroked the impressive forehead while he considered her reply.

"Ireland, perhaps," she proposed spontaneously. "Grandmother has wanted me to come for a visit for ages. Yes," she murmured purposely, a hasty plan being formulated in her plagued mind. "I shall write Grandmother without delay."

"Ireland?" Kellen sounded surprised.

Erin nodded. "Why not?" Michael is dead; there is no reason to stay where I am not wanted." The usual carefree voice sounded hollow, distant.

"I don't mean to pry, Erin, but how do you intend to finance this excursion?"

"Grandmother will send me the money for a ticket—"

"But that could take months," Kellen interrupted.

"I know, but I'll somehow manage till then," she assured him.

"You are a constant amazement to me," he murmured fondly. He cast a studious eye toward the sky to determine the position of the sun and silently calculated the number of daylight hours available to him.

"You're leaving now?" she asked softly.

"Yes." He removed his hat and slapped it against his muscular thigh. "I've tarried too long as it is. Perhaps you'll be able to straighten out this misunderstanding after I've gone," he suggested hopefully.

"No, my mind is made up," she said staunchly. "I shall go to Ireland."

Kellen certainly had to admire her resiliency. "Doubtless, you shall," he chuckled admiringly, and stepped forward to take her hands in his. "Again, I apologize for being the source of so much heartache for you, little reb." He pressed his lips against, first one hand, then the other. Then he purposefully pulled her into his embrace, entrapping her in his powerful arms and forcing her chin up till their eyes met. "But to be perfectly honest, I *never* regret the opportunity to make the acquaintance of a bewitching lady."

Before Erin had guessed his purpose, Kellen lowered his head to claim her lips in a tempestuous kiss that left her utterly and completely breathless. His lips were warm and moist as they slowly moved against hers, carefully tasting the sweet nectar of her mouth. Erin felt the muscles in his arms tighten as he crushed her against him and, quite involuntarily, she lifted her arms to encircle his neck, twisting her fingers in the strands of hair that curled along the collar of his shirt. When

160

he at last pulled his fiery lips from hers, Erin could not help but feel a little saddened that he was leaving, and she would never see him again.

"Good-bye my lovely Irish rebel." Kellen returned his hat to his head and sauntered over to Achilles and heaved himself into the saddle. Turning the animal around, he tossed over his shoulder, "I shall think of you often." He tipped his hat in a gentlemanly gesture and persuaded Achilles into a trot as they started down the long driveway.

Erin shielded her eyes from the glaring sun as she waved good-bye to the Yankee, and he was just as small speck on the horizon when she turned and walked to the door, prepared to reenter the house. But the abrupt sound of pounding hooves on the roadway made her pause and she whirled around, not knowing exactly what to expect. She was understandably puzzled to find Kellen, racing like a virtual madman back up the driveway.

"Get your things!" he commanded, pulling the reins so fiercely that Achilles reared in front of her.

"*What!*" she shrieked.

"I'll not leave you to the mercy of your insensitive brothers," he fairly shouted, trying to bring Achilles under control. "I'll pay your passage to Ireland, and see you safely on ship. I owe you that much," he explained. "Don't stop to consider the absurdity of the situation; just get your things and we'll be on our way," he urged.

Erin's heart thumped wildly in her chest and suddenly, without fully realizing it, her feet were carrying her to her room. Recklessly, she flung aside the things that she would not be able to take with her, and hastily collected some clothing and a few precious mementos. Then she rushed from the room, almost knocking over a bemused Graham.

"You're actually leaving with that Yankee?" he asked incredibly.

"Why should it make a difference to you?" she asked loftily.

"Erin, consider what you're doing." He grabbed her roughly by both arms.

"I have!" she flung at him, jerking her arms free. "*He* wants to help me, unlike my own family. *You* wouldn't even let me explain," she hurled at him accusingly.

She ran past him and scurried down the wide mahogany staircase. At the foot of the stairs, she looked up to her brother to address him for the last time, "I'm going to Ireland to be with Grandmother. She won't forsake me." And with an indignant toss of her curls, Erin presented Graham her back and flew out of the house.

Graham observed his sister's swift exodus with sincere trepidation, but as he ambled down the hallway to the door that allowed access to the gallery, a thoughtful frown crossed his handsome face. Stepping to the parapet, he watched, unobserved, as Kellen gently lifted Erin onto Lady's back. Then, recalling the affectionate glances the Yankee had cast toward his sister, he turned from the railing and mumbled to the wind, "I'll be damned. Ireland, you say? Not bloody likely."

II

The Surrender

Chapter Nine

Erin stared awestruck at the impressive four-story house in a secluded section of Georgetown. The bronzed nameplate at the gate boldly proclaimed the name of the structure to be Tiffin Square; named for his grandmother, Kellen had volunteered upon noticing her interest in the plaque. Enclosed by a wall for privacy, the chocolate red-bricked mansion stood beneath the sheltering limbs of a grove of trees while the flawlessly manicured lawn stretched out to surround the lavish structure.

At first glance, Erin was put in mind of the pictures of elegant country estate houses she had seen in the books in her father's library. To be truthful, she had not known quite what to expect when Kellen had snatched her away from Kilkieran those many days past, but somehow she had not imagined that he was from such an apparently well-to-do family.

Their journey thus far had been uneventful with Kellen playing the role of the perfect gentleman at all times. He had treated her with utmost respect and dignity, and the nights spent along the trail or in roadhouses, where available, had passed without incident. Not once had he attempted to take advantage of the situation.

Erin cast a sideways glance at Kellen as they started to move along the pebbled horseshoe drive. She had grown to admire and revere this enigmatic man as they traveled to Washington City. With each passing day the stigma of *Yankee* evaporated a little more, and she viewed him as just an ordinary man. Well, not quite *ordinary,* she smiled to herself, but a man, nevertheless, who was returning to his family after the war to begin life anew. Were they so very different after all?

Kellen could not help but notice the pensive aura that had enveloped her, and he was prompted to inquire, "What are you thinking about?"

"Hmmm?" she murmured, shaking her head to clear it of her ruminations. Then offering him her full attention, she replied, "Oh, nothing really. It's a beautiful home, Kellen. Are you certain that my staying here won't be an inconvenience for your mother?"

"Of course not," he assured her and, dismounting from Achilles, he went to assist her from Lady's back. "She's accustomed to me barging in with my old college cronies and the like." He placed her on the stoop before him, enchanted by the dazzling smile that she turned on him. Clearing his throat, Kellen continued, "However, I must admit that you are by far the prettiest house guest I've ever dragged home for Mother to pamper."

"Really, Kellen. I don't wish to be a burden," she insisted.

"You won't be."

While he spoke, Kellen tethered the horses to the hand carved hitching post, then he offered her his arm and escorted her up the long sidewalk to the house. Just before he rang the bell, he sensed her nervousness and squeezed her hand reassuringly.

"Don't worry, my sweet, Mother is sure to find your charm to be quite irresistible."

"But—"

But before Erin could openly voice her misgivings, the door was swung wide by the butler.

"Why, Mr. Kellen." The servant's stoic reserve dissolved when he recognized the caller.

"Hello, Jasper," Kellen responded cheerfully, clasping the man's hand in a firm grip. "It's indeed good to see you again. Tell me, is Mother about?"

"Yes, sir," the butler replied distantly, averting his curious gaze toward Erin. "Luncheon is presently being served. You'll find the family in the dining room. Shall I announce you and the . . . uh . . . young lady?"

"Thank you, no. I think that I'd like to surprise everyone." He grabbed Erin's hand and pulled her through the door behind him.

Kellen escorted her so swiftly through the house that Erin barely had a chance to inspect the expansive dwelling. Seconds later, they arrived at the entrance to the dining room and Kellen left her at the door while he strode inside to greet his family, thereby, giving her an opportunity to gather her wits before any introductions were made. Yet from her inconspicuous position, Erin could observe the entire proceedings.

"Tell me, Meredith, have you selected the gown you'll be wearing at tonight's festivities?" inquired a young woman who was seated at the table.

But before Meredith Sinclair could offer a response, Kellen's voice interrupted, "As I recall, Mother always looked stunning in blue."

"Kellen?" His name was a raspy whisper from the older woman's throat, and she stood up carefully and held out her arms to her son.

They both started forward at the same instant and, when they embraced in the center of the huge room, Kellen swooped her up in his arms and swung her about as though she were a small child.

"Oh, Kellen!" she exclaimed. "Put me down! I fear that I must look a dreadful sight after such a zealous welcome." A hand automatically flew to her coiffure.

"Not at all. You are as lovely as ever," Kellen said sincerely, again pulling his mother into his arms and squeezing her tightly. When at last he released her, Kellen turned to coolly address the remaining occupants of the table. "Hello, Vanessa; Geoffrey. You're looking well."

Even with his back to her, Erin could discern by the insincere tone of his greeting that the gaze Kellen turned on the couple was aloof and detached. She viewed the scene before her with sudden interest, silently wondering what had transpired previously to warrant Kellen's peculiar behavior.

Meredith Sinclair seemed to sense her son's stifled hostility, and she wisely placed a restraining hand upon his sleeve. She was understandably relieved to see the brooding scowl that blemished his face vanish when he again turned to her.

"How is Grandfather?" he asked shortly.

"Stubborn as a mule and ornery as ever," Meredith replied candidly. "He still conducts business from the house and remains ensconced in his room, insisting that he isn't well enough to venture from its confines. And we continue to set a place for him at the table, at his insistence, though he never honors us with his presence."

"He sounds the same," Kellen chortled amusedly.

"Kellen!" Vanessa called to him petulantly, cocking her head to one side and offering him a wily grin. "You're being positively mean to ignore Geoffrey and me," she scolded him. "Come and dine with us while we tell you about the gala party we've planned tonight to welcome you home."

"Tonight!"

"Yes, darling," Meredith explained. "I received your wire and, well, it has been so long since this house echoed with the happy refrains of an orchestra's serenade. We are entitled to a celebration, and I can think of no more joyous occasion than your safe return from the war. Besides, I have invited only a few close family friends."

She patted his hand lovingly and started to lead him to the dining room table, speaking as she walked, "Vanessa is absolutely right. I'll ring for the maid to set another place, then you may retire to your room to see if everything meets your approval."

168

Kellen hung back reluctantly, making no effort to join the group at the table, and he appeared to be genuinely puzzled by his mother's statement. Confusion sparkled clearly in his vivid blue eyes when he next inquired, "What? I fear there has been some sort of misunderstanding, Mother, for I shall be returning to my suite at the hotel."

Now it was Meredith's turn to appear befuddled. "But your telegram; you said to prepare a room. I naturally assumed that you intended to resume residence at Tiffin Square."

"I did not mean to mislead you, Mother." A mischievous grin suddenly highlighted his handsome face. "But I assure you that your preparations have not been in vain, for I *have* brought you a house guest."

The three pairs of eyes watched intently as Kellen stepped toward the entrance and, for the first time, they noticed the figure that huddled shyly near the doorway. Realizing the extreme awkwardness of the situation, Kellen took Erin's hand in his and gently coaxed her toward him.

"Relax," he murmured encouragingly. "No one is going to bite you."

"I'm not so certain about that one," Erin mumbled dubiously between taut lips, indicating Vanessa whose brown eyes had fastened upon her coldly.

"Don't worry about her." He squeezed her hand reassuringly and bent down to whisper softly, so that only her ears were the recipients of his next utterance. "Vanessa *is* spirited, to be sure, but I'm confident that you can adequately handle all situations involving my cousin's wife. Now give us a smile, and let me introduce you to Mother. She will surely find you as delightful as do I, and Mother, if not the others, will graciously welcome you to the Sinclair family."

Erin was given little recourse, for Kellen securely tucked her arm in his and ushered her into the room, giving her little time to fully consider the implication of his last declaration. She swallowed bravely, squared her shoulders determinedly and prepared to meet Kellen's family.

Erin sat silently in her sanctuary, nestled in the corner of the settee, and listened while Kellen recounted to his captive audience the events that had inspired him to return home with such a provocative house guest in tow. As he spoke, Erin sipped at the glass of Madeira that Kellen had conscientiously placed in her hands when the family had adjourned to the drawing room to hear the account. Erin was indeed relieved that Kellen had taken this particular task upon himself, for she did not truly know if she could provide adequate justification for the actions that had prompted her to accompany Kellen to Washington City.

"So we have you to thank for nursing our Kellen back to health." ·

Erin could not immediately determine if the acknowledgment had been issued accusingly, or appreciatively, and she turned a reserved gaze on the man who had voiced the half-hearted sentiment. She carefully scrutinized the man who casually leaned against the mantel before formulating her response.

Geoffrey Sinclair was very unlike his cousin. He was shorter and stockier built than was Kellen, but what he lacked in stature, he evidently thought he compensated for in the manner in which he presented himself. He was fairer in coloring and his eyes were a subdued shade of green; not an ounce of compassion could Erin detect in the cold orbs. Though he was not a truly unattractive man, his face seemed to be eternally shrouded by a distrustful, almost sinister scowl. Needless to say, Erin had been instantly put off by his snobbish and overbearing attitude.

Indeed, Erin contemplated ignoring the impudent conjecture, but not wishing to appear rude before Kellen's mother, she replied simply, "It was the least I could do."

"Yes," Geoffrey murmured snidely, "considering it was one of your *kind* that disabled him in the first place."

Geoffrey quickly learned that his comment was not to be received docilely, for Erin sprang from the settee to confront him. She painted rather a formidable picture; arms akimbo and fire darting from her brilliant green eyes, and Kellen made no effort to prevent the tongue lashing he realized his cousin was about to receive from his Irish termagant. Indeed, a distinctively smug expression blossomed on his face as he relaxed in his chair, prepared to thoroughly savor the forthcoming rebuttal.

Erin was not to disappoint him. "I assure you, Mr. Sinclair, that my family seldom welcomes visitors in such an objectionable fashion. However, it should be understandable how we might have been remiss in our dealings with loathsome, marauding Yankees!" she informed him curtly and, with an arrogant toss of her chestnut-brown curls, she strode angrily to the door and jerked it open.

But before she completed her exodus, Erin turned to Geoffrey to deliver one last, biting retort. "You should consider yourself fortunate that it was the Major and not you who found himself beholden to me. For you may well believe that I would not have lifted a finger to save *your* good-for-nothing Yankee hide!" And she would have executed a grand departure had Geoffrey's prompt riposte not quelled the thunderous pounding of her heart, freezing her feet where she stood.

"Major?" he scoffed, sounding very much amused, "A bit formal, don't you think, especially for one's traveling *companion.*"

A satisfied grin appeared on Geoffrey's otherwise emotionless face as the color drained from Erin's. She would have looked to Kellen for support, but she was mortified by Geoffrey's vulgar insinuation, and it was all she could do to muster the strength to gather her skirts in her hands and run from the room.

"Well!" Vanessa huffed indignantly. "Of all the nerve! Meredith, you simply cannot permit that . . . that *hussy* to remain here after such a tasteless performance."

Meredith had closely observed her son's reaction to the verbal assault on the girl's reputation, and she knew that he had exercised enormous self-restraint. But Vanessa's crude declaration had been the last straw, and he jumped to his feet furiously, the veins in his neck popping out to indicate his annoyance with the entire situation.

"Erin is not a hussy!" he began tersely. "Besides, *you* are a fine one to talk!" Kellen directed the bold accusation toward Vanessa.

Vanessa's sharp intake of breath informed Kellen that his remark had made a direct hit, but he was a little surprised at how swiftly she recouped her equilibrium.

"You've never been able to accept the fact that I chose Geoffrey over you," she stated matter-of-factly. "Rejection can be a bitter pill for one to swallow, Kellen, but it hardly warrants this unseemly display." Vanessa appeared to be thoroughly chagrined by the episode.

"Yes," Geoffrey joined the exchange, "when will you accept the fact that Vanessa loves me and *not* you?" His attitude was arrogant as he reached for the crystal decanter and helped himself to a glass of brandy.

"Vanessa doesn't know the meaning of the word," Kellen spat disgustedly. "She married you because she believes that Grandfather intends for you to control the family businesses after he's gone."

"And there is a valid reason why my wife entertains those beliefs, my good cousin," Geoffrey said smoothly. "That is precisely what Grandfather intends to do."

"We shall see about that," Kellen challenged.

"Yes, we shall." Geoffrey emptied the contents of his glass in one gulp and turned a confident sneer on Kellen. "But considering that Grandfather hasn't so much as uttered your name since you abandoned the family and went off to play soldier, I'm reasonably assured as to what his decision will be."

"I haven't time to deal with you at the present, Geoffrey, but you may believe that this matter is far from being settled." Kellen turned his back on his cousin and started toward the door, but his mother's calm voice prevented his withdrawal from the chamber.

"Where are you going?"

"To draw a breath of fresh air. I find the atmosphere in here to be quite suffocating." He leveled a brief, though nonetheless repugnant, glare at the offenders. Then he turned to his mother, a look of intense concern on his attractive features. "I must find Erin and try to console her; she was quite distraught."

Meredith stepped across the room and took Kellen by the arm and led him into the hallway, carefully closing the door behind them. "You go on to the hotel and get your things in order. I'll see to the girl and show her to her room and get her properly settled," she offered. "I think that perhaps she needs a woman to talk to right now," she added knowingly.

"Thank you, Mother, but after what just took place, I think that Erin would be happier in a hotel until I can arrange for more suitable accommodations."

"Nonsense! Would you leave your poor mother alone again with the likes of Vanessa and Geoffrey?" She tried to coax a smile from him with her lighthearted question. "Erin seems like a lovely, unspoiled girl, and I'd welcome the opportunity to become better acquainted."

"But —"

"Don't concern yourself with them." She jerked a stiff nod toward the drawing room and ushered him to the main entrance. "I can handle Vanessa and when she is content, so is Geoffrey.

"Run along now, and don't forget tonight's festivities," she reminded him. "I think that a party is just the thing to brighten your gloomy disposition."

"Perhaps," he mumbled, not thoroughly convinced.

"I know it is. Be here by seven, so you may assist me with the introductions."

"Introductions?"

"Why, Erin, of course. Don't you think she would enjoy the party?"

The wary expression that had heretofore darkened his face slowly disappeared to be supplanted by a contemplative smile. "You know, Mother," he pressed a fond kiss to her forehead, "I think that a party would be the perfect restorative for everyone's disheartened spirits." With that, he opened the door and sauntered down the driveway to his mount.

Erin rambled in and out among the tall trees that provided ample shade across the sprawling lawn. The girl was so irretrievably submerged in her own miserable thoughts that she did not notice Kellen's departure, nor was she aware of the figure that approached her from behind until she heard her name whispered softly. With a distinctively sinking heart, Erin turned to face Kellen's mother.

"I'm afraid we haven't made a very good first impression," Meredith began apologetically.

"I never should have come here," Erin mumbled glumly, her shoulders slumped dejectedly. "I simply didn't stop to consider all the consequences. I should have known that people would naturally assume that Kellen and I . . . that we . . ." Her voice faltered momentarily. Then at last she raised her eyes to meet Meredith's, and her voice rang with despair when she again spoke. "You *must* believe me, Mrs. Sinclair. Kellen and I are not *lovers!*"

"Of course, you're not." Meredith took one of Erin's hands in her own and patted it sympathetically. "Do you truly think that my son would have presented you to me if that were the circumstance?"

Erin cautiously scanned the face that smiled down at her, and her apprehension dissolved somewhat when she saw the genuine friendship that sparkled in the depths of the older woman's eyes.

"No, Mrs. Sinclair," she murmured slowly and the tense

knot in her shoulders relaxed. "I suppose not."

"What's this Mrs. Sinclair nonsense?" Meredith scolded her. "You must agree to call me Meredith, and I shall call you Erin. It's such a lovely name. I instructed Cook to brew a pot of tea before I came searching for you. Would you care to join me?" she asked politely. "I thought it would give us an opportunity to become better acquainted."

"I'd like that very much," Erin eagerly accepted the invitation and she fell into step beside the woman as she turned and started walking toward the house. But a sudden thought made Erin stop and glance at Meredith uncertainly. "Vanessa won't be joining us, will she?"

"Good gracious, no," Meredith laughed understandably, taking Erin's arm and urging her to continue beside her. They resumed their leisurely pace and, after a contemplative pause, Meredith inquired curiously, "Erin, has Kellen told you very much about his family?"

"No. We've talked about a number of things, but I guess the subject somehow never arose."

"I thought not." They had arrived at the house, and Meredith escorted Erin upstairs to her private sitting room before she continued. "The servants are busy preparing the downstairs rooms for tonight's party," she explained. "I thought that this would be more appropriate for conducting an intimate chat. Do sit down." She indicated a chair and poured each of them a cup of tea and seated herself comfortably in her rocking chair before once again addressing Erin.

"Now, where were we? Oh, yes; the family." She nodded thoughtfully. "There are certain things you should be made aware of since you are going to be staying on at Tiffin Square for a while."

"If it would mean intruding in private, family matters you need not feel obligated to explain," Erin offered politely.

"Nonsense. It's no great secret and, I fear, there will be occasions when the family is together that things might become a bit . . . awkward."

"You mean with Kellen and Geoffrey," Erin suggested.

"*And* Vanessa," Meredith added. "You noticed then?"

"One would have to be quite shallow not to sense the tension that shrouds them when they're together," she replied simply. "One could almost cut it with a knife."

"You're very perceptive, Erin." Meredith sipped at her tea, then leaned forward and placed the cup on the table. "They were to be married, you know," she said suddenly.

"Vanessa and Kellen?" Erin's interest was piqued by this revelation, and she had a faint recollection of Kellen murmuring the woman's name in his delirium.

"Yes."

"What happened?"

"The war." Meredith shrugged her shoulders frankly. "When it began, Kellen felt an obligation to join the conflict, and Geoffrey's duty lay with overseeing the family's business interests, so he *paid* someone to fight on his behalf."

"And Vanessa did not wait for Kellen to return from the war?" Erin's tone was incredulous. She could not believe that anyone could be so heartless. "How could she do that if she truly loved him?"

"I quickly learned that Vanessa's *love* was of money and security. She saw both in Geoffrey, for she believes that he will eventually come into control of the family's business enterprises." Meredith glanced toward the clock on the mantel as she concluded her explanation.

"Kellen is fortunate to have escaped matrimony to such a conniving woman." Erin had not meant to voice her opinion openly, but somehow the words tumbled from her lips, and she looked up at her hostess expectantly. But she need not have feared a reprimand from that corner.

"Indeed," Meredith readily agreed. "Oh, dear. Just look at the time. Where has the day gone? It's nearly four o'clock, and I haven't consulted the staff about the last minute preparations for tonight's affair." She stood up abruptly.

"Is there anything I can do to help?" Erin asked thoughtfully.

"It's sweet of you to offer," Meredith indicated that she should follow her from the chamber, "but you need to get ready yourself." She paused before another door just down the hallway, and before Erin could utter a response, Meredith said, "This is where you will be staying. It's Kellen's old room. I hope you don't mind the masculine decor, but it's the best I could do on such short notice. I can make other arrangements tomorrow if the room proves to be unsatisfactory."

"That won't be necessary," Erin murmured, having grown a little shy with the knowledge of the room's previous occupant. "The room will do nicely."

"Good." Meredith turned to leave. "I'll instruct Renée to draw you a bath, and she can help you dress for the party."

"What!" Erin was genuinely surprised. "Meredith, this is Kellen's homecoming party. I couldn't possible intrude."

"Don't be silly." Meredith waved the protest aside with a trite gesture. "Of course, you shall attend. We owe you a good time after this morning's travesty. Besides, Kellen would surely be disappointed if you didn't come."

"But I haven't a thing to wear," Erin insisted.

There was apparently no obstacle great enough to discourage the patient woman. "You look to be about the same size as Vanessa; just a few tucks here and there." She carefully studied Erin's svelte figure. "Vanessa has dozens of dresses, and she owes me a favor or two," Meredith mumbled shrewdly, then turned a determined smile on Erin. "I think I can *persuade* my niece to loan you a gown for this evening's party. I'll just run up to their third floor apartments and make the arrangements." With a confident wink, Meredith hurried to the staircase to complete her self-imposed task.

Erin watched until Meredith had disappeared from view, then a reflective frown wrinkled her brow as she turned to enter the chamber that had been provided for her. She had just placed her hand upon the knob when a disturbance from the corner room at the end of the corridor drew her attention.

Erin heard the unmistakable sound of glass crashing against the wall, and she watched in stunned confusion as the door was hurled open and a young woman scampered from the room amidst angry shouts from the room's surly occupant. Erin stood aside as the girl swept past her, her cheeks wet with frustrated tears, and she could not help but wonder what had occurred to warrant such a display.

"You there, girlie! Come here!"

The harsh command made Erin whirl in surprise, and she was visibly taken aback by the sight that greeted her eyes. There before her sat an elderly man, his dark hair noticeably streaked with gray and thinning at the sides. The slightly arrogant face had grown red with anger, and his crystal-blue eyes narrowed shrewdly as they carefully considered her.

Erin stared right back at those blazing eyes and knew that she had seen them before. In fact, this formidable looking creature put her in mind of another she had come to know in recent weeks, and she realized that the grumpy, old man must be Kellen's grandfather. She estimated the man to be in his late sixties, though the deep sound of his voice and the robust aura that surrounded him might deceive the careless observer. Indeed, the only thing that would be an indication of the man's frailty was the wheelchair in which he sat; the wheelchair that creaked ominously as it began to roll toward the door.

"Damn it, girl. Didn't you hear me?" he snapped hotly. "I said, come here!"

"No doubt the whole town heard you," Erin retorted unthinkingly. Though she was reluctant to comply with the old man's command, Erin stepped into the room and closed the door behind her. "What do you want?"

"To start with, you can clean up that mess." He pointed to a trail of shattered china that lay strewn about the plush carpet.

"How did that happen?" Erin demanded, remembering the

sound of splintering glass just before the girl fled from the chamber.

"Tea was too hot," he said sharply. "I simply cannot tolerate such insolence."

"Yes," Erin muttered unbelievably, giving this peculiar man a closer scrutiny. "I can certainly see how that could justify destroying perfectly good china."

"Don't get fresh with me, girlie," the old man warned testily. "Just clear that mess away and be gone with you." Then as if suddenly realizing that she was a stranger to his home, he inquired, "Who the devil are you anyway?"

"My name is Erin Richards, and I am a guest in this house, *not* a servant," she informed him haughtily. "So, I'll just leave your mess, thank you."

"A guest, are you?" he snorted, wheeling his chair around to get a better look at her. "And just *who* invited you, may I ask?"

"Kellen Sinclair."

"Kellen?" he whispered hoarsely, obviously surprised by her revelation, but he quickly masked his emotions. "Humph!" he snorted tersely. "My grandson used to amuse himself by bringing home stray puppies. It would seem he has broadened his magnanimous disposition to include impertinent young females."

"Grandson. I thought as much," Erin murmured thoughtfully.

"Did you? Yes, Kellen is my grandson. That is when he isn't running about willy-nilly playing silly war games." He turned the chair around abruptly and rolled toward a desk in the corner that was cluttered with papers.

The familiar acquaintance of Jeremiah Sinclair would have recognized his brash behavior as a dismissal, but Erin was still quite ignorant of his domineering ways. Feeling suddenly useless, Erin bent down and started to collect the broken pieces of the china cup and saucer.

"Leave it!" the harsh voice commanded her. "You're not a

servant, *remember?*" he added pointedly.

"Very well, then," Erin replied coolly, allowing the fragments of fine porcelain to slip from her fingers.

Her curiosity thoroughly aroused by the elderly man's cranky disposition, she ventured closer to the desk to see what had commanded his attention. Erin found the haphazardly strewn papers and open ledgers to be quite confounding, and she silently wondered how the man was able to work in such a disorganized atmosphere.

Jeremiah Sinclair could feel the girl's presence behind his chair and, without diverting his concentration from his task, he asked crisply, "Are you still here? Don't you have something better to do than to stand here annoying me?"

"Mmm . . . perhaps," she responded slowly, peering over his shoulder at a sheet of paper that had caught her attention. "What's this?" She plucked the half-completed letter from its resting place and quickly scanned the page.

"None of your business," he barked irritably, unsuccessfully trying to snatch the letter from Erin's fingers.

"It would appear that you alienated your secretary a trifle too soon," she correctly guessed the position the fleeing girl had filled. "Now how are you going to complete this correspondence?"

"I shall manage," he growled. "Why don't you stop pestering me with your trite questions, girlie, and leave me to my business?"

"My name is Erin," she informed him patiently. "And since I am going to be a guest in your home for awhile, I see no reason why we can't be friends."

"Friends!" he scoffed. "I don't have any friends," he said bluntly, almost proudly.

"You haven't?" Erin asked incredibly, pulling a chair closer to the desk and taking a seat. "I should think that you would be terribly lonely then."

"Well, you're wrong. Friends are a luxury I cannot afford, and I'm quite satisfied with my life, thank you," he grunted sourly, watching her movement with increased annoyance. "Just what the devil do you think you're doing?" he demanded.

"I'm going to finish this letter for you; that is *if* you'll cooperate," she stated simply, reaching across the desk to retrieve a pen. "And you needn't argue," she added pertly. "I helped my father with his correspondence on numerous occasions, and I can certainly handle this."

She sat with the pen poised over the paper and favored the elderly man with an engaging smile. "Go ahead, I'm ready."

Erin seemed to lose all track of time as she sat at the desk with Kellen's grandfather, diligently helping him create order from the chaotic mess strewn out before him. Therefore, she was surprised when the door opened a few moments later and Meredith entered the room, appearing quite distraught.

"Oh, here you are!" She was instantly relieved at finding Erin. "Thank heaven, I've found you. Come along, child. Renée is waiting in your chamber to help you with your preparation for the party. We haven't much time," she reminded her.

"I'm truly sorry, Meredith," Erin quickly apologized, "but I became so involved in helping Mr. Sinclair that I completely forgot about the party," she admitted shamefully. "You see, his secretary left rather . . . uh . . . abruptly," she began to explain.

"Yes, Erin, I ran into Amy in the foyer as she was leaving." She turned a critical eye on her father-in-law. "I suppose you'll be wanting me to schedule interviews for a replacement," Meredith suggested, but the only response she received for her efforts was a noncommittal grunt from the old man.

"Well, we shall discuss the matter later," she said softly, motioning for Erin to join her outside the chamber.

"Wait, Meredith." A thought suddenly occurred to Erin. "There really is no need to hire someone to do this, at least not until after I leave. I'd be more than willing to help Mr. Sinclair," she volunteered. "Besides, it would give me something worthwhile to do."

"Are you certain?" Meredith questioned her. "I mean, you've only just arrived."

"Nonsense. I would love doing it, that is if Mr. Sinclair has no objection." She cast a hopeful look in Jeremiah's direction, but the old man did not even acknowledge that he had heard her offer. "Would you like me to come back tomorrow, Mr. Sinclair?" she persisted.

When it became evident that he was not going to respond to her question, a dejected Erin rose slowly from her chair and started to follow Meredith from the chamber. She had reached the doorway when Jeremiah wheeled his chair around and addressed her crossly.

"Come or not; I'll be here seeing to my business affairs in any case," he said curtly.

Erin nodded understandingly, and she favored the old man with a winning smile before turning to follow Meredith from the room.

Chapter Ten

Erin stared wondrously at the image that was reflected in the mirror before her, more than a little stunned by the transformation of her appearance. Very slowly, her hands traveled down her arms to rest along her narrow waist, and she turned from side to side to make sure that everything was perfect.

The gown was made of pale blue grenadine that had narrow stripes of gold that glittered glamorously when it caught the light at just the right angle. The dress was worn off the shoulder creating a plunging back and neckline that Erin considered to be quite daring. The long, flaring full skirt was fitted snugly at the waist and was accentuated with rows and rows of dainty lace ruffles of a darker hue than the skirt. The ruffles and short, puffy sleeves were decorated with pink satin ribbons and yellow silk roses, and blue filmy drapes hung prettily from the shoulders to complete the attractive ensemble.

Erin completed her careful scrutiny, deciding that she was pleased with the way she looked and, as she turned from the cheval mirror, she noticed a familiar figure in the open doorway. She stared for a long moment at the handsome man, whose broad shoulders literally filled the doorway. He was looking resplendent in his dress uniform of blue and, if possible, his countenance was even more awesome than usual.

"Hello," Kellen murmured softly.

"Hello," Erin returned the greeting, and she felt the tingling of gooseflesh along her spine as his approving gaze swept over her.

Noticing her apparent interest in his attire, Kellen hastened to explain. "I hope you don't find my manner of dress too disturbing. Since we've only returned today, I haven't had the opportunity to report to headquarters to resign my commission. Until then, I fear this will be necessary whenever I appear in public."

"Not at all, Kellen," she assured him. "Indeed, you're looking positively . . . uh . . . handsome," she offered shyly.

"Why, thank you, little reb." He sounded delightfully surprised by her compliment then, clearing his throat, he masterfully steered the conversation to another topic more to his liking; her appearance.

"I was on my way to visit Grandfather, but it would seem that he's not receiving visitors this evening, at least not this one," he added, and Erin thought she noted a hint of sarcasm creep into his voice. "I was about to return belowstairs when your door opened and the maid exited. Then I saw you and, well, just look at you," his voice trailed off into a husky whisper. "You're stunning, absolutely stunning."

"Thank you," she murmured nervously, her eyes immediately returning to the mirror. "I suppose I don't look quite the same as I did at home," she continued awkwardly, acutely aware that his intense gaze still caressed her. "Isn't this a lovely gown? It was generous of Vanessa to loan it to me, don't you think?" she chatted on with a carefree demeanor she did not entirely feel.

"The dress is comely," Kellen agreed, "but I would attribute the overall effect more to your radiant beauty." He complimented her lavishly. "But if Vanessa loaned you the garment, you may well find yourself indebted to my cousin's crafty wife."

"Do you really think so, Kellen?" Erin adjusted the silk rose that adorned the revealing décolletage and turned to him pensively. "Actually, Meredith made the arrangements with Vanessa for the gown. But I doubt I should have to be overly concerned with Vanessa. Why, from the scathing looks she directed at me this afternoon, I sincerely doubt that she will want to *talk* with me, much less demand my servitude."

"That may be," he conceded, "but I don't like the idea that you had to *borrow* a suitable dress from Geoffrey's wife. That is an inexcusable oversight on my part, and I'll see that it is corrected shortly."

"Whatever do you mean by that?" His curious statement had understandably caught her attention.

"Never mind." Kellen tugged at the ruffled cuff of his white dress shirt, then offered her a beguiling smile. "May I escort you downstairs?" He proffered his arm in a gentlemanly gesture. "I think that the festivities are about to begin and, since I am the guest of honor, I mustn't be tardy."

"Thank you, but I'm not quite ready. Perhaps I could meet you," she suggested hopefully. "I mean, after all, I don't really know anyone else. Indeed, I think that you shall be quite bored with my company by the evening's end."

"Then you are vastly misguided by your thoughts," he said purposely then waving aside her speculative remark, he added, "Take as much time as you require, Erin, and I shall join you in the ballroom presently.

"By the way, you needn't worry about remaining friendless for long; one look at you and the whole of Georgetown will be at your beck and call," he whispered fondly.

Kellen stepped forward suddenly to take Erin's hand in his and, lifting it to his lips, he pressed a lingering kiss against the soft skin and murmured softly, "You will save a dance or two for me, won't you?"

"If you like," she answered demurely, lowering her long, silky lashes to avoid his consuming gaze.

"Indeed." He appeared to savor her reply thoughtfully. "I think that I should like that above all else." He gave her a mischievous wink and turned and left the chamber.

Kellen lifted the snifter of brandy to his lips and, as he sipped the amber-colored liquid, his penetrating gaze concentrated on the antics of a squirrel that scampered among the trees in the early evening twilight. From the muffled sound of voices in the foyer, Kellen realized that the guests had begun to arrive, but he elected not to join the festivities immediately. Instead, he moved away from the library window and poured another glass of the potent brew. Then he settled into a comfortable leather armchair to continue his reflective brooding. His solitude was not to go uninterrupted for long, however, for the door eased open to admit an unexpected visitor.

"Kellen?" the familiar voice called out uncertainly. "Are you here? I can barely see in this dim light?"

"Brad? Is that you?" Kellen stood up and strode across the room to clasp his friend's hand with a sturdy grip.

"Yes, it's me, old friend," Bradley Petersen laughed good-naturedly. "You're looking fit, I must say, considering the dire straits in which I last left you."

"Yes, I wasn't at my best when we parted ways in Virginia," Kellen admitted, turning to light the desk lamp. "Have a drink with me, Brad," he suggested and, not waiting for a response, Kellen plucked the decanter from the table and poured a glass of brandy for his friend. "Come, sit down. Let's chat for a minute."

"Actually, Kellen, your mother sent me to find you," Brad explained. "It seems that everyone is wondering what's become of the guest of honor," Brad continued somewhat uncertainly.

It was almost as if he had guessed the topic of the proposed chat, and was reluctant to enter into a discussion. But Kellen was persistent, so Brad graciously accepted the glass that his host extended and claimed a seat opposite Kellen.

"I haven't seen most of those people since the war began; a

few more minutes should be of little consequence." Kellen rummaged through his coat pocket and removed a gold case from which he extracted a slender cigar.

"I suppose you're right," Brad concurred. "I imagine you'd be wondering what happened to the mission after we left you." He correctly assumed Kellen's purpose.

"Yes." Kellen nodded. "I've only returned today, and I haven't had time to report to headquarters, so I know virtually nothing about the final days of the war."

"I'm sorry to disappoint you, old boy, but our mission did not play a role in ending the conflict as we had hoped." Brad shook his head to decline the cigar that Kellen offered him. "In fact, I hate to be the one to tell you the news, but the mission turned out to be a miserable failure."

"What?" Kellen shouted, thunderstruck. "But what happened?" He lit the cigar and jammed it into his mouth furiously, awaiting a response to his question and, when it was slow in coming, he demanded, "Well, I'm waiting."

"We . . . we were ambushed by Confederate troops just before sunset on the very day we left you." A serious frown creased his brow and his brown eyes clouded over as he recounted the gruesome tale. Brad took a thoughtful drink from his glass before continuing. "It was uncanny, Kellen, almost . . . almost as if they *knew* our every move, our exact location; *everything*. One thing I'm certain of is that they suspected the contents of the wagon."

"What became of the cargo, Brad?"

"I don't know," he answered bluntly. "I think that perhaps the war ended before the Confederates had the opportunity to utilize the explosives. Indeed, they probably blew themselves up trying to figure out how to use the tricky stuff," he mused out loud.

"Yes." Kellen puffed contemplatively on the aromatic cigar. "Since nitroglycerin is such a new substance, not very much is known about it. It's so damned unpredictable. Rather puts me in mind of a certain female I'm beginning to know quite well," he added roguishly.

"Oh, yes." Brad's eyes sparkled suddenly, and he leaned forward in his chair expectantly. "I understand that you did not return, shall we say, empty-handed. Indeed, if half of what I've heard is true, I'm almost sorry that I didn't catch that bullet on your behalf."

"Brad, I've barely returned to the city. How did you learn about Erin?" Kellen asked, feeling that the question was redundant, for he was fairly certain he knew the gossiper's identity, and Brad wasted little time confirming his suspicions.

"Who else?" Brad finished his drink and placed the empty glass on the table beside him. "Vanessa has been regaling anyone who will listen of your rather notorious association with the girl. To be truthful, Kellen, I find it quite hard to believe that sweet, innocent child I met in Virginia capable of doing half the things to which Vanessa credits her.

"However, my good friend, if Vanessa's speculations are even *vaguely* accurate, you are to be envied." He offered Kellen a discerning wink.

Kellen drained his glass and crushed out his cigar before responding to his friend's discourse. "Sorry to disappoint you, but Erin is just as you described her; sweet and innocent, a veritable unspoiled child. Vanessa's depraved attempt at character assassination won't alter that.

"Speaking of Erin, I did promise to meet her in the ballroom." Kellen stood up. "I think I should find the young lady before the local vultures converge upon her."

"As I recall," Brad also stood to leave, "she could manage herself quite handily in less than amicable situations."

"She *is* a little spitfire," Kellen laughed admiringly. "But this is supposed to be a festive occasion, and I'll not let Vanessa's vile tongue spoil it for her."

They had arrived at the door when a sudden thought made Kellen pause to inquire, "By the way, Brad, what happened to the rest of the men?"

"Dead," he responded grimly.

"Dead! *All of them?*" Kellen wheeled on him in disbelief.

"They didn't appear to be interested in taking prisoners," Brad replied dryly. "My horse reared in the confusion, and threw me. I was knocked unconscious when I hit the ground, and I guess they forgot about me in their zeal to pirate the cargo. When I awoke, well," he sighed gravely, "I cannot describe the destruction, the slaughter . . ." His voice trailed off, understandably distraught, as he recalled the ghastly tragedy.

"Sorry, Brad," Kellen muttered considerately. "It was not my intent to rekindle old memories, especially horrifying ones of that magnitude." He twisted the doorknob slowly and pulled the barrier open. "Let's join the others, shall we? We can continue this discussion at a more convenient time."

Kellen stood aside to allow Brad to exit before him, and the shocked expression on his face gradually darkened into a pensive frown as he considered the back of the man who walked away from him.

The ballroom was already a bustle of activity when Kellen made his entrance. He maneuvered through the crowd, pausing now and again to exchange cordialities with old acquaintances. All the while, his solemn gaze canvassed the room in search of Erin, but she was nowhere to be seen.

He did, however, spot one particularly pleasing face and, plucking a glass of champagne from a tray being passed among the guests, Kellen carefully picked his way through the gathering until he arrived at his mother's side.

"Hello, my lovely," he greeted her warmly, pecking her lightly on the cheek. "I thought you said you had invited only a few close, family friends," he reminded her reproachfully. "Looks as if the entire city is in attendance this evening."

"Now, don't scold me, Kellen. I told you that a party was in order, and everyone is having such a wonderful time." Meredith Sinclair looked up to find her son's resolute gaze focused

189

on the entranceway, and she correctly assumed the identity of the guest whose arrival he impatiently awaited.

"She's on the terrace," Meredith murmured softly, nodding toward the French doors that led outside.

But when Kellen turned and started to move toward the doorway, his motion was momentarily stayed by his mother's cautioning hand on his sleeve. "You might as well know, she's not in the best of spirits," she warned him.

"Brad told me. Vanessa's been wagging her tongue indiscriminately, spreading malicious lies about Erin." His eyes darkened threateningly. "I shall deal with my cousin's wife *after* I have determined that Erin is all right."

He patiently made his way across the floor, and his worrisome gaze grew even more somber when he emerged onto the verandah to find his recalcitrant waif. She stood with her back to him in the shadows, the usually proud shoulders were slumped noticeably in frustrated defeat.

Kellen approached her hesitantly, uncertain if he should intrude on her privacy. But when she turned a little, enabling him to detect the trace of tears that shimmered on her cheeks in the twilight, he knew that he could not abandon her. Stepping closely behind her, Kellen slipped his arms around her svelte waist and pulled her against him.

"It's still a bit early for stargazing," he commented on the direction of her pensive stare. "And your face is much too pretty to be blemished by this unbecoming frown." His thumb leisurely caressed one delicate cheek, and he leaned down to whisper near her ear, "What are you thinking about, little reb?"

"Home," she answered dimly. "Graham and Evan and, of course, Deborah. You know she's so frail and delicate, and she depended on me for everything. I . . . I don't know if Graham will be able to . . . cope . . ." Her voice began to crack and, not wanting to break down in front of the menacing Yankee, Erin tried to pull away from his grasp. "Please," she begged. "Go away."

But Kellen would not honor her request. Instead, he turned her purposely in his arms and held her tightly in his embrace. He said nothing for a few minutes, but appeared content to nestle her against him; his broad chest cushioning her forlorn sobs. At last, after the flow of anguished tears subsided, Kellen stood her away from him and lifted her chin, so that he could gaze into her shimmering green eyes.

"You mustn't worry about them. They'll manage," he murmured soothingly, reaching inside his coat to retrieve a handkerchief. "Here, now, we cannot allow Vanessa the satisfaction of knowing that her slanderous campaign has upset you." Kellen gently wiped at the tear-stained face that regarded him suspiciously.

"Why . . . why are you being so nice to me?" she stammered slowly.

"Because, little one," he meticulously folded the dampened cloth and returned it to his pocket, "you would not be in this predicament were it not for me. Besides, I happen to find you quite charming. Indeed, I might be persuaded to extend my neck so far as to admit that I actually *like* you, hence the reason for my attentiveness," he teased her, tucking her arm in his. "Now, might I suggest that you and I take advantage of the delightful orchestra that Mother has procured for the evening?"

He started to lead her toward the ballroom entrance, but Erin still was not convinced. "Do you truly think we should?" She cast a nervous glance toward the crowded ballroom.

"Of course!" he bellowed, walking determinedly toward the terrace door. "It's my party, after all, and I shall dance with whomsoever I please. Besides," he added shamelessly, "this will assuredly give the old fussbudgets something to buzz about."

Kellen all but dragged a reluctant Erin onto the dance floor and as the orchestra began to play a familiar waltz, she relaxed in his arms and swayed with him to the haunting melody. As the peaceful refrains of the waltz filled her head, Erin's troubled thoughts were temporarily forgotten, and she found herself concentrating instead on her partner.

He was an excellent dancer. Somehow, she had not imagined him the sort who would enjoy this particular social amenity, but his movements were faultless. In fact, Erin's eyebrows scrunched downward in a perplexing frown, *Kellen* was faultless. His appearance was immaculate, his charm unsurpassed, and there was an aura about him that commanded attention. Indeed, Erin could not imagine how anyone could enter the room and not be drawn to him instantly.

Yes, Erin sighed inwardly, since she had come to know Kellen Sinclair, she had learned that there were very few things that the man did not execute to perfection. Well, except for evading stray bullets, she added as an afterthought, and a brilliant smile suddenly highlighted her pretty face as the amusing exception sprang to mind.

"At last!" Kellen murmured in her ear.

"What?" she asked gaily.

"A smile, and a genuine one at that, mind you," he remarked as he continued to expertly lead her through the intricate dance. "Dare I ask what provoked such a comely smile?"

"You!" she teased.

"Oh, I am mortally wounded." He feigned petulance at her retort, and leaned close to whisper an outrageous anecdote in her ear which elicited an immediate titter from the girl.

As they danced, each one's complete attention focused on the other, they did not notice the disapproving stares and hushed whispers that were cast in their direction by the other couples who swept past them. Consequently when there was a pause in the music, Kellen escorted Erin toward a small gathering of old and dear family acquaintances, prepared to make introductions.

"Hello, William," he began lazily. "Beatrice." He bowed formally before the man's wife. "I don't believe you've met Mother's house guest . . ."

But before Kellen could complete the introduction, the

woman interrupted testily. "Nor do we intend to," she snapped haughtily, snubbing her nose at Erin. "Imagine, bringing home one's . . . *consort,*" she carefully selected the term, "then putting her on public display, vying for our acceptance. Your mother must be positively mortified!"

The girl at his side tensed, and Kellen sensed that Erin's immediate impulse was to flee the embarrassing scene, but he would not allow it. Instead, he tightened his grip on her hand and proudly pulled her close to him. The bitter glare that Kellen turned on the older woman was chilling, the crystal-blue orbs emulating his acute irritation.

"On the contrary, *Mrs.* Overstreet," he said coldly, his tone ominously precise. "Mother would never react so thoughtlessly, nor would she be misguided by the unsubstantiated prattle of uninformed gossipmongers like yourself."

"*Well,* I never!" Mrs. Overstreet gasped, taking umbrage at Kellen's unflattering verbiage.

"Perhaps you should," Kellen suggested crisply. He then performed a stiff bow before the astonished woman, and presented his back to her as he angrily strode away; Erin still clinging to his arm.

"Kellen?" Erin asked hesitantly, somewhat dubious of the enraged scowl that blackened his face.

"*What?*" he snapped unthinkingly then, realizing the harshness of his countenance, he turned to her gently. "I'm sorry, angel. I didn't mean to bark at you."

They had arrived at a secluded corner of the room and Kellen finally paused, easing Erin down onto a velvet covered stool.

"I know," she murmured understandably. "Perhaps . . . perhaps I should return to my room," she suggested, knowing full well that he would not entertain the notion.

"Absolutely not!" He shook his head adamantly. "You realize, of course, just who is behind this." But before she could offer him a response, he went on to explain. "That venomous witch to whom my cousin is shackled."

He beckoned a waiter toward them and, selecting two champagne goblets from the silver tray, he handed one to Erin and lifted the other to his lips and promptly drained the crystal container.

"Excuse me, won't you, Erin? But I think that it's high time Vanessa and I had a serious discussion."

"Kellen?" Erin's hand caught his sleeve worriedly.

"Not to fear." He patted her hand gently. "I'll be within shouting distance should the natives become hostile. But in the unlikely event that one of these fine, upstanding citizens accosts you in any way, you have my permission to defend yourself."

"Humph!" she grumbled desolately. "If only I had Papa's gun."

"That's my Irish girl," Kellen chuckled fondly, then he turned to take his leave of her, his eyes searching the crowd for Vanessa.

At last he found her chatting earnestly with a group of friends. Kellen immediately ascertained from their shocked expressions that Vanessa was continuing her vendetta to destroy Erin's reputation. To confirm his supposition, his observant ears picked up on the conversation as he came up behind her, making him absolutely furious.

"And they were *alone* together for weeks!" she exclaimed loudly, not caring who heard her declaration. "Why, Lord knows what went on all that time."

"And *you,* evidently." Kellen's agitated voice pervaded the air behind her, and she whirled to confront him; a rather nervous smile replacing the jubilant one that had previously molded her face. "You will excuse Vanessa, won't you?" he addressed the group that viewed the scene expectantly. "But I've come to claim our lovely hostess for the next dance."

"That's sweet of you, Kellen, but I've already promised this dance to Timothy." Her voice shook a little as she glanced pleadingly toward the young man, hoping he would come to her rescue. "Besides, won't your little *friend* become jealous of your lack of attentiveness toward her?" she inquired peevishly in an attempt to exasperate him, so that she might gain the upper hand.

"No, Erin is not as shallow as that," he replied undaunted by her trickery and, taking Vanessa firmly by the elbow, he began to lead her away from the group.

From the tenacious set of his jaw, Vanessa realized that further debate was futile, so she docilely fell into step with Kellen. But when he started to take her in his arms for the dance, Vanessa pulled away and strode gracefully toward the entranceway to the grand ballroom.

"Vanessa!" Kellen was at her side instantly, the inflection of her name dangling from his tongue as a veiled threat. "I'm warning you."

"Yes, you have done that on numerous occasions, Kellen," she answered snidely, emerging into the hallway. "Really, you needn't pretend an insatiable desire to dance with me. You want to discuss your little ragamuffin *friend,* no doubt."

"From what I've been hearing, that's the nicest thing you've had to say about her," Kellen grated icily.

"Let's step into the drawing room and discuss this civilly, shall we?" She opened the door, taking for granted that he would follow her. "You've always been easily excitable, and I wouldn't want to create a scandal and detract from Meredith's soiree."

"Since when?" he scoffed, following her into the room. "You thrive on attention, Vanessa, regardless of the source," he informed her candidly.

"Hmm, I suppose I do." She shrugged her shoulders indifferently as she moved across the room to select a comfortable chair. "Fetch me a glass of wine, won't you, darling? I have a suspicion that this is going to be the most tedious conversation."

Kellen eased the door closed behind him and moved to the wine decanter to honor her request. Handing her the glass of claret, he then stepped back and perched himself on the arm of a chair directly opposite her.

"Aren't you going to join me?" She raised her glass to him.

"No, I think I'd like to keep a clear head for this."

"At least, come and sit beside me." Vanessa suggestively patted the vacant space at her side on the loveseat, but Kellen declined the invitation. "Then do as you wish," she spat tersely.

"I usually do," he replied smugly.

"You haven't changed a bit!" Vanessa spewed angrily, jumping up from the chair so suddenly that she upset her wine goblet, sending the dark purplish-red liquid splashing across the expensive carpet. But Vanessa did not acknowledge the accident, instead she lashed out at Kellen. "You're still the same arrogant, impudent bore!" she accused, and her brown eyes grew ominously dark, almost as black as the soft tendrils that framed her face.

"I didn't come in here to debate my disposition." Kellen remained amazingly reserved throughout the confrontation. "Believe me, Vanessa, I know full well what you think of me, and I assure you that my opinion of you is no less contemptible. Now, since we both find each other's company so undesirable, let's get on with this, shall we?

"This malignment of Erin's reputation is going to stop as of this instant," he informed her staunchly, and the foreboding expression he focused on her was enough to make Vanessa wary of him.

"What . . . whatever do you mean?" She tried to force an air of nonchalance into her voice as she turned away from him.

"I'll tell you precisely what I mean." Kellen spun her around to face him and, grabbing her by both arms, he shook her roughly, bringing his lips till they were but a breath's space from her own as he issued his harsh warning. "I'll tolerate no more of your insipid little games, Vanessa. We've had our differences in the past, to be sure. I have ignored your shenanigans for the most part, but on this I shall not waver; stop spreading your malicious lies. In short, *leave Erin alone!*" He then released her, as if she suddenly disgusted him.

"And should I refuse to cower at your feet?" Vanessa demanded haughtily. "Just who are you to threaten me?"

Kellen had crossed to the door, prepared to vacate the chamber, but Vanessa's challenging riposte so embittered him that he retraced his steps in two swift strides. Taking up a dogmatic stance before her, he carefully formulated his rebuttal, delivering each word with a devastating preciseness that made her shudder.

"I'll tell you who I am," he began deliberately. "I'm the man who knows your every thought, even before you yourself think it. I'm the man who loved you *once,* so much in fact that I would have killed had it become necessary to do so. But more importantly, and you would do well to commit this to memory," he cautioned her. "I am the man who can *destroy* you."

"What? How?" Vanessa stepped backwards, her hand flying to her bosom to quell the sudden rapid pounding of her heart.

"Have you truly forgotten?" he inquired glibly, but the horrified groan she emitted sufficed as an answer to his query. "No, I thought not. Tell me, is Geoffrey aware of the true circumstances that led to our . . . uh . . . *separation?*"

"N-n-no."

"Well, I suppose it would be awkward to explain to one's husband how she had conceived a child by her former lover, then had the child destroyed before giving it a chance to enjoy life!" He had started calmly enough, but by the conclusion of his oration, Kellen's voice had reached a feverish pitch.

"Please, Kellen, don't," she pleaded, stretching her arms out to him beseechingly. "You . . . you don't understand."

"Don't I?"

"No, I . . . I was frightened," she whimpered helplessly.

"I know," he scoffed. "You were scared witless that you would be left with nothing. You refused to marry me because you feared that I would not return from the war; similarly you feared rejection from my cousin if he learned that you were carrying a child, *my* child. So, you resorted to the alternative that any self-respecting girl in your dilemma would choose; *butchery,* " he whispered loathsomely.

"At least you should be content with your present situation; lady of the manor; a loving, almost doting, husband. Yes, you stand to profit quite nicely if Grandfather selects Geoffrey as his heir," he mused aloud.

"Stop!"

Vanessa pressed her hands to her ears to block out his lucid denunciations, but Kellen ruthlessly pulled them away. His iron grip clamped around her wrists, and he held her arms to her side, forcing her to listen to him.

"A word to the wise, Vanessa." He had once again assumed a restrained demeanor. "Grandfather has a strong, insatiable desire to see that the Sinclair name continues. What do you think his reaction would be if he learned that the likelihood of Geoffrey's wife fulfilling this obsession is practically nonexistent?"

Vanessa's usual confident mien had gradually evaporated, stripped away by Kellen's heartless resurrection of her past. With shoulders slumped in apparent acquiescence, she lifted somber eyes to examine his face. Never before had she witnessed this purposefully vindictive side of Kellen.

Oh well, she sighed wearily to herself. Perhaps he feels that he is entitled for some reason. After all, she was guilty of everything of which he had accused her. She *had* spurned his offer of matrimony when he had announced that he would be going off to war.

But what possible good would he have been to me had he been killed, or worse, returned as a hopeless invalid, she reasoned selfishly.

It was then that she had turned to Kellen's cousin. He was an easy, gullible target, but even Geoffrey could not have been duped into believing the child she carried was his. So in complete desperation, she had terminated the pregnancy. It was a decision she had never had cause to regret; until now. For she had never truly thought that Kellen would be callous enough to use the incident against her.

If it weren't for that silly tramp, none of this would have happened, she thought angrily.

"All right, Kellen." She considered her plight. "You've made your point. I'll be *civil* to your little friend."

"You shall contrive to be more than civil," he told her frankly. "To begin with, there shall be no more gossip."

"As you wish," she said sourly.

"And you'll retract the lies you've already spread."

"Yes, yes! Whatever you say," she cried impatiently. "I'm sure that Erin and I are destined to become fast friends."

"Don't overdo it, cousin. Oh, is it proper for me to call you that? After all, we *are* related," he continued to taunt her. "Erin is no fool, and she'll not be taken in by your cunning ways."

"Kellen, how can you think these things of me?" Vanessa stepped forward abruptly, taking him quite by surprise. "Especially after you've just proclaimed your love for me," she purred softly.

"You misquote me, madam," he corrected her. "I believe that I said that I *loved* you once."

"Words, darling, mere words." She slipped his arms about her waist. "Besides, if you loved me once, you can surely love me again," she murmured confidently.

"No," he told her resolutely. "The Vanessa I loved no longer exists."

"Perhaps she does. Let me show you."

Before Kellen realized what was happening, Vanessa threw her arms around his neck and pressed her lips against his in a fervent gesture. Kellen's arms instinctively tightened about her, slowly creeping up her back to pull her against him. But as his lips began to accept the pressure of Vanessa's and, indeed, to return the intimate caress, he heard the triumphant groan from the back of her throat. As though suddenly dashed with cold water, Kellen realized his folly and pushed her from him in disgust.

But he had regained his wisdom a split second too late, for when he turned to stalk from the room, he found Geoffrey blocking the exit. And from the antagonistic expression that reddened his hollow cheeks, Kellen correctly assumed that he had stood witness to the seemingly passionate interlude.

Chapter Eleven

Several seconds ticked away before anyone uttered a sound. Then Kellen abruptly stepped away from Vanessa, silently cursing himself for being foolhardy enough to become thus entrapped. Casting an aloof look toward Geoffrey, he calmly awaited the verbal assault he realized his cousin was mentally formulating and, when Geoffrey began his tirade, Kellen was prepared with an adequate defense.

"Well!" Geoffrey snorted bitterly, trying to maintain a reserved facade, but the piercing blue eyes that riveted daggers at Kellen belied his enforced civility. "I wondered how long it would take you to attempt something like this," he grumbled accusingly.

Kellen endeavored to remain undaunted by Geoffrey's menacing attitude and, focusing a wooden gaze on his cousin, he offered a glib reply. "This shows every indication of turning into quite an unpleasant altercation and though I'd welcome the opportunity to put you in your proper place, present circumstances dictate that I bridle this overpowering desire to see you cower before me." He strode confidently toward the door. "Perhaps I can accommodate you another time," he added smugly.

Kellen's haughty display elicited a furious response from Geoffrey, and he stiffened angrily, reaffirming his dogmatic stance before the doorway. "How dare you!" he seethed between taut lips. "I find you forcing your attentions on my wife, and you treat it as though it were the tritest of occurrences. Well, you are sadly mistaken if you think to brush this incident casually aside. I fear that I must *demand* satisfaction!" he declared boldly.

Kellen would have laughed aloud at the proclamation had Geoffrey not adopted such an unyielding disposition. Instead, he realized that he would have to assume much the same mien in order to deal with his enraged cousin.

"On the contrary," Kellen began slowly, his speech deliberately precise, "it's you who are sadly mistaken if you truly believe that I was accosting Vanessa. Indeed, had you arrived a moment sooner, you would have been privy to a most amusing scene; that of the temptress flinging herself into her estranged lover's arms," he informed Geoffrey ruthlessly.

"That's a lie!" Vanessa shouted, rushing to her husband's side to enlist his support. "Why, the very idea! How dare you make such a lewd accusation. You, sir, are no gentleman," she informed him scornfully.

"I'd say that makes us even, Vanessa, for it's equally apparent that you are no lady," he returned the insult in full, then faced his cousin once more. "I'll overlook your challenge this time, Geoffrey. Not that I fear you, you understand, it's just that the *lady* simply isn't worth the bother," he stated matter-of-factly, and pushed past his awestruck cousin to secure his freedom.

Once removed from the drawing room, Kellen breathed a sigh of relief and, smoothing the sleeves of his sleek uniform, he reentered the ballroom. He had not meant to leave Erin alone for such a lengthy interval, and he half-expected to find that she had abandoned the festivities. Therefore he was genuinely surprised and pleased to discover that she was the obvious center of attention of a modest gathering of his friends.

"Here's Kellen now," Brad announced, dragging him toward the group. "Ask him yourself, Sally."

Kellen was maneuvered toward a girl of slight build with sandy colored hair and an engaging smile. Vaguely, Kellen mustered faint recollections of a young, freckle-faced imp who had followed him about Tiffin Square in days gone by, and he recognized the girl as Sally McAlister. The Sinclairs and McAlisters had been long time family friends, and Kellen greeted the girl cordially.

"Is it true that Miss Richards confronted you with a gun when you first arrived at her home and, when you refused to leave, she shot your hat from your head?" the girl posed dubiously.

"Yes. That's an accurate account of the incident," Kellen murmured softly as he fondly recalled the occurrence, and he wondered at the reflective expression that suddenly crossed Erin's face.

"Do go on, Kellen," Sally urged. "You must have hundreds of interesting stories about the war."

"Later, perhaps," Kellen vowed. "Right now, I believe that Erin has promised me the next dance." He started to reach for her hand, only to find that it had been claimed by another's, and she was whisked away beneath his very nose.

"That brother of mine," Sally clucked her tongue in dismay. "He's grown so bold since he served with General Grant."

"Yes," Kellen cleared his throat. "Military service ofttimes makes men of us all." He politely proffered his arm and, when the girl graciously accepted, he escorted her to the dance floor; all the while favoring Timothy McAlister with a disapproving scowl.

Following the dance, the guests were invited to partake of a buffet that was being served in the dining room, and Kellen was further chagrined to see Brad escort Erin away on his arm.

"At least *she* seems to be enjoying herself," he grumbled resentfully, more than a little disgruntled at being denied her companionship for the evening repast.

In fact, Kellen was to see very little of Erin for the duration of the party. As the guest of honor, it was only natural that he be expected to mingle among the crowd; discuss the political situation with the men, charm the matrons and favor their daughters with a dance. Therefore, the crowd had dwindled significantly, and the orchestra had begun to play the final waltz of the evening, when he again sought her company.

Kellen was standing near the doorway, bidding farewell to a guest when he caught the movement of a blue grenadine dress from the corner of his eye. Glancing toward the motion, he observed a wisp of the svelte figure before it disappeared through the French doors. His amenities concluded, Kellen turned and strode toward the exit, his gait purposeful, yet unhurried. He emerged on the terrace to find Erin situated very close to the spot where he had found her earlier, but this time her face was beaming; there were no ugly tears to mar her innocent beauty.

Erin heard the footfalls behind her and spun around to offer him a stunning smile. "I was hoping it was you," she trilled happily.

"Were you?"

"Yes. I wanted to thank you. I didn't think it possible, but I've had the most wonderful time!" she said excitedly, and Kellen could not recall ever seeing her so lighthearted, her face totally bereft of worrisome lines.

"I'm pleased that you managed to salvage most of the evening. It got off to a rather shaky start, I fear, but I'm confident that I've cleared up that particular matter. Vanessa will no longer harass you." He carefully studied the face that fairly glistened in the moonlight.

"Erin?" he said, his voice suddenly soft and warm. "Would you dance with me?"

"What? Here!"

"Uh huh." He chuckled at her reaction. "It's the final waltz, and I can think of no more pleasurable way to culminate the evening's festivities than to hold you in my arms."

He extended his hand and Erin accepted it, allowing him to

pull her into the shelter of his embrace. As they danced, their bodies swayed in perfect harmony with the music and, unbeknownst to them, a pair of hardened, aged eyes grew suddenly contemplative as they observed the romantic encounter from an upstairs window.

"Kellen?" Erin's soft whisper broke the haunting silence, for the music had long ended, yet he appeared reluctant to release her.

When she lifted her questioning gaze to search his face, Kellen found the overpowering desire to kiss the tempting mouth below him too great an enticement to resist.

"Shh," he whispered, running his thumb along her cheek.

Erin stood very still, her heart racing wildly; every instinct shouting at her to flee before it was too late. She had but to raise the slightest objection, and Erin knew that Kellen would release her. He would not force her to endure his caress.

Yet when Erin became aware of the moist lips that lightly nipped a path along her exposed shoulder to her neck, she felt her resilience falter. When the arms that surrounded her tightened instinctively, crushing her against the brawny chest, she knew that the time for protestation had passed. Perhaps more mystifying, when Erin at last felt the gentle pressure of his lips against her own, she admitted shamelessly that she had not thwarted his advances because she *wanted* him to kiss her. She *wanted* to be nestled in the security of this man's strong embrace, if only for a little while.

Kellen instantly sensed her willingness and, though he was considerably bewildered by her behavior, he did not pause to question her. Indeed, he reveled in the honey-sweet taste of her mouth and, unthinkingly, his probing tongue gently brushed aside the uncertain lips to further explore her hidden treasures.

Kellen felt her body stiffen beneath his hard fingers and, thinking he had gone too far, he started to pull away. However, he was genuinely surprised when her arms lifted quite naturally to encircle his neck, and she stood on tiptoe to return his kiss.

"Well," Kellen murmured thickly, forcing himself to terminate the pleasurable encounter. "I suppose I should see you safely inside. The air has grown quite breezy, and I, well . . ." he stumbled over his words, feeling very much like a clumsy schoolboy who had been caught in the midst of a childish prank.

"Kellen," she whispered his name softly, lifting her hand to gently stroke along his rugged cheek. "Thank you so much for a perfectly delightful evening."

Then without warning, she bobbed up on her toes and placed a fleeting kiss on his lips. And before Kellen could react to her impulsive action, she gathered her skirts in her hands and scampered into the house, oblivious to the affectionate gaze that followed her departure. She did not temper her progress until she reached the sanctuary of her chamber where she flung herself into the chair before her dressing table mirror to study her flushed expression. Pressing her fingertips to her flaming cheeks, Erin desperately tried to bring her emotions under control, as she struggled to rationalize the abrupt reversal her feelings had taken toward the disturbing Yankee.

Erin was not to see Kellen for several days, but her schedule was to be so hectic that she seldom had the chance to feel neglected. Kellen made good his promise to see that her paltry wardrobe was refurbished by dispatching a seamstress to the mansion with carte blanche privileges to provide Erin with whatever she needed. In addition, Meredith and Erin made numerous shopping excursions to purchase laces, slippers, ribbons and similar accessories.

Sally and Timothy McAlister became almost constant companions, offering to escort Erin about the city in view of Kellen's absence. And of course, she followed through with pledge to assist Kellen's grandfather with his business correspondence and similar activities.

This last endeavor proved to be a greater challenge than she had envisioned. The cranky old codger's attitude was surly at best, and Erin was rapidly growing weary trying to evoke even a simple smile from the man.

On this particular day, Meredith happened upon Erin as she emerged from Jeremiah's room, a more exasperated expression than usual blanketing her face. Erin's totally frustrated appearance prompted Meredith to suggest that they forsake their usual routine, and drive into Washington to have lunch and indulge in a bit of shopping. Upon their return to Tiffin Square, Erin found it difficult to suppress her gladness at finding Kellen's mount tethered before the house. Her face was beaming with a bright smile when she finally burst into the drawing room to greet the caller.

"Hello, Kellen," she called cheerfully. "Jasper said you were in here. I'm sorry I was out when you arrived, but Meredith invited me to go shopping, and I simply couldn't refuse."

"I see." Kellen glanced pointedly at the packages she juggled awkwardly while endeavoring to close the door. "Here, let me help you." He crossed the room in a few short strides and considerately relieved her of her parcels. "Where is Mother? Or did you barter her for these trifles?" he teased her playfully, placing the bundles on a vacant chair.

"Of course not, silly." Erin favored him with a reproving glance, though she was not truly chagrined by his banter. "Apparently, there is a problem with one of the servants that she must attend to at once. She'll join us later." She quickly removed her bonnet and lightweight cloak and, tossing them aside, she turned to him. "It's been so long since I've seen you. I trust everything is well with you."

"I'm fine," he assured her, leading her to the sofa where they would be comfortable during their visit. "And you? Are you happy?"

"I suppose." She shrugged her shoulders offhandedly.

"Meredith has been an absolute angel, I seldom see Vanessa, and Geoffrey is completely submerged in his work, as is your grandfather. And *you*, it would seem," she scolded him.

"Yes," he agreed. "Although our motives vary keenly, we Sinclairs are devoted businessmen. But I didn't come here to discuss the family's work habits." He leaned forward to retrieve the crystal decanter from the silver tray on the table before them, and poured each of them a glass of sherry.

Handing a goblet to Erin, he stretched his arm out along the sofa behind her and relaxed his powerful frame beside her. "I came to spend a relaxing afternoon with you, my bewitching angel. You see, I was under the mistaken impression that you might have withered from my inattentiveness, but just look at you. You're positively radiant."

"And you are a shameless flatterer." Erin felt the soft flush creep into her cheeks at his lavish blandishment.

"Merely an honest observer," he said simply. "So tell me. How have you managed to wile away the days since we last talked?"

"Surprisingly enough, my days have been brimming with activity," she chatted with him easily as she sipped her wine. "Mrs. Potter arrives daily with more gowns that need to be fitted. Really, Kellen, you're being far too generous. Surely, I'll not have a need for so many dresses in Ireland."

"Of course, you shall. They wear clothes in your mother's homeland, do they not?" he teased.

"Certainly!" she exclaimed, pulling away and favoring him with a remonstrative glance. "I simply meant that I'll never be able to repay you for your kind gesture."

"You already have," he assured her. "By granting aid and sanctuary to a stubborn Yankee officer who was stupid enough to get himself shot with his own weapon. Believe me, pet, a few dresses hardly seem adequate recompense for such an unselfish deed."

"Please, Kellen. I did nothing special." For some inexplicable reason, Erin had recalled the romantic kiss that they had shared on the evening of his welcome home party and, feeling suddenly vulnerable, she decided to change the subject. "But that's all in the past." She stood up and crossed to the window to gaze out at the warm spring afternoon.

"Now it's your turn," she forced a cheerful lilt back into her voice. "I suppose you've been overwhelmed with your various business interests now that you've resigned your commission and returned to civilian life."

Kellen was understandably puzzled by her statement and, as he reached inside his coat for a cigar, he said, "Ah, I see that you have been talking to Mother."

"No. Actually, it was Brad."

"Brad?"

"Yes," she replied distantly, running her fingers absently along the windowsill. "He dropped by to see your grandfather the other day, and Meredith invited him to dine with us. We had quite a lengthy chat about you. He told me all about your hotel, The Sinclairian, the horse farm, and your shipping, freighting, and railroad interests. And, well, the list goes on and on, doesn't it?" she remarked, her dulcet tone full of admiration for his achievements.

"Really, Kellen, I never realized you were such a successful business entrepreneur." Her voice trailed off, for she had turned from the window in time to witness the emotion-filled expression that suddenly crossed Kellen's face.

He had been about to light the cigar that protruded from his lips, but in the middle of Erin's narrative, he angrily extinguished the flame and jerked the cigar from his mouth in disgust. Then he stood up suddenly and began to pace in bitter frustration before the fireplace.

"Kellen?" she ventured hesitantly. "Did I say something wrong?"

"What?" He stopped pacing long enough to answer her. "No, Erin. You've done nothing. It's just rather damaging to one's ego to discover that one's grandfather refuses to see him, yet an outsider is received with open arms!" He fairly shook with fury.

"But I thought that Brad was your friend."

Kellen raked an unsteady hand through his unruly mane, and his anger had abated considerably when he next addressed her. "He is, and it was not my intent to berate him. This whole situation is so damnably frustrating." He heaved a beleaguered sigh.

"I know," she whispered soothingly, "and I . . . I'm sorry, Kellen," Erin stammered, wanting to comfort him, yet uncertain as to what she should do. "I had forgotten—"

But her next words were not to be uttered, for there came a sharp knock upon the door, interrupting their conversation.

"Come in," Kellen barked.

"Excuse me, Mister Kellen," Renée, the servant who had been assigned as Erin's personal maid, apologized and performed a polite curtsy before him, "but your grandfather sent me to fetch Miss Richards."

"Thank you, Renée," Erin responded, fearful of Kellen's reaction. "Tell him that I'll join him shortly." She quickly dismissed the girl.

Erin waited until she and Kellen were alone again, then she carefully approached him and, taking his clenched fists between her gentle, consoling hands, she attempted to offer him solace.

"I'm truly sorry," she murmured faintly. "Perhaps I can persuade—"

"Don't bother!" His tone was agitated, though Erin knew his resentment was not directed at her. "He's a spiteful, begrudging old man. I don't need him any more than he needs me," he proclaimed staunchly.

"You don't mean that," Erin gently chastised him. "He'll come around. You just wait and see." She squeezed his tense hands sympathetically. "Now, is there anything I can do to improve your melancholy disposition?"

"Yes," he said without hesitation. "Dine with me this evening," he suggested hopefully.

"Oh, I cannot tonight," she informed him apologetically. "You see, Meredith invited the McAlisters to sup with us this evening." Her brow crinkled into a serious frown, but a sudden idea occurred to her, and she lifted quizzical eyes to scan his downcast face. "Perhaps you could join us?" she offered, genuinely hoping that he would accept the invitation. "I'm certain that Sally and Timothy would love—"

"What!" he bellowed, apparently affronted by the notion. "Play second fiddle to that freckle-faced young whelp? I think not!" He whirled and returned to where he had discarded his wine glass and, plucking the goblet from the table, he quaffed the contents in a single, disgruntled motion.

"Excuse me, Miss Erin," the door reopened, and the servant again cautiously peeked into the room, "but Mr. Sinclair *insists* that he needs you immediately."

"Yes, yes, Renée. I'm on my way." She waved the girl from the room. Retrieving her belongings, Erin addressed Kellen once again. "I've made no plans for tomorrow," she began slowly. "Perhaps we could go for a ride?" she posed speculatively, but the proud back remained rigid. He did not even acknowledge her suggestion, and it was a dejected Erin who started to move reluctantly toward the door.

"Perhaps," Kellen muttered distantly. "He's a demanding old goat, isn't he?" he mumbled suddenly, and Erin detected the obvious affection that had crept into his voice.

"He's an enormous frustration," Erin conceded. "In fact, I think that you are very much like him. And," she swallowed hard, "I'm finding that I admire both of you more with each passing day."

Her words of praise were uttered hastily amidst a fluttering of skirts as she turned and hastened toward the door. Kellen was not permitted the opportunity of a rejoinder, however, for Erin ran from the room and scurried up the stairs to Jeremiah Sinclair's chamber.

"It's about time!" snapped the cranky voice when Erin flung the door open moments later and rushed inside the chamber. "What kept you?" he demanded.

Erin had not even taken the time to leave her parcels in her own room, so she situated her bundles on the bed before dignifying his presumptuous question with a reply.

"I was with your grandson," she stated pertly.

"Geoffrey?" he asked to purposely intimidate her.

"No, not Geoffrey," Erin huffed irritably. "I was with Kellen." She walked straightway to the desk to ascertain what required such urgent attention and, picking up a stack of papers, she began to peruse them, her mind not solely devoted to her task.

Erin had watched the elder Sinclair closely during her sojourn as his personal secretary, and she had subsequently formulated her own opinion of the man. She had found him to be an irascible, headstrong individual, who possessed the business acumen to create a veritable dynasty. Yet underneath this crusty exterior beat the heart of a man who felt an overwhelming love for his family.

Therefore it was an enigma to Erin why Jeremiah steadfastly refused to acknowledge Kellen. She had considered the problem for days, but knowing the man's quick temper, she had decided against voicing her opinion. But the forlorn expression she had witnessed on Kellen's face had touched her heart, and she felt that she must try to bend the old man's iron resolve.

"I think you're quite mean to treat Kellen this way," she blurted without warning.

"I don't care what you think," he replied promptly, not glancing away from the column of figures he checked for accuracy.

"I realize that, but I'm going to tell you anyway." She tossed the papers in an angry huff onto the desk and assumed a dogmatic stance beside his chair. "For some unexcusable reason, you have forsaken a grandson who dearly loves and respects

212

you. And for what? Because you feel that he in some way betrayed you by joining the war effort?" she asked incredulously, oblivious to the rising crescendo of her voice.

But Jeremiah did not act as though a single word of her narrative had penetrated his stubborn facade. Indeed, for all the apparent good her entreaty did, Erin might just as well have been addressing a brick wall. Still she persevered.

"I should rather think that you would revere Kellen for having the courage to stand up for his beliefs. Instead, you would cast your lot with a simpering Milquetoast like Geoffrey who would pay someone else to fight his battles, so that he can keep his greedy hands safe to count *your* money."

Realizing that she would not be able to work alongside him after her outburst, Erin strode across the room to gather her belongings. She opened the door to leave, but hesitated long enough to conclude her speech on an ominous note.

"You are an impossible, heartless old jackass, Jeremiah Sinclair. And one day, you shall awaken to discover yourself completely surrounded by bloodsuckers like Vanessa and Geoffrey. *Then* you will realize how much you truly need and love Kellen, but it will be too late, for he will no longer care!"

It was not until Erin had slammed the door that she realized how outraged she had become. Thinking her display to have been for naught, she hurried down the long corridor to her room to change for the evening's dinner engagement.

Erin heard the soft tapping at her chamber door but she chose to roll over in the comfortable bed and snuggle deeper beneath the coverlets rather than acknowledge the would-be intruder. But the gentle knocking persisted until she finally relented and granted the caller admittance.

"Good morning, Miss Erin," Renée greeted her cordially as she entered the room carrying a breakfast tray.

Erin returned the greeting and stretched lazily, dragging

213

herself to a sitting position. "Mmm," she emitted a lugubrious sigh. "What time is it?"

"Nearly ten o'clock, ma'am. I know the McAlisters stayed later than usual, so I took the liberty of letting you sleep in this morning. I thought you might enjoy your breakfast here, so I brought you a cup of chocolate and some freshly baked blueberry muffins." She settled the tray across Erin's lap, then crossed to the window to pull the draperies apart. "Oh, and I imagine you'll be wanting this." She reached into the pocket of her starched apron and retrieved a sealed envelope which she presented to Erin.

"What's this?" Erin rubbed at her sleepy eyes with one hand while reaching for the envelope with the other.

"Mister Kellen's servant delivered it a few moments ago, along with those." She nodded toward the vase of spring flowers that decorated the breakfast tray.

Erin's interest in the epistle suddenly increased as she eagerly ripped the envelope open, and her eyes brightened considerably as they hurriedly scanned the bold script. Her thoughts totally submerged in the contents of the missive, Erin momentarily forgot about the breakfast tray, and she bounced up and down on the bed for joy, nearly upsetting the tray.

"Careful, dear." Meredith had entered the room in time to witness Erin's jubilant reaction. "I take it that my son's message is of a pleasing nature."

"Oh, yes!" Erin assured her. Then, turning to the servant, she inquired, "Renée, did the messenger wait for a reply?"

"No, ma'am."

"I can send one of the servants with a note, if you wish," Meredith kindly offered.

"No, no. That won't be necessary. I'll just be ready when he calls for me," she said simply, unable to control the happy smile that parted her lips.

"Must I drag it from you?" Meredith stood at the foot of the

214

bed, hands on hips. "What sort of devilment has that son of mine concocted?"

"A picnic; nothing special," Erin managed offhandedly, nibbling thoughtfully on a muffin.

"Well, if that's the case, perhaps you wouldn't object if I accompanied you," Meredith suggested playfully.

"What?" Erin was so flustered by the comment that she nervously jiggled the cup of chocolate as she lifted it to her lips. "Uh, n-no, of course not," she stammered. "I'm sure that Kellen would love—"

"Then you don't know my son very well," Meredith laughed, lifting her hand to forestall Erin's half-hearted protestation, the mischievous smile that adorned her face an indication of her tomfoolery. "I was merely teasing you, my dear. I wouldn't dream of intruding on your excursion."

"But I suppose we should have *someone* accompany us." Erin contemplatively chewed on a fingernail as she deliberated the problem. "It's been so long since I enjoyed an outing such as this that I very nearly forgot that such proprieties need be observed." She glanced up in time to see Meredith's face fashion into an affectionate, understanding smile.

"Erin," Meredith spoke in a gentle, soothing tone as she stepped around the corner of the bed and sat down beside her. "I'm not so prudish as to impose such archaic mores on today's young people. No, you enjoy your day with my son." She patted Erin's hand tenderly, then stood and ambled toward the door. "Besides, if Kellen did not take advantage of your virtue when you were alone together in Virginia, he's not likely to now. No, I think perhaps my son has greater plans in store for you.

"Yes, I'd wear my prettiest outfit if I were you," she continued thoughtfully. Although Meredith was cognizant of the perplexed look that shadowed Erin's face, she elected to withdraw from the room before Erin could question her.

Meredith's curious remarks were to haunt Erin throughout the morning, but she finally managed to shrug the conversation aside, rationalizing that Kellen's mother had obviously misinterpreted the nature of their relationship. She and Kellen were merely friends, nothing more.

In spite of Meredith's tenuous conclusion regarding Kellen's purpose, Erin did select her most fashionable outfit from the wardrobe. As she sat before the mirror, while Renée arranged her hair in a becoming style, she thoughtfully considered her appearance.

She had chosen a hyacinth-blue velvet riding habit, deciding upon the heavier material because the late spring days could still be quite chilly. The high button collar of the frilly white blouse framed her face prettily, and the short jacket fit snugly at her waist to complement her shapely figure. Yes, from the highly polished black leather boots to the gently flowing ankle length skirt, Erin concluded that the ensemble was an impeccable choice.

"That's perfect!" Erin proclaimed to Renée as she lifted her hand to smooth her coiffure.

Her hair had been parted in the middle and drawn tightly across her head. Then the long, heavy tresses had been arranged in a tight chignon at the nape of her neck and draped with a net that matched the color of her riding habit.

"And we've finished just in time," Renée announced happily. "For I'm certain I heard the front knocker. Here." She handed Erin a straw bonnet. "I'll tell young Mr. Sinclair that you'll only be a moment."

As Renée hurried off to carry out her task, Erin adjusted the hat at a stylish angle and tied the broad ribbons in an attractive bow under her chin. At last, satisfied with the results of her toilette, Erin plucked her reticule from the dressing table and scampered from the room to greet Kellen.

Erin stood on the knoll overlooking Georgetown, her hands clasped behind her back. "The view is breathtaking," she turned to call to Kellen.

"I know." He exhaled slowly, giving her youthful figure a careful, leisurely scrutiny. "Would you care for some more cold chicken?" he asked considerately.

"Goodness, no!" she exclaimed. "I've done very little except eat since I arrived." She had drifted over to the blanket where he sat. "Mrs. Potter will have to let out the seams of those lovely dresses you've just purchased if I continue this gluttonous pace. I'm getting positively fat," she lamented.

"That's folderol if ever I heard it," Kellen scoffed. "If anything, you've blossomed. Why, you were skin and bones when I found you in Virginia," he reminded her.

"Yes, I remember," she murmured, kneeling beside him to help clear away the debris from their picnic luncheon.

Kellen noticed her sudden melancholia, and his hand went out to tilt her chin back, so he could see her face. "I'm sorry, Erin. I did not mean to rekindle unhappy memories." He gathered the blanket and picnic basket and placed them near the tethered horses and, when he returned, he extended his hand to her and said, "Shall we take a short walk?"

"Yes, I'd like that." She slipped her hand inside his and they strolled along the summit. "Is Tiffin Square visible from here?" Erin asked when they paused at a spot that offered a superb view of the city.

"As a matter of fact, it is." He positioned her directly in front of him, and bent down over her shoulder till he was at her eye level. Then he extended his arm, and pointed his finger at some distant point. "Do you see the church steeple?"

"Uh huh." She strained to follow the direction he indicated.

"Now, look to the left and up a little, and you should be able to see a bronze-colored roof with four corner chimneys."

"Yes, I see it. Is that it?" She raised her hand to shield her eyes from the glare of the sun.

"That's it."

"I didn't realize we had ridden so far," Erin continued to make idle conversation, suddenly aware of Kellen's close proximity.

But before she could remove herself from his reach, Kellen enfolded her in his arms and turned her around to face him. "This is a lovely accessory, Erin," his nimble fingers masterfully undid the ribbons at her chin, "but I fear it's rather a nuisance at the moment."

He tilted her head back and the bonnet slipped unnoticed from her head and came to rest gently on the ground at her feet. Erin's immediate impulse was to resist his caress, but this notion abruptly vanished when she felt the contact of his lips as they skillfully moved against her own.

Erin sensed a rush of excitement as Kellen's hands roved over her back, crushing her against him. And she became aware of a curiously delicious sensation in the pit of her stomach when his tongue swept past her lips to taste the sweet nectar that lay therein.

It was then that a soft whimpering noise penetrated her addled consciousness, and she was amazed to realize that the sounds were coming from her own throat. Caught up in the tempestuous kiss, Erin became acutely aware of Kellen's masculine nearness, her breasts that were pressed against his hard body, the hand that slid familiarly along her waist, and the fingers that had somehow managed to undo the topmost buttons of her blouse, permitting his eager lips access to her shapely neck, her earlobe; again returning to cover her lips with ever increasing fervor.

At last, regaining her reason, Erin braced the palms of her trembling hands against his shoulders and pushed him away from her, breathless, almost dizzy from the passionate encounter.

"When . . . when will you arrange for me to depart for Ireland?" she asked when she was able to recover her voice. For suddenly she understood the wisdom of Meredith's earlier remarks, and she was consumed by a panicked urgency to flee; fearful of Kellen's awesome presence and her own dwindling self-control.

"What!" he thundered, his shout reverberating in the dis-

tance. "You kiss me with such fire, such abandon, then make a preposterous request like that!" he cried unbelievably. "You cannot truly mean to leave."

"But I do," she informed him, backing away as she talked. "That is why I came with you in the first place, remember? Though there has been precious little discussion of the matter. You've been terribly busy getting reacquainted with your former routine, so I've not pressed you about it." She lowered her head and turned slightly to avoid his stern gaze. "But I think the time has come for me to continue with my original plans."

"Why? Because I kissed you?" he demanded, raking his hand through his hair in an impossible gesture.

"Yes . . . no! I don't know!" she stammered in complete exasperation, wringing her hands fretfully.

"Erin, angel." Kellen stepped forward, grasping her hands to quell their frantic motion. "You need not run from me. If you feel compelled to visit your mother's homeland, do so, but don't flee because you fear what might be developing between us. I promise that my intentions are strictly honorable." He deftly ran his finger along her cheek.

"Please, don't." She drew away from his touch.

"You know, little reb," he bent down to retrieve her bonnet, "a lesser man might be dissuaded by your standoffish attitude. But, you see, I have a distinct advantage over some other would-be suitor. I know the catalyst that prompts your hesitant behavior.

"You do not spurn my attentions because you grieve for your deceased sweetheart, nor do you find me particularly disgusting. Unless . . ." He stroked his chin thoughtfully as an unappealing idea crossed his mind. "Certainly, you have not developed a tendre for that puppy, McAlister, or Brad." His watchful gaze observed her face and he was relieved to see the negative shake of her head. "I thought not, for you see, I felt your response to my kiss," he shamelessly informed her.

"Your reluctance to my attentiveness stems rather from the fact

219

that you still perceive me as a Yankee; one of those damnable curs that pillaged your homeland." He stepped forward and, returning the bonnet to her head, he proceeded to tie a bow beneath her chin. "You must realize, my angel, that only makes me more determined to obliterate that undesirable stigma from your pretty head. Shall we go?"

He turned and sauntered toward the horses, continuing his narrative as he walked. "I'll begin making the necessary arrangements for your journey, Erin, but it will likely take a week or two, providing I can obtain passage on a suitable vessel."

He started to whistle a carefree tune as he ambled toward their mounts and, with an arrogant slant of one eyebrow, he delivered one final observation. "That is a considerable length of time, and who is to say what may yet occur? Who knows; perhaps you will undergo a change of heart, so to speak," he suggested smugly.

The return journey to Tiffin Square was made in relative silence. Though Kellen tried to lure her into conversation, Erin was not in a talkative mood. She was not angry with him, but he *had* catapulted a number of disturbing thoughts to a vanguard position in her mind, and, quite frankly, she did not know how to deal with this new emotional dilemma.

They had arrived at the mansion, but Erin was so engrossed in her thoughts that she did not notice her whereabouts. She vaguely became aware of a pair of strong hands that surrounded her waist and gently lifted her from Lady's back. By the time they had strolled up the long walkway to the door, Erin had recovered her equanimity and, deciding that she should thank Kellen for the outing, she forced a smile to her lips and looked up at him.

But, before Erin could verbalize her sentiment, the door opened and Jasper, the butler, greeted Kellen with a surprising announcement. Jeremiah Sinclair had asked to see his grandson.

Chapter Twelve

Erin watched the nervous play of emotions that flickered across Kellen's face as he hesitated outside his grandfather's door. Silently, she imagined that a hundred apprehensive thoughts must be running through his mind and, though he had literally hungered for this meeting, she could well understand his trepidation. After all, Kellen and Jeremiah shared conflicting views on practically everything, and their last disagreement had resulted in a four year separation that had nearly left the relationship irreconcilable.

Yet the bond between the two was mighty. Erin had sensed this even though she had never seen the two together. There was just something about the way each one referred to the other, and she was ecstatic that Jeremiah had finally agreed to renew his affiliation with his grandson.

"Kellen," Erin whispered softly. "I'll wait here. You go on in," she offered, sensing his tenseness.

"No, Jasper said that Grandfather specifically requested that you join us."

"But—"

"You don't want to aggravate him," he cautioned. "Grandfather can become quite acrimonious when his requests are not honored."

"All right." She relented. "I must admit that I'm more than a little curious."

"Shall we end the suspense then?" Kellen started to rap upon the barrier, but Erin's hand on his sleeve made him pause and look down at her questioningly.

"Do try to be tolerant. Don't go flying off the handle at him," she advised.

"I shall be pleasant and tactful; in short, I shall behave as usual," he informed her indignantly.

"If that be the case, perhaps it *is* wise that I am joining you. I will be on hand to intervene when your pleasant and tactful discussion erupts into a full-fledged battle," she teased him unmercifully. But before Kellen could respond to her tomfoolery, Erin knocked sharply on the door.

"Come in!" the craggy voice barked from within.

Erin's observant gaze saw Kellen's hand pause over the doorknob, and she sensed the skittish wave of anxiety that washed over him. It made her realize that, despite his usual confident, unflappable mien, Kellen experienced vulnerable moments just like any other human being. But instead of making him appear smaller in her eyes for his vincibility, Erin felt her heart swell with admiration, and she tucked her arm in his to show her support.

"Come, let's face the dragon together," she said bravely and, gently pushing his hand aside, she gripped the doorknob and swung the barrier open.

Jeremiah sat in his wheelchair, facing the doorway, the chair positioned squarely in the middle of the room. The look he directed on the pair was severe, and his tone was no less harsh when he began to speak.

"A lot of good it does me to employ a secretary who cannot be found when she is needed." His pointed look swept over Erin disdainfully. "Would it be an imposition to inquire as to your whereabouts this livelong day?"

"It's Sunday, Mr. Sinclair," Erin stated patiently, stepping across the room to retrieve the shawl that had slipped from his lap. "Even the workers on our plantation were given Sunday as a day of pleasure," she advised him pertly. "Besides, I am not under your employ. I merely agreed to assist you while I'm a guest in your home."

"Don't sass me, girlie," the man cautioned her, though the sparkle in his eyes belied his apparent perturbation. "I can quickly find a replacement for you."

"No, you can't," Erin stated matter-of-factly, returning the shawl to his lap and tucking it in. "You're not likely to find anyone else who will long endure your cantankerous disposition."

Kellen observed the exchange with genuine amusement, but he quickly smothered the laugh that threatened to permeate the chamber, for his grandfather suddenly cast a stern look in his direction and thrust an incriminating finger at his head.

"It's all *your* fault," he accused. "Whatever possessed you to bring such a troublesome wench to Tiffin Square?"

Whatever Kellen's response might have been, it was forever lost, for just as he began to speak, Jeremiah spun the wheelchair around and waved the reply aside. "Never mind!" he snapped. "The fact remains, now that she's here, must you insist upon dragging the chit away when I need her?"

"Is that why I was summoned to your chamber? Because you wished to deliver a reprimand over this petty incident?" Kellen could feel the bitterness rising in his throat but, recalling his promise to Erin, he struggled to remain calm. "It's been four years, Grandfather," Kellen reminded him softly. "Surely, we can find something more pleasant to discuss." He strode over to the desk and, turning to face his grandfather, he lounged against the sturdy piece of furniture.

"Humph!" the old man snorted. "Had you truly cared about the happenings of the past four years, you'd not have deserted your family," Jeremiah grumbled, averting his eyes from the ones that carefully observed him.

"That's a well-worn subject," Kellen sighed disgustedly. "It's evident that this little get together has been a huge waste of time. If you'll excuse me." He pushed away from the desk and would have stalked past the elder Sinclair had Jeremiah's hand not shot out to catch his sleeve.

"No, wait! Please," he murmured hastily and, for the first time, Erin noted that his voice did not possess its customary rankled inflection.

"Don't . . . don't go. At least not until I've had a chance to set things right between us."

Kellen was understandably thunderstruck by the sudden change in his grandfather's dogmatic reserve, and he dragged a chair from the desk and sat down opposite Jeremiah in a conciliatory gesture.

"All right," Kellen agreed. "Where do we begin?"

"By making a clean sweep of our past differences," Jeremiah suggested. "What's done is done, and we shouldn't let what has gone before hamper our future together."

"I see." Kellen stroked his chin thoughtfully. "And just what brought about this sudden change of heart?" he asked bluntly.

Jeremiah glanced up in the wall mirror to catch Erin's reflection and, nodding his thanks, he said carefully, "Let's just say that someone, wise beyond her years, made an impossible, heartless old *jackass* realize his folly in denying himself the pleasure of his grandson's company and the comfort of his love."

"Grandfather," Kellen began gently, reaching over to clasp the large hands that had wrinkled with age. "Our positions have varied on many occasions, but I've always valued your opinion, and I've never stopped caring."

"Nor have I," Jeremiah whispered hoarsely.

As the two men leaned forward to embrace each other, Erin slipped soundlessly from the room to allow them to continue their reunion in private. The touching reconciliation had brought tears to her eyes, reminding her of the strained relationship that currently existed between her and her brothers. Thinking that some fresh air might clear her troubled thoughts, Erin descended the staircase and made her way outside to stroll amongst the blossoming flowers.

Several days later, Erin found herself standing before the hardwood door of Kellen's suite at The Sinclairian, more than a little apprehensive about her mission. Even though Jeremiah had dispatched her to the hotel on a business errand, she still had definite reservations about visiting Kellen alone in his quarters. Nevertheless, she inhaled deeply and assumed a businesslike stance before rapping sharply upon the barrier.

From within the suite, Kellen had just concluded tucking his shirt inside his trousers when he heard the summons and, satisfied that Chin Li, his personal servant, would see to the caller, he turned to the mirror. Picking up a comb, he pushed it through his unruly hair, but the repeated knocking made him dispense with his grooming. Realizing that Chin Li had probably gone to the hotel kitchen to obtain breakfast, Kellen lithely stepped across the spacious sitting room and opened the door. The smile that swiftly spread across his lips made it apparent that he was delighted to discover the identity of his early morning visitor.

"Good morning." The smile narrowed to a lazy grin as he continued to regard her speculatively. "This is indeed an unexpected surprise, Erin. To what do I owe the pleasure?"

A door at the opposite end of the corridor opened, and a curious head popped out to observe the scene in the hallway. Erin shifted and looked at Kellen beseechingly. "Might I step inside?" she asked nervously.

"Where are my manners? Please, do come in." He stepped away from the door, so that she might enter the chamber. Once inside, Kellen took her shawl and, noticing her uneasy expression, he tried to console her. "Don't worry about Mrs. Sullivan; she's my housekeeper. She'll not wag her tongue foolishly," he assured her, gesturing toward a flowered sofa as an indication that she should make herself comfortable. "I won't be but a moment."

He disappeared into another room, permitting Erin to thoroughly examine her surroundings. She would have recognized Kellen's taste in decorating the suite intuitively. The room positively reeked of his influence; from the plush brown carpet to the exquisite paintings, porcelain figurines, oriental vases, and the expensive furniture. The furnishings reminded her of the room she occupied at Tiffin Square . . . Kellen's old room . . . and she felt a sudden, inexplicable warm glow ignite within her as she reached out to fondle a jade figurine that stood on the table beside her.

"That was a gift from Grandfather. He obtained it in his more vigorous days when he was wont to jaunt about the globe."

He had left her so that he might don his morning coat and, once suitably attired, he reentered the sitting room. But her troubled expression caused Kellen to inquire, "Still fretting over Mrs. Sullivan? Don't. Once I explain the circumstances, she'll be pacified. Which brings me to inquire . . . *again,*" he added patiently, coaxing her to look at him. "What brings you rapping on my door at this prodigiously early hour?"

"Your grandfather sent me. It seems that these papers must be dispatched at once to Philadelphia and require your signature." She extended the papers to Kellen. "A messenger waits downstairs to deliver them."

"Uh hmm," he acknowledged her statement, glancing over the papers she proffered. "I'll just take a moment to look over them." He excused himself and stepped down the hallway to his study where he sat down at his desk to peruse the documents thoroughly before affixing his signature to them.

His absence lasted several minutes and, on impulse, Erin followed him into the study. He sat at his desk, his dark, unruly curls bent studiously over his task. Deciding against disturbing him, Erin scanned the room for something that might interest her.

Noting a large table against one wall, she ambled toward it to get a better look at the drawing that lay thereon. Erin gazed thoughtfully at the monstrous structure of a house on the paper before her and, her curiosity duly piqued, she thumbed through the remaining sketches to find what were evidently diagrams of the floor plan of the mansion.

Before Kellen spoke, she knew he stood behind her. He had moved noiselessly from his desk, so his movements had not alerted her to his presence. Just the same, he was there. She could sense it; feel his virile presence, smell his masculine scent.

"That's my home," his deep voice broke the stillness behind her. "I designed it," he added proudly.

"It's lovely," she murmured. "But I didn't know you had a home outside the city. Where is it?" She glanced up into his attentive face.

"To be truthful, it hasn't been built yet. But construction is scheduled to begin soon," he said determinedly. He took her elbow and guided her toward the sitting room. "As a matter-of-fact, Brad will be dropping by later to discuss the final preparations. You see, I am but the architect; Brad is the builder. And to answer your question, my behemoth is to be built near Falls Church, away from the hustle and bustle of the city. My stables have been set up there already, as well as a small cottage for my overseer."

"It does appear to be quite ostentatious," she remarked flatly. "Why would a bachelor like yourself require such an immense house?"

Kellen laughed at her candor. "Why, Erin, my sweet. Surely, you don't think that because I am presently unattached, I intend to remain so. No, indeed. Had it not been for the war, I daresay that I should be settled there already with a devoted wife and a young one or two to bounce upon my knee."

They had arrived in the sitting room long since, yet they continued their amicable discourse. Suddenly, the clock struck eight, reminding Erin of her errand, and she reached for the papers in Kellen's hands.

"Goodness, I had completely lost track of the time. Your grandfather is sure to throttle me if these do not reach their destination on time."

But Kellen held onto the documents and stepped to the bell-cord and gave it a firm tug. Almost instantly, a servant appeared in response to the summons. Kellen murmured some instructions to the footman, then he again turned to her.

"There. The matter has been settled. Albert shall deliver the documents to your messenger and your pretty rump shall be spared a roasting . . . *this* time," he chortled wickedly at her obvious discomfiture. "Have you had breakfast?"

"No," she replied honestly. "Mr. Sinclair sent me here straightway, but I'm sure that Meredith will see —"

"Nonsense," he protested, guiding her toward the French doors that opened onto a balcony. "You shall breakfast with me, and I'll entertain no protestations to the contrary."

He whisked her out onto the balcony where table and chairs had been placed, and she was so taken with the view that she plainly forgot to offer him an argument.

"Ah, here's my man now." Kellen turned to the servant who had just returned carrying a heavily laden breakfast tray. "Chin Li," he called. "Set a place for Miss Richards. She'll be dining with me.

"And there's no need to fetch additional fare," he went on to advise Chin Li. "You always bring enough for three men. I can certainly share this with my guest."

The servant swiftly arranged a place setting for Erin and served the couple. Then recognizing the look that Kellen directed at him, he bowed silently to each of them, then reentered the suite.

"He certainly seems efficient; almost as if he knows your every wish," Erin commented as she cut into the tender beefsteak.

"Chin Li and I go back a long way," Kellen replied. "Grandfather brought him and his mother from China years ago. He is a few years older than I, but we grew up together as friends.

His mother was in Grandfather's employ as well until she passed on a few years back. Since then, Chin Li has been with me," he concluded, gazing at her fondly as she ravenously attacked her meal. "Does the cuisine meet madam's approval?"

"Oh, yes. It's delicious!" she proclaimed, biting into a slice of the freshly baked bread that she had spread generously with jam. "I had thought never to enjoy such delicacies again," she admitted ruefully.

"It's my sincerest intent to see that you never want again," he whispered purposefully. But before Erin could voice the question that sprang to her tongue regarding his peculiar declaration, Kellen pushed on. "How is Grandfather?"

"Incorrigible, argumentative, stubborn," her voice trailed off, and she offered him a woeful smile. But the twinkle in those bright green eyes indicated her feigned consternation.

"In other words; the same," Kellen laughed.

"Exactly," she concurred. "And he's full of surprises," she noted.

Kellen was genuinely taken with her garrulous mood, and he sought to continue the enjoyable interlude. "Oh, how so?" he queried.

Erin, too, was finding the exchange agreeable, and she looked at him fondly as he unceremoniously plopped a piece of steak into his mouth and chewed vigorously, apparently awaiting her response. She did not tarry with her reply.

"Take this morning, for instance. I had always assumed your grandfather to be crippled, thereby, warranting the need for his wheelchair. Imagine my surprise when I entered his chamber this morning to find him *standing* before the mirror while his valet brushed out his jacket."

Kellen nodded knowingly, taking a leisurely draft from his coffee cup. "He does lean toward the eccentric, does he not?"

"*That* is an understatement!" Erin quickly agreed. "Why does he behave so outrageously?"

Kellen shrugged. "After Grandmother passed away, he began to change; he withdrew into his room like a recluse and shunned us all. Eventually, he began to conduct family business from Tiffin Square. He ordered the wheelchair to satisfy his own fancy, and has not left the chamber since."

"He is this evening," Erin's dulcet tone clearly indicated that she was pleased with her announcement. "He will be joining the family for supper; in the family dining room, I might add."

Kellen's fork clanked noisily onto his plate, and he sat back in his chair to stare at her in awestruck confusion. *"What!* However did you manage that?" He correctly assumed the identity of the one responsible for prying the oyster from its shell.

"It was his idea actually," she replied shrewdly, her eyes twinkling mischievously. "Of course, I *did* take the opportunity to tell him what a silly goose he was; making the servants and everyone else dote on him needlessly when he is perfectly capable of caring for himself. And that preposterous ritual of setting his place at the table he never bothers to honor with his presence." She clucked her tongue disdainfully and dabbed at her mouth with the lace trimmed napkin, then set it by her plate to indicate she had completed her repast.

"For some inexplicable reason, he immediately resolved to take his evening meal in the dining room." Erin shrugged her shoulders and turned on him a feigned look of wide-eyed innocence.

Kellen laughed loudly at her narrative. "Erin, you're a pure delight," he said admirably, pushing his chair back and stepping around the table to escort her back inside. "I thank you for giving my day such a gratifying beginning."

Erin offered him a shy, tremulous smile, uncertain as to how she should respond to such lavish repartee. "A-actually it is . . . is I who should be extending my gratitude to you for allowing me to intrude on your breakfast," she stammered awkwardly.

"Not at all." He lifted her hand to his lips and pressed a lingering kiss against the soft flesh. "It isn't often my table is graced by such an enchantress."

Erin blushed. "Thank you." She gratefully accepted her shawl as he placed it around her shoulders, and she pulled it tightly about her. "I must be going. Your grandfather said something about transcribing some important letters before lunch."

"Mustn't keep the old codger waiting." He tweaked her chin and opened the door for her. "Do you have transportation back to Tiffin?"

"Yes. John is waiting for me. He's an excellent driver," she added. For the life of her she could not imagine why, but for some unfathomable reason, she was reluctant for the encounter to come to an end. "Will you be visiting your mother anytime soon?" she inquired demurely.

"I could not possibly miss Grandfather's reemergence into society," he laughed. "Tell Mother to expect me for dinner."

"I shall." She turned a beaming smile on him and, bidding him a fond adieu, Erin fairly scampered down the hall to the staircase.

Kellen watched her carefree departure and a low, appreciative whistle was heard to echo in the corridor as he gazed rather wistfully after the gently swaying skirts that scurried away from him.

The door had barely closed behind him when another knock sounded, and a wicked flicker appeared in his blue eyes as he swung the barrier open, half-expecting, half-hoping to find that Erin had returned.

"What have you forgotten, minx?" he began with a playful lilt, only to come up short when he recognized the caller.

"Colonel Langford!" Kellen could not control his surprise. "I thought —"

"I know," the colonel cleared his throat. "I saw her on the staircase. She's a pretty thing, Kellen. But I must admit, she didn't look at all the type to come calling on a gentleman unescorted, as it were."

"She's not," Kellen said dryly, standing aside to offer the man admittance. "She was on an errand for Grandfather."

"And how is Jeremiah?"

"Well, thank you." Kellen summoned Chin Li and instructed him to bring coffee. Then motioning the colonel into the study, they each took a seat, and Kellen studied the man closely.

"I know that look, Kellen," he warned.

"Oh?"

"You're wondering what the devil I'm doing here."

"I suppose I am," Kellen laughed. "I expected that I might run into you from time-to-time after I resigned my commission, just not so soon."

Chin Li appeared then with the coffee, and the colonel waited until the servant withdrew from the room before beginning his explanation.

"Out with it, Oliver," Kellen addressed the man familiarly. "A busy man like yourself doesn't usually squander his valuable time on social visits, or is this a business call?"

Oliver Langford studied him for a moment before he leaned forward to inquire, "Do you recall a fellow named Brian Taggart?"

"Taggart?" Kellen mulled the name over in his mind. "Swarthy looking character; served under me in my last campaign. Yes. What about him?"

"He showed up at headquarters a few days ago, making some accusations, *serious* accusations that the department cannot allow to go uninvestigated."

"Taggart? Impossible." Kellen shook his head firmly. "Brad told me that everyone was killed in the ambush."

"I'm aware of the report, but the fact remains; Sergeant Taggart is very much alive. And," the man paused, preparing himself for the reaction he knew that his next statement would produce, "he claims that Lieutenant Petersen was in cahoots with the Rebs in that final mission."

"The hell you say!" Kellen came to his feet angrily. "That's in-

232

sane, Oliver, and you well know it. Why, I'm surprised the incompetent oaf did not try to implicate *me.*"

"No,," Colonel Langford said frankly. "And as far as the department is concerned, you're not under suspicion of any wrongdoing."

"Thank you," Kellen snapped bitterly as he stalked to the mantel to flip open an elaborately carved box and withdraw a cigar. He seldom indulged this early in the day, but the colonel's revelation had sorely vexed him, and he needed a distraction. "I take it, then, that Bradley Petersen, my close associate and friend, *is* suspect." He rounded on Colonel Langford.

"Yes, unfortunately."

"Then my next question should come as no surprise to you." Kellen's voice was taut as he struggled to stay calm. "Why have you chosen to divulge this fairy tale to me?"

"I was . . . that is to say . . . the department was hoping to enlist your support in resolving the matter," he replied honestly.

"What? You actually expect to engage my assistance in this despicable affair? Whatever made you conceive such an outrageous notion?" Kellen asked crossly.

"As you said; Petersen is your friend. You grew up together and attended the same college, as I recollect," he said pointedly. "Certainly, you could sound the man out, quite casually of course, to see what he knows, and report any discrepancies or suspicious behavior to us."

"I repeat; what do I have to do with this? It was my understanding that my resignation released me from further military obligation," Kellen addressed the colonel stiffly.

"So it did," the colonel agreed. "But what of your obligation to your fellow man, to the memory of those soldiers who were loyal to you, who died needlessly at the hands of ruthless men with the aid of a leader they trusted. A man, incidentally, who was in command due to your own carelessness," he added for good measure, noticing Kellen's painful wince. "It occurs to me that, if for no other reason, you might want to exonerate Petersen to put your own mind to rest."

The grave expression on Kellen's face made the colonel realize that these perturbing thoughts were already plaguing Kellen's mind, and he knew that the young man wrestled with a very delicate problem. If he accepted the assignment, he risked the chance of alienating a lifelong friend should Petersen learn of the investigation and take umbrage at the insult. Or worse still, Kellen may uncover evidence that would prove his colleague guilty as charged.

Kellen stood silent for a long while, then pushing away from the fireplace, he strolled back to his chair and plopped his impressive frame down upon the leather upholstery and sighed his acquiescence. "Brief me on Taggart's story," he mumbled dully.

As the story unfolded, Kellen pushed his coffee cup aside in disgust and reached for the crystal decanter of brandy in its place. Pouring himself a generous serving of the fiery liquid, he listened intently to the colonel's narrative.

"Taggart says the Rebs were from the area, and they apparently knew Petersen, for he helped them transport the goods to the hideout and instructed them in how to handle the temperamental stuff. Taggart was able to follow them to where they stashed the cargo, and he said it wasn't so very far from where you were laid up on that plantation," Langford concluded his explanation.

"This is all very interesting drivel, Oliver, but what, may I ask, makes you so damnably certain that Taggart is telling the truth?" he hurled the question at the unruffled colonel. "Isn't it possible that Taggart is the culprit here?"

"Perhaps," Langford conceded, "though I can't for the life of me think why he'd come to the department with his tale if he were. But regardless of who is the guilty party, the allegations have been leveled and they must be investigated." He finished his coffee and stood to leave. "But let's consider the consequences, shall we?

234

"You know as well as I that the nitroglycerin you were carrying is fickle stuff. It's too new; we don't know enough about it to control it properly. It was only out of sheer desperation that the department decided to experiment with the stuff. Only we never got the chance to study its effectiveness as a weapon, thanks to your friend."

"That remains to be proven," Kellen said dryly.

"True. I'm uncertain of your feelings, Kellen, but the thoughts of that nitro sitting around like a powder keg, ready to explode at the slightest provocation—well, it frightens the hell out of me. Think of the innocent people who might be hurt." He cast Kellen a sly look from the corner of his eye to determine if his rigid countenance had wavered.

"What, pray tell, would you suggest I do?" Kellen asked blandly.

"Question Petersen for starters," he proposed. "Perhaps you could return to the scene of the ambush. The department will help you contrive some plausible reason for returning to that area if need be," he answered Kellen's unspoken question. "That would give you a chance to canvass the region; find out if the nitro is still there, been sold elsewhere, or blown some poor bastard to kingdom come. Who knows, maybe you can even clear Petersen."

Colonel Langford stepped lithely toward the door. "But I may as well tell you now that you have your work cut out for you on that score."

"Why do you say that?"

"Your mission was not the first involving the transportation of nitroglycerin. There were two others, and they also ended in ambush, albeit the cargo was destroyed due to inept handling." He opened the door to the study, preparing to take his leave. "Petersen was assigned to those patrols, too," he added solemnly.

There was a long silence in which the two men exchanged grave looks and, when Kellen made an effort to stand to escort his guest out, Langford motioned him back into his chair. "I can let myself out," he assured him. "I trust you'll let me know your decision soon."

Kellen merely offered a noncommittal grunt as a reply.

"Good day, Kellen. I'll be in touch," the colonel said before retreating from the room to leave Kellen to his thoughts.

Kellen sat gazing at the shadows the sun's reflection cast on the wall long after he heard the click of the door as it closed behind his departing guest. The problem that the colonel had laid at his feet was to plague him the entire day, causing him to be short with his serving staff and business acquaintances. And when Brad arrived for their appointment, Kellen found it difficult to conduct business as usual, such was his state of mind. Yet, when it came time to depart for his engagement at Tiffin Square, he still had not come to terms with his turbulent musings.

Kellen stared hard at the reflection that met him in the mirror as he waited patiently while Chin Li finished pressing out his evening coat. At last, slipping into the navy satin jacket, his ensemble complete, he assembled his personal effects and descended the stairs to his carriage.

As he jostled gently in the vehicle, while it made its way along the city streets, his thoughts irrevocably returned to the morning's conversation with Colonel Langford, and a pensive frown crinkled his brow. To be sure, he had not been wholly satisfied with Brad's accounting of the attack, but he did not truly think his friend capable of subterfuge. Finally, Kellen resolved that the only way he could relax and enjoy the evening's festivities would be if he made a decision and put the unhappy circumstance from his mind.

With a sigh, Kellen determined to meet with Colonel Langford the following morning and agree to accept the assignment. He had but one objective in mind: to absolve his friend of the charges that had been falsely leveled against him.

Strange, but the thought of Brad's guilt never entered Kellen's head.

Within minutes, the carriage pulled to a stop before the red-bricked mansion, his heart considerably lighter now that he had settled his dilemma. With an airy lilt in his voice, he said a cheery hello to Jasper before making his way to the drawing room to join the others who waited for him.

Bidding good evening to Geoffrey and Vanessa, Kellen bent over his mother to place a kiss on her brow, then his eyes instinctively found Erin. She was a vision, standing beside a table absently tracing abstract patterns in the polished shine of the wood. But Kellen's greeting soon caused the faraway look on her face to vanish, and she offered him a warm smile.

Erin was clad in a creamy yellow chiffon dress that complemented her alabaster complexion quite admirably. The neckline was scooped low enough in the front to expose the youthful mounds of her breasts to the discerning masculine eyes, and the décolletage was bedecked with rows and rows of bright yellow lace ruffles that successfully enhanced her youthful appearance. The sharp contrast of the bright yellow satin underskirt with the soft, flowing chiffon created a most attractive ensemble that swirled about her dainty feet when she walked.

The same ribbons that were wound intricately through the hems of the short sleeves were used to tie her hair securely at the nape of her neck. Her locks had then been brushed into a fullness and allowed to fall over one shoulder in mounds of shimmering tendrils.

The effect was dazzling, and Kellen found himself longing to nibble a trail along the one white shoulder that was exposed to his lingering gaze.

Erin felt herself flush under his lengthy examination, and the disdainful expression that spread across Vanessa's face made Erin sweep forward to greet Kellen sincerely; mindful of the scornful glare that followed her movement.

"The tart!" Vanessa whispered harshly to her husband.

"Look how the shameless hussy flaunts her wares before him."

Vanessa had not meant her comment to be overheard, but Kellen's murderous look warned her that his sharp ears had detected the slander, and she stiffened, preparing for his rebuttal.

But the door to the drawing room opened, and Jasper stepped in to announce that dinner was about to be served, and they would find the elder Sinclair waiting for them in the dining room.

With this news, Kellen gallantly proffered his arm to Erin and, when she accepted, he extended his free arm to his mother. As they strolled from the room, Kellen remarked casually, "It isn't often a man is fortunate enough to escort two lovely ladies into dinner."

Geoffrey watched their retreat with a cunning eye, then stood and held out his arm to his wife. "I should hasten to warn you to curb your venomous tongue, my pet, else we'll never be rid of her."

"Whatever do you mean? What about her plans for Ireland?"

"They've evidently been forgotten; if indeed they ever existed," he added thoughtfully. "Just look at them; observe how my dumbstruck cousin plays the besotted suitor." He nodded toward the couple just as Kellen leaned down to whisper an amusing anecdote in Erin's ear, causing her to laugh gaily.

Geoffrey shook his head and lamented, "No, Kellen will not be eager to send her away, and the old man is taken with her as well." His eyes narrowed purposefully and, when he next spoke, his tone was shrewdly calculated. "It's such a pity that one so young and vulnerable is separated from her family. Perhaps we can be of some assistance in reuniting the chit with her loved ones," he murmured slyly, and the honey-sweet smile that settled on Vanessa's lips advised him that she was in complete harmony with his thoughts.

They arrived in the dining room to discover that the others had already seated themselves; Meredith at one end, Jeremiah at the other, with Kellen flanking him on the right and Erin on the left. One look at the seating arrangement, and Vanessa's smile vanished instantly, though she did manage to conceal her rage as she strutted over to Jeremiah. With a ceremonious gesture, she leaned down and placed a kiss on the old man's cheek.

"How good it is to have you join us for dinner at long last," she purred at him. Then, assuming a haughty expression, Vanessa turned on Erin. "Why, Erin, dear, it would seem that you've mistakenly claimed Geoffrey's place. I'm sure that Jeremiah meant to have *both* his grandsons at his side."

"Stop your caterwauling, Vanessa, and sit down," Jeremiah snapped gruffly. "Erin is beside me at my request. My eyesight is not so obscure that I cannot see Geoffrey sitting a few inches from me. Besides, I find Miss Richards a damn sight prettier to look at than Geoffrey, and she's a delightful conversationalist.

"It would do you some good to broaden your repartee to include more engaging discourse, Geoffrey. As it stands, you seem besieged by talk of business and the heir to the Sinclair fortune, an heir who has not yet been proclaimed." Jeremiah motioned for the footmen to begin serving the meal. "An oversight I intend to rectify this very evening. Over dessert, I should think."

The room grew unusually silent at this conjecture, causing Jeremiah to chortle priggishly. "What, my children, no response to my much anticipated declaration? Come, you sorely disappoint an old man." His aged hand reached forward to encircle his wine glass while he surreptitiously surveyed each and every one of them.

"Kellen, of course, has shown no outward interest in his legacy," he continued when no one was quick to rise to the bait, "but you, Geoffrey, speak of little else. I must admit I'm baffled. Where's your tongue, lad? Or you, Vanessa?"

He confronted the thunderstruck girl who looked quite foolish, poised as she was, with her mouth gaping, the soup spoon suspended in mid-air between her mouth and her plate. She was obviously as surprised as the others by the unexpected announcement.

Erin was the only one who seemed unconcerned by the disclosure, but if the truth were known, she was a bundle of curiosity. But she camouflaged her interest with the propriety befitting a stranger in the midst of an intimate family discussion.

At last, Kellen's strong, impassive voice penetrated the disquieting silence. "Really, Grandfather, is this display truly necessary? I had hoped that your restoration to the family dining table might be a more cheerful occasion. *Must* you taunt us with this nonsense? If it is not your intent to reveal your successor till the final course is served, then do let us partake of the preceding ones in a more lighthearted atmosphere."

"Here, here," Geoffrey echoed his cousin's sentiments. "For once, we are in agreement." He lifted his glass to Kellen in a mock salute.

"Very well, my children; have it your way." Jeremiah smiled slyly and turned his attention to the salad that had just been placed before him.

The ensuing repast proved to be the most arduous ordeal Erin had struggled through in quite some time. Indeed, she barely took note of the vast array of succulent, palatable morsels that passed between her lips. Despite Kellen's plea for lighthearted conversation, the talk at the table was obviously forced with the topic seldom wavering from the weather, interspersed with Meredith's valiant efforts to include amusing anecdotes concerning family acquaintances.

An eternity later, dessert was finally served and, sensing the increasing tension about the table, Meredith suggested that the ladies retire to the drawing room to partake of coffee and dessert, thereby, allowing the men the freedom to conduct their business privately.

"Nonsense," Jeremiah spoke up. "I wouldn't deprive any of

you of hearing my announcement firsthand."

"Well, I, for one, see no need for our *little house guest* to be party to the proceedings. After all, *she* isn't family," Vanessa said loftily. She avoided the smoldering gaze that Kellen settled on her and turned her concentration to the tasty delicacy that sat before her.

Erin paled visibly at this unexpected assault and, placing her napkin beside her plate, she scooted her chair away from the table, apparently preparing to excuse herself from the group. "Vanessa is a-a-absolutely r-r-right," she stammered embarrassingly. "If you'll pardon me, I think I'll stroll out onto the terrace for a refreshing change of scenery," she said purposefully, turning a pointed look on Vanessa.

"No, indeed!" Jeremiah said firmly. "Pay no attention to Vanessa. She tends to forget that she is not the reigning mistress of Tiffin Square. Meredith performs that function quite adequately and, hopefully, shall continue to do so for many years to come." His lips parted in the first sincere smile that Erin had witnessed, and Meredith flushed in humble response to the praise.

Thus formally chastised, Vanessa settled into a proper sulk and Erin returned to her seat. All eyes remained focused on Jeremiah, who leisurely sipped on the champagne he had requested served in celebration of the momentous occasion. Deciding that he had tormented the onlookers enough with his shenanigans, Jeremiah sat back in his chair to consider the myriad of expressions that watched him; then he spoke.

"I know that you think me to be an eccentric, addlepated old fool," he began carefully, holding up his hand as an indication to his captive audience that he would brook no interruptions when they started to object to his disparaging self-appraisal. "Please, humor an old man and hold your comments till I've concluded my little speech.

"I have avoided choosing my successor until this moment for a number of reasons. Indeed, had it not been for the untimely passing of both my sons, this difficult selection would not be mine to make. Be that as it may, I have made my choice, and I want you all to know right now that I shall stand firm on my decision," he added staunchly.

"Geoffrey," he looked squarely at his grandson, causing a triumphant smile to spring to Vanessa's face, "has always shown a keen interest in family affairs, and has proven to be a competent business manager since I've gone into seclusion here and no longer venture into the main office."

Jeremiah paused long enough to quench his thirst with the sparkling champagne. "Kellen, however, has become quite the entrepreneur on his own.

"While I find neither of my grandsons lacking in the skills which will be required of them to assume control of the family businesses, I *do* find that I'm more than a little disenchanted with Geoffrey's avaricious inclinations, as well as Kellen's apparent nonchalance for family concerns. Therefore, I have settled upon the one solution that I feel will better serve the family's interests." He took the opportunity to scan the serious faces that were glued on him before making the long awaited announcement.

Leaning back in his chair, Jeremiah placed the tips of his fingers together in a contemplative gesture and stated simply, "The first grandson to produce a male heir shall inherit . . . everything."

Chapter Thirteen

Meredith immediately insisted that the ladies adjourn to the drawing room following this most surprising development to allow the men to converse freely. This maneuver did not set well with Vanessa, but even she knew better than to usurp Meredith's authority, and she begrudgingly followed the woman from the room.

Vanessa presently stalked about the chamber, angrily waiting for Geoffrey to join her, so that she might prod him with questions. Meredith, too, was in an anxious mood, though she gave no outward sign. But in truth, the book that lay open in her lap might just as well have been closed, for her eyes had not deciphered a single word on the page before her.

Only Erin's concentration was wholly devoted to her task. She sat on the end of the sofa near the lamp, busily working on a sampler that she was embroidering as a gift for her grandmother, should she indeed ever embark on her journey to Ireland. In her opinion, Jeremiah's solution had been the most logical one, if not particularly just; therefore, she could not fathom Vanessa's perturbation. After all, she and Geoffrey were in a more advantageous position to provide an heir than was Kellen.

"What's keeping them?" Vanessa barked impatiently, bringing her fist down on the back of the sofa with a force that startled Erin, and she nearly pricked her finger with the embroidery needle. "It's way past the old coot's bedtime."

"The *old coot* has retired for the evening," Kellen said dryly as he strode into the room accompanied by a somber Geoffrey.

He walked straightway to the decanter and helped himself to a cognac, then he turned a stony gaze on Vanessa. "In the future, I would appreciate a more civil reference to my grandfather." He did not allow Vanessa a chance to respond to his directive, but crossed to the sofa and sat down beside Erin to politely inquire of her progress on the sampler.

"Well, Geoffrey?" Vanessa crossed her arms over her bosom, and cast a severe eye on her husband. "What *did* the old . . . *Jeremiah*," she corrected herself when she detected the deadly look that disfigured Kellen's face, "have to say after we left?"

Geoffrey had settled into his favorite wing chair and, espying the evening paper, he retrieved the tabloid and absently scanned the headlines. All the while, he casually observed the couple who conversed quite amicably on the sofa. Yes, Kellen was showing definite signs of succumbing to Cupid's arrow; the girl would have to be dispatched posthaste.

With Erin out of the way, it would take his cousin months to find a suitable replacement. By that time, he fully intended to see that Vanessa was carrying the son that would guarantee his position as sole heir to the Sinclair dynasty.

Geoffrey carefully shifted his gaze to his wife, and he signed wearily. She was a beauty, of that there was no denial, but greed and selfishness were qualities that could make even the loveliest creature seem a veritable shrew. It was no different with his wife.

"*Geoffrey!*" she fairly screeched. "I said—"

"I heard you, darling," Geoffrey said sweetly, tossing the paper aside.

"Indeed," Kellen snorted. "The whole town no doubt heard you."

Vanessa bristled at the insult, but Geoffrey merely chuckled at his cousin's pettiness and, standing up, he strode over to take his wife's hand. "Come along, pet," he cooed lovingly, leading her toward the door. "Let's leave our friends to their idle chitchat. We have far more important matters to tend to.

"For instance, we shall retire to our chamber to begin fulfilling Grandfather's prerequisite for an heir." He threw Kellen an arrogant look as he swept Vanessa from the room.

But if anyone noticed the anguished expression that settled on Vanessa's face, no one spoke of it when the door closed behind the departing couple.

"At last!" Kellen cried. "I'm free to converse with my two favorite ladies."

"I fear that I must be going as well," Erin apologized, as she returned her needlework to the sewing box. "It's been a long day."

"Of course, dear," Meredith offered understandingly. "It isn't often these days that I get my son all to myself." She favored Erin with a slightly meaningful, albeit genuine, smile.

Erin stood to leave and Kellen rose to his feet to escort her to the door. He was not overly anxious to be bereft of her company, but his mother had made it obvious that she desired a few private words with him; therefore, he could not prevail upon Erin to remain. Still, he did not want her to leave without knowing when he would be able to see her again.

Erin bid Meredith a good evening when she reached the door, and she was surprised when Kellen stepped across the threshold and followed her into the hallway. She paused and looked at him, a question lingering behind the dazzling green eyes.

"I was just thinking how good an excursion to my country estate sounds. I've been meaning to ride out to check on my stables at Arcadia since I returned, but haven't found the time." He hesitated, noticing that the question behind those provocative eyes had grown deeper, and he cleared his throat before continuing. "Would you care to accompany me tomorrow? After all, it will be Saturday and Grandfather should not require your services."

"Arcadia?" Erin questioned the unfamiliar name.

"Yes, that's the name of my property near Falls Church. I named it for the ancient Grecian city. It means; a region of simple pleasure and quiet," he explained wistfully. "I think you'll understand why I selected the title once you've seen it."

Erin thoughtfully considered the handsome face that calmly awaited her response and, quite unthinkingly, she reached up to brush aside a strand of wayward hair that fell across his forehead. "I'd love to go with you," she murmured softly.

"Splendid!" Kellen captured her hand in his when she would have withdrawn it and pressed it to his lips. "Shall we make a day of it? I'll have my chef prepare something special, and we can picnic on the grounds."

"That sounds lovely," she agreed, very much aware of the warm gaze that considered her. Lowering her eyes, she asked, "What time shall I expect you?"

"Early, say nine o'clock."

"Fine," she whispered and would have walked away, but Kellen continued to hold her hand in a secure grip. "I'll be ready."

"Have I neglected to tell you how stunning you look this evening? For surely you must know that you are the most exquisite vision, and I count myself fortunate to be able to converse with you; to hold you in my arms . . ." His breath was like a warm summer breeze as it gently stroked her cheek, and she shivered expectantly when he drew her into his arms and tilted her chin back till their eyes locked.

"Kellen! Please. This isn't . . . proper. What if a servant discovers us like this?" she pleaded.

"Then he shall be witness to a very *proper* good night kiss." He lowered his head and, in the dim light of the hallway, their lips met in a gentle embrace.

246

"There." He pulled away and held her at arm's length. "Was that chaste enough for you? You see, I do not *always* behave like a lustful rogue in your presence. However, I must admit that you present quite a temptation, and a less respectable gentleman might be inclined to attempt all manner of *improper* things." His eyes fastened on the mounds of creamy flesh that protruded invitingly from the décolletage of her gown, and a wicked smile spread across his sensuous mouth.

"Kellen!" Erin stepped away from him, her hands flying to her face to shield the flush that burned her cheeks. "You're shameless!"

"Yes, and you're quite delightful. Till tomorrow, my lady." He bowed grandly before her, then turned on his heel and re-entered the drawing room.

Meredith observed the bemused expression on her son's face, and an agreeable smile immediately blossomed on her own lips. "Tell me Kellen. Does Erin know that she's quite won your heart?" she asked candidly.

But if Kellen was taken aback by his mother's forward manner, he gave no indication. Indeed, he lumbered across the floor with the hauteur of one well satisfied with himself, and settled his muscular frame in a chair beside Meredith.

"I think she suspects as much," he affirmed Meredith's suspicions, "but she's reluctant to admit that she could feel anything except complete contempt for a Yankee," he added ruefully. "I shall have to be careful in my wooing if I am to convince her that we would suit regardless of familial objections."

"What objections?" Meredith demanded. "Erin is a charming, unspoiled young lady, and I heartily approve of the match. Your taste has certainly shown marked improvement since your involvement with Vanessa," she added caustically, ignoring Kellen's beleaguered groan. "And your grandfather will no doubt dance a jig when he hears the news. Who do you fear will object?"

"Erin's family. They were quite harsh with her when they

learned that she had granted me shelter and aid when I was wounded. It will be no small feat to gain their approval." His eyes grew somber as he considered his dilemma. "And, of course, Geoffrey and Vanessa are not likely to welcome legitimate competition for the inheritance."

"What of Erin?" Meredith had a sudden thought. "Do you think she will interpret your proposal as a means for you to vie for your inheritance?"

"She might," Kellen conceded. "But, Mother, you know that I have no interest in Grandfather's companies and investments. I merely feign interest to intimidate Geoffrey. It's good for him; keeps him honest. Well, as honest as Geoffrey can be," he added with a sardonic lift of one eyebrow.

"I know, dear." Meredith sighed and slowly rose from her chair. "But somehow, I cannot help but feel that your father would have wanted his son to manage the Sinclair enterprises, not his nephew. After all, your father played a significant role in spawning the Sinclair dynasty," she said pointedly, but when Kellen made no effort to respond, she shrugged her shoulders.

"Good night, my son." She paused by his chair to place a kiss against his brow before she ambled over to the door. Before she completely withdrew from the chamber, she turned to say, "Regardless of how you choose to proceed in this matter, I want you to know that your father would be quite proud to see what a fine man you've become." She wiped at a tear that trickled down her face, then blew him a kiss and closed the door to leave him to his thoughts.

Erin sat in a remote corner of the garden, clad in a white chambray gauze gown, her hair arranged in a comely fashion to frame her lovely face. She created quite a memorable picture, seated as she was amongst the brilliant burst of color from the various flowers. But her mood did not reflect the festive scene, for Erin was quite pensive on this June morn. Neither the novel she had brought from the library, nor the cheerful melodies of the birds in the trees could rouse her from her musings.

Irrevocably, Erin's thoughts centered on a subject that had been the sole focus of her concentration for many days now; Kellen. She had not meant for it to happen; not truly thought it to be possible, but she had fallen desperately in love with him.

She felt the familiar flush as she recalled the countless times he had pulled her into his powerful embrace and covered her face with kisses; kisses that had grown increasingly demanding as their relationship grew more intimate. She remembered, quite shamefacedly, one particular encounter on the day she had accompanied him to the country to visit Arcadia.

After they had toured the new additions to the stables and Kellen informed his overseer that workmen would be arriving in a few weeks to begin construction of the house, he led Erin to an isolated glade. There they had been completely surrounded by monstrous trees that towered above them to filter the sun's scorching rays, and the only sound that permeated the stillness was the rippling brook that ran through the middle of the picturesque scene.

It was an enchanting place, and Erin was put in mind of her hideaway by the waterfall near Kilkieran and a sudden wave of homesickness enveloped her, bringing tears to her eyes.

Kellen had correctly interpreted the reason for her melancholy, and had stepped to her and placed a consoling hand on her shoulder. Thinking back, it had all seemed so natural. Erin had turned at his touch, and he had encircled her shoulders, pulling her into his arms. Pressing her face against his clean, soft shirt, she had breathed deeply of his masculine scent and, when he brushed his knuckles along her cheek, she lifted her face to receive his kiss.

Quite unexpectedly, Kellen had whisked her into his arms and carried her to the blanket that he had spread beneath a tree while they picnicked. Laying her gently on the ground, he was beside her in an instant, his hands roving expertly along her arms, her waist, until he tenderly held her glowing face between his large, capable hands; his eyes caressing her lovingly.

Before she could offer any resistance, his lips had descended upon hers hungrily, consuming her with a fierce passion she had not felt in him before. Perhaps because of her need to be comforted, or her own growing affection for this man, Erin found herself responding to his kiss with an abandon she did not know existed within her. She entwined her arms about his neck and pressed her body closer to his, thrilling in the sensation of his hard, masculine body thrust so intimately against her own.

Erin moaned breathlessly, her mouth parting slightly to give him access to the sweet nectar behind those pliable lips. He sensed her willingness and crushed her to him, as though he feared if he loosened his hold she might vanish.

Erin's mind was agog with confused ecstasy as she lay there in his arms, her head and senses full of him. At last she pulled away, panting for the breath he had devoured, and she fell back onto the blanket while he hovered above her in the flickering shade of the trees. Erin did not know what he was about until it was too late and, truthfully, she made no effort to thwart his sensuous plunderings.

His nimble fingers moved along the buttons of her jacket and, when they had achieved their purpose, he turned his attention to the buttons of her green silk blouse. His task complete, Kellen's hands purposely slid beneath the material to fondle the youthful breasts that trembled slightly at his practiced manipulation.

If Erin's thoughts had not been so jumbled, she might have thought to stop him. But as it was, Kellen was so enthralled with the lovely vision and the soft supple flesh that responded so wondrously to his touch that her protests would likely have fallen upon passion-deafened ears.

He deftly pushed the delicate fabric of her chemise aside to expose the glorious mounds to his longing eyes. A distinctive groan rumbled deep in his throat as he lowered his head, gently nibbling at the peak of one breast then the other till the nipples stood erect to taunt him, defiantly urging him on.

But when he paused to gaze down into the face that studied him in guarded anticipation, that sweet, innocent face that was alive with passion and fear, Kellen knew that he could not take her this way. Lord knew he *wanted* her! His very soul ached to feel her naked flesh pressed against his in a passionate frenzy, to feel her move against him, to feel himself inside her.

An anguished moan was torn from his throat at this last thought, and he permitted himself the pleasure of one last caress before he quickly rebuttoned her blouse. Then he pushed away from her to bring his flaming cravings under control. His equanimity restored, Kellen stood and pulled her from the blanket to stand beside him. Cupping her face in his hands, he stared into her eyes; eyes that were wide and confused.

"I-I won't apologize," he fumbled over his words. "God knows I've want to do that . . . and more . . . for the longest time. But I won't take advantage of you like this. I want everything to be perfect for us."

He noticed her eyes glaze over with tears of understanding, and he held her close. And Erin would never forget the impassioned declaration that came tumbling from his lips, as he pulled her tightly against him.

"For surely you must know by now that I love you, my darling Erin."

Erin was certain that her flush began in her toes and colored to the very roots of her hair as she sat in the garden, reminiscing over this most intimate of encounters. Ever since that day, however, nearly two weeks past, Kellen had adopted an almost brotherly attitude in his dealings with her.

"Why, just last night his lips barely brushed mine when he returned me from the theatre," she mumbled aloud. "Perhaps he does not love me nearly as much as he thinks," she sighed morosely, trying to sort out the complexities of the enigmatic man she had grown to love.

Little did she know that Kelllen's standoffishness was due to his ever increasing desire to possess her completely, and his efforts to squelch his nagging longings were in deference to her. Being ignorant of this fact, however, Erin was no nearer a solution to the reason for Kellen's peculiar behavior when Jasper came to announce that she had two visitors awaiting her in the downstairs sitting room.

Erin was positively alive with curiosity as she followed the servant along the stoned pathway to the terrace door. She could not imagine who the callers might be, unless the McAlisters had decided to drop by unexpectedly.

Although Jasper would have assuredly given me their names, she mused silently. I suppose I shall find out soon enough, she reasoned, checking her appearance in the hall mirror before pushing the door open to welcome her guests. But the perfunctory greeting died upon her lips when she recognized her callers, and she rushed forward to throw herself into her uncle's arms.

"Uncle Philip!" Her squeal of delight echoed throughout the room. "How wonderful it is to see you. Hello, Christina!" She pushed away from her uncle, but did not release him entirely, as she extended her free hand to her cousin. "I cannot tell you how glad it is to see a familiar face," Erin cried happily.

She clasped Christina's hand joyfully, the circumstances of their last meeting completely forgotten, but Erin's usually observant gaze did not notice the glint of hostility that flickered in Christina's cold eyes. She had not forgotten.

"Hello, cousin," Christina said icily, staring openly at Erin's fashionable gown, making her acutely aware of her own shabby dress. "You might as well know; this isn't a social call, nor is it a particularly pleasant one." She shoved Erin's hand away and stepped across the room to claim a seat.

Erin's breath quickened and her heart pounded in fearful

expectation of dismal news. "What is it?" she demanded, turning on her uncle, gripping his arm with surprising strength. "Something has happened at Kilkieran; something dreadful. Tell me!" She had nearly succumbed to frantic tears at this point, as her mind raced with all sorts of possibilities.

"No, Erin," her uncle whispered kindly, leading her to the sofa and gently helping her to a seat. "It was cruel of Christina to excite you." He offered his daughter a reproving look, to which Christina merely shrugged and focused her unconcerned gaze out the window.

Philip sat down beside his niece and patted her hand, a little nervously, she thought and, when he had determined that she was sufficiently recovered, he prepared to speak again.

But it was Erin who broke the lengthy silence. "I'm relieved to see that you have safely returned from the war, Uncle Philip," she mumbled considerately, then suddenly she leaned forward to clutch his hand. "Forgive my bluntness," she blurted. "But, *please* tell me what has brought you here. I assure you that I'm imagining all sorts of horrible things. Has something happened to Evan, or Deborah?"

She did not notice his obvious discomfiture at her mention of the war, such was the intensity of her concern for her family. But he quickly masked his unease when he turned to answer her.

"Everyone is well at Kilkieran," he assured her. "At least, that is the case for the time being."

"Yes?" she prompted.

"Have you heard of the taxes that are being levied on many of the South's plantations?" Philip inquired patiently.

"No. What about them?"

"Well, the short of it is, Kilkieran has been levied a property tax of a thousand dollars, and Graham has no way of coming up with the money," he explained frankly.

"A thousand dollars?" she repeated distantly.

"Yes," Christina offered snidely. "You could likely raise half that sum if you sold that piece of finery you're presently wear-

253

ing." Her eyes jealously raked Erin up and down.

"Be quiet, Christina, or you can conclude the remainder of your visit in the carriage," Philip warned his daughter. Again he turned to Erin. "Graham refused to come to you himself; that damned Irish pride you all inherited from your mother," he added fondly. "I'd offer to help myself, but it took the last of my resources to settle the taxes on Briar Cliff," he explained. "I had business in the city, so I took it upon myself to approach you with this unfortunate news, for Graham wouldn't be happy with me if he knew I was here.

"I'm sorry that our reunion has to be under such bleak circumstances, but I thought . . . that is . . . perhaps you might be able to help in some way," he coughed embarrassingly.

"You obviously do *something* that pleases that silly Yankee, else he'd have sent you packing long ago," Christina sneered. "Perhaps, if you asked him prettily, he'd give you the money."

"That's quite enough, Christina!" Her father silenced her with a threatening look. "Again, I apologize, Erin. I didn't mean for it to be this way, but Christina knew the name of the . . . er . . . gentleman you left Kilkieran with. I thought she might be of some assistance in this matter. I now realize that I was mistaken," he said sincerely.

"Come along, Christina." Philip stood and motioned his daughter toward the door. "There's just one thing more, Erin. The tax money needs to be raised quickly; less than two weeks, or Kilkieran will be auctioned to the highest bidder."

He exited the room on this ominous note, but Christina held back to offer one final insult. "A thousand dollars," she repeated purposely. "I'm inclined to think that you're not worth it. It's a wonder he still amuses himself with you, for I didn't think that men of his sort dallied with the same *mistress* for long." Christina turned up her nose in obvious distaste and strutted from the room, leaving a desolate Erin behind.

Erin wandered along the garden path in the moonlight, her

white satin nightdress flowing in the gentle summer breeze. She walked as if in a daze, totally absorbed in her thoughts. How could she ask Kellen for the thousand dollars that was needed to save Kilkieran? Two precious days had already passed since her uncle had delivered the disturbing news, yet she had not been able to bring herself to broach the subject with Kellen. He had done so much for her already. Surely, she must draw the line somewhere.

She sighed dismally, her shoulders feeling pounds heavier with this additional burden. Thus absorbed in her problems, she did not hear the footsteps on the path behind her.

"Ah, so it *is* you," Kellen's pleasant voice broke the stillness of the lonely night. "I observed you from Grandfather's window and, at first glance, thought the gardens had been inhabited by a ghostly apparition." He slid his arms around her waist and, clasping his hands beneath her bosom, he pulled her back against his chest. Leaning down, he whispered against her ear, "I should have known that such an enchanting vision could be none other."

He tilted her head forward to place a kiss at the nape of her shapely neck, expecting some sort of reply to his cajolery, but when none was forthcoming, he became puzzled. Turning her in his arms, Kellen placed his index finger under her chin and lifted her head, so he could better scrutinize her face by the moonlight.

"To be honest, Erin, I am crushed. I have been known to turn many a pretty head with my flattery, yet I cannot coax even a girlish giggle from you." He gazed deeply into her eyes and was surprised at the sadness they held. More seriously, he said, "Confide in me, little reb. What troubles you?"

But Erin could not muster the appropriate words. Instead, she merely shook her head, the unbound tresses flying wildly about her shoulders. "It's nothing," she lied. "I was tired, but couldn't sleep, so I thought that a stroll in the garden might relax me."

"And your visitors two days ago have nothing to do with your present mood?"

Erin stepped away from him. "How did you know?"

He shrugged his broad shoulders to imply that it was no great secret. "Mother mentioned it in passing. She didn't know their identity, but Jasper evidently described the lady's behavior as being 'strangely reminiscent of Miss Vanessa'," he mimicked the servant. "*That* could be none other than Christina," he chuckled knowingly. "I haven't a notion who her escort might have been," he admitted. "One of your brothers perhaps?"

"No, Uncle Philip," she offered. "He was in town on business, so he and Christina dropped by to say hello. That's all."

"I see." Kellen considered her thoughtfully, not believing her explanation for an instant, but he decided not to press her; she would confide in him when she felt she could trust him. "And they succeeded in making you homesick?" he suggested.

Erin lowered her eyes, lest he read the deception therein, and nodded slowly.

"Well, perhaps you will not have to remain so for very long," he murmured mysteriously, ignoring the inquisitive look she turned on him. "Now, on to other matters." He masterfully changed the subject.

Tucking her arm in his, he steered her along the path, chatting amicably as he guided her. Presently, they came to a secluded spot and Kellen pulled her beneath an arbor. The protective shrubs and vines had grown over the elaborate latticework to provide shelter from the hot sun, or on occasions such as this, a retreat where sweethearts might converse intimately without fear of discovery.

"Erin, I have a favor to ask of you," Kellen began hesitantly.

"Yes?" And only the strictest of upbringings kept her from adding a shameful, *anything,* to her response.

"Have dinner with me tomorrow night, *alone,* in my suite," he concluded the scandalous request.

"But—"

He placed a finger against her lips and shook his head firmly, implying that he would not accept no as an answer. "Let me finish. My intentions are honorable, I assure you, my pet." His thumb adeptly traced the outline of her cheekbone, sending delightful tremors all the way down to her toes. "But if you feel that convention must be followed, bring Renée with you. She can keep Mrs. Sullivan company, but I *must* have you alone for a time. You see, I have a very special surprise for you."

Even though she could not see the blue eyes in the darkness, Erin knew that they sparkled mischievously. "*What? What is it?*" she asked with all the enthusiasm of a five-year old, causing Kellen to laugh merrily.

"No, little reb," he tried to sound stern. "You must wait till tomorrow. It will come much faster than you think. Now I believe that it's time for me to return you to the house." He took her elbow and started to guide her out of the arbor, but Erin held back reluctantly.

"Please, I would like to remain a little longer. I'm still not sleepy; especially now that you've piqued my curiosity about tomorrow night."

Kellen hesitated, obviously averse to the notion of leaving her unattended. He pulled his watch from his pocket and glanced down at the time. *Damn,* why had he agreed to the late meeting with Colonel Langford? He was going to be late as it was and, as much as he wished, he had not the time to tarry with Erin. Besides, no mishap was likely to befall her in Tiffin's gardens.

"Then I'm off." He bent to kiss her good-bye.

Erin accepted the rather chaste kiss and, having noticed his worried reference to his watch, she could not resist the urge to say, "Anxious to be gone, are you? Tell me, Kellen, could it be to another's arms you are rushing?" She tried to sound casual, but Kellen's knowing ears caught the unmistakable jealous inflection of her voice.

He laughed, reaching beneath the arbor to pull her into his arms. "Silly chit," he scolded. "Have you not yet realized that you are more than enough woman for any man?" Then he kissed her with a passionate thoroughness that rendered her senseless to her surroundings and, when he finally released her, she found that she had to cling to the lattice to keep her watery knees from giving way.

Kellen chuckled shamelessly. "See. Man that I am, even I could not express such ardor to more than one woman." He turned and started up the cobbled pathway. "I'll send my carriage to collect you at seven tomorrow evening." With that, he was devoured by the darkness.

Hugging her arms to herself, Erin watched his retreat, contemplating all the while what a splendid man he was. *Funny,* she mused, *but just a few weeks ago I would never have made such an admission to myself.*

"Oh, well," she sighed, knowing that she would mentally count the minutes until their designated engagement on the following evening.

"How enchanting," a voice drawled sarcastically behind her. "I'm convinced I have never before witnessed a more heartrending scene."

Erin was initially startled by the unexpected intrusion, but by the time she had whirled to confront Geoffrey, she was trembling with fury. "*How dare you!* You are positively the most despicable *creature!*" she flung at him angrily.

"Perhaps," he conceded wryly. "I certainly strive to be."

Erin was devastated to think that Geoffrey had observed her encounter with Kellen, and could now stand before her and arrogantly belittle the precious moment. She was furious, but could not yet summon the necessary words to give him a proper tongue lashing; therefore, with an indignant huff, she turned and would have run the entire distance to the house had Geoffrey's next conjecture not cemented her feet to the ground.

"You realize, of course, that my cousin intends to ask you to join him in wedded bliss."

Erin turned slowly and, affixing him with a fulminating glare, seethed, "You truly are despicable. Even if that is Kellen's intention, it is thoughtless and cruel of you to purposely spoil his surprise," she admonished him, though she knew that her words had not affected him in the least.

"Actually, it should make for a most interesting, if not *loving,* union," he continued, heedless of her reproof. He appeared amused by something and, though Erin longed to know the hidden implication behind his statement, she would not dignify him with an inquiry.

"My, but aren't we stubborn?" he said sarcastically. "I was just reflecting on the chances of a successful marriage when one partner marries for money to save her encumbered estates while the other does so in the hopes of securing a financial dynasty. What happened to the carefree days of old when sweethearts succumbed to Cupid because of love?" he sighed as though he had a heavy heart.

Erin disregarded the excess drivel for what it was, but she was nevertheless intrigued by his reference to herself and Kellen, and she demanded, "How did you know about the taxes on Kilkieran? And what did you mean about Kellen's inheritance?"

"We have servants, Miss Richards, *loyal* servants who are not averse to listening at doors; especially when they know they'll be amply rewarded in their monthly pay envelope," he explained his knowledge of her financial woes. "As for the other," he regarded her closely, carefully choosing his next words, "surely, you must have noticed that Kellen's ardent pursuit did not begin until *after* Grandfather's ridiculous announcement." He shrewdly observed the crestfallen face and knew that he had successfully planted a seed of doubt in her mind.

Erin shrank away from the loathsome man and rested her throbbing head against the lattice. He had thoroughly confused her with his wild accusations, and she struggled to remain unruffled. Indeed, Kellen *had* become noticeably more affectionate in the days following that memorable dinner.

Could it be true? Was he merely courting her to better his chances at the Sinclair fortune?

No, she thought fiercely. *He loves me!* I love him. Still . . .

Geoffrey knew her to be fighting to reason everything out in her mind, and he took advantage of her despair to drive home his argument. With a graceful wave of his hand, he said, "Ah, I can just envision the intimate encounter; a romantic setting, a candlelight dinner for two, a seductive wine. He takes your hand in his and goes down before you on bended knee. Pledging his unending love for you, he asks you to become his wife, providing you present him with an heir in a suitable length of time," he added caustically.

"And you, Erin, shall you take that particular moment to request the thousand dollars you so desperately need? A trifle awkward, I'll allow, but it's to be forgiven, for I understand that time is of the essence.

"Ah, yes; romance," he concluded his monologue on a cynical note, settling his disturbing gaze on her.

"You make it all sound so sordid," Erin cried defensively.

Geoffrey shrugged his shoulders. "What can I say? Deceit is a sordid business."

"It's not like that!" she declared. "Kellen truly loves me!"

"Does he?" Geoffrey drawled indifferently. "He once *truly* loved Vanessa. A fickle thing; love."

Erin was outraged, and she stamped her foot in a fit of uncontrolled anger, her tiny fists clutched her side. "Oh, you *are* . . .

". . . Despicable," he interpolated. "So you've said. I'm quite convinced it must be so."

Erin longed for the sanctuary of her room where she could give in to her frustrations and try to sort things out, but Geoffrey was not yet finished with her.

260

"You will now understand why I must do what I *must* do," he said forebodingly.

"What?"

"Surely, you must know that I cannot permit you to become a member of our family under false pretenses. I fear I must make Grandfather aware of your chicanery." He focused his gaze on some distant star. "Yes, he will not allow the marriage. Of course, Kellen will be heartsick for a time, but he will doubtless get over it; he always does," he added ruthlessly. "Do not think for a moment that he will defy Grandfather in this matter. You recall that they have just recently come to terms with their differences, and Kellen is not likely to cause another rift, for he'll not be anxious to be out of Grandfather's good graces again."

Erin had remained silent throughout the narrative as she watched the dreams she had been building in her mind come crashing down around her ears with each word he spoke. Her chance for happiness with Kellen had been snuffed out with the utterance of a few callous phrases.

She slowly lifted cold eyes to Geoffrey, who regarded her with continued interest, and said hatefully, "Oh, how I wish I were a man, so that I might give you the thrashing you so richly deserve."

"That would be a pity, for then I would not make you the generous offer I am presently considering." He waited for her question, but Erin was not in the mood to accommodate him. "Very well, I am prepared to suffer your impertinence a little longer, albeit, I am hoping this will be the last evening I am forced to do so."

"What is your offer?" she asked bitterly.

"That you continue with your initial plan; Ireland, I believe, was your original destination." He reached into his pocket and pulled out a large envelope which he pushed into her hands. "This is your passage to Ireland; a ticket and enough cash to get you there. And this," he pulled another document from his coat, "is a bank draft in the amount of one thousand dollars, made out to your brother Graham. It's yours, *if—* " He paused to make sure he had her full attention.

"Go on."

"If you leave tonight. A carriage will be waiting at the front gate at midnight to start you on your journey. Your ship will leave New York harbor two days hence. Agree to be on it and this," he waved the paper before her nose, "is yours."

Erin considered all that he had said. She was understandably distraught by the evening's turnaround and, though her head fairly swirled with a hundred questions, she raised reserved eyes to his and merely asked, "Why are you doing this?"

"Suffice to say that it is worth my while to have you gone. But, come, you have less than two hours to prepare for your journey." He tapped his watch impatiently. "What's your decision to be?"

Erin felt the unmistakable rending of her heart as she realized what her decision must be. Kellen, no matter how much she cared for him was, after all, a Yankee. Her family would never accept him, and it was obvious that Kellen's family was as resigned against her; they would never enjoy a moment's peace. She swallowed hard, her eyes never wavering from the paper in Geoffrey's hand. Then suddenly and, without another word, she snatched the draft from his hand and ran as fast as her feet would carry her to the house.

She did not stop till she reached her room and, once safely inside, she leaned against the door and cried mournfully, "Oh, Kellen, my beloved darling. Forgive me, but it was not meant to be." Then she fell to her knees and succumbed to the tears she had valiantly withheld until that moment.

Geoffrey watched Erin's hasty flight with satisfaction, knowing that the dawn would break upon a much brighter day for him. Of course, he still had Kellen to contend with, but he would worry about that when the time came. Feeling suddenly tired, he stifled a yawn and proceeded up the pathway toward the house. He had gone but a few paces, however, when a figure stepped from the shadows to block his motion.

"Good Lord, Vanessa!" he exclaimed. "You startled me. I swear, but the gardens are quite popular tonight. I wouldn't be surprised to find the old man himself wandering about the grounds." He regarded her speculatively. "Well, my love, did you grow restless in your lonely bed and come in search of me?"

"Don't be ridiculous!" she sneered. "Tell me, husband, was it truly necessary to spend a fortune just to send the chit on her merry way?" she asked testily.

"She was not likely to leave with her family's future so insecure," he pointed out. "She's gone. It's money well spent. Forget the girl and let's retire for the night."

"No." Vanessa jerked her arm away angrily. "Don't you know he'll follow her; the transports to Ireland are the first place Kellen will look."

"She'll be well on her way before he discovers —"

"Fool!" she interrupted. "You've made a mess of things, Geoffrey. You always do. You should have let me handle it," Vanessa said crossly.

Geoffrey's amorous mood abruptly dissipated and he gave his wife a distasteful look. "It's done," he said sourly. "I'm on my way to bed, *darling*. Feel free to join me when you've controlled this annoying temper." He stepped past her, his arrogant head held high, and sauntered up the path toward the house.

Vanessa, however, did not follow him. Instead, she continued on the path away from the house, toward a destination that had been temporarily forgotten when she saw her husband conversing with *that girl*.

She hurried along the stoned path until she came to the abandoned gardener's cottage near the edge of the vast estate; a cottage that had been vacated in favor of newer accommodations, yet no one had bothered to tear down. Just as well, she thought. The cottage had served her purpose well in the years she had lived at Tiffin Square. She paused on the steps to sound the prearranged signal and the door swung open immediately.

The figure of a tall, muscular man framed the doorway, a smile glistening on his handsome face in the moonlight. He pulled her into the room, and swung the door closed in a single movement. Instantly, his hands started to undo the sash that bound the expensive robe to her, but Vanessa pushed him away.

"Not yet," she said firmly. "We have to talk."

"I didn't come here to talk, Vanessa," came the terse reply. "I'm in no mood for your games." His brown eyes flashed forebodingly.

"We'll have time later," she promised in her sweetest voice, and then her lips twisted into a sinister smile. "But, first, we must make some careful plans."

Upstairs in the huge mansion, Erin sat before the mirror and absently dabbed at her eyes with a cool washcloth. She had hastily changed into a magenta traveling dress and packed the few belongings she intended to take with her.

Then she had undertaken her most grievous task and scribbled Meredith a vague explanatory note. Next she had written a brief letter to her brother and, after carefully sealing the missive and the cherished bank draft in an envelope, she placed them atop her pillow so they might be easily found. But try as she might, Erin could not formulate the appropriate words to write to Kellen. No matter how hard she tried, the pen froze in her hand whenever she put it to paper.

She had consequently abandoned the hopeless task and resigned herself to await the stroke of midnight. It came much quicker than she anticipated. The sounding of the gong arrived almost simultaneously with that of the carriage pulling up before the house.

Erin picked up her valise and paused to look about the room one last time. Kellen's room. How many nights had she lain in the roomy bed and reveled in the knowledge that he had once slept there? She had offtimes drifted off to sleep with thoughts of their next encounter filling her head. And now?

She looked in the mirror. "Now, you're doing what you *have* to do. It's for the best."

She slipped soundlessly from the room and scampered down the steps as quietly as a mouse. Once outside, she ran as fast as her legs would carry her to the front gate, fearful that the driver might have departed when he had not found her waiting for him. But her fears were for naught, for the carriage was there, and the driver jumped down from his lofty perch when he saw her.

The man acknowledged her with a stiff nod, though he did not offer to speak. The standoffishness of the fellow did not dishearten Erin, for she was not feeling particularly affable at the moment. The man opened the door for her, tossed her valise on the seat and assisted her inside and closed the door. A few moments later, the carriage jolted forward, then it began to move more smoothly as the horses assumed an easy gait.

As the coach made its way through the deserted city streets, Erin rested her weary back against the squabs and contemplated her future; a future that did not include the man she loved. Erin huddled in the corner of the seat, her arms clasped tightly across her chest. Though the midsummer night was extremely warm, Erin found that she was quite chilled. Perhaps it was due to the impetuosity of her act, or the fact that she was being hurled into a new life when she had not truly made amends with the old; with Kellen, she lamented sorrowfully.

What would his reaction be when he learned of her decision to join her grandmother in Ireland? What would he think of her for dashing off without even saying good-bye? She shivered uncontrollably at the thought and leaned forward to

265

rummage beneath the box of the facing seat, thankfully discovering a blanket therein.

Wrapping the comforter around her, she snuggled up in the corner once again and tried to rest. She quite resigned herself to a sleepless night, for what rational person, who had suffered the tumultuous day the likes that she had, would be able to find comfort in sleep? But the increasing lateness of the hour coupled with the frayed condition of her nerves soon took their toll, and the rhythmic motion of the carriage eventually lulled her to sleep.

Chapter Fourteen

Kellen lounged in his favorite easy chair in his study, his long legs stretching out before him forming a bridge to where his booted feet rested on the edge of the desk. A brandy snifter rested in his hand and, while his fingers toyed with the bowl of the glass, his cigar lay unattended in the ashtray; the smoke swirling about his head like a billowy cloud. His resolute gaze fastened on the glass, and an outside observer might guess him to be contemplating the quality of the potent brew, while in truth, his thoughts were consumed by more profound ruminations.

Colonel Langford had not required much of his time but, even so, his brief visit had proven to be tiresome. Nevertheless, Kellen had done his utmost to answer the colonel's questions, but he knew his responses had not met with satisfaction, consequently, both men had grown testy.

Kellen took a generous draft from his glass as he reconstructed the scene in his mind. Actually, the questions had been of a general nature. Yes, he had spoken with Brad. No, he had not discovered anything particularly incriminating in Petersen's account of the incident. Yes, he would continue the investigation until the department was convinced there had been no subterfuge on Brad's part. Yes, he had begun putting a plan in motion that would return him to the scene of the ambush, but it had not been finalized.

The colonel's visit had lasted a scant twenty minutes, and he parted leaving a subdued Kellen to consider how he should next proceed with his assignment; an assignment that was made exceedingly difficult by his close association with the accused. To be truthful, Kellen could not recollect a time in his life when he and Brad had not been friends.

Brad's mother, Angela, had been widowed at an early age, leaving her with an infant son to raise alone. Accordingly, she had sought employment in the one profession in which she excelled: seamstress. She became proficient at her craft and, hence, was much in demand by all the fashionable ladies of Washington, including Meredith Sinclair.

Having no relatives to watch over her young son, it became a necessity for Angela to take Brad with her to the homes of her clients. If a customer objected to this peculiar practice, she was obliged to come round to Angela's shop for fittings. Angela was a devoted mother and, though her patrons demanded much of her attention, she was determined to see that her son received a generous portion of her time.

Since a considerable amount of Angela's expertise was required by the three ladies who resided at Tiffin Square: both Kellen's grandmother and Geoffrey's mother were alive then, Brad and Kellen had the opportunity to become good friends. Kellen willingly shared his toys and pony with his newfound comrade. They fished and hunted together and, of course, perpetrated their share of boyish pranks; Geoffrey being their favorite target. They habitually received severe reprimands for their capers, though the punishment was never so extreme that it dissuaded them from their pursuits.

They were inseparable companions, so much in fact, that strangers often inquired if the lads were brothers; such was the resemblance of one to the other. As the boys grew into men, when childhood friendships sometimes suffer the strains of time, Kellen and Brad became even closer. They attended the same schools, enjoyed the same recreational diversions and, when the war began, enlisted together. Though they were assigned to different units, they managed to keep in touch with one another, and had served together during that last campaign in Virginia.

Kellen stroked his chin pensively. He *had* noticed a change in his friend since his return to Washington. Brad did not come around as often as was his wont before the war and when they were together, Kellen sensed a certain restless aura surrounding his friend.

"Oh, well," he muttered aloud. "The war affects each of us in its own way."

The clock on the mantel chimed the hour of midnight, rousing Kellen from his reflective mood. He drained the snifter, extinguished the forgotten cigar and stretched wearily. The day had been a long one, but tomorrow promised to be glorious, allowing that Erin provided him with a favorable response to his marriage proposal.

He fingered the jeweler's box that still reposed in his coat pocket, and a contented smile curled his lips when he recalled the way she had returned his kiss only a few hours earlier. Satisfied that the impending engagement would end to his liking, Kellen stood up and left the room.

By the time he reached his chamber, however, his mind had returned to thoughts of Bradley Petersen. The evidence the army had in its possession was tenuous at best, but if the military had nothing better to do than waste its time and his on this ridiculous investigation, then he could humor them a little longer.

He pulled off his coat and hung it over the back of a chair, then sat down on the bed to remove his boots. It was then that a nagging thought which had been lurking in the back of his mind came rushing to the forefront: What if Brad *was* guilty?

Brad could not have anticipated that Kellen would have been incapacitated and left at Kilkieran to recover from his wounds. Had it not been for Deborah's hasty use of the gun,

Kellen would have been among the soldiers to die at the ambush.

Kellen emitted a thoughtful sigh as he lifted a grave contenance to the dressing table mirror opposite the bed. He was not permitted further contemplation, however, for at that precise moment there came an urgent knocking at his apartment door.

The servants had long since retired for the night, and Kellen was obliged to personally welcome his late night caller. He found himself quite bemused as he stepped through the sitting room, but never in his wildest imaginings could he have foreseen the night that lay before him.

"Mother!" he exclaimed, having pulled open the door. "What the devil are you —"

But Meredith did not allow him to finish, for she burst into the room, frantically waving a piece of paper in her hand. "Kellen, you *must* go after her!" she cried.

Kellen hastily closed the door and turned to face his mother, obviously dumbfounded by her outburst. He stared at the uncharacteristically disheveled lady who nervously paced the floor, and realized that something was terribly wrong, for it was unlike his mother to give in to such hysterics unless duly provoked.

Stepping to his mother, he took her elbow and guided her to the nearest chair. "Now, Mother. Do bring your emotions under control and tell me what has happened that would send you scurrying over here at this hour. Who must I go after?" he inquired placatingly, but his calm demeanor was to alter drastically upon hearing his mother's reply.

"Erin," she whispered hoarsely.

Kellen had started toward the decanter, thinking a glass of wine might soothe his mother's frazzled nerves, but Meredith's unexpected announcement halted him in mid stride. "*Erin!*" he thundered, and Meredith would swear later that the very windowpanes had rattled at his eruption.

Kellen erased the distance that separated them in two swift

270

strides, and clasped her shoulders between remarkably firm hands in a desperate gesture. "Erin has left? Why? Wherever has she gone?"

The panic stricken face of her son anxiously awaiting her explanation served to restore Meredith's aplomb, and she faced him calmly. "I'm not sure why, but I'm certain that Geoffrey had something to do with it. As for where; perhaps you should read this." She thrust the crumpled note into his hands.

Experiencing a gnawing sense of dread, Kellen forced himself to remain calm as he glanced down at the epistle he now clutched in his hand. The handwriting was Erin's. There was no mistaking the definitive curves of the dainty script and the elegant way the words seem to flow across the page. Parts of the missive had been smudged; tear-stains no doubt, but whether they belonged to the author of the message, or to his mother, Kellen had no way of discerning. Squaring his shoulders to prepare himself for the worst, he began to read.

Indeed, he read the letter several times, and with each perusal, his countenance grew more forbidding. The handsome set of his mouth was drawn into a white, taut line, a muscle twitched ominously in his jaw; always a sign of impending disaster, and the flesh that was exposed from the opening of the ruffled shirt to his hairline was a magnificent shade of angry red. Meredith had never seen her son in such a complete state of vexation and, just when she feared that he might succumb to some sort of seizure, he railed on her.

"What . . . what *nonsense* is this?" Sufficient words to describe the situation temporarily eluded him, but he quickly recovered his tongue. "Of all the idiotic, addlepated . . . *the simpleminded chit!*" he stormed. "When I get my hands on her—" The remainder of his threat was a strangled garble of coarsely mumbled oaths. "That slimy snake," he seethed bitterly.

"Erin?" Meredith interrupted, obviously surprised by his severe ridicule.

"No; Geoffrey," he all but shouted. "I should have been

more careful of the cur's conniving ways." He paused to consider the dilemma presented him, then muttered disgustedly, "The little *wretch!*"

"Geoffrey?" Meredith asked tentatively, finding it exceedingly difficult to follow Kellen's mumblings.

Kellen had been pacing fitfully between the sofa and window, but his tirade mellowed at his mother's perplexed inquiry. With a short laugh, he said, "They are both wretches. The only problem is, I happen to be in love with *mine,* and she is presently bouncing around in some carriage on a dark, deserted roadway. God only knows what may befall her before I find her," he added fearfully.

He stalked to the bell pull and gave it a sharp yank and, in a surprisingly scant length of time, Chin Li appeared to inquire of his employer's needs. Hastily apologizing for the lateness of the hour, Kellen assured the domestic that the summons was of the utmost urgency.

"Advise Jim to saddle Achilles." Then as an afterthought, he said, "Have him prepare a horse for you as well. I don't know what I might encounter, and I may need assistance."

"Yes, Mr. Sinclair." Chin Li bowed and went to carry out the instructions.

Meredith continued to watch her son, and the manner in which he had taken command of the situation thoroughly reassured her. Leaning back in her chair, she breathed a grateful sigh of relief and said, "Thank goodness, you are going after her. I cannot bear the thought of that poor child out in the night with no one to protect her."

Kellen had stepped into his bedchamber to retrieve his boots and jacket, but he returned in time to hear Meredith's woebegone admission. With a rueful flicker glistening behind his blue eyes, Kellen sat down opposite his mother and cast a sullen gaze upon her.

"I promise you, Mother," he stated grimly, "when I overtake our misguided wayfarer, she will have a good deal more than the *night* to fear."

"Oh, Kellen." Meredith leaned forward in her chair, a hand flying to her throat in dismay. "You cannot mean to punish the child for Geoffrey's wickedness. If I thought you truly meant to mistreat her, I would not let you go."

Kellen chuckled, a deep sound that rumbled in his chest. Shoving his foot inside his boot, he stood up and strode to the mantel to check the time. "No, I won't abuse the little baggage, but she has some accounting to do, and I cannot vow she will not be made to endure a stern reprimand."

They both fell silent then, waiting for Chin Li to return with the news that all was in readiness. As the seconds ticked away, a sudden thought occurred to Kellen, and he turned to confront his mother.

"Mother, Erin obviously did not intend for you to find this message until morning. How did you come by it tonight?"

"Oh, *that*." Meredith nodded. "There was an inordinate amount of activity about the house tonight; doors slamming, voices in the garden," she explained. "Well, I found it quite difficult to drift off to sleep, so I slipped downstairs to get a glass of sherry in the hopes that it would help me relax. It was when I was coming out of the drawing room that I caught a glimpse of Erin. She was carrying a valise and disappeared through the front door before I fully realized what was happening."

"But, surely, you tried to stop her!" he cried, disbelieving his astonished ears.

Meredith could not summon the appropriate words, but she did manage a curt shake of her head in response to his accusation.

"*What*? Why the devil not?" he demanded harshly.

Meredith was unaccustomed to being addressed in such a tone by her son, but she understood his anxiety and, therefore, overlooked his effrontery. Besides, she was deeply chagrined at her own folly, for she had made a rather scandalous assumption regarding Erin's mysterious nocturnal departure and now, forced to admit her foolish blunder, Meredith's cheeks flamed a bright scarlet.

Kellen was stunned. It had been years since he had seen his mother's cheeks emblazoned with a maidenly blush and, though the effect was most charming, Kellen knew there could be but one reason for such a reaction.

"My Lord," he breathed. "You thought that Erin was coming to me."

Meredith's eyes fell to her hands, and she nodded weakly.

Kellen muttered some unintelligible oath, then he looked at her, his eyes blazing. With a self-imposed calmness, he said stiffly, "It's indeed reassuring to learn that my own mother regards me with such high esteem. To think I would embroil that innocent creature in a clandestine relationship. Tell me, what other atrocities do you think me capable; beating little children perhaps, or even murder?" he suggested icily.

"Of course not!" Meredith gasped. She could not bear the ugly scowl that blackened his face, and she hastened to continue her explanation. "To be sure, I considered that the two of you had arranged a rendezvous, but I thought you were . . . eloping." The last word was hardly above a whisper, but it crescendoed like a cannonade about his ears.

"*Eloping*!" he roared.

"Yes, I know how you feel about the girl. You see, your father had that same devil-may-care look about him when he courted me." Her voice had grown wistful and she reflected upon happier days. "You mentioned to me that there might be objections from both families, therefore, I assumed you had decided to forego a formal ceremony and elope with Erin.

"Naturally, I realized that she would have left a note, so I hurried off to her room only to find that she had fled because Geoffrey had used his cunning to confuse her. Oh, Kellen, you must find her and bring her back."

Kellen had recovered his equilibrium by the time Meredith concluded her desperate plea, and he crossed the room and enfolded her in his arms. "Forgive me for being such a brute," he murmured softly. "I have no excuse except that I have been made most distraught by the news of Erin's flight."

A sudden movement at the door behind him caught Kellen's attention. "Ah, I see that Chin Li has come for me. Now, Mother, I want you to go home." He held her at arm's length and forced a confident smile to his lips. "Never fear. I'll collect our wayward miss and bring her safely home."

He was halfway across the floor before Meredith had the sensibility to inquire, "Kellen, what *will* you do with Erin when you find her?"

"First, I shall likely shake the little vixen until her bones rattle." And more gently, he added, "Then I shall kiss her senseless and hold her against my heart until this frantic clamoring in my chest is stilled." He flashed her a roguish smile as he grabbed his coat from the chair and disappeared through the doorway that led to the back staircase.

A very satisfied mother watched her son's departure, then she stood to make her own exit. As her hand fell upon the doorknob, she recalled his final declaration and a smile sprouted on her lips.

"Ah, yes. There is a good deal of the father in the son," she murmured faintly. Then she made her way down the dimly lit stairway to the carriage that waited to return her to Tiffin Square.

Erin awoke with a start. She had no idea what had roused her from her slumber, or even how long she had slept, but as she started to rub the drowsiness from her eyes, she experienced a sudden portent that warned her something was terribly wrong. She sat very still, her heart pounding wildly as a result of the abrupt arousal.

Then comprehension dawned on her, and she breathed a sigh of relief. "Of course, you goose," she admonished herself. "The carriage has stopped. But why?"

Erin did not think it possible, but her heart began to race

even faster, and she placed her hands to her chest and forcefully willed herself to remain calm. There was probably a perfectly logical explanation for the delay, she reasoned.

But logic failed her, and Erin's mind began to whirl with speculations regarding the unscheduled stop. She recalled tales that her brothers had recounted of carriages being held up by bandits, and her pulse quickened. How could she possibly defend herself against ruthless marauders, and what if they were not satisfied with the paltry sum of cash she carried with her? Why, they might —

Erin clamped her eyes shut and shuddered uncontrollably, as she murmured a fervent prayer. No, she must not think such ghastly thoughts. She must try to keep her wits about her and not succumb to the hysteria that threatened to overpower her. Glancing about her, Erin's eyes desperately scoured the compartment for something she might use to defend herself.

Finding nothing, she strained her ears to listen for any unusual sound and, just when she was prepared to scold herself for her excitable imagination, she heard a twig snap just outside the carriage door. Again her pulse quickened, and she leaned forward and cautiously placed her hand on the door latch.

"Driver?" she called tenuously, the tremor in her voice obvious.

Before she could open the door, it was wrenched open from without. Erin suddenly no longer had to contend with the frantic pounding of her heart, for that vital organ seemed to cease beating altogether when she came face-to-face with a masked bandit.

A startled squeak was torn from her throat as she jumped away from the imposing figure, and her eyes darted around frantically searching for a route of escape. Just as her gaze fastened on the opposite door, and she started to inch toward it, that portal was flung open to reveal yet another masked man.

"Well, well, Joey," the first man chuckled evilly. "Looks like this is our lucky night."

"Aye, Br- . . . B-B-Boss," the one called Joey stumbled over his words, but Erin was too frightened to pay it any consequence. Nor did she notice that the leader's brown eyes flickered as he shot a cautionary glance at his accomplice.

"Yep," Joey continued more carefully. "She's a pretty piece all right. I reckon old McGraw will pay a tidy sum for this one."

"Yes," the leader agreed shrewdly, his eyes boldly raking over Erin from head to toe. "McGraw will be most happy with the little lady, but he won't be leaving the inn before noon tomorrow. We have plenty of time . . ."

Erin was certain that the horrid man actually licked his lips beneath the mask in eager anticipation of his plunderings. She was equally positive that he had left his coy suggestion incomplete in an effort to frighten her.

Well, really! If that's his game, he needn't have bothered, she thought bitterly. I'm positively terrified as it is. Why the mere thought of these two ruffians even touching me is enough to make me swoon.

But Erin was to quickly learn that the rogues had a good deal more than *touching* her in mind. And a sudden movement from the leader made her realize that the insufferable waiting was over; he was about to make his move.

Erin's fingers instinctively tightened around the straps of her reticule that lay on her lap concealed beneath the blanket. Her mind raced with the alternatives available to her. In all likelihood, she realized that she would be unable to escape her captors, but she vowed not to be easily conquered. If she could manage to create some sort of distraction, perhaps she could escape the carriage and hide in the woods until morning when she could seek sanctuary with some locals.

But she would have to act quickly, for the leader had already braced his hands on either side of the door and was starting to heave his muscular frame inside the carriage, and he was saying something to his partner.

"You go up on top, Joey, and drive the carriage up the road a ways. See if you can find a secluded spot and pull off the road. I'll just ride inside and keep the little lady company," he snickered.

Erin panicked. One black boot was positioned on the floorboard. She must act now.

"What about the horses?" Joey was asking.

With an impatient grunt, the brown-eyed man snorted, "They're safe enough. We'll come back after —"

But his speech was unexpectedly preempted as Erin threw aside the coverlet and, in the same motion, swung her reticule at the unsavory villain, catching him completely unaware. The surprise of the assault, more than the actual force of the blow, sent the blackguard stumbling backwards, momentarily stunned by the clout to his jaw.

Joey had been startled by the girl's aggressive actions, but he knew that her endeavors were for naught. A mere slip of a girl could not long forestall the advances of two hardy men. He shook his head at his partner's carelessness and started to enter the carriage, but the toe of Erin's boot caught him squarely on the chin with a fierce impact that sent him careening backwards. His head struck a rock as he landed on the hard road and, just before he slipped into unconsciousness, he thought dazedly that the situation had certainly taken a bizarre twist.

Erin could not suppress the jubilant squeal that sprang to her lips, but her triumph was to be short lived. For just as she began to exit through the doorway that Joey had just vacated, her arm was grabbed from behind, and she was jerked backwards with such force that Erin felt certain her arm had been wrenched from its socket. But she was given little time to consider her injury, for the leader had entered the carriage and pinned her shoulders against the squabs.

His brown eyes flashed furiously and his voice was a raw whisper as he rasped, "*That,* my lovely, was a very foolish thing to do." The unspoken threat dangled ominously before her as he dragged her from the seat and pushed her ruthlessly to the floor. "You'll shortly discover that I'm not a man to be reckoned with," he drawled purposely, as he allowed his sinister eyes a casual perusal of the prize he would presently claim as his own.

Erin's breath caught in her throat at his last statement and, with a sudden start, she realized that she had seen this man before. She knew him! It was the eyes she recognized; those brown piercing orbs that seemed so harsh, not loving and gentle like Kellen's. Her heart felt distinctly hollow when she thought of Kellen, driving all musings of her attacker from her mind, and she moaned his name aloud.

Erin's lugubrious mumblings only seemed to amuse her assailant, as he ceremoniously pulled a rope from his pocket. "Since you've managed to render Joey senseless, I'll have to restrain you until I can safely hide the carriage from annoying passers-by." He bent over her and roughly shoved her hands behind her back and swiftly secured them with the rope.

It was when he began to bind her ankles together in a similar fashion that he heard the horsemen. There were only two riders, he surmised, but the way they were pushing their mounts could but mean one thing.

"Damn it!" he swore, while the rope slithered through his fingers to coil up harmlessly at her feet.

Erin heard the horsemen, too, and her heart leaped hopefully. Was it possible? Had Kellen somehow found out about her hasty exodus and come after her?

No, she reasoned. That was not likely.

But from the sound of things, *someone* was evidently coming to her rescue. She tried to quell the frantic stirrings of her heart, for she had seen the hateful glare in her captor's eyes, making her realize that he would not be handily thwarted. A genuine fear for the safety of the approaching horseman quickly enveloped her.

In an effort to draw the bandit off guard, Erin struggled to a sitting position, but the evil man shoved her back and her head suffered a glancing blow against the edge of the seat, temporarily dazing her. The man swung down from the carriage and slammed the door behind him, satisfied that his captive would no longer present a problem.

"Come on, Joey, before they're on us," he shouted at the unconscious man, kicking at his backside.

The stricken accomplice slowly managed to drag his weary body to a sitting position, testing first his swollen chin, then the knot at the back of his head. But the thundering sound of galloping horses forestalled any lengthy inspection of his wounds, and he scrambled to his feet.

With a frustrated oath, he turned to the brown-eyed man. "Do you think it's Sinclair?"

The leader gave a short grunt in reply. "More than likely," he grumbled, "but I do not intend to dawdle about to satisfy my curiosity.

"Get the horses, my friend," he commanded. "I'll just create a little diversion to keep our dashing young gallant suitably preoccupied while we execute our escape."

Without a backward glance at his comrade, the brown-eyed man climbed atop the carriage, released the brake, took up the whip and lashed out at the rump of the lead horse. The coach started forward with a sudden lurch and, by the time the man jumped clear of the vehicle and disappeared into the forest, the unattended carriage was lunging down the road at a very dangerous speed; its precious cargo jostling helplessly about inside.

When Kellen first spied the carriage lights, his spirits lifted considerably. He had not thought it would be this easy to catch up with his wayward miss, allowing, of course, that the stalled vehicle in the distance proved to be the one which he sought. In eager anticipation, Kellen and Chin Li urged their mounts into a faster gallop.

But as they drew near the carriage, Kellen's anticipation turned to acute trepidation as the coach suddenly careened forward to disappear around a curve in the road. In horror, Kellen realized that there was no driver atop the perch, and he spurred Achilles even faster. With a wave of his hand and a shout, Kellen instructed Chin Li to search the woods for traces of the marauders.

Kellen then urged Achilles onward with renewed determination. The horse seemed to sense his master's urgency and sprang forward with an uncanny speed, slowly but surely lessening the distance between the carriage and its stalwart pursuer. What might have normally been considered a pleasurable romp through the countryside was rapidly turning into an outlandish nightmare for Kellen.

At one point, he had nearly overtaken the end of the carriage when one wheel struck a huge chuckhole and sent the vehicle swaying precariously out of control. Kellen caught his breath, certain that the carriage would overturn, but by some twist of fate, the coach righted itself and the horses seemed to tire a little of their brisk pace, which enabled Kellen to spring around the carriage and catch up with the lead horse. Pacing Achilles beside the frightened animal, Kellen was able to reach out and grasp the harness firmly in his strong hand, finally bringing the skittish animal under control.

The coach had barely rolled to a standstill before Kellen leaped from his mount and swiftly made his way to the carriage to fling open the door. An expression of relief quickly spread across his handsome face to discover that Erin was the occupant of the runaway vehicle, but his concern returned when he saw the crumpled shape that lay like a listless rag doll on the floor of the coach.

At first glance, Kellen thought her to be unconscious, for she lay so deathly still, but the state of her disheveled appearance was another matter. Her skirt and petticoats were a tangled mess around her knees, the curls that had been so carefully brushed into place just hours ago now hung in unruly disorder about her shoulders, her bonnet lay askew at the back of her head, and her face was a lifeless shade of white.

Kellen bolted forward anxiously, but the tiny voice that managed to stammer out a faltering question gave him pause.

"H-h-have . . . have w-w-we . . . stopped?"

"Yes, infant." Kellen could not withhold the chuckle that was prompted by her tremulous inquiry. "I assure you that I'm not running alongside this conveyance," he added sardonically.

"Here, let me help you." He noticed her feeble attempts to rise and he reached inside and pulled her to a sitting position.

Erin had not trusted herself to open her eyes even when she heard the familiar voice that softly admonished her silly query. But the touch of those gentle hands that fastened around her shoulders completely reassured her, and she forced her eyes open to stare into the icy-blue ones that deliberately contemplated her. She detected the anxiety behind those penetrative spheres and, yes, the anger as well.

It was only natural that he would be infuriated with her for her foolhardy behavior, but no matter, she thought gloriously. The fact remained that he had come for her regardless of his pique.

"Kellen?" she whispered tentatively.

"Not yet, Erin."

His tone was calm enough, but she had caught the menacing ring in its inflection. Then Kellen noticed for the first time that Erin's hands had been bound behind her, and he grunted almost approvingly.

"It seems as though your would-be abductors have happened upon a most appropriate method of controlling you. To be honest, Erin," he glanced down at the small chin that quivered slightly, "I'm sorely tempted to leave you trussed up like this." Despite his lame threat, Kellen quickly freed her from the constricting bonds.

Erin regarded him gingerly. She longed to hurl her beleaguered body into the shelter of his comforting arms and let him soothe her frazzled nerves. But there was something in his countenance that guarded her against such an impulsive gesture, so she averted her attention to rearranging her disheveled gown. Then, with shaky fingers, she undid the ribbons of her bonnet and climbed up from the floor to perch her svelte figure on the edge of the seat.

Kellen had instinctively started to offer his assistance, but recalling the fright she had given him, he reaffirmed his resolve to punish the little vixen for her impetuous behavior. Still, when he saw her obvious distraught condition, he very nearly succumbed to his own overwhelming desire to drag her into his arms and kiss the great pout from her sensuous mouth. But Chin Li arrived at that particular moment, forcing him to turn his attention from Erin.

It was a subdued Erin who watched her handsome cavalier present his back to her in apparent indifference and stride over to the servant. He was gone for several minutes and, during the interim, Erin was allowed the opportunity to consider all that had transpired in those terrifying moments prior to Kellen's arrival. Throughout her reflections, Erin continued to be taunted by the notion that she had seen her brown-eyed assailant before. There was *something* about those sinister orbs that haunted her, and the voice, though he had tried to disguise it, was vaguely familiar. But as yet, she could not connect a name with the awful man.

Again, her musings were interrupted, for Kellen returned and climbed into the carriage, slamming the door behind him with a resounding bang. Without a word, he plopped down upon the seat opposite her, folded his arms across his chest, and settled a look upon her that was so cold and unfeeling that it sent a chill running down Erin's rigid spine.

Erin regarded that intense face with considerable trepidation, wanting to speak, yet not certain how to approach the brooding man. Suddenly, the carriage began to move and, immensely pacified by the gentle swaying motion of the coach, she felt encouraged. Ignoring the acerbic stare that molded Kellen's face, she ventured to speak.

"Who is driving?"

"Chin Li," he snapped. "Your coachman was nowhere to be found. Doubtless he turned tail and ran at the first sign of the skirmish."

"Where are we going?" Her voice was barely an audible squeak, but she could tell by the angry flicker in his eyes that he had heard her.

"Not to Ireland, that's for damn sure," he growled, and Erin shrank back against the seat at the harshness of his bitter reply.

Deciding that it might be to her advantage to allow his temper a chance to subside, Erin fell silent. She glanced out the window, but there was little to view, for the passing landscape was enveloped in darkness. Allowing the curtain to slip from limp fingers, she then folded her hands in her lap and pretended to be engrossed in the intricately embroidered pattern that decorated the hem of her skirt. This failing, she averted her gaze to Kellen's highly polished boots, which proved to be a mistake, for once she permitted her gaze to settle on him, her eyes quite naturally climbed to his face.

To her bewilderment, his expression had not altered and, if possible, the black glower had grown even more accentuated. Erin's countenance seemed to wither as she abruptly tore her eyes from the fulminating glare. She glanced at the floor, her hands, the door, *anywhere* to avoid the uncompromising stare that seemed to penetrate her very soul. Regardless of her efforts, Erin felt almost compelled, and her eyes were irrevocably drawn to his.

She could not endure that annoying look another instant and, in sheer desperation, she blurted, "Kellen, I-I-I'm sorry if . . . if I've—"

"Be silent!" he snapped curtly. "I'm not interested in your apologies," he informed her bluntly.

Erin sat back, the sharpness of his retort having startled her as much as if he had dashed cold water in her face. She felt utterly helpless and alone. She ached to explain how Geoffrey had cornered her in the garden and filled her head with foolish notions. Erin now realized that she had been a goose to actually believe the man, but he had sounded so convincing. If Kellen would only allow her a chance to explain, but another glance at that stern face warned her that he was not yet ready to entertain her explanations. With a heavy sigh, Erin relaxed her shoulders against the squabs and resigned herself to accept the awkwardly silent situation.

She had just rested her weary head against the carriage wall when Kellen leaned forward abruptly. Shoving his hand inside his coat in an impatient gesture, he retrieved a noticeably crumpled piece of paper which he proceeded to wave beneath her nose in a menacing manner.

"Just what sort of insane nonsense is this?" He allowed the note to flutter harmlessly onto her lap. But before she could offer a reply, Kellen hurried on. "Am I to trust that one of these innocuous missives will find its way to my door by morning?"

Erin could but offer him a blank stare and shake her head numbly. All the words she had longed to say seemed to scramble together in an unpenetrable maze, rendering her incapable of coherent speech.

"I see. I mean so little to you that I'm not even worthy of a personal farewell message," he accused hoarsely.

"No!" she tried to reassure him. "I . . . I tried to write to you, truly I did, but . . . but I couldn't," she mumbled lamely.

Kellen found that he could no longer curb his pent-up irritation, and he lurched forward and grasped her by the shoulders. Before he was even fully aware of his actions, he had seized that vulnerable body and begun to shake it mercilessly.

Erin tried valiantly to ward off the unexpected attack, but her attempts proved to be futile, for Kellen was quite absorbed in his rage.

"You little fool!" he was shouting at her. "*How dare you!* How dare you place yourself in such jeopardy?"

Kellen suddenly became aware of the pitiful creature who struggled for her freedom, and he released her as though her skin burned like a hot brick. He watched as the anguished girl shrank back against the seat and, once again in control of his faculties, Kellen jerked away from her and shoved his hand through his hair in a desperate motion.

"Good God, Erin! Don't you know what those men might have done to you?" he cried in complete exasperation. "How can you possibly justify running off like this?"

Erin sat in a ramrod straight position directly opposite him, her eyes never wavering from his. She wanted to respond to his queries, but she was, for once, unaccountably silent. Her head ached, her shoulders throbbed, and the rest of her body was bruised and battered from being jostled about during the harrowing, runaway coach ride. It was only natural for Erin to surrender to the one method of emotional release women find invaluable in situations such as the one presently facing her: tears.

Kellen observed all the telltale signs with mild disdain; the watery eyes, the sniffling nose, the protuding lower lip and the quivering chin. Yes, all the indicators for a display of feminine hysteria were in evidence, and he vowed that he would not yield to her maudlin outburst.

Determined to appear indifferent to her anguish, Kellen averted his aloof gaze and seemed to be inexplicably absorbed in a careful scrutiny of the back of one impeccably manicured hand. "I must warn you, Erin, that in this instance I shall not be swayed by such a typically feminine indulgence," he coolly informed her.

Even as he spoke, Erin's eyes filled with water and, when she could hold them back no longer, two enormous tears spilled over and rolled down her cheeks. With an impatient gesture, Erin dashed the droplets from her face, but even the hands she pressed against her mouth could not smother the choked sobs that escaped her throat.

Kellen had folded his arms across his chest and leaned back

against the seat, pushing his hat forward to shield his eyes as though he were contemplating sleep. In actuality, he continued to watch Erin and, when the sobs continued to rack her slight frame, Kellen's stand-offish resolve began to crumble. Cursing himself for being such an insensitive brute, he leaned forward and extended his arms to her.

"Come here, brat!" he grumbled, though there was no ominous inflection in his tone.

Erin did not hesitate, indeed, when she saw the open arms beckoning her into their sympathetic confines, she verily threw herself into the welcoming embrace. Once safely within the comforting haven, she began to pour out the details of her excruciating evening. She told him of her encounter with Geoffrey, how he had convinced her that it would be better for all concerned if she departed. Finally, she told him of her confrontation with the hold-up men, and she confided in him her conviction that she had seen one of them before.

Kellen questioned her at length on this matter, but no amount of deliberation could produce a positive identity. Noticing that continued discussion of the experience was causing Erin renewed distress, Kellen cradled her to him and assured her that she need not consider the subject further.

Erin accepted his kindness thankfully and snuggled closer against him, resting her head on his broad chest. Shyly, she lifted her hand and smoothed the material along the lapel of his jacket. Noting that his severe expression had mellowed somewhat, Erin ventured to inquire, "Does this mean that you are no longer angry with me?"

"I'm positively furious with you," he stated baldly. "And if you ever attempt another harebrained stunt such as this, I'll more than likely tan your pretty little backside. In fact," he rubbed his chin pensively, "perhaps I should do just that to ensure this sort of nonsense does not recur."

"Kellen?" Erin regarded him warily and prepared to execute a hasty withdrawal to the other side of the carriage.

"Sit still," he barked, and she immediately complied with

his command. "I'm not going to beat you, though your rash conduct certainly warrants some form of disciplinary action." He tilted her head back and looked deeply into the green eyes that still glistened with unshed tears.

"Oh, blast it all!" he breathed in exasperation and, giving in to his own impetuosity, Kellen lowered his lips to hers. "Perhaps this instead," he murmured.

Erin accepted his kiss willingly, indeed, she enjoyed the thrill of his caress, and was a little saddened when he pulled away. With a contented sigh, she rested her cheek against his chest and gave in to the fatigue that suddenly swept over her. But just before she succumbed to the relentless slumber that tugged at her eyelids, she felt compelled to respond to an accusation he had flung at her in anger.

"You're quite mistaken, you know," she whispered drowsily.

"Am I?"

"Yes. You don't mean so very little to me. Indeed, you are *everything* to me," she declared unashamedly.

"As you are to me," he replied lovingly, and his rejoinder brought a contented smile to her lips and, seconds later, she slept serenely in his embrace.

In fact, Erin slept so soundly that she was unaware of the flurry of activity that greeted their arrival at the Sinclairian. First, Kellen ordered a suite of rooms above his floor prepared for occupation, then he summoned a bewildered Mrs. Sullivan from her bed and requested her assistance with his newly acquired charge. Next, he sent Chin Li to Tiffin Square with a note of explanation to his mother, for regardless of the late hour, he knew that she would not rest until she had received word of Erin's welfare. Finally, he carried Erin into the chamber he had arranged for her and settled her comfortably on the bed.

Kellen adjourned to the sitting room while Mrs. Sullivan attended the sleeping girl, and he was still there, mulling over the events of the evening when his housekeeper arrived to announce that she had completed her task.

"She's sleepin' like a lamb, Mr. Sinclair," she reported. "What do you want I should do now?"

"Stay with her until morning?" he asked tiredly, the actions of the long evening finally having taken their toll on even his robust body. "I'll engage a chaperon later today." He stood up and started to walk to the door, but a sudden outcry from Erin's room led him to that chamber instead.

He lit the bedside lamp to discover Erin sitting bolt upright in the middle of bed, clutching the sheet to her heaving bosom, a look of sheer terror on her face. Without thinking, Kellen sat down on the edge of the bed and pulled her into his arms.

"There, there," he soothed her. "Had that nasty dream again, didn't you?"

Erin nodded stiffly, fighting back the tears.

"No doubt it was brought on by your harrowing encounter on the road tonight." He gently smoothed the hair that flowed across her shoulders and continued to whisper endearments in her ear.

Suddenly aware of her new and unfamiliar surroundings, she straightened and looked at him quizzically. "Where am I?" She fingered the ribbons of the freshly laundered, though rather plain, nightgown and silently wondered how she came to be so attired.

"Don't look so dismayed, my onerous wench. I haven't been up to any mischief," he vowed. "And to answer your question, you are currently residing in an apartment at my hotel. It was my housekeeper who was kind enough to tend to you, and she has agreed to stay for the remainder of the night. I couldn't, in good conscience, return you to Tiffin Square; not until I have a chance to confront Cousin Geoffrey," he added sourly.

It was just as well, she thought, for Erin did not care if she ever laid eyes on Geoffrey Sinclair again, but the sinister implication behind Kellen's last statement made her shiver. "But Kellen, I can't very well stay here so close to . . . to you," she looked away shyly, "not without a proper chaperon."

"I know that, infant. Contrary to what you may believe, I *have* been schooled in what is considered acceptable decorum where unmarried ladies and their suitors are concerned," he informed her haughtily. "I hope to convince Mother to stay with you. Her presence should curb those tongues that might otherwise spread a vicious tale. At least until I am able to make the necessary arrangements," he mused aloud.

"Arrangements?"

"Yes, for our wedding. That is, of course, if you'll have me." He stared into the bewildered face for an instant before hurrying on. "Oh, I see that I've made a botch of this. I'm certain you were expecting candlelight, flowers and a poetic proposal, and I had intended to provide all those romantic elements at our intimate dinner tonight. However, I'm afraid that your little escapade preempted my gallant intentions," he babbled, not knowing quite what to say next. "I'm even prepared to go down on bended knee if that will help you reach a speedy decision."

Erin giggled delightfully. "That won't be necessary, silly."

"Then may I assume that you accept my humble proposal?" he asked hopefully.

"Yes," she murmured softly. "I should like very much to marry you."

With a joyful whoop, Kellen dragged her into his arms again to seal their betrothal with a kiss and, when he pulled away, he emitted a throaty sigh of relief.

"You sound as though you didn't think I'd accept your offer," Erin said a little petulantly.

"To be honest, you capitulated more eagerly than I anticipated."

"Oh?"

"Yes, You see, I naturally feared that damnable Irish pride of yours might not let you forget what a horrid fellow I am.

You know; being a *Yankee*," he teased her.

Erin lowered her eyes. "I *had* forgotten."

"Good! Then let's not rekindle old memories. Shall we start our lives afresh from this moment?" he suggested.

"Oh, yes," she readily agreed. "Does . . . does that mean you can forgive me for running away?"

"Forgiven," he said simply, giving her nose an impish tweak. "But you must remember this, my darling. Now that you've agreed to be mine, I'll not let you run from me again." He coaxed her head up, so he could gaze into her brilliant green eyes.

"Nor would I want to," she whispered truthfully and, just when Kellen was prepared to culminate the conversation with a passionate embrace, Erin placed her hands against his chest to stay his movement. "Do you truly think me to be such a prideful boor?"

"Not now perhaps, but when we first met, you were positively as stubborn as a mule in regard to my northern background," he said kindly. "But as time passed and we grew to know one another better, I think you learned a valuable lesson." He smiled at her.

Erin's brow crinkled into a contemplative frown. "What lesson?"

"That pride only gets in the way when love begins to blossom." And with that, Kellen claimed her mouth in a tempestuous kiss that sent any doubts Erin might have been entertaining scattering into oblivion.

III

The Conspiracy

Chapter Fifteen

The wedding date was set for mid-July, making a jubilant
Meredith literally shriek with both joy and dismay at the announcement. She was naturally overjoyed at the prospect of
gaining such a beautiful and charming daughter-in-law, but
protested that four weeks was simply not enough time to plan
a proper ceremony. Consequently, she had ventured to suggest that the couple consider postponing the wedding for a few
weeks.

Kellen had been the one to immediately voice his objection
to the disagreeable proposal. Noting the relenting cast to
Erin's face and fearing that she might be persuaded to comply
with his mother's wishes, he quickly took charge of the situation. He politely but firmly informed his mother and fiancee
that they had very well better manage to complete the necessary preparations, for he was not willing to wait even one
minute longer than the agreed upon time to make Erin his
wife. With that lofty declaration, he had strode from the
apartment and left the ladies to their nuptial arrangements.

Meredith Sinclair had readily consented to establish a temporary residence with her soon to be daughter-in-law. Not
only did Meredith's presence add the necessary stamp of propriety to the situation, but it gave them ample opportunity to
discuss the rapidly approaching wedding, and that is precisely

what they did; morning, noon and night. There was the reception and nuptial dinner to be organized; these to be held at Tiffin Square, the invitations had to be ordered and posted, the gardener had to be consulted as to the variety and number of floral arrangements to be prepared; not to mention a host of lesser minutiae that accompany such an affair. But the singularly most important item on the agenda was the selection of Erin's wedding gown and trousseau.

Erin had balked at the latter, protesting that Kellen had recently seen to the refurbishing of her wardrobe, but Meredith had been so persistent that Erin reluctantly agreed upon a few new gowns to augment an already copious clothespress. Meredith had justified the purchases by explaining to Erin that now that she was to become a married lady, she could wear more daringly styled dresses to please her husband. And, of course, she would need lacy new underthings and peignoirs; all the delicate essentials that make a woman feel like a woman, and a man thirst for a taste of the pleasures they so provocatively enhance.

Erin had agreed upon these purchases as well, realizing that Meredith was determined to see that she was properly clothed for her son. There was one garment, however, that Erin made no pretense at objecting to: her wedding gown.

The dress was an absolute masterpiece of couture expertise; more modestly designed than many of the gowns the modiste had shown her, yet it reeked of a sublime elegance that made Erin feel like an absolute princess when she was requested to don the garment for her many fittings. The dress was an exquisite creation of silks, satins, and laces, and looked like a wisp of cloud that might drift away on a gentle summer's breeze.

The decolletage was elegantly cut in a scalloped neckline that scooped low to a daring angle that accentuated her alabaster skin. The white silk bodice was covered with a maltese lace that extended up the neck to fashion a snug collar about the bride's slender throat. The gown was secured by no less than one hundred closely sewn, perfectly shaped pearl buttons that extended from the lace collar down the back of the dress to her slender waist. These same pearl buttons were sewn along the edge of the neckline and down the front of the bodice for ornamentation.

The exquisite, billowy sleeves were made of white chiffon and billowed out from the shoulders to just above the elbow where they narrowed into a tight band of lace that extended the length of her arm and stretched into a point across her delicate hands. The sleeves were made complete by the row of matching pearl buttons that had been sewn onto the length of the lace arm band for decoration.

The white silk skirt was stretched out over the wide hoops that gave the gown its stylish shape and was covered with Brussels lace, except for the center panel, which had been cut away to reveal the luxurious white satin underskirt. The skirt was gathered in the back where a long, lace-covered train was attached and, when extended to its full length, trailed behind a regal ten feet. The skirt fell in enchanting folds that swirled about Erin's feet in a most flattering style, and the gown made such a delightful rustling sound when she walked that Erin could not resist the temptation to move about the fitting room, envisioning that she was walking down the aisle toward her beloved Kellen.

The days preceding the ceremony sped by at an uncommonly furious pace. Erin's days were spent in wedding preparations, and her evenings were happily passed in the company of her soon-to-be husband. She grew pensive whenever she allowed herself to truly consider her forthcoming marriage. For she realized that if anyone had told her a scant few weeks earlier that she would consent to become Kellen's wife, she would have laughed in their face for their foolishness. But that was before she had come to know and love, fiercely love, the man in question.

Still, Erin could not help but feel mildly apprehensive about her pending marriage, for the courtship had closely resembled a fairy-tale romance. After all, they had only met four months earlier, and not under the most propitious of circumstances. Accordingly, their precious moments alone prior to the wedding were spent in becoming better acquainted.

They shared family stories; Kellen telling her of how his father had perished in a carriage accident while he was a young boy, leaving Kellen to grow up as an only child. Erin, in turn, told him of her childhood days at Kilkieran, with four brothers who teased her unmercifully and devoted parents to love and guide her.

Of course, there were the happy childhood reminiscences. As they strolled through the city parks, lunched at popular cafes, or browsed through shops along Pennsylvania Avenue, the smitten couple poured out stories from their past.

Kellen had recounted the time he had broken his arm when he had fallen from a cherry tree that he had climbed in order to pick the succulent fruit. Despite the disabling injury, Kellen had declared that the act had been worthwhile, for Cook had baked an entire cherry pie for his enjoyment alone. After Erin's laughter had subsided, she told him of her hideaway behind the waterfall; a secret she had never confided to another living soul. Thus the betrothed sweethearts passed their days and, if possible, fell even more deeply in love.

They seldom visited Tiffin Square these days, principally due to the fact that Erin preferred to avoid any unnecessary contact with Geoffrey and his equally intimidating wife. Erin had often wondered what had transpired between the two men when Kellen confronted Geoffrey the morning after he had rescued her from the runaway carriage. Yet whenever she questioned Kellen about the matter, he would simply draw her into his arms, kiss her tenderly, and tell her that she need not worry her pretty head over such triflings; assuring her as he did so that they would receive no further interference from his scheming cousin.

Erin was not thoroughly convinced of this last declaration, but she did not think it worthy enough to entertain further discussion. But as she sat before the dressing room table, while Renee combed her hair into a becoming style, she was again consumed by her nagging doubts. Her apprehension had no doubt been rekindled in anticipation of the coming evening's engagement.

With the wedding less than a week away, Jeremiah Sinclair had insisted that the family members set aside their petty squabbles for one night, and dine together in celebration of the approaching ceremony. Erin was reluctant to accept the invitation, but Kellen had assured her that they would not linger if the situation grew too awkward for her to bear. Therefore, she finally relented and agreed to accompany him.

As she stood before the cheval mirror, adjusting the angle of her flower trimmed poke bonnet, Erin began to question the wisdom of her decision. She had not seen Geoffrey since the night in the garden when he had used his silver-tongued rhetoric to convince her that it would be to everyone's advantage if she departed. But before her confidence withered completely, Kellen appeared to escort Erin and Meredith to Tiffin Square.

The ride was pleasant and, by the time they arrived at the huge edifice, Kellen had done much to restore a lustrous glow to Erin's face. He assisted her from the conveyance, and placed his protective arm about her waist as he guided her up the steps. But Erin's worries were to have been for naught, for when the couple entered the drawing room, Geoffrey and Vanessa greeted them with their customary nonchalant hauteur as though nothing out of the ordinary had ever transpired.

Erin was surprised to discover that she found their attitude annoying; perhaps even more than a direct confrontation would have been. With a stern self-directed reprimand, Erin resolved to put the vexing couple from her mind, for after all, they were Kellen's relatives, and she must at least strive to be civil when forced to suffer their company.

Erin gratefully accepted the glass of claret that Kellen proffered, and she had just selected a comfortable seat when Vanessa casually inquired as to the progress of the wedding plans. Erin began to reply to the half-hearted question, but Jasper appeared in the doorway and coughed loudly, apparently preparing to make some sort of announcement.

"Dinner will be delayed," the butler proclaimed formally. "The elder Sinclair has expressed his desire to have a private interview with Miss Richards before the family convenes in the dining room."

Erin remained in her chair for a moment, silently pondering Jasper's rather strange declaration. She frowned. What could the crotchety eccentric be up to now? She shot Kellen a furtive glance which he correctly interpreted as a plea for help.

"Don't be intimidated, love," he whispered encouragingly. "You are familiar with Grandfather's ways by now. It's probably the tritest of matters, but I'll accompany you if you like." He stood and offered to escort her from the room, but Jasper quickly dispelled any such notion.

"Begging your pardon, Mister Kellen," the servant maintained a dauntless facade, "but your grandfather particularly emphasized his wish to speak with Miss Richards *alone.*" Jasper stood aside to allow Erin to pass through the door before him.

Erin moved as if in a daze and she did not witness the curiously hopeful looks that Geoffrey and Vanessa exchanged. Nor did she heed the contemplative expression that shrouded Kellen's face as he deliberated his grandfather's peculiar request. Indeed, the only observer who seemed nonplussed by Jeremiah's summons was Meredith, who sat quietly sipping her wine; a smile of reminiscence twitching at her lips.

Erin climbed the steps slowly, scarcely able to imagine what sort of devilment Kellen's grandfather might have contrived this time. She rapped sharply upon the door to announce her arrival and, not waiting for a summons, she turned the knob and thrust the door open. Jeremiah stood before the mirror while his manservant adjusted the slant of his tie, and he carefully slipped into a dark colored jacket before he turned to acknowledge her presence.

With a negligent wave of his hand, Jeremiah dismissed the servant, and settled his piercing gaze upon Erin. "You certainly took your own sweet time getting here," he snapped crankily.

"On the contrary, I came as soon as I received your summons," she promptly informed him and, closing the door, she came fully into the chamber. Coming directly to the point, she asked, "What is it you wished to discuss with me that needs to be conducted in this clandestine manner? I assure you that the occupants of the downstairs drawing room are simply agog with speculation."

"I'm not the least bit concerned with what others might think, as you well know," he said testily. "Since you've sequestered yourself in that damned hotel, you've made it virtually impossible for me to discuss the terms of the marriage contract with you."

"Marriage contract?" she repeated faintly, genuinely confused. "Kellen has said nothing about a contract."

"There is a simple explanation for that, my dear. Kellen knows nothing of the matter. I, and I alone, handle the family's legal affairs." Jeremiah walked to his desk and extracted an official looking document from the layers of papers that were strewn across the table top. "If you'll be so good as to sign this, we can go down to dinner."

"But why? What does it say?"

"I should have known you'd be a difficult one; demanding all sorts of explanations," he sighed wearily. "Very well, to answer your questions in reverse order; this document stipulates the terms of the marriage and, because, if you do not affix your signature to the contract, I fear that I cannot permit the marriage to take place." Jeremiah proffered the paper toward

301

Erin for her perusal and patiently awaited her response.

But Erin was too shocked to make much sense of the legal jargon, and she cast a beseeching look at Jeremiah. Feeling a sudden trembling in her legs and, fearing the loss of their valuable support, she sank down upon the edge of the bed. Her gaze was still transfixed upon the imposing man, but her eyes had lost much of their sheen, and her voice was a mere whisper when she again found her tongue.

"But I . . . I love Kellen," she murmured weakly. "There is no need for such a contract." Then her eyes grew suddenly cold, and her voice bitter, when she demanded, "Why are you doing this?"

"To protect the family's interests, of course. I already have one grandson shackled to a greedy parasite. I shall make sure that Kellen displays better judgment."

"Does that mean you do not approve of his choice?" she bristled noticeably at the man's brash demeanor.

"Not at all." Jeremiah strode over to the dressing table where he thoughtfully fingered a leather case. "You have exhibited great spunk and resiliency; attributes that are to be admired and respected. They are also prerequisites if one is to survive the rigors of the Sinclair family," he informed her bluntly.

He regarded her favorably, then a slight frown creased his brow as he continued, "I must admit that I have found displeasure with your behavior on but one occasion, but that single impetuous act has prompted me to take precautionary measures to ensure that this union is given a fighting chance."

"But what did I do?" she asked desperately, clutching her hands in her lap.

"Surely, you must know," Jeremiah's voice grew uncharacteristically soft, though his countenance remained unchanged. "Kellen needs a wife who will be a constant force in his life, not one who will turn tail and run at the slightest provocation. To be sure, I thought you were made of sterner stuff," he added as an aside.

"You mean *this*," she waved the paper about in a frantic gesture, "is because of that, *that* — " Erin could not think of a sufficiently reprehensible term for Geoffrey, so she vented her anger by crumbling the document and hurling it across the room. "I cannot fathom why I am to be punished for that scoundrel's wicked behavior," she hissed furiously.

"The marriage contract is not meant as a chastisement, my dear; rather a safeguard against repeated instances of a similar nature. And, of course," he bent to retrieve the wadded document, "should this alliance prove intolerable to either party, provisions have been made for the dissolution of the marriage."

Erin grew unusually quiet as she struggled to maintain her equanimity, but the white knuckles of the hand that gripped the bedpost belied her calm exterior. "Just what, may I ask, are the terms of this asinine agreement?"

"It's very simple. You agree to remain with Kellen for a period of two years. If, by the end of the agreed upon time, you have managed to provide my grandson with an heir, you may remain, should you be so inclined." He paused, apparently engrossed in pressing the crinkled folds from the legal contract.

"And if I am remiss in my wifely responsibilities?" Erin asked caustically. Her plucky demeanor having gradually been restored, Erin was now prepared to engage in battle with her formidable adversary.

"Then you shall free Kellen from the marriage, so that he may seek an alliance which will produce a suitable heir."

"What will happen if I refuse to sign this wretched piece of paper?" she challenged.

"Did I neglect to tell you of the settlement I am prepared to bestow upon you for your acquiescence in this matter?" He regarded her closely for her reaction, but Erin did not so much as bat an eye. "I happen to know that Kellen paid the taxes to save your family's plantation from the auction block, but it will take a great many resources to set things aright. Be that as it may, I am quite willing to make the investment, allowing that you agree to the terms as I've outlined them."

Erin's lovely face grew black with fury. "You pompous, evil old man!" she all but shouted. "You cannot *buy* my servitude. *Damn you,* and damn your money! You, sir, may go to the devil!" She leapt from the bed and bolted across the room to the door, as though planning to take her leave of him.

"Doubtless, I shall," he countered dryly. "Though I'm certain you can appreciate my concern to see that the family is reasonably established before my ornery soul is cast into the fiery depths of hell." He offered her a wry smile and, noticing her progress toward the door, he called, "But where are you going, my girl? We have not yet concluded our transaction."

"Oh, yes we have," she retorted, pausing by the door long enough to fling the old man a hateful glare. "I have no intention of accepting your money." As an afterthought, she added, "It's indeed easy to determine from whom Geoffrey inherited his loathsome ways; you both seem to think that any means can be achieved by merely flaunting your fortune. Well, I for one, am not so handily purchased," she stated grandly. "Nor will I sign your cursed contract. What do you say to that?"

"That I shall forbid the marriage."

"Kellen will not heed you."

"You sound very sure of yourself, but you have forgotten one very important factor. I am still head of this family; Kellen *will* honor my wishes in this instance," Jeremiah said with such conviction that Erin was persuaded to turn away from the door and face him.

"Why?"

"Because of his inheritance, of course."

"No," Erin declared. "Kellen cares not a whit about your dynasty. He is a successful businessman in his own right. You'll have to do better than that."

"Perhaps Kellen did not care in the past," Jeremiah conceded, "but Geoffrey's recent indiscretion toward you has wrought a peculiar change in my younger grandson. It would seem that Kellen suddenly possesses an insatiable desire to usurp Geoffrey's ascension to chief executor of our vast fortune."

Erin became very quiet; her eyes downcast as she silently absorbed all that had been said. "So you see, Erin," Jeremiah continued more gently, "Kellen will abide my decision because he does not wish to be held in disfavor."

The old man carefully crossed to stand before her and, taking her limp hand in his, he led her to the desk. Jeremiah smoothed the wrinkles from the crumpled piece of paper, produced two more copies, and handed her a pen.

"Sign these," he whispered softly.

Erin accepted the proffered pen and stared blankly at the paper. "You are . . . are quite certain that Kellen knows nothing of this?" Her voice trembled in anticipation of his reply, for she could not bear to think that her beloved would be a conspirator in such a vulgar scheme.

"He doesn't know, nor need he."

Jeremiah coaxed the unsteady hand onto the paper, and Erin hastily scrawled her name across each document. Upon completion of the loathsome task, she flung the pen onto the desk and turned a fulminating glare on her soon-to-be in-law.

"You needn't take umbrage, my girl." Jeremiah meticulously folded the legal papers and tucked them inside a desk drawer. "Two years isn't such a long time, after all."

But Erin was in no mood for his attempts to smooth over the deplorable situation. "I meant what I said about the money," she reiterated. "I'll not have one cent of your funds spent on Kilkieran." She squared her rigid shoulders and met Jeremiah's gaze with an undaunted determination of her own.

"As you wish, but the offer shall stand if you ever have reason to change your mind."

"I shan't, thank you. May I go now?" she asked impatiently.

"There's one thing more." Jeremiah returned to the

305

dressing table and retrieved the elongated jewel case he had fingered earlier.

"What is it? Shall I sign another paper swearing that I'll abide by the terms of the first?" She rounded on him irritably.

Jeremiah wisely chose to ignore her emotional outburst. "The others are certain to be curious regarding the purpose behind this little . . . ah . . . tete-a-tete. We shall tell them that I wished a private interview, so that I could present you with this." He flipped open the case to reveal an exquisite emerald necklace.

Under normal circumstances, Erin would have accepted such an extravagant gift with alacrity, but the present situation was far from normal. Therefore, she barely managed to mumble a civil thank you to the old man.

"This belonged to Kellen's grandmother," he explained lovingly, lifting the flawless gem from the velvet lined case and dangling it so that it sparkled in the light from the table lamp. But when Erin continued to show no enthusiasm over the jewel, he walked over to her.

"May I?"

Erin stood stiffly as he fastened the necklace about her throat. Without further ado, she swept past the man and, without a backward glance, fled from the room. She flew down the stairs to the drawing room, but paused before the door to catch her breath and restore her composure. She forced a smile to her lips and pushed the barrier ajar. As she stepped across the threshold, one thought coursed through her beleaguered mind: Kellen must never learn of the contract that Jeremiah had just persuaded her to sign.

Kellen changed positions in his chair and pulled his watch from his pocket to glance at the time. He repocketed the timepiece while the fingers of one hand resumed their relentless drumming against his muscular thigh. A serene, almost peaceful smile curled his lips as he scrutinized his opponent with a fastidious gaze.

Erin sat opposite him, elbows propped upon the table, her chin resting in her hands. A particularly serious frown crinkled her brow as she studied the chessboard that was spread upon the table between them. A good twenty minutes had elapsed since she had assumed control of the board, and Kellen had long since realized from her haphazard, careless moves that Erin's concentration was not entirely devoted to her play.

Kellen's eyes narrowed considerably as he continued to observe the delicate features of the exquisite creature opposite him. Perhaps if he watched her long enough, he might be able to discern what was troubling her, for it took no great genius to see that something plagued Erin's mind. But what? Meredith had assured him that it was nothing more than a case of pre-nuptial jitters, but Kellen was not wholly satisfied with that explanation.

A sudden movement caught his eye, and he turned his attention to the chessboard. Apparently, his opponent was finally going to make her move. He observed as one slender hand reached forward; the other still serving as a prop for her chin. With a negligent shrug and a sigh, Erin picked up the queen and moved it to the decided upon position.

Kellen immediately leaned forward to study her move and calculate his own. "Ah ha," he murmured, stroking his chin in a thoughtful gesture. Then his eyes lit up with mischief and a victorious smile spread his lips. "Erin, darling, I fear that your heart is not in this. You've left your king quite unprotected. In fact, I believe; yes, I have you at checkmate," he proclaimed grandly.

Erin did not seem desolated by the loss. She merely collected the discarded pieces and returned them to the velvet lined case. "It's a silly game in any case." She shrugged her indifference.

307

"Silly, is it? I'll have you know that I'm considered a masterful strategist."

"Oh, not so *very* masterful," she baited him, "else you would have conquered my king much sooner."

"But, alas, my love," Kellen murmured tenderly, "*that* was my strategy; to prolong the game, so that I might share your company a little longer."

Erin laughed gaily at his banter, a musical, lilting sound that had been alien to her lips since her encounter with Jeremiah. "You're incorrigible."

"Yes, I believe that I am," he freely agreed. As he watched her, his expression grew suddenly amorous, and his voice was husky when he said, "Come here, wench! I have a desire to collect my winnings. A kiss will suffice, I should think."

A slightly wicked flicker danced in the green eyes that sparkled at him, and she rose from her perch and dutifully stepped around the table and placed a deliberate perfunctory kiss against his cheek. "As you wish, m'lord," she said obediently, fluttering her lashes demurely. And when she would have scampered from his reach, Kellen's hand shot out to capture her slender wrist, and he dragged the mildly protesting girl onto his lap.

"Brat!" he growled, giving her rump a good-natured slap.

"*Sir!*" she gasped, placing a hand to her insulted backside. But try as she might, Erin could not assume the proper air of effrontery his actions warranted. "You take liberties of a very personal nature."

A hearty chuckle rumbled in Kellen's chest. "Madam, lest you forget, tomorrow we shall become man and wife; a glorious event which will entitle me to take all manner of liberties with your very lovely person," he whispered softly, a roguish gleam twinkling behind the crystal blue eyes. "I may as well warn you that the chaste kiss you so graciously bestowed upon me will do little to assuage *my* lascivious appetite."

Erin feigned a pout. "How unchivalrous of you to berate my lovemaking."

308

"You accuse me unjustly, my love." Kellen tilted her chin back, and gazed adoringly into her soulful green eyes. "I never berate a young lady's romantic overtures, however, can you fault me for desiring a somewhat more . . . uh . . . zealous response? Something on the order of this . . ."

Kellen then proceeded to cover her mouth with his in a passionately possessive kiss that completely squelched any notion Erin might have harbored at remaining passive in this virile man's arms. Quite without thinking, she entwined her fingers in the hair that curled at the nape of his neck, and clung to him in a breathless frenzy; returning his kiss with an abandon that thoroughly surprised her. A little moan reverberated in her throat as his lips masterfully moved over hers, and she sighed delightfully when she pulled away and rested her head on his shoulder.

They remained so engaged for a long while; both silent, each obviously content to reflect upon personal musings. Finally, Erin stirred in Kellen's embrace, thereby, breaking the magical spell of the tranquil moment.

"Kellen?" she murmured hesitantly, rubbing her hand along his rugged chest.

"Yes, little reb." He lifted the slender appendage and pressed a kiss into the palm of her hand.

"Are you certain . . . about tomorrow, I mean?" she asked carefully. "There is still time to change your mind if you're inclined to do so."

"What nonsense is this?" Kellen positioned her on his lap, enabling him to obtain a better look at her face. "Has Geoffrey been bothering you again?" he asked suspiciously.

"No," she assured him, lowering her gaze, for she could not bring herself to look him squarely in the eye. "I just thought . . ."

"Then, by all means, don't think," he told her bluntly, settling her against his chest again. "I assure you, my darling, that I could not be more pleased with the way things have turned out. I'm thrilled beyond imagining that you have consented to be my wife; unless . . . tell me, are *you* having second thoughts about our marriage?"

"No," she whispered softly. "I'm happier than I ever thought I could be."

"Good." He thrust his hand into his pocket and withdrew his watch. "Then I trust that we shall not have to broach this subject again." He cast a watchful eye toward the timepiece.

"I'll not mention it again," she promised and, noticing his concern with the time, she said, "Kellen, you've shown an unnatural interest in the time this whole evening. Why, you must have consulted your watch a dozen times alone during our chess game. Counting down the remaining hours of your bachelorhood, are you?" she teased him unmercifully, as she leaned forward to press a spontaneous kiss against his mouth.

"Not at all," he protested, holding her close. "I am expecting a caller is all," he offered obliquely.

"A caller?" she exclaimed. "At this hour? Why, it must be ten o'clock."

"A quarter past."

"What sort of man conducts business at this hour of the night?" She chewed on a fingernail thoughtfully. "Knowing you, it is probably something totally unscrupulous," she baited him, hoping to elicit some clue as to the identity of the anticipated visitor.

Further speculation on Erin's part was preempted, however, by a sharp knock at the apartment door.

"It would seem, madam, that all your questions are about to be answered." He pushed her from his lap and nudged her toward the door. "Go on, brat. Be a good girl and open the door. The servants have long since retired, and I am much too weary to acknowledge the summons." He lifted a hand to his mouth under the pretense of stifling a yawn.

Erin was not fooled for an instant by Kellen's sly behavior, but she was similarly aware that he was impossible to deal with when he adopted this contrary disposition. With a recriminating glance at her fiancé, she hurried off to see to the stranger at the door. She turned the knob and opened the door but a crack, enabling her to peer into the corridor, but a squeal of unmistakable delight presently filled the chamber as Erin flung the door wide and hurled herself into her brother Graham's open arms.

Kellen allowed brother and sister a few moments of privacy before he sought to interrupt the happy reunion. Indeed, the couple was not even aware of his presence until he spoke.

"Won't you step inside, Graham, where we can converse more freely?" he offered kindly.

Graham nodded stiffly, as Erin all but dragged him across the threshold and led him into the spacious sitting room. Once she had deposited him in the room's most comfortable chair; a chair that was Kellen's favorite, that gentleman noted with a fond smile, she perched herself on the edge of the sofa. Kellen had seen that look before, and he realized that Graham was about to undergo a rigorous inquisition. Thinking that the young man might require sustenance after his long journey, Kellen stepped forward and placed a gentle hand on Erin's shoulder.

"Perhaps your brother would care for some refreshment," he suggested. "I instructed Chin Li to leave a platter of sandwiches in the kitchen and, if you look, I'm fairly certain you will discover a decanter of wine, so that we may properly celebrate this special occasion."

"Forgive me for being so thoughtless, Graham," Erin hastily apologized. "You surely must be ravenous after your long trip." She jumped up and scurried off toward the kitchen.

Kellen waited until the rose-colored gown had disappeared behind the door before he addressed the visitor and, when he spoke, his voice was genuinely friendly. "Thank you for coming. You cannot imagine what your presence at the wedding will mean to her. Why, I've not seen her so happy since . . ." He gazed after her wistfully. "Well, to be truthful, I've never

311

seen her so completely contented. I find myself indebted to you," he said humbly.

"There is no need to feel that way," Graham assured him. "I'll not deny that I resented you for a long while after you spirited Erin away from Kilkieran, and I've cursed myself a thousand times over for my shabby treatment of her; that is, until this very moment," he added softly and, looking across to the sofa where Kellen had taken a seat, he met his gaze squarely. "I fear that you credit me wrongly, for the enchanting glow that brightens my sister's face was put there by you, Mr. Sinclair, not I."

"Thank you. I'd like to believe that to be true. But please, you must agree to call me Kellen," he urged. "We are to be related, after all."

"Very well, Kellen. I never thought that I'd be willing to admit this, but I believe you will be very good for my little sister."

Kellen smiled gratefully as he stood and proffered his hand to his future brother-in-law. "Your generous attitude is more than I had hoped for; indeed, more than I had a right to expect under the circumstances. I do love Erin, and I shall do everything within my power to provide for her and make her happy," he sincerely promised.

"I believe you shall." Graham clasped the extended hand in a firm handshake. "Let's put the past behind us, shall we? Allow me to formally welcome you to the Richards family," he said earnestly.

"What of Evan?" Erin had returned from the kitchen in time to witness the exchange between Kellen and her brother. "Does he share your sentiments?" she asked skeptically.

Graham considered his response a full thirty seconds before he replied. "No, Erin. I fear that he does not," he answered honestly. "But you must remember that Evan's wounds were severe and will require much time to heal properly. He'll come around in time. I did," he added encouragingly. "But come, let's talk of happier things. Your wedding is tomorrow and,

312

thanks to Kellen's invitation, I've come to give you away."

Kellen stepped to Erin to relieve her of the cumbersome tray, and he directed her back to the sofa. He assumed the responsibility of pouring each of them a glass of wine, and soon the three of them were nibbling on the delicious sandwiches and chatting amiably. Erin told Graham about the wedding plans and inquired about the welfare of her acquaintances back home. It was with reluctance that she asked of Deborah's progress, and she instantly regretted her inquiry, for his attitude grew ominously somber.

Several pregnant seconds ticked away before Graham spoke again and, when he did, his voice was hesitant, almost stilted. "That's . . . that's one of the reasons I came. I have an enormous favor to ask of you . . . *both* of you."

Erin leaned forward expectantly. "Yes? Anything."

"Hear me out, Irish, before you make such an unselfish commitment." Graham reached out to pat her hand affectionately. Then he stood up and walked over to the fireplace where he rested his foot on the hearth, staring aimlessly into the grate that had not held a fire in weeks.

Erin was understandably concerned by his troubled expression, but when she would have gone to comfort him, Kellen placed a restraining hand on her arm. She looked at him pleadingly, but he shook his head firmly; his silence speaking volumes. Graham would confide in them when he was ready. Thankfully, they did not have long to wait.

"Deborah is no better," he began slowly, purposefully choosing his words. "I thought she might improve when I returned but, if anything, she despises me even more."

"No," Erin insisted. "Deborah loves you."

"I know, but she worships you, sis, and she blames me because you left Kilkieran. Not that she's wrong, for Lord knows I did precious little to encourage you to stay," he berated himself.

"The situation *was* awkward," Kellen offered sympathetically.

313

"No one is to blame for my coming with Kellen," Erin defended her actions. "Besides, everything has turned out for the best; I am going to marry the man I love." She offered Kellen an adoring smile. "Perhaps if I were to write Deborah a letter, telling her how happy I am, she might feel less hostile toward you."

"Perhaps," Graham muttered dubiously. *"Damn it all!"* he suddenly swore, crashing his clenched fist against the mantel. "What I'm trying to say is that I . . . *we* need you. I'm doing my level best to put the plantation back together, but I can't do that, as well as successfully deal with a childlike wife *and* a brother who is embroiled in his own self-pity. On top of that, many of our former slaves have returned seeking shelter and employment. Quite frankly, I don't know how I'll be able to provide for everyone." His shoulders slumped under the weight of his personal dilemma, and the room fell silent except for the ticking of the clock on the mantel.

Finally, Graham turned from the fireplace, his hazel eyes scanning them hopefully, and his voice was soft when he said, "I know I have no right to ask you this, but will you come home, Erin?"

Erin turned immediately to consult her fiancé, fully expecting him to balk at the suggestion. Therefore, she was elated to hear him say, "I can deny the brat nothing when she turns those bewitching green eyes on me. Of course, we will come. That is, if I am to correctly assume that your invitation includes the dashing bridegroom."

"Certainly."

"Then it's settled," Erin cried jubilantly. "When shall we leave?"

"Whoa there, little lady!" Kellen playfully scolded her. "There is a matter of a honeymoon to be settled first, lest you've forgotten."

Erin blushed painfully. "I haven't forgotten," she murmured sheepishly. "It's just that it is so lovely at Kilkieran this time of year; I simply thought we might honeymoon there."

"Yes," Kellen mumbled dryly. "I had always envisioned that I would conduct my honeymoon in the midst of a throng of curious family members. I shall no doubt have to contract some malady just to see you since you will be lavishing your attention on Deborah and Evan," he pouted.

"And you," she promised.

"Nevertheless, I must attend to my business affairs and check on the construction of the house at Arcadia before we go off on a jaunt." He mentally calculated the time he would require to complete his business transactions. "I see no reason why we cannot be ready to leave by next Wednesday."

"Oh, darling, thank you so much!" Erin threw her arms about his neck and hugged him fiercely.

Kellen wrapped his arms about the tiny creature and pressed a kiss to the top of her head. "You're quite welcome, my love," he murmured tenderly.

The remainder of the evening was spent in idle chitchat, and it was approaching midnight when Graham rose to leave. Bending over Erin, he placed a brotherly kiss against her brow.

"Goodnight, Irish. Christina and I will see you at the church tomorrow."

Erin bolted forward on the sofa, not believing her ears. "Did you say Christina will be accompanying you?"

"Yes."

"Whatever possessed you to bring that . . . *creature* with you?" Erin asked.

Graham patted the top of her head as though soothing a petulant child. "She asked if she might accompany me, and I could not refuse her. She sees so few people at home, and I thought this trip would be a bit of an adventure for her. Aunt Lydia and Uncle Philip were in agreement with me, and could see no harm in it."

"Humph!" Erin grumbled. "No more harm than giving the fox the key to the henhouse."

Graham chuckled at her pettiness. "You exaggerate, Irish.

Take pity on our poor cousin. All eyes will be on the beautiful bride tomorrow, and she will be but a lonely face in the crowd, wishing no doubt that she were as lucky as you."

Erin softened a little; but she still did not feel completely charitable toward Christina; not after the spiteful way she had behaved at their last encounter.

"Very well," she relented. "But tell me, where is our deprived cousin this evening?"

"I saw that she was comfortably settled at our hotel before coming here. She was worn out from the journey, poor girl. Besides, I wanted to talk to the two of you privately." He strolled over to the door. "Well, I'm off."

Kellen stood to show him out and, at the door, he took Graham's hand and pumped it vigorously. "Thanks again for coming. I'll send my carriage round for you tomorrow, so you can escort Erin to the church. My mother will be happy to pick up Christina. Now, if you'll just tell me where you're staying—"

Erin could not clearly make out the faint mumble of their voices, nor was she overly concerned with the context of their speech. She was immersed in her own thoughts; indulging herself in a bout of self-pity.

"What are you thinking that should provoke such a woeful expression on the eve of our wedding?" Kellen inquired solicitously, reclaiming his seat beside her and drawing her into the crook of his arm.

"Vanessa and Christina," she moaned lugubriously.

"Yes? What of them?"

"They both hate me, yet they will be in attendance at our wedding. Oh, why didn't we elope?" she sighed her consummate frustration.

"I sincerely doubt that the girls *hate* you. They might envy you, of course, for making such an advantageous match. I was much sought after by the ladies of Washington, you realize," he added wickedly, ignoring the unimpressed scowl Erin turned on him. "And we did not elope because I have always contended that couples who do so have something to hide; something for which they are ashamed," he said seriously. "I love you, Erin; deeply, more passionately than I've loved any other woman. I am not ashamed of my love for you, and our wedding tomorrow is my way of bellowing that fact to the world."

"I love you, too, you know," she whispered faintly.

"I know." He stood up, pulling her to her feet beside him. "Come, my angel, it's time I escorted you back to your own apartment. Blessedly, after tomorrow, we shall not have to worry about separate chambers ever again."

"Oh, did I not tell you that I expect a separate bed chamber after we're married?" she playfully taunted him, fluttering her eyelashes in a coquettish manner.

"The hell you say!" he thundered, dragging her into a crushing embrace and kissing her so completely that Erin realized that she never wanted to be separated from this man; not for any reason.

Chapter Sixteen

The wedding was proclaimed an overwhelming success by everyone who was in attendance. Even Vanessa and Christina kept their churlish remarks at a minimum, and seemed to find enormous enjoyment in each other's company, no doubt targeting much of their guarded discourse at the unsuspecting bride. Indeed, the only guest to suffer a disquieting experience was Graham, and it had befallen him quite by accident.

Deciding that he was in need of a brief respite from the crowded reception, Graham had wandered into the garden. As he approached the arbor, his thoughts irrevocably focused on the unstable situation at Kilkieran and, consequently, he overheard much of a hushed conversation before he had even realized that he had stumbled upon a private meeting.

Graham hurriedly stepped from the path, but barely had time to conceal himself behind a large shrub before the two conspirators emerged from the arbor and strolled back toward the mansion. He did not recognize the man in military dress; a colonel, but there was no mistaking his companion.

Graham's wooden gaze bored into Kellen's back as it was devoured by the darkness, and he struggled to recall the snatches of conversation he had just overheard. What was it the colonel had said? Oh, yes.

"Granted, the mission means a great deal to the department, Kellen, but we didn't mean for you to *marry* the chit to ensure its completion. Damned noble sacrifice, I must say."

Graham had grown understandably scarlet with rage. He did not take note of Kellen's cryptic riposte, but that was of little consequence. It was obvious that the bastard had an ulterior motive for marrying his sister. But what could it possibly be?

"Oh, my sweet, guileless sister," he whispered on the wind. "I truly believed that Sinclair loved you, but now I fear he is going to break your heart," he mumbled morosely, as he deliberately made his way back to the crowded ballroom where he promptly commandeered a glass of champagne from a passing waiter.

Erin presently sat stiffly before the dressing table mirror in Kellen's chamber, blindly pulling a brush through her hair. Renée had diligently assisted her from her wedding gown, taking special care to hang it in the armoire, and had seen to Erin's evening toilette before retiring from the room. Now Mrs. Sinclair sat alone in the mammoth room, nervously awaiting the arrival of her husband.

"Husband," she murmured faintly. How odd the term sounded.

A sudden shuffling sound in the corridor made her jump, and she subconsciously held her breath while her eyes flew to the doorknob to see if it turned. But there was no movement, and she slowly exhaled and lifted her eyes to the mirror.

"Goose," she hissed at her wan reflection. "It isn't as though he is going to *ravish* you. He is your husband, and will certainly behave accordingly," she emitted a low, lugubrious moan.

How *did* a husband behave?

She returned the brush to the table and walked to the foot of the bed, but to stare at that awesome piece of furniture made her heart quiver, so Erin wisely turned aside and began to pace the length of the room. While she paced, she reflected upon the events of the hectic day just spent; her wedding day.

The day had dawned gorgeously sunny and clear, and Erin had been surprisingly calm during the brief ride from the hotel to the church. Once inside the church, however, it had been impossible for her to recall much of the ensuing ceremony, for when her eyes locked with Kellen's all time had stood still for her. She had veritably floated down the aisle on her brother's arm, and had repeated her vows as if in a trance.

The remainder of the day was a much more vivid blur to her. There had been the countless guests to receive, followed by a lavish reception at Tiffin Square. There had been dancing and music, and their happiness had been toasted with gallons upon gallons of iced champagne. The reception had been followed by an intimate family dinner, after which, the bride and groom had been driven back to The Sinclairian.

Erin halted her pacing and cast a disparaging look toward the door. "What can be keeping him?" she muttered, totally exasperated by her errant spouse.

Suddenly her eyes fell on the small package that her brother had slipped into her hand while they danced at the reception. With a determined toss of her chestnut-brown curls and a forced swallow, Erin plucked the parcel from the table and went to search for her groom.

Kellen sat in the leather desk chair in his study, elbow propped on the armrest, his head resting thoughtfully in his hand. His mood was somber; not what one would expect of a groom on his wedding night. Kellen, too, was indulging in a round of intense contemplation of the day's activities, but, unlike his distracted bride, he could recount every minute of the wedding ceremony in graphic detail.

Closing his eyes, he visualized Erin as she had looked when she walked down the aisle on Graham's arm, and his breath caught in his throat as he recalled the impact of her appearance. She was the most exquisite creature he had ever seen; so innocent and trusting. And now this lovely young thing had made safeguarding her welfare his responsibility. Not that Kellen truly doubted his ability to care for her, but there was another problem that loomed prodigiously in the forefront of his mind. How would she receive him tonight?

After all, Erin had been the victim of a vicious assault, and rape, he knew, could leave a permanent scar on one's mental perspective.

A tortured groan escaped his throat, and he mechanically reached for the bottle of whiskey he had retrieved from the liquor cabinet when he began his sojourn in the study. "God, but I love her, and I want her; want her more than any woman I've known. But . . ." He ran his hands through his unruly hair in obvious uncertainty and, pouring himself a generous portion of the potent brew, he unceremoniously quaffed the contents of the glass.

It was as he leaned forward to refill the container that Kellen noticed a slight movement near the door and, training his gaze in that direction, his eyes fell upon Erin. She looked an absolute angel, draped in white satin and chiffon and, as he gaped at the enticing vision, it began to glide gracefully across the floor toward him.

Erin observed the usually unfaltering hand tremble a little as he tilted the bottle over his glass, and it somehow made her own apprehension subside when she realized that Kellen was experiencing the same qualms as she. It was when some of the amber-colored liquid sloshed down the side of the container he was filling that Erin placed her hand over his to steady its motion. Consequently, she was the first to break the awkward silence.

"I always thought it was the bride who suffered from nervous anxiety on her wedding night," she whispered demurely.

"Aren't you?" he inquired candidly. Returning the bottle to the table, Kellen casually reclined in his chair, but his eyes

never wavered from her glowing face as he awaited her response.

"I'm quaking like a sapling in a windstorm," she admitted.

Kellen smiled and his tense body seemed to relax. "Then perhaps I can prescribe some libation to help alleviate this nervous malady of yours. A glass of wine should serve nicely." He prepared to fetch the suggested beverage, but Erin made a fleeting gesture to forestall him.

"What are you drinking?"

"Whiskey."

"Then that is what I shall have," she proclaimed.

Kellen frowned his uncertainty of her judgment. "Are you sure, little reb? You might find it a bit strong for your taste," he cautioned.

"Surely, a sip or two won't be so awful."

Erin observed as Kellen poured a small quantity of the liquid into a second glass, and she stepped around the desk to stand in front of him. Shyly, she accepted the glass that he proffered and, under his watchful eye, she lifted the vessel to her lips and drank. Almost immediately, Erin came to regret her impetuous decision, for her tongue fairly reeled with the pungent taste, but she bravely squared her shoulders and swallowed the fiery brew. The subsequent spontaneous reaction made Kellen chortle merrily, for her eyes filled with tears, and she was consumed by a spasm of coughing that caused her to double over. Placing a conciliatory arm about her shoulders, Kellen guided her toward a chair.

"Care for another glass?" he asked playfully.

Erin's sputtering came to an abrupt halt as she gazed up into her husband's mirthful face. "No, thank you. I wouldn't want to become addicted to the stuff."

"True." Kellen chuckled fondly at her banter. "Actually, I am feeling particularly neglectful, for a proper wedding night should doubtless include champagne."

"Oh, I drank quite enough of that at the reception," she chatted gaily, hoping that her quivering chin did not betray her. "Meredith is such an efficient hostess; the food was splendid and the champagne flowed endlessly."

"Yes, it was a grand affair," he concurred.

They both fell into an uneasy silence, Erin avoiding his intense gaze by pretending an inordinate interest in the carpet's design while Kellen turned his eyes toward the window. An interminable length of time had ticked away when, as luck would have it, the porcelain clock on the mantel began to chime the hour. No longer able to endure the thundering silence, Kellen went down on his knee before her, taking her hand gently in his.

"Erin, sweetheart," he began uncertainly. "It's all right. I mean, I understand if you'd rather not —"

He halted in mid-sentence, for Erin reached out to place a silencing finger against his mouth. "You don't understand, my darling." She meaningfully stroked the rugged contour of his face. "I think perhaps that I truly rather *would*. But first, I have something for you," she whispered mysteriously.

She withdrew a small jeweler's box from the package on her lap and lifted the lid to expose a handsome gold ring with an even more remarkable diamond setting.

"It belonged to Papa," she explained.

"It's certainly an impressive ring." He admired the gem. "But surely your father would have wanted one of his sons to have this."

"No, Mother's wedding ring will go to Evan's bride, and this," she took his right hand and gently pushed the ring onto the third finger, "is to be my husband's.

"There," she declared satisfactorily. "A perfect fit. I thought as much, for Papa had hands such as yours; large and strong."

"In that case, I shall be happy to accept your generous gift. However, I fear that you shall have to wait a day or two for your wedding present. When you see it, you will understand why I could not present you with it tonight." He laughed at the inquisitive frown that crinkled her brow, but Kellen bestowed upon her a look that warned he would brook no lengthy interrogation this night.

"Erin?" he murmured as he examined the ring thoughtfully, an enigmatic sparkle beginning to dance behind his brilliant blue eyes.

"Yes, dearest."

"If this is some sort of family tradition, am I to assume that a daughter of ours would inherit the ring to present to her husband on her wedding night?"

Erin nodded, causing her unbound tresses to flutter about her shoulders in a charming manner.

"Well, then," he leaned back, slapping his knee, "we must do all that is humanly possible to ensure that this marvelous custom does not expire with our generation." He favored her with an adoring look that made her shiver with its intensity. Then he stood and scooped her into his arms and swiftly carried her to their chamber.

The bedclothes had been turned back by the maid, so Kellen wasted little time settling his agreeable burden against the pillows. Then, he, too, sat down on the edge of the bed. Neither of them spoke, but when his hands began the meticulous task of undoing the various ribbons and sashes that bound her nightclothes to her, Erin placed her hands on his to protest.

"The light. Please," she begged.

Kellen could understand his bride's shyness, but he was not willing to completely deny himself the luxury of beholding her splendid body. To compromise, he reached across her and dimmed the bedside lamp, so their first encounter might not be a glaring embarrassment for her, yet it set off their silhouettes in enticing shadows.

"Better?"

"Yes," she answered, hardly aware that she had spoken, for Kellen's hands had resumed their inquisitive exploration of her youthful body.

With an ease she did not recognize as expertise; the result of experience, Kellen managed to slip her nightdress up and

324

over her head, then casually discarded it on the floor beside the bed. Erin lay motionless while the blue eyes traveled over her exposed flesh; so forceful was his perusal that Erin could almost feel the trail they blazed.

They started at her eyes, then slowly wandered downward across her plentiful bosom, the tips of which were already taut with anticipation of what was yet to come. Further downward they roamed, sweeping past the flat stomach to the softly rounded hips, further still to the wondrous triangle that gave way to the shapely legs and ankles, finally pausing at the perfectly shaped toes to exhale a very shaky breath. As if he wanted to ensure that he had not overlooked even a single inch of the exquisite vision, his eyes leisurely and carefully retraced their journey.

When his eyes once again held hers, he murmured huskily, "You're even more beautiful than I imagined."

Erin found herself blushing under his lavish appraisal and, a little uncertain as to what was expected of her, she extended her arms and timidly pulled his head down until their lips caressed. He kissed her gently at first, but as his passion became more acute, so did the fervency of his kiss.

Erin was in a state of blissful euphoria as Kellen's masterful exploration left her flushed with excitement. Purposefully, Kellen's strong arms encircled her, pulling her against him. As his hands became familiar with the supple flesh along her back, his lips began to map out a trail from her mouth to her throat, gently nibbling a sensuous path to the tempting mounds that proved to be his ultimate destination.

Kellen moaned his delight as the pink tips responded to his practiced ministrations and, with a breathless sigh, he pushed away from her. Reaching out to smooth her cheek with the back of his hand, Kellen gazed at her longingly.

"Do you wish me to stop?"

"N-n-no," she stammered and, when she would have said more, he deftly silenced her with yet another kiss.

Then he pulled away and stood up to remove his own restrictive garments and, when he turned toward her, it was Erin's turn to intimately scrutinize her husband's naked physique. She could not prevent the little gasp that escaped her lips as she beheld the impressive sight.

Her demure gaze traveled from the blue eyes that regarded her speculatively to the broad shoulders, then to the long, sinewy arms, across the expansive chest that boasted a multitude of dark, curly hairs. She continued her perusal on downward across the trim belly to the muscular thighs, creeping back till they came shyly to rest on the already passion inflamed manhood that was obviously eager to proceed with the romantic interlude. Erin actually gulped as she tore her eyes from the intimidating spectacle; this glorious specimen that was her husband.

Laughing softly, Kellen stretched out on the bed beside her and pulled her into his embrace. Without hesitation, he resumed his intimate fondlings; touching her arms, her breasts, her thighs; expertly preparing her for the ultimate encounter that would truly unite them as man and wife. His lips traced a pattern of kisses from her mouth to her ear and, as he gently nibbled on the lobe, he whispered loving endearments as he carefully positioned himself above her.

Erin lay beneath him, her body a sensual bonfire of excitement. She felt his moist lips as they determinedly tugged at the nipple of one breast, the hand that slid along her waist while the other persistently urged her thighs apart. She delighted in the array of sensations that engulfed her, and she struggled to differentiate each one and store it in her memory, so that it might be savored at some later time.

Then suddenly, the moment she had once regarded with extreme trepidation came and went with just the slightest bit of discomfort tingling between her thighs. Glancing up into Kellen's awesomely handsome face, Erin thought she detected an undeniable frown. But the notion of questioning him quickly vanished, for she became keenly aware of a host of other sensations, and she felt him inside her; felt his powerful body as it began to move against hers.

Quite by instinct, Erin encircled his neck with her arms, and she clung to him fiercely as she struggled to match his motion. The faint whimpers of pleasure, echoing in the depths of her throat, grew into moans of heady rapture as Kellen continued to thrust deep within her, skillfully weaving an intoxicating magical spell that consumed her with its severity. Erin gave herself up to the flood of sensuous tremors that inundated her, and she had a strange feeling that she was about to experience some final, exquisite phenomenon when Kellen's body trembled suddenly, and the thrilling adventure came to an abrupt culmination.

Looking down into the luminous face that nervously avoided his penetrating gaze, Kellen placed a finger beneath her chin and gently persuaded her to look at him. "It can be uncomfortable at first," he whispered sympathetically, "but it will get better."

"But it . . . it was wonderful. *Truly,*" she assured him, the long, silken lashes fluttering closed to shield her eyes from his careful scrutiny, for she was more than a little embarrassed by her wanton admission.

Kellen chuckled at her response and, rolling to his side of the bed, he extinguished the lamp then returned to pull her into his arms. "Believe me, my love, it *will* get better." He lovingly stroked the luxurious tendrils that cascaded about her shoulders.

"But—"

"Shh," he commanded softly, but firmly. "Go to sleep."

"But my . . . my nightdress," she murmured pleadingly.

Again she heard the wicked chortle that rumbled in his broad chest. "Oh, my darling, innocent wife. It shall be a very long time indeed before you require that particular garment again." He wrapped her more securely in his embrace, and held her in his arms until she drifted off to sleep.

But Kellen did not quickly succumb to a restful slumber, for his mind was astir with a sorely perplexing development.

He lay on his back, his arms folded behind his head, as he thoughtfully studied the flickering shadows that the moonlight cast across the ceiling. His face was an unreadable mask of somber contemplation, as he reflected upon the discovery that the evening had wrought. Erin had come to him a virgin, for there was no denying the slight, albeit, unmistakable resistance he had encountered during their first coupling.

"But how can that be?" he mumbled beneath his breath. "Certainly, she would have no reason to contrive such a horrendous tale." He mentally recalled the nightmares that had tormented her at Kilkieran. "No, she truly believes that she was raped."

Thoroughly puzzled, Kellen rolled to his side and rested on one elbow above his slumbering bedmate. Peering down into the flawless features, Kellen plucked a heavy curl from her shoulder and gently traced a fleeting pattern along her cheek.

"What *really* happened to you, little reb? What took place that was so dreadful that you would prefer to believe your nightmares rather than the actual occurrence?" He brushed the curl against his lips before allowing it to slip from his fingers, and he sighed uneasily. "Perhaps this return visit to your home will turn out to be for the best after all. For the solution to this puzzle, as well as my own, doubtlessly lies there," he mused aloud and, dropping a kiss to Erin's brow, he rolled to his side and fell into a deep, comforting sleep.

Erin awoke the following morning with a startled gasp; more than a little disoriented by the unfamiliar surroundings, not to mention the impressive figure that lay serenely beside her. As her sleep-muddled head began to clear, she was consumed by a rush of delicious memories of the evening just spent. Savoring her recollections with languid contentment, Erin twisted to her side to steal a long, uninterrupted look at the man who slept peacefully beside her. It was difficult to imagine that this now sanguine figure had been the same who had lifted her to unimaginable heights of passion in the dark, lonely hours before dawn. She had pleasured him, too, she smiled coquettishly to herself, as she recalled his throaty cries of delight that still seemed to echo throughout the chamber and, vaguely, she wondered if she would ever experience that ultimate sensation that had consumed her husband.

Once again, her thoughts turned to Kellen, and her gaze focused on him. He lay on his back, one arm thrown carelessly across his chest, the other curled above his head. The sheet had been tossed aside in defiance of the sultry July heat, allowing Erin an unihibited view of his lean, powerful body. With a curious uncertainty, Erin extended her hand and traced an abstract pattern along the muscular shoulder, down his arm and across his broad chest. On impulse, she raised herself on her elbow and placed a fleeting kiss against his lips.

Even as she started to pull away, the sleeping figure began to stir and two brawny arms reached out to entrap her in their unyielding confines. Stealthily, one sun bronzed hand crept up her back to become hopelessly entangled in the heavy tresses that tumbled down her back. He gently forced her head down until their lips came together again in a more ardent encounter. When at last he permitted it, Erin drew away to observe the smugly satisfied grin that adorned Kellen's face.

"Good morning," she whispered faintly.

"Indeed. It certainly shows every promise of becoming one," he murmured huskily, as he allowed his hands to wander down her silken back to linger along the rounded curves of her bottom, which he proceeded to squeeze familiarly.

"Kellen!" she squealed in protest, as she tried to wiggle from his grasp.

Kellen, however, was not willing to relinquish the cherished possession, so he merely reaffirmed his grip and rolled with her until she lay beneath him. Erin was still very much an ingenue to the intimacies that a husband and wife shared, but one did not have to be an expert to recognize the passion that inflamed the blue eyes that presently burned into hers.

"You know, my lovely enchantress," his voice held a lazy, dulcet tone as his teeth nibbled provocatively at one inviting earlobe, "I could grow accustomed to awakening in just such a fashion."

"I fervently hope so, for I must warn you that I have not the slightest desire to go elsewhere." Erin wrapped her arms around his torso and ran her fingers along his back, reveling in the play of his hard, rippling muscles. "I fear that you are quite ensnared within my clutches."

"I assure you, madam, there is no other place I'd rather be." He kissed her upturned face and allowed his hands to begin a leisurely fondling of her supple flesh.

"Kellen!" She endeavored to remain nonchalant though it was apparent that her resiliency was rapidly crumbling. "Is it not time for breakfast?"

"Later."

"But . . . but, aren't you hungry?"

"Oh, my darling." He chuckled earnestly. "I'm positively ravenous, but no mere mortal cuisine can compare with the ambrosia I presently have before me."

Erin giggled merrily at his rhetoric, but her laughter halted abruptly with a hoarse intake of breath, and her eyes flew to her husband's dancing ones. As their eyes locked together, Kellen's adept hand began to meticulously stroke the sensitive area between her thighs that his nimble fingers had instinctively captured.

With considerable effort, Erin tore her eyes from his and allowed herself to wallow in the sensual frenzy he masterfully summoned within her. But when Kellen's own desire grew too great to withstand, he took her with a fierce passion that made her cry out with unbelievable pleasure. Erin reached out to clasp him to her, and she lurched upward to crush her breasts against his hard chest, as though she would meld their bodies into one, undefinable configuration.

Kellen reveled in the wild abandon she exhibited, and he

slipped his arm beneath her hips and pulled her against him, instructing her in the motion she should follow to achieve maximum enjoyment. Then, somewhere in the midst of this sensual upheaval, Erin became aware of a faint pressure deep within her. It was just a scant bud that began to blossom and grow, spreading out to encase her with a fiery splendor that suddenly erupted into a glorious explosion of incredible sensual satisfaction.

During the course of the amorous interlude, Erin's rather subdued murmurings grew into obvious moans of contentment that finally culminated with an unmistakable cry that made her partner realize that she had at last experienced the ultimate joy of womanhood. Drawing her closer to him, Kellen relaxed his furious pace and his movements became more rhythmic and methodic. Erin braced her arms against his broad shoulders as she continued to strain against him, her heart pounding wildly in her chest. And it seemed an eternity later before Kellen, too, found blissful release and came to an exhausted rest atop her, his flaming passions temporarily satiated.

Staring down into the beautiful face, Kellen favored her with a knowing smile. "I told you it would get better," he reminded her, a roguish chuckle reverberating in his chest.

Erin returned the smile and tightened her arms about him possessively, wishing that the moment might never end. "So you did," she murmured shyly, then more reasonably, she added, *"Now,* shall we have breakfast?"

They dined on a delicious breakfast of ham and eggs, freshly baked biscuits that were accompanied by an assortment of jams and jellies, and they topped off the meal with a bowl of fresh fruit. It seemed to Erin that her spouse barely took note of the scrumptious victuals, however, for his head was buried in the morning paper. Erin watched in mild amusement while the large hand groped for the coffeepot, the blue eyes still glued to the news of the day.

With a small sigh, Erin reached across the table to push aside the faltering appendage and filled his coffee cup for yet a third time. As though suddenly aware of his oversight, Kellen folded the tabloid and tossed it aside.

"Forgive me, darling," he glanced at her impishly, "but, I fear, some old habits are difficult to break. You shall have to launch a dauntless campaign if you are to properly train me to be a suitable mate."

"No need." She shrugged indifferently. "Lest you forget, we shall be leaving for Kilkieran day after tomorrow. You'll not find daily newspapers so readily available. It is lamentable, I know," she forced a sympathetic lilt into her voice, "but you shall have to content yourself with staring at my plain face across the breakfast table."

"A sight that shall never cease to delight me, I assure you, my pet." His hand stretched across the table to encircle hers. "Have you any idea how much I love you?" he asked softly.

Erin's eyes suddenly glistened with unshed tears as she responded to the look of pure adoration with which he favored her. Swallowing the sob that threatened to choke her, Erin returned his impassioned gaze and nodded slowly. "Yes, I believe that I do."

But further discourse was made impossible, for Chin Li chose that particular moment to inquire after the couple's needs. The intrusion lasted only a few moments, but it was long enough to shatter the captivating spell that had previously enveloped them. Returning his attention to his breakfast, Kellen cleared his throat and endeavored to embark upon a less romantic conversation.

All too soon the delightful encounter came to a conclusion, for Kellen stood to announce that he had several business matters to address before they could depart for Kilkieran. Erin watched as he disappeared inside their chamber and, with a morose shrug of her shoulders, she dabbed at her lips with the linen napkin, then rose and silently followed him into the room.

Kellen had already donned his trousers and was shrugging into a snowy white shirt when Erin entered the room. He observed her humdrum expression in the mirror's reflection where he stood combing his hair; a futile gesture since the unruly mane seemed to have a will of its own. Kellen continued to watch her as she wandered about the chamber, undertaking a number of trivial tasks; rearranging the flowers in a vase on the whatnot table in the corner, and meticulously folding a shirt that he had discarded for the laundry.

With an amused shake of his head, he concluded his personal grooming and stepped across the room to pull her into his arms. "What's this?" He cupped her chin in his hand and forced her to look at him. "Can it be that you find life with me tedious after but a single day of wedded bliss?"

Kellen received a sunny smile for his efforts at cajolery, but Erin was quick to assure him that she found no displeasure with his company. "Don't be silly," she chided him, gently extricating herself from his grasp. "It's just —"

But the explanation for her melancholia died upon her tongue when, as she turned, her eyes came into contact with a blotchy stain that blemished the sheets of the unmade bed. Erin unwittingly emitted a garbled cry while one hand shot out to grasp the bedpost for support.

Kellen, aware of the untimely discovery, stepped forward to offer her comfort. "Honey," he murmured softly, placing a hand upon her shoulder.

Kellen, however, was unprepared for Erin's vehement response as she jerked away from him, viciously slapping aside the compassionate hand he proffered. *"You knew!"* she rasped hoarsely. "Why . . . why did you not tell me?" She glared at him accusingly.

Kellen, momentarily stunned by the severity of her assault, was no less harsh with his vitriolic retort. "Forgive me my oversight, madam, but I was quite *preoccupied* at the time of my . . . er . . . discovery, and a declaration of your virtue was quite the last thing on my mind," he drawled glibly.

Kellen noticed her cringe at his rhetoric, but he was unable to refrain from one last sarcastic jibe. "Take heart, Erin. I'd wager that many a damsel would be delighted to show her husband such overwhelming proof of her innocence."

Kellen heard her strangled cry of anguish, and his behavior altered accordingly. Upon further contemplation of her chagrined face, he silently admonished himself for his impulsive words. "I'm truly sorry, angel. I did not mean to screech at you. It's just that I love you beyond distraction; I care not about what lies in your past." His voice was soft and held a distinctive quiver and, thinking it might be wise to leave her to her suffering, Kellen prepared to leave.

He had taken but two steps, however, when Erin's faltering admission halted him in mid-stride. "And I *adore* you." Her knees buckled beneath her, forcing her to sink down upon the bed. "But don't you understand what this means? The Yankees did not . . ."

Finding herself unable to complete the staggering realization, Erin covered her face with her hands and succumbed to the rush of tears that engulfed her. "Oh, why can't I remember what truly happened that dreadful day?" she sobbed uncontrollably.

Kellen carefully retraced his steps and, sitting down beside her, he tenderly coaxed her into the shelter of his secure embrace where he nestled her against him and murmured comforting endearments in her ear. "Shh, my darling. Perhaps one day you shall remember, but try not to think of it now. It sorely distresses me to see you in such turmoil."

"But . . . but my nightmares," she persisted. "They seem so real; they *are* real!" she cried, burying her face in the fold of his shirt.

"Dreams often appear frightfully accurate," he agreed. "But the fact remains, my little reb, that you were somehow rescued from the terrifying ordeal, yet your mind continues to play you a cruel trick. Do your nightmares still haunt you?" he asked quietly, smoothing the hair from her tear streaked face.

Erin gratefully accepted the handkerchief he proffered, and she hurriedly blotted away the tears that streamed down her cheeks before she answered him. "No," she admitted. "Not since the night you rescued me from the bandits."

Satisfied that she had sufficiently recovered her equanimity, Kellen stood to button his shirt. "If memory serves me, that is the night you agreed to be my wife. Perhaps," his voice grew suddenly tender, "your acceptance of my proposal was a portent of things yet to come. For surely you must realize that keeping you safe shall be my utmost concern from now on. And that, my lovely, includes protecting you from your nocturnal apparitions."

He walked over to her and gently pulled her to her feet. "I have to go. Are you going to be all right?"

In response, Erin summoned a fleeting smile and nodded briskly.

"Good. I hate to leave you, but it cannot be avoided." He slipped his broad shoulders into his coat and stooped to place a parting kiss upon her generous mouth. "I'll send Renée to prepare you a warm bath and, when I return, we'll go for an afternoon drive in the park and dine out this evening. I know just the place to accommodate star-crossed newlyweds like ourselves. Then, tomorrow we shall undertake the monumental task of purchasing supplies and any gifts you might like to take home to your family. Does that sound pleasing to you?"

"Yes, Kellen," she murmured softly.

Erin watched as he gathered his personal effects from the dressing table and sauntered toward the door. Enveloped by a staggering sense of contentment, Erin wandered to the window where she stood till she saw Kellen emerge on the street below her. How like him to take command, to be in complete control of every situation, she thought admiringly. A somber frown suddenly flickered across her pretty face as the full impact of her married status registered, and Erin realized that she would gladly face the days ahead with Kellen by her side, regardless of what may lie before them. He was so wonderful, and they were blissfully happy; if only life could remain thus uncomplicated.

The night before their scheduled departure for Kilkieran, Erin found that sleep would not come easily. She no sooner shifted to one position than she would tire of it and flop on her side, her back, or to her stomach, creating a most distracting bouncing motion that made her husband vaguely wonder if he had taken a jackrabbit for a wife. Needless-to-say, it was an excessively weary Kellen who came face-to-face with a wide-eyed Erin as both of them rolled toward the center of the roomy bed at the very same moment.

"Erin, my sweet." Kellen propped an elbow against his pillow, arching one eyebrow into an indulgent scowl. "Does *something* pain you, or is it your customary habit to thrash about like a dying fish out of water?"

Erin was instantly all contrition as she hastened to express her apology. "I'm sorry, Kellen, but for some reason, I cannot seem to fall asleep. Did I wake you?" she inquired considerately, reaching out to caress the worn lines around his eyes.

"No," he responded truthfully, "for every time I would be on the verge of sleep, the bed would begin the most annoying motion." A wolfish grin suddenly parted his lips and, even in the dimly lighted room, Erin could detect the wicked sparkle in the blue eyes that lovingly regarded her. "Since I appear destined to forego sleep this night, I should think it only fitting that she who is responsible for my discomfiture provide me with some form of *entertainment*." He shrewdly pulled her into his arms and lowered his head toward her, his intentions quite obvious.

"Not again!" she roared, feigning disdain at his amorous

conjecture. "I should think that you'd had your fill of *that* for one night."

"Never!" he cried and, bellowing mightily, he buried his head in the heavy tendrils that cascaded across her shoulders, nipping at the white skin that lay underneath.

In retaliation, Erin playfully sank her teeth into the sensitive flesh of his earlobe and, when he jerked away in surprise, Erin tweaked his nose and started to roll away from him. Kellen recovered quickly, however, and two strong arms clamped about her tiny waist and propelled her backwards.

"So, my naughty miss wishes to play." His hoarse chuckle rumbled in his throat and, before she knew what was happening, Kellen delivered a half-hearted slap across her rump.

"Kellen!" she screeched in abject indignation.

Further remonstration was made quite impossible, for Kellen abruptly flipped her over and the couple proceeded to roll and cavort about on the bed like uninhibited wild things. Their laughter echoed throughout the chamber, and it was several minutes before they concluded their gamboling and came to a breathless halt; a blissful configuration of intertwined naked limbs.

Erin lay sprawled across his chest, her hair spilling across her face in tangled disarray. Kellen's loving hands lifted to brush the hair into place, and he gasped in surprise as Erin lurched forward to kiss him with an innocent thoroughness he had only dreamed possible. When she pulled away, Erin folded her arms on his broad chest, cupped her chin in her hands, and gazed at him contentedly.

With a languid sigh, she breathed, "Shall it always be like this?"

"I hesitate to disillusion you, pet, but knowing that Irish temper of yours, I feel certain that we'll have our share of disagreements. In fact—"

"My temper!" She jutted out her lower lip in an exaggerated pout.

"In fact," he reiterated, "there will probably be occasions

when you rue the day you married me." He noted with fondness the insistent shake of her head, and he wrapped his burly arms about her and held her tightly against him. "But I can promise you this; I'll never cease to love you as much as I do at this moment," he murmured softly, gently running his hands up and down her back.

"You're uncertain about returning to Kilkieran, aren't you?" he whispered suddenly, reasonably confident that he had correctly guessed the basis for her restlessness.

"I suppose so." Erin nodded reluctantly, forever surprised by his uncanny ability to read her thoughts.

"Ah, I see. You're afraid the locals might turn on you for attaching yourself to a good-for-nothing *Yankee.*"

"Just as long as *you* don't turn against me." She snuggled against him.

"You need never concern yourself on that score," he said, continuing to stroke the velvety soft skin along her back.

Neither of them spoke for a long time and, just when Kellen decided that she must have drifted off to sleep, Erin stirred, a sudden thought prompting her to ask, "When did you realize that you had fallen helplessly in love with me?"

There was an airy inflection in her voice, but Kellen could feel the tenseness in the little body that was entwined with his, and he knew that his answer meant a great deal to her.

He laughed at the impish smile she turned on him and shifted to a more comfortable position before he attempted to reply. "Well, let's see." He thoughtfully stroked his chin. "You would not believe me if I said that I have loved you from the moment I first clamped eyes on you; though I must confess that I was definitely fascinated after our first encounter. I'll never forget the way your green eyes spewed daggers at me, nor the defiant way you wielded your father's ancient rifle. And how could I forget the spiteful way you glared at me and called me *Yankee?*" He chuckled to himself. "Then, there was that memorable morning I awakened from my fever to discover a rather fetching vision stretched out beside me; *au na-*

turel, I might add. I must admit that my interest piqued considerably after that."

"Cad!" she scolded him. "How like you to remind me of *that* embarrassing incident."

Kellen pecked her tenderly on the nose, his countenance growing abruptly serious and, when he next spoke, Erin knew that he was sincere.

"I cannot pinpoint the exact moment of my total capitulation," he murmured honestly. "I only know that I awakened one day to the realization that I never wanted to face a future that did not include you."

"I love you, too, you know," Erin whispered softly. "I think perhaps that you knew it before I admitted it to myself." She pushed away from him to slide to her own side of the bed, cradling her pillow against her. "I think I can sleep now. It's a relief to know that nothing my family might do or say can destroy our love for one another."

The words were barely from her lips when Kellen heard the rhythmic sound of her breathing; an indication that she had finally succumbed to a peaceful slumber.

Chapter Seventeen

Despite their restless night, Kellen and Erin were up early the next morning to begin their rigorous excursion. Erin was to quickly learn that her husband did not dawdle when preoccupied with matters involving an extensive journey. Therefore, with much cajolery and prompting from him, Erin found herself descending the stairs on Kellen's arm, and being handed into their waiting conveyance less than two hours after being rousted from her comfortable bed.

Their entourage consisted of two carriages; Erin and Kellen occupied the lead vehicle, along with a goodly portion of their luggage. The second carriage held the remaining trunks and baggage, as well as Renée and Chin Li. Erin had protested about dragging Renée away from Meredith, insisting that Maisie could sufficiently care for her needs once they reached Kilkieran, but Kellen had remained adamant. Consequently, there was little for Erin to do save yield to his wishes.

As she was being escorted toward the carriage, Erin noticed with some interest that Achilles was tethered to the rear vehicle, though he was obviously none too pleased with this restriction, for he whinnied and pranced about, nervously chomping at the bit. Following one prodigious snort from the indignant animal, Erin was prompted to comment, "Achilles appears to be somewhat skittish this morning. Are you not going to ride him?"

"Later, perhaps." Kellen flashed her a wily smile. "We have another stop to make before we can fully embark on our journey. Until then, I shall content myself to ride inside with you."

It was then that she thought to question him about Lady's whereabouts, but Kellen had turned to converse with the drivers of both vehicles. And by the time he had completed issuing last minute instructions to his housekeeper and the manager of The Sinclairian and climbed in beside her, the errant mare had slipped from her thoughts.

A few moments later, the carriage began to roll forward and Erin settled back against the cushioned squabs, resigning herself to the long, tedious journey that lay before them. Without really thinking of her actions, Erin reached beside her to take Kellen's hand in hers, and casually inquired, "How far shall we travel today?"

Erin, believing that she had voiced a perfectly valid question, was in a quandary to understand her husband's comical reaction, for he threw his head back and literally howled, his laughter filling the tiny compartment. Casting him a stern look, she stated baldly, "I fail to see the basis for these histrionics, Kellen." She tried to extricate her hand in a peevish gesture, but he held her steadfastly.

"How like you to ask when we shall be stopping for the night when we have barely begun our travels," he explained his outburst, then leaned closer to whisper a wicked suggestion in her ear. "Dare I hope that your zeal stems from an eagerness to be held in my arms again? For, if that be the case, I can assure you that we need not postpone our frivolity. As you can see, we are quite concealed and can safely while away our confinement in any number of pleasurable pastimes."

Erin had understandably felt herself flush when Kellen began his nefarious speech, but by the time he concluded the scandalous proposition, her cheeks were as red as the scarlet plume that adorned her stylish bonnet. Assuming a composed hauteur, Erin carefully retracted her hand and made quite a fuss about brushing a piece of nonexistent lint from the skirt of her traveling gown. She fought to retain an affronted mien, but, if truth were told, she found his rhetoric quite diverting. But after all, they were still newlyweds, and she did not want him to think her a total wanton. Therefore, Erin primly folded her hands in her lap and cleared her throat before attempting to address him.

Yet, despite her efforts, Erin found herself squirming under his close scrutiny. "Pray, do not concern yourself with my entertainment. Meredith had the foresight to loan me several books and, of course, I brought my needlework along to help me pass the time."

"Yes," Kellen chuckled wryly. "I can certainly understand why you would prefer pricking your fingers in a jostling carriage to my lovemaking."

"Must you speak of it in such casual terms?" Erin softly chastised him, and, though her voice was not terse, Kellen detected its somber inflection. He had to strain to hear her remaining discourse, however, for Erin's gaze had fastened on the passing landscape. "I truly cherish the times that you and I are . . . are together." She lowered her head shyly. "Indeed, I hold them most precious and dear."

"And you must think me the most odious, inconsiderate of creatures to appear indifferent about our intimate life," he interpolated.

Erin favored him with a lopsided grin. "Well, not *odious*, perhaps."

"Then I shall strive to be a more considerate husband, my love." He patted her knee affectionately, then averting his attention to the morning paper that lay on the seat opposite them, he drew a heavy sigh and said, "Albeit, I must confess that you are much to blame for my lecherous tendencies." He adopted a nonchalant demeanor as he negligently scanned the headlines.

"*What!*" Erin drew herself up, offering him a reproving

glare. "What could you possibly mean by that remark?"

"Hmm?" He pretended to be particularly engrossed in his tabloid, and, without looking at her, he began to explain, "Well, you see, most newlywedded couples are granted an acceptable length of time following the ceremony to . . . uh . . . *cavort,* as it were, in blissful seclusion."

"You speak of a honeymoon, I believe," Erin said dryly, not for a moment duped by his shenanigans.

"Ah, yes; a honeymoon." Kellen snapped his fingers in exaggerated comprehension. "Quite a marvelous tradition, or so I am told. I fear that I shall never experience the luxury of such a custom, for here I am; a scant three days since I allowed myself to become shackled to a bewitching seductress, about to be foisted upon a bevy of in-laws who harbor no great affection for their *Yankee* relation." He assumed a wounded expression, as he endeavored to sound put upon.

"And how does your woebegone plight make *me* culpable for your lecherous antics?"

"Quite simple, my lovely." He turned his most beguiling expression on her.

"Oh?"

"Had I been permitted a respectable . . . er . . . *get acquainted* period, perhaps I would now be weary of holding you in my arms and could exhibit a proper enthusiasm toward this excursion. Yes," he nodded, warming to his own banter, "just think of all the pretty Southern ladies I've yet to captivate with my irresistible charm," he boasted, meticulously refolding the paper, preparing to toss it onto the seat.

But the journal was not to be thus discarded, for Erin snatched it from his hand and began to pummel his unsuspecting head with earnest vigor. "Grow tired of me, will you?" she cried with feigned perturbation. "I'll show you, my pompous blowhard. In case you have failed to notice, I'm no missish schoolgirl who will tolerate a philandering husband."

Throughout her outburst, Erin continued her merciless assault, but, with minimal exertion, Kellen managed to render his assailant defenseless. The unread paper fell harmlessly to the floor of the carriage as Kellen purposefully pulled her toward him, a distinctively roguish expression highlighting his handsome face.

"Missish? You? Ha!" he fairly howled. "No, princess, that is a term I can safely wager no one has ever directed toward you. You're a troublesome wench, that's what you are, and I'll tell you this, my beautiful spitfire." Erin's half-hearted struggles came to an abrupt halt as she felt the warmth of his sigh a mere breath's pace from her lips. "I've known from the moment I first laid eyes on you that you would be a handful for any *normal* man," he whispered huskily. "How lucky for you that I happened along when I did."

"Humph!" Erin scoffed, though she made no effort to wrench herself from his grasp. "I suppose you feel that you've made quite a noble sacrifice; saving the general male population from such a bothersome female." She hunched her shoulders and stuck out her lower lip in an obvious pout.

Kellen chortled heartily at the picture of righteous indignation she presented, and, giving a bemused shake of his head, he murmured tenderly, "I must love you quite dearly to be willing to suffer such abuse. It's fortunate that you have one or two redeeming virtues that make the effort worthwhile." He smiled at her fondly while one hand automatically lifted to caress her cheek.

"What?" she asked glumly.

"Well, for instance, you have the most kissable mouth; especially when you insist upon thrusting out your lower lip as would a chastised youngster." Kellen fastened his arms about her in a secure embrace. "Tell me, wife, would I be forever branded a boorish lecher if I enticed a kiss from you?"

"I shouldn't think that one kiss would matter very much," Erin said softly, lifting her face for the promised endearment.

As their lips touched, Kellen heard her sweet sigh of languor as she nestled comfortably against him. Erin, however, was oblivious to everything except the pressure of his mouth and the protective grip that melded her to him. But somewhere in the foggy recesses of her contentment, she became vaguely aware of his expletive regarding her headgear, and, in the next instant, the fashionable accessory was sent spiraling to the floor.

While the conveyance continued its leisurely pace away from the awakening city, the couple inside concluded their romantic interlude, completely unaware of the events that were currently being planned that would severely test the depths of their love.

On the crest of a hill on the outskirts of Washington, a lone rider diligently prodded her mount along a deserted road. Few travelers were out and about at this early hour; that is precisely why the woman had chosen the secluded location for her clandestine rendezvous. Realizing that she was late, she spurred her mount into a swifter gait until she reached a trail that led deeper into the forest. She followed this route to a fork in the road, then selected the lesser traveled path without the slightest hesitation.

A quarter of an hour later, after dodging tree limbs that scraped at her face and arms and nearly being scared witless by a fox that skittered across the road before her, Vanessa Sinclair guided her mount into a clearing and jumped down from her perch to run into her waiting companion's arms.

"I'm sorry to be so late, darling," she hastily apologized, noticing the impatient gleam in the brown eyes that fastened on her. "But I waited to make certain that our travelers departed on schedule."

"Did they?" asked the emotionless voice.

"They were on their way by seven o'clock." She laughed smugly. "The new bride must be anxious to show off her fine catch to her family." She pulled away from him and went to retrieve the rolled blanket from her saddle.

"Could be," the man mumbled in agreement.

His attention was drawn to Vanessa, who had spread the blanket on the ground and stood beckoning him toward her. With an amused chuckle, the brown-eyed man began to saunter in the direction of the attractive woman.

"I'm curious, Vanessa. Does Geoffrey even suspect your . . . uh . . . *exploits?*"

"My husband thinks of nothing but his work, *and* producing the first male heir, so that he may thwart Kellen in their quest for control of the Sinclair enterprises," she added sullenly. "And, if you'd strive to be a bit more accommodating this morning, we should get to work on the latter."

"You know what the doctors have said," the man reminded her. "The chances of your bearing a child are —"

"Doctors, *doctors!*" Vanessa spat hatefully. "Are they never wrong?" she demanded hotly. "If our plans are not to go awry, I must have a child. *I must!*"

"And so you shall, sweetheart." Vanessa found herself being pulled into her lover's arms. "Besides, there are ways to obtain children without needlessly disfiguring this lovely body," he said vaguely, then more bitterly, he added, "That old coot certainly made a shambles of our carefully conceived scheme when he announced how his successor would be named. It would have been much simpler had Geoffrey received the entire inheritance." He bent over her and kissed her with a ruthless passion, and, when he would have walked away, Vanessa clung to him.

"You cannot mean to leave me now!" she cried in disbelief.

"As much as I'd like to spend the morning languishing in your arms, I fear that I must be off."

"But Br—"

"*Don't,* Vanessa!" The man gripped her arm hurtfully. "I need to keep an eye on our quarry." He released her abruptly and ambled across the clearing to his horse.

Vanessa raced after him. "But, why are you following Kellen to Virginia?"

"Let's just say that I left some unfinished business there,

and I need to make sure that Mr. Kellen Sinclair doesn't go sticking his nose where it doesn't concern him." He adeptly climbed atop his mount.

"And if he does?"

"Then I suppose I shall have to cut if off," he stated matter-of-factly. "Go home, Vanessa. I'll get in touch with you some-how, and let you know how our scheme progresses, and how you can help bring about its successful completion."

With that optimistic declaration, the mysterious brown-eyed rider blew her a fleeting kiss, then he coaxed his horse into the forest. Vanessa watched him disappear into the thick foliage, a serious frown tugging at her pretty face. If only she could feel as confident that their plans would not go amiss.

Erin wandered along the drive that led to Arcadia, aim-lessly dangling her bonnet by its ribbons as she patiently awaited the reappearance of her husband. Kellen had insisted on this stop, explaining that he could not leave for an ex-tended period of time without first checking on his stables and the progress of the house that was under construction.

The sudden sound of hammering diverted Erin's gaze to-ward the massive structure that was beginning to evolve, causing her to muse aloud, "Whatever possessed him to build such a monstrosity?"

"Perhaps he intends to fill its spacious chambers with chil-dren," answered an amused voice behind her.

A crooked smile fashioned upon her lips as Erin turned to stare up into the pair of radiant blue eyes that gazed lovingly into hers. "Building an orphanage, are you?" she quipped.

Recognizing the playful lilt in her voice, Kellen adopted a similar mien. "No, imp. It shall be my *wife's* responsibility to accommodate me on that score. Remember that, and strive to do an adequate job, else I might be persuaded to find myself a more indulgent companion." He tweaked her nose and turned to lead her back toward the overseer's cottage, but Erin remained rooted to the ground.

Kellen turned to her, completely ignorant of the fact that his candid speech had inadvertently jolted Erin's memory of the contract that Jeremiah had forced upon her. Totally incognizant of her harried expression, Erin's hand flew out to clutch his sleeve.

"What is it, honey?" He gave her a curious look, then added tenderly, "If it's about what I just said, surely, you must know that I was merely joking."

"I know," she murmured low, but there was a distinctive glimmer of doubt shrouding her green eyes when she lifted them to his face. "But I *do* want to have your children."

"And so you shall, my darling, but there is no great rush. After all, we've not been married a week. We have plenty of time to plan a family. Let's get to know one another first, shall we?" He patted the hand that still clung to his arm, and, placing his hand under her elbow, he coaxed her to walk with him. "Come along. I have a surprise for you."

Erin's apprehension was immediately replaced by her natural feminine curiosity, and she cuddled against him. "You have something for me?" she cooed, flashing him a coquettish smile.

"Yes, it's your wedding gift," he explained. "I mentioned such a token the other evening, but we became . . . ahem . . . *preoccupied* with other matters, and I daresay that it must have slipped your mind."

Erin heard his throaty chortle, but chose to ignore it. "What is it?" she inquired nonchalantly.

"Ah, piqued your interest, have I?" They had arrived at the cottage, but Erin was so engrossed in their discourse that she did not notice that another horse had been tethered beside Achilles. Kellen placed his hands on her shoulders and persuaded her to look up at him, and his voice was warm when he said, "What should make you happy?"

"I don't know," she replied honestly. "You've given me so

much already; I cannot think of anything that would make me happier than just being with you."

"Erin, you are like no other woman I know," he laughed good-naturedly, turning her so that the horses were in her line of vision. "I hope my choice pleases you. In truth, I was not certain as to the particular trifle a wife might enjoy, but I finally settled upon a duchess: a duchess for my princess," he added adoringly, bending down to kiss the top of her head. "Go make friends with her." He gently pushed her toward the animal.

Finally comprehending his purpose, Erin hurried forward to do as he suggested. Her voice was soft and gentle as she purred sweetly at the animal to gain her confidence, scratching it lovingly behind one ear. A bedazzling smile was Kellen's reward for his efforts when Erin turned to face him a few moments later.

"Is she truly mine? Did you say that her name was Duchess?" Her questions came in a breathless rush, as she again devoted her attention to the animal. "Isn't she a beauty?" she whispered whimsically, stroking the regal forehead.

"Yes; on all three counts." Kellen walked to stand between the two thoroughbreds. "I took the liberty of sending the carriages ahead, but it shouldn't take us long to overtake them. Would you care to ride?"

"I'd love to!" she replied happily, stepping toward him. "But first, I would like to thank you for my gift."

She reached up to encircle his neck with her arms and urged his head downward to allow her accessibility to the sensuous lips that eagerly awaited her caress. The couple remained thus engaged for quite some time, neither conscious of the construction workers who observed the scene in amusement. Indeed, had it not been for Achilles' rather impatient snort, the newlyweds would have been content to wile away several more minutes in just such a fashion.

Kellen reluctantly pulled away, though he continued to cradle her against him, and he breathed in her fresh, sweet scent.

Again, Achilles voiced his abject disapproval, causing his master to growl, "All right, Achilles. We're going." He carefully placed Erin atop Duchess, then went to settle himself astride his own surly mount.

"Oh, I nearly forgot," Erin commented. "What have you done with Lady?" She meticulously anchored her bonnet atop her coiffure while she awaited his response.

"Lady is receiving a much deserved rest." Kellen pointed toward an expanse of enclosed pasture, and, in the distance, Erin could make out the shape of her beloved horse running freely across the crest of a hill.

"She looks so happy; so . . . peaceful," Erin mumbled faintly.

"Then why do *you* look so glum?"

Erin gave her shoulders an allusive shake. "I suppose I feel guilty about leaving Lady behind when she could be so useful at Kilkieran. We have very little livestock, you know."

"You are not to worry your pretty little head over such niggling matters. Besides, perhaps you shall discover that circumstances are not as dire as when you left," he added enigmatically, nudging Achilles away from the tethering post.

Erin followed his lead, deciding to let the matter drop, but then another thought occurred to her, prompting her to inquire, "Are you satisfied with the progress they're making on your house?"

"*Our* house, darling," Kellen corrected her. "Yes, though I was disappointed that Brad was unable to meet with me. Apparently, there was a mix-up on some of the materials, and he stopped at the supplier to set things aright. What about you? Does Mrs. Sinclair approve of her future home?"

"It's truly magnificent. I shall love living here with you," she said adoringly.

"Good. Then, perhaps I can persuade you to undertake the task of decorating and furnishing our somewhat august domicile."

They had arrived at the end of the driveway and Kellen

drew his mount to a halt. Glancing askance at Erin, he could ascertain by her wistful expression that she found his suggestion most appealing. In fact, he was similarly correct in his assumption that ideas for color schemes, material swatches and furniture decor had already begun flittering through her head.

"I should like that very much!" she exclaimed with alacrity.

"I thought as much," Kellen groaned, fleetingly wondering if he had taken leave of his senses. "You must realize, sweetheart, that what I just offered you is the heart's delight of every woman, and every man's nightmare."

Erin had been about to follow Kellen onto the roadway, but the woebegone sound of his voice made her pause and gaze at him curiously. "Oh, and what might that be?"

"Unlimited utilization of her husband's pocketbook!"

Erin's pleasant laughter filled the air around them and, without further ado, she urged Duchess into a lively gait; passing Kellen to assume the lead. "Don't worry, dearest," she called over her shoulder, favoring him with a devilish smile. "I'm not likely to make you a pauper, *yet*."

Then, with a light tap of her riding crop across Duchess' rump, Erin spurred forward to create a wide void between them, knowing full well that Kellen would not permit it to remain so for long.

Maisie was the first to see the small assemblage slowly making its way up the long driveway in the late afternoon shadows. She had been sweeping the front porch when she became alerted to the carriage wheels on the drive, and had not been surprised when she glanced up to see the familiar figure on horseback who rode ahead of the two vehicles. Indeed, the only thing the old servant considered peculiar was the fact that her mistress did not ride beside her husband.

A brilliant smile beamed across Maisie's face as she scurried to fling open the front entrance to announce the arrival of their eagerly awaited guests. "Dey's hyah!" she proclaimed happily, then ran down the steps to be the first in line to greet the travelers.

"Hello, Maisie!" Kellen called cordially. "Bet you never expected to see my mangy hide again, did you?"

"Oh, yes, ah did. Massah Gra'am done tole me how you up'n married mah Miz Erin, but ah knowed it wuz a cummin', coz ah seen how you eyed her whilst you wuz hyah, mendin' yore busted leg," the old woman informed him baldly, looking past him to the approaching carriages. "Where iz she, Maj'r? How iz de chile?"

Kellen was about to reply to the sincerely expressed inquiry when a sudden commotion drew his attention toward the porch. The frown of dismay that shrouded his handsome face as he glanced over the reception line that formed to greet them did not go unheeded by the observant domestic, and Maisie hurried to offer an explanation.

"Dey just wanted ter welcum Miz Erin back home."

Kellen's shrewd gaze flitted across the line of spectators once more, and he scoffed openly when his eyes passed over Christina. "I daresay that some of them might not possess such a selfless kindred spirit in their motives for being here," he mumbled beneath his breath, and, stretching one leg up and over Achilles, Kellen lithely swung himself to the ground.

He tethered Achilles to the hitching post before turning to address Maisie again. "I recognize Graham, of course, but who are the other three?"

"Dat shy, li'le thing whut's shakin' lak she's about ter die from fright iz Miz Jenn'fer Wells, Miz Christina's friend."

"Ah, yes. I remember that she came to visit, though I never met her. Poor thing," he added sympathetically. "Does she think I mean to harm her?"

"Naw, dat's how she always acts. Dem othah two iz Miz Christina's mamma and papa."

"Philip and Lydia Richards?"

"Yes, Maj'r."

352

"Please, Maisie," Kellen laughed. "I'm no longer affiliated with the army; major no longer signifies."

"Whut should ah calls you den?"

"How about Mr. Sinclair, or perhaps you could be persuaded to address me as Mister Kellen. I should like that even better; it might make me feel more like family." He offered her a winning smile, but the arrival of the carriages made a worried frown reappear to mar his otherwise flawless features.

"Damn!" he swore softly, scanning the faces of the onlookers who lined the porch. "I had hoped this would be easy for her."

Turning again to Maisie, he confided in the faithful servant, "Maisie, I'm going to need your help. Your mistress is not feeling quite the thing today. Do you think that you can help me get her past that crowd without allowing them to further upset her? She needs to lie down and rest for awhile," he explained.

"You jest watch'n sees if ah cain't," Maisie replied determinedly. "Ah has always looked aftah Miz Erin, an' if rest iz whut de chile needs, rest iz whut she'll git!"

"I knew that I could depend on you," Kellen said warmly, as he turned to open the carriage door.

The ashen face that peered out at him was no less pale than when he had placed her inside that morning. "Come, sweetheart. You're home." He slipped a sturdy hand beneath her elbow and assisted her from the conveyance.

Erin gratefully accepted his strong, supportive arm about her waist, and she favored him with a faint, appreciative smile. The smile faded, however, when she noticed the group of well-wishers that waited to greet her.

"Oh, Kellen." She clutched his hand tightly. "I cannot face them; not just yet."

Kellen gave her waist a reassuring squeeze. "I know, honey. Just leave everything to me. Maisie is going to take you to our room, so that you may lie down and compose yourself. I'll make the necessary explanations to your family."

He nodded for Maisie to follow, then he escorted Erin onto

the porch, past the confused onlookers, and into the wide foyer. Erin did manage to murmur a faint greeting to her relatives before Kellen relinquished her into Maisie's capable hands, and she was whisked abovestairs to the peaceful quiet of her room without further ado.

Even before Kellen turned to confront his bewildered audience, he realized that the reception he was about to receive would be tenuous at best. Therefore, he decided that it would serve his frayed spirit to better advantage if he immediately took charge of the situation.

He turned slowly to face the group, and, without the slightest hesitation, he addressed them, "I must apologize, but the trip has been strenuous for Erin, and I fear that she is exhausted." Then to Graham, he said, "May I have a private word with you?"

"What's happened? Can it be that my cousin is already having second thoughts about marrying you, Yankee?" Christina's haughty question was meant to taunt him.

Kellen directed a stony gaze toward the speaker, but his mien remained undaunted. "Everyone is welcome to stay to supper. I'm certain that Erin will be sufficiently refreshed to receive you then." He indicated that the group should make themselves comfortable in the front parlor and motioned for Graham to follow him.

The two men walked in silence to the bluff overlooking the stream that flowed behind the august mansion. Suddenly, Kellen paused and knelt down along the precipice to pluck a wild flower, which he twirled loosely between his fingers while he stared thoughtfully into the depths of the shimmering water. Then, muttering a lugubrious sigh, Kellen heaved his broad shoulders and cocked his head upward, ready to speak to his brother-in-law.

"Has Erin discussed the events that transpired on the day of the raid with you?"

"So, *that* is what's troubling you." Graham's impassive face suddenly assumed an embittered shade of red, misconstruing the basis for Kellen's question. "None too pleased to discover that you've received damaged goods, are you? Well, you can thank your Yankee comrades for that!" he spat vindictively.

The expression that darted across Kellen's face was no less enraged than was the one that stared down at him. With an angry oath, he crushed the flower beneath his foot and stood erect to face Graham.

"First, Christina, and now you. I did not expect this to be a trouble free endeavor, but I had hoped to enlist your support at least, considering that we share a common dilemma."

"What do you mean?"

"Your wife, I believe, suffered a severe setback as a result of the events of that day," Kellen pointed out.

"The two situations are hardly comparable," Graham commented dryly. "Erin has nightmares, whereas, Deborah . . . well, it's just different," he muttered helplessly. "What's this all about anyway?"

"Contrary to Christina's lofty assumption, Erin's curious behavior is not to be attributed to any discord in our relationship," Kellen informed him matter-of-factly. "It all began yesterday when we stopped to have lunch. We were just concluding our meal when we heard the refrains of a marching band, and Erin became so excited to discover what was about that I let her run ahead to investigate while I settled the bill."

Kellen grew suddenly somber, and he clasped his hands behind his back in a furtive gesture, averting his gaze toward the distant horizon. "When I went to look for her," he continued, "I discovered that the festivities had ignited the town's interest, for the streets and sidewalks were crowded with curious spectators. It seems that a traveling troupe of some sort was setting up its tent show on the outskirts of the town, and they were staging the parade to drum up business.

"I had maneuvered my way through the crowd to find Erin just as one of the jesters ran up to her and began to prance about. He was wearing a hideously decorated mask, and, just as I reached her side, he jerked the mask away to reveal his grotesquely painted face."

"What happened?" Graham asked softly.

"The jester ran on his merry way to play his prank on some other unsuspecting onlooker, but Erin grew so pale and wan that I truly thought she was going to faint. She's been a jumble of nerves ever since, and, last night, her nightmares started again," he concluded his narrative on a solemn note, mentally recalling the anguished cries that had awakened him in the darkness.

"They had stopped?"

There was a lengthy pause, then Kellen nodded slowly and turned to face his brother-in-law, his expression grim. "Graham, Erin has told me all that she can remember of the incident, but yesterday's occurrence has got me thinking, and I am persuaded that *something* must be done to help release the girls from this mental turmoil that plagues them."

"What do you propose to do?"

"I don't know yet," Kellen responded honestly. "But, if a plan materializes, I would like to think that I could count on your assistance."

Graham's reply was momentarily preempted by a faint singsong voice that floated across the lawn to command their attention, and both men were drawn to watch the pathetic creature that ran in and out of the afternoon shadows, as she made her way toward the mansion. An understanding look passed between them, then Graham gave a curt nod of his head before he turned to follow his wife inside the plantation house.

Kellen hesitated in the hallway before the chamber that had been prepared for Erin and himself, and a roguish smile fashioned upon his lips as he entertained fond recollections of the last time he had occupied this particular room. Suddenly consumed by the desire to hold his wife in his arms, Kellen's hand

356

encircled the doorknob, but his amorous thoughts were quickly dashed when the sound of girlish laughter, emanating from within the chamber, enveloped his ears.

He opened the door to find Erin sitting up in bed, looking much improved, with Deborah perched on the edge of the structure, happily clutching a new poke bonnet to her bosom. Kellen was about to withdraw into the corridor, to allow the girls to complete their chat in private, when Erin spied him.

"Hello, darling," she called brightly, stretching out her hand toward him. "Do come join us."

Kellen could not help but notice the drastic change in Deborah's attitude, for her carefree smile immediately vanished upon his emergence upon the scene. With a speculative glance toward Deborah, Kellen quickly stepped across the room to place a tender kiss against Erin's brow.

"Feeling better?" he asked softly.

"Oh, yes! Deborah and I have been having a cosy talk, and I'm feeling much more the thing. Aren't you going to say hello to Deborah?" Erin offered him a beseeching smile, and Kellen could not refuse her.

Facing the timid girl, Kellen performed a gentlemanly bow and cheerfully said, "Hello, Deborah."

"Hello, Yankee," came the begrudging reply.

Kellen would have emitted a frustrated groan, but Erin quickly intervened. "Now, Deborah. You must remember what I've been telling you. Kellen is my husband; he's not the beastly ogre you believe him to be. Why, it was he who suggested that I bring you the pretty bonnet. Try it on and model it for us," she encouraged the girl, casting her spouse a hopeful look to enlist his support.

"By all means, please do," he responded to Erin's gentle prodding.

The look Deborah turned on Kellen was clearly distrustful, but her own wish to see herself in her new gift won out, and she meekly set the bonnet atop her head and began to fumble with the ribbons. "Could you help me, Erin? It's been so long

357

. . ." Her voice trailed off to a faint murmur.

"Here, let me." Kellen stepped forward abruptly. "I'm becoming quite adept at such formalities." His nimble fingers quickly completed the simple task, and he guided her to the mirror, so that she might survey his handiwork.

Kellen and Erin watched in silence as the girl carefully considered her reflection, and they observed the glimmer of tears that sparkled in her eyes when she lifted her hand to brush her fingertips against the mirrored image. Several moments lapsed before Deborah concluded her curious self-examination, and, when she turned to face them, there was a distinctively incandescent glow about her face that made Erin's heart leap for joy.

"Thank you, Erin," she whispered hoarsely, as her fingers lovingly stroked the broad silk ribbons, "and you too, Yank . . . uh . . . K-K-Kellen," she shyly altered her name selection. "Would you excuse me, I want to show Graham right away." She flew across the floor to enfold Erin in a clumsy embrace, then hurriedly scampered from the room.

"Oh, Kellen!" Erin looked at him excitedly.

"Don't rush it," he warned, correctly reading her thoughts. "And don't get those Irish hopes of yours up too soon."

"I won't," she promised. "But I do think that we can help her get better."

"Perhaps, but it will take a great deal of time to undo all that has happened."

"I realize that," she murmured, then a sudden thought caused her to clap her hands together gleefully. "I can hardly wait to give her the new dresses we brought her." She patted the space beside her as an indication that he should join her on the roomy berth.

Kellen did not wait to be invited a second time. He stepped to the bed and leisurely stretched out beside her, instinctively wrapping his arm about her shoulders. "Am I truly a beastly ogre?" he asked petulantly.

"No, silly. Deborah was merely a little frightened of you,

but things are sure to change if you just give it a little time. Besides, didn't you notice that she addressed you by your Christian name? That's quite a breakthrough in itself." She heard his disgruntled snort and cocked her head at an angle that allowed her to better scrutinize his face.

Reaching up to caress his cheek, she lovingly stroked the unbecoming frown that turned down at the corners of his sensuous mouth. "Poor darling. Has my family behaved badly toward you?" she whispered sympathetically.

"Not really, but I'd give a king's ransom to know what is going on behind the eyes of those who are presently ensconced in the downstairs parlor. I fear that if looks were lethal, you would have been left a widow upon our arrival." He shook his head lamely. "And you must remind me to ask Mother if I've been mistaken all these years, and she christened me *Yankee* at birth rather than Kellen." He gave a stoic chuckle.

"Poor darling," she repeated. "Is there anything I can do to compensate for my family's shabby treatment of you?" she purred suggestively, as she snuggled against him in the crook of his arm and turned her face up to receive the kiss she knew he would bestow upon her.

A mischievous twinkle immediately brightened the dull cast in his eyes as he warmed to her coquettish play. "I can think of perhaps one or two things." His mouth parted in a sinfully wicked grin, and he lowered his head to claim the lips that anxiously awaited his caress.

But a sudden, sharp knock at the abutting chamber door caused the couple to spring apart, startling Kellen so that he lost his balance and slipped from the bed to land on the floor with a resounding thud. Erin was immediately all concern, and she scrambled to her knees to see if he had injured himself in the fall. Her fears were quickly put to rest, however, for she could ascertain from the expression of pure outrage that adorned his face that only his masculine pride had suffered an injury. Erin clamped her hands to her mouth to smother the titter that threatened to bubble out, and she felt a genuine pang of remorse for the unsuspecting soul behind the door, who patiently awaited the summons to be acknowledged.

"Hell and damnation!" he thundered, and, jumping to his feet, he stomped to the door and jerked the barrier open. *"What is it?"*

It was a bewildered Renée who was the unfortunate recipient of this harsh greeting, and she shrank away visibly to perform a rather awkward curtsy before the enraged man. "B-b-beggin' your p-p-pardon, Mister Kellen, but Miss Erin asked me to wake her when it was time to get ready for the evening meal."

Erin noticed the frightened tears that filled the young servant's eyes, and she soundlessly slipped from the bed to stand beside the formidable figure that continued to glower at the helpless girl.

"Thank you, Renée," she said gently, offering the girl a comforting smile. "Be a dear and lay out the rose chambray gown, and I shall join you in a few minutes." She quietly returned the door to its former position, and, turning to rest her shoulders against the sturdy portal, she folded her arms across her bosom and settled a reproving look upon her husband. "Careful, my love, lest the servants label you with a term much worse than Yankee," she jokingly chastised him.

"I'm sorry," he mumbled, running a hand along the back of his neck in a frustrated gesture. "I don't know what came over me."

"I do." She took him by the hand and led him to a comfortable chair. Once he had seated himself, Erin moved behind him and began to massage the tenseness from his neck and shoulders. "It's called fatigue, and I know just the remedy. I'll summon Maisie to prepare you a nice, hot bath. Does that sound pleasing to you?"

"Only if you agree to stay and wash my back," came his nefarious reply.

"Another time, dearest," she promised, bending down to kiss his cheek. "Right now, I must see to Renée's wounded feelings and change for supper. Besides, Chin Li has been patiently waiting to unpack your things." She strode gracefully to the door, and, with her hand on the knob, she turned to face her taciturn counterpart. "Don't judge my family too harshly," she said softly. "Give them half a chance, and I know they'll warm up to you. I certainly did," she added shamefully, then slipped inside the adjacent chamber.

Erin had been wise in prescribing a soak in a hot tub for her husband, for his mood showed a marked improvement when she next encountered him. He stood before the cheval mirror, patiently retying the silk stock that refused to heed his diligent labors.

"Doesn't Chin Li do that for you?" She lounged in the doorway of the abutting chamber, a wifely smile dressing her face as her fond gaze drifted over him.

"No, I'm quite particular when it comes to my stock, but I seem to be all thumbs this evening." He abandoned his efforts in disgust and turned a waspish grin on her. "You go on without me. I sincerely doubt that I'll be missed in any case. Perhaps you could persuade Maisie to bring me the table scraps. I think she's beginning to like me."

"Of course, she likes you." Erin came into the room and walked over to him. "But you need not forego supper over this paltry matter; especially when you have a very capable wife." She pushed his fumbling hands aside and quickly accomplished the bothersome task. Then, she turned him around, so that he might view her expertise. "Does this meet your rigid standards?"

Kellen leaned closer toward the mirror and gave his appearance a thorough scrutiny. "Perfect!" he proclaimed, turning to favor her with an affectionate gaze. "However did you become so accomplished?"

"You forget that I come from a predominately male family," Erin reminded him, linking her arm in his and tugging him toward the door. "Many was the time I came to the rescue when clumsy fingers became entangled in their task," she chuckled softly, but her fond recollections halted abruptly when she noticed that Kellen made no effort to follow her.

Turning a quizzical expression on him, she found that his stormy gaze rested on the adjacent chamber, where Renée presently scurried about, putting things in order.

"Kellen?" she asked hesitantly, wondering what could be going on behind the turbulent blue eyes to cause such a sour countenance. "What's wrong, darling?"

"Nothing. I was just considering the thoughts of separate bedchambers," he remarked wryly. "How positively maudlin," he grumbled, as Erin laughed and pulled him out into the corridor. "Tell me, am I truly expected to honor such an archaic custom?" he asked peevishly.

"No, silly. I'm simply using the chamber as a dressing room. Lord knows, if we both tried to accomplish that feat in the same vicinity, we'd never be heard from again," she giggled delightfully, wrapping her arm more securely in his. "You're smiling again. Good. I'm afraid that I shall have to endure any number of gloomy faces across the supper table this evening. It's reassuring to know that there is one face that will not glower at me."

"It shall always be so, my pet." He patted her hand tenderly and escorted her down the wide, mahogany staircase.

They appeared in the drawing room just as Maisie arrived to announce that the meal was ready, therefore, Erin had but a moment to exchange greetings with everyone before being whisked away on Kellen's arm to the dining room. The meal progressed much more smoothly than Erin had imagined possible, and, aside from Christina's obvious distant countenance, she was quite pleased with the proceedings. She was spared from much of Christina's discourse, for Jennifer Wells sat beside her cousin, and the two girls seemed content to engage in quiet conversation throughout most of the repast.

Deborah had even joined the group at the table, and,

though she contributed virtually nothing to the conversation, Erin realized that this was an important step toward her eventual recovery. Graham seemed happy, too, and he displayed his satisfaction by including Kellen in the earnest discussion he was having with his Uncle Philip. The only blatant damper on the evening's festivities for Erin was the fact that Evan refused to acknowledge her homecoming, and had elected to dine alone in his chamber.

One problem at a time, she thought to herself, and, with a lighthearted shrug, she turned to her aunt to inquire, "How is Kevin getting along these days?"

"Quite nicely, thank you," Lydia replied. "You know, of course, that he and Charlotte were married just as soon as he returned from the war."

"Yes, and they're living in Richmond, I believe."

"That's right. Charlotte's family resides there, and they insisted that Kevin become a part of their business. I'm so —"

But further discourse was momentarily preempted by a thunderous crash that emanated from the second floor.

"Good heavens!" Erin literally jumped up from her chair. "What was that?"

"Evan," came Graham's complacent reply.

Erin was immediately full of concern for her impaired twin. "Do you suppose he's injured himself?" she asked anxiously, and was infinitely shocked that her family did not share her concern.

"Not likely," Christina scoffed.

Erin shot the girl a cold look, but the scathing retort she was prepared to unleash on her cousin was overruled when a second, more prodigious noise convinced Erin that something was terribly amiss abovestairs.

"Sit down, Erin," Graham advised softly. "I'm sure that Evan is all right. The servants are probably busy in the kitchen and haven't had time to take his supper up to him," he explained simply enough.

"What!" she demanded incredulously. "Does he never come to the table to receive his meals?"

"He never leaves his room at all," Jennifer informed her sadly.

"And you tolerate this behavior?" Erin threw her brother a critical look.

"He's an invalid, Erin," Graham replied helplessly.

"Fiddlesticks!" she snapped impatiently. "He's bamboozled the lot of you. Well, he shall presently learn that I will not fall victim to his shenanigans." Erin tossed her linen napkin onto the table and stalked determinedly toward the door.

"For pity's sake, Erin." This time, it was her uncle who addressed her. "The boy's been through a hell that you cannot possibly conceive. Can't you leave him to his misery?"

"That's just it, Uncle Philip. Evan is no longer a boy; he's a man. Granted, he's not the same man who went away from Kilkieran four years ago, but then the war has changed us all in one way or another," she said solemnly.

"James and Matthew were taken from me, but Evan was spared for some merciful reason, and I don't believe that it was to spend the remainder of his days wallowing in self-pity," she concluded brokenly, and, jerking the door open, Erin hurried from the room.

It happened that Maisie was just passing by the door with Evan's supper tray when Erin bolted from the dining room, and she surprised the old servant by snatching the tray from her hands and bounding up the stairs to confront her cloistered brother.

Chapter Eighteen

Erin did not truly know what she might expect when she hurled the heavy door aside, but the horrified expression that quickly masked her face clearly indicated that she was consummately shocked by the scene that gradually unfolded before her eyes. The chamber was in virtual darkness except for the light that filtered through the open entranceway, and, although her vision was somewhat impaired, Erin was distraught by what she could see.

Heavy, black draperies hung across the window, thereby, giving the room a semblance of intense foreboding. Articles of clothing lay strewn haphazardly about the room, while books, papers, and other notions showed every inclination of having received a similar dismissal. Moldy scraps of food sat in containers in various stations around the chamber, and bits of broken glass from discarded whiskey bottles cluttered the plush carpet.

The room itself reeked of a foul stench that Erin surmised must be the result of improper ventilation, coupled with the intermingling of odors that included spoiled food, whiskey, unwashed flesh, and human perspiration. In short, the chamber was in a state of chaos, and, though Erin was understandably thunderstruck, she became even more chagrined when her eyes finally came to rest on the pitiful figure who reclined against the headboard of the large bed.

At first, Erin believed Evan to be unconscious, for he had made nary a move since her appearance at the door, and she had remained in the entranceway for several moments while she surveyed the debacle before her. The figure on the bed did not remain complacent, however, when he realized that the unwelcome creature in the doorway was apparently intending to intrude upon his privacy. Bolting upward, he threw up a restraining hand to prevent any such maneuver.

"Leave the tray and take yourself off," he commanded gruffly in a voice that indicated he would brook no action to the contrary.

Erin made no effort to enter the chamber, indeed, she was so overwhelmed by the entire situation that she could barely find her tongue.

"Well?" he demanded. "Why do you stay?"

Erin swallowed hard, and the dishes on the supper tray jiggled noisily in reaction to her apprehension. "Evan," she spoke his name softly. "It's Erin. I've . . . I've come to —"

"*What? You?*" he screamed at her viciously.

Even in the semidarkness, Erin could detect the look of pure fury that distorted his face, and there was a savage hatred burning in the green eyes that raised their fulminating gaze to consider her.

"So, you've come sniveling back to the scene of your debauchery," he spat at her, his voice laced with contempt. "Well, don't expect me to welcome you and that Yankee bastard with open arms. Graham may do as he sees fit, but you can very well stay the hell away from me. I want no part of you!"

"Evan, please. I want to help —"

"I don't need your help!" he shouted bitterly. "And the only thing I *want* is to be left alone . . . completely alone. Can't any of you understand that? Go away! Just . . . just go away." His wrath apparently spent, Evan sagged back against the headboard.

But his anger was quickly rejuvenated when he noticed that his sister obviously refused to comply with his wishes, for she remained rooted in the doorway. With an infuriated oath, Evan rolled out of the bed and began to slowly drag himself across the floor toward the open portal.

Erin watched aghast as the invalid deliberately and purposely inched along the carpet, painfully dragging his body across the debris littered floor. The look of raw determination on his face made Erin's heart ache, and she longed to comfort him as she had done when they were children. But, just when she summoned the courage to step across the threshold, regardless of Evan's heated protestations, her brother arrived at the door and promptly slammed the barrier in her anguished face.

Erin stood as if in a daze, staring blankly at it, not fully believing the events that had just transpired. She vaguely became aware of voices in the corridor behind her, but still she remained immobile. Presently strong but gentle hands reached around her to relieve her of the supper tray that somehow had managed to survive the ordeal unspilled.

Kellen handed the tray to Maisie, and, placing a consoling arm around Erin's waist, he coaxed her away from the chamber. Erin's hand trembled on his arm as she struggled with the conflicting emotions that flooded her. A portion of her longed to confront Evan and force him to face the embittered monster he had become, yet she experienced a similar desire to hold him in her arms and console him with a sisterly compassion. She could do neither, however, until she recovered from the impact of her discovery and Evan's subsequent hateful reaction.

Holding tightly to her husband, Erin whispered chokingly, "Did . . . did you witness that . . . that awful display?"

"Most of it," he replied kindly. "Come along, sweetheart. We'll deal with your brother another time." Turning to Maisie, he said, "Tend to young Richards, Maisie; I'll see that Erin is safely settled in our room."

"Maisie?" Erin paused and focused her distraught expression on the loyal servant. "How long has he been like that?"

"Since de day he come home, Miz Erin. He done locked hisself in dat room, and he doan talk to nobody or sees nobody. All he does iz eats and drinks and throws hissy fits when we doan do whut he wants t' suits him," Maisie explained sorrowfully. "He woan even let me stay aroun' long enuff t' cleans up dat rat hole of a room. It's lak a pigpen, ah knows, but whut's a body t' do?" she sighed helplessly.

"I don't know, *yet,*" Erin murmured slowly, then, with renewed vigor, she squared her shoulders and faced her husband. "But we will think of something, won't we, darling?"

Kellen observed in wonder as his disconcerted wife changed from a nervous bundle of insecurity to a bulwark of grim determination in the span of but a few seconds, causing him to chuckle wryly. With a bemused shake of his head, Kellen tucked her arm in his and led her down the hallway.

"Doubtless we shall, little reb," he said admiringly as he escorted her down the wide mahogany staircase, so that she might bid farewell to their guests.

In the days that followed her turbulent homecoming, Erin devoted much of her time to supervising the restoration of the plantation house. Erin, Deborah, Maisie and the other servants made certain that each and every room, other than the one occupied by the surly invalid, received a thorough cleaning. Floors and walls were scrubbed, furniture was polished and repaired, windows were shined until the sun verily glistened through them, and precious heirlooms that Erin had hidden away against the possibility of scavenging Yankees were returned to their proper stations throughout the mansion.

While Erin directed the activity within the august plantation house, Kellen assumed the responsibility of supervising the exterior work that was to be done. The house and outbuildings received a fresh coat of paint, broken shutters were mended, roofs were replaced and new fences installed. In addition, the sprawling lawn was landscaped with fresh shrubs and rosebushes, and a new white picket fence was erected around the family cemetery.

Following one particularly grueling day of housework, Erin relaxed in a luxurious tub of temperate water, and allowed the soothing restorative to caress her aching muscles. She reclined against the back of the tub, eyes closed, and permitted her mind to wander aimlessly. Therefore, though she did hear the door between the chambers open, she did not react suddenly, for she naturally assumed that Renée had come to see how she progressed with her bath.

"Renée," she murmured faintly. "Please ask Maisie to have a supper tray sent up. I'm positively exhausted, and believe that I shall eat a bite and fall into bed."

"And what might your husband have to say about that?" breathed a husky voice behind her. "I should think that he might be disappointed if he were denied the pleasure of your company after his hectic day."

Erin did not turn around, nor did she open her eyes, but Kellen knew that a devilish smirk dressed her face, for she quickly replied, "Oh, *him?* I shouldn't concern myself about him. What with the way he has been gallivanting about the countryside the past week on his *mysterious* errands, he'll not likely notice my absence from the supper table." Her voice took on a sudden petulant tone as she continued. "I must admit that I'm beginning to feel quite neglected. In fact," she rolled the words on her tongue as though contemplating some perplexing quandary, "I'm rather persuaded to believe that my husband has cast his fancy elsewhere."

"Balderdash!" Kellen erupted with gay laughter. "You do love to prattle, don't you, brat?"

He stepped to the side of the tub and knelt down beside her, and, taking a satiny tendril of hair between his fingers, he dipped the end into the murky liquid and began to trace lazy patterns along her collarbone. Erin sat very still while Kellen drew an abstract design with his makeshift paintbrush, and, when his plunderings at last led to the rosy red nipple of her breast, Erin opened her eyes to confront her playful suitor. It was then that she observed the truly fatigued expression on his face, and she raised a gentle hand to smooth away the lines that creased his brow, giving him a moody appearance.

"Poor darling," she cooed sympathetically. "Have you had a strenuous day?"

"Uh huh," he sighed tiredly. "I'm positively bone weary."

"You're pushing yourself much too hard," she scolded. "Graham tells me that you're doing the work of three men, and now he says that you've concocted some crazy notion about reopening the sawmill."

"It's not crazy," he said softly, and, allowing the heavy strand to slip through his fingers, Kellen rose and stretched his arms high above his head to relieve the pressure along his aching back. "If this plantation is going to thrive again, some changes will have to be instituted. Reactivating the sawmill is but one of my plans. I've discussed them with Graham; he's skeptical, but he's no fool. He knows that things cannot go as they did before, and he's willing to try my ideas."

When he began his narrative, Kellen stepped to the washstand to cleanse himself of the day's accumulation of dirt and grime. As he spoke, he stripped off his shirt and began to splash himself with the cool, refreshing liquid. Meanwhile, Erin slipped from her bath, and, wrapping herself in a fluffy towel, crept closer to him.

Standing behind him, she listened intently to his reasoning before quietly asking, "Why are you doing this?"

Kellen did not immediately respond to her inquiry, for he presently groped about, blindly searching for something with which to mop up the excess soap and water from his face. Realizing that she had used the only available towel, Erin shoved the cloth into his hands and hurriedly donned her dressing gown. Kellen turned in time, however, to catch a glimpse of the provocative naked flesh before it was concealed beneath the folds of the satin robe, and an impish grin lightened his face as he reached out and dragged his wife into his arms.

"Because, my lovely, the sooner your family is situated, the sooner we can return to Arcadia and begin living like ordinary, married folk."

"But you're wearing yourself to a frazzle the way you've been carrying on," she pointed out, and, slipping from his embrace, she sat down at the dressing table and began to brush the tangles from her hair. "Take today for example; where have you been?"

Erin paused in midstroke and focused her curious gaze on his reflection in the mirror. She did not truly believe that he had developed a tendre for another woman, but his frequent prolonged absences had brought comments from Graham. Erin saw the blue eyes grow cloudy with dismay, and, not wanting him to think her a meddler, she quickly offered him an apology for her interrogation.

"Nonsense." He shrugged his broad shoulders and sat down on the edge of the bed to watch her. "I simply went into Braxton to make sure that the livestock would be delivered tomorrow as promised, then I ordered additional supplies."

He paused for a moment to consider the green eyes that shrewdly calculated his explanation, and he silently pondered just how much he should tell her. It sorely plagued him to deceive her this way, but he felt it was necessary. A letter from Colonel Langford had been delivered shortly after their arrival at Kilkieran informing Kellen that Taggart would meet with him at the tavern in Braxton, and he should make appropriate arrangements for a rendezvous.

Kellen had no way of knowing the exact date of Taggart's arrival, therefore, he had made a habit of riding into Braxton every day for the past week. He had been about to leave the tavern that very afternoon when Taggart finally made his appearance. Consequently, the two men had ridden to the site of the ambush, then Taggart had led Kellen to the cave where he had seen the Confederates stash the cargo; only to discover that the plunder had been moved. But given the state of disorder at the cave entrance and the contiguous area, the two men concluded that the evacuation of the stolen goods had recently taken place.

Kellen blew a low whistle, and, deciding that he should not embroil Erin in such complicated and potentially dangerous matters, he coughed and said, "Then I had lunch at the tavern and spent my afternoon exploring this vast estate of yours."

He averted his gaze, hoping that Erin would not detect his distortion of the truth, but she was not to be so easily duped. Even though she did not pester him further, Erin knew instinctively that her husband was holding something from her.

Deciding that a change of subject would better conceal his fraud, Kellen inquired, "Have you encountered any success with Evan?"

"No," she mumbled in reply, her shoulders slumping in dejection.

"Well, don't fret, pretty one. You'll think of some masterful ploy to reach him. Just look at how you coaxed my dragon grandfather from his cocoon," he reminded her encouragingly, and, a twinkle returning to his eyes, Kellen crossed the room and took up a stance behind her.

Lowering his large hands over the front of her dressing gown, he deftly parted the folds and began to fondle the amply proportioned flesh of one tantalizing breast. "Meanwhile, perhaps we can devote our immediate attention toward a more pleasurable pastime; something that requires considerably less conversation." His roguish suggestion was a warm breath against her neck.

Erin found it difficult to ignore the pulsating sensations that rushed through her, and she did not resist the mouth that captured hers, nor the forceful tongue that hungrily parted her lips and lunged inside to caress her own. Rendered almost dizzy by his sensuous assault, Erin became vaguely aware of the warm breeze that wafted across her naked flesh, as Kellen

372

effortlessly removed her dressing gown and lifted her in his arms. He swiftly carried her across the threshold to their roomy bed, and, throwing aside the coverlets, he placed his desirable burden upon the fresh smelling sheets.

It was then that Erin fully realized his purpose, and, turning a flirty smile on him, she murmured, "I thought that you were bone weary."

"So I am, albeit I am never too taxed to make to love to you, wench," he whispered throatily. "Besides, though my bones are weary, I assure you that my passions are functioning quite adequately." He indicated the growing bulge that strained to be free of the constricting trousers.

In less time than it took Erin to wiggle to the far side of the bed and open her arms to him, Kellen had discarded the remainder of his clothing and slid into the berth beside her, instantly wrapping her in his sinewy embrace. Erin's coquettish laughter and whimpers of delight soon filled the room, and, outside the chamber, Renée withheld the knock she had been prepared to sound. Instead, she made an abrupt turnabout in the corridor, and returned to the kitchen to advise Maisie that the newlyweds would not be taking supper in the dining room after all.

The intense situation that had been smoldering between Erin and her twin was to come to a tumultuous climax the very next day. The morning started out as usual and advanced peacefully, and by mid-morning, Erin decided to take a break from her busy routine and stroll out to the fields to see how the men progressed with the fence that was being erected around the south pasture.

Deciding to take the shortcut through the woods, Erin spotted her husband immediately upon emerging from the dense undergrowth of woodland foliage. Having discarded his shirt in deference to the sweltering August heat, he stood with his back to her. As she approached, Kellen cast aside the digging apparatus he had been using and bent down to retrieve the heavy fence post, and, heaving a satisfied grunt, he positioned the stake in the ground. Erin gazed in admiration as the hard muscles rippled across his back and shoulders in response to the physical exertion, and she was a little embarrassed to be caught gaping at him when he turned around seconds later.

With a casual smile in her direction, Kellen stepped to the nearby shade and procured a ladle of cool water which he proceeded to drink thirstily. Allowing the scoop to splash noisily in the bucket, Kellen ran his forearm across his mouth to wipe away the excess moisture before bending to collect his shirt. Slipping into the garment, he motioned for Erin to join him in the shade.

"Has my lazy brother deserted you?" Erin asked jokingly, noting that Kellen appeared to be alone in his endeavors.

"No," he laughed good-naturedly, and, stretching out on the green earthen carpet beneath him, he pulled Erin down beside him. "Two more of your former laborers returned seeking shelter and employment, so Graham took them back to the house to get settled. The others went to collect another wagon load of fence posts," he explained.

"Two more mouths to feed," she sighed. "However will Kilkieran be able to support everyone?"

"There are jobs aplenty to keep everyone occupied, and Kilkieran will be able to sustain them all, provided Graham adheres to my advice," he added. "But, then, your brother has proven to be one of the more level-headed Confederates I've encountered." Crossing his arms behind his head, he braced his broad shoulders against the tree trunk and settled an inquisitive gaze upon her. "I trust that your morning has been suitably active."

"That's an understatement," she groaned. "I had forgotten how tedious housework can be." She lifted a hand to smooth an errant strand of hair back into place, thereby, permitting

Kellen the chance to notice the unsightly smudge that streaked her forehead.

With a short chuckle, Kellen dampened the cuff of his shirt sleeve and leaned forward to wipe the blemish from her pretty face. "There. Now no one need ever suspect that I've wedded a humble chamber maid." He eased back against the tree, but he became understandably dumbfounded by Erin's sudden sharp intake of breath and the look of sheer bewilderment that abruptly crossed her face.

"Erin, sweetheart, what—"

But the question he had been prepared to sound died on his tongue, and his confusion changed to acute chagrin when he deciphered Erin's strangled cry.

"Michael!" she rasped, clutching one hand to her throat while the other clamped Kellen's wrist with a vise-like grip.

Erin's pulse raced as she baldly stared at the image that had stepped from the forest not ten feet away from where they sat. She blinked wildly, thinking that her mind was playing some cruel trick on her, but the vision remained transfixed before her disbelieving eyes. As if mesmerized by the unexpected intruder, Erin braced trembling fingers against Kellen's shoulders and climbed to her feet, and, somehow, her quivering legs carried her toward the man she had been led to believe had died in the war; the man she had once loved.

"Michael?" she repeated more clearly, though her voice was full of anguish, and his subsequent reply left her head reeling.

"Yes, kitten. It's Michael. I've finally come home to you." He stepped forward as if preparing to draw her into his embrace, but Erin placed a restraining hand against his arm to forestall the impetuous movement.

"Then . . . then you're not . . . not d-d-dead," she stammered hoarsely.

"What! Good Lord, no; I'm not dead, though I very nearly was. I fear that life in a prisoner of war camp did not resemble that to which I was accustomed at Fox Bush." He effortlessly pushed aside the hand that inhibited him and pulled her close to breathe in the fresh scent of her hair. "Many was the time I wanted to give in to that bastard, death, but I'd close my eyes and see your pretty face and know that I had to survive all that misery, so that I could come home to my kitten."

Erin threw her head back to stare upward into the once familiar face that now seemed so foreign to her. She stared blankly at the auburn hair that lay in unruly curls about his head, the striking blue eyes, and the sensuously full mouth that had curled into a hopeful smile. Vaguely, she became aware of his arm tightening about her waist, and, just as his head began to lower toward her lips, Erin pushed away from him abruptly, stumbling backwards.

"No, Michael! You . . . *we* mustn't," she cried, desperately choking back the sobs that constricted her throat.

"Erin, honey, what's wrong? Don't pull away from me; I need to hold you in my arms. It's been so very long."

Erin saw the sorrowful look that shadowed his confused face and it took every ounce of self-control she could muster to deny him his request. "No, Michael," she repeated softly, though firmly. "You don't understand. We cannot be together . . . ever."

"You're right. I don't understand. Why can't we be together?" he demanded.

She faltered, not knowing precisely how to divulge the heartbreaking news to the man who watched her with guarded anticipation. But the sudden pressure of Kellen's strong hand upon her shoulder gave Erin the strength to continue. Clutching her husband's arm for reassurance, Erin lifted tortured eyes to Michael. It grieved her to be the one to inform him of the shattering news, but it would be cruel to allow him to continue to believe that the dreams they had once shared could at last be fulfilled.

Swallowing hard, Erin forced the words from her lips. "Because . . . because I'm married." The final word was uttered as a harsh whisper, but the intended recipient experienced little difficulty interpreting the statement.

"Married!" His deafening outcry discomfited a cluster of starlings, sending them scattering toward the heavens.

Erin's eyes immediately flooded with tears of compassion as she observed the painfilled expression that contorted Michael's handsome face. "Yes," she managed weakly, pulling Kellen beside her. "This is Kellen, my . . . my husband."

The newcomer glanced helplessly back and forth between the couple, until finally, his incredulous gaze rested on Erin. "No," he moaned pitifully. "That can't be true! What about us? What about the plans *we* made?" he asked feebly, stumbling sideways, the force of Erin's declaration stunning him as much as a blow to the face would have.

Seeing his distress, Erin rushed forward to clasp his huge fists in her tiny hands. "I'm so sorry, Michael," she sobbed. "But I believed that you were dead; truly I did. Evan said—"

She halted in mid-explanation, and Kellen was perplexed by her abrupt change of behavior. For Erin suddenly released Michael's hands and stepped away from him, hastily dashing aside the tears that stained her cheeks. Her pretty face was no longer shrouded with despair, indeed, it had grown scarlet with undeniable fury.

"Evan!" she hissed crossly, and, lifting her skirts in her clenched fists, she turned and bolted toward the house.

Both men watched Erin's speedy retreat with mixed emotions, but it was Graham, arriving in time to witness his sister's departure, who spoke first. Tearing his surprised gaze from Michael, he gestured toward Erin's fleeing back and inquired of Kellen, "What's happening?"

A bemused smile flickered across Kellen's face, and, scratching the back of his head, he shrugged and said, "Offhand, I'd say that all hell is about to break loose."

Erin ran as fast as her tremulous legs would carry her across the rolling pasture, through the thick grove of trees, and up the long graveled driveway. She created quite a spectacle in her furor, causing more than one laborer to stop working and gape after her. Erin was impervious to their stares, however, as she ran up the front stoop and threw open the door to the plantation house. She rushed inside, visibly gasping for breath and clutching at the sharp pain that ravaged her side, to confront a bewildered Maisie.

"Lawd-o-mercy, Miz Erin!" the housekeeper exclaimed. "My, but you looks fit t' be tied."

"I am!" she panted breathlessly, leaning against the doorjamb while she struggled to regain her composure. "Summon Ruth and any of the servants who aren't otherwise occupied and send them to Evan's room. Bring brooms, mops and lots and lots of soap and scalding water," she ordered, and, before Maisie could question the peculiar instructions, Erin had darted up the staircase.

She ran straightway to Evan's room, and, without hesitating, flung the door aside and barged into the chamber unannounced. In an instant, she crossed to the windows and yanked the heavy black draperies from their anchor, sending them crumbling to the floor and flooding the room with brilliant sunlight. She whirled with a vengeance to face her bedazed brother, who painstakingly struggled to achieve a sitting position on the bed.

It was a formidable figure he prepared to battle, for Erin's eyes flashed like a fireworks extravaganza at a Fourth of July celebration, and she stood with her feet planted squarely on the carpet, hands on hips, her resolute expression positively scathing. Nevertheless, Evan tipped the whiskey bottle he cradled in one hand to his lips and settled a repulsive glare upon her.

"Get out," he growled.

"No. *You* are the one who will presently get out," came her blunt retort.

"The hell I will!" he shouted.

"So be it. You may come willingly or shrieking like a deranged lunatic, but rest assured, you will soon be dislodged," she informed him matter-of-factly. "This slovenly pigsty is going to receive a much overdue cleansing and so, dear brother, are you."

"I think not," he droned indolently, returning the bottle to his lips to secure another lengthy draft of the potent brew. "Go away," he repeated, tilting the bottle to his lips yet again.

With impatient rancor, Erin marched across the room, jerked the nearly empty container from his hand and hurled it across the room. The chamber reverberated with the clatter as the bottle made contact with the wall, and the room subsequently filled with an unmistakable pungent odor as the brown liquid formed a blotchy stain on the wallpaper. A series of thunderstruck expressions twisted Evan's face; chief among them being incredulity, but, more predominantly, his attractive features grew black with uncontrollable rage.

"How dare you?" he seethed hotly, and, in a rebellious action, he reached for the bell to summon a servant to fetch another bottle.

"Don't bother." Erin snatched the bell from his reach. "You shall have to retrieve your own poison from now on, for the staff will no longer be permitted to assist you with your insane attempt to destroy yourself. You've been mollycoddled and pampered long enough. It's time someone reminded you that you're a man; though a poor excuse for one at the present, but a man nonetheless, and you've certain family responsibilities," she informed him bluntly.

"And you see yourself as my self-appointed savior?" His hollow laugh echoed in the chamber, and he settled a murderous glare on her. "Why, you sanctimonious, little slut; I'd sooner —"

But the remainder of his vitriolic retort was to remain forever a mystery, for Erin deftly silenced him with a resounding slap across his face. Momentarily dazed by the vicious blow, Evan could do little more than gawk at the termagant before him in genuine stupefaction.

"You're vile!" she hissed coldly. "And this deranged bitterness you've nurtured since your injury is going to be put to rest as of *this* instant. If you want to die that badly, go ahead, but be kind enough to spare the rest of us your histrionics. And, while I'm on the subject, you can very well stop punishing those who love you for the severe blow you've been dealt." She turned and retraced her steps to the window to focus her smoldering gaze on the horizon.

After a moment of silent reflection, she continued, "It was cruel and heartless of you to lead me to believe that Michael was killed in battle. You see, I saw him today," she murmured sadly.

"Erin, I—"

For the first time, there was a hint of regret in his voice, but she waved aside his appeal with an abrupt gesture.

"I know that you meant to hurt only me, but your rash conduct has affected the lives of three innocent people. Yes, *innocent*," she reiterated at his scoff. "Your misplaced bitterness caused me to abandon the man I loved and accept shelter from a veritable stranger. Had I but remained at Kilkerian . . ." She did not complete her musings, but turned a truculent countenance on the invalid. "I shall *never* forgive you!" she rasped hoarsely.

Maisie and the others arrived in the open doorway soon after this impassioned declaration. Uttering precise directives, Erin instructed the servants to scrub the room from top to bottom, *including* its sullen occupant, and she sent Paulie to fetch Doc Wilson, so that a thorough examination of Evan's injured leg might be conducted. Satisfied that her orders would be sufficiently carried out, Erin heaved a heavy sigh and started to leave the room.

At the door, she turned to address Maisie. "One final instruction, if you please."

"Yes'm?" The faithful servant regarded her with round eyes, amazed that the girl had accomplished that which had bamboozled everyone else.

"Set a place at the dining room table for Master Evan. He

shall henceforth take his meals with the rest of the family."

It was a visibly dispirited Erin who emerged from her chamber several hours later, and mechanically made her way to the front parlor to congregate with the rest of the family before going in to dinner. She silently pushed open the door, and, unbeknownst to the occupants therein, made a sweeping surveillance of the room before stepping inside.

Graham stood with his back to the entranceway; his preoccupation centered on pouring each of them a pre-dinner glass of wine from the crystal decanter. Evan, meanwhile, sat on the sofa beside Deborah, looking thoroughly disgruntled with the entire proceedings, the crutch that was propped against the fireplace a constant reminder of his anguish. The sight of her brother proved to be a hollow victory, however, for the absence of another promptly caught her attention.

Erin gently closed the door, then sought out Chin Li to inquire if he was aware of Kellen's whereabouts. Upon learning that, not only Chin Li, but the entire staff had not seen Kellen since his departure for the fields that morning, Erin grew concerned.

It was a pondering expression that creased Erin's brow as she silently deliberated her husband's mysterious disappearance. With a vague mumble, she instructed Chin Li to advise the kitchen staff not to delay supper for her, then she wandered out onto the front porch to continue her musings. As Erin's pensive reflections surrounding the events of her hectic day continued to taunt her, she ambled along the sprawling lawn, hands clasped behind her back, completely lost to her thoughts. As of their own volition, her feet directed her to the back of the house, along the well-worn path beyond the barn and other outbuildings, and across the meadow to the rippling brook.

At this point, Erin seemed to awaken from her hypnotic state, and she stared blankly into the shimmering water, wondering how

381

she had managed to ramble so far from the main house. Then, suddenly, her eyes lit up with comprehension, and she turned and trudged onward, following the stream into the thick undergrowth of foliage that led to her secret hideaway.

She was not truly surprised to find Kellen there. After all, she had often fled to this sanctuary when she needed to be alone to think more clearly. And here he was, obviously deep in thought, for he stood on the far bank of the pond facing her, his feet planted firmly, arms crossed, his head barely visible through the swirling clouds of smoke his cigar created. His unreadable gaze was focused on the water, as though he would penetrate the depths of the blue abyss, and Erin would have left him to his musings had it not been for the brooding expression that darkened his handsome face, causing her some concern. Without further contemplation, she stepped into the clearing and quickly made her way to his side.

"I've been looking for you everywhere," she called, forcing a carefree lilt to her voice and a smile to her lips. "Chin Li tells me that you did not return to the house for lunch, and now you're forsaking supper as well." She clucked her tongue at him in a motherly fashion, and, tucking her arm in his, she tried to coax him to accompany her. "I won't have you starving yourself just because—"

"Is Cahill as you remembered him?" Kellen interjected softly, never wavering from his stance.

"Whatever are you talking about?" Erin laughed uneasily, hoping to avoid the subject he was determined to raise. Tugging on his arm again, she said, "Come along, darling, the others are—"

"To hell with the others!" he exploded angrily, and, shaking off her hand in disgust, he stalked away from her. "This is one problem I'll not let you tuck away in some obscure corner of your mind as though it never happened. You're hurting. Good God, *everyone* around here is hurting for one reason or another," he exclaimed his frustration. "But you and I . . . *we* . . . are going to face this together, so stop pretending this extremely awkward situation does not exist, and answer my question. Is he as you remembered him?"

Erin stared at the rigid back presented her, trying desperately to read Kellen's beleaguered thoughts. It would do little good to continue to appear unaffected by the day's happenings, for he would easily see through her charade. The forced smile melted away, and, in a distinctively weary voice, Erin said, "I suppose Michael is the same. He's lost a good deal of weight, of course, and he looks tired and wan."

"That's most likely attributed to the dysentery," Kellen mumbled, turning to face her. "You see, Cahill and I had a lengthy chat after you scurried off. It seems that after his release from the prisoner of war camp, he spent several weeks recuperating from the affliction in a northern hospital."

He paused as though reluctant to proceed, then he placed his hands on her shoulders, and, taking a deep breath, he said, "Honey, the hospital was located in Washington."

Erin's hands flew to her mouth to smother her strangled cry, but she could not prevent the anguish from clouding her eyes, no more than she could keep her trembling legs from buckling beneath her. Placing a considerate hand beneath her elbow, Kellen led his distressed wife to a fallen tree and eased her down onto the log.

It was with considerable trepidation that Kellen observed the various emotions that played across her face. It was only natural that she experience a feeling of remorse for having been so close to Cahill yet, in her ignorance, was unable to go to him. And, if he knew his wife, he felt certain that she was silently condemning herself for the merry life she had led in Washington while Cahill lay bedridden and friendless in an overcrowded hospital with no one but strangers to care for his needs.

Erin hung her head in her hands and moaned, "Had I only known."

With a purposeful gesture, Kellen snuffed out his cigar with his boot and tilted Erin's head back, compelling her to look at him. "It grieves me to see you in such despair, little one, but I cannot say that I wish things had turned out differently. In fact, had I been aware of Cahill's presence in Washington, I cannot truthfully say that I would have delivered you to him," he informed her candidly.

Then, bracing himself for the answer to a question he was loath to voice, Kellen forced himself to inquire, "Do you still love him?"

"Kellen, please," she begged, placing a weary hand to her forehead, "this is hardly the time—"

"You're quite mistaken, Erin," he prompted. "This is precisely the time. Now, *answer me!*"

Though his tone was harsh, Erin read the dreaded anticipation that dulled the crystal blue eyes, and she hastened to reassure him.

"Kellen," she began carefully, meticulously selecting her words. "To be honest, at this instant, I'm not certain how I feel about Michael, but I do know this. I married you because I love you, and our marriage is a commitment I do not take lightly. I . . . I don't want Michael's reappearance to jeopardize our life together." She had looked him squarely in the eye as she delivered her impassioned declaration, and her chin was quivering when she finished as she struggled to fight back her tears. "I do love you, Kellen," she cried as he wrapped her in his consuming embrace.

"That's all I wanted to hear," his warm whisper caressed her cheek. "For now that you're mine, I certainly have no intention of letting you go." He held her close for several moments while the pent-up tears from her nerve-racking day soaked the front of his shirt.

Erin was the first to pull away, though she did not release him entirely. "Kellen, take me away; back to Washington. We can stay at The Sinclairian until our house is finished. Please!" she beseeched him. "I'm so frightened!"

"No, little reb. Now is not the time to run. Our business is not quite settled here," he reminded her. "Soon, we shall go. Until then, there is no need for you to be frightened, my love, for I shall protect you from everything; with one possible exception," he added, a rakish lilt creeping into his voice.

Kellen's hands moved leisurely up and down her arms, and it did not take Erin long to understand what sort of devilment sparkled behind the blue eyes that had recovered much of their brilliance. Erin held her breath as his nimble fingers moved to the front of her blouse, and she put her hands atop his to stay his motion.

"Kellen," she tried to sound scandalized though, in truth, she longed to be in his arms, to share the warmth of his hard masculine body against hers, to be driven bereft of all reason by the thrill of his masterful lovemaking.

"Surely, you cannot mean to—*not here!*" she exclaimed, yet she did not thwart his plunderings as his thumbs slowly and methodically massaged the tips of her breasts till the nipples stood erect, struggling to be free of their bonds.

"Oh, I most certainly do. What could be more natural, or beautiful?" he breathed thickly.

Erin was not allowed the opportunity of a rebuttal, for Kellen swiftly undid the buttons of her blouse and buried his face in the voluptuous mounds of sensuous flesh. Erin sensed his urgency, but when she tried to help him with the ribbons of her undergarments, her fingers became entangled in the satin strands, snarling them in hopeless knots. With an impatient grunt, Kellen pushed her useless hands aside, snapped the threads in two and pushed the delicate material apart to grant him access to the enticing bounty.

She stood motionless, as if in a daze, while Kellen undressed her and shed his own clothing, then enfolded her in his arms and resumed the amorous interlude. One by one, he removed the pins from her hair and ran his fingers through the heavy tresses to brush them to a shimmery fullness, finally arranging it around her shoulders like a silky blanket.

Their eyes met for a split second before Kellen lowered her to the ground. His face was emblazoned with such raw desire that Erin moved against him provocatively, anxious for the glorious moment when he would make them as one. Kellen sensed her eagerness, and he took her quickly as though he dared not take the time to cosset and pamper her lest the heavenly body writhing beneath him somehow vanish unexpectedly.

To Erin, it was the most exquisite splendor she had ever experienced. Her senses were full of the sounds of the forest surrounding them, the sky above, and the hard earthen blanket beneath them. And, of course, the muscular phenomenon that held her in a relentless embrace, thrusting between her velvety thighs with a passionate fervor that made her cry aloud and cling to him desperately as she endeavored to match his ardor.

As the enthralled couple languored in the throes of their passion and their throaty cries of rapture echoed throughout the clearing, their uninhibited cavorting did not go unobserved. For two pairs of eyes, one brown and one blue, watched the tempestuous scene from a place of concealment from within the cave behind the cascading waterfall. But it was very different emotions that characterized each observer's eyes.

Michael Cahill's blue eyes were filled with pain and anguish while those of his mysterious brown-eyed associate were calculatingly shrewd. As the two men continued to watch the carefree lovers, the brown-eyed observer was prompted to comment, "I suggest that we implement our plan quickly if we are to achieve our respective goals."

With that, the two men silently retraced their steps through the dark and clammy cavern to emerge at a rear entrance that few people knew existed.

Chapter Nineteen

The ensuing fortnight passed without major incident, a phenomenon for which Erin was prodigiously grateful. She occupied her time in a variety of pleasing ways, however, for now that the house had been restored to order, Erin discovered herself with an inordinate amount of leisure time at her disposal.

She and Kellen had grown accustomed to exercising their mounts every morning after they had breakfasted, unless business matters otherwise preoccupied the latter. They attended Sunday services at the local church and accepted and returned numerous social calls from area residents. Erin's aunt and uncle became regular visitors to Kilkerian, for Philip had heard of the improvements Kellen had implemented at the plantation, as well as those yet to be undertaken, and he was anxious to discuss every new and innovative idea with him.

There remained one, however, who continued to regard Erin with such resentment and open hostility that even she was stumped as to how she might go about penetrating Christina's iron resolve. Friendship and camaraderie came from a totally unexpected quarter in the shape of Jennifer Wells.

In truth, the girls had been long time childhood companions, but had drifted apart in recent years. It was indeed good to renew old acquaintances, Erin thought, though she entertained a nagging suspicion that it was not solely her own companionship that Jennifer sought during her frequent sojourns at Kilkieran. For it had not taken Erin long to determine that Jennifer was quite hopelessly in love with her brother Evan.

Erin had even experienced a modicum of success in breaking through the impenetrable barrier her twin brother had erected about himself. Though she could not honestly admit that Evan had grown particularly affable or garrulous in his dealings with the other residents at Kilkieran, at least he no longer lashed out at them like a crazed lunatic.

The one person Erin steadfastly contrived to have as little contact with as possible proved to be the man she had at one time thought to spend the remainder of her life. She realized, of course, that it would be virtually impossible to avoid Michael entirely, for Fox Bush, the Cahill plantation, bordered Kilkieran. In addition, Graham and Michael had always been great friends, and she could not expect their acquaintance to wither simply because her own plans had undergone a significant change. Consequently, Michael became a frequent guest at Kilkieran, and, quite naturally, endeavored to engage her in private conversation on countless occasions.

But in order to maintain the harmonious marriage she was building with Kellen, Erin would greet Michael cordially at these social gatherings, then discreetly seek out her husband, thereby, avoiding any painful confrontations. At least, that had been the case thus far; Erin had no idea how long she could continue to deny Michael the confidential interview he so fervently desired.

On this particular day in late August, Erin was enjoying the companionship of two of her closest and dearest friends. She, Jennifer, and Deborah were closeted in the upstairs sewing room where numerous materials, threads, laces, patterns, and fashion plates had been scattered about the chamber, giving the room a distinctively disheveled appearance. The girls chatted gaily throughout the morning, reminiscing over childhood memories as they diligently perused the latest designs.

"Here, Deborah." Erin indicated a stylish pattern. "This would look wonderful made up in the yellow taffeta; the one with the tiny white flowers. What do you think Jennifer?" Erin turned to her guest when Deborah showed no outward interest in the suggestion.

"I think it would make a lovely gown," Jennifer heartily voiced her approval of the selection, and both girls turned worried eyes toward Deborah.

"You know, I was just remembering," Deborah murmured faintly, her svelte fingers lovingly caressing the yellow material. "I wore a gown, very much like this one, to the Saunderson's spring cotillion. It was the first time that Graham asked me to dance; the first time he ever really noticed me." She glanced over at her sister-in-law with bright tears brimming her eyes. "Do you remember, Erin?"

Erin reached over and patted Deborah's hand. She had been quite satisfied with the progress that Deborah had made since she had returned to Kilkieran. Deborah had begun to take pride in her appearance and had, to Erin's profound relief, halted her ramshackle attacks on her hair. Consequently, left unmolested, her raven locks could now be fashionably dressed in a style that flattered her creamy complexion. The girl had renewed a similar interest in her mode of dress, for her gowns were always clean and freshly pressed. And Deborah had begun to allow bits and pieces of the past to filter through her disturbed thoughts; treasured memories that she had considered forever buried.

"Yes, Deborah," Erin whispered gently, "I remember. As I recall, my roguish brother claimed you for *three* dances that evening, including two waltzes. Scandalous!" she clucked her tongue in feigned disapproval.

"Yes, I think that we fell in love the instant that our eyes met; our hands touched . . ." Deborah's voice trailed off unsteadily, and she shook her head to clear it of her sentimental recollections. "I'm sorry. I didn't mean to prattle on so."

"Not at all," Erin assured her, giving her hand an affectionate squeeze. "You certainly don't have to apologize to me for being in love with my brother. Just remember that he loves you quite dearly, too."

Jennifer had remained quiet throughout the exchange, but a sudden thought prompted her to volunteer, "Do you know what I remember about that particular cotillion?" Try as she might, she could not control the mischievous gleam that sparkled in her eyes.

"No. What?" Erin asked curiously, kneeling down to rummage through a box of old patterns that Maisie had brought down from the attic.

"Really, Erin!" Jennifer focused wide, exasperated eyes on her friend. "You cannot have forgotten the spectacle of Christina sprawling in the Saunderson's fish pond."

A soft titter began to warble in the back of Erin's throat, and, by the time the entire episode had flooded her memory, she had collapsed onto the floor in a fit of uncontrollable giggles.

"Oh, yes!" she cried joyfully, but noticing that Deborah had not joined in the frivolity, Erin quickly explained, "Don't you recall, Debby? Christina had worn a particularly revealing gown that evening; the dècolletage was shockingly indecent, even for her," she added as an aside.

Jennifer resumed the tale at that point. "She attracted her usual numbers of admirers, or *gawkers,* I should say, for what man with eyes can ignore Christina when she sets out lures? Anyway, Christina and her bevy of devotees strolled out to the garden, and there, beneath the budding limbs of a maple tree, she met her fate," Jennifer announced somewhat dramatically, at last succumbing to her own laughter.

"Now, I remember!" Deborah chimed in, anxious to be included in the recounting of the long forgotten tale. "As I recall, a horrendously large caterpillar fell from the tree and landed right between . . . well . . . uh . . . that is to say, in a

390

most distracting location." She blushed vividly at the thought of the wormlike creature helplessly lodged between Christina's voluptuous breasts.

"I'll say," Erin chortled nefariously. "And let's not forget how her undaunted admirers nearly trampled each other in their zeal to extricate the tiny beast from its resting place."

"They needn't have bothered though, for our Christina discovered her own method of ridding herself of the pest — drowning," Jennifer offered. "I shall never forget the sight of Christina frantically waving her arms and screeching like a veritable shrew, then the next instant there was a terrible splashing sound as she toppled headlong into the fish pond." All three girls lapsed into spasms of hilarious laughter at this juncture and it was several minutes before they managed to compose themselves.

"I've always considered it uncanny how the caterpillar managed to drop from the tree at just the right moment," Deborah mused thoughtfully.

"Oh, it's not as uncanny as one might think." Erin smiled smugly, as one would when acquainted with all the facts. "Especially when one has a brother who scoured the woods for three hours the day of the cotillion searching for just the right specimen," she giggled knowingly. "Evan was the culprit."

"He never was!" Jennifer exclaimed. "You mean to say that he actually *told* you of his chicanery?"

"There were few secrets between Evan and myself in those days," she reflected sadly, but refusing to let this admission dampen her spirits, Erin changed the subject. "But really, girls, it is quite naughty of us to express such merriment over Christina's distress," she sputtered despite her attempt to sound penitent.

Temporarily chastised, the girls returned to their contemplative surveillance of the sewing materials, but it was not long before Jennifer caught Deborah's eye and the two began to chortle again. One look in their direction was all it took for Erin to succumb to the infectious giggling, and soon the room reverberated with their combined uninhibited laughter.

Kellen cast a quizzical glance toward the staircase when he entered the foyer, for the tittering from the sewing room could be heard echoing throughout the house. His sensitive ears detected Erin's musical laughter above the others, and, had it not been for the fact that he had been summoned to the mansion with the news that a visitor awaited him in the front parlor, Kellen would have been sorely tempted to investigate the basis for his wife's carefree behavior. Kellen was, however, immersed in thought as he contemplated the purpose for Brian Taggart's unexpected visit, and a bemused expression highlighted his face as he entered the parlor.

"Hello, Taggart," he said shortly, his voice bearing no welcoming tone. "I thought we agreed that we would conduct our business from the Braxton tavern. I trust you have adequate justification for disregarding that understanding." Kellen's blue eyes took on an ominously smoky luster as they settled on the man.

"I do." Taggart was equally succinct with his reply. "I wouldn't come here if the matter were not urgent, but we weren't supposed to meet again until tomorrow, and I think you'll agree that the matter cannot wait." He reached inside his coat to retrieve a newspaper clipping which he thrust toward Kellen.

Kellen quickly read the account of an attempted bank robbery in Fredricksburg that had been thwarted when the would-be thief was killed in a mysterious explosion. The article went on to explain that the authorities were looking into the incident, but there were few clues to study, for the body had been burned beyond recognition. Kellen read the article several times and his countenance had darkened considerably by the time he next addressed his guest.

"Do you believe that some of the nitro has surfaced?" he asked somberly.

"Can't say for sure till I check it out," Taggart answered, brusquely. "But I'd say it's a safe wager. That's why I rode out here today. I'm on my way to Fredricksburg now to see what I can find out. Could be that the idiot who blew himself to hell had an accomplice who can be persuaded to tell me where he obtained the stuff."

"Do you want me to go with you?"

"No. You just keep an eye on things around here." Taggart settled his hat on his head and walked to the door to pull it open. "I'll send you a note to meet me at the tavern when I return," he assured Kellen, and the statement was barely from his mouth when he turned and nearly toppled over Erin, who, in her zeal to enter the chamber, had not noticed the man.

Erin's audible gasp of surprise caught Taggart offguard, and he hurriedly doffed his hat and mumbled an apology before scurrying from the room. Kellen was by her side in an instant to lead her to a comfortable chair, for Erin was obviously quite shaken from the impact of encountering the brown eyes that served to revive so many haunting memories.

"What . . . what was that despicable creature doing here?" she demanded, unknowingly crumbling the journal she held between taut fingers.

"He came to discuss a matter with me," Kellen explained tenderly. "I'm sorry, Erin, for I know he must have given you a tremendous fright, but, unfortunately, it was necessary for him to contact me here."

"You can never mean to say that you are actually engaged in some business venture with that . . . that wretched scoundrel?" she screeched her incredulity.

"You're distraught," Kellen pointed out needlessly. "Let me ring for Renée. Perhaps you would care to lie down and compose yourself," he offered, hoping to avoid a lengthy interrogation, but Erin was not to be so obliging.

"No, I would not!" came her indignant reply. "I *insist* upon knowing why my husband has chosen such a disreputable business associate. Now, answer me!" she persisted.

393

Kellen's eyebrows shot heavenward at the brusqueness of her speech, and he bristled instinctively at her impertinence. Realizing that her uncharacteristic behavior had been ignited by Taggart's appearance, Kellen shrugged aside his wife's blatantly offensive outburst and took a seat beside her on the settee. Wresting the mangled pamphlet from her fingers, he tossed the publication onto a side table and took her trembling hands in his. He was loath to admit complicity with the likes of Taggart, but, similarly, he refused to contrive a plausible deception to appease her.

No, he mused to himself. Better to be evasive than conjure up an out-and-out falsehood.

Tilting her chin upward, he sighed wearily and said, "Yes, love, Taggart and I are working together on a project. Hopefully, our affiliation will not be a lasting one, but, regardless, I vow that you shall never be subjected to another encounter with the man," he said sincerely, and the speaking look he bestowed upon her made Erin realize that this was not an idle promise.

Erin remained unconvinced. "But, *why him?*" she demanded.

Kellen released her hands and stood to take a turn around the room. Had anyone else dared to question his rationale for selecting a particular associate, he would have informed them, in no uncertain terms, that his concerns were none of their affair. However, this was hardly a normal situation, and he could not censure Erin after the shock she had just incurred. Allowing her this one condescension in regard to his judgment, Kellen returned to stand before her.

"Suffice to say that circumstances were such that made our collaboration necessary," he began carefully, but the forlorn expression on her pretty face made him dispense with his efforts.

"How could you?" she asked despondently, as though she felt singularly betrayed by his actions. "After what he tried to do to me." She lifted such a desolated countenance to him that

394

Kellen was prompted to return to her side and draw her within the protection of his reliable embrace.

"Erin, sweetheart," he whispered, cradling her against him, "Taggart's behavior toward you was totally inexcusable and *quite* unforgiveable. In no way do I condone his actions, you understand. It's just that men at war often behave abominably," he offered lamely. "Nevertheless, I assure you that our temporary connection *is* unavoidable."

Erin was by no means satisfied with the situation, but she would gain little by inviting his rancor by voicing continued disapproval over this one isolated incident. "Well, as long as you do not make a habit of associating with known ravishers of innocent maidens, I shall not protest too strongly, *this time.*" She emphasized her conciliation by waving a stern finger beneath his nose; an indication she would not look favorably upon future ventures of a similar nature.

"You have my solemn promise on that score, my lovely." He kissed her upturned face, then, settling her more comfortably against him, he said, "I caught a glimpse of your cheerful expression before it withered upon your recognition of Taggart. I take it that you had something of a pleasing nature to discuss with me."

"I did," she confirmed his suspicions, "and still do." Squirming from his embrace, Erin retrieved the discarded periodical and plopped it unceremoniously into his lap. "This arrived today," she began by way of an explanation, "accompanied by a letter from your mother. It seems she thinks we might be interested in furnishing that monstrosity you're having built for us, therefore, she forwarded the latest furniture catalog for our perusal."

"I see," he murmured understandingly, absently riffling through the pages. "She grows anxious for our return to Washington."

"As do I," Erin reminded him faintly.

"Soon, my sweet. Very soon," he promised softly, and a loving smile passed between the couple as two heads bent together to study the furniture drawings spread before them.

Erin graciously clasped the hand that Kellen extended as he offered to assist her from the wagon. She had gladly accepted his invitation to accompany him into town, and her exhilaration over the excursion had become more pronounced during the drive. Consequently, she had kept him entertained with a lively stream of chatter throughout the ride. By the time they arrived in Braxton, she was bubbling with such anticipation that Kellen was persuaded to chuckle aloud at her antics.

Erin withdrew her hand and favored her husband with a guarded look. "Have I done something to amuse you?" she strived to sound annoyed, but the flickering smile that pulled at the corners of her mouth belied her consternation.

"No, beloved." He fastened his hands about her slender waist and effortlessly lifted her from the conveyance. Once on the ground, Kellen tucked her hand under his arm and started to lead her toward MacPhearson's mercantile. "It's just that I am forever amazed at the exuberance with which you females undertake a mere shopping expedition."

"I shouldn't think you'd be overly surprised at my enthusiasm in any endeavor," Erin murmured thoughtfully, cocking her head at a more advantageous angle, thereby, enabling her to witness his reaction to her next conjecture. "Why, if memory serves, it was just last evening that you gave me every reason to believe you considered my . . . uh . . . *exuberance* to be most gratifying." She fluttered her eyelashes at him coquettishly.

"My, but what a brazen, little hussy you've become," he chastised her scandalous reference to their lovemaking, but the affectionate squeeze of her hand implied that he was not offended by her banter.

They had arrived before the mercantile and Kellen drew her to one side, so they would not impede the progress of others along the sidewalk. "I shall leave you here to place our supply order and browse around while I run my errands at the telegraph office and bank. My business shouldn't take long." He glanced down at his pocketwatch. "I'll return for you in an hour, then we can have lunch before returning to Kilkieran. Does that meet with my lady's approval?"

"Oh, yes!" she replied gaily. "An hour should prove a sufficient length of time to render you penniless."

"Hardly," he scoffed good-naturedly, and, opening the door of the store, he placed a familiar hand against her backside and pushed her across the threshold before turning to take his leave. "Behave yourself, infant," he cautioned playfully over his shoulder as he casually sauntered down the wooden steps and across the street to the telegraph office.

Kellen's hand had encircled the doorknob, but before he pushed the barrier open, he felt a sharp yank on the tail of his jacket, causing him to whirl around to confront the perpetrator of this unusual summons.

"You be Kellen Sinclair?" demanded a young lad of indeterminate age, wiping an overlarge, dirty shirtsleeve across a similarly unkempt face.

Kellen regarded the boy warily, yet a glint of laughter registered in his blue eyes as he rested his shoulders against the doorjamb and crossed his arms in front of him. Favoring the disheveled waif with a purposefully obscure expression, Kellen mumbled noncommittally, "Could be. What concern is it of yours if I am Kellen Sinclair?"

"Coz, if'n you be Sinclair, I've gotta message fer ya," the boy mumbled laconically, as he shoved his hands into his pockets and traced an imaginary pattern on the dusty sidewalk with the toe of his ragged shoe.

"I see," Kellen drawled, thoughtfully scratching his chin. "And just what might that message be?"

"It'll cost ya," the boy announced grudgingly, thrusting out a grubby hand. Once a suitable number of coins had been placed in the greedy appendage, he turned and pointed a directive finger toward the tavern. "Over there. Mr. Ridgeway wants a word with ya."

Kellen watched in guarded amusement as the boy deposited the recompense in his pocket and scampered across the busy thoroughfare to spend his newly acquired funds at MacPhearson's mercantile. His demeanor altered sharply, however, as he pushed away from the doorway and made his way to the tavern. And by the time Kellen reemerged from the dimly lit room a quarter of an hour later, a distinctively contemplative frown could be detected upon his handsome face.

The forbidding expression had deepened significantly by the time he rendezvoused with Erin at the appointed time before the mercantile. In fact, his attitude had undergone such an extreme reversal since their separation that Erin was prompted to inquire if his business errands had gone awry.

Kellen shook his head to clear it of his pensive reflections, and he summoned a smile to his lips as he focused his gaze upon her. "No, my sweet, all went well. And you? Did you manage to fritter away all of your pin money?" He looked down at her fondly and was genuinely surprised to discover her hands empty save for two small parcels. "Is this everything?"

"The supplies will be loaded onto the wagon while we dine," she explained. "And I did not 'fritter away' my allowance, dear husband," Erin retorted haughtily. "Unless, of course, you consider the cigars I purchased for you to be a frivolous extravagance. Wait here, and I'll just return them." She made as if to suit her actions to her words, but Kellen's firm grip on her wrist stayed her movement.

"I'll never understand what possessed me to take such an onerous wench to wife," he grumbled playfully, placing her arm in his. "Perhaps you would care to refresh my faltering memory over a light collation at the coffeehouse?" He began to lead her away from the storefront.

"All right," she willingly conceded. "Then you can tell me about your conversation with Mr. Ridgeway." She glanced up at him expectantly, but if Kellen was perplexed by her knowledge of the impromptu meeting with Ridgeway, he gave no outward indication. "I was not aware that you were acquainted with him," she added offhandedly.

"We have talked on occasion at the tavern," he explained nonchalantly. Then, his curiosity getting the better of him, he asked, "How did you learn of my encounter with Ridgeway?"

They had arrived at the coffeehouse, and Erin waited until Kellen had seated her at the table before embarking upon an explanation. "I was engaged in an ardent discussion with Mr. MacPhearson about the outrageous prices he insists upon charging.

"You know, Kellen," she momentarily deviated from her purpose, "someone should do something about that man. Anyway, we were engaged in an earnest debate when this unsightly little urchin ran in demanding to be waited upon."

"Impertinent little baggage," Kellen commented negligently, as he settled his gaze on the menu a waiter had placed in his hands.

"Indeed. But I assure you that his atrocious manners were not nearly as difficult to tolerate as was the pungent aroma that enveloped him." Erin wrinkled her nose disdainfully as she, too, pretended to focus her concentration on the coffeehouse menu. "Mr. MacPhearson seemed dubious of the lad's ability to pay hard cash for the goods he requested, and he was quite astounded when the boy produced the required sum. I was certain that Mr. MacPhearson was going to accuse the boy of obtaining the money dishonestly, when he boasted how he was able to finagle a gratuity out of—'that no-good Yankee'—his words, not mine, darling," she hastily inserted, "for a message that Mr. Ridgeway had already paid him to deliver," Erin concluded her lengthy narrative and glanced up at him over her menu.

Kellen placed their order with the waiter, then returned his full attention to his companion. "Ridgeway wanted to buy me a drink," he said simply.

Erin's expression clearly indicated her skepticism, but she merely commented disapprovingly, "A bit early in the day for that sort of thing, don't you think?"

"That depends," he retorted noncommittally. "Some individual's days begin earlier than others." He noticed her frown deepen, and reached across the table to clasp her hand between his. "All right, infant. Don't pout at me. You're not the only one concerned with the exorbitant prices MacPhearson places on his goods." He thought quickly, thankful that in her narrative, she had provided him with the ideal ploy to satisfy her curiosity.

"Ridgeway owns the vacant building on Main Street on the north end of town," he explained offhandedly. "I've decided that MacPhearson could stand a little honest competition, and intend to open a store of my own. I broached the subject with Ridgeway this morning, and we decided to meet again this evening to discuss the project at length."

"But," Erin began to protest, but Kellen held up his hand to forestall the bevy of questions he knew to be formulating in her mind, for their meal had arrived.

Grateful for the interruption, Kellen addressed Erin patiently, "Mustn't pelt me with your quandaries now, pet. I'll explain everything in due course. I, for one, am weary of business discussions," he announced pointedly, "and would now content myself with this delicious looking repast and your delightful conversation. Now, tell me, what other trifles did you purchase?"

Erin was by no means pacified by Kellen's obtuse behavior, yet she did not wish to invite his anger by harping on a subject he had made clear he had no desire to discuss further. Consequently, the return ride to Kilkieran was made in virtual silence as each one withdrew into silent deliberation. And it was a thoroughly disgruntled Erin who watched from the upstairs gallery that evening as her husband rode off to keep his appointment with Mr. Ridgeway.

Kellen's countenance grew even more somber as he maneuvered Achilles along the deserted roadway that led to Braxton. His thoughts had seldom wavered from his morning encounter with Ridgeway, and, as he made his way along the dusty, winding thoroughfare, he silently calculated how far he should allow himself to trust the man. After all, the fellow was little more than a casual acquaintance.

Therefore, Kellen had been thoroughly intrigued when Ridgeway informed him that he could provide evidence that would prove conclusively that one of the men who had served in Kellen's regiment had been a Southern sympathizer.

"Why should that interest me now?" Kellen had inquired, his manner aloof.

"Because, that means your man was a traitor, and, while the military will tolerate many things from a soldier during a war, treason is not among them," Ridgeway had spoken candidly.

"Very well. How do you figure this concerns me?" Kellen asked suspiciously, declining the drink Ridgeway offered to pour into his glass.

"Because the backslider has turned up in Braxton." Ridgeway quaffed his own drink and brought his empty glass down onto the table with a thud. "Now, I've got my own reasons for telling you all this, but if you want to know the whole story; meet me in my vacant building on Main Street at eight o'clock tonight."

"I know the place," Kellen nodded.

"Good. Of course, you realize that you'll be expected to pay, and pay dearly, I might add, for the information I'm going to provide you. But I'm confident you'll be more than willing to do so." With that, he flipped a coin onto the table and sauntered from the tavern.

Kellen grunted sourly as he reconstructed the scene in his mind, and he was further puzzled by Ridgeway's implication that the traitor had returned to the area. Headquarters still insisted that Bradley Petersen was the chief suspect, yet the biweekly telegrams Kellen dispatched to his friend were always answered promptly. The situation was certainly taking an interesting twist, for now the guilty finger seemed to be pointing toward the very man Colonel Langford had sent to assist Kellen: Brian Taggart.

Kellen had long since arrived at his destination, but he was so engrossed in his musings that he did not immediately dismount. Finally, realizing that the solution to the jumbled puzzle lay inside the vacant building before him, Kellen heaved a conciliatory sigh and swung his muscular frame to the ground.

He secured Achilles to the tethering post and placed a boot upon the first step. There he paused and reached inside his pocket to retrieve one of the cigars that Erin had purchased for him earlier that day. He proceeded to light the aromatic tobacco, then he resumed his progress toward the front door of the building. But just as he reached the top step, the air was rent by a thunderous blast that sent him careening backwards to the hard street.

Momentarily stunned by the unexpected eruption, Kellen lifted his hand to feel for the trickle of blood that had begun to flow from the cut on his forehead, and he winced at the pain the movement produced in his shoulder. He watched in dazed wonder as the structure before him literally exploded into a wall of flames, sending debris showering down around his head and shoulders. Vaguely, Kellen became aware of shouting in the distance, and, as the sounds of charging footsteps echoed in his ears, he slipped into blessed unconsciousness.

Erin was dozing in the front parlor when a commotion of undetermined origin jolted her from her salubrious dreams. Casting a chagrined glance toward the mantel clock, her fears grew when she noted that the time was fast approaching midnight and Kellen had not yet returned from his meeting in

Braxton. She stretched and slowly began to uncurl herself from the divan when an urgent pounding at the main entrance made her realize that it had been raised voices from outside the house that had rousted her from her sleep.

Her heart lurched violently, and, suddenly overwhelmed by a discomfiting sense of dread, Erin bolted from the divan. Completely heedless of the various sewing articles that scattered in her reckless evacuation, she flew to the parlor door and succeeded in wrenching it open just as Graham arrived to respond to the late night summons.

The ensuing scene that unfurled in front of Erin's startled eyes provoked a terrified scream from her throat as the door burst open to reveal her uncle and former sweetheart supporting the slumped, almost lifeless frame of her husband between them. Erin swallowed her fear and stepped forward bravely, realizing that a display of hysterics would be of little use.

"What happened?" she asked in remarkably composed tones.

"There was an explosion at Ridgeway's building in Braxton," Philip Richards hurriedly explained.

"Damndest thing I ever saw," Michael added. "The whole building just vanished in one violent blast. It was awesome."

"Yes," Philip concurred. "Kellen is one lucky fellow. He was apparently just going up the steps when it happened, and the force of the explosion threw him clear of the fire."

"Then he's not . . . not . . ." She faltered, unable to continue, her knees weakening with relief beneath her. She had fully expected to be told the worst possible news, therefore, it was incredible for her to believe that the limp figure in front of her still lived.

"No, Irish. He's not dead," Graham whispered kindly, slipping his arm about her shoulders for support.

"No, Erin," her uncle quickly assured her. "He's mighty shaken up, that's all. Most of the townfolk were engaged in trying to bring the blaze under control when we left, but I did

403

send someone to fetch Doc Wilson. Where do you want us to put him?"

"Forgive me for making you stand in the open doorway," she apologized. "I fear that your arrival has quite stunned me."

The wall sconces had long since been extinguished, so Erin retrieved a brace of candles from the hall table to light their progress up the long staircase.

"Follow me," she directed somberly.

Maisie had been wakened by the disturbance as well, and, after one look at the wounded man, she scurried off to collect the necessary articles to treat his injuries. Erin was indeed grateful for the servant's timely arrival, for the next several moments of her time were concentrated on seeing that Kellen was comfortably settled in bed. She was absorbed in her ministrations, but as she struggled to remove Kellen's boots, Erin became aware of her brother's muffled inquiry.

Erin turned slowly from her task to confront the three men who stood huddled near the mantel, earnestly discussing the tragic events of the evening. "Well?" she demanded, placing her hands on her hips. "Answer Graham's question. Was anyone killed?"

"Erin," Michael began patiently. "We didn't mean for you to overhear."

"Obviously," she retorted dryly, referring to their hushed murmurings.

"Truly, sis, this isn't a story fit for feminine ears," Graham defended Michael.

"On the contrary." Erin remained staunch in her resolve to be told everything. "My husband was very nearly killed tonight, and I want to know why."

"Very well," Philip conceded. "I'll tell you what I know." He pushed away from the mantel and came to stand in front of his niece. "Arthur Ridgeway's horse was found tethered in the alley behind the burning building, but he was nowhere to be seen. If he was inside the building when the explosion occurred, well, there is no way that anyone could have withstood such a blast," he ended dully.

Erin nodded her understanding, and, turning, she grasped the bedpost and stared down at the unconscious man who slept on, oblivious of his surroundings. "But what could Kellen have to do with all this?" she mumbled puzzledly.

"That's something that only he can tell, and I'm certain he'll explain everything when he awakens," Graham whispered behind her.

Additional discussion was made impossible, however, for Doc Wilson arrived at that moment and immediately dismissed the group from the chamber. Even Erin was excluded while the doctor examined his patient, and, although she was reluctant to leave Kellen, her head was whirling with confusion, making further debate quite hopeless.

The sun had crept from behind the horizon the following morning before Kellen demonstrated any definitive signs of awakening. His eyes fluttered open as he struggled to attain a sitting position, but the pain the movement ignited made him pause to reconsider his actions. Gradually, the events of the previous evening began to filter through his cloudy memory, and he lifted his hand and gingerly tested the bandage that covered his right temple. It was then that a slight rustling sound at the foot of the bed caught his attention, and, forcing a lopsided grin to his lips, Kellen murmured a tenuous greeting to his wife.

The response he received was hardly gratifying, however, for Erin simply muttered some unintelligible phrase and stepped to the window to thrust apart the draperies, thereby, flooding the chamber with brilliant rays of sunshine. Kellen winced as the glaring light momentarily blinded him, and, though he swallowed the oath that sprang to his tongue, his smile quickly withered as he observed his unusually recalcitrant wife pacing fitfully about the room.

Kellen sighed dismally. His head ached, there was a throbbing pain in his shoulder, and an even more relentless ache in his side. Having just awakened, he had not yet had the time to fully reconstruct the events of the previous evening. In short, he was not ready to entertain an intensive interrogation from Erin.

Hoping to cast her attention elsewhere until he had contrived a suitable explanation, Kellen began to speak, "Have you no good morning kiss for your husband, wench?" He endeavored to force a playful lilt into his voice.

Erin, however, was in no mood to be cajoled. "No," she answered coldly.

Kellen's eyebrows arched at a surprising angle as he shrewdly regarded the defiant little creature that had taken up a dauntless stance at the foot of his bed. With considerable effort, he managed to maneuver himself to a comfortable position, utilizing the backboard as a brace for his broad shoulders. Then he crossed his arms in front of him and assumed a somber expression as he prepared to confront her.

"I see," he grunted sourly. "Well, let's have done with it, shall we? I'm certain that I'll not encounter another moment of peace until you've had your say, so go ahead. I assure you that I am quite at your disposal," he added dryly with a sweeping gesture to indicate his indisposed condition.

The embittered gaze he received for his rhetoric was consummate, and Erin's tone was frosty when she spoke. "To be honest, I'm much too furious to discuss this sensibly," she informed him sharply. "Besides, you'll only lie to me, as has been your habit as of late. So, you might as well be warned at the outset," she waved an ominous finger at him, "I'll not be satisfied by another of your flimsy excuses. I want the truth, and I want it now!" She stamped her foot to accentuate her demand, but before Kellen could respond to her outburst, Erin hurried on, "Don't you see? The next time you might not get by with a dislocated shoulder and a few bruised ribs. *You might be killed!*" she cried, placing her hands to her mouth in an attempt to smother the tortured sob that rose in her throat.

Kellen's mood changed drastically from defensive arrogance to genuine contrition as he absorbed the essence of her speech. The events with which Erin had been forced to contend since their marriage had been arduous enough to test the patience of the veriest saint. She had dealt admirably with Deborah's problem, Evan's obdurateness, and Michael's unexpected reappearance from the dead. But now, when subjected to her own husband's near disastrous accident and subsequent reluctance to confide in her, it was only natural for Erin to succumb to her pent-up frustrations.

His expression was tender as he extended his uninjured arm toward her. "Come here, little reb," he urged, a relenting smile fashioning his lips. "I shall tell you everything, but you must promise that what I am about to share with you will be kept in the strictest confidence," he cautioned.

Erin bobbed her head affirmatively to his condition as she scurried around the side of the bed and carefully slipped into the bed beside him. She clasped his free hand between both of hers and patiently listened as he recounted the events that had led him to agree to assist the military in its investigation of Bradley Petersen. He told her of the contents of the disabled wagon that had first brought him to Kilkieran, of Taggart's accusation which had resulted in the current investigation, of his surveillance of the local countryside and his cooperation with Taggart, concluding with his somewhat hazy recollection of the happenings of the previous evening.

Erin listened intently throughout the lengthy narrative, and her brow had crinkled into a contemplative frown when she looked up at him. "I still don't understand the need for so much secrecy."

"Because I didn't want Brad to suspect anything out of the ordinary." He placed an impetuous kiss against the tip of her upturned nose. "Besides, I explained that some locals were implicated in the theft; I didn't want to incur your wrath if you learned that I was questioning your friends."

"But, Kellen," she persisted. "The ambush of your wagon was an act of war. Certainly, any Southern involvement cannot be considered criminal now."

"Not unless one of them was involved in last night's little bonfire," Kellen murmured thoughtfully. "Murder, my love, is still very much a criminal offense," he reminded her.

"True, but why would anyone want to kill Arthur Ridgeway?" Her frown deepened, and she cocked her head at an angle to better study her husband's serious face.

"Because, dear little one, he knew the identity of the traitor within my regiment, and was prepared to divulge that information to me. Unfortunately for Ridgeway, he underestimated the treachery of my nameless adversary," Kellen murmured contemplatively. "Now, I fear, I know as little as before."

Erin instinctively reached up to smooth away the scowl that shadowed Kellen's soulful blue eyes. "Do you still suspect Brad?"

Kellen shook his head slowly. "My heart would never truly allow me to believe that Brad was involved in any of this," he admitted. "Besides, I received a telegram from Brad in Washington yesterday afternoon. As far as I'm concerned, that should be sufficient evidence to absolve my friend of this nasty business."

He fell silent for a moment, apparently lost in concentration; content to caress the tiny hand that rested trustingly in his. "You know," the troubled look returned to his face, "I have never been able to understand Taggart's motive for implicating Brad. It's all so very confusing, but I'm persuaded to believe that he concocted this ruse out of some demented scheme for revenge."

Erin shrugged her slim shoulders, as perplexed by her husband's tale as was he. "The man was obviously resentful of your command, and, realizing that you would be eager to clear Brad of any charges, he embroiled you in his unsavory strategem in the hopes that he could catch you off guard and

. . . and *kill* you." She shuddered at the mere speculation, causing Kellen to draw her close to comfort her.

"Perhaps," he murmured pensively.

"Well," Erin's voice was considerably lighter, "now that you know Taggart is your man, the completion of your mission should be relatively simple. All you need to do now is apprehend the scoundrel and—"

"Whoa!" Kellen interjected good-naturedly. "It isn't *that* simple, sweetheart." He tweaked her chin playfully. "I have no conclusive proof that Taggart is indeed the villain; just a gnawing suspicion. And that, my love, is not enough to convict the man." He suddenly began to ease himself toward the edge of the bed, moving gradually as he tested the extent of his injuries.

Erin sprang forward to protest his premature withdrawal from bed. "Just what do you think you're doing?" she demanded sternly, hands on hips.

"There's much to be done," he answered simply, reaching for the shirt and trousers that lay neatly folded on the cedar chest at the foot of the bed.

"But you mustn't," Erin insisted, and she darted around the bed to snatch the clothes from his grasp. "You're still badly shaken from your mishap."

"Nonsense!" he scoffed. "I'm not about to let a few scratches make a slugabed out of *me*. Unless, of course," he favored her with a devilishly wicked grin that made her flesh tingle with excitement, "you are willing to help me while away my confinement in a more diverting manner."

"You are in no condition to undertake *that*, sir!" She endeavored to appear unaffected by his bold suggestion but, in truth, she was relieved to note the tension-free lilt in his voice.

"Madam, you sorely underestimate my capabilities." He feigned indignation at her repartee. "But no matter, for the fact remains that I do have pressing business to conduct, and I shall not be mollycoddled into shirking my responsibilities by an óverprotective wife." He successfully wrested his clothes from her and donned them as quickly as his pain-racked body would allow.

"What can be more important than your well-being?" she cried desperately.

"Yours," came his soft reply.

"I don't understand." She shook her head vaguely.

"I intend to make arrangements today to send you back to Tiffin Square to reside with Mother for a few days. Then I shall instigate a thorough search for Mr. Brian Taggart," he explained.

"No!" she exclaimed her protest. "I won't leave you. You might need me."

By this time, Kellen had concluded dressing and returned to his seat on the edge of the bed. Taking Erin by the hand, he gently pulled her onto his lap and coaxed her chin up, so that their eyes met.

"Honey, listen to me. If Taggart is determined to cause me some distress, there is no more complete way that can be accomplished than through you. You must know by now that I adore you, you little wretch." He stroked her cheek devotedly. "I would be totally desolated should some mishap befall you because of me. I want to be certain that you are safe, therefore, you shall do as I bid," he informed her in a voice that warned he would brook no argument to the contrary.

Yet Erin remained adamant. "But if he wants me, he'll only follow me to Washington," she reasoned.

"No, the nitro, or what is left of it, is still here. I need it as evidence, and Taggart knows that. But more importantly, I want him," his tone grew dangerously ominous, and Erin shivered intuitively at the harsh slant of his eyes. "I must be getting close to something, and I'll not rest until I have unraveled this mystery. Now, run along and pack a few things, and I'll begin making your travel arrangements."

He started to push her from his lap, but he needn't have wasted the effort, for Erin leapt to her feet in a rage. "No!" she shouted. "I won't go? There is nothing, *nothing* you can do or say to make me. Kilkieran is still my home, and you cannot force me from it. I shall stay here to ensure that you don't get that stubborn Yankee hide of yours killed. *That* I promise you!" She concluded her tirade in a huff and disappeared through the chamber door amidst a flurry of swirling petticoats.

The slamming of the door was still ringing in Kellen's ears when he slowly lifted his aching body from the fourposter and wandered over to the window. He was completely absorbed in his thoughts when his eyes focused on Evan, who was valiantly struggling toward the barn with the aid of his crudely shaped crutches. Suddenly, Kellen's blue eyes sparkled with mischief, and he turned a confident gaze toward the door through which his wife had recently stormed.

With a soft chuckle, he spoke aloud, "Nothing I can do, you say? We shall just see about that, my fiery, Irish termagant."

Chapter Twenty

Erin stood on the gallery overlooking Kilkieran's vast expanse of green lawn. Ordinarily, the spectacular view of the winding, tree-lined driveway and the distant horizon brought joy to Erin's heart, but on this particular October morning, she was not in complete accord with her world. Her eyes focused intently on the pair of carriages that were being prepared for the journey to Richmond, and, for at least the thousandth time, she silently cursed her husband's cleverly construed scheme.

As Erin leaned against the balustrade, her observant ears detected the faint click of the French doors behind her. If she harbored any uncertainty as to the identity of the unannounced intruder, her doubts dissolved when she felt the familiar arms slip around her waist and pull her back against a rock hard chest.

Kellen locked his arms securely beneath Erin's bosom and leaned down to breathe deeply of her sweet-smelling scent. "Still angry with me, princess?" he murmured in her ear.

"Consummately," she replied without hesitation. Yet, despite her obvious perturbation, Erin could not repress the tingle of excitement that engulfed her at his touch.

"Odd," he began thoughtfully, as though mulling some perplexing dilemma in his mind, "but your anger dissipated long enough last night to allow you to accept *and* enjoy my romantic overtures. And surely, it was not out of bitterness that you awakened me just prior to dawn to engage in that delightful bit of diversion you so masterfully initiated." He laughed heartily as a distinctive flush colored all the way to Erin's dainty earlobes.

"Come, Irish, admit it. You are not nearly as vexed with me as you would have me believe." He gave her a fierce squeeze as he proceeded to lift her from the floor of the gallery.

Erin squealed frantically at his antics, and she slapped at his hands in an attempt to gain her release. "Kellen!" she pleaded. "What do you think you're doing? Do you want the servants to see?"

"I want the whole world to see!" he bellowed as he lowered her, turning her round to face him. "I am not ashamed for others to witness my devotion. You must realize by now that I am quite passionately attached to you, my little love," he breathed hoarsely.

"Humph!" she pouted, refusing to meet his overpowering gaze. "You love me so much that you're willing to cast me adrift, so that you may pursue that madman about the countryside at your leisure." Erin pushed away from him, her frustration acute, and she marched further down the gallery before whirling to confront him again. When next she spoke, her eyes glittered brightly. "I shall never forgive you for duping me with this ridiculous plan you have concocted."

"It's not ridiculous, infant," Kellen gently reproved her. "I cannot truly believe you insensitive enough to deny Evan this chance to be a whole man again."

"Of course, I'm not!" Erin gasped, shocked by his accusation. "But—"

"Besides, you credit my genius to excess," he continued, ignoring her protest. "I merely approached Graham with my idea to open a mercantile in Braxton and install Evan as the proprietor. Graham considered this an excellent notion, for not only would it provide MacPhearson with a little honest

413

competition, but it would furnish Evan with a useful occupation. Yet, we both realized that your prideful twin would balk at any suggestion I might offer, relying on his impediment as an excuse." Kellen strolled forward and casually leaned against the balustrade facing his petulant wife.

"It was then that I recalled reading about the advancements that are currently being made with artificial limbs, and, upon further discussion with Doc Wilson, I was able to obtain the name of a competent physician in Richmond. The remainder was fairly simple." He suavely polished his manicured nails against his lapel in a gesture that Erin found particularly maddening. "Graham explained to Evan that I planned to expand my freighting line to provide service to Braxton and neighboring communities, thereby, helping offset the expenses of reopening the sawmill and constructing the new store. He then pointed out to Evan that the salary he would earn as storekeeper could help the plantation thrive again."

"I have heard all of this before," Erin interrupted impatiently.

"Yes, I know," Kellen droned tritely. "But considering your dauntless pertinacity, I thought that the explanation warranted repeating." He favored her with an indulgent smile that did little to improve Erin's disposition.

Breathing an embittered oath, Erin stamped her foot in a rage and thrust out an accusing finger at Kellen's regal head. "You cannot deceive me, Kellen Sinclair. You conceived this scheme, knowing full well that Evan could not undertake such a lengthy sojourn unattended."

"True, but, if you recall; it was Graham, not I, who suggested that you accompany Evan on the journey," he reminded her.

"How *convenient* for you!" she snapped as she folded her arms across her bosom and focused her unyielding gaze on the sun-drenched horizon.

Kellen drew a long sigh as he pushed away from the railing and moved to stand in front of Erin. Grasping her tenderly by the shoulders, he compelled her to look at him.

"Don't frown so, pet," he whispered lovingly. "You are not nearly as pretty with this ugly scowl marring your lovely face." He affectionately caressed her cheek with his fingertips. "We shan't be separated for long, I promise; just long enough for Evan to be fitted for and instructed in the use of the prosthesis. I will conclude my business with the nefarious Brian Taggart, then dash off to Richmond to join you. Then we shall repair to Arcadia to enjoy our first holiday season together.

"Which reminds me, brat." Kellen suddenly tucked her arm in his and led her through the French doors to the chamber they shared. "What progress have you made toward furnishing our modest domicile?"

"I shall see what may be found in Richmond, and charge it to your account, you may be sure," she replied shortly, breaking away from him to collect her bonnet and traveling gloves.

Kellen winced automatically at her response as he mentally calculated the stress about to be placed upon his bank account. His grimace vanished, however, as he selected a chair and fondly observed as Erin securely tied an elaborate bow at her chin and pulled on her gloves. With a sudden pang, Kellen realized just how much he would miss this lovely vision during the coming weeks. Thus motivated, he soundlessly crept across the floor and pulled Erin into his arms, and he would have kissed the great pout from her mouth had the brim of her poke bonnet not hampered his purpose.

"Damn these infernal headpieces you insist upon wearing!" he swore beneath his breath, starting to turn away.

"You exasperate too easily." Erin murmured softly, and, catching him by the sleeve, she cocked her head at an angle that provided Kellen with ready access to the treasure he sought.

Much later, Erin could be heard to emit a languid sigh as the tempestuous embrace ended, and she rested her cheek against his broad chest, vastly comforted by the rhythmic beating of his heart. "Kellen?" she faintly whispered his name.

"Yes, love?"

"You will be cautious in your dealings with that unsavory fellow, won't you? You won't do anything foolish? Promise me," she sniffed brokenly.

Kellen smiled knowingly as he strengthened his embrace about her and murmured the appropriate endearments. "I shall exercise the utmost discretion, my darling," he assured her. Then tilting her chin back, he stared into the misty green orbs and said fondly, "Now, let's dry those eyes, and I expect to see a brilliant smile upon your lips by the time we reach the carriage.

"You don't want Evan to think that you are loath to accompany him, do you?" he asked kindly.

"No," she agreed as she collected her reticule from the chair before the fireplace. "Actually, since I have had this little jaunt foisted upon me, I intend to make the best of the situation by trying to resolve my differences with Evan." She graciously accepted the arm that Kellen proffered, and they started to exit the chamber, but she lingered in the doorway to scan the room one last time.

A sudden cold chill sent shivers racing up and down Erin's spine as an omen of foreboding enveloped her. Noticing the questioning glance her husband turned on her, Erin quickly pulled the door closed and obediently allowed Kellen to escort her down the corridor. As she walked, Erin pressed a hand against her stomach to suppress its violent, inexplicable lurching. But try as she might, Erin could not eradicate the suffocating premonition that very little good would come from his enforced separation from Kellen.

Erin's brief sojourn to the city of Richmond was to gradually grow into an extensive visitation. She had not foreseen that there would be any difficulty obtaining an appointment for Evan to be examined by the celebrated Doctor Gallagher, but the man's practice had tragically quintupled since the war, making his expertise much in demand. Once the coveted interview had been granted, there had been countless measurements, days of waiting, and, finally, hours of relentless instruction and therapy in the use of the artificial limb.

The experience had been an arduous endeavor for Erin as well as her brother, but she stalwartly stood by his side; offering words of encouragement as he struggled to conquer the towering obstacle. But the tedious hours of work and dedication had culminated that very morning in triumph in Doctor Gallagher's office. For relying on naught but the hand carved cane that Erin had purchased for him, Evan was able to walk from the physician's office to where his sister awaited him, showing but the slightest indication of a limp.

Brother and sister had embraced joyfully on the street, heedless of the indignant stares their unbridled display evoked from passing strangers who were not privy to the situation. With trembling fingers, Erin dabbed the jubilant tears from her eyes and literally dragged her twin inside the carriage, proclaiming that a celebration was in order. Accordingly, she delivered Evan to the house they had rented for the duration of their stay in Richmond. Then she scurried off to arrange for a gala evening of entertainment.

Erin gratefully accepted the coachman's proffered hand as she alighted from the conveyance. She hastily scampered up the short walkway to the row house on Franklin street, and let herself inside. She was standing in the foyer removing her bonnet when the butler entered the corridor from the parlor.

"Pardon my absence from the hall, Mrs. Sinclair, but I had just gone to present the young lady to Mr. Richards when I heard the carriage pull up," the servant explained.

"Don't be a goose, Mallory," she gently scolded the butler, waving the oversight aside. "I am certainly capable of opening a door for myself," she declared, a question furrowing her brow. "But what young lady did you announce to my brother?"

Mallory dutifully commandeered the parcels that Erin patiently began to stack on the hall table. "I'll just have these sent up to your chamber," he offered solicitously, stepping to the bell pull to summon a footman. "Oh, yes, the name of the young woman is Wells; Miss Jennifer Wells. I was reluctant to admit her to the hall, considering she arrived on the doorstep unescorted, but the young miss was quite persistant," he prattled needlessly to an empty corridor, for the moment Erin had learned the identity of the visitor, she had bounded down the hallway and flung open the parlor door.

"Jennifer!" Erin exclaimed gleefully, pausing on the threshold long enough to request that Mallory have refreshments sent in right away. Then she verily flew inside the chamber to embrace her friend. "What brings you to Richmond?" she asked happily.

Jennifer flushed a little as she cast a glance at Evan, then she pulled away from Erin to smooth a wrinkle from the skirt of her gown. "Well, I came to enjoy some shopping and a bit of a holiday mostly, but I also came in the hopes that I can prevent any unpleasantness," her voice trailed off obliquely.

Erin and Evan exchanged inquisitive looks. They were both understandably intrigued by the latter portion of Jennifer's admission, but Erin considerately led her guest to a comfortable chair before beginning her interrogation.

"Whatever can you mean by such an ominous pronouncement? What sort of unpleasantness are you talking about?" Erin asked lightly as she selected a chair opposite her friend.

"The kind that Christina creates wherever she goes," Jennifer stated matter-of-factly.

"Christina!" Erin's incredulois cry echoed throughout the chamber. "Will she never give me a moment's peace?"

"Christina has always proven to be a particularly annoying creature, but I sincerely doubt that our cousin came all the

418

way to Richmond to purposely antagonize you, sis," Evan patiently chided his sibling.

"I wouldn't be surprised if she did just that," Erin sulked peevishly.

Evan could not suppress the grin that his sister's exaggerated pout spawned. "Well," he cleared his throat, "Richmond is a big city. There is an excellent possibility you won't have to endure her company. Besides, Irish, we'll be going home in a few days," he reminded her.

"Home?" Jennifer's spirits brightened. "Does that mean that everything has . . . uh . . . has w-w-worked out to your satisfaction?" she stammered uncertainly, directing her question to Evan.

"Well, yes; I suppose it does," he replied, shifting uncomfortably in his chair, for he was still quite self-conscious about his impairment.

Erin sensed his acute embarrassment and swiftly came to rescue. "Pay no attention to my modest brother, Jennifer, for he greatly belittles the wonderful progress he's made. In fact, to celebrate Evan's achievement, we are going to attend the theatre this evening. A New York traveling repertory company is in town to perform *Hamlet.*"

"Speaking of which," Evan inserted, reaching for his cane. "I think I'll just leave you ladies to your chitchat while I find Chin Li and see if he was able to remove that unsightly spot from my favorite jacket." He carefully made his way across the room and bent down to place a brotherly kiss against his sister's brow. "It was damned thoughtful of that husband of yours to send his man along to assist me." The smile was genuine when he turned to bid farewell to Jennifer. "Will you be attending tonight's performance?"

"No." Jennifer could not control the disappointment that infiltrated her voice. "We only arrived this morning. Christina has time to consider little except shopping and making the acquaintance of eligible young men," Jennifer sighed her explanation.

419

"Then perhaps you could be persuaded to join us tonight," Evan offered kindly, affixing the young lady in question with a hopeful look.

"Oh, yes!" Erin quickly voiced her approval. "There will plenty of room in our box. Please, say that you will come, Jennifer!" she urged her friend.

Erin had to say little to convince Jennifer, for the girl happily bobbed her head up and down in eager acceptance of the invitation, and the disheartened frown that had previously dressed her face blossomed into an ecstatic smile.

"Good." Evan resumed his advance toward the exit. "Just give Erin the directions to your residence, and we shall call for you at seven." He had arrived at the door, but he paused at the threshold to address a parting comment to his captivated audience. "It shall indeed be a pleasure to escort two such lovely and charming ladies. I shall doubtless be the envy of all the gentlemen in attendance."

Erin waited until the door closed behind her twin before she turned to witness the lustrous glow on Jennifer's face. But she was permitted no opportunity to comment on the situation, for Jennifer descended upon her excitedly.

"Oh, Erin! Can you believe it? I can hardly believe it myself. I've waited so long for this moment." She observed Erin's circumspect frown, and hastened to reassure her friend. "I know that tonight's invitation is no declaration of love, but it is a start. I was beginning to think he'd never notice me at all," she admitted in a small voice, lowering her gaze to her hands that nervously knotted the straps of her reticule.

"Jennifer," Erin began slowly. "When Evan left for the war, he was little more than a prankish youngster, and he returned an embittered young man. The past few months have been excruciating for him, and, for a time, I truly believed he might never accept his fate. But the weeks I have spent with him here in Richmond have proven to be rewarding, for I think he is beginning to feel like a whole man again, and is ready to accept the responsibilities of manhood.

"I cannot make any promises, you understand, nor do I wish to give you false hope, but I do know that Evan thinks highly of you. Just be patient with him," she murmured gently. "The old, personable Evan is just beginning to resurface, and, given a little time along with a little inside encouragement; who is to say what might happen?" A decidedly conspiratorial grin lit up Erin's pretty face.

"Oh, no, Erin. You mustn't!" Jennifer hurriedly objected. "I don't want Evan to think that I'm *chasing* him."

"Pooh!" Erin scoffed. "What man does not enjoy a harmless flirtation? Besides, if you follow my suggestions, I'll wager my dear brother will soon be an avid pursuer."

"Do you really think so?"

"We'll see," Erin replied noncommittally. "Now, why don't you fill me in on all the gossip from home? Did you see Kellen before you left?" she asked hopefully.

"Yes. He sends his love, and says to tell you that he'll be seeing you soon. He misses you dreadfully; I could tell. It must be wonderful to be so completely cherished," she sighed romantically.

"It is," Erin whispered hoarsely, suddenly consumed by an overwhelming loneliness for her absent spouse.

"Oh, how silly of me. I nearly forgot," Jennifer said suddenly, reaching inside her reticule to withdraw an envelope. "Kellen asked me to give this to you."

Erin accepted the missive, longingly examining the bold script before tucking it inside her pocket to peruse when she had sequestered herself alone in her chamber. The door opened at that moment to admit Mallory with the requested tray of refreshments, and the two girls contented themselves for the remainder of the afternoon by nibbling on the scrumptious delicacies and indulging in a tireless round of girlish gossip.

Erin did not consider the performance that evening to be

particularly enthralling, for her thoughts were irrevocably focused elsewhere. The missive she had received that day from Kellen had merely served to accentuate her homesickness and had attributed greatly to her present downcast mood. And though her eyes were trained on the stage in apparent fascination, the images that flitted through her mind were of a very different configuration.

With a discontented sigh, Erin shifted in her seat and hugged her arms to herself while she permitted her memory to wander freely. She languished in the glorious recollection of Kellen's warm breath against her skin, the lazy inflection of his voice, and the gentle strength of his hands as they masterfully stroked her flesh, arousing her to unbelievable heights of ecstasy.

Erin flushed as the direction of her reminiscences acutely reminded her of the celibate life she had led the past few weeks, and, as she began to fan her scarlet face with the theatrical program, she detected a muffled chortle from the brother who sat beside her. In dismay, she turned to confront Evan's laughing eyes, and had she any doubt about the reason for his taunting expression, it was quickly dispelled when he spoke.

"It would seem, dear sister, that your concentration lies quite decisively elsewhere, for I've witnessed nothing on the boards thus far to warrant such an impassioned reaction," he teased unmercifully.

"Evan!" She winced painfully, her flush deepening, for he made no pretense at denying he had guessed the contents of her musings. "Others may hear you," she pleaded.

"I fear that your reverie was so complete that you've not yet noticed that it is now intermission. Perhaps a cool libation would serve to . . . ahem . . . *soothe* your somewhat flustered condition." Evan barely avoided the indignant hand that shot out to render him a severe reprimand for his impertinence. But the caustic retort that sprang to Erin's lips was to go unspoken, for he leaned close to whisper sympathetically, "You truly love that pesky Yankee, don't you, Irish?"

"Yes," she murmured. "And I miss him awfully."

"I know you do." Evan reached out to pat her hand affectionately, his mien growing suddenly somber. "I've never said as much, but I want you to know that I appreciate the sacrifice you've made by attending me here in Richmond. Your kindness is more than generous, especially when one considers the despicable way I behaved toward everyone.

"No, let me finish." He waved aside the protest Erin began to interject. "I'm not particularly proud of the things I said and did, but I promise that the world shall be subjected to a very different Evan Richards from now on. I also promise to return you to the arms of your husband as soon as the necessary travel arrangements can be made.

"Meanwhile, Jennifer and I are going to procure some refreshments before the play resumes. Would you care to join us?" He stood up carefully, offering his hand to Jennifer.

"No, you two run along," she answered, exchanging a meaningful look with the girl who stood at his side.

"Very well. We'll bring you a glass of iced champagne," Evan offered kindly, holding aside the curtain, so that Jennifer might exit in front of him.

Erin watched as the curtain fell behind them, and she experienced a pang of envy when she recalled how Evan had taken Jennifer's hand during the performance and had leaned close to whisper some fleeting comment in her ear. Both had been very simple gestures, yet they had made her yearn for her husband's embrace. Thus reminded, Erin's thoughts again turned to Kellen, but the faint touch of a hand on her shoulder startled her, and she looked up expectantly. But her hopeful smile dissolved when her eyes met the ones that gazed soulfully into hers.

"Michael!" she exclaimed. "Whatever are you doing here?"

"You sound surprised to see me."

"I am!"

"Well, to be honest, since you refused to receive me at Kilkieran, I decided to follow you to Richmond. I *must* speak

with you, Erin. May I sit down?" he asked, nodding specifically toward the chair beside her.

Erin glanced anxiously over her shoulder, then with a
shrug, she said, "Of course, you may sit down. After all, we've
been friends for years." She offered him a tentative smile. "When
did you arrive? How are you?" she asked pleasantly.

"I haven't time to exchange banalities, Erin," Michael replied glibly, his manner serious. "I've never been one to beat
about the bush, and I'll not start now. I want you to come away
with me. I still love you. You must come away with me.
Please, say that you will."

Erin could not check the slight gape of her mouth, nor the
blank expression that met his urgent gaze. "Michael," she began uncertainly, thoroughly stunned by his declaration. "You
cannot be thinking rationally. You don't truly expect me to
leave Kellen!"

"Yes, I do," he stated baldly.

"Well, I won't, and I don't intend to discuss the absurd notion further," her retort was as equally succinct, and she
turned from him, discouraged by the unfortunate outcome of
their meeting. "The play will resume shortly. Perhaps you
should return to your seat."

Michael glanced around the bustling auditorium, and realized that Evan and Jennifer would be returning soon; he
would have to hurry if he were to successfully achieve his purpose. "Very well," he conceded. "I will go, but I still need to
talk to you. Have lunch with me tomorrow," he suggested
abruptly, coaxing her to look at him again.

Erin hesitated, not wanting to cause him further anguish,
yet knowing that was precisely what would happen should she
continue to encourage him. Finally, she said, "I . . . I don't
think that would be wise. I *am* sorry, Michael, but Kellen
would not understand—"

"I don't give a damn about that worthless Yankee!" Michael
thundered, his blue eyes growing dark with rage, and he
clenched his fists to bring his ire under control. His equanim-

ity restored, Michael again spoke, "You once claimed to love me, Erin, we were going to be married. It was not I who destroyed those dreams by marrying another," he added pointedly, causing Erin to hang her head sorrowfully. "I hardly think that dining together in a crowded restaurant can be construed as infidelity," he said dryly. "You owe me this much. Say yes."

Erin glanced into the handsome face, the once familiar features that now seemed so foreign to her, and knew that she could not deny him this innocent request. Besides, she reasoned, what possible harm could come from a friendly luncheon date?

Meeting his gaze, she nodded her acquiescence.

"Good. Shall I call for you at noon?"

"No!" she quickly objected. "I . . . I have a number of errands to run in the morning. It will be more convenient if I meet you."

"Very well." Michael stood to take his leave. "I'm staying at The Bristol. Meet me in the foyer at noon." He bent over her hand and pressed a kiss against the delicate appendage. "Till tomorrow," he murmured wistfully, then disappeared through the blue velvet curtains just as Evan and Jennifer prepared to reenter the box.

Evan gave his sister a curious look, but Erin glanced away hastily, determined to make a concentrated effort at enjoying the remainder of the performance. But her resolve quickly withered as her thoughts drifted to her promised engagement with Michael.

Erin's ponderings were no less confused the following day as she made her way along the busy city street toward Michael's hotel. Indeed, much of his discourse remained an unreadable blur to her, except, of course, for his unforgettable declaration of love. Had she taken the time to thoroughly consider her actions, Erin probably never would have consented to the rendezvous, for she realized that she was taking a risk. Kellen would never condone such a meeting, especially with Michael.

"Oh, well," she mumbled to herself. "I shall make absolutely certain that Kellen never learns of this little indiscretion," she vowed determinedly. "But Michael must be made to accept the fact that I love Kellen, and that I will do *nothing* to jeopardize my marriage."

Erin looked up suddenly to find that she had arrived at The Bristol. She paused for a moment on the sidewalk to renew her courage, and, peering through the window, she could see Michael pacing about the lobby. Swallowing resolutely, Erin prepared to enter the hotel, but a disturbance outside a neighboring building made her pause.

Glancing up expectantly, Erin saw a young street urchin dart from the doorway and sprint up the sidewalk toward her. In hot pursuit of the grubby lad was the store proprietor, who wielded a broom ominously and shouted coarse threats at the fleeing thief. Many pedestrians along the corwded thoroughfare scampered out of the way of the charging duo, and Erin was about to adopt a similar course of action when the young prankster suddenly swerved toward her. Before she realized what was happening, the boy crashed into her, sending her sprawling clumsily onto the hard sidewalk.

Erin was momentarily stunned by the mishap, but her immediate recovery was impeded by the crush of do-gooders who crowded around to determine the extent of her injuries. Thus surrounded, Erin did not see the lone figure standing on the opposite side of the street who viewed the scene with obvious satisfaction. An evil smile spread Vanessa Sinclair's lips, and, with a contented swirl of her petticoats, she turned and sauntered away from the skirmish, reasonably assured that the remainder of the carefully conceived plan could now be accomplished.

Meanwhile, Erin struggled to attain a sitting position, but her maneuverability was severely hampered by a sharp pain that tore through her ankle. Leaning back, Erin lifted a trembling hand to readjust her askew bonnet. Feeling slightly humiliated and decisively bruised, she assured those who hovered about her that she was perfectly fine; wishing all the while that Kellen was there to take command of the situation.

But the concerned blue eyes that met hers when the crowd finally dispersed did not belong to her husband; they were Michael's.

He had witnessed the incident from the hotel doorway, but when he would have come to her rescue, he found his way substantially blocked by a swarm of curious bystanders. He at last managed to shoulder his way through the crowd, and a look of relief framed his face when he beheld Erin's somewhat amusing state of dishevelment. For though she had been understandably shaken by the accident, the profound look of consternation that adorned her pretty face warned him that only her pride had suffered a devastating blow.

He considerately retrieved the parcels that had scattered willy-nilly from the force of the impact, then he returned to offer her his assistance. "Hello, kitten," he said softly, extending his hand to her, so that she might rise.

"Oh, Michael!" she cried, "Did you see that dreadful, little boy?" Erin grasped the proffered hand and carefully climbed to her feet, though she teetered somewhat unsteadily on her rapidly swelling ankle.

"You're hurt!" Michael acknowledged her faltering movement.

"It's nothing serious; just a wrenched ankle," Erin assured him. "But it is throbbing painfully. Would you please summon a carriage for me?"

"Nonsense! You're in pain and badly shaken. I'll just take you up to my room, so that you can freshen yourself and rest that ankle for awhile," he said practically.

"No!" she balked at the scandalous suggestion. "I will be fine. Truly, I will," she insisted. "But I want to go home, *now!*"

But her escort staunchly refused to heed her pleas. Instead,

427

he shoved the parcels into her hands, then bent and gathered her in his arms. "And so you shall. But first, I want to make absolutely certain that you're all right. Now, you can come along quietly, or screeching like a lunatic. Personally, I should think that the former would create a less memorable scene, but the decision is yours."

He swiftly carried her through the lobby and up the staircase to his second floor apartment before Erin could offer further protests.

"Michael, this isn't at all proper," Erin said disapprovingly, as he struggled with the key while holding her firmly within his grasp.

"Don't worry, kitten," he chided her.

Michael finally succeeded in heaving the heavy door aside, then he carried her across the threshold. He hesitated for a moment, as if deliberating where he should deposit his precious burden. Then with a shrug, he kicked the door closed and strode purposefully toward the bed. After he had carefully placed her there, he considerately assisted her from her cloak and bonnet.

He started to take a seat beside her, but Erin's bewildered expression and frantic objection made him pause. *"Really,* Michael, I think I'd be more comfortable in a chair!"

"No, you wouldn't," he retorted bluntly. Then more patiently, he added, "I didn't bring you here to ravish you, if that's the reason for your distress."

"Of course, you didn't!" Erin returned hastily. "It's just that . . . *Ouch!"* Her explanation was preempted by a stabbing pain in her ankle.

Erin propped herself up on her elbows and extended her leg, struggling to obtain a better look at the throbbing joint. But even as she strained to reach the rapidly swelling area, more composed hands pushed hers aside to thoroughly inspect the afflicted ankle.

"It's not so bad," he said eventually. "There is a good deal of swelling, however, and the boot needs to be removed, so that the ankle can be wrapped in a cool compress," Michael suggested wisely.

"Can you take me home first?" Erin pleaded, the inappropriateness of the situation plaguing her as much as her ailing limb.

"No," he informed her brusquely, "it cannot wait. Now, I suggest that you take a deep breath, for this is certain to be quite painful."

Michael's prediction proved to be extremely accurate, and, though Erin had to bite her lower lip to keep from screaming, she was grateful when the leather walking boot had been removed. Erin sighed thankfully and sank back against the soft coverlets, silently watching as the brooding man tended her wounded ankle. First, he dipped a cloth in cold water and carefully swathed the tender joint, then he propped her foot on a pillow for added comfort. After determining that she was adequately settled, Michael went to pour her a glass of wine.

"Here, drink this," he ordered, proffering the glass.

Erin dutifully accepted the drink, and, as she sipped at the flavorful liquid, her eyes climbed to his, and she offered him a sheepish smile. "Thank you, Michael. I am feeling much better now." She settled the empty glass upon the beside table. "Do you think that you could take me home now?" Her voice was calm, but her apprehension was rekindled when Michael sat down on the bed beside her.

"In a little while," he murmured noncommittally, romantically clasping her hand between his. "We haven't dined yet, and I did promise you a luncheon," he reminded her.

"But I couldn't eat a bite at the moment, and I am certain that Evan must be wondering where I am," she explained, nervously pulling her hand from his.

Erin endeavored to put some distance between them by squirming to the opposite side of the bed, but her efforts proved futile, for she suddenly found herself the recipient of a rather ardent embrace.

"Michael!" Erin cried her acute dismay. "Please! You

mustn't. You don't know what you're doing."

"Yes, I do," he said plainly, establishing her more securely in his arms. "I'm about to make love to you," he bluntly informed her.

"*What?*" Erin shrieked. "*No!* Oh, Michael. This is madness. You *must* let me go!"

Until now, Erin's objections had been half-hearted, for she did not truly believe that he meant to compromise her. But as the arms about her tightened possessively, and Michael's mouth descended upon hers hungrily, Erin became alarmed, and she stiffened in his embrace. She lay rigid as he pressed kisses against her lips, her eyes and brow, hoping that her obvious disinterest would discourage him.

Instead, her indifference merely served to spur his own desire to ignite her passion, and, while his mouth returned to hers, his hands began to roam familiarly up and down her back and along her arms.

Erin's flustered mind verily spun as she tried to think of some way out of her predicament, but when Michael's insistent tongue forcibly entered her mouth to initiate its sensual probing, she sprang into action. Summoning all her strength, she managed to pull her arms free and push him away from her.

"*Michael!*" she hissed sternly, waving a trembling finger beneath his nose. "Don't you *ever* do that again! Do you hear me?

"*No!*" She furiously slapped away the hand that relentlessly endeavored to caress her cheek. "Please, take me home, Michael. And then . . . then, I think it would be wise if we didn't see each other again."

"You don't mean that!" he protested vehemently.

"Yes, I do. At least . . . at least until you can accept the fact that I am happily married and totally committed to Kellen," she delivered her ultimatum with such finality that Michael went rigid beside her.

The room grew awkwardly silent and several pregnant seconds ticked away before either of them spoke. Michael was the first to speak, however, his words only served to revive her anxiety.

"That doesn't matter, because I still love you, and I want you. I've been obsessed with the notion of having you since the day I saw you by the waterfall . . . *our* waterfall . . . with that bastard you foolishly married." His blue eyes grew dangerously sinister as he recounted this bit of information to her, and he grabbed her roughly by the shoulders and pulled her toward him. "I want you to cling to me the way you did to him that day! I want you to tell me that you love me!"

"But I love Kellen. I *belong* to him," Erin persisted, and, though she was shocked to learn that he had observed her passionate encounter with her husband, she did not think to rebuke him for his distasteful surveillance. For she was trying desperately not to succumb to the hysteria that threatened to consume her at any second.

"You won't after today, not after *this.*" He easily shoved aside her defiant hands to allow him access to her voluptuous bosom.

Within seconds he had undone the buttons of her blouse and pushed the delicate material apart to reveal the pink tipped mounds that heaved violently against her sheer undergarments. Exhaling a throaty sigh, Michael impatiently rent the flimsy material and began to fondle the enticing flesh that trembled fearfully beneath his touch. Sensing Erin's reluctance, Michael placed a gentle kiss upon each breast, then he crushed her against him and captured her lips with a brutal kiss.

When at last he pulled away, Michael eased her back against the covers and tenderly stroked her cheek. "Don't be afraid, kitten," he whispered hoarsely, his voice thick with passion. "I'll be gentle. I won't hurt you."

"But you *are* hurting me," Erin whimpered pitifully, vainly trying to ignore the hand that had returned to caress her exposed breast. And in one final, desperate plea for her freedom, she cried, "Have you any idea what Kellen will do to you if he learns of this?"

"Offhand, I'd be willing to wager that he would be mighty tempted to kill the son-of-a-bitch," came a precisely calculated answer to her question.

Painfully aware of the untimeliness of the discovery, and equally cognizant of the identity of the intruder, Erin frantically shoved Michael aside. She quickly searched the face of her husband as he leaned negligently against the doorjamb, but if she had expected to find understanding in Kellen's murderous expression, Erin was to be sorely disappointed. For there was no compassion glistening in the vivid blue eyes that raked over her; only acute disgust.

Chapter Twenty-one

Achilles had barely come to a halt when Kellen vaulted from the steed's back in front of the row house on Franklin Street. He securely tethered the animal to the post before the residence and ran up the narrow sidewalk to sound an impatient knock upon the door.

He had not wired ahead to inform Erin of his impending arrival, thinking instead that he would surprise her. Therefore, it was he who received the surprise when the butler announced that Mrs. Sinclair was not presently at home.

Swallowing his disappointment, Kellen offered the servant a pleasant smile and said, "You must be Mallory. My wife has mentioned you in her letters," he explained his identity. Then stepping into the foyer, he asked, "Could you have someone tend to my horse and carry my belongings to my wife's chamber? I would like to freshen up a bit before she returns."

"Certainly, Mr. Sinclair," Mallory replied, undaunted, as though he was accustomed to acknowledging instructions from perfect strangers. "Perhaps you would care to wait in the drawing room with the others," he suggested.

"Others?"

"Yes." Mallory dutifully helped Kellen from his overcoat. "Two young ladies arrived a short while ago, and requested that they be allowed to wait for Mrs. Sinclair.

"I was just about to serve tea," the butler continued. "Would you care to join them, sir?"

"Ladies?" Kellen murmured speculatively, not convinced that the notion of spending his afternoon being regaled by a group of prattling hens appealed to him. Still, he reasoned, if Erin had made new acquaintances in Richmond, he should at least exchange cordialities with his wife's guests.

"Yes, Mallory," Kellen sighed his acquiescence. "I suppose that I *should* say hello. Do you know their names?"

"Yes, sir." Mallory stepped along the wide corridor to the drawing room door, and, just as he opened the portal, he answered, "They are Mrs. Geoffrey Sinclair and Miss Christina Richards."

Too late, Kellen realized that Mallory had already swung the door open and stepped across the threshold to announce his arrival. Almost immediately, Kellen came to regret his decision to greet Erin's visitors, for Vanessa swept across the room to stand before him.

"Why, Christina. Look who's here," she cooed sweetly. Then to Kellen, she said, "Hello, Kellen. This is quite a surprise."

Casting a beseeching look at Mallory, Kellen quickly surmised that he would receive little assistance from that quarter, for the butler had discreetly exited the chamber; apparently having gone off to collect the aforementioned refreshments. Resigning himself to his fate, and silently rendering his absent wife a thundering scold, Kellen squared his shoulders and prepared to suffer through the dreaded encounter.

"Hello, ladies," he said pleasantly, though not particularly sincerely. "I might say the same of finding you here; *that* is indeed surprising."

Reluctantly stepping across the threshold, Kellen selected a comfortable chair and sat down. He stretched his long legs in front of him, then, leveling a suspicious glare at Vanessa, he demanded, "What are you up to, Vanessa?"

"Why, Kellen. Whatever do you mean by that remark?" she

asked innocently. The completely guiltless look that Vanessa assumed was so ridiculous that Kellen had to forcibly restrain the chuckle that rose in his throat.

"You know very well what I mean," he informed her tersely. "What are you doing in Richmond, and, more specifically; what are you doing *here?*"

Vanessa took a seat beside Christina on the sofa before dignifying his questions with replies. "Christina and I became such good friends at your wedding," she began, "so, when she wrote to tell me of her plans to visit her brother in Richmond, I decided to join her, so that we could renew our acquaintance. Then when Christina informed me that our Erin was also in residence, it was only natural for us to call on her."

"Naturally," Kellen droned caustically, his expression plainly revealing that he did not believe her explanation for an instant.

Vanessa correctly interpreted his cynicism, prompting her to castigate him. "Really, Kellen, sometimes you can be the most distrusting creature."

"A quality that has doubtless spared me a great deal of misfortune," he countered. Then suddenly weary of their company, and satisfied that he had adequately completed his duties as host, Kellen rose to take his leave of them.

"Don't tell me that you're going to abandon us so soon," Christina protested.

"Lamentably, I must. I would like to wash away some of this trail dirt before Erin returns." He sauntered toward the door. "Mallory should be returning momentarily to serve tea, so I'll just leave you ladies to your chitchat." He reached for the doorknob, but Vanessa's next inquiry gave him reason to delay his departure.

"Tell me, Kellen. Is Erin expecting you?" she asked casually.

"No, I was hoping to surprise her," he said purposefully, curiously noting the secretive murmurings the girls exchanged upon hearing his reply.

"Oh, I'm confident you will do just that," Vanessa purred mysteriously. "In fact, I think that I can safely speculate that your wife may have a surprise or two of her own for you."

"Just what is that supposed to mean?" Kellen sighed tiredly, but Vanessa merely shrugged her shoulders noncommittally.

Christina, however, was more willing to elaborate. "I think that Vanessa meant to say that had Erin been aware that you were arriving today, she never would have accepted Michael's luncheon invitation."

"Michael!" Kellen abruptly forgot his eagerness to be free of his guests, and he stalked across the room to stand directly before Christina. "Are you telling me that Cahill is in town as well?" he demanded harshly.

"Y-y-yes," she stammered, shifting uncomfortably in her seat as she grew increasingly wary of the fierce looking man who loomed over her.

"And Erin is with him now?" he shouted incredulously.

"Well, yes," Christina answered. "That is, I assume so. You see, I ran into Michael this morning, and he happened to mention that he had invited Erin to take lunch with him."

"*Where?*"

"Now, Kellen," Vanessa chided him. "You're starting to sound like a very jealous husband. I'm certain that Erin's luncheon engagement with her former sweetheart is quite . . . innocent."

"I'm not interested in your suppositions," Kellen informed her bluntly, and, turning on Christina, he thundered, "I said, *where are they?*"

Christina found it exceedingly difficult to maintain her composure under Kellen's foreboding countenance, but she somehow managed to reply, "I believe that Michael mentioned that Erin was going to meet him at The Bristol; that's where he is staying. The Bristol *is* reputed to have one of the finest eateries in the city. Perhaps you will find them there."

But Christina's final conjecture was made in vain, for Kellen turned and stormed from the chamber upon learning his wife's direction. The two ladies who remained behind exchanged congratulatory nods, then stood to emulate Kellen's example.

"Do you truly think we should follow him?" Christina asked worriedly.

"Of course. I wouldn't miss this for the world." A vindictive smile spread Vanessa's lips. "Besides, our mission is not quite finished," she added meaningfully. Then with a sweeping gesture, she strode across the floor to exit the room, with Christina closely dogging her tracks.

Kellen's withdrawal was executed with such haste that he very nearly bowled over Mallory as the servant maneuvered a heavy silver tea service toward the drawing room. In fact, Kellen was so completely lost to his fury that he had traveled a block from the row house before he stopped short; suddenly realizing that not only had he forgotten to don his overcoat and hat, but he was not acquainted with the address of The Bristol. Thus reminded of his oversight, he was forced to return to the house to consult with Mallory, and he had just obtained the desired information when Vanessa and Christina emerged from the drawing room and overheard him request that the servant summon a cab for him.

Seizing upon this most opportune moment, Vanessa explained to Kellen that her carriage was parked just outside, and it would be no trouble to drop him at The Bristol. "Besides, I shouldn't want to delay your reunion with your lovely wife," she added sweetly.

Swallowing the bitter rejoinder he was tempted to voice, Kellen jammed his hat upon his head and stalked out the door ahead of them. He reasoned that time was of the essence, and, while he might derive personal satisfaction in exchanging insults with Vanessa, his immediate priority was to find Erin and purge himself of the nagging sense of dread that presently consumed him.

The ride to The Bristol was made in virtual silence, for though both girls were reasonably smug in their confidence of what awaited Kellen at the hotel, they similarly realized the folly of openly voicing such an innuendo to the enraged man.

The carriage had not come to a complete stop before Kellen threw the door open and jumped from the conveyance. Without a backward glance at the ladies who intently watched after him, Kellen raced across the sidewalk to the hotel entrance. A cursory inspection of the dining room did not reveal what he sought, therefore, Kellen's countenance had grown positively black by the time he approached the desk clerk.

The young man who was stationed behind the desk took one look at the awesomely foreboding gentleman who towered over him, and wasted little time giving Kellen the direction of Michael Cahill's room. Even Kellen's closest comrade would not have anticipated that his already foul disposition could grow even more ominous. But when he eased open the unlatched door to find his wife locked in a seemingly passionate embrace with her one-time suitor, Kellen's demeanor became frightfully intimidating.

The couple had immediately separated upon hearing Kellen's glib response to Erin's hushed question, but his wife's glaring state of dishevelment did little to assuage Kellen's rapidly escalating fears. Emitting a guttural cry of obvious repugnance, Kellen kicked the door closed and came full into the room.

"Well, well, well," he droned icily as he strode purposefully toward the bed. "It would seem that my dear wife has not suffered from a lack of entertainment since her arrival to the city." Kellen stared pointedly at Erin's naked bosom and the masculine hand that still rested dangerously close to that voluptuous region, and when he spoke, his tone was deadly. "Cahill, you will, I think, understand that I must insist you move away from my wife."

Michael's immediate reaction was to balk at Kellen's hostile attitude, but since everything was proceeding to his advantage, he decided that it would be simpler to acquiesce. So, with a conciliatory gesture, he retired to an inconspicuous corner of the room.

Realizing that she would be the focus of Kellen's attention, Erin hastily rearranged her clothing and threw her husband a beseeching look. "I . . . I know how this must look to you," she began tentatively.

"Believe me, Erin. You cannot sufficiently imagine how disgusting you look at this moment," he ruthlessly informed her.

"Oh, Kellen!" she cried weakly. "Please, listen to me, for I promise that I can explain everything." She struggled to a sitting position on the edge of the bed and stretched out her hand to him.

"You know, I sincerely doubt that you can," he seethed coldly, ignoring the hand that pleaded for his touch.

Erin took one look at the unyielding set of Kellen's jaw, and her heart sank. She rationalized that he had every right to be upset with her, and it was understandable that he would think the worst, considering the incriminating circumstances in which he had discovered her. If she could only persuade him to listen to her, she was positive that she could make him believe her. But sitting in the midst of Michael's bedchamber was hardly the place to conduct such a delicate conversation.

Her hand fell limply to her lap, and she murmured desolately, "Would you please take me home?"

"Now, there's an idea." Kellen's voice was rich with sarcasm. "Had you the foresight to stay there in the first place, this distasteful scene could have been avoided. Lord only knows how long this has been going on," he mumbled wretchedly. "Tell me, Erin, are there other lovers with whom I may have to contend?"

Justifiably incensed by Kellen's churlish remarks, Erin snapped back at him, "You're being quite ridiculous about—"

But before she could complete her statement, Kellen grasped her by the shoulders and jerked her to her feet. *"I'm*

439

being ridiculous!" he thundered incredulously, but the excruciating grimace that shrouded Erin's face made him pause. "What is it?" he barked unsympathetically.

"My . . . my ankle. This wretched little boy pushed me down earlier, and I twisted it. Michael was merely . . . merely *helping* me . . ." Her voice trailed off, and she cast an imploring look toward Michael, begging him to corroborate her story, but he made no effort to speak on her behalf.

"You must forgive my skepticism, Erin," Kellen began snidely, "but even if what you say is true, it appeared that Cahill was administering a most peculiar treatment for your infirmity." He stood by while Erin forced her swollen foot back into her boot, then he snatched her discarded coat and hastily wrapped it about her shoulders. "Come along," he ordered crossly. "We will discuss this bit of indiscretion at home in private." He shot a loathsome glance at Michael.

Kellen stalked angrily toward the door, leaving a helpless Erin no alternative save to limp along on her injured foot. Embarrassing tears of anguish welled up in Erin's eyes as she hobbled after him, but she had managed only a few faltering steps when Michael rushed to her assistance.

"I'll help you, kitten," he murmured softly, extending her a considerate hand. Then returning Kellen's scornful look in full, he added, "Now that this insensitive bastard has shown his true colors, it will be much easier for you to come away with me."

"The hell you say!" Kellen roared murderously.

In two swift strides, he lessened the distance that separated him from his adversary, and, clenching Cahill's arm in a vise-like grip, he ruthlessly shoved him away from Erin. Michael recovered quickly, but, too late, he correctly interpreted the enraged man's purpose just as Kellen's precisely aimed fist caught him squarely on the jaw and sent him toppling backwards over the sofa. Michael wisely maintained his rather humbling position while he observed his attacker turn and swoop Erin into his arms and carry her from the room.

Kellen hurriedly descended the narrow staircase, but he came up short when he emerged from the hotel and came face-to-face with Vanessa and Christina. He heard Erin's startled intake of breath and felt her stiffen in his grasp, and, though he was not feeling particularly solicitous of her feelings at the moment, he did share her sentiments about their awkward circumstance being viewed by the scheming pair.

"Excuse me," he said abruptly as he started to shoulder his way past the meddlesome twosome.

"You needn't be so brusque," Vanessa chided him. "And surely, you cannot mean to carry Erin all the way back to Franklin Street." She smiled complacently as she watched his eyes skirt up and down the thoroughfare for a vacant cab.

Finding nothing available, he fastened his frosty stare upon her and droned, "What do you suggest?"

"That Christina accompany Erin home in my carriage while you and I have a little chat." She noticed the contemptuous twist of his sensuous mouth and hurried on. "I *do* have some rather interesting news to impart from your grandfather. I promise that it will be worth your while to hear me out," she added mysteriously.

Kellen focused a decisively cynical look at the smugly confident face that awaited his reply, and he silently wondered what her reaction would be if he told her to go to the devil. But, despite himself, he had to admit that his curiosity had been duly piqued. With a nonchalant shrug, Kellen stepped to the carriage and deposited Erin inside, then he turned to confront Vanessa.

"Very well," he consented. "Just where do you propose we have this . . . *chat?*"

Erin was understandably outraged at being abandoned in this ruthless fashion, for regardless of what Kellen might think of her, he had no right to treat her so abominably. And before Vanessa could voice a reply, she interrupted irritably. "But I thought that *we* were going to talk," she objected indignantly.

"Oh, we shall talk, my sweet. You may rest assured of that," he said, a menacing scowl twisting his handsome face.

Then he handed Christina into the vehicle, and the closing of the door resounded in Erin's ears as she watched her husband stroll away from the conveyance with his one-time lover.

Erin sat numbly before her dressing table mirror, staring blankly at her pale reflection. Almost without realizing what she was doing, her hand lifted to smooth her hair, and, for the hundredth time, she wondered why the tears that welled behind her eyes would not fall.

With a disheartened sigh, Erin let her hand fall to her lap. What good would tears do her anyway? For a display of feminine hysterics could serve her little during her forthcoming encounter with Kellen. She *must* remain calm and composed while she carefully prepared her defense, so that she might convince Kellen of her innocence.

That particular thought elicited a tortured groan from Erin's throat as she recalled the look of sheer abhorrence that had contorted his handsome face upon his discovery of her in Michael's chamber. The blue eyes that had always regarded her with gentle reverence or playful mischief had grown uncharacteristically cold and harsh; a sight she hoped never to witness again.

Even as she sat in her chair, fretfully rehearsing her speech, Erin knew that the task that lay before her was going to be an arduous one. Still, she was determined that she would make Kellen believe that the scene he had stumbled upon was nothing more than a horrible misunderstanding; that she had not betrayed his love, and that she would never purposely do anything to hurt him or jeopardize their happiness together.

Feeling substantially rejuvenated, Erin released her wet hair from the towel that she had wrapped about her head following her evening bath, and began to pull a brush through the tangled locks. But a soft knock upon the door caused her to jump with dreaded anticipation, and, swallowing the nervous lump in her throat, she turned to face the barrier.

"Come in," she squeaked faintly.

Her mouth was dry and her heart was pounding so fiercely in her chest that she feared she might be driven mad by its incessant thumping before her caller made his identity known to her. Finally, the door eased open and Evan stepped across the threshold.

"Oh, Evan," she breathed gratefully, returning to her task. "It's only you."

"Well, that's a fine how-do-you-do." He feigned effrontery at her blunt greeting. Then closing the door, he crossed the room to stand behind her chair, and, placing his hands on her shoulders, he gave them an affectionate, brotherly squeeze. "Hiding out, are you?" he intentionally teased her.

"As if that would do me any good," she lamented.

Evan took a seat on the edge of the bed, and, though he tried to maintain a lighthearted mood for Erin's benefit, he knew that the situation that existed between her and Kellen was grave.

Watching her closely, he said, "You're right about that, little sister. Knowing my brother-in-law, I'd say your chances of avoiding a showdown are minimal at best."

Focusing an icy look on her sibling, Erin droned sarcastically, "Thank you. It's so kind of you to stand by me in my hour of need. And just when did you become such an expert on my husband's capabilities?" she demanded peevishly.

"I'm not. But it doesn't take a genius to realize that the brooding gentleman, who is presently sequestered in the downstairs drawing room, will not be denied an explanation. And from the sound of things, I'd make it a damned good one, if I were you."

"Kellen's here?"

"I don't believe that Mallory is wont to admit strangers indiscriminately to the hall, *or* allows them unlimited access to

443

the liquor cabinet." He scrupulously brushed a piece of unsightly lint from his lapel.

"Oh, do try to be serious!" Erin unthinkingly stamped her injured foot at him, causing her to wince painfully.

"I am."

"He's drinking, then?" She chewed a fingernail anxiously.

"Yes."

"How long?"

"He arrived about two hours ago, requested a bottle of the cellar's best, then proceeded to lock himself away in the drawing room. He's been pacing and thumping about like a caged animal ever since." Evan's somber gaze met and held his sister's in the mirror. "I must be candid with you, Erin. I don't find your present situation a particularly enviable one."

"Oh, Evan," she cried lugubriously, burying her face in her hands. "What am I going to do?"

Evan stood up, and, grasping his cane in one hand, he returned to Erin's side. "Here." He offered her the use of his arm for support. "I suggest that you retire to the chaise lounge, so that you may dry your hair before the fire. You don't want to appear like an unkempt hoyden before your husband; not tonight in any case."

Erin nodded in agreement, and, after she was comfortably seated, Evan sat down beside her and took her hand in his. "Quite simply, you are going to tell Kellen the truth."

"It isn't *that* simple," she insisted. "What if he doesn't believe me?"

"Then you shall have to convince him. He seems to be a reasonable sort, for all that he *is* a Yankee." He glanced down at his pocketwatch and stood up abruptly, obviously preparing to abandon her.

"You aren't deserting me?" she wailed.

"Yes, I am," he answered shortly. "Jennifer has consented to dine with me this evening, and I shall have to hurry if I'm going to fetch her on time." He glanced down into Erin's distraught face and said softly, "Don't worry, Irish. I don't suppose he intends to *beat* you." Then as an afterthought, he added, "Though, if a wife of mine ever behaved so foolishly, I certainly would."

"Evan!" Erin groaned. "You are doing precious little to strengthen my confidence. You *know* that I was not unfaithful to Kellen."

"I know," he whispered. "But I am your brother. Kellen, on the other hand, is your husband, and, like it or not, he is presently entertaining some serious doubts about your fidelity. He feels threatened by today's episode because of your past association with Michael. Oh, he'll bellow at you for a time, but when the smoke clears, I think he will believe you."

Erin watched in solemn silence as her twin executed his departure, and, as the door closed behind him, she mumbled forlornly, "I do so pray that you are right, dear brother."

Meanwhile, a thoroughly disgruntled Kellen seethed bitterly in his self-imposed prison in the drawing room. He presently sat in a wing chair before the fireplace, his long legs stretching out in front of him to be warmed by the fire's glow. But the raging blaze might just as well have been little more than smoldering embers for all that Kellen took note of it, for his concentration was singularly devoted elsewhere.

His hand automatically reached for the near empty bottle of brandy on the table at his side, and, uttering an undecipherable grunt, he poured the remaining contents into his glass. As he raised the snifter to his lips, his eyes fell on the wrinkled paper that lay in his lap; the document that Vanessa had so *graciously* bestowed upon him earlier that day. His lips narrowed into a thin, taut line, and a muscle in his neck twitched menacingly as he recalled the distasteful encounter.

Vanessa had sat across from him in the coffeehouse, a suspiciously jubilant smile highlighting her face. Thinking back on it, he remembered that he had considered it odd that Vanessa had not offered some churlish comment regarding the scandalous scene she had just witnessed. But he was to quickly learn that Vanessa had more pressing matters on her mind; matters that included presenting Kellen with a copy of the marriage contract that Erin had signed to appease Jeremiah before he would consent to the marriage.

Again, Kellen's eyes fastened hatefully on the paper, and, with a furious gesture, he cast the document aside and stood up to rest his elbows on the mantel. Lowering his beleaguered head into his hands, he closed his eyes and tried to sort out the complexities the day had wrought.

At first, he had merely thought that Vanessa was up to one of her old tricks. But his faith in his wife's loyalty had already been badly shaken, therefore, Vanessa experienced little difficulty persuading Kellen to read the contract.

Kellen could vividly recall the mingled feelings of humiliation and outright fury that had swept through him like an uncontrollable blaze raging through an arid forest, as his eyes had scanned the legal document. But when he beheld the signature; that delicately configured script which was so characteristic of Erin, he experienced a rage so intensely incredible that he had momentarily feared for his sanity.

Kellen's wrath was so consummate that he was unsure which of the ladies he despised more at that exact moment; Vanessa or Erin. Yet, outwardly, he gave no visible indication that the contents of the document had disconcerted him in the least. In fact, he meticulously refolded the contract, tucked it inside his jacket, politely thanked Vanessa for bringing the matter to his attention, then he stood, and, executing a perfunctory bow over her hand, he withdrew from the restaurant.

Kellen had not bothered to hire a cab to return him to the house, but had completed the journey on foot. Then just as Evan had indicated, he barricaded himself in the drawing room in the hopes that he might drink his tortured soul into a state of blissful indifference. But unfortunately, that was not to be the case, for, if anything, the liquor had only served to amplify his misery.

A light tapping at the chamber door suddenly drew his attention from his personal dilemma, causing him to grumble crossly, "What is it?"

Kellen focused a foreboding glare at the portal as it cautiously opened to reveal Mallory, who continued to maintain his stoic reserve, despite the fact that the tumultuous events of the day had the remainder of the household staff buzzing speculatively.

"Excuse me, Mr. Sinclair," the domestic began formally, "but Mrs. Sinclair dispatched me to inquire if you might be needing anything."

"Did she, now?" Kellen drawled cryptically.

"Yes, sir," Mallory continued, undaunted. "Mrs. Sinclair requested a modest supper tray in her chamber, but she was concerned that you not go unattended."

Kellen appeared unmoved with this pronouncement as he sauntered back toward his chair, and, Mallory, thinking his services were not required, made as if to leave. But when Kellen's eyes beheld the empty liquor bottle on the table, he motioned for the butler to remain.

"Since my wife is concerned that I should want for nothing, why don't you fetch me another bottle of this?" He carelessly tossed the empty vessel toward the servant, then claimed a seat, safe in his assumption that his request would be swiftly honored.

Settling his broad shoulders against the back of the chair, Kellen placed his fingertips together while a contemplative expression furrowed his brow. "So, my darling wife is pondering the essence of our inevitable *chat*. Why else would she cower within the confines of her chamber?" he mulled aloud. "She is doubtless imagining all sorts of horrible things.

"Well, let her," he snarled bitterly, his fist coming down viciously upon the arm of the chair. "She would do well to fear me, considering the despicable facts I learned today."

447

He concluded his tortured musings as the door opened and Mallory returned with the brandy he had been instructed to retrieve. Kellen sat patiently while the domestic filled his glass with a generous portion of the amber-colored liquid. Then with a negligent wave of his hand, he dismissed the butler for the night. Warming the snifter with his hands, Kellen's unreadable gaze rested on the dying flames of the fire, and he resolved that Erin could very well deliberate his purpose a little longer.

The last flickering flames of the fire had sputtered in the grate when Kellen finally dragged his weary body from the chair, deciding that the time had come to confront his cunning wife. Recorking the half empty bottle of brandy, he tucked the vessel under his arm and ambled from the room. Slowly and determinedly, he made his way along the dimly lit corridor and up the narrow flight of stairs, arriving at last before Erin's chamber.

Without hesitation, and not allowing her the courtesy of a knock, he carefully eased the door open and stepped across the threshold. A cursory inspection of the chamber revealed his wife in peaceful repose on the chaise lounge before the comforting glow of the fireplace, apparently having succumbed to an unencumbered sleep. The mere idea that she could dismiss the wretched situation that festered between them with such casual aplomb infuriated Kellen beyond imagining, and, in a fit of pique, he slammed the door so furiously that it actually rattled the hinges.

This action brought about immediate results as Erin bolted upward, clutching her hands to her bosom. Blinking the sleep from her eyes, she glanced about wildly to determine the source of her abrupt awakening, and, when her eyes fastened upon the imposing figure who lounged against the door, she gulped nervously, realizing that the insufferable waiting was over.

"Kellen," she managed weakly. "It's . . . it's you."

"So it is," came his glib retort. "Sorry if that disappoints you. Were you expecting someone else?"

"Of course not!" she vehemently denied the coarse accusation. Then more calmly, she added, "You . . . you frightened me, that's all."

"Did I? Perhaps I meant to," he said stonily.

He pushed his tall, agile frame away from the door and strode toward her, a distinctively menacing scowl blackening his handsome face. Feeling particularly vulnerable, Erin swallowed bravely and tried to recall the carefully worded explanation she had rehearsed while drying her hair. One look at the unyielding man who now towered over her, however, was all it took to drive the essence of her speech from her tongue.

Instead, she blurted suddenly, "Kellen, I can explain!"

"Can you?" he asked doubtfully.

"Yes. I know you must think me the most reprehensible of creatures—"

"You're being generous with your adjectives," he interrupted dryly. "For believe me, my dear wife, what I presently think of you is far less charitable. Continue."

Determined to withstand his dogmatic countenance, Erin squared her shoulders and met his unnerving gaze. "I realize that it looked as though Michael and I were . . ." she faltered momentarily, ". . . were locked in a passionate embrace, but I promise you that it was simply the most dreadful misunderstanding."

Once she had regained her confidence, her words came in a rush. She told him of her encounter with Michael at the theatre and, subsequently, how she had come to accept his luncheon invitation. She recounted every minute detail of the time she had spent alone with Michael in his chamber, including how he had declared his love for her.

"And what was your answer to that?" Kellen inquired, his manner detached.

And though he contrived to appear indifferent, Erin knew that it was essential that she convince Kellen of the infallibility of her response. Her eyes never wavered from his as she said, "I told Michael that I love *you*, that I belong to *you*. And it's true! I don't know why Michael did this awful thing, but I swear to you that absolutely *nothing* happened. I have not been unfaithful to you!" she concluded brokenly, her eyes anxiously searching his for some indication that he believe her innocent of any wrongdoing.

But she was not to be immediately made privy to the thoughts that hovered behind the brooding blue eyes, for he turned his back to her and strode over to the fireplace. Placing the brandy bottle on a side table, Kellen rested one elbow on the mantel and focused a shrewd gaze on her. Several pregnant seconds were consumed by the night, and, just when Erin thought she would be driven mad by his silence, Kellen began to speak.

"You know, I could *almost* be persuaded to believe you."

"Almost?" Erin's voice quivered noticeably.

"Yes. Were it not for this," he reached inside his jacket to retrieve the marriage contract, "I'm certain that I should."

"What . . . what is that?" she asked reluctantly, suddenly consumed by a nagging sense of apprehension.

"This?"

He casually unfolded the legal contract and dangled it carelessly in front of him. But the icy glare he focused on her clearly belied the aloof exterior he tried to maintain.

"Since your dainty signature is scrawled all over it, I should think that you would be thoroughly acquainted with the document," he said accusingly, and, crossing to the chaise lounge, he ceremoniously dropped the paper into her lap.

Erin's heart was in her throat, and her hand trembled noticeably as she retrieved the document and scanned the first few lines. Her worst fears came to fruition when she recognized the paper as the marriage contract that Jeremiah had foisted upon her.

Glancing up into the face that regarded her resentfully, she whispered hoarsely, "Where did you get this?"

"What's this? Not even a half-hearted attempt to deny the obvious?" he baited her.

Erin was rapidly losing her taste for the entire proceedings. *"Where?"* she demanded angrily.

"Vanessa."

"Vanessa!" Erin cried her bewilderment. "I might have known. That spiteful witch has resented our relationship from the outset. It is apparent that she will do anything to destroy the happiness we have found together," she spewed bitterly.

"You credit Vanessa to excess, for I must hasten to point out that you have managed to accomplish that feat quite nicely on your own." Kellen's mocking laugh sent a shiver of portent racing down Erin's erect spine.

To Erin's dismay, Kellen reached for the bottle of liquor that he had discarded earlier. He glanced around for a glass, but finding none readily available, he tipped the bottle to his lips and drank thirstily.

"Haven't you had enough of that?" Erin asked disdainfully. For she had never seen him in this severe state of intoxication, and she doubted her ability to cope with him should he succumb to the wicked spirits.

"No," he informed her bluntly and to accentuate his point, he quaffed another generous draft of the fiery brew. "Tell me, my darling wife, did you mastermind this clever scheme on your own?" He suddenly crossed to the bench and sat down beside her, making Erin tense nervously.

"What do you mean?" She shook her head uncertainly. "There was no *scheme;* only another of your grandfather's eccentric demands. He insisted that I sign the contract, or he threatened to forbid our marriage."

"How utterly predictable you have become," he droned sarcastically, "for that is precisely the excuse that Vanessa said you would offer."

"Her again!" Erin spat in exasperation, and, were she not

451

still hampered by her sprained ankle, she would have paced irritably about the room. "How can you believe that vile—"

"Tut, tut," Kellen clucked his tongue in mock admonition. "I would think twice before slandering Vanessa, were I you. For in many ways, you are from the same mold."

Erin decided to ignore the blatant insult, at least temporarily, for she wanted to hear the remainder of Kellen's interpretation of the contract. "Oh, and just what did *dear* Vanessa tell you?"

"Nothing. After all, Erin, I *can* read," he said pointedly. "And one does not have to be a legal expert to define the terms of this despicable piece of—" His final declaration was little more than a garbled oath as he snatched the contract from her hands and hurled it across the room.

When he turned back to her, his eyes flashed bitterly. "I suppose that you are not entirely to blame. Lord knows, you did little to hide your hatred of all Yankees, but I was just stubborn enough to think that I could make you forget your miserable past and begin a new life with me."

"And you did." Erin's comment was a mere whisper as she reached out to grab his arm in a desperate gesture, truly fearful of the conclusion she felt certain he was about to make. "Kellen, please, let me explain."

He angrily wrenched his arm free and stood up and stalked away from her. "It really isn't necessary, for I am no longer interested in your lies! The facts are quite clear.

"You saw our marriage as a means to save your floundering family estate. And you were wily enough to include a few safeguards in the contract to ensure that you did not have to remain shackled to me forever. Tell me, Erin," he snarled hatefully. "Could you not wait until the specified length of time had transpired before you selected a lover? Do you despise me that much?"

"*No!* Oh, Kellen, don't!" she pleaded. "It's not like that! You must believe me! Jeremiah *made* me sign that accursed piece of paper; I swear it!"

452

"Oh, Grandfather doubtless was a willing accessory, but why? What does Grandfather have to gain by this union?" he speculated aloud. "All the advantages are yours; the money."

"I have never accepted any recompense from Jeremiah!" she wailed.

"Well," he shrugged indifferently, "I suppose there was really no need, not with me squandering a substantial fortune on the refurbishing of Kilkieran.

"What else could it be?" He paced fitfully as he spoke. Then his eyes fell upon the legal document, and, bending over, he plucked the discarded paper from the floor.

He glanced down and a particular section verily leaped out at him. "Ah, yes. The heir." He mulled this revelation over in his mind. "How remiss of me to forget Grandfather's incessant quest for a suitable heir."

The room grew unbearably silent for Erin as she studied Kellen's emotionless face while he continued to stare at the unfortunate piece of paper. She wanted very much to be able to say something to comfort him, to reassure him of her unquestionable love for him. However, her compassion suffered a thundering blow when Kellen next spoke to her.

"Do you realize what you have done?" he asked purposefully. "You *sold* yourself to me in marriage for financial profit. In my book, that makes you little better than a common *whore!*" he spat disgustedly.

The blood instantly drained from Erin's face, and, completely forgetting about her ailing limb, she flew off the chaise lounge to confront him. She managed only a few faltering steps before she realized her folly, but her quarry was but a few inches from her, and sheer fury spurred her onward. She was limping quite painfully by the time she drew herself up in front of him, hands on hips, obviously prepared to engage in battle.

"How dare you!" She seethed uncontrollably. "That remark was wholly unconscionable."

"Perhaps," he conceded. "but then, your behavior this afternoon can hardly be considered less than contemptible.

"You were careless with Cahill, my sweet, for whether you realize it or not, Grandfather does possess certain scruples, and I'm quite positive that he expects any child you might bear to be sired by me," he added caustically.

Erin literally gasped for breath, the impact of his brusque denunciation overwhelming her as if he had struck her in the face. The thought of verbal retaliation never entered Erin's head, for, in truth, she could think of nothing vile enough to call him. Instead, the clenched fists that rested on her hips were suddenly called into action as she lashed out at him; pummeling his face and chest with vicious blows.

Kellen was momentarily taken aback by the severity of her attack, but with minimal exertion, he was able to render her defenseless. He swiftly captured her hands in his, but she squirmed and kicked at him, struggling to gain her freedom. Laughing evilly, Kellen effortlessly forced Erin's arms behind her back and crushed her against his chest, forcing her head back, so that their eyes met.

Erin correctly interpreted the savage passion that clouded the blue orbs, and it took no great genius to surmise his purpose. But she resolved that he should not have his way.

How could he? she thought. How could he possibly want to make love to me after the despicable things he just said?

"No!" she rasped breathlessly, recoiling from his touch.

"Do you truly think you can prevent me from taking what I want?" he scoffed at her tenacity.

"No, but I shouldn't think that you would want me; not if you truly believe that I am guilty of your vile accusations," she countered.

"Under ordinary circumstances, I wouldn't, but there is the matter of the contract to be settled, and I shouldn't want Grandfather to be disappointed." He lowered his head meaningfully to claim her mouth in a tempestuous kiss.

Erin's determination to disregard his sexual overtures abruptly dissipated when the lips she had longed for in past weeks melded against her own, reigniting a burning passion of which she had only keen recollection. Finding her hands inexplicably free, she wrapped her arms around Kellen's neck and pressed herself against him familiarly, moaning her delight as she reveled in her own rekindled desire. She eagerly parted her lips to accept his thrusting tongue and caress it with her own, and, just when the memory of their bitter argument had been driven from her thoughts, Kellen pulled away, his eyes washing over her scornfully.

"Tell me, *darling,* did you fall this easily into Cahill's bed?" he taunted her.

Without considering her actions, Erin drew back her hand and rendered him a vicious blow across the face. *"Bastard!"* she spewed venomously, and turned to limp away from him, tears of humiliation gathering at the corners of her eyes.

She had taken only a step or two when Kellen's hand came down upon her shoulder, and he spun her around to face him. Erin's confident mien withered considerably under the murderous glare that burned into her flesh, and she immediately regretted her impetuous behavior.

"Kellen," she began shakily, trying to apologize.

But he would have none of it. Emitting a guttural cry of anger, he stepped forward and jerked open the sash that bound her dressing gown to her. Then in one precise motion, she stood before him, attired in the sheerest of nightgowns.

Kellen stared lustfully at the lovely vision who tried desperately to shield her nakedness from his flaming gaze. Their eyes met and he held her gaze as he slowly and meticulously began to remove his own clothing. But as he watched her, Kellen found himself consumed by a strange sense of ambivalence as he discovered that he was simultaneously attracted to and repulsed by the enchanting seductress.

Erin stood frozen to the floor, not knowing what she might next expect from her explosive husband. She was not kept in suspense for long, however, for once he had dispensed with the perfunctory task, Kellen focused his undivided attention on her. Stepping to the chaise lounge, Kellen sat down and reached out to take Erin's hand and tug her toward him. "Come along. I find myself almost anxious to renew our intimate life; especially with today's revelation."

"What . . . what do you mean?" Erin asked distantly, allowing him to drag her to a standing position before him.

"Well, there are certain things that a man cannot expect from his wife," he explained vaguely, reaching up to fan the thick, satiny tresses about her shoulders, "but you have proven that being my wife is not a role that particularly enthralls you, so the possibilities available to us are now limitless."

"I . . . I don't know what you're talking about." Erin shook her head confusedly, causing the luxurious curls to flutter seductively about her face.

"Never fear; you shall quickly learn," he chuckled wickedly.

Without warning, Kellen pulled her down onto his lap, and coaxing her chin up with his thumb, he covered her mouth with his. His kiss was not as she had remembered; not gentle and loving, but cold and vindictive. It was as if he had completely eradicated all memory of their love for one another in his zeal to punish her for the wrongdoings of which he had already convicted her.

His kiss was brutal as he ruthlessly brushed her lips apart with his hard tongue and thrust it inside to ravage the sweet tasting splendor of her mouth. As he bruised her lips with his relentless embrace, his hands roamed along her shoulders, down her arms, and across her bosom. He could feel the taut nipples as they strained against the delicate fabric, and, muttering an inarticulate groan, he plunged his hand beneath the flimsy garment and intimately fondled the hardened rosy tips between his practiced fingertips. Then gathering the sheer material in his fist, he virtually ripped the nightdress from her.

The sound of rending material frightened Erin, causing her to stiffen in his embrace, and, placing her hands on his broad shoulders, she managed to push away from him. "That really wasn't necessary," she rebuked his harsh action.

But Kellen was not in the mood for conversation, and, turning her in his arms, he eased her back against the chaise lounge. As he moved, his foot caught the edge of a bowl of ice that Renée had brought so that Erin might better control the swelling of her tortured ankle, and a distinctively roguish gleam flickered in the blue eyes that drank in her naked splendor.

Straddling the narrow bench, he grasped Erin's legs and slid her forward, so that her thighs overlapped his; his already passion enflamed manhood positioned enticingly close to her femininity. Reaching down, Kellen selected a sliver of ice, and glancing into Erin's expectant face, he began to trace slow, methodic patterns across her flat stomach. Erin's sharp intake of breath made Kellen chuckle evilly, and his sensual gaze captured hers as he purposefully maneuvered the ice cube across her silken flesh.

The ice blazed a contrasting trail of freezing goose bumps and sensual fire from her stomach to the valley of her breasts, where Kellen extended the ice and allowed a few droplets of the melting cube to trickle between the luxurious mounds. Then he intentionally ran the cube around the base of one breast, creating a number of wide circles that gradually grew smaller and smaller until he arrived at his ultimate destination. And he felt Erin's thighs contract violently against his as the devastating contact of the ice against the sensitive nipple made her shiver uncontrollably.

"Please . . . stop!" she cried out, wriggling frantically beneath his touch.

Since the ice had finally dissolved, Kellen was more than willing to comply with her request. Besides, his own desire had grown quite persistent, and he was anxious to culminate the amorous adventure. Sliding his arms beneath her back, Kellen lifted her forward and carefully positioned her astride him.

Kellen saw her eyes widen with surprise, and he grunted his understanding. "Just wrap your legs about my waist and follow my instructions."

Erin was too overcome by her own desire to say anything in reply; she merely nodded and did as he suggested. She clasped her legs about him tightly, and buried her face in his shoulder. She reveled in the tremors of sensual excitement he masterfully summoned within her as his skillful tongue flicked at the nipple of, first, one breast, then the other. And by the time he finally lowered her onto his throbbing shaft, Erin was so caught up in the euphoric spell he had woven, that the distressing situation that existed between them was temporarily obliterated from her consciousness.

As Erin waited in breathless anticipation, Kellen's sensuous hands slid down her back to rest on her hips. Once there, they began to rotate her back and forth with a methodic rhythm that Erin felt certain was meant to deprive her of her sanity. Unable to contain her whimpers of delight, and suddenly discontent with his sluggish pace, Erin began to move against him, creating an exhilarating motion that thrilled Kellen as well.

Encircling his neck with her arms, Erin clung to him fiercely, for she recognized the unmistakable signals which warned that the exquisite conclusion to this monumental experience was clearly attainable. Relaxing her feverish motion, Erin once again relied on Kellen's expertise; an expertise that quickly brought her the rapture she sought.

Erin's throaty cries of pleasure alerted Kellen that she had achieved the ultimate of sensations, yet his own sexual craving remained undaunted. He consequently slackened his pace for a moment to allow Erin an opportunity to recover her equanimity, and, just when she thought the encounter had ended, Kellen enthusiastically resumed his sensuous plunderings. She clung to him desperately, her breasts crushed tightly against his chest as she struggled to remain atop the thundering ocean swell that crashed again and again, leaving her weak with its awesome intensity.

When, at last, Kellen's demanding fervor had been satiated, Erin collapsed against him, as helpless and lifeless as a child's rag doll. Saying nothing, Kellen carefully lifted her in his arms and carried her across the room to the bed. Pressing her against the turned down sheets, he drew the coverlets up and over her, but the hand she placed against his arm prevented him from withdrawing. Staring down into her beautiful face, he detected the tears that had begun to trickle down her cheeks, but he refused to respond to such a typical feminine emotion.

"Where . . . where are you going?" she asked chokingly.

"Don't worry," he replied gruffly. "I'm not leaving. After all, the evening is still quite young." To accentuate his point, Kellen slipped his hand beneath the coverlets and slid it along her inner thigh.

Erin bit her lip to keep from sobbing aloud, and, when he finally withdrew his hand, she felt compelled to make one last attempt to bridge the enormous gap that loomed between them. "Please, Kellen. I love you so. Don't . . . don't hate me!"

"Hate you? Why, madam, I quite despise you," he spat loathsomely. "It galls me to the very core to think that I allowed myself to be taken in by your unspoiled innocence. Ha! You may have been an innocent once, but you perpetrated your scheme with the calculated shrewdness of a whore. Well, you have made your bed, my sweet, and now you shall very well lie in it; at least until you no longer amuse me."

Erin watched dejectedly as Kellen ambled back across the room to collect his forsaken liquor bottle. Then he settled his muscular frame in the chaise lounge; probably to consider the variety of ways he intends to torture me, Erin thought dismally. Then gathering her pillow to her breast, she turned on her side and succumbed to the heartbreaking sobs she had heretofore valiantly restrained. Thus spent, she soon drifted off to sleep.

Erin awakened just prior to dawn with a startled gasp, and an intensely awkward feeling that something was amiss. Blinking wildly to adjust her eyes to the morning twilight, she quickly ascertained the cause of her abrupt arousal as she focused on two very familiar crystal blue eyes poised directly above hers. As the events of the previous evening flooded her memory, Erin resolved that she would not handily yield to his practiced ministrations this time. Thinking she would put any such notion from his head at the outset, Erin started to push him away from her. It was then that she discovered the reason for the smugly arrogant expression that dressed Kellen's face.

"Oh!" she squealed her surprise, becoming keenly aware of the stiffened manhood that was already nestled snugly inside her. "K-K-Kellen!" she stammered nervously.

"Good morning," he cooed huskily. "Sorry to awaken you so early, but, you will, I think, appreciate my urgency."

Then giving a hollow laugh, he began to move against her, plunging deeply inside the velvety crevice. There was no tenderness or compassion in his lovemaking this morning; only a primitive desire to satisfy his own lustful yearnings. Erin's attempts to ignore his kisses proved futile, for he forced her to endure his caresses, just as he suffered her to withstand the masterful thrusts that penetrated her being; thrilling her beyond imagining and lifting her to rare heights of ecstasy despite her efforts to disregard them.

Afterwards, Erin lay quietly in the mammoth bed, feeling very much like the paid whore that Kellen had declared her to be. She watched silently while Kellen washed and dressed, and he was just concluding his grooming when Erin braved a question.

"Where are you going?"

"To breakfast," he replied simply. "I will have yours sent up, if you like. Afterwards, I suggest that you start preparing for the return journey to Kilkieran. I intend to speak with Evan this morning, and, if he is ready, we shall leave tomorrow."

"Will you be returning with us?" she asked hopefully.

"For a time. I still have a few matters to tend to; the mill and the store, *and* Taggart," he offered noncommittally.

"I see," she mumbled glumly, but her heart sank even deeper when she observed him turn and stride toward the door. Clutching the sheet to her bosom, Erin climbed to her knees, and stretching out her hand to him in a beseeching gesture, she blurted, "Kellen! Wait. Please, don't go. Tell me, what is to become of us?" she dared to pose the question that had plagued her since the moment he had discovered her in Michael's arms.

Kellen's hand was resting on the doorknob when he turned to face her, his expression cold and unfeeling. "To be perfectly honest, Erin, I don't know, and, at the moment, I truly don't give a damn," he informed her bluntly. Then he exited the chamber, leaving a somber Erin to contemplate the shambles in which her life currently lay.

IV

The Awakening

Chapter Twenty-two

Erin gathered her heavy cloak more securely about her as she trudged along the frozen roadway. It had perhaps been foolhardy of her to embark upon her excursion on foot, but the winter had been fierce, thereby, forcing her to remain indoors much of the time. Therefore, with the promise of a moderately warm February day before her, Erin had understandably succumbed to her own desire to experience an uninhibited day out of doors.

She had no predetermined purpose in mind as she set out on her walk; unless it was to temporarily purge her heart and soul of the devastating predicament in which she had found herself in recent weeks. The unfortunate situation that existed between Kellen and herself had not improved since their return from Richmond. If anything, he had grown even more distant and remote, choosing to devote his time and energy toward the solidification of the various business enterprises he had set in motion, rather than attempting to salvage the crumbling pieces of their faltering marriage.

Though they seldom shared more than a courteous word or two in passing these days, Erin had begun to notice the telltale signs of his restlessness. The mill had opened, and, with the abundance of spring timber, was assuredly destined to flourish. Similarly, the store in Braxton would be ready to open within the week, what with the daily arrival of supplies on Kellen's freighting firm. With the single exception of the Taggart incident, Kellen's mission was complete, and Erin could foresee that the moment she had dreaded since that awful day in Richmond was not far in the offing; the day that Kellen would take his leave of her forever.

An uncontrollable shudder raced down her spine at this conjecture, causing Erin to pause in the roadway and glance about her. Much of her exercise had been conducted in the midst of a contemplative trance, therefore, Erin had paid little attention to the direction she had traveled during her jaunt. But now that she recognized her surroundings, Erin genuinely regretted that she had not been more mindful of her wanderings.

Finding herself on the driveway that led to Fox Bush, Erin promptly turned herself about and swiftly retraced her steps. She was nearing the main road again when she noticed a lone horseman perched at the end of the drive. One fleeting glance was all it required for Erin to distinguish the identity of the rider, for the image of this remarkable man would forever be emblazoned in he thoughts and in her heart.

She was standing directly beneath him now, and still he could not bend his iron resolve to extend a cordial greeting. Fighting back the embittered tears that sprang to her eyes so easily these days, Erin pulled her cloak about her and swept past Achilles, determined that she could be just as stubborn and pigheaded as her husband.

Kellen, however, had no intention of maintaining a subdued countenance, and, tearing his murderous gaze from the direction of the Cahill plantation house, he focused his attention on Erin. Nudging Achilles forward, he quickly closed the gap that separated them.

"My, my," he droned icily. "Isn't it peculiar how the merest hint of spring can rekindle all those smoldering passions that have lain dormant all winter?" he taunted her, making casual reference to the fact that they had maintained separate bedchambers *and* beds since their return from Richmond.

But Erin did not acknowledge his speech. Indeed, she merely squared her shoulders and marched determinedly onward.

Knowing Erin as he did, Kellen realized that she was exercising enormous self-restraint; still he could not resist the temptation to further torment her. "I must admit that you surprise even me. I mean, a midday rendezvous. Have you and Cahill no shame?" He immediately misconstrued the reason for finding her on Michael's estate.

No longer willing to endure his unwarranted ridicule, Erin stopped dead in her tracks and favored him with her most fulminating glare. "You odious wretch," she hissed. "You're beneath contempt."

She delivered the setdown succinctly, then turned and stepped into the forest, deciding to take an alternate route home. But she had accomplished only a few steps when Achilles crashed through the sparse woodland undergrowth and circled around in front of her to block her path. Undaunted, Erin turned to select a different route, only to have the same thing happen.

This continued, until finally, in a fit of pique, Erin placed her hands on her hips and stomped her foot angrily. "Stop it, Kellen!" she screamed at him, tears of frustration brimming her eyes. "You are being quite childish."

Kellen did not appear to take umbrage at her remark. Instead, he simply extended his hand toward her and said, "Come, I will escort you back to Kilkieran."

"I'd rather walk, thank you," she replied tersely.

"Now, who's being childish?" he scoffed. "The sun is fading and the air grows colder, Erin. Be sensible," he chided her. "Besides, I don't truly think you realize how far you have roamed. Now, come along," he said patiently. "Achilles grows impatient to be off."

Erin stared up into the rigid face and knew that further argument was useless. With a conciliatory sigh, she stepped for-

467

ward and permitted the powerful arm to swoop down and lift her onto the mount in front of him. Under ordinary circumstances, Erin would have delighted in his nearness, but the storm that plagued them remained suspended overhead like a thundercloud ready to unleash its unspent fury.

The ride to Kilkieran was made in complete silence, thereby giving Erin a chance to consider a great many solutions to her plight. Though she realized that Kellen considered their relationship to be quite irreconcilable, Erin could not as yet abandon all hope.

She took great comfort in the arm that rested complacently about her waist, yet she knew it was there only as a means to keep her anchored securely in front of him. Still, since he had forced her to accompany him, Erin decided that it might be to her advantage to remind him of the warm and loving wife he had so ruthlessly cast adrift. Accordingly, she leaned back against him, pressing her body against his familiarly and resting her cheek against his broad chest.

Even through the thick layer of his heavy overcoat, Erin could hear the steady rhythm of Kellen's heart, and she grew suddenly melancholy. Without thinking, she placed her hand over his arm and adjusted it to a more satisfactory position across her stomach. And as Achilles plodded relentlessly along the rapidly darkening trail, Erin thought wistfully of the child that grew within her . . . Kellen's child.

She vaguely wondered what sort of reaction the news would elicit from him, if indeed, she decided to tell him. For knowing Jeremiah's ways, the old man would certainly try to do everything within his power to make her adhere to the terms of that odious contract. And should Kellen truly abandon her, Erin feared that his grandfather might demand that the child be raised in the Sinclair household, and that was a thought that completely terrified her.

In the days since her discovery of the baby, Erin had wrestled with the notion of Kellen's eventual departure. Should he decide to truly abandon her, Erin knew that she would be totally devastated, but she had derived enormous solace in the knowledge that a part of Kellen would live on forever with her through the child they had created. Yet, she similarly realized that she would lose all will to carry on should the baby be denied her as well.

Realizing that she was no nearer a solution to her problem than when she had set out on her walk, Erin pressed Kellen's arm more tightly against her abdomen, content to jostle lazily against him. She reveled in his nearness, and tried desperately not to think of the disturbing circumstances that presently tormented her life.

Kellen sat in the comfortable wing chair before the window, his pensive stare targeted on the star studded heavens. It was late. He was uncertain of the exactness of the hour, but the remaining occupants of the mansion had already retired, for he had detected their muffled shufflings through the corridors ages ago. The only sounds that had since penetrated his consciousness had been the crackling of the fire in the grate and the customary noises of the house settling for the night.

He was alone, with nothing more than his cigar and the diversions of his own tempestuous thoughts for company. At last, the motionless figure stirred and leaned forward to flick the cigar butt against the ashtray. Kellen quickly regretted his action, however, for his reflective gaze quite naturally settled upon the door to the abutting chamber, causing his thoughts to focus on the one subject he had fervently tried to avoid: Erin.

"Damn it!" he swore. "Will I never be able to dismiss that conniving temptress from my mind?"

Kellen extinguished the cigar with an impatient gesture, then stood up and began to pace fitfully about the chamber. As he walked, he struggled to contend with the conflicting array of emotions that plagued his disconcerted mind. Up until a very few days past, Kellen had considered there to be but one solution to the awkward situation in which he currently found himself; nullification of the marriage. But now he discovered, to his own amazement, that the notion no longer sounded as appealing as it once had.

He halted his purposeless ambling as his thoughts inadvertently returned to the day he had found Erin strolling near the Cahill plantation, and a host of tantalizing recollections inundated his memory. He could still recall how the gently wafting fragrance of her scent had enveloped his nostrils, instantly rekindling a multitude of overpoweringly heady sensations. Kellen coughed nervously to drive the tormenting vision from his head, but how could he forget the provocative way she had pressed her body against his; almost as if she *dared* him to ignore her.

This last rumination provoked a lugubrious moan from Kellen, for the direction of his musings had quite naturally summoned the familiar stirrings in his loins; a gnawing passion that had gone unheeded for several weeks. Silently cursing the one he felt responsible for his predicament, Kellen turned a scathing look on the connecting chamber door. Then, on impulse, he walked over to the barrier, eased it open, and quietly stepped across the threshold.

He soundlessly crept to the side of the bed and paused to stare down at the beautiful face that was illuminated by the pale moonlight. A closer examination of the slumbering figure revealed a face ravaged by tears, and a pillow still damp from the watery deluge; she had obviously cried herself to sleep.

Kellen stood over her for several minutes, his expression obscure. Unthinkingly, he reached down to pull the coverlets more securely over her exposed shoulders. The impulsive action caused her to stir and roll to her back, giving him a clearly uninhibited view of her flawless face.

She looked an absolute angel with the soft shadows of the moon lazily flickering over her, and Kellen found himself possessed with an irresistible yearning to hold this exquisite crea-

470

ture in his arms. And he very nearly yielded to the temptation, but the image of this same enchantress, locked in a searing embrace with another, suddenly drove the relenting expression from his eyes.

"Ah, my deceitful wench," he breathed hoarsely. "You'll not take me in again. I have endured enough of your kind to last me a lifetime; first with Vanessa, and now you. I'll not likely succumb to your cunning wiles again." He turned abruptly and stalked to the door, but he paused at the threshold to cast one last resentful glare in her direction. "Women! Bah!" he spat disgustedly and reentered his own lonely chamber.

Kellen realized that he was probably destined to suffer another sleepless night, still he angrily stripped off his clothing and climbed into the roomy berth. He had been abed for only a short time, however, when he became aware of the garbled mumblings from Erin's room, and he quickly surmised that she was in the midst of one of her nightmares. As he listened, her frantic murmurings grew more intense, eventually erupting into one ear-piercing cry, followed by her uncontrollable sobbing.

He slipped noiselessly from his bed and moved to the connecting door, and, just when he had decided to go to her, Graham entered his sister's chamber to offer her solace. Curiously, Kellen eased the door open a little, so that he might better hear their conversation.

"There, there, Irish," Graham gently soothed her. Sitting down on the edge of the bed, he tenderly enfolded her in his arms and held her until her tears subsided. "Had that nasty dream again, didn't you?"

Erin nodded, and, pushing away from him, she wiped at her tear stained face with trembling fingers. "I'm sorry," she sniffed. "I didn't mean to wake you."

"You didn't," he said kindly, his careful gaze searching her face, and he was truly surprised by her distraught expression. "Erin, honey, are you all right?"

"No," she admitted, the bright green eyes again clouding

with tears. "I am quite miserable," she sobbed.

Graham was aware of the stressful situation that existed between Kellen and Erin, and, though he was loath to see his sister in such despair, he could not help but think that it might be for the best. For Graham still remembered the conversation he had overheard on their wedding day, and, even though Kellen had proven to be an exemplary brother-in-law, Graham found that he could not allow himself to completely trust him because of the one incident.

Besides, he reasoned, Kellen was still a Yankee.

Graham again pulled the stricken girl into his arms and cradled her against his chest. He gently rocked her back and forth and brushed aside the errant strands of hair that shadowed her face.

"Everything will be fine, sis," he murmured softly. "The nightmares will eventually cease to torment you—"

"Oh, Graham. You don't understand," she cried desperately, and, jerking away from him, she climbed out of bed and crossed to the dresser to select a hanky from a bureau drawer. As she mopped up her tear-streaked face, she explained, "It's not the dreams; I'm learning to cope with them. It's Kellen. He won't believe anything I tell him. He's being so unreasonable."

"Perhaps he feels he has a right to be."

"But he doesn't," she insisted. "Well, I suppose it *was* irresponsible of me to meet with Michael, but I had no idea that he was going to behave like such a lecher.

"Oh, what am I going to do?" she lamented sorrowfully. "I feel so helpless. I'm losing him forever, and there is absolutely nothing I can do to prevent it." She had wandered over to the French doors during her narrative and presently stood staring out at the moondrenched horizon.

"You think he intends to leave you, then?" he asked solemnly.

The proud shoulders slumped in dejection, and she sadly bobbed her head. "I'm certain of it."

472

Graham blew a low whistle. "I didn't realize the situation was so completely irreversible, honey." He crossed to her and placed his hands on her shoulders. "Is there no one who might be able to convince him of your innocence?"

"I don't know." She shook her head dismally. "Michael was no help when Kellen found us together."

"Have you seen him since then?"

"*No!* Nor do I intend to," she said staunchly.

"Anyone else?"

"Only Jeremiah. Kellen's grandfather is the one who orchestrated that sordid business about the marriage contract, yet I was blamed for that as well," she muttered glumly.

"Well, Irish." Graham considerately led her back toward the bed. "Perhaps it is more advantageous for Kellen to condemn you as a faithless wife than seek out the truth," he mused aloud.

"I don't understand. What do you mean?"

"It's nothing." Graham waved the comment aside. "It certainly is a puzzle, and I know you'll not find this an acceptable consolation, but you must believe that things will work out for the best.

"Now, try to get some rest." He coaxed her into the bed and carefully tucked the coverlets in around her. "Just remember that you shall always have a home here at Kilkieran." He brushed his lips against her forehead, then slipped from the room.

Meanwhile, it was a very subdued Kellen who gently closed the door between the chambers and made his way back to his own bed. He painstakingly recounted the conversation he had just overheard, and, by the time he gave himself up to a restless sleep, he had reached a decision that would ultimately settle the fate of his failing marriage.

The day that Erin had dreaded was to dawn much sooner than she anticipated. It was the morning after Graham had consoled her following her nightmare, and Erin had promised Doc Wilson that she would undergo a thorough examination to ensure that the pregnancy was progressing satisfactorily. On her return from the doctor's, Erin decided to stop at the waterfall to put her meandering thoughts into perspective before returning to Kilkieran.

There was a light powdering of snow on the ground, and the hem of Erin's gown created abstract designs as she ambled about the clearing. Duchess had been allowed to roam freely as well, but a nervous whicker from the animal alerted Erin to another's presence. Retrieving the reins, she murmured soothing words to calm the fidgety horse, then turned to confront the intruder.

Kellen sat astride Achilles just beyond the clearing, and, as she watched, he dismounted, tethered the animal to a nearby bush, and started walking toward her. Erin, however, barely took notice of his purposeful stride, for her eyes were steadfastly glued to the bulging saddlebags and blanket roll that rested atop Achilles.

Kellen saw the direction of her gaze, and he endeavored to force a casual lilt into his voice when he addressed her. "I thought I might find you here, though I am baffled as to why you would venture out in this weather."

"What?" she asked distantly, tearing her eyes from the disheartening sight. "Oh, I was just on my way home from Doc Wilson's," she explained.

"Doc Wilson's?" There was a distinct hint of concern in his voice, and, for the first time, he noticed her pale complexion. "Are you ill?"

Erin glanced up into the brilliant blue eyes that were obviously full of concern, and, for one split second, she toyed with the idea of telling him about the baby. The notion quickly passed, however, and instead, she allowed Duchess' reins to slip through her fingers, and she turned from him and began to stroll toward the frozen pond.

"What would it matter to you if I were?" she accused.

"That isn't fair, Erin." Kellen followed her, and, when she paused, he placed his large hands on her shoulders. "Granted, we haven't been the ideally enraptured couple as of late, but I wish you no ill will," he murmured sincerely.

Erin felt the gentle pressure of his strong hands, and she instantly regretted her terse retort. Lowering her gaze from the distant horizon, she shook her head and sighed, "No, I'm not ill."

They were silent for a very long time, until, unable to endure the smoldering anxiety that enveloped her, she turned to confront him. "You're leaving me, aren't you?"

Kellen met her amazingly composed gaze, and nodded abruptly. "Yes, I'm leaving."

Erin had wondered how she would respond to the news when it came, and she found herself consumed by emotion. Without thinking, she flung herself forward into his surprised arms. "Oh, Kellen! Please, don't go! You *must* give me another chance to prove how much I love you," she begged.

For a brief instant, Kellen gathered her against him, but just as quickly, he summoned his reason and carefully put her from him as he turned away. "Don't!" he whispered harshly. "Let's not make this any more painful than necessary, shall we?"

"Painful!" she hissed. "Kellen, I'm fighting for my life . . . *our* life together. I'm sorry if that distresses you, but I cannot believe you capable of forsaking me so callously. Have you truly considered what you're doing?"

"I have thought of little else since Richmond," he murmured sadly, turning to face her. "I know you will find this bitter comfort, little reb, but you must believe that what I am doing *is* for the best.

"Well," he coughed awkwardly, "I must be off. Chin Li is waiting for me on the roadway. Good-bye," he muttered faintly, lumbering off toward Achilles. He did not trust himself to look at her again, fearing that if he observed her crestfallen expression, his determined countenance might wither.

No, he thought resolutely. I *must* know the truth. Otherwise, I shall always question her devotion.

Erin's heart sank as she watched the man she adored stalk across the clearing, preparing to exit her life forever. Without fully realizing it, her trembling legs began to stumble after him, desperate to prevent the inevitable from happening.

"Kellen, please, wait!" she cried breathlessly. "There is something you should know."

Kellen had reached his mount by this time, but his ascension into the saddle was impeded by the hand that clutched his sleeve. Heaving a conciliatory sigh, he gazed down at her anxious face.

"What is it?" he inquired patiently.

"I'm . . . I'm going to have a baby," she murmured faintly, her hopeful eyes searching his face.

But if she had expected to read compassion in his expression, she was to be sorely mistaken, for the blue eyes grew suddenly distant, and his voice was calculatingly cold when he said, "Oh, and have you told the father?"

The hand that rested on his arm was snatched away, and she gasped at his ruthless conjecture. Her yielding disposition rapidly deteriorated, and her eyes were flaming when they next met his.

"You may go; *gladly* and with my blessing," she spat hatefully. "It was stupid of me to think that *our* child would mean anything to a heartless cad like you. You're nothing but a selfish, spiteful, good-for-nothing *Yankee,* and I curse the day that fate led you to my door.

"I truly hate the monster you have become!" She concluded her fiery tirade, then presented her back to him and raced off toward Duchess.

Kellen watched in grim silence as she mounted the patient animal amidst a flurry of swirling petticoats and flailing limbs. Without so much as a backwards glance, Erin slapped the horse across the rump and bolted from the clearing.

Kellen continued to gaze in the direction of the fleeing figure long after she had disappeared from view. Finally, he shook his head sorrowfully, heaved his large frame into the saddle, and, muttering some undiscernible phrase, he gently prodded Achilles into motion and guided him from the clearing.

Erin, however, did not lessen her furious pace until she entered the stableyard at Kilkieran. Paulie observed in genuine amazement as his mistress dismounted the horse before it had completely come to a stop, and tossed the reins in his direction. Assuming that the boy would stable the animal, Erin sprinted across the rolling lawn; slipping in the snow in her fervor to reach the haven of her room.

She was grateful that the foyer and corridor were void of spectators to witness her harried flight up the staircase, for she could not endure an interrogation about her grieved behavior. At last ensconced within the boundaries of her own chamber, Erin quickly closed the door and sagged against the barrier as she gasped for breath.

Her heart was still pounding fiercely, however, when she hurled aside the connecting chamber door to survey the now empty room that she had once shared with Kellen. She stared at the chamber in disbelief; almost as if she had considered the disastrous occurrences of the day to be the events of one of her horrible nightmares, and she had fully expected to find Kellen seated in his favorite chair by the fire. But sadly, that was not the case.

Swallowing the hopeful lump that had lodged in her throat, Erin dazedly stepped across the threshold and began to wander about the room. Amazingly, she had not yet succumbed to the torrent of tears that hovered behind her eyes. But when her gaze fell on the diamond ring that reposed on the dresser, the ring that Erin had given Kellen on their wedding night, she was suddenly inundated with an overpowering sense of loss. Clutching the ring in one hand, Erin staggered a little, and, reaching out to grasp the bedpost for support, she slowly dropped to her knees and surrendered to her misery.

Kellen sat on the sofa in the Tiffin Square drawing room, his long muscular legs stretched out in front of him; crossed at the ankles, his arms folded across his chest in a pensive gesture. His nonexpressive stare was fixed on the brandy decanter that rested on the table before him, and he suddenly leaned forward to pour himself a glass of the amber liquid. His hand had just encircled the crystal container, however, when a voice from behind stayed his movement.

"From what Chin Li has been telling me, I should think that you have had enough of *that* to last you for quite some time to come," the voice informed him disapprovingly.

Kellen turned to meet his mother's severe scrutiny, and, giving his shoulders an obscure shrug, he said, "I shall have to remind Chin Li of the position he fills as my employee." Nevertheless, he withdrew his hand from the decanter and returned to his chair.

"Chin Li also tells me that you have been in Washington for an entire week." She moved to stand in front of him, and waved a remonstrative finger beneath his nose as she demanded, "Why did you not let me know that you were here?"

"My, my, Mother," Kellen droned icily. "I was unaware that you were wont to spend so much of your day gossiping with the hirelings. You must tell me all the juicy tidbits you unsurfaced during your tête-à-tête."

"Don't take that fresh attitude with me, young man," she warned. "I am still your mother, and I'm not wholly adverse to the notion of taking a strap to your cantankerous backside."

Kellen could not restrain the smile that sprang to his lips at her outrageous threat, and his dismal temperament seemed to wane as he took her hand and pulled her onto the sofa beside him.

"Forgive me, Mother. I didn't mean to behave like such a bear," he apologized. "I have been swamped with business matters since I returned from Virginia, and have had a great deal on my mind," he added distantly.

"Erin?" Meredith ventured a guess.

Kellen regarded his mother carefully, then said, "It would appear that my servant has quite a chatty tongue indeed."

"Don't be angry with Chin Li. His concern lies with your welfare and happiness, as does mine," she murmured softly. "What can I do to ease your troubled mind?"

"To begin with, you can inform Grandfather that I would like a word with him." Suddenly discontent with his idle state, Kellen got up and began to wander about the room.

"He's resting at the moment. Couldn't I help you instead?" she offered.

"Perhaps." Kellen plunged his hand inside his jacket and withdrew the document he had grown to despise. "Are you familiar with this?"

He extended the legal papers to her and continued to pace about while Meredith perused the contract. But he stopped short and whirled to face her, his expression thunderstruck, when he heard her reply.

"Yes, I am," she whispered wistfully.

"What? You are?" he shouted incredulously.

"Well, not this particular contract," she explained, "but a similar one. You see, Jeremiah insisted that I sign a marriage contract before I married your father; Geoffrey's mother had to do the same, as did Vanessa. I am told that this unique Sinclair tradition has been in existence for several generations. Supposedly, its purpose is to keep the couple legally bound to one another over those first stormy months of marriage when it might be simpler to abandon the relationship." She paused and glanced down at the document lovingly, her eyes misting over with reflective tears.

"I know that it's an absurd custom, but Jeremiah is adamant that it be observed." She gave a short laugh as she recalled the incident surrounding her own pre-nuptial confrontation with Kellen's irascible grandfather; totally oblivious to the figure who had slumped into a nearby chair and hung his head in abject despair. "I balked at first," she admitted, "as I'm certain Erin did, but I loved your father so completely that I would have stood on my head and recited the Declaration of Independence had the old codger but requested it."

Meredith painstakingly refolded the legal contract and truly looked at her son for the first time since beginning her narrative, and she was duly shocked to observe the distraught creature that greeted her eyes.

Almost immediately, she correctly interpreted the reason for his despondency, and she cried, "Good Lord, Kellen. You cannot mean to tell me that you deserted that sweet, innocent child over this trifling matter."

Acutely affronted by what he considered the unjustifiable accusation, Kellen leveled his haughty stare on his mother. "I'll have you know that I found that . . . that *sweet, innocent child,* as you so generously refer to her, in bed with another man," he said dryly.

"No!" Meredith exclaimed, scandalized by his blunt declaration. "You never did."

"Yes," Kellen insisted.

"Well, then it must have been some perfectly horrible misunderstanding. Tell me the whole story, dear." Meredith smoothed the skirt of her gown and folded her hands in her lap, her contemplative expression apparently focused on the oriental vase on the mantelpiece.

"Mother!" he bellowed. "You can't possibly mean for me to —"

"Yes, I do. Now, get on with it." She tapped her foot impatiently.

Kellen recognized the defiant set of her jaw, and, with a relenting shake of his head, he quickly and succinctly related the events of that disastrous day in Richmond.

"I see," Meredith murmured thoughtfully, carefully considering all that he had said. "And you say that Vanessa and Christina led you to the hotel where you found Erin?"

"Yes."

"Convenient, don't you think?"

"I can hardly believe my ears," Kellen shouted his surprise. "I am saddled with an unfaithful wife, and you side with her."

"Come, now, my foolish darling," she scolded. "Aren't you the one who sat in this very room and told me that you feared opposition from Erin's family? From what you have told me, Christina harbors no great affection for Erin. And Geoffrey and Vanessa are no better where you are concerned. They would like nothing better than to see your marriage crumble."

"But, Mother," he protested, "I *saw* them —"

"Did you never stop to consider," she interrupted, "that perhaps you saw that which you were *meant* to see?" she said meaningfully.

"No, I know what I —"

"How did you learn about the marriage contract?" Meredith inquired suddenly, impervious to his adamant protestations.

"Vanes . . ." he began, but as the essence of realization began to uncloud his beleaguered thoughts, he found that he need not complete the vixen's name.

"Precisely," she said pointedly. "Vanessa knew that you were not acquainted with Jeremiah's bizarre custom, and she fully expected you to react as you did."

Kellen woefully observed the knowing smile that parted his mother's lips, but he could not yet rejoice in the knowledge of Erin's innocence, for he vividly recalled his ruthless treatment of her. His lugubrious moan echoed throughout the chamber, and he shoved his hand through his hair in a desperate motion as he mumbled, "Oh God! What have I done?"

Meredith noted his despairing countenance, and she quickly moved to his side and reached down to pat his shoulder sympathetically. "You obviously behaved like a man very much in love with his wife; a bit impetuous perhaps, but besotted, nonetheless."

"But you don't understand, Mother," he groaned. "I said

and did some unforgivable things," he lamented.

"You aren't giving Erin much credit," Meredith gently chastised him. "You have doubtlessly hurt her quite deeply, but she loves you, my son. And I think that you will quickly discover that a loving embrace and a sincere apology will contribute greatly toward healing the wounds you have opened.

"Go to her, Kellen," she urged softly.

Kellen sat silently for several moments, meticulously deliberating the matter that had been brought to his attention. Geoffrey and Vanessa would have to be dealt with once and for all before he could return to Erin and remove her to the safety of Arcadia where they could raise their child in peace.

At last, he lifted his face to his mother's. "I shall indeed go to her, but first, there is an urgent matter I must settle," he said with such finality that Meredith dared not rebuke him.

"Shouldn't you at least wire her, so that she will know that you are coming home to her?"

Kellen mulled this suggestion several seconds before shaking his head firmly. "I think not. I got myself into this mess. I believe it is only fitting that I confront Erin personally and beg her forgiveness."

"Preferably, on your knees," Meredith added, more seriously than her lighthearted tone indicated.

"If that is what it takes," Kellen chuckled, lovingly patting her hand. "And knowing my little spitfire, that is precisely what she will demand."

Feeling substantially rejuvenated, Kellen rose to guide his mother from the room. "Do you think that Cook could scavenge some lunch for me? Suddenly, I am possessed with a ravenous appetite." The smile that had been alien to his face as of late lit up the blue eyes that sparkled down at his mother.

"Yes," she replied. "I think that something can be arranged." She entwined her arm in his, and permitted him to escort her from the room, her own mood vastly improved.

Kellen strode about his bedchamber at The Sinclairian, haphazardly grabbing articles of clothing and stuffing them into his saddlebags. Unbeknownst to him, Colonel Oliver Langford rested against the doorjamb, a bemused smile flickering across his face as he watched the preoccupied young man.

"I thought that you paid someone to do this type of thing for you." He sauntered into the room and bent to retrieve a shirt that had fallen to the floor unnoticed, and extended it toward its owner.

"I do," Kellen grunted, accepting the garment and tossing it carelessly onto the bed. "But I have dispatched Chin Li on a number of other errands, as I am anxious to begin my journey."

"Is that why you asked me to meet you here at this ungodly early hour?" the colonel questioned.

"Yes, but we need not conduct our business in my bedchamber." Kellen stepped past the colonel and motioned for him to follow him to the sitting room. After they had seated themselves, Kellen wasted little time in getting to the heart of the matter. "I want out," he stated simply.

"Out?"

"Don't play coy with me, Oliver. I have been investigating this nonsense for months, and am no closer to a solution now than when I started."

"Do you still believe that Petersen is guiltless?" Colonel Langford selected a periodical from the table in front of him and absently thumbed through the journal as he awaited a reply.

"I have uncovered no evidence to the contrary," Kellen informed him tartly.

"Perhaps you're not looking hard enough," Langford dared to suggest, knowing full well that he would ignite Kellen's ready temper.

Accordingly, Kellen favored the colonel with his sternest expression, and his voice was reserved when he spoke. "Are you implying that the department is dissatisfied with the way I have conducted my investigation?"

Colonel Langford dispensed with his forced interest in the journal, and, returning it to the table, he met Kellen's steadfast gaze. "No, Kellen. Your reports have been complete and informative, albeit, I do think you've been a bit presumptuous in assuming that Brian Taggart is the guilty party."

"Humph!" Kellen snorted indignantly. "The man is a notorious rake."

"So you've told me," Langford sighed. "Tell me, have you spoken to Petersen lately?"

"You know that I have been in Virginia."

"Precisely."

"What is that supposed to mean?" Kellen demanded.

"Nothing," the colonel replied vaguely.

"I maintained constant communication with Brad while I was away. He promptly responded to every telegram," Kellen painstakingly informed him. "I explained everything in my reports; how Taggart disappeared just before Ridgeway was murdered, and hasn't been seen since. Why, I received a wire from Brad the very afternoon of the murder."

"Did you? Are you certain the response came from him?" the commander asked casually. *"Anyone* can send a telegram, Kellen. An accomplice, perhaps," he suggested offhandedly, noticing the contemplative frown that suddenly creased Kellen's brow. "Have you seen your friend since you returned?"

"No," Kellen admitted. "My . . . my thoughts have been elsewhere."

"I understand," Langford murmured sympathetically, standing to take his leave. "It's just as well that you didn't try to see him, for you would have wasted your time. You see, Petersen left town the very day you and your bride departed for Virginia, and he hasn't been seen in Washington since."

Colonel Langford waited several minutes while Kellen digested this tidbit of information, then he asked, "Do you still want out?"

Kellen carefully considered his response, then, with a weary gesture of surrender, he said, "No. I will continue to delve into this mystery, but only until the end of the month. If I have uncovered no new evidence by then, I shall wash my hands of the entire matter," he stated unequivocally, rising to show his guest to the door.

"Fair enough," Langford agreed.

The two men shook hands, then the colonel walked to the door. But as he stepped into the corridor, he turned to address one final comment to Kellen.

"There *is* one piece of information that I think you should know."

"Oh, and what is that?" Kellen asked doubtfully.

"Here." The colonel pulled an envelope from his coat and thrust it toward Kellen. "Read this. I think you'll find the contents pertinent to your investigation."

"What is it?" Kellen accepted the proffered material.

"Newspaper clippings that tell of three more explosions that are quite likely connected with our nitro. We weren't so lucky this time, my friend, for at least one innocent bystander was killed in these recent blasts." Cognizant of the brooding expression that suddenly clouded Kellen's face, Colonel Langford added softly, "Find him, Kellen. You must do your level best to solve this perplexing riddle before others suffer by his hand."

Kellen nodded grimly, and watched as Colonel Langford quietly withdrew down the corridor. He remained rooted in the entry for several minutes, however, while his troubled gaze carefully perused the news articles that the colonel had moments before placed in his hands. His demeanor was somber as he reentered his private chamber to swiftly conclude his packing. For with the news just presented him, Kellen was consumed with a compelling urge to return to Kilkieran.

Yet, Kellen realized that he could not immediately embark upon his journey, for there was one important matter that remained unresolved. And a distinctively resolute grimace covered his attractive face as he collected his belongings and left the apartment.

Geoffrey Sinclair sat behind the ornate desk at his business office, meticulously reviewing the correspondence his secretary had just finalized for his signature. The day was progressing along its routine, almost mundane, schedule; therefore Geoffrey found himself pleasantly surprised when his secretary came to announce that Kellen Sinclair was in the outer office, requesting a conference with his cousin.

A satisfying smirk twisted at the corners of Geoffrey's mouth as he nodded stiffly toward the girl who waited to carry out his instructions. "Yes, Mary. Do show him in. I rather think that a stimulating discussion with my churlish relative might prove to be a welcome distraction to this otherwise monotonous day."

He casually leaned back in his comfortable leather chair, and, when Kellen stepped across the threshold a few moments later, Geoffrey was quick to launch an offensive. "Well, well, cousin. How unlike you to observe protocol by *requesting* an interview. I'm surprised you didn't merely slither beneath the door like the low reptile I know you to be," he drawled caustically.

But if he had hoped to ignite his cousin's easy temper, he was to be sorely disappointed, for Kellen scarcely acknowledged the jibe. Assuming a disdainful posture, Kellen doffed his hat and strode into the room, his superior bearing immediately casting Geoffrey in the shade.

Selecting a seat opposite the desk, Kellen settled himself in the chair and leveled a castigating scowl at his cousin. "Tut, tut, Geoffrey," he admonished the man. "I must hasten to criticize your professionalism, or is it your habit to treat potential business associates with such tasteless decorum?"

"Associate?" Geoffrey scoffed. "Whatever are you talking about?"

"To be honest, as much as I would like to exchange insults with you, I simply haven't the time today," Kellen informed him tartly. "I have come to discuss an important business matter with you, then I must be off to Virginia."

"Ah, decided to overlook the hoyden's indiscretions, have you?" Geoffrey quipped, but he was to instantly regret his spontaneous conjecture.

Kellen was on his feet immediately, and he positioned his hands on Geoffrey's desk and leaned forward, his countenance fierce. "Geoffrey," he began ominously. "It would serve your purpose to limit your comments to those relative to business. Do try to wag a civil tongue, lest I be persuaded to reconsider the magnanimous offer I am about to make."

Geoffrey swiftly pulled a handkerchief from his pocket and dabbed at the beads of perspiration that had appeared on his upper lip. "Very well," he grumbled, gesturing Kellen back into his chair. "Just what is the nature of this noble sacrifice, and what makes you think that I would be remotely interested in any of your schemes?" Geoffrey drawled his indifference.

"Because, dear cousin, in return for your cooperation in a matter that is quite precious to me, I am prepared to relinquish all claim to the Sinclair fortune," Kellen stated laconically.

"What!" Geoffrey was genuinely taken aback by Kellen's totally unexpected announcement.

"Do stop gaping at me," Kellen commented impassively. "I assure you that I haven't taken leave of my senses."

"Grandfather will never permit such a maneuver on your part," Geoffrey pointed out, reluctant to believe his profound good fortune.

"Grandfather cannot force on me that which I no longer desire," Kellen countered.

"Nevertheless, he is certain to voice his opposition to such a plan," Geoffrey insisted.

"I can deal with Grandfather," Kellen assured him.

Geoffrey thoroughly considered his cousin's response, but

his expression was nonetheless bewildered when he exclaimed, "But, *why?*"

Kellen leaned back in his chair, crossed his long legs, and focused his nonchalant gaze on the impeccable manicure of one hand. "I did imply that I expect something in return for my generous concession," he assiduously reminded Geoffrey.

"Yes, you did. What do you want?" he inquired suspiciously.

"Might I suggest that you ask that lovely secretary of yours to fetch us some liquid refreshment? I must confess that this particular business transaction has rendered me quite parched." Kellen offered Geoffrey a noncommittal smile. "Then I shall accommodate you with a complete explanation.

"Afterwards," he continued, "if you are in harmony with my proposal, we shall adjourn to my attorney's office where the appropriate legal documents can be drafted." He noticed Geoffrey's incredulous grimace, and hastened to put to rest any doubts the man might be fostering.

"You needn't appear so distrustful, Geoffrey," Kellen assured him, "for I promise you, once we are in complete accord on this matter, we shall be rid of one another once and for all," he concluded meaningfully, noting, with considerable satisfaction, that Geoffrey rose and went to request that his secretary bring them a decanter and glasses.

Chapter Twenty-three

Erin sat alone in the spacious confines of the sewing room, busily stitching a garment for the child she carried. Kellen had been gone from her life for nearly a fortnight, and though thoughts of him still caused her enormous distress, she found that the mental anguish was less intense if she focused her concentration on other activities.

She paused in her endeavors and lifted her forlorn face to the window and stared listlessly at the beautiful sundrenched spring day. Her melancholy gaze never truly fastened on a particular object, but her wandering thoughts were abruptly summoned to the present when she became alerted to a persistent fluttering sensation in her abdomen.

"Yes, child," she murmured lovingly. "I am aware of your presence." She ran a soothing hand across her slightly rounding belly, oblivious to the fact that she had been joined by a curious observer.

"Is the baby moving?" Deborah whispered softly.

Erin glanced up suddenly, momentarily taken by surprise by her unannounced visitor. "Yes. He grows more active every day."

"He?" Deborah questioned.

"Oh, that's just an expression," Erin explained. "I will be perfectly happy with the baby, regardless of its gender." She stiffened suddenly, startled by the renewed stirrings inside her. "Quickly, Debby, come here." She beckoned the shy girl forward. "I don't know if it's strong enough yet, but place your hands here." Erin carefully positioned her sister-in-law's hands on her stomach. "There! Did you feel that?" she asked sunnily, but when she lifted her face to Deborah's, she was genuinely puzzled to see that the girl's eyes had misted over with tears.

Erin was immediately full of concern, and she clasped Deborah's hands between hers and considerately inquired, "Deborah, honey; what is wrong?"

Deborah hastily pulled her hands free and dashed aside the salty droplets that slithered down her cheeks. "It's nothing," she managed shakily. "I guess I'm just a little envious; that's all."

"But there is no need for that. You and Graham will have a family someday," Erin said encouragingly.

"I suppose," Deborah muttered glumly, and, locking her hands behind her back, she strolled over to the window. Staring out at the distant horizon, she said, "I'm sorry, Erin. I didn't mean to be such a gloomy goose. I'm truly happy for you."

"I know, and you needn't apologize, Debby. Lord knows, we all experience the doldrums from time to time. Just look at how I have behaved lately," she muttered sadly.

"But with good reason," Deborah objected. "Why, if that no-good Yankee—"

"Please," Erin interrupted. "I'd rather not embark on a lengthy discussion of Kellen. I . . . I am trying to forget that he was ever a part of my life." Even as she voiced her impassioned plea, her hand mechanically returned to caress her abdomen. "Let's talk of more pleasant things, shall we? For instance, what are you doing here? I thought you would be on your way to the mill by now, or has Graham decided to return to the house to partake of his noon meal?" she asked, forcing a smile to her somber lips.

"No," Deborah answered slowly. "In fact, that's the reason I came to see you. I was wondering if you might like to go with me when I take Graham's lunch to him. The snow has melted and it's such a bright, cheerful looking day. We could take the buggy," she added hopefully, trying to coax Erin from her self-imposed hideaway.

"Forgive me, Debby, but I am not in the mood for an outing today," Erin sighed tiredly, raising her eyes in time to see Deborah's expectant expression replaced by one of acute chagrin, thereby, prompting her to inquire, "What's wrong, Debby?"

"It's nothing." the girl mumbled dejectedly, turning to walk to the door.

But Erin was not about to let her depart without an explanation for her odd behavior. "Deborah," she said in a scolding, motherly tone. "You have been rendezvousing with Graham over lunch every day since the mill opened. You have never requested a chaperon before," Erin reminded her teasingly. "Why the sudden yearning for a companion?"

"It's nothing, really," Deborah insisted, reaching for the door handle, but before she could withdraw into the corridor, Erin crossed to her side to prevent any such maneuver.

"Tell me," she said softly, leading Deborah away from the door and into a nearby chair.

"I saw a man watching me in the woods," Deborah blurted suddenly, desperately grasping the arm of the chair for support.

"A man?"

Deborah nodded.

"When?"

"You mean you . . . you believe me?" Deborah's frightened eyes rose to find Erin's, and she felt remarkably reassured by the understanding expression that she encountered.

Erin seated herself on the footstool facing her sister-in-law, and patted her hand in a consoling gesture. "Of course, I believe you," she murmured. "When did you see the man, and where?"

"I saw him for the first time a couple of days ago when I was coming from the mill. I had just emerged from the forest onto the path that winds along the creek when, suddenly, there he was." She shuddered uncontrollably despite the gentle hands that reached out to comfort her.

"Were you able to get a look at his face?"

"Only a glimpse," she admitted. "When the man realized that I was aware of his presence, he turned and disappeared into the forest."

"But you implied that you have seen him since then," Erin reminded her kindly.

"Yes. I saw him again yesterday," she explained. "He followed me to the mill and back again."

"Did the man say anything to you, or behave as though he meant to harm you in any way?" Erin asked, her countenance growing serious.

"No. He just followed me and . . . and watched me. Erin, I could almost *feel* his eyes burning into my flesh. It was the most frightening sensation," she wailed, burying her face in her hands.

"I am certain it was," Erin murmured sympathetically. "Have you told Graham about the man?"

"N-n-no," she stammered. "I was afraid that he wouldn't believe me." She lifted her eyes to scan Erin's face, her unhappy expression speaking volumes.

"Of course, he would," Erin whispered earnestly, correctly guessing the basis for Deborah's reluctance to confide in her husband. "You fear that Graham might think you are suffering some sort of a setback," she offered gently, and, noting the weak nod of Deborah's head, she continued. "I understand your trepidation, but I think that perhaps you are selling your husband short," Erin softly chastised her friend. "After all, you are so much better than you were when Graham first came home," she pointed out. Then standing, she began to walk toward the door.

"Come along, Debby. You run ahead and instruct Paulie to ready the buggy for our outing."

"Then you'll go with me?" Deborah asked, a relieved smile highlighting her pretty face.

"Certainly," Erin said determinedly. "Graham needs to be informed of this situation immediately, and I am not about to let you go off all by yourself. Get your things, and I'll meet you in front of the house in ten minutes."

Deborah observed the grim look on Erin's face and it caused her some concern. "But where are you going?"

"To fetch Evan's pistol," she answered directly. "Should our mysterious stranger reveal himself to be a scoundrel, he shall quickly discover that it's not two missish simpletons that he has chosen to harass," she said staunchly, and exited the room before Deborah could voice her objection to the impetuous plan.

As Deborah had indicated, the March day was mild and appeared to be the perfect weather for a jaunt. Erin held the reins loosely between gloved fingers as she expertly maneuvered the horse along the muddy trail, and she endeavored to maintain a lighthearted conversation with her companion while she surreptitiously scanned the woods for signs of anything out of the ordinary. Silently, she wondered if Brian Taggart might be the man that Deborah had seen, but her reflective musings came to a halt when she glanced askance to witness the moody frown that blemished her sister-in-law's face.

"What is it, Debby? Have you seen him again?" Erin asked anxiously.

"What? Oh, no. I was just thinking," she began hesitantly. "It's been so very long since I handled the reins. Do you think I could drive the rest of the way?"

"I don't see why not. We're less than a mile from the mill, and I should think that you could manage that," Erin said fondly. "In fact, I believe that Graham will be very pleased to see how intrepid you've become."

They were traveling along a relatively straight stretch of roadway, so Erin carefully handed the leather straps over to the excited girl. Deborah had barely assumed control of the horse, however, when Erin became alerted to a commotion in the forest to her left. Startled by the abrupt noise, Erin's eyes darted toward a clump of trees just as a lone horseman crashed through the woodland foliage and onto the path. And the ensuing events occurred in such a whirlwind fashion that, when questioned later, the girls were hard pressed to piece together the particulars surrounding the incident.

Erin watched in horror as the masked assailant maneuvered his mount alongside them, fixing his evil gaze on her for a brief moment, he gave a diabolical laugh. Erin was permitted only a short glimpse of the man's face, but the split second glance was enough to strike her with an impending sense of doom. For, although she was denied a clear look at the man, because of the kerchief that camouflaged much of his face, she did witness the threatening cast to his brown eyes; the same brown eyes that had been the source of so much torment for her.

Erin's heart lurched with unbridled panic, and she frantically shoved her hand inside the pocket of her heavy cloak to retrieve the pistol she had brought along for their protection. Her reaction proved to be for naught, however, for, in the next instant, the unsavory man produced a whip, and, giving a loud whoop, he delivered several vicious blows against the backside of their horse.

Understandably frightened by the malicious assault, the animal gave a nervous whinny and began to run at a swifter pace, hoping to avoid any further abuse. Spurred into a precarious gallop along the narrow trail that followed the course of the creek bed, the animal raced on, heedless of the furious tugs on the reins that commanded him to quell his frenzied pace.

Erin noticed that Deborah's face was white with terror as she struggled to bring the runaway vehicle under control.

And though she wanted to offer her some assistance, Erin found that she could not pry her fingers from the seat where they clung in sheer desperation. She closed her eyes as the buggy rounded a curve on two wheels, but as the conveyance righted itself and continued to swerve along the treacherous course, Erin reopened her eyes to behold an even more frightening sight: a felled tree blocked the roadway just a few yards ahead of them.

Thinking quickly, Erin wrested the reins from Deborah's fists, hoping that her more experienced and authoritative hands might persuade the animal to abandon this wild ride before it ended in disaster. Erin's skillful ministrations proved futile as well, however, and, in complete desperation, she was prompted to shout, *"Jump,* Debby! We have to jump!"

"No! I can't!"

"You must! Go ahead. I'll be right behind you," Erin cried, still struggling with the jerking reins.

Erin glanced sideways in time to see Deborah gather her cloak tightly about her and leap clear of the runaway buggy. Deborah grimaced in anticipation of her painful confrontation with the hard earth, but, thankfully, the muddy creek bed successfully cushioned much of the impact. When she had rolled to a stop, Deborah anxiously climbed to her knees to watch for Erin, but the scene that greeted her eyes made her cringe: Erin was still in the buggy.

As Deborah watched, helplessly, the horse veered to avoid the fallen log, sending the conveyance crashing into the obstacle. The horrible noise of the splintering wood directly coincided with the even more horrifc sound of Erin's terrified scream as the force of the impact dislodged her from her perch and sent her sailing from the disabled vehicle.

Even before Erin landed on the muddy ground, Deborah started to scramble toward her stricken sister-in-law. Fully expecting the worst, Deborah was none too surprised by the deathly white pallor of Erin's face. Emitting a strangled cry of despair, she scurried down the embankment and dropped to her knees beside the unconscious girl.

"Erin!" she cried hysterically. "Please, talk to me! You've got to be all right. You've just got to!" she sobbed wildly, clutching Erin's limp hands to her breast. "Oh, why didn't you jump?"

As Deborah's beleaguered eyes settled on Erin's face, the lifeless figure began to stir. Erin's eyelids fluttered open, and she moaned painfully, pulling her hands free to rub along the bump that had begun to swell on the back of her head.

"I couldn't jump," she mumbled an answer to Deborah's delirious question. "I . . . I didn't . . . have time."

"Oh, good!" Deborah shouted happily. "You're awake. I was so afraid that . . . that—"

"No, Debby," Erin consoled the worried girl. "I'm all right," she assured her, but when she tried to shift to a more comfortable position, she was staggered by a crippling pain in her ankle. But, more frighteningly, the movement had rendered her momentarily weak with nausea, and, fearing for the life of her child, she gripped Deborah's hand with an awesome strength that startled the girl.

"What is it?" she asked, alarmed by Erin's abrupt behavior.

"The baby!" she replied excitedly. "I'm afraid something might be wrong. Oh, Debby, you must go on to the mill and bring Graham back to me."

"No! I can't leave you alone," Deborah protested. "That awful man might come back."

"Honey," Erin said urgently, feeling a sudden twinge in her abdomen, "you must leave me. I've reinjured my ankle as well. I couldn't possibly make the journey with you," she explained. "Besides, I'll be all right." She reached into her pocket and withdrew the pistol. "And this time, I'll be ready for the scoundrel, should he be foolhardly enough to return."

"Okay," Deborah reluctantly agreed, her eyes darting toward the destroyed buggy. "The horse appears to be uninjured; I'll . . . I'll ride him to the mill. Don't worry, Erin, I'll bring Graham, and he'll get you to Doc Wilson's," she said reassuringly, turning to clamber back up the steep incline.

"Deborah," Erin called suddenly to stay her motion.

"Yes?"

"Be careful," she warned.

"I will." Deborah smiled bravely, but before she could resume her climb, Erin again called out to her. "Yes, Erin. What is it?" came the remarkably composed reply.

"Please, hurry!"

"I will," Deborah promised, and, scampering up the embankment, she quickly disappeared from view.

Clutching the pistol to her bosom, Erin reclined against her muddy mattress, and silently prayed for Deborah's swift return. Her equanimity momentarily restored, Erin relaxed her tense muscles, and, finding her eyelids abnormally heavy, she once again slipped into unconsciousness.

Erin had no idea how long she had remained incapacitated, but when she awoke, she immediately became alerted to the plodding of a horse's hooves on the roadway. Thinking that Deborah and Graham had returned for her, Erin started to call out, but common sense prevailed, and she wisely held her tongue. She listened closely as the rider brought the mount to a halt, and, moments later, she heard the undeniable sounds of a man's footfalls tramping along the muddy ridge above her.

Erin's heart pounded, for surely if Graham had arrived he would call out to her, she reasoned.

Vainly trying to remain calm, Erin's slender fingers instinctively found the pistol nestled in her lap. When next she dared to glance toward the ridge, she discovered a pair of booted feet planted squarely not ten feet from her eyes. Swallowing the frightened lump that constricted her throat, Erin courageously leveled the weapon at the unknown intruder. With bold determination, she carefully cocked the pistol, and, just when she would have discharged the gun, the man addressed her.

"Damn it, wench! Do you welcome all newcomers to Kilkieran in this annoying fashion, or is this a ritual that you have devised especially for me?" asked a familiar voice in a derisive tone.

The fingers that tightly gripped the pistol abruptly grew limp, and the weapon fell harmlessly to the ground. "Kellen?" she whispered hoarsely, blinking her eyes in disbelief. "You're here?"

"Yes, infant," he murmured softly, moving to kneel by her side.

"But, what are—" She faltered, for as she spoke, she endeavored to struggle to a sitting position, but the throbbing pain in her head gave her reason to reconsider her action.

Greatly concerned by the unsightly grimace that appeared on her pretty face, Kellen tenderly assisted her back to her former location. "Stay put," he advised. Then sitting down beside her, he carefully positioned her so that her head could repose in his lap. "Better?" he asked considerately.

"Mmm," she moaned her contentment, then suddenly consumed with curiosity, Erin felt compelled to inquire, "How did you know where to find me?"

"I was at the mill when Deborah came riding up shrieking like a woman possessed by a demon," he began candidly, his expression serious. "She was babbling so incoherently at first that even Graham encountered some difficulty interpreting her hysterical ravings. Once she calmed down, though, we were able to determine that there had been an accident, and that you had been hurt, prompting me to dash off to your rescue." He paused to look down at her, his hand lovingly stroking her cheek.

"Kellen, there was a man," she began, becoming unduly agitated, causing Kellen to place a finger against her lips to forestall any further attempts to explain what had happened.

"Shh, honey," he cooed dotingly, pressing a kiss to her brow. "There will be time for explanations later." He gently rocked her in his secure embrace.

Erin, however, would not allow her heart to believe that Kellen had returned to attempt a reconciliation. He's probably come back to complete his mission for the department, she reasoned dismally, refusing to meet the gaze that she felt certain regarded her with contempt. No, she continued her silent musings, he has only come to console me until the others arrive.

In a deliberately hollow voice, Erin asked, "Where are the others?"

Kellen's observant ears detected Erin's disheartened tone, but he attributed her peculiar behavior to the severe trauma she had just suffered. Consequently, he adopted a more solicitous manner. "Graham and Deborah have gone off to fetch Doc Wilson; he'll be waiting at the house for us," he assured her. "And one of the men from the mill is bringing a wagon, so that we can safely transport you home."

"But can't you take me on Achilles?" Erin asked plaintively. "I'm so very weary of lying here in the mud," she sighed her frustration.

"I know," he whispered soothingly. "However, you must remember that you've experienced a tremendous shock, and I'll not take any unnecessary chances with your life, or that of our child's. The last thing you need is to be jostled about atop my horse.

"Take heart, princess," Kellen murmured softly. "I think I hear the wagon approaching us now."

He stood up and carefully lifted her in his stalwart embrace, then, making sure of his footing, he swiftly carried her up the embankment, accomplishing his task just as the vehicle arrived. Kellen gently placed his burden on the floor of the wagon, then, tethering Achilles to the rear of the transport, he climbed into the wagon with Erin. He thoughtfully removed his own protective overcoat and wrapped it snugly about her for added warmth, and, settling down beside her, he again offered her the use of his lap as a pillow. Then with a wave of his hand, he signaled the driver to begin the short journey to Kilkieran.

"Slowly," he cautioned the man. "This is precious cargo you're transporting." He favored Erin with an adoring look, but she was oblivious to his devoted expression, for she had once again lapsed into unconsciousness.

Kellen paced fitfully about the spacious parlor as he awaited word from the doctor on Erin's condition. As he had promised, Doc Wilson had been waiting on them when they arrived at the mansion. Kellen had quickly delivered Erin to the comfort of his old room, and been properly confounded when the physician dismissed him, so he could conduct a thorough examination of his patient, "without a meddlesome husband getting in my way," the physician had informed him pertly.

There had been no reasoning with the crotchety old man, therefore, Kellen was left with little recourse save to comply with the good doctor's wishes. But that had been hours ago, and still there had been no word from the man concerning the seriousness of Erin's injuries.

"Damn!" he swore aloud. "What can be keeping him?" He stepped to the bell pull to summon a servant to bring him yet another pot of coffee.

His hand had just encircled the satin rope, however, when the door to the chamber opened, and whirled toward the entranceway expectantly. But his hopeful expression dissolved when he recognized the arrivals as Evan and Graham. Masking his disappointment, Kellen let the cord slip from his fingers and strode across the floor to greet them.

"How is Deborah?" Kellen inquired solicitously.

"Her nerves are badly shaken, but Doc Wilson says she'll be fine," Graham replied wearily, falling into the first available chair. "He gave her something to help her sleep. She's resting now."

"Has there been any word about Erin?" Evan asked worriedly, for having just returned from the store in Braxton, he was still very much in the dark about the accident.

"No," Kellen moaned miserably. "Come and sit down, Evan. I was just about to order a pot of coffee from the kitchen. I fear that our vigil is not quite over."

"If it's all the same to you, Kellen, I'd just as soon have something a bit stronger," Graham said matter-of-factly.

"I quite agree." Kellen went to pour each of them a serving of whiskey, and he was just handing out the brimming glasses when the parlor door reopened and Doc Wilson sauntered into the room.

"I sincerely hope that one of those is for me." He offered them a wan smile, and, placing his medical bag on a chair near the entrance, he settled himself on the divan next to Evan.

Kellen politely extended the glass he had prepared for himself, and quickly voiced the question that had haunted him for hours. "How is she, Doc?"

Doc Wilson permitted himself a leisurely draft of the fiery liquid before he bothered to put Kellen's tormented mind at ease. Finally, he said, "She's bruised up a bit, and she'll most likely have a nasty headache for a day or two, but she's going to be fine," he assured the three pairs of anxious eyes that were trained on him.

"And the child?" Kellen prompted, almost fearful of the physician's reply.

"You mean to say that you knew about the baby when you left her?" Evan interrupted, his face red with indignant fury. "And you think that you can waltz back in here —"

"Evan, this is a matter between Erin and Kellen. Let's let them settle their affairs privately, shall we?" the doctor gently reproved Evan's impetuous remarks, then turning to Kellen, he said, "Erin is strong and healthy. I've prescribed a few days of bedrest as a precaution, but I found nothing during my examination to indicate that the child is an any danger."

The doctor heard Kellen's thankful sigh of relief and, in anticipation of the younger man's next question, he favored him with a beleaguered smile and nodded. "Yes, you may see her. But don't you go upsetting her," he ordered, waving a stern finger at Kellen. "She's suffered a tremendous shock today, and right now, she's mighty apprehensive about the reason for your return. Now, I'm betting that you've come back to try to make amends, but if I'm mistaken, and you're here to cause her more anguish, then I'll withdraw my permission and suggest that you see her after she's had a chance to recover from today's mishap."

"Don't worry." Kellen hastened to reassure the doctor. "The truth is, a very wise person made me realize what a complete jackass I've been, and I have come to set things aright; that is assuming the little firebrand will have me."

"Oh, she'll have you right enough," Evan spoke up, his anger having subsided when he heard Kellen's admission. "She'll like as not lead you a merry chase for awhile, but I believe I'm relatively safe in saying welcome back to the family, brother-in-law." He extended his hand, and Kellen shook it firmly before leaving the room.

He had progressed no further than the stairway, however, when he heard his name called, thereby delaying his reunion with his wife. Casting a regretful glance up the wide staircase, Kellen turned to face the individual who had summoned him.

"Yes, Graham?"

"I know you're anxious to see Erin, so I won't detain you, but something has been nagging at me for the longest time, and I'd like you to satisfy my curiosity before you go to my sister. Because you see," his voice grew uncharacteristically grave, "if I'm not appeased with your explanation, I'm going to override Doc Wilson's decision to let you see Erin. For I'll not let you hurt her again, Yankee."

Kellen instinctively tensed at this last jibe, but he managed to keep his temper in check. After all, it had been a long, tedious day, and, from the looks of things, it was far from over. He

502

was tired and weary, and only wanted the chance to hold his wife in his arms and kiss away the sadness that wrinkled the corners of her beautiful green eyes. Therefore, it was a precarious countenance he turned on his brother-in-law.

"All right, Graham," he sighed his acquiescence. "What's troubling you?"

"Something that I overheard at your wedding reception."

"What!" Kellen could hardly believe his ears. "Why am I standing here listening to this rubbish when I could be holding Erin in my arms?" he asked of no one in particular.

"Please, hear me out," Graham said patiently, and he went on to repeat the portion of the conversation he had overheard between Colonel Langford and Kellen in Tiffin Square's garden.

"I see." Kellen nodded understandingly. "And you naturally assumed that I had some underhanded reason for marrying Erin."

"Yes."

"Well, the truth is, I *am* conducting an investigation for the military that involves this vicinity, but I hardly had to marry Erin to return to the area. In fact, I want to discuss the matter with you at length, but not tonight," he added purposefully. "You told me once that you would assist me if I should devise a plan that might help Erin remember what truly happened on the day of the raid."

"I recollect making such a promise." Graham nodded.

"Good. I'll come round to the mill tomorrow to fill you in on everything," Kellen informed him, but before he continued his journey up the staircase, he addressed Graham one last time. "Oh, and Graham. I had but one motive for marrying your sister. It's because I love her, passionately, more completely than I had ever imagined possible. And I promise you this," he continued, his voice growing somber. "It's my sincerest intent to see that Erin never suffers again."

Kellen concluded his explanation and turned to bolt up the staircase, lest anyone else decide to pelt him with insipid questions regarding his return to Kilkieran. For, in all honesty, there was but one individual he cared to provide with that particular information, and he found himself suddenly consumed by an unfamiliar emotion: fear. He was genuinely afraid that Erin might shun his attempt at a reconciliation.

Kellen paused outside his chamber for a moment to collect his thoughts, then he carefully pushed the door open and stepped across the threshold. A perplexed frown suddenly crinkled his brow, however, for the room was in total darkness. Kellen paused near the entranceway, allowing his eyes time to adjust to the dim light, but he became further chagrined when he discovered an empty bed.

His gaze intuitively fell on the door that connected his room with Erin's, and, feeling decidedly intimidated, he crossed to that portal and opened it. The soft glow of the lantern illuminated Erin's slender frame on the bed, but from his vantage point, Kellen could not yet ascertain if her eyes were closed in slumber.

Maisie sat in a chair at the foot of the bed, diligently keeping vigil over her mistress, but when she saw Kellen standing in the doorway, she came to her feet. "Come on in, Mistah Kellen." She beckoned him into the room.

Kellen closed the door behind him and went to stand beside the servant. "Is she asleep?"

"Jest dozin'," Maisie answered. "She's been askin' aftah you. Why doan you sits yoreself down hyah till she wakes up?" the domestic suggested, obviously intending to leave him alone with his wife.

"How is she?"

"Fidgety and a mite fevahish, but de doctah says she'll be good as new in no time atall." She noticed Kellen's pensive frown, and she hastened to comfort him. "Doan you worry none, Mistah Kellen; Miz Erin is a fightah."

"I know." He fastened an affectionate gaze on his wife. "Perhaps a dose of your famous bitters would do her some good," he commented offhandedly.

"Mah bittahs ain't no good fer whut ails dat chile, Mistah Kellen. Dey woan fix no broken heart. Seems t' me dat only *you* can mend dat," she informed him, then shuffled from the room.

The door had barely closed behind the departing housekeeper when Erin's eyelids fluttered open, and she focused a rather drowsy gaze on her husband. "Kellen?" she managed weakly.

Moving to the bed, Kellen sat down on the edge and smiled down at her. "Hello, little reb. How are you feeling?"

"Tired," she murmured.

"Would you like me to leave, so that you can rest?" he offered, though he was loath to leave her alone.

"No," she murmured. "Besides, if I adhere to Doc Wilson's instructions, I shall be getting a good deal of rest." She averted her eyes, feeling suddenly awkward at being alone with him.

"Oh, you will most certainly follow the doctor's orders, my sweet. I am here to promise you that. But evidently you think that you cannot get sufficient peace in the master chamber," he casually made reference to the fact that she had elected to spend her recuperation period in her own room. "I apologize if my choice of accommodations offended you."

"It didn't, Kellen," Erin began tentatively. "It's just that you will be sleeping there. I . . . I thought that you would rather not . . . not have me around," her voice trailed off sadly, and she would have turned her face into the pillow had Kellen not placed his fingers under her chin and forced her to look at him.

"Well, my darling, permit me to quickly dispel that idiotic notion, for I assure you that I do indeed want you — more than ever, if that is possible." He tenderly caressed her cheek with the back of his hand. "But more importantly, I need you," he whispered throatily, his blue eyes misting over with tears of remorse.

505

"Kellen," she breathed his name compassionately, but he would not tolerate her interruption.

"No, let me finish," he said determinedly. "To say that I am sorry for the anguish I have caused you the past few months would be a gross understatement. My conduct was totally reprehensible, and I have no valid excuse to justify my actions other than the fact that I was blinded with jealousy," he admitted.

Kellen paused for a moment, then exhaled a harried sigh before continuing. "Mother was instrumental in helping me realize what a perfect ass I have been." He quickly recounted the conversation that had taken place with Meredith. "When I finally discerned that I had been cleverly duped by Vanessa and Christina's little charade, I came rushing back here to beg your forgiveness.

"I am even prepared to grovel on my knees if that would help influence your decision to my advantage," he concluded with this impassioned admission.

"I don't think that will be necessary," she whispered gently, offering him a wan smile.

"Damn!" he grumbled frustratingly, shoving his hand through his hair in a frantic gesture. "I would not blame you if you had my mangy hide tossed from your home."

He turned away from her, unsure of the reaction his inadequate apology would elicit. But if he had ventured to glance at the beautiful face that stared at him in wonder, he would have realized that total surrender was just seconds away. Vaguely, he became aware of the slight pressure of her hand on his arm, inducing him to look at her.

Her voice was soft and forgiving when she eventually spoke. "Now, why should I want to behave like a silly goose; especially since I love you so very much," she murmured shakily, cognizant of the tears that had begun to trickle down her cheeks.

But before she completely yielded to the tension-purging emotion, Erin extended her quivering arms to her husband. "Hold me?" she whispered hopefully.

A lustrous smile immediately spread Kellen's sensuous mouth, and he swiftly enfolded her in a fierce embrace. Neither of them spoke for the longest time; each apparently content to rejoice in the pleasure of one another's caress. At last, Kellen nuzzled his face in her hair and breathed deeply of her fresh, clean scent.

Pressing an affectionate kiss against her brow, he pulled away to stare down into the exquisite face that was marred only by the tears that stained her cheeks. In a considerate gesture, Kellen tenderly brushed away the few remaining tears, yet his hand lingered along her cheek.

"God, I have been frantic with worry," he sighed heavily. "I didn't know what I would find when Deborah told me that you had been hurt. And then to be kept waiting for hours with no word on your condition; well, this day has been sheer agony for me, I assure you."

"There is no need to fret, my love," Erin quickly assured him. "Doc Wilson says that I will be fine after a few days of rest."

"I know." He looked down in time to witness the startled expression that briefly crossed her face. "What is it, honey? Shall I summon Doc Wilson?"

"No," she laughed a little nervously. "It's much too soon for that."

"What?" he asked, genuinely perplexed by her banter.

"It was just the . . . the baby," she explained, glancing away. "I fear that I am not quite accustomed to its stirrings."

"Ah, yes, little mother," he breathed, his adoring gaze sweeping over her. "I had nearly forgotten that the responsibility of fatherhood awaits me in but a few short months." He carefully slipped her hand beneath the coverlets and purposefully slid it across her nightdress till it came to rest on her rounding stomach. "My, my, but that is an exceptional bulge, my lady. Do you think it might be twins?" he asked suddenly, hoping that his genuine interests in the child would encourage her to forget the ugly accusation he had hurled at her by the waterfall. It did and, for his efforts he received one of her most dazzling smiles.

"Heaven forbid!" she shrieked. "I feel positively fat as it is," she bemoaned her fate.

"Unfortunately, my lovely, that goes with the territory. But you can take heart in the knowledge that yours is a purely temporary condition," he said teasingly, preparing to remove his hand.

But he was completely taken by surprise when Erin meaningfully covered his hand with hers and gently coaxed it upward to caress her breast. Correctly interpreting her intent, Kellen was quick to squelch her amorous plunderings. With considerable effort, he managed to check his own rising passion as he confronted her.

"Erin, my sweet," he coughed awkwardly. "I hardly think that now is the time—"

"But, I don't understand," she mumbled petulantly, her eyes anxiously searching his face. "I . . . I want you to make love to me; that is, of course, unless you don't want me." She looked away, dreading his response.

"Not want you?" he bellowed. "I've thought of little else for days! But you have experienced a severe shock today, and you need your rest," he informed her in no uncertain terms. "Now, I am going to extinguish the light, but I will entertain no more of this nonsense, do you understand?"

He solemnly acknowledged Erin's contrite nod of acquiescence.

"Good. Now, do be a good wife, and follow your loving husband's advice; go to sleep, little reb. I promise that there will be plenty of time to . . . ahem . . . *cuddle* once you have sufficiently recovered your strength."

And with his nefarious chuckle still echoing in her ears, Erin succumbed to the first truly peaceful sleep she had encountered in weeks.

Chapter Twenty-Four

Erin sat before the dressing table mirror in her chamber, meticulously pulling a pearl handled brush through her hair. As she contemplatively fingered the heavy tendrils, a decisively pensive expression shadowed her pretty face, for her thoughts had quite naturally centered on Kellen.

It had been three days since his return to Kilkieran, and, in that time, he had barely managed to spend as much as five minutes alone with her at any given time. Much to her chagrin, Kellen had resumed his investigation into the Taggart affair, and, having taken Graham into his confidence, she learned that her brother was wont to accompany him as he scoured the countryside for any clue that might help him solve the confounding mystery.

His endeavors kept him from the house from the early morning hours until late at night, severely limiting the time they were able to spend together. Consequently, Erin had come to believe that if she was ever going to see her vagabond husband again, it would be up to her to contrive some sort of rendezvous.

Thus reminded of her purpose, Erin carefully arranged the décolletage of her dressing gown at a daring angle. Then giving her head a careless toss, she allowed the satiny tresses to settle about her shoulders in a seductively alluring fashion.

Satisfied with her handiwork, Erin next applied a generous portion of her favorite perfume behind each earlobe, and, on impulse, dabbed a few droplets between the voluptuous mounds of her breasts. Once she was satisified with her appearance, Erin stood and went to await her husband in the privacy of his chamber.

She did not have to wait long, however, for she had barely settled herself in the leather wing chair when the door was flung aside, and he trudged into the room. Finding the chamber in virtual darkness, except for the glow of the fireplace, Kellen's initial instinct was to light the lantern. But as he reached for the lamp, his nostrils became suddenly inundated with a maddeningly familiar fragrance, causing him to forego this action.

He turned from the dresser, a roguish grin pinning back the corners of his mouth, and favored her with an adoring look. "Hello," he murmured softly.

"Hello, yourself," she replied saucily. "Tell me, sir. Are we acquainted? My husband used to inhabit this chamber, but he has been so preoccupied since his return from Washington that I have scarcely laid eyes on him. Why, I'm not entirely certain that I would recognize the scoundrel if he did condescend to grant me a few minutes of his precious time," she said peevishly, thrusting out her lower lip in an obvious pout.

Kellen could not repress the chuckle that rose in his throat as he beheld the caricature of righteous indignation she so magnificently portrayed. With a mischievous gleam twinkling behind the crystal blue eyes, he sauntered over to his wife and casually dragged her into his arms.

"Feeling neglected, are you, brat?" His warm whisper sent rivulets of delicious shivers tingling along her spine.

"Yes," she answered tersely.

"Well, it is good to see that your tongue has recovered much of its sting." He laughed at her petulance. "How about the rest of you? Are you feeling better?"

"I am fine, Kellen," she replied, articulating each syllable precisely.

"Good!" he said pleasantly, and, releasing her suddenly, he strode over to the washstand. Stripping off his shirt, he began to splash water on his face and arms in an attempt to rinse away the day's accumulation of dirt and grime. "Perhaps we can celebrate your recovery by riding into Braxton tomorrow. I would like to see how Evan is getting along at the store."

"I was rather hoping that we might *celebrate* this evening," Erin countered, her meaning quite explicit.

"Oh, I fear that it is much too late to go riding tonight," he taunted her by feigning ignorance at her coy suggestion.

From her vantage point, Erin could not see the playful smile that fashioned Kellen's lips; he was deriving immense pleasure from her coquettish attempt at seduction. Turning toward her, his consuming perusal swept over her, giving him the opportunity to truly notice her attire for the first time.

She wore a yellow silk dressing gown that was inlaid with a tiny, intricate pattern; the exact design of which was undiscernible in the flickering light. However, the billowy sleeves, flowing skirt, youthful ruffles, and plunging neckline all combined to create a most attractive ensemble.

"That's a fetching piece of finery you're wearing, my dear," he complimented her. "I don't recall seeing it before."

"This is the first time I have had the occasion to wear it," she explained vaguely. "You see, I purchased it in Richmond, so I have had little reason to wear it lately."

"It's lovely, as are you," he murmured huskily, and tearing his eyes from her breasts, he returned to his ablutions. "Am I to assume that you also procured a matching nightdress."

"Yes."

"Good. I look forward to seeing it."

"I'm not wearing it at the moment. As a matter-of-fact, I'm not wearing anything underneath my dressing gown," she announced baldly, deriving excessive gratification as the bar of soap splashed noisily into the porcelain bowl.

Erin noted his shocked expression with amusement, and she had to bite her lower lip in an effort to maintain a nonchalent hauteur. "Are you hungry?" she asked, abruptly changing the subject.

"Famished!" came his automatic reply.

"There is a plate of sandwiches on the table, and cold milk. Or" she placed a finger to her cheek as though considering an important alternative, "there *is* champagne, but then you don't appear to be interested in celebrating this evening." She started to drift toward the door of the connecting chamber.

"Where do you think you're going?"

"To bed." She pretended to stifle a fatigued yawn.

"Blast it, wench! *Come here!*" he bellowed, throwing open his arms to her.

In an instant, Erin flew across the room and hurled herself into his welcoming embrace. She lifted her face to his and sighed her contentment as they kissed, eagerly, passionately. When at last they separated, Erin slipped her hand into his and led him to the table. Pushing him down into the chair, she placed the plate of food in front of him. Then she handed him the chilled bottle of champagne and patiently waited until the container had been opened. After she poured each of them a glass of the refreshing beverage, she curled up in the wing chair to watch him.

They chatted amicably while Kellen devoured his flavorful repast, and, by the time he had concluded the late night collation, they were on old terms again. It was as if Richmond had never happened.

"Delicious," Kellen proclaimed, reaching across the table to pour the last remaining drops of champagne into Erin's glass. Then leaning back in his chair, he raised his arms high above his head to stretch his weary muscles.

"Tired?" Erin asked considerately.

"Just working out the kinks in my neck and shoulders," he explained.

"Perhaps I can be of some assistance," she volunteered, and, slipping from the chair, she beckoned him to follow her to the bed. Throwing aside the coverlets, Erin instructed him to lie down.

Mildly intrigued by his wife's behavior, Kellen stretched out on his stomach on the wide berth. He had anticipated that she intended to massage the tenseness from his exhausted body, but the technique she selected through which to perform the intimate task thoroughly surprised and delighted him. For Erin suddenly climbed atop the bed and carefully positioned herself astride him.

Resting her knees on either side of his muscular body, Erin purposely moved her hands along his back and shoulders, deliberately kneading the hard flesh with her gentle fingers. She carried out her agreeable chore effortlessly, creating a sensual, rhythmic motion that Kellen could not ignore. That, coupled with the incredible sensation of her naked thighs pressed tightly against his sides caused him to moan pleasurably.

Without warning, Kellen wriggled to his back, taking special care not to dislodge his delicate passenger. And his voice was understandably thick with desire when he next addressed her. "You handled that problem quite nicely; quite nicely indeed," he whispered huskily, his hand slipping beneath her robe to slide up and down her slender waist. "So, I was wondering if you would care to direct your attention to another rather . . . ahem . . . urgent dilemma," he casually made reference to the stiffened organ that presently strained to be free of his trousers.

"Perhaps," she murmured, her mouth assuming a demure smile. "What did you have in mind?"

"Let me show you." His hands instinctively found their way to the front of her gown, and he began to fumble with the sash at her waist.

At the same instant, Erin reached down to grapple with his belt buckle, causing him to entangle the delicate ropes in hopeless knots. Gnarling his lips in bitter frustration, Kellen prepared to break the dainty threads between his anxious fingers, but calmer hands prevailed.

"Oh, no, my impatient darling," Erin gently scolded him. "You shall not get the chance to ruin this one." She quickly unknotted the sash, and, giving a seductive shake of her shoulders, the elegant garment was sent slithering to the mattress behind her.

Kellen exhaled a heady breath as he allowed his thirsty eyes a leisurely reunion with his wife's exquisite body, and their eyes locked in a knowing embrace while Erin's nimble fingers returned to swiftly accomplish her previous task. That settled, Kellen promptly kicked off the remainder of his clothes, finally enabling him to initiate a thorough exploration of the lovely creature who hovered above him in the faltering firelight.

Kellen's large hands slowly crept up her arms, across her shoulders, eventually sliding downward to capture her trembling breasts. He expertly massaged the sensitive peaks until they grew hard between his fingertips; the firm tips straining urgently against his masculine flesh. Kellen marveled as he felt the familiar stirrings in his loins, reminding him how much he had missed this splendid vision.

Wrapping his arms around her, Kellen gradually coaxed her forward, until their lips came together in a caring embrace. The kiss began as a tender encounter, but the gentle pressure of her mouth on his quickly reminded him of the recent months of their separation, during which he had spurned all thoughts of romance. His passion thusly rekindled, Kellen guided his adept hands down her back to her hips where he deftly fondled the tantalizing flesh.

Erin was acutely aware of the glorious, tingling sensations his precise ministrations had ignited within her. Still, it was her sincere wish to give him pleasure as well, and, breathing a languid sigh, she managed to force her lips from his. Then she began to press a trail of feathery soft kisses from his mouth to one ear; where she playfully nibbled at the lobe with her teeth.

514

Altering her course somewhat, her moist lips blazed a path across his broad chest, her tongue lightly flicking at the hard flesh, causing the blood to surge through him like liquid fire. Thrilling at the sensual tremors that racked his body, she continued her downward progression until an unexpected ploy from her husband caused the breath to catch in her throat.

Her eyes quite naturally returned to Kellen's face, and she was none too surprised to witness the smugly satisfied grin that was on his lips. Unable to tear her eyes from his, Erin found that she could do little but cling to him as she gave herself to the wildly delirious sensation he had successfully summoned within her. Erin moaned her delight, momentarily content to bask in the tempestuous feeling of his hand methodically stroking her femininit . But when she became reminded of the throbbing shaft that was pressed against her inner thigh, she grew restless, for she was impatient to proceed with the romantic encounter; to feel his hard masculinity nestled snugly inside her.

The mere thought prompted a lugubrious moan from her lips, causing her to plead, "Take me. Please. Now." But when she would have tumbled onto her back against the mattress, Kellen caught her between his unyielding hands. "But," she began to protest.

"Shh," he whispered soothingly.

If Erin had any doubts about his purpose, they soon disappeared, for in the next instant, he lifted her and effortlessly positioned her atop his pulsating manhood. She was vaguely cognizant of his wicked chortle when he beheld her startled expression, but her gnawing passions had gone unheeded for so long that she could concentrate on little save the thundering shivers of excitement that inundated her very being.

Her eyes again found his, and she actually gulped at the intense devotion she read in the impassioned blue spheres. As he compelled her to look at him, his hands slid down her back, and he began to rotate her hips, creating a sublime motion that she felt was meant to leave her bereft of her few remaining sensibilities. Thus inspired, Erin began to move against him, the two of them generating such a diversity of excruciatingly pleasurable sensations that she was persuaded to pace her movements, so that the glorious adventure might be prolonged.

The spacious chamber echoed with her soft whimpers of delight, but as she strained against him, struggling toward the ultimate fulfillment, her rather submissive murmurings grew into throaty cries of unbridled rapture. Kellen reveled in her display of uninhibited abandon, and, thoroughly gratified by her apt ministrations, his hands were now free to undertake more pleasurable matters. Quite instinctively, his sensitive fingertips crept along her waist, sliding across her velvety soft flesh until they arrived at the bountiful globules that heaved in breathless anticipation. He continued to hold her gaze in the enraptured trance as he, ever so gently, began to stroke the vibrant nipples with his thumbs.

The precious moment continued with Erin losing all sense of time and her surroundings. But as she rode the crest of one tremulous wave after another, the thrilling sensations that had previously been scattered throughout her being suddenly came rushing together in one staggering explosion of sensual bliss.

Kellen heard her strangled cry of emotional relief, and a few moments later, he was able to satisfy his own lustful appetite. Their passions assuaged for the time being, Kellen tenderly caressed the cheek of the rare treasure that lay in an exhausted heap atop his chest. They lay motionless for a very long time, each content to languor in the memory of their tempestuous lovemaking.

Kellen was the first to stir, and he carefully lowered her quivering body onto the bed beside him. Then he wrapped his arm about her, and, drawing her close, tenderly brushed aside the strands of hair that cascaded across her face.

"I love you," he whispered hoarsely, his voice thick with emotion.

"Oh, Kellen!" She buried her face in his chest. "I was so afraid that I had lost you forever. Please, don't ever leave me again. I truly think that I should die if you did."

"Never fear, princess. I'm back for good," he assured her, his hand softly stroking her shoulder. "Go to sleep," he murmured lovingly. "I shall be here when you awake."

But Kellen was the first to succumb to a restful slumber, and, on impulse, Erin scampered from the bed and stepped to the dresser to rummage through the top drawer. It took her only a moment to find that which she sought, then she turned and hurried back to the warmth of her husband's bed. Taking care not to disturb his sleep, Erin lifted his hand and carefully slipped her father's diamond ring onto Kellen's finger. Then smiling happily to herself, she snuggled against him and drifted off to sleep.

Erin awoke the following morning to find Kellen leaning over her, a beguiling smile highlighting his handsome face. Upon closer examination, she determined that he had already shaved and dressed, causing a distressing frown to shape her mouth.

"Are you leaving already?" she asked, unable to keep the disappointing lilt from her voice.

"Not for awhile," he comforted her. "I thought that we could breakfast together before I leave. I do want to talk to you about something." He bent to retrieve her dressing gown and considerately extended it to her. "Maisie will serve us here, so that we may talk privately."

He leaned over to press a kiss against her petulant mouth, then murmured seriously, "Please, don't frown at me, angel. You know that I am determined to find Taggart, and, as much as I would like to spend the day languishing in your arms, I fear that I cannot. I will not take the chance that the rogue will try to harm you or Deborah again. I *must* find him."

"I understand," she mumbled, her eyes downcast. "It's just

517

that I wish that you would not drive yourself so hard. I worry about you."

"All wives worry about their husbands," he laughed good-naturedly. "Now, get dressed. I really cannot dally much longer."

Erin quickly donned her dressing gown, then slipped into the adjoining chamber to run a brush through her tangled locks and splash cool water on her face. She returned a few moments later to find that their breakfast had arrived, and Kellen stood behind her chair, waiting to assist her to her seat.

After he had seated her, Erin reached across the table to fill his coffee cup, then her own. But when she lifted the cover from her plate, she was given reason to sigh in dismay, for huge mounds of food had been piled upon her dish.

Kellen had already plopped a piece of the juicy beefsteak into his mouth, but his wife's outburst prompted him to inquire, "What's wrong, angel?"

"Just look at this! I cannot possibly eat all this food," she exclaimed, pointing to the huge portion of steak, eggs, grits, and biscuits and honey.

"Well, I did mention to Maisie that your appetite had returned." A smile spread over Kellen's mouth.

"Even so, I could never eat this much." She diplomatically chose to ignore his sly inference to their lovemaking.

"Perhaps your condition inspired Maisie to be a bit presumptuous. After all, you *are* eating for two; possibly three," he added mischievously, taking great delight in her beleaguered expression.

"I am not having twins!" she insisted. "And I refuse to discuss the matter further," she informed him in no uncertain terms. "Now, what did you want to talk about?" She started to pick at the food on her plate.

"I realize that this might be an imposition, considering your recent accident," he began slowly, carefully choosing his words. "But I was wondering if you were feeling up to entertaining some company?"

"Company? Who?"

"Mother."

"Of course! I would love to see Meredith," she squealed happily. "Does she know about the baby?"

"Yes, I told her when I was in Washington. I know that she is anxious to get here, so she can help you organize the nursery," he said fondly, his admiring gaze drifting to her face.

"Wonderful! When will she arrive?" Erin asked excitedly.

"Next week," he replied offhandedly, refocusing his attention to his plate. Moments later, as he chewed thoughtfully on a biscuit, Kellen again addressed her. "Honey, I was just thinking. Do you think it might be possible to plan some sort of party while Mother is visiting us?"

"A party?" She mulled the idea for several seconds. "Why, yes; I suppose so. We used to have a spring barbecue every year; nearly everyone in the county would come." Her eyes grew bright with remembrances of happier times. "Oh, yes. Let's do have a party!

"I will meet with Maisie right after breakfast to start making out the invitation list." Her mouth puckered into a pensive frown. "Oh, dear. I wonder what sort of affair I should plan."

Kellen shrugged his shoulders in apparent indifference. "I don't know. We men really are not as astute as you ladies when it comes to these things. However, a masquerade ball sounds diverting, don't you think?" came his casual suggestion. "We could have food and champagne and music. I can hardly wait to waltz with you in my arms again," he murmured tenderly.

"A masquerade?" She thoughtfully considered his offering. "Yes, that does sound like fun," she agreed. "Although, now I am faced with the additional quandary of selecting a suitable costume."

Having completed his meal, Kellen rose from his seat and went to stand beside her, placing a loving hand against her stomach. "Well," he chuckled wryly, "if Maisie continues to serve you such outrageous portions, you could always come as a pumpkin." He quickly covered her mouth with his to obliterate the vitriolic retort that sprang to her lips.

"Just teasing, my darling." He tweaked her nose before he started toward the door. "I shall return in time to have supper with you. Meanwhile, would you be a dear and inform Maisie that she should prepare two of the guest rooms for occupation?"

"Two?" Erin looked up from her plate, a quizzical expression wrinkling her brow.

He nodded, and, heaving a belabored sigh, he turned to her, plainly dreading his forthcoming admission. "Geoffrey and Vanessa will be accompanying Mother."

"*What?*" Erin jumped up abruptly, sending her fork clanking noisily onto the table. "You mean to tell me that you invited that . . . that viper and his . . . his—"

"Yes, Erin, he replied calmly. "I did. Geoffrey and I have a business venture to conclude, and, like it or not, Vanessa *is* his wife. I could hardly suggest that he leave her at home, now could I?" he asked glibly.

"No!" she shouted at him, stamping her foot to accentuate her ire. "I will not have that . . . that *woman* in my house!"

"Yes, you will, Oh, it will be awkward, to be sure, but I am confident that you will welcome my family cordially, and conduct yourself with the gracious deportment befitting my wife," he stated simply, his meaning explicit.

"Why?" she demanded. "Give me one good reason why I should be nice to that witch."

"Because, my darling, if you are not, I shall be forced to turn you over my knee and soundly wallop your pretty little rump," came his infuriating retort.

"Ooohhh!" she snarled angrily, but, before she could respond to this blatant threat, Kellen withdrew from the chamber, leaving a decisively irritate wife behind.

In a fit of pique, Erin picked up the plate cover from the table and promptly hurled it against the door. Then she turned and marched straightway to the adjoining chamber and jerked the bell pull to summon Renée to the room. Her eyes were flashing brightly as she plopped down in front of the dressing table and began to pull the brush through her hair with furious strokes.

"Humph!" she snorted. "Spank me, will he? We shall just see about that!" she vowed. But as her anger gradually subsided, her thoughts irrevocably returned to the night just spent in Kellen's arms, and a soft smile highlighted her eyes, and she rejoiced in the knowledge that her husband was home to stay.

At least the weather proved to be agreeable on the date of the scheduled masquerade ball, for the sun shone gorgeously throughout the day. The same could not be said, however, in regard to the temperament that prevailed among the inhabitants of the stately mansion.

Erin, of course, was preoccupied with last minute preparations for the gala evening ahead. She had spent the days during the past few weeks juggling her time between making plans for the party, and seeing to the needs of her guests; the latter proving to be no easy task.

Geoffrey and Vanessa were naturally accustomed to the hustle and bustle of Washington, and, consequently, considered life at Kilkieran to be a dreadful bore; a fact that Vanessa took enormous delight in repeating at every opportunity. Kellen had done his part as host by including Geoffrey as he went about his daily routine, and thankfully, Vanessa had renewed her friendship with Christina, thereby, relieving her of the responsibility of hostess at least a portion of the time.

Meredith, on the other hand, had proven to be a delightful companion, and Erin knew that she would miss Kellen's mother terribly when she returned to Washington in a few days. A sudden frown turned down at the corner of her mouth as she recalled Meredith's harried expression over the breakfast table that morning. Erin sat at her desk in the back parlor, silently perusing the list of things that had to be completed before the guests arrived, and she had just made a mental note to question Meredith about her peculiar disposition when Maisie scurried into the room, angrily wielding a butcher knife.

Erin took one look at Maisie's indignant countenance and emitted a weary sigh. "What has Vanessa done now, Maisie?" She correctly guessed the reason for the servant's distress.

"Ah'll tell you whut. If'n dat uppity lady complains 'bout mah vittles once moah, ah'm gonna give her whut foah," the servant declared irascibly. "She done said dat mah biscuits were lak stone, an' you knows dat ah makes de flakiest biscuits in de whole county."

"I know; Maisie. You are a wonderful cook." Erin laid down her pen and tiredly rubbed her eyes. "Pay no attention to Vanessa; she has nothing better to do with her time, I fear." She stood up, and, placing her arm around the faithful servant, she walked with her to the door. "Be patient; Vanessa will be leaving in a day or two."

"Dat woan be none too soon t' suits me," Maisie sourly grunted her approval.

"Me either," Erin concurred with the housekeeper's apt evaluation of the situation, and, opening the door, the two women stepped into the corridor. "Run along, now. I am certain that you have a mountain of things to do before the guests arrive."

"Jest keep dat woman outta mah kitchen, Miz Erin, else ah cain't be held 'countable fer mah axshuns." She made a menacing gesture with the butcher knife before shuffling off toward the kitchen.

"Allow me to speculate," Kellen's husky voice chuckled behind her, "Vanessa has been badgering Maisie again."

"Yes," Erin sighed, turning to face him. She offered him her lips, and they kissed. Then linking her arm in his, she strolled with him toward the majestic staircase. "I'm not certain how much more Maisie can endure."

"Vanessa *can* be an enormous trial," he admitted.

"That's an understatement," she muttered beneath her breath.

"Speaking of my infamous relatives; where are they?"

"Christina stopped by earlier to ask Vanessa to drive into Braxton with her; probably to purchase the finishing touches for her costume," she conjectured. "And Geoffrey requested a horse and went off for a ride."

"Where is Mother?"

"In her room. I'm concerned about her, Kellen," she confided in him. "Did she seem distant to you this morning?"

"Not really, but I will check on her later," he promised. "Where are you going?"

"To lie down for awhile. I don't want to fall asleep before the unmasking at midnight." She ran a loving hand across her protruding stomach. "Besides, your son is reminding me that it is time for a nap."

"How can you be so certain that the child is a boy?" he whispered, placing his hand on her abdomen to feel the baby's slight kicking motion.

"Only a boy would carry on like this," she reasoned. "But then in only three more months, we shall know for certain." She smiled up at him.

"Erin?" he murmured her name, and the serious inflection of his voice caused her to regard him curiously.

"What is it, darling?"

"Is it such a dreadful ordeal; having my child?" he asked somberly.

Erin reached up to capture his face between gentle, adoring hands. "Oh, my love," she breathed softly. "It's not an ordeal. Indeed, it is a most precious and beautiful experience. I'm just a little tired; what with all the activity surrounding the party," she explained. "It is nothing to worry about. It's perfectly normal."

"Go on upstairs and rest," he suggested considerately. "I shall see to things down here. I was about to enlist the aid of a

523

few of the servants to rearrange the furniture in the parlors, so there will be plenty of space to accommodate our guests." He pressed a kiss to her brow and sauntered off toward the kitchen. "But remember," he called over his shoulder, "the first waltz belongs to me."

"As does the last," she promised, and turned to continue toward her chamber.

It seemed to Erin, however, that her eyelids had barely closed when Renée came to help her dress for the party. She stood patiently before the cheval mirror while the servant carefully slipped the elegant gown over her head.

Erin had chosen a dress fashioned after the Empress style that was made of sheer India muslin and embroidered with gold thread in diagonal stripes. The dress was high waisted with a narrow, floating skirt that convincingly concealed her rapidly expanding abdomen. It was very scanty, with a scooped neckline and short, puffy sleeves that barely capped her slender arms. She completed the ensemble by stepping into gold kid slippers and white evening gloves, then she sat down at the dressing table, so that Renée could arrange her coiffure.

She sat quietly while the girl expertly brushed her hair to a shimmering luster. Then she parted the chestnut-brown locks in the middle and pulled it back tightly to create a smooth appearance. Next she piled the heavy tresses in an attractive configuration at the crown of her head, permitting some of the curls to hang loosely. She then pulled a few curls free to frame Erin's lovely face, and finalized her work by weaving a series of gold threads through the arrangement.

Erin was thoroughly pleased with Renée's handiwork, and she praised the girl heartily as she reached for her jewel box. On impulse, she selected the emerald necklace that Jeremiah had bestowed on her upon her engagement to Kellen. She quickly fastened the gem about her throat, selected the gold fan from the table, then stood, prepared to make her way below stairs to greet the guests who would be arriving at any moment. But as she stepped toward the door, Renée rushed after her.

"Miss Erin," she said hastily. "You're forgetting your mask."

"How silly of me." Erin gratefully accepted the rhinestone studded, gold half mask. "One can hardly attend a masquerade without a disguise." She tied the satin threads about her head, taking special care not to disturb her coiffure, and, her costume at last complete, she descended the staircase in anxious anticipation of the coming evening.

The last guest had been greeted, and the musicians were just beginning the refrains of the first waltz when Erin began to make her way toward the gaily decorated ballroom. She had taken but a few short steps, however, when her progress was interrupted by a sharp tap on her shoulder. She whirled, startled by the abrupt summons, and came face to face with a pair of striking blue eyes, shrouded by a black half mask.

"Excuse me, Mrs. Sinclair," a familiar voice drawled huskily, "but I believe that this particular dance is mine."

Erin's response was to whip her fan open and flutter it in front of her face in a coquettish manner. "Sir," she began, affecting an affronted tone. "Just what makes you so certain that *I* am Mrs. Sinclair?"

"Ah, wench," he breathed wistfully, drawing her close. "For one thing, you have a maddeningly distinctive fragrance. And for another," his hand intuitively moved across her bulging stomach, "I fear that your . . . ahem . . . *condition* quite gives your identity away," he chortled wickedly.

"Yes, well, I assure you that I have my husband to thank for that," she countered, deriving considerable pleasure in their banter.

"Believe me, madam," he whispered, a sinful grin fashioning his lips as he escorted her to the ballroom. "Your husband is constantly amazed and gratified with the enthusiasm through which you express your appreciation." And before she could respond to his nefarious rhetoric, Kellen pulled her into his arms, and began to whirl her about the dance floor in perfect harmony with the haunting melody.

As hostess, it was Erin's duty to mingle with the various guests. Accordingly, she danced with her uncle, Doc Wilson, her brother Graham, and a few other gentlemen of whose identity she was uncertain because of their disguises. She had been a little surprised to find that Michael had accepted her invitation, but deciding to put the past behind them, she had even graciously honored his request to partner him for the Virginia Reel.

She was sitting in an obscure corner of the parlor, reveling in a scrumptious plate of food from the plentiful buffet when she next encountered her husband. The musicians had paused with the other guests to partake of the enticing repast, and they had just returned to tune their instruments when Erin glanced up to find Kellen's smiling face staring down at her.

"Hello, my lovely," he greeted her warmly. "Are you enjoying your party?" He settled his muscular frame in the chair next to her.

"Oh, yes!" she replied gaily, biting into one of Maisie's delicious pastries. "Do you think that our guests are enjoying the festivities?"

"Well, some more than others, perhaps." He nodded pointedly toward the French doors through which Evan and Jennifer were about to exit. "Tell me, my beautiful matchmaker, do you believe that a wedding is in the offing?"

"I certainly hope so," she replied excitedly. "They would be so good for one another." She put her plate aside and turned to him. "Have you seen your mother, Kellen? She disappeared when the members of the reception line went off to dance, and I haven't seen her since. I feel as though I have completely ignored her today."

"Nonsense. She is having a wonderful time," he said casually, averting his gaze. "I believe that she has just gone upstairs to the powder room to . . . well, to do whatever it is that you ladies do." He stood up suddenly, preparing to leave. "I think that I see Graham conversing with your Uncle Philip. Will you excuse me, darling? I just recalled something that I need to discuss with them."

"Certainly."

"What do you say we give Evan and Jennifer a few moments to complete their . . . uh . . . *stargazing,* then meet me on the terrace," he suggested, a mischievous sparkle twinkling behind the sensuous blue eyes.

"But, Kellen. The sky is overcast this evening," she reminded him. "I am quite positive that we will not find a single star in the heavens this night." She feigned ignorance at the ultimate purpose behind his romantic proposition.

Kellen reached down and squeezed her knee familiarly. "I know, angel. But just think of the fun we can have trying to find one. Meet me in half an hour," he instructed, then strode off, confident that she would yield to his fanciful proposal.

The terrace was deserted when Erin emerged from the house at the appointed time, but the cool April breeze that wafted over her soon gave her reason to understand why few of her guests had ventured from the warmth of Kilkieran's parlors. She paced back and forth, clasping her arms tightly about her in a desperate effort to keep warm, and she had just decided to return inside to collect her wrap when a sudden movement in the distant shadows caught her attention.

She turned toward the noise, fully expecting to find her husband. "Kellen, it is positively freezing—"

But the severe reprimand died on her tongue as she inhaled sharply, stepping backwards, staggered by the sight that greeted her eyes. She watched in unbridled horror as a man stepped forward to be illuminated by the light from the mansion. It was not the man, however, that was the source of her fear, but rather the costume in which he was clad, for the figure was wearing a uniform of the Union Army with a brightly colored bandanna to shield his face from recognition.

"Who . . . who are you?" she demanded, clutching her hands to her throat. "What do you . . . you want?"

But the sinister looking man did not respond to her inquiries. Instead, he began to walk toward her with a measured, purposeful stride.

"No!" she cried, whirling to run toward the safety of the house, but another figure stepped from the shadows, causing her head to reel in disbelief. *"Mother!"* she gasped, teetering precariously on weak knees, shaking her head vehemently to make the ghostly apparition vanish.

But the haunting vision did not disappear. Indeed, it began to glide forward, moving determinedly toward the menacing Yankee. Erin's initial instinct was to run, but she found that her feet were rooted to the terrace, and she gripped the back of a garden chair for support, helplessly doomed to witness the ensuing confrontation.

As she watched, the woman stepped boldly to the Yankee, and, reaching up, she grabbed the bandanna and ripped it from the man's face. The masquerader proved to be Geoffrey Sinclair, but in that initial instant, when the mask was torn free, Erin's mind was flooded with the memory of another man's face.

"No!" she shrieked, hysterical tears beginning to roll down her cheeks.

The ornamental fan she carried fell from her limp fingers to clank noisily on the terrace floor, and the distraction served to ignite her into action. She pushed away from the chair and stumbled toward the house, but the unsettling experience had served to render her quite dizzy. Just as she feared that she was going to succumb to the blackness that threatened to engulf her, two compassionate arms caught her in their powerful embrace. Then all became blessed forgetfulness as she slumped against her husband, the victim of a disabling faint.

Erin stirred, weakly lifting her hand to push aside the cool compress that had been placed against her brow. Her eyes fluttered open very slowly to find the worried expression of her husband focused on her. He sat on the edge of the bed beside her, and, as her muddled thoughts gradually cleared, she was reminded of the evening's catastrophic revelation.

Suddenly, she lurched forward to hurl herself into Kellen's arms. "Oh, Kellen!" she cried pitifully. "I remember. *I remember!*" She buried her face in his chest.

"I know, honey," he cooed tenderly, holding her against him. "I am so sorry that I had to put you through such a frightening ordeal, but I knew of no other way to help you. For now that you have remembered, perhaps the past will be easier for you to forget," he murmured sagaciously.

"But . . . but, I don't understand." She frowned. "What did *you* have to do with it? I *saw* my mother and —"

"No, Erin," Meredith whispered, stepping forward from a corner of the room.

Erin had thought that she was completely alone with Kellen, but as she glanced around her, she discovered that several anxious faces were scattered about the chamber.

"Graham gave me a photograph of your mother, so that I might fashion my hairstyle after her, and Maisie gave me one of her gowns. It was a cruel trick, I know, darling, but Kellen assured me that he had your best interests at heart," she explained quietly.

"But it was Uncle Philip!" Erin blurted abruptly, clutching Kellen's arm in a fierce grip. *"I saw him!"*

"The man you saw tonight was Geoffrey," Kellen informed her gently. "But the man you saw all those years ago, and have since blocked from your memory, the man who led the raid on Kilkieran was indeed your Uncle Philip," he was quick to affirm her accusation.

"What?" Evan was the first to react. "Why, that's preposterous!"

"Is it?" Kellen asked dryly, and, easing Erin back against the pillows, he stood to face the accused man. "Why don't we ask your uncle? Tell us, Philip. Is Erin mistaken?"

All eyes turned on the man who leaned negligently against the closed door, and several tense minutes passed before he gave any indication that he was going to respond to the inquiry. Finally, the man could be heard to breathe a beleaguered, almost relieved sigh, and he shook his head slowly.

"No," he said at last. "Erin is not mistaken."

"But, why?" Erin cried her incredulity.

But before Philip Richards had a chance to answer her impassioned question, Graham rushed forward, and, grabbing his uncle by the lapels of his jacket, he pinned the older man against the door. "My God, man! Don't you know what you've done?"

Kellen crossed the room in three long strides, and successfully separated the two men. "Graham, I know that this is difficult for you, but let us hear the man out. I, for one, am extremely interested in what he has to say."

Thus chastised, Graham shook off Kellen's restraining arm, and returned to stand by Evan. Satisfied that an altercation had been temporarily averted, Kellen rejoined Erin on the bed, taking care to slip her hand into his. Understandably, all eyes turned on Philip Richards.

"Believe me, Graham," Philip began sadly. "I have relived that horrible day a thousand times over in my mind. I realize that to say I'm sorry is hollow consolation, but I swear to you that I never meant to harm anyone."

"What happened?" Kellen prompted him softly.

"Our sole purpose in coming to Kilkieran that day was to intimidate my brother, so that he would abandon his neutrality policy and let you boys get involved in the war. That is why we dressed as Yankees; to convince Joseph that he could not remain detached forever." Philip paused for a moment to collect his thoughts.

"And you wore disguises?" Kellen questioned.

"Yes."

Kellen nodded. "That is the portion of Erin's description of the raid that I always found puzzling."

"We only meant to frighten the women and ransack the house and property," Philip continued, for now that his deception had been revealed, he was anxious to purge himself of his evil involvement in the despicable affair. "We just wanted to create enough mischief to spur Joseph into action. But when Maura stripped away my disguise, some of the men panicked, and things got out of hand. No one was supposed to get hurt," he repeated his earlier statement.

"But the fact remains that people *did* get hurt," Graham snapped bitterly. "Our mother died during that raid, and Deborah; my God! When I think of what those animals did to her—" He clenched his fists in a concentrated effort to keep his hands from encircling his uncle's throat.

"I know, believe me, and I'm . . . I'm sorry," Philip mumbled lamely.

"Stop saying that!" Graham shouted wildly. "You cannot atone for your loathsome crime by the mere utterance of that meaningless phrase."

"Graham." Evan placed a consoling hand on his brother's shoulder. "I know it's difficult, but let him finish."

But Graham was not to be easily subdued, and, angrily pushing Evan's hand aside, he strode toward his uncle. "You may continue to listen to his *explanation*, if you want, but I have heard quite enough, thank you." And with that, he shoved Philip from the doorway and stalked out of the room.

"Graham!" Erin called after him, but Kellen placed a gentle, restraining hand on her arm.

"He will be all right," he assured her. "Please, Philip, continue."

Philip Richards shrugged his shoulders disconsolately, and moved to stand at the foot of the bed. "There's not much more to say except that I never should have trusted that damn Yankee." His surprising admission left the others momentarily speechless.

Kellen was the first to find his tongue. "Yankee? What do you mean?"

"It hardly matters now," Philip sighed lamentably.

"It might," Kellen advised him. "What Yankee?"

"Oh, my men took him prisoner one day after we skirmished with his regiment," he explained indifferently. "He was a brown-eyed, silver tongued devil who quickly talked his way out of a hanging by telling us a few Yankee secrets.

"As I recall, he overheard some of the local men discussing their ire over Joseph's decision to remain impartial to the war that was raging around us, and he suggested the idea of the 'mock' raid with my men wearing the uniforms of his former comrades.

"Yes, the Yankee turncoat proved to be a valuable resource during the war, for his loyalty could be purchased quite handily as I recall. Why, he even arranged for the ambush near here of a shipment of nitroglycerin and medical supplies that was headed for Richmond." He paused, having concluded his narrative.

But his final statement had served to pique Kellen's curiosity. "An ambush of nitro, did you say?"

"Why, yes; that *would* have been your platoon," Philip nodded his understanding.

"Tell me, were there other locals who took part in the raid, or the ambush?" Kellen asked purposely.

"Yes, a few, but most were outsiders."

"Was Arthur Ridgeway involved?" Kellen continued his interrogation, trying to piece together the fragments of the puzzling tale.

Again, Philip nodded.

"Anyone else?"

"Michael Cahill is the only one who is left from this area," he answered, cognizant of Erin's strangled cry of disbelief. "The others were either killed in battle, or returned to their homes when the war ended," Philip explained.

"And this Yankee; have you seen him around here lately?"

Kellen asked, his eyes never wavering from the other man's face.

"No. Can't say that I have," he replied truthfully.

Kellen blew a long, frustrated sigh, then he had the presence of mind to inquire, "You wouldn't happen to remember the fellow's name, would you?"

"As a matter-of-fact, I do. His name was Br—"

But the name of the evil man was to literally die on his lips, for the French doors were suddenly kicked aside, and a knife was hurled through the opening, catching Philip squarely in the chest. As the man stumbled backwards into the dresser, the other occupants flew to his aid. But by the time Kellen had managed to extricate himself from his wife's frantic grip and darted through the doorway, the assassin had vaulted over the parapet and disappeared into the night.

Chapter Twenty-five

Death, in all cases, is difficult to understand, but in the instance of a senseless, cold-blooded murder, acceptance becomes a virtual impossibility. Consequently, the Kilkieran plantation was pitched headlong into a state of emotional upheaval in the days immediately following the murder of Philip Richards. To worsen the foul situation, the identity of the assassin had yet to be determined.

Erin stood beside her husband in the church cemetery, her solemn expression focused on the coffin that lay in the narrow trench. The words of the minister barely penetrated her tempestuous thoughts, for her head was filled with memories of her uncle. Uncle Philip; her father's brother, a sweet, gentle man who had always treated her with loving affection. Why, he had given her the very first pony she had ever ridden. How could he? How could he have taken part in such an evil, wicked thing?

She sighed glumly, reaching for Kellen's hand. Sometimes, it was so very hard to be forgiving.

Kellen gave the delicate appendage a comforting squeeze, and, the service having concluded, he escorted her away from the cemetery toward their waiting carriage. Deborah and Evan had already seated themselves in the conveyance, and Kellen was about to hand his wife into the vehicle when Erin was distracted by her aunt's anguished sobs as she was assisted from the gravesite by her children; Kevin and Christina.

"Oh, Kellen," she murmured compassionately, her heart going out to the distressed woman. "Perhaps I should go to her. I must let her know that we don't blame her for what Uncle Philip did."

"I know, sweetheart," came his understanding reply. "Do you want me to come with you?"

"No, thank you, darling." She offered him the first carefree smile she had felt in days. "I won't be but a moment."

The last of the mourners had extended their condolences to the grieving widow and were moving away when Erin approached her aunt. Unsure of what her exact words should be, she swallowed hard and whispered Lydia's name. But she was not to be given a chance to address the woman, for Christina abruptly stepped in front of her, blocking her progress.

"What do *you* want?" Christina demanded bitterly.

"Christina," Erin began patiently. "We have all been under a tremendous strain the past few days. I have no quarrel with you. I have come to talk with Aunt Lydia. Kindly let me pass." She started to move past her cousin, but Christina grabbed her by the arm, her fingers digging harshly into Erin's delicate flesh.

"Oh, no, you don't. You're not going to badger my mother with your lies," she snapped scornfully.

"Lies?"

"I don't care what the sheriff says; my father could not have done all those terrible things; he couldn't have!" she screamed. "Instead of damaging the memory of an innocent man, the authorities should be looking for Papa's murderer. And, as far as I'm concerned, they can start by questioning *your* brother," Christina said viciously.

"What?" Erin exclaimed.

"You heard me! Oh, I know all about how Graham stormed out of your room in a rage, and then, minutes later, my father was dead." Christina paid no heed to the gently restraining

535

hand her brother placed on her shoulder. "And just where is Graham today? I'll wager that he is too afraid to show his guilt-ridden face in public," she charged.

"You're hysterical," Erin hissed, and, pulling her arm free, she whirled to return to her own carriage.

Lydia Richards had stood witness to the very ugly scene, and she instructed Kevin to assist his sister into their carriage, then she hurried after her niece. "Erin, wait. Please, forgive Christina's rudeness. She's taking her father's death quite hard."

"I realize that. It is an awkward situation, but I just wanted you to know that I love you, and want to help in any way that I can," Erin stated sincerely.

"I know. You're such a dear. Just give us a few days to mourn our loss, then come for a visit. You are always welcome at Briar Cliff," Lydia said kindly.

"As are you at Kilkieran." The two women hugged each other, then Erin quickly made her way to Kellen who promptly lifted her into the carriage.

Kellen then swung himself in beside her and signaled for the driver to begin the drive home. But the coach had barely begun to jostle down the roadway when Deborah spoke up.

"I heard the awful things Christina said about Graham. They simply aren't true!" she insisted.

"We know that, honey," Erin murmured consolingly, yet her mouth puckered into a decisive frown. Graham *had* been furious with Uncle Philip, and rightly so. But was he capable of committing murder? she mused silently.

The remainder of the journey was completed in silence, each of the passengers choosing to engage in silent contemplation rather than verbal speculation. When they arrived at the mansion, Deborah and Evan scurried off to attend to respective matters, leaving Erin and Kellen alone in the foyer.

Kellen considerately assisted Erin from her wrap, then, linking her arm in his, he began to lead her toward the staircase. "It's been a taxing morning, young lady. I think that you should lie down for awhile," he suggested solicitously, yet his manner plainly indicated that he would not accept no for an answer.

"I am tired," she admitted.

"I will bring lunch up later, so that we can dine alone in the privacy of our chamber. I'll make the appropriate excuses to our guests." He pressed a kiss to her brow, then turned and entered the front parlor.

Erin had taken only two steps down the wide corridor when the idea of a nap suddenly lost its appeal. On impulse, she went to collect her cloak, deciding that a walk in the cool, refreshing air might help rejuvenate her dampened spirits.

Erin's hands were clasped tightly behind her back as she strolled along the banks of the pond beside the cascading waterfall. She had not meant to wander so far from Kilkieran, for Kellen had grown quite protective of her since the buggy accident. But her head was awhirl with an abundance of confusing speculations, thereby attributing greatly to her faulty sense of direction.

Besides, she reasoned, she could always think more clearly in the quiet solitude of her hideaway. It was so peaceful here.

Her thoughts this afternoon were irretrievably situated on the vile charge that Christina had leveled against Graham, and she sat down on a rock to pursue her flustered musings. She was well acquainted with her brother's hot-blooded temperament, but she truly doubted that he was Philip's assassin. Kellen, she knew, believed the culprit to be Brian Taggart.

The mere thought of the evil man sent cold shivers racing down her spine, and, feeling suddenly uncomfortable, she decided that it was time to return to the house. As she rose from her seat, Erin glimpsed a clump of brightly colored wild flowers at the edge of the forest. On impulse, she walked over to the blossoms, thinking that a bouquet of the vivid blooms would do much toward improving the glum state in which her spirits lay. But when she went to gather a bunch of the fragrant petals, a pair of black boots suddenly stepped from the forest and planted themselves within inches of her fingertips.

Erin jumped back, startled by the abrupt interruption. She glanced up at the intruder, prepared to deliver a severe reprimand to the one who had given her such a fright. But when her eyes came into contact with the brown ones that seriously pondered her, she gave a squeal of sheer terror and sank back on her haunches, the flowers scattering about her feet.

"Erin?" a vaguely familiar voice spoke her name. "I'm sorry. I didn't mean to alarm you."

Erin blinked wildly, and, focusing her eyes on the man's face, she blew a sigh of relief. "Oh, Brad." She recognized Kellen's friend. "You *did* startle me, but I am all right now." She gratefully accepted the hand he proffered to assist her from the ground. "Whatever are you doing here?"

"Didn't Kellen receive my telegram?" Bradley Petersen asked offhandedly.

"He didn't mention it."

"That's odd," he murmured, thoughtfully stroking his chin. "I wired him of my impending visit. It was certainly not my intention to drop in on you unannounced."

"That's no problem," she assured him. "I am sure that Kellen will be pleased to see you." Her mouth suddenly puckered into a curious frown. "But what are you doing *here,* and afoot?"

"My horse threw a shoe," he explained, "and I thought I'd try to find a shortcut through the woods. I've been wandering about for hours, it seems, so it's fortunate that I should happen upon you like this." He smiled down at her.

"Yes, it is," she replied pleasantly. "Now, if you will follow me, I'll lead you to my husband."

Erin started to escort him from the clearing, but a commotion behind them caught her attention, and she spun around to investigate the source of the disturbance. But she could not control the gape that fashioned her pretty face, nor the terror that gripped her heart, for she turned in time to see Brian Taggart emerge from the forest. Unthinkingly, she fell back against Brad, thoroughly frightened by the unanticipated appearance of the unsavory man.

"Oh, no!" she gasped. "It's that dreadful man! Kellen has been looking everywhere for him."

"Mr. Taggart and I are acquainted," Brad drawled casually.

"An admission I'm none too proud of," Taggart countered, watching Brad closely.

"What are *you* doing here?" Erin asked anxiously.

"I think that Petersen knows the answer to that, ma'am," Taggart replied. "Now, you run on home to your husband, and leave us to our business," he suggested, his menacing stare raking over Brad.

"Don't listen to him," Brad whispered harshly. "He'll only try to kill me, then follow you through the woods. Your only chance is to stay with me."

Erin was positioned in front of Brad, and, using her as a shield, Brad surreptitiously removed a revolver from his pocket, a smug sneer appearing on his face.

"Mrs. Sinclair, please," Taggart continued to address Erin. "I don't want you to get hurt."

Taggart took a step forward, but he could proceed no further, for Brad abruptly leveled his weapon at the man and fired. The bullet caught him in the chest, and the force of the impact sent him staggering to the ground.

Erin screamed and covered her ears with her hands, the sound of the unexpected explosion still ringing in her ears. Her hysterical eyes watched as Brad stepped across the clearing and bent down to examine the stricken man. Then with a grunt, he shoved the unconscious man aside and returned to her.

"Is he . . . is he dead?" Erin asked reluctantly.

"He soon will be," Brad replied indifferently, and, taking her by the arm, he prepared to guide her from the clearing.

"Aren't you going to help him?" Erin cried incredulously,

helplessly glancing over her shoulder at the wounded man.

"No," came the heartless retort.

"But . . . but you just can't leave him here to . . . to die," she stammered her disbelief, pulling away from him.

"Oh, yes I can," he assured her, and the ruthless leer he turned on Erin made her blood run cold. "In fact, I have done so on one other occasion; right after I helped your Southern friends bushwhack that shipment of nitro that Kellen has been scouring the country for. I made a mistake last time, but," he threw a look over his shoulder, "I'm confident that I am rid of the bastard for good this time.

"Now, I have but one final nemesis with which to contend, then I can leave this wretched place once and for all," he growled, his countenance sinister.

Then he clamped his hand around her arm in a vise-like grip and dragged her into the forest, taking her further away from Kilkieran and Kellen.

Kellen sat in a chair in the parlor, his long legs stretched before him, his chin propped in his hands in a contemplative gesture. Like his wife, he was submerged in deep thought, reflecting on all the aspects of the perplexing dilemma with which he was faced. He did not believe for an instant that Graham had been involved in Philip's murder. No, he was quite confident that he knew the identity of the villain. The problem was coming up with a foolproof plan to coax him out into the open.

As he considered his alternatives, Kellen rose from the chair and strolled over to the window. He stood there for several moments, his gaze never truly focusing on anything. And he was about to turn from the casement when a peculiar occurrence commanded his attention.

While he watched, Vanessa suddenly appeared around the corner of the house and walked directly to the clump of bushes that lined the terrace beneath Erin's chamber. She then began to pick through the shrubs, moving the limbs this way and that, as though diligently searching for something.

Finding himself thoroughly intrigued by her antics, Kellen folded his arms across his chest and continued to peer out the window. He observed as Vanessa conducted an exhaustive search of the area, and, just when he suspected that the woman was about to abandon her task, she snatched something from beneath one of the bushes and shoved it into her pocket.

His curiosity duly aroused, Kellen stepped to the French doors and pulled them open. "Hello, Vanessa," he called lazily. "Would you mind stepping in here a moment?"

The satisfied smile that had previously adorned Vanessa's face swiftly vanished when she looked up to discover Kellen lounging against the doorjamb. "As a matter-of-fact, I would," she snapped spitefully.

"It's a pity that you feel that way, for I fear that I really must insist," he informed her, the square set of his jaw an indication that he would brook no argument to the contrary.

Vanessa recognized his undaunted scowl, and realized that it would do her little good to argue with him. "Oh, very well," she sighed petulantly. "What do you want?" She pushed past him and plopped down on the sofa in a huff.

"To begin with, you can show me what it is that I just saw you conceal in the pocket of your skirt." He surprised her with his candor. "No, don't try to deny it." He correctly interpreted the indignant pout that immediately dressed her face, and, closing the door, he moved to stand in front of her, his countenance threatening.

It was Kellen's turn to be disconcerted, however, for Vanessa suddenly reached out to clasp his hand. "Oh, Kellen. Why are you always so mean to me these days? We used to be so . . . compatible," she purred sweetly, climbing to her feet to encircle his neck with her arms. "Can't we be friends again?" she begged, pressing her body against his suggestively.

Kellen pretended to be contemplating her conjecture,

when in actuality, he was merely plotting his next move. While Vanessa endeavored to coax his head down to hers, Kellen eased her down onto the sofa. He heard her deep sigh of languor as he slid his hand along her waist. But when he plunged his hand inside her pocket to successfully seize the sought after article, Vanessa's passion changed abruptly to acute rancor, and she raked her nails across his cheek.

As Kellen jerked away to nurse his wounds, Vanessa righted herself. "My, but what a cunning bastard you've become," she spat in disgust.

"I had an excellent instructor," he countered pointedly.

"You're vile!" she hissed between clenched teeth. "How I wish that Geoffrey might have witnessed your little performance just now. I know I could have convinced him that you had compromised me.

"Oh, how I would have loved to observe the look on your face when he demanded satisfaction," she screeched hatefully.

"Frankly, Vanessa," Kellen began, his voice purposefully bland, "I sincerely doubt that Geoffrey could derive satisfaction from anything he might find in this room." He looked at her specifically before casually glancing down at the item he clutched in one hand.

His inquisitive gaze fastened on the fine linen handkerchief, and he began to twist and turn the masculine accessory in his hands as though giving it a thorough scrutiny. And he was just about to toss the insignificant item aside in frustration when he beheld the elegantly embroidered initials of the absent owner.

Vanessa observed the series of contrasting emotions that played across his face, and, deciding to take advantage of his temporary distraction, she started to creep from the room.

"Stay where you are!" Kellen ordered. "I'm not quite finished with you," he added with such hostility that Vanessa was prompted to sink into the nearest chair.

Several tense minutes were to be consumed by the clock before Kellen again addressed her, for his sole concentration was focused on the glaring revelation. B.P.; the initials read: Bradley Petersen. Suddenly, Kellen understood a great many things. Brad *was* the blackguard that the department sought, and not Brian Taggart.

Kellen silently absorbed the shock of the painful discovery, then settled his smoky expression on Vanessa. How was she involved in Brad's loathsome schemes?

Yet, before he had completed the pensive conjecture, a knowing grimace crossed his face. "Of course," he mumbled beneath his breath.

"Would you care to explain this?" he asked casually.

"Explain what?" she snapped insolently. "I simply found that silly rag while I was strolling on the lawn," she answered with a trite wave of her hand.

"Really?" he droned dubiously. "Perhaps you could be induced to reconsider that statement; especially when I tell you that I observed your little scavenger hunt from the window. You were quite obviously searching for a specific object." He suddenly dangled the handkerchief in front of the agitated woman. "Tell me, Vanessa. Does this belong to your lover?"

"What!" she exclaimed, nervously clutching the throat of her silk blouse. "I . . . I don't have the slightest notion of what you're talking about," she protested.

"On the contrary," he drawled icily. "You are perfectly acquainted with the facts of which I speak. And you are going to tell me what I want to know, or . . ." He did not bother to complete the menacing statement, choosing rather to intimidate her with the threat.

"You'll what?"

"I shall not hesitate to make Geoffrey aware of my suspicions," he informed her bluntly. "Granted, my cousin can see very little beyond his avaricious nose, but I think that even Geoffrey would take exception with the news that he is being cuckolded.

"Now, I am struggling to piece together the full extent of your involvement in Brad's chicanery, but regardless of the

543

outcome of this little tête-á-tête, I am certain that you don't want Geoffrey snooping into your *affairs,* so to speak." Kellen selected a chair, and, lowering himself into it, he placed his fingertips together in a contemplative gesture and focused his smoldering expression on her. "So, what is it to be? Will you cooperate with me, or shall I summon Geoffrey from his chamber?"

"Oh, very well," Vanessa grumbled bitterly. "Brad and I are friends. What of it?" She looked away from him, fastening her haughty stare on the ornate mantelpiece.

"Friends!" he scoffed. "My dear Vanessa. I am quite persuaded to believe that your relationship with Brad supersedes the boundaries of mere camaraderie."

"Again, what of it?" Vanessa turned a stony countenance on him. "Geoffrey means nothing to you. Why should you concern yourself with my harmless flirtations?"

"To begin with, I'm not entirely convinced that your escapades are wholly innocent," came his blunt retort. Then noticing her riding habit and dust covered boots, he hurled an accusation at her. "You've just come from Brad, haven't you? He feared that someone would discover this incriminating piece of evidence that he carelessly left behind when he jumped from the gallery after killing Erin's uncle. So, he asked you to retrieve it for him."

"No! Brad didn't kill him; Graham did," she insisted.

"That's what Brad would like everyone to believe," Kellen said harshly.

"No, it's true! Brad merely dropped the handkerchief when he came to see me the night of the masquerade ball, and, knowing that you would jump to all kinds of crazy conclusions should you discover the rag, he asked me to get it for him." She leveled a hateful scowl at him.

"I must hasten to caution you, Vanessa," Kellen stated explicitly, unaffected by her ridiculous explanation. "If you continue your efforts to thwart my investigation of this case, you might very well find yourself charged with complicity." He did not mince words as he delivered the vitriolic speech, and he derived immense satisfaction from her frightened gasp.

Convinced that he would encounter minimal resistance forthwith, Kellen continued. "Where is Brad?"

"I don't know," she replied tartly.

"You're lying."

In a rage, Vanessa flew from the sofa and stamped her feet in a flamboyant gesture. "Damn you, Kellen Sinclair," she shrieked at him. "I will not remain here and let you badger me this way. I don't know Brad's whereabouts!" she reiterated.

"But he *is* in the area, and you *did* meet with him today?" Kellen persisted, and, though her beleaguered expression told him that his assumption was correct, Vanessa remained closemouthed. "Very well," he murmured, deciding upon another approach. "How long have you and Brad been . . . uh . . . *friends?*"

"Since you abandoned me," she blurted angrily. Then her curiosity getting the better of her, she was prompted to ask, "Why?"

"Because, that piece of information helps me understand a number of things," he explained noncommittally, leaning forward in his chair. "Sit down." He motioned her back into her chair.

"Allow me to speculate, if you will," he continued, after Vanessa had returned her sullen frame to the sofa. "After I enlisted in the army, you turned to Geoffrey, for you naturally assumed that even if I managed to survive the conflict, Grandfather would disinherit me because I had disregarded his explicit instructions to remain impartial." Kellen held up his hand to forestall her halfhearted protests to the contrary.

"Please, let me finish before you regale me with your indignant denials," he sighed tediously. "Now, where was I? Oh, yes. Somewhere along the way, you and Brad developed a tendre; that was perfectly understandable since he was a frequent visitor to Tiffin Square. But knowing, as I do, your preoccupation with the almighty dollar, as well as Brad's fi-

545

nancial limitations, you quickly learned that he could not offer you the extravagant life to which you had grown accustomed with Geoffrey.

"Therefore, it would seem that the two of you concocted a scheme to remedy your dilemma." He leveled his menacing glare on Vanessa. "Tell me, did you plan to do away with my unsuspecting cousin once the inheritance was safely his?"

"You seem to be the one with all the answers," Vanessa snapped resentfully. "You tell me."

Kellen mulled his speculation over in his mind for several moments before he honored her with a reply. "Yes," he murmured pensively, "I think you did. For as Geoffrey's sole beneficiary, you would stand to inherit his entire fortune. Thus endowed, and following an acceptable period of mourning, of course, you would have been free to marry Brad. An excellent choice, I might add, for he has always been a particular favorite of Grandfather's."

Kellen stood up suddenly and went to pour himself a glass of brandy from the crystal decanter on the mantel, and, resting his shoulder against the narrow shelf, he proceeded. "It was unfortunate for you that I returned from the battlefield unscathed, for not only did my reconciliation with Grandfather inspire him to alter the method through which his heir would be selected, but I brought along with me a very real threat to your eventual domination of the Sinclair dynasty: Erin," he stated matter-of-factly, his expression becoming less brooding as he thought of his wife, who he believed to be resting comfortably in their chamber.

"This is all quite boring drivel, Kellen," Vanessa huffed irritably. "Would you please get to the point? If indeed, there is one."

"Directly," Kellen assured he as he continued to unravel the mystery that had plagued him in recent months. "Realizing that I intended to make Erin my wife, Geoffrey cunningly convinced her to go ahead with her plans to visit her grandmother in Ireland. But that wasn't good enough for you, for you knew that I would only follow her and bring her back." He paused for a moment to take a lengthy draft of the amber-colored liquid.

"I recall that Erin mentioned she thought she had seen one of her assailants before, but the comment had completely slipped my mind, until now." Kellen returned the empty glass to the mantel, then positioned his menacing frame in front of Vanessa. "Brad is the one who attacked Erin on the north road that night, isn't he?" Kellen demanded.

But Vanessa had grown suddenly taciturn, and she merely favored him with a glib expression, saying nothing.

Kellen quickly became infuriated by her continued imperturbable hauteur, and, giving a hoarse growl, he grabbed her by the shoulders and shook her roughly. *"Answer me!"* he thundered, a murderous gleam flashing in the blue eyes.

"All right!" she screamed, trying to avoid his painful grasp. "Yes! Yes! It was Brad. We wanted to make sure that you were unable to find her until . . . until—" she faltered.

"Until what?"

"Until I was able to convince Geoffrey that I was carrying his child," she muttered lamely.

Kellen released her suddenly and straightened. "You're barren, Vanessa. There can be no children," he murmured tiredly.

"Geoffrey doesn't know that. There would have been a child," she informed him instantly. "Brad had a plan."

"Ha!" Kellen scoffed. "It would seem that my friend possesses an uncanny ability for masterminding clever, underhanded schemes. He no doubt intended to make some backalley arrangement to obtain an infant," he commented offhandedly. "But tell me, Vanessa. Would you have actually feigned a pregnancy to convince everyone that the child was Geoffrey's."

"If need be," she replied stonily.

Kellen placed a weary hand to the back of his neck, and rubbed a consoling hand across the tension riddled area. "I can only assume that Brad followed us here to continue his efforts to separate me from Erin."

Vanessa nodded.

"And you answered the telegrams, making me think that he was in Washington," Kellen posed, amazed at how thoroughly he had been duped by the man he had called friend since childhood.

Again, Vanessa nodded.

Kellen turned away, shaking his head in disbelief. "I must applaud your efforts, Vanessa, for your chicanery very nearly succeeded." He was reminded of the harried weeks following Richmond. "You and Brad chose well in your accomplices; Cahill doubtlessly cooperated out of his genuine love for Erin, and Christina, well, she *is* a jealous creature.

"Only one thing puzzles me." His brow wrinkled into a confused frown. "The charade in Richmond had to be perpetrated with pinpoint timing. How did you know when I would be arriving?"

"Brad wired me the day you left Kilkieran," she offered, wishing very much that the disgusting interview was over. "We were uncertain of the time of your exact arrival, but Michael was instructed to do whatever was necessary to keep Erin in the room with him until you discovered them together," she explained sourly.

A somber expression shadowed Kellen's handsome face, and, finally satisfied that he had learned the full extent of Vanessa's involvement with Brad, Kellen turned and lumbered toward the door.

"But, where are you going?" she asked, perplexed by his abrupt behavior.

"To find your clever lover and ask him a few probing questions about such things as murder and treason," he said, his manner foreboding.

"No, that's not true! Brad would never do anything like that!" Vanessa cried, jumping to her feet.

"I used to believe the same thing," came Kellen's hollow reply. "But no longer.

"As for you," he redirected his attention on Vanessa, "be grateful that your unsavory plans for Geoffrey did not materialize. Granted, adultery *is* a totally reprehensible offense, but it is hardly criminal.

"You were fortunate this time, Vanessa," he said bluntly. "And now that I have denounced any claim on Grandfather's businesses, Geoffrey stands to inherit everything. Now, if I were you," he advised her carefully, "I'd take every precaution to ensure that your husband lives a long and prosperous life." He paused at the door to deliver one final warning. "Remember, I shall be watching."

He stepped into the corridor and closed the door behind him, and, thinking that he should look in on Erin before instigating a search for Brad, he started to climb the wide staircase. He had progressed only halfway up the steps, however, when he encountered Maisie, who was just returning from Erin's room.

"Mistah Kellen," she greeted him familiarly. "Has you seen Miz Erin?"

"Is she not in her room?" Kellen asked, puzzled by the question.

"No, suh, an' ah wuz wantin' t' asks her 'bout de farewell dinnah fer yor momma t'morrah," she explained. "Ah done looked dis hyah house ovah, but ah cain't seems t' find her nowheres. Could be, she done went out fer a breath of air. She's had a powahful lot on her mind lately." The loyal servant speculated offhandedly before continuing down the stairway.

"Yes," Kellen murmured thoughtfully. "Perhaps she did."

He quickly descended the staircase and marched to the front door. Stepping out onto the porch, Kellen cast a watchful eye skyward as he considered his wife's truancy. Then, on impulse, he shoved his hands into his pockets and started to trudge toward the barn to collect Achilles.

"She's probably at the waterfall," he mumbled to himself as

he saddled the patient stallion. "I'll just check on her before I start looking for Brad." That decision made, Kellen swung lithely into the saddle and spurred Achilles in the direction of Erin's secret hideaway.

The frantic pounding of Erin's heart had finally subsided, and she now sat nervously in a straight-backed chair in the sparsely furnished sitting room at Fox Bush; Michael Cahill's plantation house. It was odd that the thought should cross her mind at this distressing time, but she could not help but think that it was a shame that the stately mansion had been allowed to lapse into such a state of disrepair.

Sighing disconsolately, Erin shifted on the hard seat and chanced a look at her captor. He sat in the wing chair opposite her, and, though his calculating gaze was trained on the window which gave him an uninhibited view of the long driveway, Erin realized that she could not hazard an attempted escape; especially in her clumsy condition. Her only hope was that the evil man might succumb to the foul smelling whiskey he had been swilling since their arrival, and lose consciousness long enough for her to slip unnoticed from the house.

Erin's hands instinctively flew to caress her rounded abdomen as the baby began to flutter about inside her, and, feeling suddenly disillusioned with her uncomfortable confinement, she slowly rose to her feet.

"What are you doing?" Brad asked suspiciously.

"I have to move about. I . . . the baby . . . well, I simply cannot sit another moment," she explained, reddening with embarrassment.

"Just don't do anything stupid," he cautioned her, shaking his revolver at her in a meaningful gesture.

Erin nodded understandingly and gratefully began to wander about the room. She placed a comforting hand against the small of her back as she moved, but a sudden thought made her turn to question him.

"Does Michael know that you are using his home for your evil purposes?" she posed daringly.

"Yes," Brad answered simply. "As a matter-of-fact, I have spent my entire sojourn here at Fox Bush."

"Here?"

"Yes," he laughed triumphantly. "I assure you, it did my heart good to watch that snobbish husband of yours traipsing about the countryside willy-nilly when I was right here under his nose all along."

Erin was stunned. "But that would mean that Michael is involved in all this," she whispered hoarsely. "I can't believe it."

"Believe it," Brad droned snidely.

Thoroughly bemused by the revelation, Erin weakly asked, "Why would Michael assist you in your wicked endeavors?"

"You heard much of the explanation from your Uncle Philip." Brad shrugged his shoulders offhandedly. "Michael was among the rebels that raided your home."

"A raid that *you* masterminded," she reminded him.

"As you wish." He tilted his head in a condescending gesture. "Anyway, I quickly realized that Cahill was quite anxious that your family never learn of his participation in that little escapade, and understandably so." He stood up suddenly and walked to where she was standing. "In return for my silence, Michael agreed to help me conclude some business matters I had in the area."

Erin hung her head, thoroughly disenchanted with Brad's narrative. "I still find it hard to conceive that Michael would be a part of such despicable goings-on."

"Don't be so hard on the young man, Erin," Brad laughed perversely, and, placing the tip of the revolver under her chin, he forced her head up. "Actually, had it not been for Michael's timely intervention at Kilkieran, Kellen would have received a slightly . . . uh . . . despoiled wife upon his nuptial bed. But then, you wouldn't remember, because you fainted just before your valiant champion burst upon the scene."

"You!" Erin hissed, recoiling from his touch. "It was you who tried to —"

"Yes," he interpolated. "I've always regretted the fact that Cahill spoiled my opportunity to experience the thrilling sensation of your womanly charms." He leaned closer, the rancid stench of his breath making her head reel dizzily, and breathed thickly, "You're a handsome wench, all right. Why, even now I find myself stirred to passion with the thoughts of possessing you." He glanced down at her protruding stomach.

"No!" Erin cried pitifully, and she shrank away from the vile man, frantically searching the room for a route of escape.

"Don't worry," he chuckled at her reaction. "I might be a ruthless blackguard, but even I possess a few scruples. I am not given to the ravishment of women in your obvious condition. Besides, there will be time for that in the days yet to come," he added enigmatically, and, lifting the whiskey bottle to his lips, he drank liberally.

"What . . . what do you mean?" she asked hesitantly, uncertain if she truly wanted an answer to the perturbing question.

"You shall see, my lovely. You shall see," he replied noncommittally, returning to his chair. "Well, have I sufficiently satisfied your curiosity?"

"Not quite."

"By all means. Ask your questions." Brad leaned back in his chair and crossed his arms behind his head in an indulgent manner.

"Why did you try to kill Deborah and me? It *was* you who caused the buggy accident, was it not?" she bravely leveled the accusation, meeting his unnerving gaze.

"Yes, it was. You know, Erin, you should have gone off with Cahill when he asked you in Richmond. For as long as you were married to Kellen, I couldn't take the chance that you would remember your uncle's participation in the raid," he explained. "When Kellen left you, I thought that my plans were safe, but when Vanessa telegraphed me with the news that

Kellen was returning to Kilkieran to make amends with you, I knew that I had to do something.

"I started watching for you in the woods, for I know you frequent the waterfall. Unfortunately, your sister-in-law sighted me in the woods, and I feared that she might recognize me from your room on the day she shot Kellen, therefore, it became necessary to silence the both of you," he concluded with a nonchalant wave of his hand.

"You're an evil, *evil* man," Erin hissed.

"Well, we all have our little faults," he countered glibly. "Unhappily, my carefully thought out schemes went awry, for you did recall the actual events of that day, forcing me to take alternative steps," he added purposefully.

"Then you *did* murder Uncle Philip!" she exclaimed, aghast at the appalling man's seemingly limitless capacity for wretchedness.

"Guilty," he replied, leaning forward to retrieve the discarded whiskey bottle.

"But why have you done all these awful things? Why are you holding me prisoner?" she blurted desperately.

"You, my dear, are bait," he informed her frankly. "I've been waiting for just such an opportunity, for I am going to use you to lure your precious husband into my trap."

"Why, so that you can kill him, too?" she demanded, feeling suddenly fearful for her husband's safety.

"Yes."

"But why? Why do you hate Kellen so much?" Erin cried hysterically.

"Why? Why? Why?" he parroted her. "I'm growing excessively weary of your insipid questions," Brad snapped irritably.

"That's a pity," announced a reserved voice from the doorway. "For I assure you that the answer to that question is of particular interest to me."

Erin could hardly believe her astonished ears, and she whirled toward the sound of the voice to find her husband leaning negligently against the doorjamb. In an instant, she bolted across the room to be enfolded in Kellen's reassuring embrace.

"Ah, Kellen. Do come in," Brad drawled casually. "I see that you discovered the trail I left for you from the waterfall."

"Oh, Kellen!" Erin said excitedly. "It was Brad all along. Taggart was completely innocent, and Brad shot him and left him to die by the waterfall."

"I know, angel," he whispered softly. "In fact, I have learned a great many things about my friend here today. You see, I had a long, informative talk with Vanessa this afternoon." He looked pointedly at Brad. "Then I found Taggart. It seems that he returned to the vicinity some time ago, but he was afraid to approach me, for he realized that I suspected him in Ridgeway's murder. He hoped to apprehend Brad and bring him to me, so that the matter could be cleared once and for all," he explained, holding Erin close.

"You mean, he isn't dead?" Erin asked, pushing away from Kellen to stare up into his handsome face.

"No." He smiled down at her. "He's in bad shape, though, and I had to drop him at Briar Cliff before coming to your rescue, else I would have been here sooner. He was quite concerned for your safety, as was I.

"Are you all right? Has he mistreated you, my darling?" he murmured lovingly.

"Not really." She shook her head, snuggling against him. "And I am fine now that you are here."

Growing weary with their romantic drivel, Brad chose that moment to inquire, "Just how long have you been standing there?"

"Long enough to hear you confess to a number of crimes that should suffice to send your despicable hide to the gallows," Kellen informed him candidly.

"Good," Brad droned lazily. "Then I won't have to waste my time with monotonous repetitions. Do move away from the door, Kellen," Brad directed, leveling his gun at Kellen's chest. "Oh, and please be so kind as to remove your revolver from your inside pocket. Carefully," he warned as Kellen slid his hand inside his coat.

"That's a good fellow." Brad observed as Kellen withdrew the weapon and laid it aside, then he beckoned the couple toward him.

Kellen slipped Erin's hand into his and led her back into the room. He considerately seated her in the chair she had previously inhabited and took up a stance behind her, placing his hands on her shoulders.

"You were, I believe, about to tell Erin why you harbor such an unnatural dislike for me," Kellen prompted.

"Dislike!" he scoffed. "Let me assure you, Kellen, that I quite despise you," he said succinctly.

"But Kellen has always been your friend. Why are you treating him like this?" Erin demanded.

"Friend? Bah!" Brad spat in disgust. "He was a constant reminder of the things I could never hope to achieve because of my low birth: wealth, power, success."

"That's not true, Brad. You could have had all those things," Kellen advised him, his voice soft.

"Yes, if I groveled at your feet," he snarled. "You have no idea what it was like to grow up in your shadow, do you? To bask in the glow of your triumphs and conquests; to have to beg for the slightest acknowledgment from *anyone* while the mere mention of the Sinclair name brought about immediate attention." His face twisted with anger as he unleashed his pent-up hostilities, and Erin feared that he would lose control and discharge the weapon.

"I . . . I didn't realize that you felt this way, Brad," Kellen said gently, trying to maintain a calm facade so as not to further antagonize the deranged man.

"I know," Brad grumbled sourly. "You were always too preoccupied with your own interests, and couldn't bother yourself with the concerns of insignificant ne'er-do-wells the likes of Bradley Petersen. But that doesn't matter now, for I shall presently send you to the fiery depths of hell. Apt recompense for your arrogance, don't you agree?" He leaned forward, a crazed look distorting his attractive features, and his next utterance completely horrified Erin. "And you shall die with the agonizing knowledge that your wife shall be left behind to atone for your high-and-mighty ways."

Brad noted, with considerable satisfaction, the tortured play of emotions that crossed Kellen's face, and he hastened to strengthen his grip on Kellen's heart. "Ah, yes. I can almost feel the wench writhing beneath me now," he added, his lustful gaze raking over Erin.

"You disgusting son-of-a-bitch!" Kellen rasped through taut lips. "I'll see you in hell first!" he cried, taking a threatening step toward the man he had once considered to be his closest friend.

"That's an ill-advised maneuver, my friend," Brad warned ominously. "Just consider; the gun might go off, and there's no telling who might be hit." He nodded pointedly toward Erin. "Besides, are you quite certain that your curiosity has been satisfactorily assuaged. I'd certainly regret it if you were to wander through eternity not knowing the full range of my debauchery." He gave a malicious laugh.

"As a matter-of-fact, I would like to know why you felt it was necessary to murder Arthur Ridgeway."

"He was a member of the regiment that attacked Kilkieran and later bushwhacked the wagon load of nitro," he explained. "Unfortunately, he discovered Cahill and I as we were relocating the nitro from its hiding place in the cave by the waterfall to the cellar here at Fox Bush. When Ridgeway drew the unhappy conclusion that I intended to sell the chemical to several of my more nefarious acquaintances, he made the mistaken assumption that I would pay him a share of the profits in return for his silence." Brad paused long enough to quench the thirst that the lengthy tale had spawned, then he continued.

"Then Mr. Ridgeway made the unwise decision to acquaint you with the facts—"

"And you used a portion of the nitro to silence him forever," Kellen interjected.

"Precisely," Brad concurred. "You were supposed to perish in that blast as well," he admitted. "Had you been cooperative then, I would now be spared the unpleasant task at hand."

"You'll never get away with this," Erin whispered hoarsely.

"You think not? That has yet to be determined." He pointed out. "Would you care to hear my plan?" He received no response to his inquiry, yet he proceeded to enlighten them, impervious to the stares of his captives.

"You see, Cahill is presently imprisoned in the cellar," he began. "Once I have disposed of you, Kellen, I shall see to him, making it look as though the two of you murdered each other. Most of the county residents are aware of Erin's indiscretion in Richmond, so they will naturally assume that you finally came to settle the score."

"And how will you account for Erin's disappearance?" Kellen posed.

"Everyone will recall her past history of mental deterioration under stress, and, having discovered the bodies of her husband *and* lover, will think that she wandered off in a state of shock," he stated simply.

"There is one very significant flaw to your plan," Kellen pointed out, and, before Brad could question the nature of the defect, Kellen deigned to favor him with an explanation. "Brian Taggart still lives, and I promise you, he will not rest until you've been tried and punished for your evil doings," Kellen vowed.

"My trail shall have long since cooled by the time Taggart's wounds have healed," Brad scoffed. "I grow weary with all this talk," he suddenly announced. "It's time to complete my task, so that I may be on my way. Move away from her, Kellen. I wonder, shall you die like a man, or will you plead for your life like a low coward?"

"No!!" Erin shrieked, desperately flinging herself into her husband's arms, tears of anguish streaming down her cheeks.

"Not to worry, my darling," Kellen whispered so that only her ears could hear. "I've been waiting for just such an opportunity."

As he cradled her in front of him, Kellen's hand surreptitiously slipped inside his pocket to withdraw the second revolver he had concealed there before entering the house. But Kellen was not to be permitted the occasion to utilize the secreted weapon, for the surprising appearance of Michael Cahill at the door stayed his movement.

Brad noticed Kellen's quizzical expression, and, when he turned to discover Michael, his own countenance withered substantially.

"What do *you* want?" Brad demanded crossly.

"Drop the gun, Petersen," Michael ordered, ignoring the question.

"Why, *you!*" Brad hissed spitefully, taking an angry step toward the man.

"Don't!" Michael commanded, carefully extending a small box in front of him. "I think you can guess what this box contains, and you are similarly aware of its capabilities. Furthermore, I assure you that I won't hesitate to use it. This is but a portion of the cache that remains in the cellar, so you can well imagine the havoc I can create if I grow clumsy and release this box," he said purposefully.

"Now, drop the gun, Petersen," he repeated, his voice threatening.

Brad glanced anxiously toward the box of nitroglycerin, and gradually lowered the weapon to the floor. Thus disarmed, and no longer a menace to Erin, Kellen started to move across the room to apprehend the villain.

"No!" Michael shouted. "Stay where you are! This is between Petersen and myself," he declared, the vibrant blue eyes alive with fury.

"Let's not be hasty, Cahill," Brad began nervously. "Perhaps we can talk this out."

"I have nothing to say to you," Michael said coldly, but the expression he turned on Erin was tender and sorrowful.

"Michael," she murmured his name softly.

"Shh, Erin; let me talk," he whispered, his eyes filling with tears of remorse. "I've certainly made a fine mess of my life, haven't I, kitten? The only thing I ever wanted was to love you, to build a home and life together with you," he said painfully, his fingers beginning to tremble as they fiercely clutched the box of nitroglycerin.

"I know," she said sympathetically, but Michael continued heedless of her attempts to comfort him.

"It's because of this bastard that I shall never realize that happiness with you." He cast a scornful glare at Bradley Petersen. "God, I never meant to hurt you, Erin," he moaned pitifully. "You believe me, don't you?"

"Of course, I believe you, Michael," Erin said consolingly. "But, Michael, please; put the box down. It's all over now. Let Kellen turn Brad over to the proper authorities, so that he can be punished for his crimes," she pleaded. "Please, let's not hurt anyone else."

"I'm afraid I can't do that, kitten. There is only one thing I can do to compensate for the anguish I have caused you." He refocused his bitter gaze on Brad. "Believe me, when I'm finished here today, Petersen will no longer be a threat to anyone.

"Take her out of here, Sinclair," Michael abruptly shouted at Kellen.

"Michael, wait." Kellen endeavored to reason with the determined man. "Consider what you're doing."

"I have. Now, *go!*" Michael screamed hysterically.

Fearing for Erin's welfare, Kellen clamped his hand firmly about her wrist and ushered her from the room. His objective was to carry her a safe distance from the mansion, then return to prevent Cahill from carrying through with his reckless plan. He half-dragged-half-carried Erin through the twilight, until, having traversed a sufficient distance from the house, Kellen suddenly stopped. He helped her to the ground, then turned back toward the plantation house.

"Where are you going?" Erin cried.

"To stop him."

"No!" she shrieked hysterically, clinging to him to prevent him from leaving her. "You'll be killed!"

Kellen didn't have time to argue with her. Instead, he merely shoved her hands aside and began running toward the house.

Frantic with worry, Erin scrambled to her feet and began to stumble after him. "Kellen! Come back!"

Kellen stopped in his tracks and rounded on her. "Stay there, Erin!" he commanded sternly, resuming his progress toward the mansion.

He had traveled only a few feet, however, when the night was rent with a tremendous blast, the force of which lifted him from the ground and hurled him backwards through the air.

Erin was completely thunderstruck as the stately mansion literally exploded in front of her eyes, scattering bits of broken glass and splintered wood on the wind. As she watched, the house was totally enveloped by a ravaging wall of yellow and orange flames that cast foreboding shadows against the darkening sky. The shock of the terrifying ordeal finally began to subside, and, of their own volition, her quivering legs began to carry her toward her husband's stricken body.

Twenty-six

Kellen's eyes snapped open abruptly, but a soft smile gradually spread his lips as he identified the source of his premature awakening. Erin lay on her side pressed closely against him, her very pregnant stomach nestled familiarly in the small of his back. His smile broadened as the gentle kicking motion grew into a persistent thumping, causing him to turn over and rub a soothing hand along her abdomen.

"Shh, little one," he whispered in the dim morning light. "Let your mother sleep. Now that she is no longer haunted by her nightmares, it seems a pity for you to disturb her rest."

But even as he spoke, Kellen heard Erin's lugubrious moan and looked down in time to see her eyes flutter open. A drowsy, lopsided grin curled her lips when she observed his handsome face above hers in the semi-darkness. She reached her arms high above her head and stretched, then she encircled his neck and pulled his head lower, so that their lips met in a gentle, loving embrace.

"What time is it?" she yawned sleepily.

"Much too early for you to think about rising, my darling. Indeed, I, myself, had hoped to play the slugabed today, but this little rascal would have none of it." He ran a devoted hand across her protruding belly. "Do you think it will be much longer?" he asked tenderly.

"I hope not," she sighed heavily. But her concern with his fatigued expression prompted her to slide her fingers along the lines that creased his brow. "What time did you get home last night?"

"Very late," he replied tiredly. "My meeting lasted longer than I anticipated. I don't recall the exact hour, but you were deep in slumber, gently snoring away, by the time I crawled into bed."

"I don't snore!" she retorted indignantly, jerking her hand from his face in a peevish gesture. But her petulant frown was short lived, and she commented offhandedly, "I almost wish we had remained at Kilkieran. At least, I got to see you occasionally there."

"Are you saying that you are not satisfied with the lavish home I have provided for you? My, what an ungrateful wife you are," he said tritely, feigning effrontery at her statement.

"No, of course not, silly. I truly love it here at Arcadia," she quickly assured him. "And it was so thoughtful of Graham to let Maisie tend me until after the baby comes. It's just — "

"Yes, princess?" He pressed a loving kiss to her brow.

"Oh, I suppose I am just being a silly goose, but I received a letter from Deborah yesterday, and it made me a little homesick," she explained.

"I see." He nodded understandingly as he settled her in the crook of his arm. "What is the news from Kilkieran?"

"The mill is booming, and Evan's mercantile is doing such a prosperous business that MacPhearson has had to lower his prices in order to compete," she informed him, noting the triumphant smile that immediately adorned his face.

"I knew that those two enterprises would be good investments. Were you aware that you had married such a brilliant entrepreneur?" Kellen assumed an appropriate arrogant expression.

"No," she murmured thoughtfully. "But I *did* know that you were a pompous blowhard," she teased him unmercifully, but her frantic attempt to wiggle from his grasp was greatly impeded by her advanced stage of pregnancy.

With minimal effort, Kellen pinned her hands above her head, and favored her with a mischievous scowl. "My, my, but what an onerous wench you are at six o'clock in the morning," he clucked his tongue in a scolding manner. "I might even add that you owe a debt of gratitude to our unborn child, because were it not for him," Kellen glanced down at her stomach, "you would presently be receiving a very richly deserved spanking." He covered her mouth with his to smother her scathing retort, and, when he pulled away, he tweaked her nose and climbed out of bed to pull on his clothes.

"Where are you going? Surely, you cannot mean to go into the office on a Saturday," Erin cried disappointedly.

"No, angel," Kellen chuckled. "I am your devoted companion for the day. I merely thought I would run down to the kitchen and see what sort of goodies Maisie has prepared. Does breakfast in bed sound appealing?"

"Wonderful."

"Good. While I am dressing, you can regale me with the news from Deborah's letter," he suggested.

"Well, it would seem that Evan finally summoned enough courage to ask Jennifer to be his wife," Erin said brightly. "They plan a September wedding."

"And you would like to attend the ceremony?" Kellen voiced Erin's unspoken sentiment.

"Very much."

"We shall see, pet. Much depends on how you progress after the child is born." He shoved his feet into his boots, then stood to tuck his shirt into his trousers. "Any more news?"

"Yes. As a matter-of-fact, it appears that the family will increase in number again next spring, for Deborah is pregnant," Erin said happily.

"Do you think she is ready to cope with the responsibility of motherhood?" Kellen asked seriously.

Erin chewed thoughtfully on a fingernail while she considered her reply. Eventually, she said, "I think so. She showed a significant improvement during our stay at Kilkieran, and when I was injured in the buggy accident, she spent the days afterward doting on me. Perhaps a child will help her put back together those pieces of her life that are still dangling."

"Perhaps," he agreed. "Anything else?"

"No. Why?"

Kellen, having concluded his morning ablutions, strolled over to the bed and sat down. "Because, I learned something yesterday that I think you will find interesting, if not down-right amusing."

"What?" she inquired, thoroughly intrigued with his conversation.

"You are aware that I had a meeting with Colonel Langford and Brian Taggart yesterday to officially close Brad's case," he began slowly.

"Yes," she murmured, reaching out to cover his hand with her sympathetic one, for she knew that memories of Brad were still quite painful for him.

"You know, Erin; I was very wrong about Taggart," he admitted ashamedly.

"Really? I find that hard to believe," she mumbled doubtfully.

"I know, honey," he murmured sympathetically. "He was none too kind in his treatment of you, but, as it turns out, he was assigned to my regiment by the department to test my integrity, more or less."

"I don't understand."

"It seems that headquarters had become suspicious of Brad long before he was placed with my unit," he explained. "And knowing of our long time friendship, they wanted to determine if I might be connected with Brad's crimes."

"So Taggart tried to rape me?" she cried incredulously.

"As ludicrous as it sounds; yes. Oh, Taggart had been a thorn in my side throughout the mission," he admitted, a deep frown suddenly furrowing his brow. "You know, sweetheart, I always considered it strange that Taggart had made such a

564

ruckus that night at Kilkieran. And yesterday he confirmed that he had purposely wakened me, so that I would be aware of his destination."

"And if you had not proved to be the honorable man that you are, and come to my rescue, would he have carried out his reprehensible act?" she demanded.

"I truly don't know the answer to that, Erin," Kellen replied honestly. "But the fact remains, I did thwart his plunderings. And because Taggart reported that he could find nothing remiss in my command, the department decided to ask me to conduct the investigation to determine the exactness of Brad's crimes.

"You see, my wily friend had managed to successfully camouflage his unlawful doings, and Colonel Langford felt that he might slip up around a close associate."

"Is it officially over now?" Erin inquired softly, aware of his brooding countenance.

Kellen nodded, his expression subdued.

"But what of this amusing anecdote you were going to tell me?" she questioned lightly, wishing to avert his concentration from the unhappy course it had taken.

"Oh, yes. After our meeting, Brian took me aside to tell me that he is also about to forsake his bachelorhood for the married life." He paused to brush a piece of lint from the sleeve of his jacket.

"Oh, anyone we know?" she asked indifferently.

"Uh huh," he answered, his manner aloof.

"Well, who is it?" she demanded, her curiosity piqued by Kellen's odd behavior.

"Christina," he murmured slyly.

"Christina!" she shrieked in astonishment. "But, how . . . when . . ."

"During his recuperation at Briar Cliff, I suppose," Kellen shrugged his rugged shoulders.

"But . . . but . . . *why?*"

Kellen gave a hearty laugh when he beheld Erin's incredulous expression. "I'm at a loss as well, my love, but then, who am I to explain the mysterious ways of Cupid? After all," he lifted her hand to his lips and gently pressed a kiss against her palm, "I'd wager that there were those who questioned the wisdom of our union, but I think that we have adequately proven that two opposites can eke out a compatible existence."

"But *Christina?*" Erin still could not believe her ears.

"Well," he began thoughtfully. "Perhaps her irascible temperament will disintegrate once she becomes a contented married lady." Then a distinctively wicked grin spread his lips, and he added, "Yours certainly did."

Before Erin could respond to his playful taunt, Kellen pecked her on the cheek then ran out to collect their breakfast.

Erin lay still for several moments, a wistful expression clouding her eyes. Then deciding that she would slip into her dressing gown and prepare the table on the balcony, so they could breakfast outside, Erin started to climb out of the bed. But she had moved only a few inches toward her destination when an unexpected pain in her lower abdomen left her quite breathless. Erin gripped the sheets between white knuckles until the spasm subsided, and she had just fallen back against the pillows to catch her breath when Kellen returned with their meal.

Noting her unusual expression, Kellen quickly asked, "What is it, princess?"

"N-n-nothing," she stammered, not wishing to excite him lest she be mistaken in her suspicions. "Mmm," she sighed. "That certainly smells scrumptious." She settled herself against the pillows while Kellen placed the tray across her lap. "But I thought that we would dine on the balcony," she suggested, glancing up into his handsome face. "It's so lovely outside."

"You will be more comfortable where you are," he advised considerately. "I'll sit here at the table." He draped the linen napkin across her stomach, then removed his dishes from the heavily laden tray.

Erin favored him with an endearing smile before turning her attention to her own food. But when her eyes fell on her plate, she grew curious at what she found.

"What is this?" She plucked the beribboned scroll from the tray and regarded it quizzically.

"A present," he muttered noncommittally.

"Oh?"

"Yes, I rather thought that you might like to burn it," he explained, thereby, further puzzling her.

"Burn it? Whatever for?"

"Because, it is the marriage contract that Grandfather forced you to sign."

"I see," she murmured, carefully studying the document she had once treated with contempt. Then giving a shrug, she placed it on the bedside table and turned to sip from her coffee cup. "I think I'll just keep it."

"Keep it?" he fairly shouted.

"Yes, as a memento."

"A memento? Erin, that wretched document nearly ruined our marriage," he reminded her. "Burn it!"

"Kellen, it's July," she pointed out needlessly. "Hardly the time of year to build a fire in the grate. Besides, I should like to keep it," she said simply. "I cannot explain my feelings, but women like to keep things like this that will remind them of their youth when they are wallowing in their dotage. Now, eat your breakfast, and don't think of it again," Erin whispered gently.

Then following her own suggestion, she began to nibble on a piece of toast when a sudden thought prompted her to inquire, "You know, Kellen, you never did tell me how you managed to enlist Geoffrey's assistance at Kilkieran. How did you persuade him to masquerade as a Yankee?"

"How do you think?"

Erin shrugged her shoulders. "I don't know. Money, I suppose."

"Close," he laughed, then abandoning his breakfast, he returned to sit with her on the bed. "Promise you won't be angry with me?"

"Promise," she murmured adoringly, running her fingers through his hair.

Thus reassured, he ventured to explain. "In return for his assistance, I gave up any claim on Grandfather's inheritance."

"What?"

"Yes, it's true." He nodded slowly. "I realize that you probably think that I behaved irrationally, but I wanted to make certain that we were free from my meddlesome cousin and his wife for good. Additionally, I hoped to coax those tortured memories of yours out into the open." Kellen hung his head in remorse. "I'm sorry I had to put you through that, Erin."

"I know, sweetheart," Erin purred lovingly. "You only did what you thought was best for me. I shall always love you for that."

"Well, be that as it may, now that I have forsaken Grandfather's inheritance. I fear that we shall have to muddle along on the pittance that I make for us through my own enterprises. We may be poor, but we shall be free from meddling relatives," he breathed a grateful sigh.

Erin glanced around at the extravagant chamber in which she currently lounged, and her voice was laced with sarcasm when she droned, "Yes, I can well image that we shall lead a very deprived life."

"You aren't angry then?"

"Of course not. And I should think that Vanessa is ecstatic with the news," Erin chuckled knowingly.

"Oh, she has become quite the doting wife, I assure you." He shared her laughter. Then his countenance grew suddenly sober, and he started to withdraw from the fourposter, but Erin grabbed his hand to stay his motion.

"You're thinking of Brad, aren't you?" she questioned softly.

Kellen nodded, saying nothing.

"I know that you blame yourself, and you mustn't." She squeezed his hand devotedly. "He was blinded by jealousy."

"That's just it," he cried his frustration. "I loved him as a brother. We were inseparable comrades; we did everything together. My family tried to make things easier by helping him through financial difficulties, but I never realized he resented us for it. I guess I'll never understand how Brad could throw his life away like that," he sighed dismally, then angrily thumping his fist against his thigh, he shouted, "How could I be that trusting of someone and not know that he was capable of committing such despicable crimes? How could I not sense his hatred of me?" Kellen shook his head sorrowfully.

"He disguised his feelings well," Erin offered feebly, aware that her lame explanation did not assuage his tortured thoughts. "Don't think of it now, darling," she urged. "It grieves me to see you berate yourself for something over which you had no control.

"It was a horrible, frightening ordeal, and, God willing, we shall never endure anything like it again. Both Michael and Brad died in that awful explosion, and I thought that I had lost you as well." She shivered uncontrollably as she recalled her husband's lifeless form in the flickering shadows of the burning house.

"We both have fond recollections of our respective friends; remembrances from a time that was not overshadowed by the horrors of war. Let us try to think of them as the carefree, loving friends we once knew, and not the embittered, angry young men who died at Fox Bush," she murmured wisely.

"My, but what a sagacious young woman you've become," Kellen said admiringly, and, setting the breakfast tray aside, he drew her into his arms. "The smartest thing I ever did was to make you my wife," he breathed thickly.

Erin reveled in his embrace, but the return of the strong, relentless spasm in her abdomen made her smile nervously, and her eyes brimmed with tears.

"And unless I am mistaken, I believe that I am about to make you a father." Her unexpected declaration caught him completely by surprise, and he pushed away to gape at her.

"W-w-what?!" he exclaimed. "You mean . . . you mean, it's . . . it's time?!" Kellen's usually unflappable mien withered with the staggering news.

"Yes, darling," she answered.

"Does it hurt?"

"No," she giggled at his absurd inquiry. "At least, not yet."

"But, but you're crying." He pointed at the wet paths that marred her cheeks.

"These are happy tears, silly," she explained, clutching his arm as she was consumed by the strong contraction.

"Honey?" Kellen gazed uneasily into her anguished face. "What do you want me to do?" he asked anxiously.

"First, you can make Maisie aware of what is happening," she said calmly. "She'll know what to do until the doctor arrives."

"I'll do that right away!" He started to run for the door, but Erin refused to release him.

"*Then* you can sit yourself down and have a tall glass of brandy to help you relax," she suggested thoughtfully.

"The hell you say!" he balked at her notion. "I'll get Maisie, then I am riding for the doctor," he told her in no uncertain terms.

"Kellen, this is my first baby. It will probably be hours before it is finally born," she insisted.

"Nevertheless, I'm going for the doctor, *now*," he said emphatically. "Then I will sequester myself in my study and swill an entire bottle of the stuff. Now, release me, so that I may be on my way," he commanded.

"Kiss me first," she murmured softly.

"Erin!" He gaped at her in amazement. "You're being completely ridiculous."

"Please?"

He noted her tortured face, and realized that she was experiencing a great deal of pain, consequently, he leaned forward and pressed a loving kiss against her mouth. But when he endeavored to pull away, Erin caught his face between her gentle fingertips. Tenderly caressing his cheek, she whispered throatily, "I love you, Yankee."

"And I love you, little reb, but at the moment, I am frightened out of my mind with concern for you," he admitted solemnly. "Let me fetch the doctor, then I will come and sit with you for awhile," he promised.

Erin nodded relentingly and watched while he quickly exited the chamber. Breathing a low sigh, she leaned back against the pillows, and resigned herself to accept the rigors of the long day ahead of her. Yet, regardless of the outcome, she knew that she could look forward to facing a long future with Kellen. He was her strength. With him she had found a contentment and a happiness that she knew could not be duplicated by any other, and, as a warm smile fashioned her lips, she closed her eyes and dreamed of the wonderful life before them. The turmoil that had scourged the early months of their marriage was over, and what lay ahead was but a joyous treasure of experiences yet to be realized.

HISTORICAL ROMANCE AT ITS BEST!

by KATHLEEN DRYMON

TEXAS BLOSSOM   (1305, $3.75)
When Sorrel's luscious curves silhouetted the firelight, Mathew felt lust and desire like he never felt before. Soon, he was enmeshed in her silvery web of love—their passion flowering like a wild TEXAS BLOSSOM!

WILD DESIRES   (1103, $3.50)
The tempestuous saga of three generations of women, set in the back streets of London, glamorous New Orleans and the sultry tropics—where each finds passion in a stranger's arms!

TENDER PASSIONS   (1032, $3.50)
While countless men professed their adoration for Katherine, she tossed her head in rejection. But when she's pirated away by a man whose object is lust, she finds herself willing!

by CAROL FINCH

RAPTURE'S DREAM   (1037, $3.50)
By day Gabrielle is the insufferable waif who tests Dane Hampton's patience; by night she is the phantom lover who brings him to the heights of ecstasy!

ENDLESS PASSION   (1155, $3.50)
Brianna was a sensuous temptress who longed for the fires of everlasting love. But Seth Donovan's heart was as cold as ice . . . until her lips burned his with the flames of desire!

DAWN'S DESIRE   (1340, $3.50)
Kathryn never dreamed that the tall handsome stranger was wise to her trickery and would steal her innocence—and her heart. And when he captured her lips in one long, luscious kiss, he knew he'd make her his forever . . . in the light of DAWN'S DESIRE.

Available wherever paperbacks are sold, or order direct from the Publisher. Send cover price plus 50¢ per copy for mailing and handling to Zebra Books, 475 Park Avenue South, New York, N.Y. 10016. DO NOT SEND CASH.